Twisted Fairytales

TONY WALKER

Ged bu mhath an cala dh'fhàg sinn,
Seachd feàrr an cala fhuair sinn

TRADITIONAL SCOTTISH GAELIC

Contents

PART FOUR
LONDON

PART FIVE
WALES

PART SIX
BRITTANY

PART TWO
THE TOWER OF KER-ZU

PART ONE

Yorkshire

The Poisoned Rose

THE BIG HOUSE stood back from the minor road. It had been hard to find and Edward was glad he had the benefit of the taxi driver's local knowledge. Not that the man knew Hackthwaite Hall itself, but he was familiar with the general area, which was more than Edward was.

Edward had got a taxi from Knaresborough as it was nearly ten miles to Hackthwaite from the station, and the walk would have been a hard one in this frost, still unthawed by the early winter sun.

Edward saw the sign on the gatepost that read 'Hackthwaite Hall'.

"In here, yes, I think." Diffident as ever, Edward's voice was quiet and the taxi driver struggled to hear him.

"Beg your pardon, sir?"

"Here."

"Yes, I'm not blind. It says Hackthwaite on the pillar, there." The man pointed over his steering wheel.

Edward was rather taken aback by the man's tone, but then he remembered that Yorkshiremen were famous for being brusque, so it was probably a joke.

The entrance to Hackthwaite Hall was like a photograph that draws your eye in — the twin entrance pillars topped with stone flowers — a rose on the left, and a lily on the right, and then a long gravel drive swallowed by trees leading to the house itself, which was invisible from the road.

The car turned and entered the drive and the sound changed as the wheels crunched over the gravel.

Edward mused. "I always think ivy is unfairly treated."

"Sorry, sir?" the driver said, not looking back.

"In the song: *The Holly and The Ivy*. The song's named after both plants, but it's the holly that gets all the praise."

"As you say, sir. Never thought of it like that."

"I mean all the pricking thorn, the blood of Jesus, the crown."

"Yes, sir."

"But I suppose the scarlet berries of the holly are more resplendent than the green ones of the ivy. Even so, I prefer the ivy, I think; it's more discreet."

"There it is, sir." The driver lifted his left hand from wheel and indicated the house, his gloved finger like an arrow.

And so, Edward Smith first saw Hackthwaite Hall.

He remembered his reading about it in the Victoria County History of Yorkshire:

Original Tudor manor house, much remodelled in Jacobean times to its current look: parapets, intricate stonework, featured windows to make it like an antique piece of art, or a cake of sculptured stone. Right hand side features ill-judged Victorian accretion, but otherwise the place is symmetrical.

As they neared the Hall, Edward thought the central porch looked like a mouth with its stone wings on either side like enfolding arms.

"Shepherd's warning," the driver said.

"Sorry?"

It had been dark when they set off from Knaresborough Station, and now it was light. The sun, not visible, blocked by the stone of the house, had risen and though the orb itself was out of sight, its rising had coloured the air with the vibrant red of a poppy in June.

It was an unhealthy glow, Edward thought: like a furnace at work out of sight, or blood spilled in the dawn. Of course, the colour meant nothing. Colours were just themselves: white was white, red was red, yellow was yellow. They had no meaning beyond their hue.

The car passed the large pond in front of the house, where water was hardened to ice. The dawn silhouettes of ducks wandered grumpily across it; the trees around stood mournful and bare.

They drove further down the path to the turning circle in front of the porch with its great oaken door. A stone fountain, lichen etched, ivy leaves hoar-frosted with white, stood silent in the centre of the gravel circle around which the taxi driver turned.

The driver brought the car to an expert, smooth stop. "And here we are, sir."

The driver named his price and Edward fumbled with his wallet, not finding it at first in the depths of his pocket, then giving the man the fare and a tip, calculated as close to twelve per cent as his change would allow.

"Thank you kindly, sir. I'll get your bags."

"I don't have much."

"No, indeed, you don't sir. How long are you planning on staying?"

The man passed out of earshot on the other side of the car so Edward got out, his brown brogues crunching on the gravel. The sharp pebbles, flecked with moss, pricked through the thin, city-street soles of his shoes. He waited until the driver was close enough, Edward's bag in his hand and then replied to the question.

"Erm, not sure — a week or two, I suppose."

The driver glanced at the closed oak door. "Nobody's come. Want me to wait?"

Edward wondered if the driver thought there was no one in and he would have to take Edward back to Knaresborough with him.

Edward laughed. "No, no. I am expected."

"It's no trouble. It's a long walk back, especially on such a cold and frosty morning. Very seasonal though."

Edward thought that the weather wouldn't actually make the walk any longer, but he guessed the man meant that it would seem further because it was cold. He said, "Very kind, but I shall be fine, I assure you."

"Very well, then. I wish you good luck, and thanks for the tip."

So, Edward Smith waited for the taxi to start, because he believed that doing so was good manners, and he watched it drive away past the frozen pond with its ring of winter trees, away down the long drive, away out of the gateway with its guardian lily and sentinel rose.

He felt one knock might not be heard and three knocks might be rude, so he lifted the heavy iron ring of the door-knocker, and brought it down twice on the massive door.

Then he waited.

Chapter 2

The heavy thump of the iron door-knocker was devoid of any echo, as if the hall beyond was solid with no room for the sound to escape into.

Minutes went by. Perhaps twice hadn't been enough? Edward thought of knocking again, but he didn't. They were expecting him, though perhaps not as early as this. He didn't want to put them out, so if they didn't answer, he supposed he could go for a walk and come back later. He pulled up the collar of his overcoat in anticipation of a chilly stroll to kill time.

Then, without any warning via the sound of footsteps, or a shouted greeting, the door opened inwards.

Edward backed off the top step, and then the second, until he stood on the gravel. He knew it was impolite to stand on someone's step.

The man who opened the door there did not seem surprised to see him despite it not being even nine a.m.

Edward said, "Sorry to be so early. I caught the milk train from York to Knaresborough. It was either that or trying to sleep in York Station waiting room, so, I thought I'd make a start. Hope you don't mind."

The other was a man in his mid-to-late fifties, his hair longer than current fashion, his suit brown and pressed, of good quality cloth but not flamboyant. His tie was narrow and also brown. The man had a trimmed goatee beard, flecked with grey, and his temples were touched with the same colour but his brown eyes appeared youthful. There was something eager in them.

"Mr Smith!" he said. "How lovely to make your acquaintance at last. After all our letters, I almost felt I knew you, but now I have a face to put to the handwriting."

"Pleased to be here, Dr Lovegrove, and thank you for your invitation."

Lovegrove stepped back and gestured with his arms like a magician inviting a theatre-goer on stage to take part in some dishonest conjuring trick. "Come in, come in. It's cold out this morning."

Trying to be positive, Edward said, "At least there's no more snow."

"No, that would have made your journey harder. How was it, in any case?"

"Not too bad. I came up from Cambridge yesterday and stayed in York last night. I had business with Andrew Ferguson. Do you know him?"

"I'm afraid not."

"He works at the Minster Library."

As they spoke, Lovegrove gestured again in welcome and Edward stepped over the threshold of Hackthwaite Hall, gripping his paltry, battered suitcase.

Lovegrove closed the door behind them. The winter was shut out but the stone-flagged hall was still cold. The place did not appear to be heated.

"Welcome to Hackthwaite," Lovegrove said. "I hope you enjoy your stay for as long as you are with us, and I hope you stay with us as long as it is pleasurable."

"I'm sure I shall. I'm keen as mustard to get cracking with your collection."

"Pah! the library can wait. A man needs sustenance first. Have you eaten breakfast?"

"No, it was too early at Knaresborough, nothing was open, but don't worry."

"I do worry. I can't let my new cataloguer perish before he starts. I shall ring to ask Mrs Edmundson to lay on an extra setting for breakfast. We weren't expecting you so early, but we always have plenty in."

"I'm sorry if I've put Mrs Edmundson out."

"Don't worry. She loves to feed visitors. We get so few. Come through to the dining room. There's coffee on the table. You'll be pleased that I haven't drunk it all yet."

"Oh, no, it's your coffee. I don't mind if you've drunk it."

"Well, I haven't. Follow me."

Antique statuary lined the back wall of the Entrance Hall with aspidistras and other plants in large terra-cotta pots standing here and there on the brown and tan tiles.

There were doors to the left and right of the hall, and directly ahead of them was a big wooden staircase that rose to a landing, and alongside the stairs, to the right, was another corridor that branched off into the hall itself.

Dr Lovegrove had already walked over to the door that led deeper into the house, and stood waiting.

Edward took a minute to orientate himself.

Behind him was the large front door, of oak, reinforced with black-painted iron studs and bars, probably Jacobean.

On either side of the large door were mullioned windows that let in sufficient daylight so that artificial lighting was not needed, though the room remained gloomy.

Edward saw electric lights on the walls and a large chandelier, also converted to electricity, hung in the centre.

He was not much of an expert on wiring, but the light switches and wiring looked to date from the 1930s.

"Chop chop! Come through," Lovegrove said.

"Of course. Sorry. I was just admiring your entrance hall."

"I'm glad you like it." Lovegrove took him along the passage to the right of the staircase and opened the first door on the right.

This led into the dining room, which was set for breakfast with two settings, both pristine, with linen and silver cutlery.

In the middle of the table was a silver bowl with white sugar lumps and silver tongs, a glass jar of Seville marmalade, a butter dish and silver jug containing milk. There were two porcelain coffee cups.

Lovegrove said, "You sit in Susannah's place. She won't be up for hours and the girl can bring fresh cutlery for her when she does get up."

Lovegrove walked to the wall and yanked a bell pull. "Still works, despite the age of the house" he said.

Edward heard a bell tinkle far away in the depths of the house.

He sat at Susannah's chair. He guessed she was Lovegrove's wife, or his daughter, or perhaps just a female friend. He was embarrassed to ask but wondered whether he should.

Lovegrove sat down opposite him. A minute later, a middle aged woman, dressed in an unfussy blue dress with an apron indicating she was probably the housekeeper, opened the door.

As she came in, Lovegrove said, "Good morning, Mrs Edmundson. This is our guest, Mr Edward Smith of Cambridge University. He has arrived earlier than anticipated. I hope that doesn't inconvenience you?"

"Not, at all doctor. You know we're ready at Hackthwaite for any eventuality. Mind you, it's a good job he did get here early. I just saw out of the kitchen window that it's started to snow again and the wireless say it's forecast heavy."

Lovegrove beamed at Edward. "Luck is with you, Mr Smith. This is Mrs Edmundson, a very good cook. Bacon, eggs, toast, coffee suit you?"

Mrs Edmundson added, "The eggs are our own. We can offer bacon and sausages, both local from Fletts at Hackthwaite village. Butter and milk are from Mr Harrison at Low Rigg. Even the bread's only come from the baker at Burton Leonard. Sometimes we bake, but not this week due to us being busier than usual."

"Sounds splendid," Edward said.

"It'll be ready in twenty minutes. In the meantime, do you need more coffee?"

Lovegrove said, "A fresh pot would be lovely."

"I'll send Ruby with it presently."

When she had gone, Edward said, "How many servants do you have here?"

"Two at the moment. We'll get you fixed up with breakfast, then show you to your room to leave your things and give yourself a quick wash, and then I hope you don't mind my getting straight to it. I've thought of nothing else since we agreed you would come."

"Of course, I'm as excited as you are, Dr Lovegrove. What a collection!"

Lovegrove said, "I've only been at Hackthwaite since just after the War. Before I came back to the UK in the 30s, I was in Hong Kong, but of course, I've been collecting for many years. I've amassed quite a few books," he laughed, "including some rare volumes. I was lucky to get Ripley's collection in 1929, which is the core of what I have."

"And it's never been catalogued?"

"No, not as a collection *per se*. It's a dreadful mess. I am afraid that I do not have a tidy mind, Mr Smith. I know where the books that I want are, but I am older now and won't be here forever, so I wanted them ship-shape. Susannah can decide what she wants to do with them when I'm gone — either keep them or sell them, though she does have quite an interest in the same kind of esoteric matters as I do."

"Well, women are on the up and up," Edward said. "These are egalitarian days, Dr Lovegrove."

"Harold, please, though not Harry, if you don't mind." Lovegrove laughed again.

A slim young girl, blonde-haired, rather pretty, about eighteen years old, came in with a pot of coffee. She put it down on the middle of the table and left without raising her eyes or speaking more than a mumble.

"These young girls are so shy," Lovegrove said, "Though she usually manages more words than that. I fear she may have been put off by your sudden appearance."

"Oh, I'm sorry."

Lovegrove waved away his concern. "She's a good girl. Just a little shy, and in awe of people from outside her limited rural circle. Coffee?"

Edward took his without milk. Raising the thin rim of the delicate cup to his lips, he sipped and said, "Yes, I'm looking forward in particular to the alchemical books. I think I said I had a special interest? My doctorate, not yet awarded, but awaited, was a review of Richards-Luard's work, most especially manuscript G.g. 1.8, which has some very interesting alchemical entries reminiscent of Nazari."

Lovegrove said, "I am familiar with Nazari, of course, and it was the subject of your doctorate that caused me to seek you out. You were recommended by a friend of mine at Caius."

"Oh? Who?"

Lovegrove gave a thin smile. "That would be indiscreet."

"Sorry, of course."

"By the way, how much time can you spare us?"

"Well, it's three weeks to Christmas. I was hoping to have it wrapped up by the twenty-third, and travel home on Christmas Eve."

"I hope that is possible."

At that moment, the door opened, and Edward Smith beheld the most beautiful young woman he had ever seen. She stood in the doorway, her fair skin giving off a light glow, her face painted with subtle pinks. Her gorgeous red hair fell in soft waves around her face, framing it perfectly. Her eyes were like precious emeralds that glittered from the inside, making it impossible not to look at her. And her lips, which were a soft shade of pale pink, were slightly parted, as if she were about to smile.

"Susannah, you're up early."

"I heard something, father, and I guessed our visitor had arrived, so I came down to see if he had."

Smith stood. He blushed bright red.

Lovegrove gestured. "Mr Smith, meet my daughter, Susannah, the rose that adorns Hackthwaite Hall."

Susannah walked gracefully to the table and sat. She did not offer to shake hands, which Edward was rather grateful for as his hand had become clammy on her appearance. Seated, she smiled at him, clear-eyed, intelligent and warm.

Edward sat down after Susannah, shifting his chair slightly away from her.

He scanned the table, seeing four chairs positioned around it but only two place settings.

"I'm afraid I've taken your seat," Edward said.

Resting her chin upon the back of her hand, Susannah reassured him, "Don't fret. Mrs. Edmundson will see to it that I am well cared for. Besides, losing my seat is a minor price to pay for the pleasure of meeting a new person."

Her eyes drifted to the window. "And it seems you may be here for a while. The snow appears to be coming down heavily."

Chapter 3

It was shy, young Ruby Mumberson that got the job of showing Edward Smith to the bedroom on the second floor, where he would stay while at Hackthwaite Hall.

She took him back to the Entrance Hall, and up the broad oak staircase. The stairs rose straight up from the entrance hall to a landing. When they arrived at the first landing, the window showed a sky full of falling snow. On either side of the landing, further risers of four steps led off to the wings. Ruby indicated for them to go left.

"Do you live in?" Smith said, following her.

"In the Hall? Yes, sir. Both Mrs Edmundson and me live here."

"I'll wager you're glad you don't have to walk home through all that after finishing work tonight."

"Yes, sir."

Edward always found it easier to talk to people who were younger than him and those that might be considered by less progressive people than he, as his social inferiors. He felt ordinary, working people didn't expect things from him, and that made him more comfortable.

She saw him glance at the falling snow. "It doesn't look like it's going to stop soon." Ruby said.

After that, she said barely anything, leaving them walking in awkward silence as they went up the stairs and along the landing until they arrived at the door of the room where Edward was to lodge.

As they'd walked saying nothing more, Edward revised his

opinion and considered perhaps it wasn't as easy as he'd thought to converse with *country* people.

"This is the blue room, sir," Ruby said, opening the door with outstretched arm.

Smith stepped inside, meagre case in hand.

Powder blue curtains, patterned after a William Morris design with cheerful yellow blossoms, hung at the window of Edward Smith's new bedroom. An antique four-poster bed, draped in coordinating blue fabric, stood at the centre of the room. At its feet lay an ornate oriental rug with azure and cerulean hues, depicting a blue sky and blue fountains contrasting with a mass of crimson and carmine roses that together portrayed a Sultan's perfumed garden.

"Bokhara?" Smith said.

"Sorry, sir?"

"The carpet. Just wondering where it was from."

Ruby looked baffled. "Harrogate, maybe?"

"Well, it's lovely."

The quilt on the bed was also blue. The water jug and basin for washing were Chinese willow pattern, blue, of course. Edward thought there was rather a lot of blue; it could give a chap a headache.

"The bathroom's down the hall. Will that be all, sir?"

He looked at Ruby. She really was quite pretty, in a village girl kind of way — wavy blonde hair, blue eyes (that matched the room), a hint of red flushing her cheeks, though that might be from shyness as much as her natural colour.

He supposed she was of Danish stock — many of these Yorkshire dales-folk were.

"I think that's it. Dr Lovegrove said to meet him in the library, didn't he, as we were going out?"

"Yes, sir."

"Trouble is, I don't know where that is."

"Do you want me to wait to show you, sir?"

She still hadn't met his eyes.

He said, "No, I'm sure you're very busy. I just need to wash my hands and face after the journey. If you tell me where it is, I'm sure to find it."

"Very well, sir. But the library is on the third floor, at the end of the east wing corridor. Go back to the landing, then up the opposite passage until you get to the east stairs. Go up and that's where it is."

"Capital. I'm sure I can find that from your splendid directions."

Ruby turned to leave.

"Thank you, by the way," Smith called to her retreating back.

He heard a muffled, "You're welcome, sir," as she spoke, not turning round, hurrying away.

Edward Smith put his case on the bed, then removed it, wondering if it was bad manners to place one's case on a made bed and concluding it was.

He wasn't much used to family ways. His mother and father had sent him home from Ceylon to school and he'd spent all the terms and most holidays back in the tropics with his family, and then later at Cambridge, living in college with other young men.

His mother and father had been rather distant, so families and women were both a mystery to him, and he'd had no sisters nor female friends. He'd had to learn the social rules of mixing with others laboriously rather than having had it taught him by his parents.

Edward took off his wire-rimmed spectacles and pulled a white cotton handkerchief from his pocket. He brought the glasses up to his mouth, breathed on them, and then rubbed away the mist. That was better. He could see better now. Then he went to the window.

By his reckoning, this window faced the middle of the house, while the one on the other side of the room looked over the pond to the front.

The window was a mosaic of small glass diamonds bedded in thick lead piping. He touched the glass, and it was cold to his fingertips.

This glass was old and not uniform, some thick and some thinner, with bubbles and infirmities showing it was a hundred years or more old.

Through it, even with his clean spectacles, he could only vaguely see the snow falling, and so he twisted the catch and pushed the window open, letting the frigid air in. He smelled the winter's cold, but stuck his head out anyway and peered down.

This window looked onto an open quadrangle in the centre of the house.

In the middle of the quadrangle was a surprisingly sizeable garden, about the size of a tennis court, and full of luxurious greenery.

The rest of the house was so neat that Edward would have expected this quadrangle garden to be tidy too, but not a bit of it. Plants grew in profusion, despite the season, and among them, wild-looking rose bushes, with arms of briar and thorns and still, even in December, red roses bloomed, heads down, heavy with snow, intoxicated and numbed by its chill touch.

Edward shivered and closed the window, pressing down the catch hard so the window would not come open again.

He thought a wash and brush up would do him good, so he left his blue room and wandered along the long, wood-panelled corridor until he found the bathroom, three doors after his own, on the opposite side. He presumed the other doors led to other guest rooms. He also presumed they were locked, but he didn't check.

After a wash and a comb of his hair, he tried to follow Ruby's directions to the library but found himself lost.

He was sure he was in the correct wing of the building, but these old buildings were so convoluted with accretions added on down the years. Edward remembered seeing the Victorian additions from outside and wondered if that was the part of the building he was in now.

He kept on going and found a pleasant-looking room in a tower. There was a stained-glass window of Victorian provenance that showed the front of the hall and the frozen pond with its mournful ducks. It was rather well done for Victorian glass.

Through the window he observed that the snow was indeed still falling, and more heavily. There were three or four inches down now and any marks left by his taxi, made not much more than an hour before, were obliterated beneath it.

The odd thought came to him that he had not just arrived, but that he had been here at Hackthwaite forever, but it was such a silly idea that he laughed and left the room and stepped back into the gloomy corridor.

He was still lost.

The walls of the passage were adorned with landscapes, but they were dismal and lacked any sense of reward or beauty. The oil paintings appeared neglected, as if they needed a thorough cleaning to restore their true essence. It was difficult to determine whether their sombreness was intentional or a consequence of neglect.

To the left of Edward, a door stood slightly ajar, beckoning him with a sliver of light seeping through. It wasn't the entrance to the library, yet something about the room beyond intrigued him. Perhaps it held a large window, offering a glimpse of the outside world. Curiosity stirred within him, urging him to explore further. And deep down, a part of him longed to witness the snow once more.

There was an ethereal quality to the snow, as if it possessed a heavenly power to cleanse and transform. It seemed to bring an end to the old and herald the arrival of the new, its pristine whiteness shimmering in silence.

Again, silly, poetic thoughts — very unlike him.

As Edward entered the room, he immediately recognised it as

the music room. The space was filled with an air of anticipation, caused by chairs arranged awaiting a grand concert. In the centre stood a majestic grand piano, its presence commanding attention.

Driven by curiosity, Edward circled around the piano, drawn to the open lid, revealing the intricate inner workings of the instrument. It was as if the piano itself yearned to be played, its keys awaiting the touch of skilled hands. On the thin arms of the music stand, a book of sheet music lay open, displaying Schumann's *Winterreise.*

Edward imagined the soul-stirring music that had filled the room. It was a scene that evoked a sense of both beauty and melancholy, as if the printed music whispered of emotions and stories yet to be told.

Edward could not play the piano, but like everyone who cannot play the piano, when they find one with no one around to hear, they plonk the keys. He reached out and played.

The notes rang out singly into the empty room.

He did not know the keys, and though he had piano lessons at school until they gave up on him, could not read music. Was that a C? A D?

He kept trying until he had a run of notes — a pleasant, if stilted, melody. He was quite lost in his playing.

"Ah, Mr Smith, you found the music room."

Dr Lovegrove stepped into the room. "I had wondered where you'd got to, but it seems you have been exploring."

Edward blushed, his cheeks turning rose red. "Oh, I'm so sorry. I shouldn't have. I was looking for the library and I got a bit lost."

Lovegrove frowned. "Did Ruby not wait to show you the way?"

"No, it's not her fault. I told her to go. She gave me good directions. Directions I was unfortunately too stupid to follow. I'm so sorry to intrude in your private rooms. I saw the door open, and I thought perhaps this was the right way."

"You thought it was the right way — really? But in any case, these rooms are not private. Do not apologise. I too am easily diverted by music. Do you play?"

Smith gave a brief laugh. "Erm, no. As you may have heard."

Lovegrove smiled. "I thought you might have been warming up. In any case, come and I will show you the library."

Chapter 4

Dr Lovegrove led Edward up the east stairs from the second floor to the third floor and then a short way to the library, which was the end room of that wing.

The library, once spacious, now felt cramped and constricted due to the overwhelming presence of bookshelves. These shelves lined the walls and obstructed the window, limiting the influx of natural light. Books occupied every available space, stacked on shelves, piled atop free-standing bookcases, and even adorning chairs. Towers of books precariously stood here and there on the floor, threatening to collapse at any moment.

"You see what I mean?" Dr Lovegrove said.

Even a cursory glance showed the books on the shelves were out of order. They were not arranged alphabetically by author, nor in subject order, and neither were they in order of date of publication

"You have a lot of books."

Lovegrove sighed. "It's an obsession, a love, a sign of a mind that wanders and never focuses, because here we have novels, and there poetry and there history and here, going down that shelf, Greek and Latin and Hebrew and here German philosophy and over yonder books on gardening and mineralogy and ornithology and physics and mathematics."

"Quite a breadth of information."

"By inclination, I am a jack of all trades and I cannot keep my mind from wandering and I cannot throw any of these books away, even though there are some here I first read when I was twenty, have never opened since and will never open again. But I cannot leave them and wherever I have moved in my life, I had these ungainly children lugged along with me in tea chests, upstairs, downstairs, across bridges, on ships —everywhere. It is a sickness, I know, but I am incurable."

"Is collecting books something to do with your work? Are you an academic?" While he said this, Edward gazed around, calculating how long it would take him to catalogue these unruly heaps, not to mention the truculent rows on the shelves. It would not be a short job.

"I should like to say, yes, but no. Some of them are related to my work, but very few."

"What is, or was, your line of business, Dr Lovegrove?" Edward felt he was teetering on the edge of impertinence, but Lovegrove did not show any sign of being offended.

"Mainly, I was an industrial chemist, but my wealth, such as it is, came from another hobby of mine."

"Fascinating, please do tell."

"Well, Mr Smith, are you familiar with automobiles?"

"Yes, of course. Not that I have one, but perhaps one day."

"Hmm. And you know that cars have wheels?"

"Yes."

"And that those metal wheels are ringed round with India-rubber tyres?"

"Yes, I've seen them." Edward said.

"And those tyres are full of air, and not to bore you further, the air is held in by a small valve, and I own the patent to that valve. I have invented many things, but that was by far the most lucrative. I have a patent for its design, though I have rival valve-makers who seek to encroach, both in the British Empire and its Dominions and the United States of America."

"Do you still work as a chemist?"

"Because of the patent, I have not needed to work for over a decade and instead devote myself to buying books."

"And reading them?"

"Absolutely! I don't judge a book by its cover, although I must admit that the occasional captivating cover has caught my attention. Nor do I acquire a book based on its monetary value or rarity. Instead, I value a book for the wisdom and knowledge it holds within its pages. Perhaps we have something in common in that."

Here Lovegrove grew silent, stroking his beard, as if thinking, then said, "It's as if I hope that in one of these books I will find the secret that will fill up the emptiness inside me."

Edward wasn't aware of an emptiness inside him, so they did not have that in common.

Lovegrove smiled. "Perhaps I have said too much. Now, you know all about me. You should tell me something of yourself, Mr Smith, and soon to be Dr Smith, if I heard you correctly at breakfast."

"I hope to be awarded my doctorate soon. I want to be a librarian. I like books. I would like to be paid by an employer to read and catalogue books."

Lovegrove smiled, "We might say that your mission is to bring order to the world's knowledge?"

"I am very interested in cataloguing systems, so I suppose we might say that." Edward pushed up his spectacles with his middle finger.

"Well, my library is a good place to start."

"If you don't mind, I propose to order them by subject matter and within subject matter by author, alphabetically. I would like to use the Dewey Decimal system, if you have no objection to Dewey. Some prefer James Duff Brown."

"Dewey or don't he? Being honest, I don't mind what system you use."

"Very droll, sir."

"I would suggest you start right away. I'll ask Ruby to bring you up a cup of tea in due course. Milk and sugar?"

"Ruby is the young blonde girl?"

"That's her."

"She seems very shy."

"Indeed, but that soon goes when she gets to know you."

Chapter 5

In fact, it was Mrs Edmundson who brought up his cup of tea and some biscuits: a fig roll, a gingersnap and a custard cream.

Putting down the tray, she said, "It's cold in here, Mr Smith, you'll catch your death. The fire's laid. Do you want me to light it?"

Edward said, truthfully, "I hadn't noticed the cold."

She smiled. "I see you're another one who gets drunk on books. You and the Doctor are well suited. I'll kindle the fire now for you, before you go blue and find yourself numb and unable to call for help."

He muttered, "I don't think it would come to that."

"You never know. It's a big old house and no one would hear you calling from up here."

She leant down and struck a match. It flared and she touched the yellow flame against a curl of newspaper. This newspaper roll lay at the bottom of the rest and on top of the tightly twisted papers was a wigwam of sticks and on top of those a bed of small coals. There was a coal scuttle and brass tongs and a shovel. She said, "You can add more coal to it once it catches."

"I thought young Ruby was the maid."

"Aye, she is, but I've got her preparing vegetables for dinner."

"Oh."

Mrs Edmundson wagged her finger. "Don't you go upsetting Ruby. Be careful, Mr Smith. Ruby's has had her heart broken once. Treat her like eggshells! Keep at arm's length!"

"No, I didn't mean that."

"In any case, I wanted a look at you myself."

"A look at me? What do you mean?"

"You're a serious one, aren't you? But I think you'll do. Looks like you'll have to, and we'll have to get used to you because I don't think you'll be leaving too soon. The snow's heavy. Not much is moving on the roads now."

She left Smith to his journey among the books. He found *The Observers' Book of Airplanes* (New York, 1942), next to Oswald Spengler's *Der Untergang des Abendlandes: [The Decline of the West]*, original German edition, (Munich, 1918), and that stuffed in next to a volume of poetry by Siegfried Sassoon.

The books were in complete disarray, lacking any semblance of order. It appeared as though someone had haphazardly grabbed armfuls of random volumes, as if in a hurried raid on a second-hand bookshop, and carelessly placed them on the shelves. And this was only for the books that had actually made it onto the shelves. The ones scattered on the floor were even more chaotic and disorganised.

In the library, the fire crackled, the room warmed: Edward Smith loosened his tie. A minute later, he even took off his jacket and rolled up his sleeves.

An old wooden ladder in one corner allowed access to the higher shelves. What treasures lurked up there? Edward sighed heavily. He had to be systematic, so he decided he would work from the bottom up and he left the ladder where it stood.

The books at hand level ranged from modern paperbacks by Daphne Du Maurier and Graham Greene and Victorian novels by Captain Marryat and Thomas Hardy to old, leather-bound books that emitted a musty scent as evidence of their age and the many hands that had held them over the years.

The books ranged from academic tomes on subjects such as psychology and zoology, to works of poetry, art, and nature. Along with these were also history books, detailing the grand events and discoveries of times long past.

Edward found *Historiae* by Tacitus, *The Histories* by Herodotus, *The Aeneid* by Virgil, *The Republic* by Plato as well as *Meditations* by Marcus Aurelius, all clumped together indicating at some point someone's mind, perhaps Lovegrove's in a fit of orderliness, had put some order on this collection. Unless of course, Lovegrove had bought them together as a job lot and they had not strayed from one another's side since.

He found some first editions that might be worth something: *Brave New World* by Aldous Huxley from 1932, and even *Ulysses* by James Joyce printed in Paris in 1922.

There were also a surprising number of books on the occult, including the *Corpus Hermeticum*, *The Kybalion*, and the *Hermetic Philosophy and Alchemy* by A. E. Waite.

He even found two by the infamous devil worshipper Aleister Crowley: *Magick in Theory and Practice* from 1929 and *Liber AL vel Legis* from 1909. However, these occult texts were placed alongside a book on flower arranging and another on Italian cookery. Edward realised that drawing conclusions about Dr Lovegrove's character based solely on these books would be unwise. Perhaps the doctor had merely acquired them out of curiosity, like a magpie attracted to shiny objects, without necessarily endorsing their contents.

Edward shifted a heap of books including one about tank warfare, another about vegetable gardening, and a novel by Kathryn Mansfield, and sat. It became clear that this work would take planning. He took out his pencil, his notepad and drew a diagram of the library and began to sketch out where each section would go: history, biography, poetry, philosophy, novels in English, novels in German, even novels in Russian. It appeared Dr Lovegrove was quite the linguist as well as the inventor.

And so the short December day passed. Ruby came up with some ham sandwiches and a bottle of Brown Ale at 1 p.m. but didn't say much though he tried to engage her in conversation. She came back with coal at 2 p.m. and filled the scuttle which Edward had half-emptied by stoking the fire.

At one point, while she stood by him, coal shovel in hand, her bare arm touched his. He jerked away. The touch of her silky skin was like sensual electricity. He stood, dumbfounded and rubbed his forearm where she had brushed against him.

"Do you need anything else, Mr Smith?" She said.

He found it difficult to respond to her as a sudden lightheadedness washed over him. The sensation was accompanied by a surge of heat, leaving him feeling rather peculiar. "No, thank you," he stammered.

"Another bottle of beer?"

"Maybe a cup of tea later."

And she was gone again. Despite the unsettling feelings that her touch had provoked, he wished she would have stayed longer.

He turned his mind to his work. The library was pleasantly warm now. He had begun to assess his monumental task. Initially daunting, he now found solace in the progress he had made. The vision of a completed library by Christmas, once deemed improbable, now seemed within reach.

As the clock struck four, Edward flicked on the electric light and the chandelier illuminated the shelves. The books he had catalogued, once in disarray, now seemed to stare at him with a mix of resignation and melancholy. It was as if they mourned the loss of their untidy state, reluctantly accepting the order that was being restored within their ranks.

Shortly after, he went to draw the curtain, but first he gazed out onto the white world outside, where sat the gardens of Hackthwaite Hall, giving way to trees and fields that climbed to the stark white hills and the sky. Then he closed the outside world out.

Turning his gaze to the room, there by his hand, and he didn't know why he hadn't seen it before, was an old volume. How had he missed it? It was octavo size, bound in leather. He picked it up. It was entitled:

"Discourses on the Essence of Poisons and Physic: Written by Cornelius Fludd, Esq."

He thought it must be quite rare. He turned the pages, and read:

The pharmakon is two-fac'd, like the Roman Janus. In the pharmakon is its secret, it is both deadly poyson and sublime healing. All ills are cur'd by this tincture, but those who are cur'd require the price of another. For this mystery, those who study, shall discover its truth.

Edward scratched his head. The words made little sense, but was typical of alchemical texts. He knew all too well that enigmatic language was the hallmark of such manuscripts. On reflection, there were a surprising number of books on alchemy, both ancient and modern: from *The Emerald Tablet of Hermes Trismegistus, The Alchemical Wedding of Christian Rosenkreutz* to a very recent copy of Carl Jung's *Psychology and Alchemy.*

Edward thought that while Lovegrove may have a background as an industrial chemist, his true passion lay in the realm of alchemy.

Chapter 6

After many hours cataloguing books, Edward's stomach started to rumble. He thought it was probably nearly time for dinner, so he made his way downstairs. Descending the stairs, his gaze was drawn towards the Dining Room door. Through the partially obstructed view, he caught sight of an intriguing scene unfolding. Two women were positioned near a stepladder, their hands gripping it firmly, while another woman stood atop the ladder.

They were decorating the house for Christmas, stringing up chains of coloured paper across the ceiling and draping the chandelier with gold tinsel. Edward recognised Ruby standing by the stepladders, holding the wooden legs to steady them, while Susannah, Dr Lovegrove's daughter, perched on the topmost step, stretching to stick the end of the red and yellow and blue paper chain into the corner of the room with a drawing pin.

Mrs Edmundson rummaged through a worn cardboard box

of Christmas decorations, her hands sifting and choosing baubles from Christmases past, and handing up the decorations as Susannah needed them. This she did with great care, and Edward wondered whether the decorations were heirlooms or valuable, though they looked ordinary enough.

The women turned and looked as he entered the room. Unaccountably, Ruby blushed, Mrs Edmundson nodded and went back to her sorting through the decorations, and Susannah Lovegrove smiled down at him, though, as she turned to smile, she overbalanced and the ladder rocked.

Instinctively, Ruby stretched out to steady Susannah, her hand jerking forward. Yet, just before making contact, Ruby abruptly pulled her hand back.

In the event, Susannah managed to readjust her balance, and the ladders settled once again, but it was no thanks to Ruby, and Edward wondered whether perhaps there was some secret dislike between the two women — certainly, it seemed Ruby would rather Susannah tip over than grab the ladder to help her.

As he watched, Susannah darted a glance at Ruby, and their eyes briefly met, as if they both realised they had almost given away something that should remain secret. Ruby blushed in response, and Susannah quickly glanced at Edward and smiled to bring things back to normal.

Edward had the feeling that something odd had just happened, even though he did not know what it was. He said, "Is it near dinner time?"

Susannah said, "I bet you're hungry. I should think it's hungry work trying to put some shape on daddy's books."

"I've been absorbed. I forgot the time."

Susannah turned back to Ruby, who carefully handed her a chain of coloured paper hoops. Once again, they were careful not to touch.

Susannah stretched until she pressed the drawing pin home and secured her paper chain. That was the second one up.

Looking beyond them, the dining room table was beautifully set, but Edward couldn't detect the aroma of cooking food. His heart fell. Then he remembered the kitchen was located on the other side of the large house, out of the range of his sense of smell.

Susannah said, "Daddy's in the sitting room, reading, if you want to join him and wait for dinner."

"Dinner won't be long," Mrs Edmundson said. "Half an hour. We always eat at six."

It was already dark outside and the red satin curtains of the dining room were already drawn to.

"The Sitting Room is where again, sorry?" Edward asked.

Susannah had descended, and Ruby moved the ladders to let her past. Susannah grinned and pointed. "Go there, to the entrance hall, then go through the doors straight ahead. The sitting room is the first door on the west wing corridor. Really, this house is too big for us. I don't know why Daddy bought it. Most of the rooms are unused."

Susannah's long auburn hair and striking green eyes were unnervingly attractive. Something about her exuded a fresh, invigorating scent, reminiscent of fresh leaves and fragrant flowers.

Edward's lack of experience with women heightened the unsettling effect of having three of them so close, though Mrs Edmundson, given her age, didn't count.

In contrast to the company of men that he was used to, these two women possessed a radiance that worked like gravity to draw his gaze and made him want to linger in their company.

Perhaps, he pondered, all women had always possessed this inherent power, but he simply hadn't recognised it.

Edward smiled foolishly and thought he would much rather stay here than talk about books with Dr Lovegrove. It would be very nice to watch these women, Susannah and Ruby, transform the house with tinsel and paper chains and dress it for the Season.

However, he was not so callow that he did not realise that lingering too long could be considered impolite. So, blushing, with a muttered, "Thank you," he turned and hurried off in the direction of the distant sitting room.

However, as he was walking away, he heard Susannah say, "He seems very nice," and Mrs Edmundson reply, "He's very shy. I imagine he's led a very cloistered life."

As it happened, Edward found the Sitting Room easily enough. It was just as he'd been directed. It faced the west side of the house, though by now the curtains were drawn here: full-drop gold satin drapes.

The room was conventionally appointed — a gilt mirror over the marble fireplace where a coal fire burned. There were five or six armchairs, a coffee table, a sofa, and in an armchair, reading Country Life, sat Dr Lovegrove.

The Sitting Room had already received the ministrations of the three women and was adorned for the Christmas. A six foot Christmas Tree stood in the corner, replete with coloured glass baubles, green branches wrapped in silver tinsel like a society lady wearing a stole, garlanded with coloured lights that were threaded among its dark, spiky branches, glittering red, yellow and blue.

Dr Lovegrove sat forward. "Edward! Come in and sit down, old chap."

Edward looked from chair to chair.

Lovegrove pointed. "Here, near me.." He patted the arm of the chair next to his. "Do sit, dear boy. Give me a report on your progress at ordering the chaos I bequeathed you. Would you like a sherry?"

Edward nodded and stood as Dr Lovegrove got up and stepped over to the drinks table upon which stood several cut-glass decanters, one of them apparently containing sherry.

Seeing Lovegrove do it himself, rather than ring for a servant to pour the drinks, Edward stuttered, "I.. I didn't mean to put you to any trouble, Dr Lovegrove."

"Nonsense, old fellow, you're my guest and I've got you

working hard for my benefit. The least I can do is fetch you a sherry."

Dr Lovegrove had previously said that Edward should call him Harold, but it felt too familiar. How should he address him then — doctor? That seemed safest.

Lovegrove handed Edward, who was still standing, the sherry glass, and both men sat.

"Dinner will be beef, I should say." Dr Lovegrove said. "It's Thursday, so we generally have beef, carrots and potatoes. Mrs Edmundson occasionally throws me with Cottage Pie on a Thursday, though Cottage Pie is *usually* Monday and fish pie is Friday. Do you like fish pie, by the way, Edward?"

"Not so much, sir, no."

Sir? He'd thought he was going to call Lovegrove, 'doctor'. How did 'sir' come out of his mouth?

Lovegrove seemed not to notice.

"Ah well, we will have to see if we can deflect Mrs Edmundson from her iron routine for Friday. I will ask Susannah to make discreet suggestions. What would you like instead?"

"Erm, anything, really."

"Anything except fish pie, of course."

"No, not fish pie. Though I could try it."

"Thought you didn't like it?"

"I don't think I do."

"Then why try it?"

Edward cleared his throat. He noticed his hands were trembling and his mouth unaccountably dry. "I'm not sure."

"So not fish pie, nor fish of any kind, I should think."

"No, I'm not a fish lover."

"I'd suggest sausages."

"Sausages would be an excellent alternative."

"Good! Now, the books?"

"Well, Professor, I've got a plan and I've made a start. Would you like to see my sketch of how I foresee the new arrangement?"

"Of course. Very interested."

Lovegrove pulled the coffee table closer between the two men's chairs. The carriage clock on the mantelpiece chimed the quarter hour. They studied Edward's sketch of the new shelving arrangements under the Dewey Decimal System.

Lovegrove said, "Hmm. I didn't realise I had so many books on the occult."

"You have quite a few, sir."

Lovegrove laughed. "I see that from the space you've allocated."

"Primarily, alchemy."

"Ah, well, that makes me feel slightly better. Alchemy is not strictly occult. Some famous scientists were alchemists — notably Isaac Newton."

"I would have to disagree respectfully. Though now considered merely a forerunner of chemistry, in general, alchemists hid their practice to avoid persecution by the Church. Therefore, it was occult."

Lovegrove grinned. "I retract what I said and agree with you. Alchemy was, and is, of course, an occult practice where 'occult' simply means hidden."

"Of course."

Lovegrove continued. "And we must hide our work from the eyes of those who would misconstrue it and see it as something darker than it really is." He looked deliberately at Edward. "And from those who simply do not have the understanding to appreciate the benefits it can bring."

The benefits the long-debunked quasi-scientific, pseudo-science of alchemy could bring — what on earth did the man mean?

Dr. Lovegrove contemplated Edward, gently stroking his beard. "You may know that for the alchemist, prayer held as much importance as the alembic itself. They believed their retorts and equipment could not function without spiritual devotion to the

Great Work."

Edward nodded politely. When he spoke, his voice was skeptical. "Yes, indeed, sir. But in that belief, they were mistaken. Surely, you agree?"

A soft chuckle escaped Lovegrove's lips. "The alchemists possessed a peculiar, but significant, notion that the prime materials they worked with held a spark of life, an awareness. They believed these substances were sentient, collaborating with them in their experiments."

Edward's brow furrowed. "But that is pure nonsense. Merely fanciful musings. Of course, if you're Roman Catholics…"

He realised the audacity of what he had said, and his mouth clenched tightly shut. Edward had never stayed with a Catholic family, and he feared he had crossed an unspoken boundary. Who knew what odd, superstitious beliefs Catholics had?

Unfazed by Edward's momentary discomfort, Lovegrove smiled. "No, we are not Catholic, though we do not fit neatly into the Protestant category, either. We exist in a space that transcends those traditional boundaries."

"You are a free thinker, then? Or Jewish?"

His anxiety escalated. If he already felt bewildered by Catholics, unsure of the right words and behaviours, how could he navigate the customs and sensitivities of a Jewish household without causing offence?

"Jewish? Not as such. Keep fishing, you'll find it in the end."

Edward's face burned red. "I'm sorry, sir. I was being impertinent."

"You were being curious. I can always forgive an enquiring mind for any social faux pas." He sipped his sherry while Edward sat, feeling the heat rise in his cheeks.

"You know there are different types of alchemy?" Lovegrove said.

"You mean Chinese alchemy and Arabic alchemy? I know a little about those."

"Of course, those are different, though remarkably similar in some senses too to European alchemy, but no, I meant *mineral* alchemy versus *vegetal* alchemy. Mineral alchemy is most famous, of course.."

Edward said, "All that silliness about transmuting lead into gold, et cetera."

"Yes, yes — creating the philosopher's stone, the elixir of life. But what can be achieved through minerals can also be achieved through plants."

Edward frowned. His intellectual curiosity displacing his embarrassment for the man. "Really? So if the goal is to turn lead into gold in traditional alchemy, what is the goal state for vegetal alchemy?"

"Well, the ultimate goal remains the same—immortality. But on the path to that lofty aspiration, consider the possibility of discovering a process, or a flower of that process, capable of healing all ills. Imagine a cure for every disease, no matter how profound. Would that not warrant years, even a lifetime, of study?" Lovegrove smiled indulgently. "But tell me, Edward, are you truly interested in these ramblings of an old man?"

Edward nodded politely. "All new knowledge is nourishment to me. Please go on."

At that moment, Ruby knocked on the door of the Sitting Room. "Dinner's ready, Dr Lovegrove, Mr Smith."

Lovegrove rose from his seat, comforting Edward with a reassuring remark. "Fear not, Edward. The secrets of the ages can wait until after dinner, saved for when we can savour them alongside a glass of port."

Chapter 7

The dinner table had four chairs, but was only set with three places. The tablecloth was of fine white linen, Edward could see the quality of it. Each place had three crystal glasses: a flute for white wine, a goblet for red wine and a third, smaller glass for a dessert wine.

Sterling silver cutlery flanked the place setting: a soup spoon, a small knife and a fork, and inside those a larger knife and fork, while, at the top, like a lintel bridging two uprights at Stonehenge, lay a dessert spoon.

Ruby Mumberson was the waitress, shuffling in and out of the room, while out of sight in the kitchen, Mrs Edmundson cooked.

Edward sat at his place, opposite the empty chair, as directed by Lovegrove.

Susannah looked ravishing. She wore a cerise evening gown that hung loosely off her shoulders, and her vibrant auburn hair tumbled around her neckline like tongues of flame. Her emerald eyes shone with a secret amusement as they regarded Edward, though he was unaware of what he had done to warrant such interest from her. It was almost as if she knew something about him that he himself did not suspect.

Ruby served the soup from a tureen — cream of chicken soup with crusty farmhouse bread. Edward was hungry but tried to eat slowly and politely while Susannah provided him with small snippets of conversation about their neighbourhood.

"When did you get back to Cambridge?" Lovegrove said.

Edward was puzzled. "Get back?"

"I presume you served, given your age. Unless you were excused for ill-health?"

Edward shook his head. "Ah, I see what you mean. No, I'm fully fit."

"Good!" Susannah said, as if he had just answered a question correctly in a job interview.

He continued, as they had asked him the question. "I was in Burma. I was with the Dorsetshire Regiment. My family settled in Bridport after coming back from Ceylon, so I joined my county regiment."

"With Slim?"

"Yes."

"Were you at Kohima?"

Edward sipped his soup, then nodded. "I was. And when it was all over, I left the jungle and the excitement…"

"And the death," Susannah said.

"Of course. And the death. And came back to be a librarian."

"A rather qualified librarian — an academic. And your plans?"

Edward shrugged. "I'd rather like to stay at Cambridge and look after one of the college libraries."

"Will that be that possible?"

"Yes, it's possible. I think that's what I shall end up doing."

"Don't you think you'll get bored?" Susannah said.

"I shouldn't think so. I love cataloguing books."

"We have books here," Susannah said. "You might even decide to stay with us."

Lovegrove laughed. "Don't mind her. My daughter is joking. However, I knew I had the right man for the job."

Edward knew it was normal to ask about the other person once they'd asked about you, so he began, "And yourselves? Were you here during the war — at Hackthwaite?"

"No," Lovegrove said, "I've only been here a few years. I was in London initially until September 1940, then when that became rather hairy, I must admit, discretion became the better part of valour and I retreated to Somerset for the remainder, and when I was tired of Glastonbury, up here to Yorkshire."

"And where did you spend the war, Susannah?" Edward asked.

Lovegrove interrupted before Susannah could speak. "She was with me. When I say 'I', that is merely a habit formed from my self-preoccupation. I mean 'we', of course."

Soup finished, Ruby cleared away and then brought beef braised in red wine gravy with mashed potatoes, carrots and brussel sprouts.

The conversation paused briefly as they all enjoyed the dinner.

"And how do you fill your time, Susannah?" Edward said. He realised he was talking to her more than to Lovegrove. He didn't like to meet her gaze, it was too unsettling. It made him feel strange, like he was a bottle of Champagne, full of bubbles held in place by a cork.

She didn't answer immediately. He glanced up at her. She was staring at him, still amused. Her rapt attention made him rather uneasy, though strangely thrilled. He felt himself blushing again.

"I read," she said.

"I approve of that." He felt bolder. The wine helped. "Anything else?"

"I garden."

He raised his eyebrows. "Garden? In December. I know little about gardening, but I thought the earth slept through the winter and there wasn't much to do."

"Our garden's rather special." She raised her wineglass to her lips and sipped the claret. "It's somewhat exotic."

"I didn't think Yorkshire folk approved of the exotic."

She said, "I'm not a typical Yorkshire person. I don't have any Yorkshire blood, as such. "

"Oh, and where do your kin hail from?'

"I have a smidgeon of Yorkshire blood," Lovegrove said.

Lovegrove was as if he had been observing the conversation between the two young ones, studying their budding relationship. He continued, "Yes, my grandfather was a Moorcock — from Hawes."

Edward said, "Then you must have a little Yorkshire blood, Susannah."

She laughed. "I suppose I must. Though I don't much like the weather here. I'm a flower that prefers the sun and heat."

"Not that we get much of that here at this time of year," Lovegrove said.

They finished the beef and Ruby brought the pudding, which was Eton Mess, with freshly whipped cream.

After dinner, they all three retired to the Sitting Room where Edward had previously been with Dr Lovegrove. Susannah sat next to her father on the sofa. Despite their obviously good relationship, she left space between the two of them.

As the men took sips of port, Susannah took the cup of coffee that Ruby brought in for her. After placing the cup down, Ruby addressed Dr. Lovegrove. "Will that be all, Dr. Lovegrove?"

Lovegrove said, "Of course, and thank you both for giving us such a lovely meal."

"Thank you. That being all, I shall tell Mrs Edmundson we're done. I will turn off the lights in the other rooms, and if it's just as well with you, go to bed."

"Of course, Ruby. We'll see you in the morning, then."

"Yes, Dr Lovegrove. Goodnight, Miss Susannah. Goodnight, Mr Smith."

Before she left the room, Ruby gave Edward a lingering glance. He thought she was pretty, but in a far less sophisticated way than Susannah.

Why were these women paying such attention to him? He'd never been the focus of female interest in his life.

On reflection, he thought it must because young men were rare visitors to Hackthwaite Hall. Heaven knows, he might be the first for months and months. Years even.

Ruby left. Lovegrove shifted back in his seat. He was smiling. "And now I think it's time I told you the tale of the ghost of Hackthwaite Hall."

"Hackthwaite has a ghost?"

"You don't believe in alchemy, so I take it you don't believe in ghosts."

"You're correct; I don't, but that doesn't mean I don't like ghost stories. I'm fond of M. R. James. Please tell me the tale of the ghost." Wine and port made Edward feel rather amenable. It helped with his anxiety of not knowing what to say to people.

Lovegrove paused, looking at his hands like an actor preparing to deliver his lines, then began, "Though the house is much older — going back to medieval times, it was remodelled in the seventeenth century by a man called Cornelius Fludd? Have you heard of him?"

"I think I saw one of his books in your collection. But, otherwise, no."

"He was one of those who signed the death warrant of King Charles I, but he was a well-renowned natural scientist and alchemist. His alchemical affairs were kept secret at that time — 'occult', you might say, but the scholar Frank Sherwood-Taylor has shown that Fludd was a keen and committed alchemist. I must admit it is me who adds Fludd to this ghost story. The traditional tale doesn't mention him, but I believe the ghost and Fludd are closely linked."

While still listening to Lovegrove, Edward's gaze shifted slyly from his port to Susannah. Her green eyes, sparkling with an undisclosed intrigue, remained fixed on him as she sipped her coffee. Her gaze had an enigmatic quality to it, but its full mystery was hidden behind the delicate porcelain rim of her cup.

Lovegrove continued with the ghost story. "It is said that many centuries ago, a Lord of Hackthwaite dabbled in the dark arts and that he was a bachelor with no children, so his considerable fortune was spent on his experiments with magic. This is a memory of Cornelius Fludd, I believe."

"It would make sense," Edward said, "if any of it were true."

Lovegrove smiled. "If any of it were true, indeed, but bear with me. It is said that in his dark summonings, this lord created an elemental creature from flowers and roots and imbued it with life. He raised the creature and taught it on a daily basis, and eventually, it took the form of a beautiful young woman and the sorcerous lord claimed it as his daughter."

Susannah caught Edward's eye. The ghost story was an obvious allusion to her and her father. He gave her a shy smile, and she smiled back at him, but always with that knowing behind her eyes. Were she and Lovegrove teasing him in ways he didn't realise?

Lovegrove continued, "Yes, this young and beautiful creature became the delight and treasure of the old magician."

"The great tragedy, however, was that she could never leave the house where he had produced her in his laboratory below stairs because of the precarious nature of the magic that had created her."

"And is there such a laboratory?" Edward said.

"Oh, yes. Though it is now my laboratory."

"Perhaps it's a true story after all, then, " Edward said, finding himself smiling.

Lovegrove wagged his finger. "If you believe country superstitions, which of course, Edward, you do not."

"I did not before you began, and I still do not, even though you tell the story well."

"The vegetal spirit loved the garden best, but as it could not leave the walls of the house, the magician, whom we will call Cornelius Fludd, created a garden for her in the central courtyard, and there she loved to stay, tending the plants."

"But! There was a young servant, a gardener who occasionally came in to tend the quadrangle garden and Fludd had not anticipated that his young flower woman would have desires like any other young woman, and she fell in love with this youth, and he with her, for she was very beautiful and full of life."

Edward sipped his port. "Don't tell me — they tried to elope, and he killed the boy?"

"Edward!" Susannah hissed. "You're spoiling the story!" She was laughing though.

Lovegrove said, "Well, you're right; they tried to elope but news of this plan came to Fludd's ears from another servant, for it amused him to favour first one servant then another and so to pit them against each other."

"Oh, dear. What an unpleasant chap."

Susannah laughed. "Yes, that's what I think, too. What a horrible old man!"

Lovegrove shot his daughter a glance that Edward did not understand and she shrugged and grinned and made a moue of mock shame, though it did not seem she really was shamed, because when her father looked away, she winked at Edward as if to say: 'we two at least are on the same page.'

Lovegrove continued, "And Cornelius Fludd intercepted the young man and killed him and buried him in his beloved rose garden in the quadrangle, where he became blood and bone meal for the flowers."

"How dreadful!" Edward said. He smiled because he did not believe a word of this tale and thought that Lovegrove had made it up on the spot. "And this unfortunate boy is the ghost of Hackthwaite Hall?"

"Indeed, he is. He is said to be the source of the strange noises, the creakings and groanings in the night and the cause of doors opening and closing on their own."

"And what happened to the daughter — the flower girl? Did Fludd kill his own creation in a fit of rage at her disobedience to him?"

Lovegrove smiled and shook his head. "Oh, no."

"Then what happened to her? Did she pine away and die from a broken heart once her father killed her beloved?"

Lovegrove shook his head again. "Oh, no."

"Then what?"

Lovegrove said, "She still lives."

"Still lives! And there your story falls apart. That was hundreds of years ago. Nothing lives that long."

"The Rose Child did. If you remember, in the story, she was not born of woman, but was created through plant alchemy. As she was not naturally born, she can not naturally die."

"Very interesting." Edward finished his port with a final swig. The grandfather clock struck ten.

Dr Lovegrove stretched. "I'm afraid I'm a boring old coot. It's my bedtime."

"He gets up terribly early to do his exercises,' Susannah said. "But I'm not tired. Will you stay down here with me, Edward? You can tell me all about Cambridge. I've never been."

He felt awkward at the thought of sitting here alone with her. "Oh, I don't know. I've had rather a long day myself," Edward said. "I'm sure I'll sleep like a log." Then he stood. "If you'll excuse me."

"Oh, you're both so boring!" Susannah said.

Edward stood. "Good night both. See you tomorrow."

Dr Lovegrove still sat in his chair. "I hope the ghost boy doesn't keep you awake."

Chapter 8

Edward performed his nightly ritual of washing his hands and face before changing into his pyjamas and slipping into bed. Exhaustion quickly overtook him, and he fell into a deep sleep.

However, he forgot to draw his bedroom curtains.

In the dead of night, when silence possessed the house, Edward jolted awake. The brilliance of the midwinter moon poured through the bedroom window, spilling through the open curtain, casting a silver glow over the room, illuminating the blue quilt, the Persian rug and the antique bed. Waking suddenly, the dazzling light disoriented and startled him.

He remembered hearing that those who awaken under the moon's pale gaze succumb to madness. Dazed, rather than rationally dismissing this silly idea, he fell prey to unreason, which after all is the domain of the Moon, and panic gripped him.

He jumped up and out of bed, hardly knowing where he was. That sobered him somewhat. The floor was cold under his feet. He stepped over to the window and yanked the curtains shut, blocking out the baleful moonlight.

He began to regain his composure, rationality now prevailing.

He was a man of reason, after all. It was simply moonlight.

Still discomfited, he surveyed his surroundings, slowly piecing together his memories: the icy journey to Hackthwaite, the library and its books, Dr. Lovegrove, and his captivating daughter; they all came flooding back to him.

Edward reached for his watch on the bedside table. By its glowing hands, he saw it was a quarter to three. As if to emphasise the lateness of the hour, a distant clock chimed, its echoes resonating through the depths of Hackthwaite Hall.

His eyes shifted towards the window, the curtains now drawn. He sighed. He couldn't allow a foolish fear of moonlight to dominate him. Still, he was reluctant to pull back the curtains and allow in that dreadful, cold glare.

But he must. It was simple psychology. He must face his fears, like getting back on the horse that threw you, so he climbed out of bed. Off the rug, the floorboards chilled his bare feet and he hopped rather than walked to the window.

There he slowly drew back the curtain.

See! That wasn't too bad.

Through the frosted glass, he gazed out onto the moonlit landscape. The sight that greeted him was of the rose garden blanketed in snow.

The pathways were covered with a glistening layer of white, while the vibrant red roses, seemingly unaffected by the winter's chill, swayed under the weight of delicate snowflakes. Bathed in ethereal moonlight, they appeared divine, red and white, a surreal sight to behold.

Suddenly, a figure moving amidst the bushes, tending to the flowers, drew his attention. Who was out there in such cold, at such a time of night?

Edward's heart skipped a beat as he remembered the ghostly boy, buried in the Rose Garden—the spirit of Hackthwaite. But it wasn't the boy at all; it was a woman. In the shadow it was hard to tell who she was. She was young and slim, but the moonlight stole all shades of colour so it was impossible to tell what hue her hair was. It looked merely dark.

More disconcertingly, the woman wore a nightgown, translucent in the moonlight. Though the ghostly moonlight shone on her, her tumbled locks hid her face, but even half seen, she was a vision of a lunary paradise, an angel of the dark hours of night.

It is likely that seeing any young woman in a nightdress might have stirred Edward's blood in ways for which his early life and education among chaste and book-preoccupied men had not prepared him.

But there was something more to the thrill he felt than the merely sensual. He knew the word numinous but had never applied it to any inner state he felt, mainly because he had never had such feelings. But this was what he felt now.

The girl emerged fully from the shadows, engrossed in her task of cutting and collecting flower heads. Edward could not tear his gaze away. He was filled with curiosity and trepidation. What could she be doing in the garden at such a late hour on a freezing December night?

But before he could think any further, she seemed to know he was there. She raised her head and met his eyes through the cold glass.

Her skin shone as white as the glistening snow, and though all other colour was bleached from that scene of snow-white and ink-black, the roses she held somehow kept their colour. They glowed vibrant red, a red of the same shade as blood.

And here was a strange thing — it was not so much that the girl's hands clutched the roses, as it was that roses held her hands, petals flowering around her, briars branched to create a flowery cage so that, as he looked, the flowers seemed to extend all about her and she and the roses were one.

Standing with the roses in her delicate, moon-kissed hands, standing in the snowy garden, staring up at him, she smiled.

Edward backed away from the window, embarrassed that he had been seen — an intruder stumbling across a private interlude. But he did not retreat to bed, for as much as he was mortified that he had been caught looking, he could not leave the scene and he went back to the window again, but this time, when he looked, she was gone.

Chapter 9

Edward lay awake for what seemed hours after seeing the woman in the rose garden. Was it Ruby, or could it have been Susannah? Or was there a possibility of a third presence—a manifestation of the fabled Rose Child described in Lovegrove's eerie tale?

Such thoughts run riot during the hours of darkness when the rationality of the sun is eclipsed by the madness of the moon.

He reasoned it must be one of either Ruby or Susannah, but what either would be doing out there in that cold at that time of night was inexplicable.

Edward lay staring at the ceiling. How long he lay he couldn't tell because minutes were hours, and hours seemed like minutes, but at some point he slept, and in this sleep, he stumbled into a deep, dark, and ominous dream where a nameless, crawling figure of briars and thorns pursued him through the passages and cellars of Hackthwaite Hall.

This sleep was not restful, and he woke late and still tired. Realising he was late, he washed and dressed and hurried down the wooden staircase, getting momentarily lost but then finding the Dining Room. By the time he got there, the Dining Room was empty.

A spot of mustard on the otherwise pristine linen tablecloth indicated somebody had already breakfasted. One place setting remained untouched of the three set and Edward guessed that Susannah and Dr Lovegrove were now about their daily business, whatever that might be.

At first, Edward did not sit. He stood, stared at the table and didn't know what to do. He was still disturbed by seeing the woman in the Rose Garden the previous night and then the horrible dream of the creeping creature of thorns and briars that hunted him down the corridors of Hackthwaite Hall.

He walked to the window. Looking out, he saw the morning was bright with cold white clouds and cold white snow. Snow was no longer falling, but what had fallen had frozen during the night creating a frigid cloth over all the garden, hanging in heavy white blankets in the trees, and locking the pond with its door of ice.

No one came. Edward wondered what he did now. There must be a bell-pull to call the servants, but he couldn't see it. He bit his lip, awkwardly looking at the table, glancing at the door, gazing back at the table, but still not sitting, and then blonde-haired Ruby arrived with a plate.

"Breakfast, sir," Ruby said, and lifted the napkin with her left hand from the centre of the place-setting so she could put down his white breakfast plate with her right. Eggs nestled by bacon beside mushrooms next to twin sausages and above them, a fried tomato.

Edward hurried to the table and sat down.

"Would you prefer tea or coffee sir? And toast?"

"Tea, please and toast would be splendid."

Yes, she was perhaps nineteen, he thought. He was only twenty-five. And indeed, she was 'bonny', as he guessed they said up here.

"Sorry to be late," he said. "Dr Lovegrove and Susannah have been and gone, I guess."

"Yes, sir."

He tilted his head. "What have they gone off to do?"

"I don't know, sir. You'd have to ask them that yourself, sir."

"Of course, sorry." He hesitated. He didn't know if it was manners to start his breakfast while Ruby still stood there. She wasn't quite a servant, not like the servants in his parents' house in Ceylon. And she showed no sign of leaving so he made conversation.

When he was a boy, he had been so unsure of how to behave in conversations that he'd memorised lists of polite questions and rehearsed them in front of a mirror. He was older now and more confident, but still struggled finding things to say that felt easy and natural.

He cleared his throat. "Are there only you and Mrs Edmundson here?"

"Working here? Yes, sir. Now."

"Now? Were there more staff before? It does seem a big house for two of you to manage."

"We used to have a gardener, Ned."

"I suppose he left." Edward frowned. That sounded rude — 'left'. Perhaps he should have said 'departed' but that sounded unnatural. He ploughed on. "Still, I don't suppose there's much to do for a gardener in the winter."

"He's dead," she said.

He hadn't been expecting that. People did die, of course — in the War, of diseases, of old age though Ned couldn't have been so old. How awkward. "Oh, goodness," he said. "I'm sorry to hear that. When did that happen?"

He was asking questions he didn't really want to ask, but he had no idea how to stop the conversation, other than simply shutting up and that would be even more strained.

"Last summer," she said.

"I'm very sorry. I suppose he was a local lad so you must have known him well — not like a colleague in a city job, where you might not know them very well at all."

He was full aware he was talking nonsensical and inappropriate tosh.

She seemed to want to talk about him. "He was my sweetheart. We would have been married. That's what we hoped."

He probably didn't die of old age then, if he was her sweetheart and she was only nineteen or so.

It was hard to read her expression. Probably that meant she

was about to cry, which was understandable now she'd been reminded of her late lover.

Crying. What should he do? Should he offer her a handkerchief? He had one in his pocket. He went to reach for it and then stopped in case it wasn't the right thing to do.

In all his previous life, his emotions had been subdued: not spoken about at all at home, covered up with male brusqueness at school and university and of course in the army, where death became a brutal joke — the blacker the joke, the funnier and easier to process.

He said, "I can't imagine how you feel." He'd heard people say that in similar situations, but it was true. Imagination was not his strong point.

"They say that the Lord giveth and the Lord taketh away, Mr Smith."

He felt relieved. She had come to terms with it. He even smiled. "They do say that, Ruby. I hope your Faith gives you comfort."

"I'll fetch you your tea and toast." She said, "Tuck in, you don't want it to be getting cold."

Chapter 10

Ruby left. When she'd gone, Edward thought there really was something rather special about her. Even though she had almost cried, she'd been so self-possessed and calm. She'd had no education and socially she was just a maid - if any modern person even noticed such things, but for all that, she was rather charming.

He ate his breakfast and enjoyed it.

Ruby came in again and brought him tea and toast, smiling now. His mouth was full, so he didn't converse, but what lovely golden hair she had. Toast delivered, she left the room.

After he'd completely finished his breakfast, Edward sat and took off his spectacles, polishing them on his handkerchief. They never seemed to remain clean for long.

With no sign of Ruby returning to clear the plates, something he had to admit he'd hoped would happen, he stood and left the Dining Room.

Edward had been up and down to the Library a few times now, but still was not wholly confident of the way. He knew he had to go up the main staircase and then turn left, was it?

He was his way along the quiet corridor, when he heard the sound of people talking. How strange to hear people in this empty old house, where so many rooms were vacant. He didn't know where Dr Lovegrove and Susannah went during the day but it must be them talking of course.

Edward knew walls and doors cut out all the high frequencies, so all he heard was the lower muffled tones of a man. The higher tones of a woman, and a young woman at that, were harder to hear.

They were in the room with the piano he'd stumbled across before. He was outside the door. He remembered the way to the library from here, but still he hesitated.

It was Dr Lovegrove and Susannah, and they were talking quite earnestly about something — it wasn't just a chit chat about the weather. From the tone if it, there seemed to be something wrong.

He heard Susannah say, "He's very slow. He's not taken the bait yet."

Then Lovegrove replied. "There's time, my dear. Don't be so impatient."

"As you say, daddy. But I can't help but want it to work."

Edward had the idea they were talking about him. Then he checked himself — listening outside doors was not the act of a gentleman. He hurried on to the Library.

He found the stairs to the third floor and then at the top, headed confidently to the library door.

The library hearth had been cleaned and had the makings of a new fire in it — twisted curls of newspaper, kindling wood and coal with more coal in the scuttle.

He took the box of long cook's matches and lit the newspaper twist, watching the blue and yellow flame curl and consume, transforming it to the flimsiest black and then to ash and then to smoke. Such is the process of combustion, he thought, a kind of alchemy where one thing feeds another but in doing so is utterly changed.

There he went — his mind running on alchemy again! It was all alchemy here. Even his dream could be considered alchemical.

After feeling the fire's warmth radiate out into the air of that old room and rubbing his hands in front of it, Edward raised himself from kneeling and set about work.

Today, he had set himself the task of getting some kind of shape on the modern novels: Hemingway, D H Lawrence, Somerset Maugham, Hugh Walpole et cetera, et cetera.

The Library warmed quickly. He began his labour. At times, as he worked, he glanced out of the window at the frozen scene to the house's east side and away over woods and fields to the bare fells beyond. It was quite a grim landscape, but rather magnificent in its grimness.

The exercise of moving armfuls of books in the warm room made him sweat, and he took off his jacket and rolled up his sleeves.

Ruby arrived with a tray of tea around 11:30. He was pleased to see her.

She laughed when she saw him with his sleeves rolled up. "Who'd have thought books were so physically demanding," she said.

"Well, there *are* a lot of them!"

"There are indeed, Mr Smith." He put down the tray. "Here's some tea. Milk, no sugar — that's right, isn't it? And a piece of Mrs Edmundson's Victoria sponge."

"Thank you, Ruby."

She smiled him.

"I suppose I seem quite eccentric to you, do I?" he said.

She shook her head. "I'd be hard put to say what was eccentric about a Cambridge Scholar. I haven't met enough of them to know what's normal for them."

"The doctor's an educated man though."

"The doctor's the doctor, and there's no one like him. Just shout if you need anything more."

"You won't hear me from up here."

She grinned. "The walls have ears."

"What?" he began.

"There's a bell-pull over there." She pointed.

"Ah, yes. Sorry, I didn't see that."

"Too busy with your books, I'd say."

"Something like that. Bye, Ruby. I'll see you later, I suppose?"

"I should think so, Mr Smith."

"Edward, please."

"Well, I don't know if it's correct I should be calling you by your first name. You being a scholar from away and me a house servant."

"I don't mind. I'm a Socialist."

"A Socialist?" She laughed out loud and left.

Edward banked up the fire, sat in an armchair that was now clear of books, sipped the tea and munched Mrs Edmundson's delicious Victoria sponge cake. As he sipped, he surveyed his work. A little was done, much more was to do.

He drained his teacup, then went to look at more novels, putting the last of the cake in his mouth. So many novels! Surely the man couldn't have read them all? But some were old editions, so if he'd kept every book he'd ever bought over the past thirty years, then perhaps Dr Lovegrove had indeed read them all.

With six books under the crook of his left arm, reaching for a Virginia Woolf with his right, Edward overstretched and *The*

Years slipped through his fingers and dropped down behind an armchair.

Cursing mildly, Edward put the books in his hands on the top of a bookcase, and went back and pulled back the chair to retrieve the errant volume of Woolf. There it lay on the wooden floor. He reached, and as he reached, he saw behind it, previously hidden by the armchair a small set of doors that looked like they housed further bookshelves.

And so they did. The books here were older, and looked rarer.

Edward ran his finger along the spines of the books. They were in Latin and Greek with one or two in Hebrew, which he couldn't read.

The volumes looked sixteenth century in style — leather bound with faded gilt lettering. He drew one volume out. The paper was of thin cardboard, stiffened with starch, as was normal for the period.

He took the book out, opened it in his left hand and riffled through the pages with his right. There were perhaps forty pages, printed in blackletter. The pages carried annotations in ink and pencil, all faded, in several different hands. Between the blocks of printed text were figures of glass retorts and alembics and drawings of the petals and stamens of flowers. It seemed to be a book of botany.

And then as he examined further, Edward realised it was a book of alchemy, and from the copious illustrations of roses and lilies, diagrammatic and detailed with figures of explanation and names in Latin, he realised it was actually a book of botanical alchemy, so-called vegetal alchemy.

This was Dr Lovegrove's secret hiding place then. Or perhaps not secret — after all the doors had not been locked. The books had been concealed due to the confusion of the library, rather than being deliberately hidden.

Did Lovegrove even know he had them still, or were they so

long out of mind they had been put here when the Lovegroves moved in and forgotten ever since.

Edward checked the book's title page. It was called *Liber Rosae Venenatae*, 'The Book of the Poisoned Rose' and had been published in Leiden in 1610 by Abraham de Pape. Very interesting. Edward knew of Pape.

Just then there was a muffled bang from outside, a muffled but loud bang.

Edward put the book aside and rushed to the window. He couldn't see much, but something had happened on the road outside — some kind of motor accident. Black smoke rose in curls. He heard shouting and the sound of the house door opening. It all seemed rather serious.

Edward put on his jacket and left the library, hurrying downstairs to see what all the commotion was about. It seemed unlikely he could help, but, like many otherwise rational people, he had a morbid curiosity about accidents.

Chapter 11

Edward emerged at the top of the main stairs, ran quickly down them, then hurried to the front door where he found Mrs Edmundson with Susannah beside her.

Mrs Edmundson stood at the door with her hand to her mouth. "It's terrible. There's been an accident!"

Susannah was also there, standing near Mrs Edmundson but did not reach out to comfort her.

Edward said, "What's happened?"

Susannah said, "The coal van skidded on the ice and hit a tree. My father and Ruby are out there with them. Perhaps you could go and see if you can offer assistance?"

"Of course." At her word, Edward rushed out of the door, feeling the bite of the winter cold. He'd only gone three paces when he slipped on ice in his haste and went down on one knee.

Pushing himself up, hoping he didn't look a fool, he saw the coal waggon on the road beyond Hackthwaite's gateposts. It appeared that the snow had blown over a frozen puddle right at a kink in the drive and turning its wheels to negotiate the bend, the waggon had skidded into the tree.

The bonnet of the vehicle was buckled up and steam hissed into the air before the slight breeze blew it away. One of the coalmen stood by the passenger side, and Ruby stood beside him, without her coat. This was the passenger. The man looked dazed and blood ran into his eye from from a cut above his eyebrow, but he was in a better state than the driver.

Dr Lovegrove had the driver's door open and was talking to the man who wasn't responding. It looked like he'd been jerked forward by the impact and smacked his head against the windscreen.

Lovegrove yelled, "Edward, come, please help. Let's get him out."

Edward hurried over to the driver's side. The man was slumped forward and unresponsive, blood seeping from his right ear.

"He's unconscious," Lovegrove said.

"I think he's..." Edward bit his tongue. He was no doctor, but he'd been in the War. The man looked dead to him.

Lovegrove acted as if there was some chance of saving the unfortunate, though, by the way the man's head lolled on his shoulders, Edward judged the chance to be slight.

Lovegrove was insistent that they move him, so Edward inserted himself between Lovegrove and the stricken man, who fortunately was only slight.

Despite his slender frame, the man hung like a sack of potatoes between them. He didn't help or move in the slightest and with sweat breaking on their brows, even in the bitter winter cold, the two men heaved him out.

"Support him, Edward, and we'll walk him to the house."

Lovegrove lifted the driver under his left armpit with Edward on his right.

"Is he okay?" the passenger said.

He turned to Ruby. "It's Davey Wilson from Outerside. You know Davey."

"Aye. I know Davey, Jack, and you too. You come in and we'll get you a cup of tea."

Ruby followed Edward and Lovegrove with the passenger coal-man as walking wounded. Ahead, Lovegrove and Edward lugged the other man, his head rolling on his shoulders in a most macabre and concerning manner. They took him along the front drive and to the house door.

As they went in, Mrs Edmundson came to help them carry the body of Davey Wilson. Ruby was fussing about the bleeding man.

Only Susannah seemed calm. "Take him into the Morning Room," she said. The two men, now with Mrs Edmundson offering moral if not physical support, dragged their burden through to the Morning Room.

"Put him on the floor," Susannah said.

They laid him down. He did not move.

Edward said, "Shouldn't we call a doctor?" But answered himself before anyone could reply. "Though, I suppose..."

Lovegrove turned his head. "Susannah is a healer. She will do better than any doctor."

Edward sighed. "Though, poor chap. I think... I mean I saw enough poor lads who'd bought it in Burma to know when they have a chance, and I fear this fellow's too far gone. A doctor could certify death."

Susannah said, "You two leave me now."

She laid her hand gently on the man's snow-pale face. She brushed her fingers over his blue lips. This was the first time Edward had ever seen her touch anyone.

Dr Lovegrove caught at his sleeve. "Come on. Let's leave her. Let's see how the other fellow's doing."

They found Mrs Edmundson comforting Jack Greggains in

the Sitting Room. The family did not normally use the Sitting Room in the morning as it was on the west side of the house and didn't get good light until afternoon.

Jack Greggains sat, head in hands, an untouched cup of tea steaming on the table beside the chair. He was softly weeping. "Davey was a good lad. Who'd have thought it? Just out for our normal run, and then this. We were talking about the football. It's all so senseless."

Mrs Edmundson stroked his arm. "Never you mind, Jack. Miss Susannah's special."

Ruby said, "Just leave it to Miss Susannah. She's got a rare gift."

Jack Greggains looked up. "Did you see him though? He wasn't moving. He banged his head right hard."

Edward sighed. The man was right. But the women were fervent in their reassurance that Miss Susannah was a healer, so he bit his tongue.

Lovegrove was behind him. "Cup of tea, Edward?" He turned to Mrs Edmundson. "Mrs Edmundson, if you wouldn't mind?"

"It's all right. I'll go," Ruby said, and Mrs Edmundson nodded at her as if even in this situation, people should know their role, and fetching tea was the maid's job.

Edward watched her go. What a competent, unfazed young woman Ruby was. Many other girls of her age would be in bits after seeing all of this.

They sat a while then the coal-man stood suddenly. "I feel sick. Can I use your bathroom?"

"I'll take him," Mrs Edmundson said and she accompanied the man out of the Sitting Room.

"What a terrible thing," Edward said.

Lovegrove said, "The ice of course. It's lethal when it's covered by snow and right on that bend too. He must have felt the waggon skid and then braked too hard and lost control."

"It's such a shame, that driver chap was so young," Edward

lamented. "I know you mentioned that Susannah has some knowledge of medicine—"

"That's not exactly what I said," Lovegrove smiled. "I said that Susannah is a healer."

"Not a doctor, though."

"No, a healer."

"What do you mean exactly? You mean like a faith healer?" Before he could answer, Edward replied. "I'm afraid I can't put much stock in that. You don't really believe in all that spiritualism nonsense, do you?"

"It's not spiritualism, Edward," Lovegrove said. "But I caution you against dismissing things that you don't fully understand. There is a life force that flows through all things, a force that can be harnessed by those with the right attunement."

"Are you referring to vitalism?"

Lovegrove's eyes were bright with enthusiasm. "Susannah possesses a rare gift, Edward," he said. "She has the ability to channel this vital life force and heal the sick and wounded."

Edward leaned forward. He was an uncertain man socially, but when it came to facts, he was firm in his opinions. He probed, keen to demolish such wooly-headed thinking. "But what do you mean by 'life force'?" he asked.

Lovegrove said, "It is the in the flowers, in the grass, in the birds in the beasts — even in the wind and stone," he said. "Susannah has a unique connection to it, and she can use it to heal the body and mind."

Edward raised an eyebrow. "So you believe this is some sort of supernatural power?"

Lovegrove shook his head. "Not at all," he said. "It is a very real, very physical force. It is the energy that keeps us alive and healthy. Susannah has simply learned how to tap into it and direct it where it is needed."

Edward was silent for a moment. What poppycock! Not that

he could say that in so many words. "And you, Dr Lovegrove, do *you* actually believe she can heal people with it?"

Lovegrove nodded. "Yes, she has healed many people in the village. But she is careful not to exert her powers too often. It can be taxing, both physically and mentally. Also she cannot use it outside this house. Her patients come to her."

"Hmm," Edward nodded. A silence fell between the two men, Edward uncomfortable and inwardly scornful, Dr Lovegrove smiling benignly.

Lovegrove rubbed his hands. "I wonder where that tea has got to?"

Wanting something to do, Edward stood. "I'll go and see."

Lovegrove watched him go.

Edward was half way down the passage on the ground floor that he was relatively confident led to the kitchen, when he saw Ruby Mumberson coming the opposite way with a silver tea tray upon which was a silver teapot, two cups and saucers and a gingerbread cake.

She laughed. "Careful where you're going Mr Smith. This way leads to the servants' quarters and if we find you there we'll give you a job."

"I have a job, thank you, Ruby."

"But not a proper job — books isn't a proper job. What kind of work is that?" Her eyes twinkled.

"It is a proper job—." He stopped. "Oh! You're teasing me."

"Got it in one, Edward!"

He must have looked startled because she said, "You did say I could call you Edward, though I thought I'd best only use your first name out of sight of our elders and betters in case they thought we were friends."

"I hope we are friends."

She grinned. "Come on, back to the Sitting Room for your tea and cake."

Edward followed her, trying to match her brisk pace along the passage.

"Terrible do, all that," he said.

"The crash? Yes, terrible."

"I mean I think that poor chap is a goner, to be fair," Edward said. "Of course, no one likes to say that, but…"

Ruby stopped and hesitated as if she shouldn't be speaking. Then she said, "You shouldn't underestimate Miss Susannah. She has gifts not given to others."

He couldn't take the scepticism out of his voice. "They must be considerable gifts if she's to bring the dead to life."

Ruby shrugged. "You'll see for yourself soon enough." She was about to go and then said, "Did anyone tell you not to touch her?"

"Not to touch Susannah? No. What do you mean?"

"I just thought Mrs Edmundson might have spoken out of turn. She means well, but she likes to talk."

"It's not my habit to touch strange young women."

Ruby laughed out loud. "Isn't it? Poor you! Poor them!"

He blinked. How should he react to this? It seemed like more teasing. Should he laugh? Or, was she laughing at him, in which case should he be upset?

Seeing his bafflement, she shook her head. "Come on, come and get your tea."

Edward followed her in silence to the Sitting Room.

Lovegrove clapped his hands. "Tea and gingerbread too!"

The coal-man and Mrs Edmundson sat together on the sofa. She was patting his hand. She said, "Jack here's my cousin's boy."

Ruby set out the cups.

"Should I get Susannah?" Edward said.

Lovegrove shook his head. "No, she'll come back to us when she's finished what she has to do."

Edward still hadn't sat down. "I think if I can't help down here, I'd better be getting back to work."

Lovegrove smiled. "As you wish, dear boy. But do take a piece of gingerbread up with you."

Chapter 12

Even though he'd gone back to the library out of a sense of diligence, Edward couldn't settle his mind on the work of cataloguing books. He stared out of the window onto the snowbound scene though he couldn't see the dented coal waggon from here.

What rot Lovegrove had been speaking. The man was dead. He really thought they ought to inform the authorities, or whatever served for authorities in this rural wilderness, locked down by the weather as it was — the police he supposed.

Edward ate the gingerbread standing. He set the fire to blaze then sat.

He just stared at the rows and rows and piles and piles of books. Then he stood, pushed away the armchair to reveal the hidden cupboard, opened it and drew out *The Book of The Poisoned Rose*.

He took it to the seat by the hearth so he could benefit from the fire and opened the tome. The book smelled old, leather and paper and wood and ink long ago created by those long ago dead. How strange that marks on a page should convey knowledge. It seemed to him that others often took for granted the great technological invention that was writing that made it possible for knowledge to be passed from generation to generation without the need to rely on fallible memory.

This book in his hands was four hundred years old, and though he treasured the words it contained and prized the illustrations and even adored the smell its pages gave of former times, he did not believe what it said.

Edward was a thoroughly modern twentieth century man who'd seen the horrors and the gifts of science and knew that good or bad, used for evil, or used for good, the knowledge provided by the scientific method was the one bedrock upon which to base one's faith.

Not like this book that overflowed with superstition and half-truth: alchemy, a misleading and therefore dangerous pseudo-science.

As he turned the stiff pages, reading the Latin and the antiquated English, he translated to himself:

'All prayers and devotions, spirits and æthers, angels and roses: the divine life of plants conjured forth.'

The book spoke of creation of an alchemical child, not of gold or salt or mercury, but instead of petals and stems, and more disturbingly, blood and bone — the Rose Child.

And this Rose Child was the same as the *pharmakon*.

Pharmakon was a Greek word — the root of our word 'pharmacy' — that conveyed the idea of medicine, but there was more to the *pharmakon*: it was double-faced thing, like the god Janus. The pharmakon was magical and could heal any ill, even bring the dead forth again from the underworld so they might walk among the living once more, their previous death remembered only as a dim dream, a forgetting and a sleep.

In that, the pharmakon was wonderful, but the pharmakon was also dreadful because, paradoxically it was panacea and poison together — that which heals and that which harms.

'Those who are dead it will bring back to life: those who are living it will slay.'

All nonsense of course. Pretty, poetic nonsense, paradoxical and therefore meaningless.

The whole of Western logic was based on Aristotle's idea of the excluded middle. To find a paradox, was to find an impossibility.

Edward sat in the armchair by the fire, surrounded by shelves and shelves of books. He had always abhorred paradoxes.

It was too chaotic, too illogical. He preferred a world of black and white, of true and false, where everything had its place and nothing was left to chance.

But as he looked at this *Book Of The Poisoned Rose*, Edward couldn't help but feel a sense of unease.

He read:

Verily, the magistri of alchymie doth know the craft of transmutation and the fashioning of tinctures by means of the philosophical fire, as hath been writ by Hermes and Geber. For lo, the Philosophers' Stone, which hath been sought by many for ages, is found in the hidden chambers of nature, and by its grace, the common rose is transformed into the mighty Rose Child, which hath a dual nature. It is both the cure for every ailment and the bane of all, for it containeth both panacea and poison in its essence. Such is the wisdom contained within the pages of the Liber Rosae Venenatae, which doth instruct the diligent student in the ways of the vegetal alchemy.

Hearken ye, O ye seekers of the alchemical art! Know ye that the great work is not for the faint of heart, nor for those who lack skill and knowledge. For behold, the creation of the Rose Child is a task that demands great diligence and patience. Yet, for those who possess the wisdom and skill of the sages, the labour shall bear fruit, and the alchemist shall behold the great miracle of the Rose Child, born from the womb of the earth and nourished by the essence of the heavens, and the blood of a man.

With artful hands and keen mind, the alchemist must gather the purest elements of the earth, and through the secrets of vegetal alchemy, he shall distill the essence of the Rose. For the rose is the key to the creation of the Rose Child, the panacea and the poison, the bane and the antidote. In the vessel of the alembic, the rose shall be transmuted and purified, and the alchemist shall witness the emergence of the Child, born of the union of fire and water, flesh and leaf.

Edward scratched his head — beautiful language but what utter tripe. He closed *The Book Of The Poisoned Rose*. He was curious to see what was going on downstairs, and whether the dead really did rise again.

Chapter 13

There was no one about. The door to the Morning Room was still closed and despite his brave thoughts about debunking superstition, he had no stomach to open it and see the dead man lying there.

Lovegrove was probably back at his work, whatever that was, and Ruby and Mrs Edmundson would be in the kitchen and had taken the coal-man, her cousin's boy, to sit there with them there, where it was probably warmer in any case.

Edward sighed. It was freezing. Someone must have left a door open. He could see no fire lit in any of the rooms that he passed so he decided to fetch his coat from the Entrance Hall where it hung on a hook with all the other coats. His shoes were there too.

After putting on his coat he also put on his shoes, he thought he'd get some fresh air. He opened the front door and was struck by a blast of frigid air. It was snowing again, just a few feathery flakes coming down but the ground underfoot was frozen and slippery with ice under the fallen snow. His smooth-soled town shoes weren't up to walking far in that. He could still have a walk around the house, but he'd probably go over on his ankle. Despite this, he craved to be out of doors.

Then he remembered the quadrangle and its internal garden, set out like the cloister of an old monastery. He'd never seen the garden up close and was intrigued at how luxuriant and green it had looked last night even in the moonlight, even in mid-winter.

He turned round and instead of exiting the house by the front door, he turned and followed the passage that ultimately led to the kitchen and scullery. On the passage, he'd seen a glass-paned door when he'd wandered past before, though it was a door he'd never opened. He guessed that was the door out to the inner garden.

He found the glass-paned door again, and opened it.

As Edward Smith crossed the threshold of the cloistered garden, he was immediately transported to a world of vivid colours and lush foliage. Despite the grip of winter, the garden was in full bloom. The roses were especially striking, with shades of carmine, burgundy, and crimson that seemed to pulse with life against the cool grey of the limestone walls.

The garden was bounded by sandstone slabs which formed a outer walkway under the house walls. The garden was luxuriant and overgrown. He could have walked round the perimeter and seen it from all sides, but for some reason that would not do.

Edward was drawn deeper into the garden. He found a stone-flagged path which led between the bushes and flowering shrubs. As he got further in, he discovered strange, exotic plants twisting and curling among the rose bushes. Though he could not identify them, he was amazed by their beauty and the way they twined with the roses to create a tapestry of colours and textures.

The rose bushes themselves were varied and abundant, with differing shades of red. In fact, there were only red roses there, and each bloom was plump and perfect. Edward reached out. The petals were velvety to the touch but the thorns were sharp and drew blood.

He drew back his hand and sucked blood from his scratched finger.

The heady perfume of the roses overwhelmed his senses. It was so strong and summery, despite the cold winter air.

Edward walked deeper into the garden along the laid out stone path. Among the rose bushes here were twisted vines of a deep green, with vibrant yellow berries that looked distinctly poisonous.

The garden was not a formal maze, but the plant growth was so riotous it would have been easy to get lost. Eventually he came to the garden's heart. In the centre here stood a small gazebo, its intricate design and ornate details a testament to the skill of the craftsmen who had built it.

Inside the gazebo, surrounded by a sea of blooming flowers tied to the wooden lattice behind her, sat Susannah. Her eyes shone with pleasure at the sight of Edward, and her smile was warm and welcoming. "Hello, Edward!"

"Sorry to disturb you," he said.

She smiled. "You're not disturbing me."

He looked around, marvelling. "What an extraordinary place this is," Edward said. "All these flowers. The roses, I recognise, at least as roses, but these other ones look decidedly foreign."

Susannah laughed. "Yes, they are rather exotic. Don't touch the vines or their berries!"

"No, I wouldn't. They look like nightshade or something."

"There are various types. Somehow they create a harmony with the roses, don't you think? But they are all poisonous."

Edward felt like an intruder in her garden. He hovered, unsure whether to sit.

She patted the wooden bench next to her. He sat. Then he asked about the driver of the coal waggon.

"He's resting."

He raised his eyebrows. "Resting? I thought he was past resting."

"I know what you mean, but I have helped him."

"Your father said you knew some medicine." Edward knew he was being unkind now, but he persisted. "Where did you train?"

She tilted her head. "I think you guess, that as a woman, it would be difficult for me to train as a doctor."

"There are women doctors."

"I know. But few, and I am not one of them."

"Then are you a natural healer? A sort of traditional—" he searched for the word.

She completed his sentence "—witch? Wise woman?" She shook her head. "No, not that either."

"I'm just curious where you learned how to heal."

She eyed him intensely, her eyes glittering now greener, her lips redder against her pale skin. "I did not learn healing," she said.

"I don't know what that means."

"Did you learn flesh, or are you flesh?" She said.

"What? It's not the same thing."

She paused. "Isn't it? Do you really want to know what I am?"

"I know what you are. You are Dr Lovegrove's daughter. I was only asking how you can heal people. I wasn't being impertinent about your origins."

"You've read my father's book? It was placed for you to find."

"I've looked at many of your father's books."

"You know the one I mean: The Book of the Poisoned Rose."

"Ah, yes the alchemical tome. I've flicked through it."

"Then you know what I am."

He paused. This was awkward. He didn't want to embarrass the poor girl who seemed to have some odd beliefs. He said, "I'm sorry. I don't follow."

"I will tell you then."

He wasn't sure he wanted to continue this conversation, but it would be too awkward to leave abruptly so it seemed he had little choice. He cleared his throat and said, "Please do."

She said, "I have come to those who seek to be healed, and I am ready for those who want the blessing of the Goddess Flora."

"The Roman goddess of flowers and gardens? Are you sincerely telling me you are a devotee of some half-remembered pagan goddess?"

"I am not she, but I am of her kind."

Susannah did not take her eyes off him. "I am the Pharmakon, the honoured one and the scorned one. I am both virtuous and venomous. I am she who is blamed for illnesses and the one who is praised for their cure. I am she who heals. I am she who gives birth to new life, and I am she who eases the pain of death with the milk of poppies. I am she who opens the door of death with the juice of nightshade."

Edward sat back. He was still staring at her. She was so beautiful when she spoke with such passion, even though she was talking drivel. But she clearly believed all this stuff. She was mad. There was no other explanation. Lovegrove should take her to see a doctor.

She tilted her head. "You doubt me, I see it."

"Well, not wishing to be rude, but all this is absolute tripe. Science has wiped the earth of such nonsense. Those who believe it still are..." He didn't finish his sentence.

She laughed. "Surrender. Cease doubting, Edward! Become one of those who believe ! Become the servant of the Pharmakon and help me heal the sick. Or be its enemy, and accept the consequences of that."

Edward was silent. How embarrassing.

She smiled. "Truly, I am the Pharmakon: The Poisoned Rose, created by my father."

"Your father created you? Harold Lovegrove?"

"My father was Cornelius Fludd."

Edward didn't know whether to feel sorry for her, or ring for a doctor to have her committed. As usual, he felt embarrassed. "I just hope you have been able to help the driver, though I don't see how you could."

"The man lives," she said.

Edward said. "He was clearly dead."

"He was dead, but now he lives again."

Edward stood abruptly. "Well, I think I should be getting back to the house, I've got rather cold sitting here."

Susannah reached out as if to stop him leaving. She went to grab his wrist. There was no force behind her touch and, he was sure it was an innocent gesture, but the feel of her fingers on his flesh sparked a strange, almost overpowering sensation. He suppressed a gasp. His head spun.

But along with the sensual thrill, came a sharp sting, like being pricked by a rose's thorn.

Edward pulled back his hand with a yelp and glanced down to where she'd touched him. Her slender nails had left behind a set of fine rakes on his wrist. Drops of blood welled up from the shallow scratches, glistening against his skin.

His gaze moved from his bleeding wrist back to Susannah. She was smiling still. He looked at her hands. Her fingernails were sharp and painted the same shade as the roses surrounding them. Such soft, feminine hands; they looked harmless, delicate even, but the evidence of her assault was dripping from his wrist.

Soon, an overwhelming heat began to radiate from the site of the scratches.

Edward's heart pounded in his chest as if attempting to break free from its bony prison. His palms were slick with sweat, and anxiety sent a ripple through his spine. His thoughts started to blur, his surroundings melting into a disorienting amalgamation of blooming flowers and creeping vines.

He backed away from her and felt a sudden, desperate need to escape the maze-like garden, to flee from Susannah's enchanting and threatening presence.

Barging through the tangle of exotic flora, without saying goodbye to her, Edward was overwhelmed by the overpowering scent of the flowers, intensifying his panic. The riotous garden seemed to close in on him from all sides. The smell was intoxicating and narcotic. It threatened to undermine his reason with its primal life.

He thought, we did not make the flowers; they came before us. They represent life itself, not our human life, overlain with conceptions and perceptions, thoughts and plans and dreams. They were like the life of the body, over which we have little power. They were a life of petals and blood, earth and bone.

Anxiety unmanned him as the thorny underbrush snatched at

his clothing. It wanted to pull him back towards the gazebo, towards Susannah.

Every gasp of the perfumed air felt suffocating, every step intended to help him escape, instead led him deeper into a labyrinth he feared would consume him. The world spun. The vibrant colours of the garden melted into one another as the edges of his vision started to darken.

He would faint. He would fall to earth and then the plants would grow over him, bury him in their foliage.

But he had some strength left — both physical and mental. He mustered every ounce left within him, and propelled himself forward, desperate to find an exit from this blossoming nightmare.

And then through the thorny thicket, he saw the stone perimeter of the rose garden, the safe flags where no plants grew. He stumbled towards them, pushing his way through thorn and briar and vine.

And as he staggered out of the garden, hidden among the green leaves and stems of the flowers, protruding from the snowy earth, he saw three fingers of a human hand.

Even as he broke out of the vegetation, he turned and looked.

Was he hallucinating? It was as if a corpse had been buried standing up and was reaching out from the depths, the cadaver buried with only its fingers breaking the surface.

"Good God!" He yelled. What fresh horror was this? He was ill. He was so hot.

The fingernails were masculine, and there was dirt under them and they were stained with the earth.

Edward was bleeding from lacerations on his face and hands. He did not feel at all well, but he had to know if this was real.

He stooped then fell to his knees, reaching out to scrape away the snow that obscured the fingers as they sprouted from the cold soil. He touched them. They were real. A man was dead here.

Chapter 14

Edward entered the house and went looking for others. The first person he came across was Mrs Edmundson dusting in the hall.

He said, "Mrs Edmundson, we need to call the police straight away."

"Calm down, Mr Smith! What's got into you? Everything has been done properly about the crash earlier. We don't need the police."

She studied him. "Oh, you are in a lather. You look like you're feverish and your face is covered with scratches. And your hand is. You're bleeding quite bad from that wrist."

She pointed to where Susannah had scratched him.

"No, it's not that. Something else. In the rose garden."

"What? In the Rose Garden? What's happened there? I didn't hear anything. Is Miss Susannah all right?"

"No, she's well. It's not her. I've seen something terrible. There's a body buried in the rose garden."

Mrs Edmundson went suddenly quiet, then her face changed, as if she was playing a part. "I don't think you're quite yourself, Mr. Smith. What do you mean?"

"A human hand is buried in the Rose Garden!"

"What were you doing in the Rose Garden, anyway?"

"I just went to get some fresh air. I bumped into Susannah and she regaled me with a whole lot of insanity. And then, walking out, I saw it sticking out of the soil – a hand. Someone has been buried there. I don't know when. Probably before you came here."

"I've been here a long time."

"In any case, we must call the Police."

Mrs Edmundson shook her head. "We don't want to be calling the Police. This isn't something that the police get involved in. Listening to you, they wouldn't believe you anyway. You're raving. Why don't you sit down and I'll get you a glass of water?"

"I am not delirious. There are human remains there. Please ring for the police."

She shook her head. "I won't be doing that."

Edward was stunned.

Mrs Edmundson said, "What did Miss Susannah say about herself to you? Did she explain?"

"She said she could bring the dead back to life — pure insanity."

"You don't believe that, but you do believe you saw a severed hand in an ordinary English country garden. That sounds more like insanity to me."

"You tell me you think that Susannah actually can bring the dead to life?" Edward said, "Come on. You're a down to earth woman — a country woman. You weren't born yesterday."

Mrs Edmundson said, "There are things in this world that you don't understand, Mr. Smith. The truth is that Miss Susannah's been here a long time in this house — long before I came here and I've known this house all my life. It was empty for a long time on account for the tales of it being haunted. And it is haunted, though not by ghosts. Then, after the War, Dr Lovegrove came and he was a man who understood. He called forth the spirit of the garden and adopted her as his daughter. She's an ancient thing, but she has taken on modern shapes and manners as he has taught her."

"You can't really believe this too?"

"I do. She raised my son from the dead, when he was killed by a horse, aged five years old. Now he's a strong young man out in the world. Of course, I believe. You will believe too when you see it with your own eyes."

"You say she raised your son from the dead? Do you realise how insane that sounds?"

Mrs Edmundson continued. "There won't be any police coming here, Mr Smith, for the police don't deal with miracles, and what you will see today is a miracle. It is up to you whether you believe, whether you believe and become one of us."

Edward paused. "You're telling me that she's brought this coal driver back?"

"She has. He's sitting with Dr Lovegrove and the other lad drinking tea and eating cake like it was all a bad dream. They might have to leave the waggon until the tow truck can get here later on, but they're both fine."

Then Edward said, "Ruby told me she had a sweetheart who worked here."

"Yes, Ned."

"The gardener."

"He was."

"But he died. Is that who it is in the garden?"

Mrs Edmundson nodded. "He was Ruby's betrothed but he became impatient with her. She's a chaste girl, and he wanted more so when she wouldn't give him what he wanted, he started fawning around Miss Susannah."

"Sometimes working class men struggle to restrain their passions. I hate to say it, but it's breeding."

"No, you're not understanding me. Ned touched her, you see? Miss Susannah is beautiful and you couldn't blame any man losing his head, no matter how nicely brought up— just like you might have done just now in the Rose Garden."

"What do you mean?"

"I seen the scratch marks on your wrist. If you'd gone to grab her, then she'd be justified in scratching you. Just like she scratched Ned."

"Please do not conflate me with that lecherous oaf!"

She continued, "We always told him that he mustn't touch her, but he did and he was poisoned. Her touch is life and her touch is poison. She brings the dead to life with her touch, but she will strike the living down with the same touch. Ned never believed. And he paid the price. Miss Susannah didn't kill him.

He killed himself. And now you can see why we can't call the police."

"This is all poppycock. How can it be true!"

"Hereabouts, we don't deny the truth; we see it."

Then the garden door opened and Susannah stepped in. She said, "I'm so sorry, Edward, about my little speech. I do get carried away sometimes. I hope I didn't upset you. Goodness me, you're cut."

He put his hand to his face, suddenly overwhelmed that she was here again. Her presence was like wine or like opium, it overpowered him. "It's nothing," he stammered. "The roses."

Susannah winced for him. "So pretty, and yet their thorns are so painful."

He rubbed his moist forehead. He felt nauseous. He knew now he would get no sense in the matter from Susannah and Mrs Edmundson. He had heard of contagious hysterical beliefs among women. It could run rife where females were cloistered together. He would speak to Dr Lovegrove. He was a man. He would surely take what Edward had found seriously. He must. Human remains on his property! He'd want the police to know as soon as possible.

"It must be nearly time for lunch, Mrs Edmundson," Susannah said. "I'm looking forward to your cottage pie. Is my father around?"

"No, miss. He's busy. He said to eat without him."

Chapter 15

Edward wasn't hungry. He made the excuse of feeling unwell, and, in truth, he did feel unwell, and he retreated to the library and sat for a while among the books. There was a refuge among books. The books were ordinary — ordinary titles by well-known authors, novels, fripperies, entertainments. The books at least seemed sane.

What was he to make of the claims that Susannah could bring a man, clearly dead, back to life? Or rather what was he to make of the fact that these women believed those claims?

Edward rose from his chair and strode over to the cupboard and from there, with the tips of his fingers, withdrew *The Book of the Poisoned Rose.*

He read again the account of the creation of the Rose Child. It was as Susannah said. This child was poison and healing together: the Pharmakon. He was familiar with the idea of the pharmakon from previous reading at Cambridge.

The book said in its antiquated English and passages in Latin that the Rose Child was created from flowers and earth and from blood and bone and from tears and prayer.

A child could not be created from petals and bone, from tears and prayers. The place was affecting him, the isolation, stuck in this strange house, kept here by snow and bad weather.

He remembered that Susannah had said her father was not in fact Dr. Lovegrove, but that, she, the Rose Child, was created by Cornelius Fludd four centuries previously.

If this were so, then Lovegrove had come here and found his so-called daughter, and she was his daughter in imagination only. Edward remembered how Lovegrove always talked about his previous life as 'I', not as 'we', even though Susannah must surely have been with him for some of that time.

And Susannah looked twenty-five not four hundred and twenty-five. She was not a wizened corpse, but a living, vibrant young woman.

The door budged open. "I hope I'm not disturbing you."

Edward looked up from his book, guilty to have been caught with that particular volume open on his lap. He snapped it shut.

Lovegrove entered. "Ah, you found it. I thought you would. And what do you think of it?"

"It's very rare, obviously. Leiden 1610. It must be worth a fortune."

"Indeed, but its monetary value is not its real value. The knowledge contained within is worth more than a whole world of gold."

"Where did you get it?"

"I got it here. It came with the house."

"Really? It was here. What a find!" He realised he was talking to Lovegrove as if nothing odd had happened.

"It belonged to Cornelius Fludd. The caretakers of the house in the intervening centuries ensured it was safe and I inherited it with the house."

"It's a nice book, but the contents are total guff."

Lovegrove sat down on a chair opposite Edward and crossed his legs. "Is it? On the contrary, I believe every word of it is true."

"Then you are far more credulous than I thought, Dr. Lovegrove. How can you make a child of petals and roots, of dried blood and bone meal? It's poetry — figurative, not literal."

"And yet you have seen her. The Rose Child walks amongst us."

"She is your mortal daughter, Susannah, not a creation of some long-dead alchemist. How could she be? I was hoping, Dr Lovegrove, that you would speak more sense than I've heard from the women of this house. One expects perhaps that women, being frailer and more imaginative creatures than men, might more easily fall prey to superstition and fancy; they always have and they always will. But you, Dr Lovegrove, you are a scholar! How can you believe this fairytale?"

Lovegrove plucked at his beard. "Fludd began the work, and I was called here to finish it."

"Finish it? What are you talking about?"

"Have you heard of a man called Samuel Liddle Macgregor Mathers?"

"Vaguely. An occultist? Something to do with The Golden Dawn?"

"Exactly. Well, I knew him in Paris, when I was a young man. He introduced me to a chap called Fulcanelli. That wasn't his real name of course. He was an alchemist."

"The author of *The Mystery of the Cathedrals*?"

"Well done, Edward. You do know your books."

"We had a copy of it at Cambridge."

"Did you read it?"

"No. I can't read all the books I catalogue. I save my time for reading worthwhile ones."

Lovegrove said, "Ah, no. For you, books are not flowers to smell, but cows to be corralled. Such a pity. But in any case, in Paris after the First War there was a cabal. I think that is the correct word, better than conclave. We studied, not mineral alchemy of lead and salt and mercury, but vegetal alchemy of roses, and violets and crocus. And in my studies, I learned of Cornelius Fludd, who was also a vegetal alchemist, which was unusual for his time with its obsession with the Philosophers' Stone. And I learned that Cornelius Fludd had completed the Great Work and created the Rose Child, here at Hackthwaite, his country house in remote Yorkshire."

"And so I came to see if she remained. And she did, languishing in the garden he made in the centre of the house, but so small, curled in the leaves of the briars. And so I fed her with my own blood and she grew."

"By the way, Edward, be careful of the Rose Garden, it is full of deadly poisons: nightshade and aconite, foxglove and cuckoo pint. But perhaps you know that already?"

Edward snorted.

Lovegrove went on. "In the summer the roses smell so sweet, so heady, and that is where she lived until I fed her and she become sufficiently strong that she could come into the house."

Edward interrupted him. "Dr Lovegrove, I am not sure I can remain here any longer."

Lovegrove cocked his head. "Is the work not to your taste?"

"No, the work is interesting."

"Then, perhaps, the house not comfortable enough for you?"

"No, no. The house is warm and sheltering. I cannot complain."

"Then the food?"

"No. Not the food. You know what I mean."

"I'm not sure I do. Perhaps it is the company. I am afraid there is only me and Mrs Edmundson, and of course Ruby and Susannah. Perhaps it is the young women that frighten you? So many young men these days are terrified of women."

"Not at all. It is that there is an atmosphere of madness in this house. None of you seem to live in the real world. You live in a land of dreams and myths, and some of the dreams approach nightmares."

Lovegrove was impassive. "Oh, well that is a pity. I'd be sorry to see you go. Especially as your work here is hardly begun."

"Still, I think we are at odds. The gulf is too wide. Our views of the world are too dissimilar."

Lovegrove shrugged. "When do you propose to leave?"

"As soon as possible."

"But you'll stay for dinner?"

"If I do, then that will make me too late to leave tonight."

"Then perhaps you could leave tomorrow morning? That might be more sensible. You'd have the whole day ahead of you and it's a long walk to the station in this cold."

"Walk? I'd thought a taxi."

Lovegrove grinned. "The roads are iced up. You've seen how dangerous they are with the snow fallen on the ice, and more snow is due. I doubt anyone will come to pick you up."

Edward frowned. "I see."

"Perhaps you had better stay. You might come to enjoy our fairytale."

"I doubt that, to be honest."

"But in any case, I came to make a proposal."

"A proposal?"

"A little extra collaboration."

Edward sat back. "I'm busy enough here." He gestured at the books. "I've no time for more. Even if I wasn't leaving."

"And you're leaving the job undone, so it doesn't seem you have such a strong commitment to my poor books. Surely, you have time to help me with a little something."

Edward cleared his throat. "What is it?"

"Well, I had thought I'd show you my laboratory. It's downstairs in the cellars. I'm in the middle of a delicate experiment and I could do with a male eye. You've already alluded to the over-imaginative minds of women, and there are only women here apart from you and I. I would benefit from your masculine brain and vision."

Edward hesitated. "What kind of thing is it — this experiment?"

"I'd rather not say. My work here is confidential, and if you decide not to take me up on this offer, I'd prefer not give you full details of this personal work I am doing. Why not sleep on it? Have dinner with us tonight. You don't have time or light enough to walk to Knaresborough today, so no need to make a decision until tomorrow, but I promise you, you will be intrigued and amazed at what I am achieving in my little laboratory. Everyone is."

Chapter 16

Edward felt queasy. He hated falling out with people and would much rather have been on his way, except what Dr. Lovegrove had said was true. It had been too late in the day to walk to Knaresborough safely by the time he'd decided to leave. He would have to stay one more night.

Though he would have preferred to have hidden away in his room, Edward went to dinner out of politeness. The meal was served and only the sound of genteel eating broke the silence. Three of them sat around the table: Dr Lovegrove, Edward and of course Susannah. She looked radiant in a red gown with a pendant of ruby at her throat and bangles of garnet around her wrists.

Edward presumed she knew his plan to leave and guessed also that she knew why. The marks on his wrist throbbed.

Eventually she broke the silence, "Do you like gardening, Edward?"

It seemed a non-sequitur.

He shrugged. "I know little about it. I've never had a garden."

"Surely, your parents had a garden when you were younger?"

"I was away at school, and you don't really have gardens in Ceylon."

"I suppose the tea planation was a huge garden," Dr Lovegrove said.

"I suppose so." Edward did not laugh. Tea plantations were not gardens. They were full of snakes for one thing.

"I've promised to show Edward my laboratory tomorrow." Lovegrove said.

Susannah looked at Edward and met his eyes. "Before he leaves, of course," she said.

"If he leaves." Lovegrove smiled like a kind old uncle.

"If I leave? I assure you, my mind is made up."

Lovegrove said, "Edward, look at the weather."

Susannah said, "It really would be sensible to wait a few days until traffic starts moving on the roads. Otherwise, you will have to walk."

She put down her knife and fork and lifted her glass of red wine to her lips, and after sipping it, she said, "I still don't understand why you've made this sudden decision. I thought you liked the library."

Edward blushed. "I do."

Susannah teased him. "Then it must be the food."

She was playing with him with the exact same words her father had used.

"No, it's not the food. The food is excellent."

She grinned. "Then me? Have I offended you in some way?" Her emerald eyes sparkled and Edward wondered whether there was something not altogether human smiling through her green eyes.

"No, of course it's not you."

"Then why leave?"

Edward stopped eating. He took off his glasses, removed his handkerchief from his pocket and polished though them even though they were quite clean. "Has your father not told you?"

Susannah remained silent. The silence grew and became tense as a bubble that eventually broke. "It's the occult. The irrational."

"The occult?"

Edward said, "I'm not a particularly religious man. I'm not pious. I'm not evangelical. But I am a Christian."

"Interesting," Lovegrove said. "I thought you were a Socialist."

"A Christian Socialist."

"Intriguing!" Susannah said.

He sighed heavily. "You both seem to believe these mythological, folkloric stories of alchemy. It's at odds with my rational world view."

"I thought you said you were a Christian?" Susannah said.

"A rational Christian — a modern Christian."

"Ah," Lovegrove said, "Surely, when you remove the irrational from Christianity you're left with a dried-up, everyday philosophy of simply being nice to people?"

"What's wrong with that? What's wrong with being nice to people?" Edward said.

"Nothing, of course, but if that's all it is, it has lost its connection with numinous. And here in this house, we retain that," Lovegrove said.

Edward shook his head. "We all know that alchemy has been superseded and that its beliefs have been revealed as medieval superstition, but you still seem to believe it has value."

Lovegrove looked at Susannah. They were both grinning like Cheshire cats. "We do. Don't we, Susannah?"

She nodded. "We do."

Edward said, "So, I must either conclude that you are fools, which you clearly are not. Or..."

Lovegrove raised an eyebrow, still grinning that infuriating grin. "Or?"

"Or you are insane."

"Insane." Susannah covered her mouth with the back of the hand to suppress her laughter, but she failed and sat back roaring.

Lovegrove laughed too. He banged his silver spoon on the table in time with his guffaws.

Edward frowned. "I do not see what is so amusing about this."

For the first time it occurred to him he might not be safe in that house with these two people who were so different from anyone else he'd ever known.

He glanced at the windows where curtains shut out the winter night. The weather outside was freezing cold and he couldn't leave tonight on foot; he'd die of hypothermia. No taxi would come for him either over the treacherous slippery roads.

He would lock his door that night, and leave after breakfast, walking to Knaresborough. It might take all day but at least he would be away from Hackthwaite Hall.

Ruby Mumberson appeared. "You called, Dr Lovegrove?"

She looked bewildered to see them laughing and hardly able to respond to her.

"Ah!" Lovegrove said. "The spoon!" He found that hilarious.

Susannah was gasping for breath between laughing.

"I was banging the table!"

Ruby shook her head. "I'm sorry, Dr Lovegrove. Do you not want anything?"

"No, no. I was just banging the spoon because Mr Smith is so funny."

Ruby creased her brow. "I'm not sure I understand."

Edward shot her an appealing glance, thankful that someone

sane was here. The Lovegroves were mad, but Ruby was normal. At least there would be someone staying in the hall that night who retained her judgement.

"Can I bring the pudding yet, Dr Lovegrove. It's apple crumble and custard."

"Oh, yes, please, Ruby. My favourite!"

"For everyone?" Ruby looked at Edward whose plate was hardly touched.

"For everyone!" Lovegrove said.

Chapter 17

Inside his room, Edward stood by the door looking at the lock. The old-fashioned iron key stood out from it. He put his hand on the cold metal of the key. He had determined to lock the door, but now he stopped, rubbed his chin and walked away. If he locked the door, he would be giving into the irrationality he so despised. There was no real threat here, natural or supernatural. There was no need to lock his bedroom door.

Since his arrival, most of his clothes and other possessions had remained in his case, so it took him little time to stow those he had taken out, razor, face flannel, tooth power and tooth brush, back in the case, and get ready to leave in the morning.

That done, he prepared for sleep. He took off his watch and laid it on the bedside table, checked the time—a quarter to eleven—and picked up his book. It would be dark until around 9 a.m., and so dawn would not wake him. He hoped to be ready to go at first light.

He had no alarm clock, so he'd just have to try to will himself to wake up early. He had a better chance of waking if he got to sleep early, so he decided not to read and switched off the bedside light.

He had already drawn the heavy satin curtains closed to keep the moonlight out, and as he switched off the light, the room was plunged into absolute darkness

He didn't feel too well, actually. He hadn't managed the apple crumble. He put his nausea down to the awkward situation and the stress of falling out with the Lovegroves.

Surprisingly quickly, he slipped into a dream. Edward's dream was filled with swirling colours and strange, unfamiliar symbols. He was actively manipulating them, trying to combine them in different ways to create something new. It was like an alchemical experiment—a mixture of science, art, and magic.

He felt dizzy as the symbols blended together before his eyes. He wasn't sure what he was trying to achieve, but he continued for what seemed like hours. His dream became more intense as time went on; it was like a race against the clock as he struggled to complete some unknown task before waking up again.

Deeply asleep, he did not hear the door open, but in his slumber, he turned on his side to face the wall and away from the intruder and continued to sleep.

The intruder came closer. He dreamed on.

Edward's dream shifted, and he found himself walking through the long corridors of Hackthwaite Hall. He felt something was wrong but could not pinpoint what it was. The walls seemed to close in around him, oppressive and menacing.

In the dream, at the end of a corridor, he noticed a dark figure standing in the shadows. It seemed to be observing him as he slowly made his way towards it. As Edward approached, he realised that instead of human features, roses were snaking across the figure's face and its very female body.

The briars moved and twined about, on the floor, writhing closer to him, trying to engulf him in thorns and petals. He panicked and tried to run away, but the briars seemed alive, crawling towards him with eager intent. They twisted around his ankles and held him fast.

When the quilt was dragged off him, he almost woke, almost surfaced from sleep. But the dream gripped him with tendrils of ivy and bramble.

The intruder got into the bed beside him.

She stroked his head. Her breath was hot against his ear when she whispered to him "Let me take you to a place where you can be safe, where things won't hurt you anymore..."

He felt a strange warmth spread through his body.

He finally woke when her silken skin pressed against his own and felt her long fingers on his arm and chest, snaking down. He felt her heavy hair on his face and chest as she rose above him, and moved her legs to straddle him.

Edward had never been intimate with any woman, but his instincts responded with the same knowing that teaches birds to build nests, and newborns to seek the nipple. Such things are deep in the flesh, waiting to be awakened by life.

And so Edward knew his part in this ancient dance. The woman wrapped around him and rolled on him, and he felt her flesh against his, soft and yielding. Her lips were upon him, and even through the darkness, he knew those lips were red as they laid kisses on his face.

At first, he'd thought he was still asleep but now he knew he was awake. The body that lay with him was real from her warmth. At first he forgot where he was.

Then he remembered, and said, 'Susannah.'

The woman did not speak. And, in any case, they had now progressed beyond words, the animal had caught him, and he was no longer a person but a player in a process of darkness and procreation.

In time, the business came to its urgent end, and then she whispered, "Thank you, Edward."

He sat up with a shock. The voice was not the polite pronunciation of the Lovegroves, but instead pure Yorkshire. She got out of bed, and as she padded across the floor, she pulled aside the curtain to let the moonlight in, but in its pallid glare, he could not tell who the woman was.

Chapter 18

After the woman left, still naked, Edward did not sleep again.

What had he done? The experience itself had been something he would never forget. It had consummated his life. It was as if he had waited all down the years for this woman in this bed that night. It shook him. What had happened was not amenable to reason. It made no sense. Could it be Ruby he had slept with?

At first, he had been convinced it was Susannah, and then when the voice had not been the polite tone of an English lady, but that of the Yorkshire lass, he'd thought it must be Ruby. Of course, Susannah could easily disguise her voice to trick him.

He lay awake until dawn came. She had left the curtains undrawn, and what heat there had been in his bedroom seeped out through them. Even with the pale daylight, the room did not warm up significantly. It was mid-winter after all, he told himself. The weather was natural and normal for the season, and so was everything else.

When he finally rose and went to the window to check the weather, ice had crusted on the inside of the glass and he could see his breath in the air. Outside, the weather was unchanged. Snow was falling still.

He walked to the bathroom down the quiet corridors of the house. The cold seeped in everywhere, but he heard the hot-water pipes that ran along the passages gurgling as they began to heat the house.

The water in the sink was hot, thank God. He washed and shaved and when he was clean, he dressed and went down to breakfast.

Ruby was there setting the table. He had hoped she wouldn't be there.

"You're early," she said.

He listened for the telltale tone that would reveal whether it had been really her and not Susannah who had come to his bed the night before. Surely she would say something, hint at their shared intimacy, but there was nothing.

Ruby set the table as he imagined she did every morning. In

the end, she turned and tilted her head. "Are you all right, Edward? You look like you've seen a ghost."

He nodded and sat still without speaking.

"Tea or coffee?"

He cleared his throat. "Coffee, please."

"Righty-oh. I'll be right back."

Edward watched her leave and sat silently in front of the table with its linen cloth and silver cutlery, its butter dish and butter knife, its jar of Seville marmalade next to its jar of blackcurrant jam.

He did not hear Susannah enter. "Hullo, Edward," she said.

He turned his head, his reverie broken as she seated herself opposite. He blushed.

"Has Ruby been in?" she asked.

He nodded without looking at her. What did she mean by saying that? A minute went by.

"Are you all right, Edward?" she said. "You seem rather distant."

He studied her, his gaze moving from hair to emerald eyes to red lips held in a concerned smile.

He didn't answer. What was there to say? If it was her, then she'd know. If not, then it wasn't the sort of subject a gentleman brings up over breakfast.

"I suppose it's because you're leaving us," she said. "You realise how sorry we are to see you go? We've become quite fond of you, even in the short time you've been here."

"I still mean to go."

"You don't have to leave, you know."

"I do."

"Do you hate us so much?"

He shook his head. "No, I don't hate you. It's this place. I feel like I've fallen asleep and am dreaming. It's so heavy on me — so strange."

She laughed. "You're not the first to say that about Hackthwaite Hall. It is rather a dreamy place, though, myself I love to live in dreams.”

He said, “Have you always lived in grand old houses?”

She said, “I’ve always been here. I don’t remember anywhere else.”

She was maintaining the charade then.

Then Ruby entered. She brought a silver coffeepot and a silver milk jug.

Susannah said, “Coffee for me.”

Ruby pointed at the jug. “I’ve brought enough for two. I guessed you would want coffee. I heard you coming in from the garden.”

“Oh, you are a love, Ruby.”

Ruby laughed and Edward watched the two of them; the lily and the rose like two pre-Raphaelite maidens in a painting by Edward Burne-Jones. They were so familiar with each other, so easy, almost as if they were sisters.

But then he thought there was so little company here that inevitably, two young women would gravitate together. But socially, they were so different. What did they talk about, other than local trivia and the weather, he wondered?

He said to Susannah. “Have you been out in the garden already?”

She nodded. “Yes, why?”

“But it’s freezing.”

She said, “My darlings need care at all times, especially in the snow.”

Ruby said, “I see it’s snowing again.”

“Delightful!” Susannah said. “I simply adore the snow.”

Ruby walked to the door, with one hand on the crystal door-knob, she smiled. “Breakfast will be here soon. Mrs Edmundson is hard at work.”

When she’d gone, Susannah said, “Are you determined to leave, Edward?”

"I am."

"But, as Ruby said, it's snowing again, quite heavily. Where are you headed for?"

"Knaresborough — the station."

"But that's miles. You'll freeze to death. Let me look at your shoes."

She ducked beneath the table, lifting the cloth and peering at his feet. "Do you have any boots?"

He shook his head.

She said, "Those shoes you have will soak through. You'll have frostbite before you've done a mile."

A masculine voice spoke. "I would lend him some boots, but I don't want to encourage him to leave." Dr Lovegrove entered, taking his seat, unfurling the napkin with a flourish and then stretching for the coffeepot. The rich dark aroma of the coffee, its steam, its warmth, lifted from his cup. "Please don't go, Edward."

"I must. I shall go insane if I stay."

After he'd eaten, he went to fetch his case from his room and then went to the lobby where his coat hung with hat and scarf and gloves.

Lovegrove and Susannah were waiting to see him off.

As Edward dragged on his coat, wrapped his scarf around his neck and pulled on his leather gloves, Lovegrove opened the door and the wind blew in a whirl of snowflakes. "Brrr!" Lovegrove said and shivered theatrically.

Susannah was beside him but she didn't seem to mind the cold even though Edward felt the frigid air right through his coat.

Putting on his hat, picking up his case, he went to the front door. Behind him, Ruby and Mrs Edmundson emerged from the passage. "We just came to see you off," Mrs Edmundson said.

"I know it's not my place," Ruby said, "But I don't think you should leave today. Wait until it thaws, then the taxi will be able to get through. Some of them drifts are three feet deep."

Edward turned to her, his brown eyes lingering, locking but

then leaving her blue ones. He said simply, "If I don't go now, I never will."

"This is very foolish, old man," Lovegrove said.

"Yes, Edward, please stay," Susannah said. "If this is all just a dream, what harm can it do you?"

"It's not a dream. It's a nightmare."

Shaking his head, he said, "I'm leaving now. All of you have been incredibly kind, but..."

His words gradually faded away. Suddenly, he found it was difficult for him to put into words why he was leaving. Maybe they were right. Had a woman really come into his bed? Had a man really been brought to life? Had another man really been killed and buried here? Surely, it was just the flow of a dream. He'd seen strange things indeed, but the more rational explanation was that he'd been hallucinating.

But a deeper part of him knew that, despite the house's warmth, food, and comfort, his very survival depended on his departure. He looked out the window at the relentless snowfall and admitted that the outside environment looked more dangerous. But, although he was afraid to leave Hackthwaite Hall, he was even more fearful of remaining inside its walls.

He didn't look at them. He stepped out and his feet sank in new snow. He heard the crunch of his steps, felt the slight slip underfoot as he trudged through the snow and within five paces his feet were wet, the cold ice-water seeping in through the stitches in the leather.

They were not expensive shoes. They were never meant to be worn in weather like this.

He didn't turn back to look at them, though he knew all four were standing watching him.

And then, when he got to the turn in the drive, he stopped, twisted his head and saw the front door of Hackthwaite Hall was closed. They had gone back inside and left him alone out here.

The snow fell as he walked. He had got only a hundred yards

before his feet were soaking and cold. The snowflakes slid down his neck past the collar of his coat. The icy wind found its way around the tops of his gloves. His feet were numb already. His departure was proving a bitter one.

He breathed in the frigid air, and it burned his mouth and lungs. The snow fluttered onto his lips, turning instantly to water in his mouth, and he slogged on.

Edward reached the main road and recollected the route the taxi had taken. Opting to follow the same direction, he began his journey down the road. It was clear from the untouched snow that no vehicles had traversed this route for quite some time.

Various animal footprints marked the snow, birds, a fox, a badger. Beyond these echoes of life, there was only the gently falling, drifting snow. The silence it brought seemed to hush the entire world, making everything tranquil and dead.

He arrived at a junction marked by a cast-iron fingerpost with the inscription 'Yorks North Riding C. C.' in black and white. He read the directions by clearing away the ice-hardened snow from the sign with his gloved hand. It said "Knaresborough 15".

It dawned on him that he could never cover that distance. A wave of dread washed over him. He would perish in the bitter winter landscape long before he arrived in Knaresborough, his body undiscovered. The snow would bury him, providing him with an eternal, icy slumber, and he would remain hidden until the thaw.

He could almost see the newspaper headline describing his tragic demise. He imagined Dr Lovegrove telling the Knaresborough Post how he'd strongly advised him against embarking on this perilous journey. His life would be reduced to the status of a cautionary tale.

He ploughed on past the sign for another hundred yards and then stopped. He stopped and looked back towards Hackthwaite Hall.

Chapter 19

Mrs Edmundson answered the door immediately. "You silly boy!" she said, then she turned her head and shouted into the house, "He's back, Dr Lovegrove."

Within seconds, Lovegrove appeared as if he had been waiting. "I was going to give you another fifteen minutes and then come after you. I knew you'd never make it, but you wouldn't listen to reason, so you had to be allowed to make your own mistakes before I came to rescue you."

Edward stepped into the entrance hall and between them, Mrs Edmundson and Dr Lovegrove stripped him of his sodden and snow-caked coat, hat and gloves and left them in a heap on the stone-flagged floor.

They supported him, rubbing his arms to return warmth and circulation into them as his teeth chattered. He shivered uncontrollably as they led him into the morning room, where they sat him in an armchair in front of the fire.

Ruby appeared. "You are an idiot, Edward. What on earth were you thinking? But you wouldn't be told. Anyway, I'm glad you're back."

"Bank the fire, Ruby," instructed Mrs Edmundson.

Edward heard the scrape and gritty clatter of the coals as Ruby obliged. Using the shovel, she heaped the coals from the scuttle into the already blazing fire. The coals were covered in clouds of coal dust, which were quickly drawn into the hungry flames, sparking and crackling as the dust was caught, burned, and consumed.

Despite his conflicting emotions, Edward found himself grateful for the warmth emanating from the blazing hearth as he sat in the Morning Room. The room held a strange significance; it was in this room that the coal waggon driver's body had been laid out — the same man who had been declared dead and then apparently resurrected.

Lovegrove poured golden liquid into a cut-glass tumbler from a crystal decanter on the walnut drinks table. He brought it and thrust it into Edward's hand, which shook so much from the cold that Edward couldn't raise it to his mouth without spilling.

He shivered even more as he warmed, but he clamped the glass to his lips and tipped it, drawing the burning whisky into his mouth and gulping it down, burning like fire in his gullet.

"He'd be better off with a hot cup of tea," Mrs Edmundson said.

"Probably, Mrs Edmundson, but this is what I had to hand."

"I'll make tea and get him some toast." Mrs Edmundson hurried from the Morning Room, calling, "Come on, Ruby."

Ruby stood there half a minute longer, her eyes lingering on him. Then she bent in and kissed his temple. "You are such an idiot, Edward."

Lovegrove watched her, but if he disapproved of such familiarity from his servants, he said nothing, not reprimanding her but watching her go and then turning, smiling, to Edward. "I've got some clothes you can borrow. You need to get out of these wet things."

Steam rose from the legs of Edward's trousers as he sat in front of the fire. "Thank you," he muttered.

"And when you're warmer and drier, you can come and look at my laboratory."

Edward had forgotten about the laboratory. He gazed stupidly at Lovegrove, his mind still half-frozen.

Lovegrove wagged his finger, grinning. "You see, you don't get away so easily!"

An hour later, having consumed tea and toast and been at the centre of Mrs Edmundson and Ruby's careful attention, Edward began to recover. Ruby, ever so considerate, had brought him a tartan blanket, draping it over his knees. Gradually, his shivering ceased. His body was warm again, albeit uncomfortably so, with his trousers now unpleasantly damp and the sleeves of his jacket giving off a faint steam.

Lovegrove appeared with a set of old-fashioned tweeds and a shirt and woollen tie.

"They should fit, though they're a bit old. They date from when I was a little slimmer, about your size."

Edward gazed at them.

Lovegrove said, "Ladies, if you would leave us a while, Edward is about to disrobe."

Something in Edward made him hesitate. He stared at the clothes in a pile now on the sofa, and the attentive Lovegrove nearby. "I can leave, if you'd prefer privacy to change," Lovegrove said.

"No, I don't need you to leave."

"Then chop-chop. Hurry and get out of those wet things."

But still Edward hesitated as if by taking off his own clothes, he would lose something of himself, some tangible reminder of who he was before he'd come to Hackthwaite.

"Come on, you silly boy. Are you quite well?" Lovegrove studied him.

"I'm not sure," Edward said. "I feel strange."

"It's the cold. Change your clothes and then we can go downstairs. I'm certain you'll find what awaits you quite intriguing," Lovegrove said.

"All right," Edward agreed, standing up. As he removed his woollen waistcoat and started to unbutton his shirt, he could feel the comforting warmth of the fire. He bent over and pulled off his socks.

Upon looking at his arm, something seemed off. He touched it, and the skin felt smooth, oddly numb. "What's this?" he asked, puzzled.

Lovegrove looked equally confused. "What's what, old chap?"

"My skin. It's too smooth, and I can't feel it." Edward scrutinised his arm, then noticed another similar patch on his stomach. "It's discoloured. It doesn't look like my skin anymore."

Lovegrove shook his head. "I can't see anything."

Edward jabbed at the discoloured smooth patch on his left forearm. "Here."

"Oh, there." Lovegrove shrugged. "Haven't you always had it?"

"No. My skin's never been like this before."

"Is it sore?"

"No. It just doesn't feel the same."

"Well, I wouldn't bother about it. If you're still troubled by it once the snow thaws, I can get the doctor over. Dr Poppe, a decent chap. But don't worry about that now. Come and see my lab!"

Lovegrove led Edward down the passage to a door that Edward hadn't noticed before. It was painted black and looked old. Lovegrove took a cast-iron key from his pocket and turned the lock. He opened the door and revealed stone steps that led down. Lovegrove flicked a switch and electric lights came on. "All mod cons in my lab, you see."

Edward felt strangely anxious. "Do I have to go down?" he said.

"You'll be very interested in my work, Edward. You have such an inquiring mind."

Following Lovegrove, feeling he had no choice, Edward put his hand to the wall as he walked down the stone steps. He was light-headed and unsteady.

As he descended, an unexpected warmth enveloped the underground space, and the air was filled with a faint acrid scent. Edward recognised the distinct odours of ammonia and sulphur.

Lovegrove went ahead, Edward trailed behind, rounding the passage corner into a large space.

The cellar he found himself in was walled by grey limestone that bore the imprints of age and absorbed the glow from the overhead electric lights, deadening everything. The floor was laid out with flagstones, their surfaces smooth from years of use but bearing irregular cracks and scratches from their long history.

Tables of various heights and sizes were scattered throughout the room, some as long as six feet, and others with more modest dimensions. An impressive display of scientific and alchemical apparatus was arranged across the tables. There were many retorts and alembics, some delicately crafted from glass, their transparent bodies revealing an assortment of brightly coloured concoctions.

Glass jars lined the surfaces of the tables, filled with a variety of substances ranging from mundane to bizarre. Some contained coloured powders, while others held liquids that shimmered in artificial light. There were also containers containing what appeared to be small organic specimens in a clear solution, perhaps once human.

Sturdy wooden shelves were attached to the walls, sagging slightly under the weight of large glass containers. These contained an even more diverse assortment of items. Some held intricate miniature moss and fern landscapes, others swirling, iridescent liquids, and a few rocks and crystals, their surfaces gleaming with a mesmerising sheen.

"This is where I do my work."

"Which is?"

"I make tinctures from the plants that Susannah grows. I feed her with them."

Lovegrove turned to face Edward, his expression undeterred by the disbelief that etched the younger man's features.

"I understand," he replied, his gaze moving back to the wonders on his tables. "It's a difficult thing to grasp, especially if you're not accustomed to such pursuits."

His hand motioned towards a series of flasks on a nearby table, their contents glowing with hues of violet, orange, and the palest green. They were like miniature worlds filled with unearthly light, captivating and almost otherworldly in their vibrancy.

He then gestured towards a collection of bottled oils resting on the same table. Their colours varied, some as clear as crystal, while others were of a deep, rich hue. Each bottle was a testament to careful distillation, their contents gleaming under the overhead lights.

Lovegrove moved his attention to the white crystals heaped in a small ceramic dish, their structure sharp and defined, a product of slow evaporation and meticulous measurement. "These are salts, a critical component in my work," he said, lightly running his fingers over the crystals.

Next, his gaze fell on a fat-bellied glass tube where a mess of leaves was simmering slowly in clear liquid. The leaves gave off a fragrant aroma, pungent and earthy, as their essence was methodically extracted.

"This is where I prepare the sustenance that will nurture the Poisoned Rose, until she gains the strength to sustain herself," Lovegrove explained, his voice filled with a strange mix of scientific determination and fatherly tenderness.

Edward shook his head. "None of this makes sense to me."

"And that's perfectly reasonable, Edward," Lovegrove replied, his voice steady, "Not all truths are meant to be understood at first glance. Sometimes, we must delve deeper, look beyond the superficial to see the marvel that hides beneath."

Edward looked around. "This place is so old."

"It was Cornelius Fludd's laboratory, although I have modernised the equipment somewhat."

"I don't feel well. It is the fumes?" Edward said.

"There is natural ventilation. I don't think it's the fumes."

Edward steadied himself against a solid wooden table. His hand brushed against several jars, filled with varying substances, causing them to wobble precariously. Lovegrove moved swiftly, securing the containers with a steady hand.

"Careful, Edward."

Edward stood. He was light-headed. If not the fumes, then perhaps the whisky? But he'd only had one.

Lovegrove said. "For over two years after I came, I thought I would succeed where Fludd had failed. He had created the Rose, but she was bound to the living earth as a plant is." He rubbed his beard. "I had some success. I managed to uproot her, but she can not go far from the earth she was born in, and every night has to return to the earth and sink her roots deep into it to nourish herself."

Lovegrove motioned towards the myriad of vials and flasks filled with luminescent concoctions, his face etched with despair. "This alchemical sustenance is but a meagre substitute for the nourishment the Rose needs, and, sadly, an inadequate one." Lovegrove sighed, a sound heavy with regret. "I've reluctantly accepted that the Rose cannot ever free herself from the confines of Hackthwaite to bestow her healing gifts upon the world, a world so desperately in need of healing after the horrendous war."

"I am not well," Edward said. "I feel ill."

Lovegrove continued, almost as if he was musing to himself rather than talking to Edward, "She herself is not free from the house, but what if the Rose had a human child? Or a half-human child, to be more correct."

Edward said, "This, Lovegrove, is all gibberish. Why not channel your energies into a noble field, such as medicine or chemistry?"

Lovegrove studied Edward for a moment, concern casting a shadow over his eyes. "Edward, you are indeed looking decidedly unwell."

The heat coursing through Edward's body was now a raging inferno, turning his skin numb.The acrid smell of the chemicals was overpowered by a sweet floral scent. He turned to see Susannah.

She picked up a vial of rose coloured oil, took out the rubber bung and was about to drink it.

Edward's head was spinning. Was he becoming delirious from the hypothermia? He hadn't heard Susannah come down. Was she really here, or was he imagining her?

"Edward, you need to sit," Susannah said, her voice softly commanding.

Lovegrove reached out to steady him, clutching his arm. As Susannah moved to take his other arm, she paused, her gaze locking with her father's. Lovegrove gave a slight nod, smiling at his daughter. "It doesn't matter anymore," he said.

She nodded and took his other elbow. He felt her fingers through the cloth of the borrowed jacket. They were warm. She was fragrant.

Together, they led him to the end of the laboratory. Here, a small anteroom had been dug out of the earth. The spartan room was furnished with an armchair, a lamp, and a table – an apparent sanctuary for Lovegrove amidst the chaos of his experiments.

"In here, Edward. Just sit here." Lovegrove led him to the chair, and he and Susannah lowered him into it.

"I... I'm so exhausted, yet I feel odd..." Edward's voice dwindled to a murmur.

"Just take it easy, old chap. There's nothing you need to worry about," Lovegrove replied, his voice a comforting balm.

Edward's consciousness ebbed and flowed. He watched through blurry eyes as Lovegrove and Susannah retreated towards the door. He heard the creak of the hinges as it closed, followed by the final, ominous click of the lock.

Chapter 20

Endless hours slipped away. The frigid temperature of the cell gnawed at Edward, making him shiver as his breath materialised into tiny wisps in the dim light. Unable to bear the biting cold of the chair, he rose and began pacing the room in a futile attempt to generate warmth. As more hours ebbed away, the cold seeped deeper into his bones.

His attention, previously unfocused, was now drawn to the

peculiar design of the door. It was disturbingly reminiscent of a prison cell door, fitted with a small window flap that could only be opened from the outside.

A chilling thought struck him: had this room previously served as a prison for others? The memory of what he'd seen in the garden, of Ned, the young gardener, surfaced, making the notion even more disconcerting.

Mrs Edmundson made no secret of the fact that Ned had died, and they had spun a fanciful tale about him falling victim to the Rose Child's poison, but Edward was now piecing together the grim reality. He surmised that Ned's life had been snuffed out by Lovegrove and his daughter, his body concealed where they believed no stranger would stumble upon it.

The motivation for such a monstrous act was beyond his comprehension, but perhaps the motives of murderers aren't always rational. Sometimes the act of killing provides a perverse pleasure, like the case of George Joseph Smith, who drowned his brides for nothing more than enjoyment.

Edward deduced that Ruby and Mrs Edmundson were mere pawns in the Lovegroves' malevolent game. Their simple, rustic minds had been effortlessly manipulated by the smooth-talking Dr Lovegrove and his daughter. Certainly, Susannah, with her angelic beauty, could easily disarm any suspicions of her capacity for murder. It's a common misconception that beauty and evil are mutually exclusive, a belief that Edward now had proof couldn't be further from the truth.

He now knew it was no hallucination. He'd seen those fingers stretching through the frozen soil.

Time seemed to blur in the dim light, the hours as indistinguishable as the surrounding shadows. So long went past that he thought it must now be evening.

The rattling of a pin drew his attention to the window. The tiny flap swung open, revealing Ruby's worried expression.

"Oh, Edward," she murmured, her eyes welling up with tears. "I'm so sorry."

His brow furrowed. The look on her face convinced him she had been taken in by Lovegrove. She held a bowl of soup. He wondered whether she'd brought him food because they told her to, or from her own basic decency, once she'd found out they'd locked him up here.

His appetite had been buried beneath layers of anxiety, his stomach knotted in nervous knots. "I don't feel much like eating," he said.

"But you need to eat, Edward," Ruby insisted, holding the bowl of soup in her hands.

"Ruby, what excuse did they give for locking me in down here? Surely you can see it can't be right." His voice echoed against the stone walls.

Ruby looked as though she might cry at any moment. She swallowed hard and replied in hushed tones, "Miss Susannah said you assaulted her."

"What?" he said, his voice suddenly loud, echoing off the stony walls.

"And she thinks she's carrying your child." He thought he heard a tremor in her voice. Even she must see how ridiculous and wicked this was.

He raked his hand through his hair. "This is ludicrous."

But he remembered a woman visiting him in the middle of the night. He had first thought it was Ruby, then Susannah, then Ruby. Now, it was clear that it had been Susannah. But the accent.

He studied what he could see of Ruby's face, listened to her voice. No, it had not been Ruby. She was too pure. Pure, but she'd fallen for this nonsense. But perhaps because she had become enamoured of him, she was jealous and believed Susannah's vile tale. Though even a country girl must know it was too soon for Susannah to know she was pregnant, and that fact in itself proved the whole thing a tissue of lies.

Ruby's voice pulled him back from his racing thoughts. "I know you wouldn't do something like that, Edward, but Dr Lovegrove is furious."

"When he left me, he didn't seem angry. He's a dreadful liar, Ruby. You mustn't believe him."

"Dr Lovegrove says one thing and does something else. The house staff know that. He's not the pleasant, straightforward man he appears to be," she said.

He felt he was winning Ruby round. He looked around him. "What does he do down here, in this...laboratory?" he said, his voice tense.

"I'm not sure. I never dared to ask," Ruby confessed.

He begged her, his voice trembling with desperation. "You have to help me, Ruby. You must know I have never abused a woman."

"I really want to believe you," she admitted. "I believed you were a gentleman. But, some men do do things like that. Did you and she...?" she faltered, unable to find the right words.

He shook his head emphatically.

Ruby continued, "I'm not saying you forced her — of course, you didn't. But were you...close?" Her cheeks flushed at the implication of her words.

He'd never forced himself on a woman, and he never would. Yet his mind was conflicted—one part believed he had never been intimate with a woman at all, while another part knew full well that he had slept with a woman right here in this very house. He held both notions in his head simultaneously, a falsehood and the truth. But because he preferred it, the lie prevailed. Now he had convinced himself of the truth of a lie; in his soul, he felt virginal and pure.

For all his vaunted rationality, he opted to believe what he wished to be true over what truly was.

"No," he said emphatically. "No, we weren't. We didn't do that. You must understand that I am not that kind of man."

Ruby said, "Of course. Of course. You're not like that."

As he spoke these words, vivid visions of his trial and vindication flashed through his mind — a court filled with righteous rage, Lovegrove revealed as a treacherous scoundrel, and twelve honourable jurors finding him innocent. He had never had sexual relations with any of the women at Hackthwaite Hall! How dare they suggest it! He urged the imagined jury to find him innocent. He withdrew himself from the imagined future courtroom that would vindicate his honour, back to the coldness of the present locked cellar.

"We must call the police, Ruby," he said. "They will release me from this place, and Lovegrove will get his comeuppance."

Ruby did not reply.

"The police must be called," he repeated.

Ruby sighed. "But what if Dr Lovegrove is just protecting Susannah as he sees fit? I'm sure that all this can be sorted out without the police. If she's making it all up, he'll have to face the truth and reconcile with you."

He wouldn't be put off. "How soon can the police be here?"

"When it thaws?"

"I'm sure they will come sooner. They are the police, after all. A little ice on the roads shouldn't stop them."

"There's been a lot of snow down, Edward."

"Has he called them? If he thinks I've done what he says, then he should have."

"I don't think so."

"That proves his lie. Can you call them for me — to end this rigmarole?"

She frowned. "Me? No, I..."

He sighed. "Ah, you're worried you'll lose your position."

"Yes."

Hie wheedled. "But I don't have lots of time, Ruby. It's freezing down here. I'll die of cold."

"I can bring a blanket."

"But that's not enough, Ruby. I am so cold here. I can't wait days. I don't have days."

"I know. I know." She was crying.

"Can you let me out?"

"I...I would get into serious trouble," she stammered.

"I could pretend to overpower you, or... I don't know. All I know is that I need to escape. I swear as soon as I reach town, I'll turn myself into the police, and they can untangle this absurd situation."

"But you couldn't make it through the snow last time you tried." Ruby reminded him.

"This time it's different. The stakes are higher. I must get out." He was determined now, his face grim. "And you, Ruby, must help me. For the love of all that's human, you can't leave me to die here."

"Believe me, Edward, I don't want you to suffer," Ruby said.

"Do you know where the keys to this cell are?"

She nodded. "He keeps all his keys on a hook near the door at the bottom of the stairs."

"Go and fetch them."

She hesitated. "I can't just now. We can't attempt an escape now. It's not late enough. Dr Lovegrove and Susannah are still awake. Besides, Dr Lovegrove keeps a gun," Ruby said, her voice barely above a whisper.

"He'd never use it."

She remained silent.

Edward pleaded. "When can you let me out, then? Please, the sooner the better."

He saw the terrible conflicted expression on her face.

"Please."

He was obviously winning her round. She hesitated, then said quietly, "I can come down in the night. But not till midnight."

Edward was not oblivious to Ruby's suffering. "I wouldn't want you to lose your job because of this," he remarked. "I realise there isn't a lot of work in these rural parts, but the pursuit of justice is more important than money. I know you appreciate how serious this situation is for me."

"I do, Edward." She paused before continuing. "Would you mind taking me with you when you return to Cambridge? I'm sure I could find something to do there. Perhaps we could even—"

Edward knew what she was implying. He frowned. "I'm not sure that's a possibility, Ruby. You know, it would be improper for you to live in my rooms. It would be unacceptable and unseemly. I'm thinking of you, of course. Your reputation would suffer greatly as a result. You must preserve your reputation in order to be employable in good households. You see that, don't you?"

She averted her gaze; her dismay obvious. "Yes, I suppose you're right."

"Please understand, I'm not being unappreciative."

"No, I understand. I'm only a girl in service; I'm neither a lady nor an intellectual. I understand we can't be together. But I could still make my own way there. I could get by in Cambridge, don't worry. And perhaps we could meet up now and again?"

He sighed. "Perhaps. After you release me, we could certainly travel together to Cambridge, and I could offer you some money to help you find a place to stay when we got there."

She gave him a forlorn smile. "That would be wonderful. Thank you very much. Don't worry — I'll be back at midnight. I'll bring your coat, gloves, and hat with me."

"Thank you so much, Ruby. You are exceptionally gracious."

"Even if graciousness is the limit of our relationship," she said, then turned and walked away.

She was a fine girl, he thought. He was clearly breaking her heart, and he was sorry about that, but what would his friends say? No, they could travel together to Cambridge, and there their ways would part.

Edward looked at the bowl of soup. It had cooled so much as to be unappealing, but given his hunger, he ate it anyway.

Chapter 21

Inside his frigid cell, Edward's thoughts began to meander. He found himself in a peculiar mental state. He had once read that individuals on the brink of hypothermia often experienced a tranquillity, followed by confusion, then an overwhelming urge to lie down. Alarmingly, this is exactly how he felt.

In an attempt to shake off the growing numbness, he paced back and forth across the room, slapping his sides with his hands. The smooth, green patches on his skin, which had initially appeared small and isolated, were spreading. Each patch was about the size of a two-shilling piece, and where before there had been only two or three, there were now at least half a dozen.

Edward knew he was sickening; he needed medical attention, but it was clear that would not be possible until he could escape his current confinement.

The bitter cold was relentless. Edward resorted to star jumps in a frantic attempt to retain body heat. He lost all notion of time as the hours blurred together in the freezing chamber. Then, unexpectedly, the window in his cell door opened, revealing the face of Susannah.

"Edward, my heart aches for you in this situation," Susannah began.

"Regrettably, your sympathy doesn't make the air any warmer," he said, then abruptly, "Why on earth does your father think I assaulted you?"

She shook her head. "I'm afraid that Father has got it into his head that you crept into my room and had your way with me."

"Then let him call the police," Edward said.

"He intends to, once the snow melts."

"I might not survive that long in this cold," Edward said.

She laughed, perhaps mistaking his tone for humour.

"I'm deadly serious, Susannah. I'm gradually freezing in this cell. If I'm left here, I won't last the night. I'm begging you, help me out of here."

"I'm afraid I can't. My father would never forgive me. You see, he believes he's protecting me."

"But he's not. I'm not that kind of man."

"No, you're not."

"Then if you haven't come to let me out, and you haven't brought me any food–"

"–that's Ruby's job."

"Indeed. But if neither of those two things, what have you come here for?"

"I felt the need to share a bit of news: The Rose has blossomed."

"What?"

"She is with child, Edward. A direct result of your actions."

"The Rose? You're still clinging to this absurd notion."

"You should be proud of yourself, Edward. You managed to fulfil your role as a man — finally, and I am sure so many thought you never would, what with your head in your books and your awful stilted shyness, the odds were against you."

His cheeks burned crimson.

She continued, "Of course, you had a little help. You had to be guided down the flower path as it were, but we got there in the end."

"I'm not feeling well, Susannah. I've developed some sort of skin condition, unlike anything I've experienced before. I need medical attention. I'm unsure whether it's a result of the cold or something I've contracted, but I urgently need to see a physician."

"You will see a doctor, Edward. All in due course."

He scoffed. "When it thaws?"

"Possibly sooner. But now it's time to rest. I just wanted to share the joyous news that you're about to become a father."

She closed the window and left Edward alone.

He sat in the dark in the cell beneath Hackthwaite Hall. Susannah generally went to bed about ten and that meant it was about two hours short of midnight, and at midnight, Ruby would come, but only if her courage didn't fail her.

He trusted Ruby's innate good nature and sense of what was right. He had to. He was at her mercy and he could only hope she would follow through on her promise and that she was a decent enough girl that she wouldn't allow him to freeze to death in this infernal chamber of ice and cold.

He was dozing, his mind drifting, his dreams winding round like a spiral staircase, when the rattle of the chain and the wooden click of the window shocked him awake.

Ruby hissed. "I have the key. Stand back, I'll open the door."

The door creaked open, allowing the feeble glow from the cellar to infiltrate the stark blackness of the cell. He squinted, feeling as if he were an actor on stage, caught unprepared as the house lights come up and the play begins.

Rising to his feet, his knees protested, numb and painful. Ruby stood in the doorway, holding out his belongings, as he stumbled on his stiff legs.

"Here's your overcoat and hat," she said, handing them over.

Awkwardly, he reached out, clumsy fingers tangling in the items before his hat slipped from his grasp. Ignoring it for the moment, he pulled the heavy woollen overcoat onto his shoulders, and the immediate return of trapped body warmth seeped into his chilled skin.

Bending, he retrieved his fallen hat. "Thank you, Ruby. I can't thank you enough," he said. Then, on impulse, he lunged forward, wrapping her into a hug. He felt her shoulders and arms and her breasts pressed against him. As the realisation of his action dawned on him, he hastily stepped back. "Sorry, I'm just... so relieved."

Ruby gave him a wide grin in response to his sudden hug, teasing him, "I never knew you had such boldness in you!"

"Sorry!" he said again.

"It's too late for you to be sorry," she said cryptically.

"What do you mean?"

She chose to ignore him. "Susannah and the doctor are asleep," she said, whispering like she was telling him secrets. "Mrs Edmundson as well. We're the only ones awake now. You and I."

He was already looking for a way out of the dimly lit cellar. "Which way?"

"Just follow me up the stairs and be as quiet as a mouse," she said. "Be brave, Edward."

They ascended the stairs with an almost theatrical stealth, tiptoeing to keep the ancient wooden boards silent. Upon reaching the top, Ruby eased the door open with a soft click. A welcoming warmth enveloped Edward as they emerged from the cellar's icy embrace into the heated parts of the house.

Hope kindled within him, the flickering flame of survival. Edward's thoughts raced toward Knaresborough, then further, with the roaring wheels of a train whisking him to York, and ultimately back to Cambridge.

He was just glad to get away and decided he probably would not now speak to the police. He just wanted to forget all this madness.

In his gratitude, he whispered to Ruby, "Are you still wanting to come to Cambridge?"

She nodded. "I've been wanting to leave for so very long."

"Well, you can't stay with me in Hall, but my colleague's wife takes in lodgers. Her rent is very reasonable."

"That would be splendid, Edward."

Chapter 22

It was pitch black in the corridors of Hackthwaite Hall.

"Which direction to the front door?" asked Edward.

Ruby responded by placing her hand on his shoulder. He had hugged her and somehow this initiated a new level of contact between them, making touch an accepted language. She led him forward, her fingers wrapping around his forearm in gentle insistence, soft taps on his elbow serving as unspoken directions. On an impulse, she brushed away the hair that veiled his eyes.

"With your hair like that, it's a wonder you can see at all," she teased, her laughter echoing softly in the quiet night.

She seemed too light-hearted. Something was wrong.

She'd told him that the doctor's room was above the main door, and explained they shouldn't risk going that way that in case they woke him.

"Which way then?"

"There's a back way. We have to go out into the quadrangle."

"Through the Rose Garden?"

"Yes, that's quickest. Then there's a small door that leads to a passage that opens up at the other end to the outer gardens. It's not long. The gardeners use it."

"Used it," Edward corrected without much thought, the old habit of precision overpowering any delicacy for the feelings Ruby might hold for her lost lover.

"Used it," she agreed, falling into a thoughtful silence.

Edward shut the warm, shadowy comfort of the house behind him, the click of the garden door echoing as it closed and they stepped into a world painted in radiant silver and deep black. Above them, the moon held court in the cloudless sky, the faint twinkling presence of Jupiter and Mars as her minor attendants.

The chill was biting. Edward buttoned up his coat. "Which way now?" he asked.

"Stay on this path," Ruby guided him again, with hand taking his wrist.

Edward fell in step behind Ruby, plunging into the labyrinthine paths of the Rose Garden. All dressed up in moonshine, the stunning tapestry of plant life bore the surreal, midwinter spectacle of roses in full bloom, an impossibility in the natural course of things.

Vibrant clusters of woody nightshade made a brazen show of their bright-red attire, while the lustrous black berries of deadly nightshade added a dangerous allure to the nocturnal beauty; their dark leaves stood in stark contrast to the glistening, frost-kissed paths they bordered.

Between the rows of nightshades, Cuckoo Pints stood vigil, their arrow-shaped leaves piercing the silvery moonlight. Their green and purple speckled hoods rose from curled spathes like the heads of strange lurking creatures.

Foxgloves, in uniform, serried rows, towered along the pathways, their bell-shaped flowers defying the harsh winter. The clusters of flowers, usually pinks and purples, were tonight, under the pale luminescence of the moon, ghost-white, their colours leached by the unearthly glow.

The rose bushes around them rose to a height of six feet, their thorny branches intertwining to form an almost impenetrable wall on either side of the path. They could see nothing on either side and hardly anything ahead. In daylight, their complex network of paths had confounded him, turning a casual stroll into a disorienting maze. Tonight, Edward relinquished any attempt at navigation. He had to trust Ruby and that she knew where she was going.

"Drat it," she said. "I've come the wrong way."

"Perhaps we should have gone around the maze, even though it is further."

"No, no," she said. "We have to go through the Rose Garden."

He hissed, "We need to get out of this house. You want to come with me, don't you? Then we need to hurry before we're caught."

She wasn't listening. She stopped again. "I think this is the right way."

The rose bushes grew higher here and their height meant he and Ruby stood in deep shadow where the moonlight did not reach. She didn't move. It was like she was waiting for something.

He was losing patience. "If it's the right way, why don't you go forward?"

Her voice changed. "I'm frightened, Edward."

He was exasperated. "Frightened? Why have you suddenly got frightened?"

"Up there, amongst the shadows," she pointed. "Someone's standing there."

He peered into the dark. He saw nothing. He said, "I thought you said Lovegrove was in bed? Who could it be? You're imagining things. Let's go."

"I think it *is* Dr Lovegrove..."

Edward stepped in front of Ruby, peering past her to look into the ink-black, midnight-black dark. Then he stopped, torn between his desire to escape and his terror of what might be standing just ahead in the dark. He was suddenly terrified that it might be Lovegrove, even though reason told him it was impossible.

It was hard to see anything. He stared, pulled back. There was a shadow, but it must be the shadow of a plant that looked like a man.

He sighed. "There's no one there, Ruby. Let's hurry."

She wouldn't move. "No, Edward, there is someone there."

He raised his voice. "Don't be a hysterical woman. Come on, we have to go."

She grabbed at his arm. "I'm frightened, Edward."

He'd had enough. "Well then, you can stay. The garden door to the passage that leads outside is the other side of the maze. Is that right?"

She nodded.

"And I don't need a key to get out?"

"No. It's never locked."

"Then I'm getting out of here."

"You'd leave me?"

"I'm very grateful that you let me out, Ruby, but I must go."

She was silent. She was probably going to cry.

He said, "It's not that you're not attractive, it's just we're of different classes. It wouldn't have worked."

"No, I suppose you're right," she said. "Thank you for saying I'm not unattractive. It's the greatest compliment you've ever paid me."

"Goodbye, Ruby." He turned and walked along the path, into the dark and, despite her saying she was frightened, she followed him. But he didn't care about her now, he just wanted to escape this dreadful house and this dreadful maze.

But then, in an area where moonlight bathed the limestone path with a pearl-white glow, he saw Dr Lovegrove.

"Leaving like a thief in the night, eh?" Lovegrove said.

Edward puffed himself up, filled with righteous anger. "Dr Lovegrove. You have no right to keep me here. I don't know what you think I've done to Susannah, but I assure you…"

Lovegrove waved away Edward's hollow piety. "That was all a pretext, dear boy. Whatever you did and whomever you did it with, it was always my plan, not yours. I had hoped you would be man enough to court her yourself, but that was not to be, I quickly realised that, and so we set it up between us."

"A pretext? What for?"

"Initially, to be my little pollinator. That done, to fertilise the waiting soil. That meant to get you here in the garden under the waxing moon before the Solstice, a most auspicious time."

"An auspicious time for what?"

"All those books you've read and you've never come across anything on gardeners' lore?"

Edwards mouth dried and his palms grew moist. He stammered, "Let me leave. I don't know what you're talking about."

"What I'm talking about, dear boy: blood and bone meal — very good for the roses. And if I want my flowers to flourish, then this is the most opportune time to apply it."

Edward heard a noise behind him. He spun round to see Ruby standing on the path in the soft glow of the ivory moon.

"Ruby?"

But this was a version of Ruby unlike any he had seen before. She was standing off the path on a bare patch of earth. Her shoes were discarded, leaving her feet exposed. Her toes, curling downwards, dug into the frost-laden soil as though they were roots seeking nourishment.

Lovegrove said, "Behold the poisoned rose!"

"Ruby? But, I thought..."

"We played quite the trick on you, my dear boy," Lovegrove said. "A sleight of hand, as it were."

And then to the side of Lovegrove, Edward saw Susannah. She too was rooted in the ground, drawing sustenance from the dark earth of the Rose Garden.

Lovegrove grinned. "I have two daughters, you see. But I need a son."

Edward was stunned, his mind unable to understand the terrifying reality unfolding before him. As he turned his head to run, Lovegrove's hand closed around the shaft of his gardener's spade. He said, "The touch would kill you eventually, but I have never been a patient man."

Lovegrove swung the spade with all his strength, bringing the edge cutting down on Edward's head.

The blow drove Edward spiralling into darkness, and pain erupted throughout his body. Blood spurted from his lacerated scalp, scalding hot, steaming up into the December night. Blood ran through his hair, blood ran down his forehead and cheeks, and blood ran into his eyes, then, still hot, it pooled on the ground and the dark cold earth drank it up.

Edward collapsed into a tangle of bindweed, and lay surrounded by tall foxgloves and roses, disoriented and weakened. The prickly briars wrapped themselves around his damaged body, their curved spines digging into his flesh like venomous barbs, securing their grip. He gasped there, his life force leaking out.

In his agony, Edward's gaze was drawn to the surrounding plants. The moonlight exacerbated the toxic sheen of monkshood and nightshade in his hazy eyesight. In a bizarre twist of fate, a new bloom sprouted from the damp soil, nurtured by his life blood. It was a strange creation, a hybrid rose he'd never seen before, its petals a haunting shade of blood-red, dripping with a menacing milky fluid.

Edward died, but a new Rose Child was to be born — one with a human father who could break free of Hackthwaite, and with its grandfather, walk the world.

Chapter 23

Yorkshire in May has a great beauty to it. The sweet scent of hawthorn blooms haunts the air, and the lively voices of little birds fill the daylight hours, serenading the awakening countryside.

Hackthwaite Hall embraced the spirit of summer, with tables on the grass that gently sloped down towards the lovely pond on its front lawn.

Water lilies grew on the placid surface, creating a peaceful haven for coots, moorhens, and ducks as they manoeuvred the floating duckweed.

Dr Harold Lovegrove sat in the idyllic scene with his daughter Susannah, sipping cool Pimms as the sun warmed them. Mr Mortimer, their new guest, oozed youthful vigour, his cheeks slightly reddened by the sun's caress.

"I am delighted you have finally arrived, Mr Mortimer," Dr Lovegrove said cheerfully.

The young man settled back into his seat, sipping his drink and taking in the atmosphere. "What a wonderful site this is. What a charming antique house. Is it Jacobean?"

Dr Lovegrove laughed. "Some of it is older, but significant remodelling occurred during the Jacobean period. In the seventeenth century, it was held by a man named Cornelius Fludd."

"The alchemist?" Mr Mortimer's interest was piqued.

Susannah's eyes glowed with curiosity. "Do you know who he is?"

"Only in passing," said Mr Mortimer modestly.

"You will find my library quite fascinating, Mr Mortimer," Dr Lovegrove said. "It holds a lifetime's worth of treasures."

Mr Mortimer's excitement was evident. "I can't wait to start cataloguing it. I believe it has never been done before?"

"No, it has remained uncatalogued until now."

"What a delightful undertaking!" Mr Mortimer gushed.

Mrs Edmundson, the housekeeper, arrived on the lawn with a platter of sandwiches. Ruby, bearing a baby in her arms, accompanied her.

Mr Mortimer's gaze was drawn to the radiant mother, entranced by her beauty. Nonetheless, his interest in the infant itself was small. He couldn't help but note how keen ladies were to show off their children.

"And this is our distinguished team. I thought it would be appropriate for you to meet them," Lovegrove said.

"Very nice to meet you, sir, " Mrs Edmundson said.

Mr Mortimer rose from his seat and extended his hand to Mrs Edmundson. "It's a pleasure to meet you, Mrs. Edmundson." "How about you, Mrs...?"

"Mrs Smith," Ruby said with a friendly smile. "My husband is the gardener around here." She gave the baby a kind look. "He adores our little Rose, but I suspect he loves his rose garden even more."

"He rarely strays from it," Dr Lovegrove added.

Susannah laughed. "Indeed, Edward is quite devoted to his horticultural haven."

Mr Mortimer's curiosity was peaked. "You said the rose garden is in the quadrangle. I expect I'll meet Edward when I visit the enchanted kingdom of the roses."

Susannah nodded to reassure him. "I am confident you shall, Mr Mortimer." She looked very beautiful that day. She said, "Do you have children yourself, Mr Mortimer?"

He shook his head. "No, not yet."

Susannah smiled. "Not yet? Then you hope to have one soon."

"Not soon, but someday."

Ruby grinned. "I'm sure we can help you with that."

PART TWO

Cumbria

The Bewcastle Fairies

IT WAS CHRISTMAS 1653, not that there was a real Christmas that year since Oliver Cromwell and his Puritans had banned Christmas as a pagan festival. Instead, we were to have a 'silent contemplation' of the birth of Christ.

Silent contemplation, my arse. I needed ale. So, I set off Christmas morning leaving my good wife Jane with the plucked goose and my sons and daughters to do the work needed before I returned to eat. Myself, I got my old bay mare Jenny. The fact that the horse is called a similar name to my wife is a cause of some confusion to me at times, especially after a few pints sunk.

I clip-clopped on Jenny along the road to Bewcastle. The road is rough. You couldn't get a cart over the ruts and stones in the winter mud. But Jenny managed it just fine.

I arrived at the King's Head, a rough, tumble-down sort of place, but very close to my heart to be greeted by Ned, the landlord. 'What are you doing here today Alexander Armstrong? Shouldn't you be having a silent contemplation of our Lord's birth?' He cackled.

'I'd rather do it over a pint of your best ale. I can contemplate while I'm looking into the bubbles,' I said.

And so I drank one. I drank another one from my leather tankard, which I take with me everywhere on the off chance I may call into an alehouse. Then I sank yet another. There was no one in the pub that Christmas Day but me. At least Ned had the fire on.

'Banned Christmas, eh?' Ned said as way of conversation.

'Cromwell,' I spat.

'You a Royalist then, Alex?'

I shook my head. 'I'm an Armstrong. We Armstrongs look after each other. Not English, not Scotch, not Royalists not Parliamentarians. Just Armstrongs. We live here in the Debatable Lands and we see to ourselves. So, no Neddy. I'm no Royalist. And I don't care whether Christmas is banned. I never cared for it much, anyway.' I looked around. 'Seems it scared the rest of your customers away.'

Ned said, 'No, never had many in Christmas morning. Usually they choose to be with their families.'

He was making some point. I said, 'Maybe they have wives better favoured in the looks department than my Jane.'

He looked like he might say something more but I was a good customer so he spat into the fire instead.

After five pints, I was feeling a little unsteady.

'You having a goose?' he said.

'Aye.'

'You'd better be off, hadn't you?'

'Suppose.'

'Well, Merry Christmas,' he said, standing.

I stood too, with a little wobble. The beer had gone to my head. 'Merry Christmas, Neddy.' I gave him a big hug which took him aback rather. He showed me to the door. He held it open so I could go out. The cold wind blew in, fluttering the fire, rattling the pots and squeaking through all the holes in the wainscotting. It was snowing.

'Very Seasonal,' said Ned.

'Aye.'

'You've a bit of a ride home.'

'Aye. But Jane's a good horse.'

'You mean, Jenny,' he said. 'Jenny's your horse. Jane's your wife.'

I laughed. 'Thanks for reminding me, Ned.'

The poor old mare stood shivering, hitched outside. In Bewcastle nothing moved as I rode through the snow. It got in my face, cold and wet, and down my neck. I leaned over the saddle and trusted Jenny to take me home.

But the snow grew to be a blizzard, and we could hardly see. Jenny was struggling because the snow had grown so deep, and I was getting cold now and shivering with the wet. I wished myself home and thought of the goose waiting for me. I regretted my comments about Jane's looks. She was a dutiful wife and cooked a fine goose. If rather plain of face and fat of arse.

We came into a stand of trees. Snow clung to them and whipped across my face. I'd ridden this road a thousand times, nay, ten thousand, in my years, but this place looked strange to me. The snow was in heaps and still blowing, whipping across. Jenny's mane had snow on it. My fingers were blue with cold and numb. My hat had a crust of snow as did my shoulders and even into the turn-ups of my sleeves.

The wood went on a while, perhaps because our progress through the snow was difficult and slow. I began to think I would freeze to death before I got home.

And then behind the flitting curtain of snow, I saw a light: a golden light. It came from beyond the trees. I'd never seen a light like it before. It was like the sun rising on a beautiful summer morning, but in the middle of the snow and the trees.

We struggled through the weather and the path took us towards the light. As we got closer, the snow faltered and then vanished as if it were banished by the golden light. As if we'd crossed a curtain. And now, I could see the source of the light. It came from a hill I recognised as the one they call Skelly How. They say it is an ancient place and the old folk shun it saying it is the home of the fairies. But they are idiots.

I thought nothing of such stupidity, but the change in the weather was odd. I looked around amazed at the golden glow. It was as if the sun had suddenly chased away the snow, and we stood within an enchanted circle.

Jenny neighed and shook her head to clear the ice from her mane. I took off my hat and shook it and then I saw a man. I didn't see how he appeared; it was as if he had just appeared.

He was the strangest-looking fellow. Tall and thin with white hair as fine and crisp as if it were made of spun sugar. His complexion was bone white too with a sharp nose and black lips. His eyes were the deepest violet with no pupils, just enormous violet irises which blocked out the whites completely. He wore a long gold brocaded coat of blue satin — hardly suited to the weather I had just been travelling through, though more fitted to this warm place I found myself in now. From his look, I wondered if he was French.

He spoke English like a gentleman from down south, not one of us country folk. 'Alexander Armstrong, is it?' he said quite pleasant.

I nodded. 'Who asks?'

'My name is Mr Spindledrift Goodfellow.'

I cleared my throat. 'I'm not familiar with that name, Mr Goodfellow. Where do you hail from?'

'Here and there.'

I peered at the strange-looking man. 'Where is that exactly?'

He laughed. 'Under dale and over hill.'

I grew suspicious. 'I'm not familiar with that place. It seems to me that you are being rather evasive, Mr Goodfellow.'

'Oh, no. Not at all, Mr Armstrong. ' He seemed to be keen to change the subject. 'To cut to the chase, Mr Armstrong, I find myself in need of someone to take a particular object off my hands. Think of it as a trade..'

'A trade?' Here it was. Typical Frenchman.

'Yes. Here it is.' He reached into his coat and pulled out a golden sphere. A soft glow emanated from it and I thought it was humming to itself, though I could be mistaken.

'What's that?' said I.

'It's an egg.'

'An egg?' and when I looked at it, it did now seem that it was egg-like. Not shaped like an egg, no it was perfectly round. But something egg-like inhered to it. 'What kind of egg?'

'A magic egg.'

I threw back my head and laughed. He was surely jesting with me for there is no such thing as a magic egg. 'And what will it give hatch to?' said I.

'Your fortune.'

I laughed. 'My fortune?'

'Riches beyond your dreams. Are you interested?'

I looked at the egg. It might even be made of gold and if he was foolish enough to trust me with something obviously valuable, then that was his loss.

I tilted my head. 'So, what's the catch?'

He looked innocent. 'No catch. Why would there be a catch?'

'Because strangers don't normally give me golden eggs for nothing in return.'

He said, 'I didn't say for nothing. But it's for almost nothing.'

'What is the cost?' said I.

'Just a tiny thing,' said he.

'A tiny thing? What tiny thing?'

'Just a drop.'

'A drop of what?' I felt he had something to hide.

He smiled a crooked smile. 'Just a tiny drop of your blood. It'll be easy enough to get. Just a scratch.'

'That's a most extraordinary request.'

'It's a most extraordinary egg.'

'And it will give me riches?' It would give me a few shillings at least if I sold it, that's for sure.

'Whatever you want.'

'And all this for a drop of blood.'

'Yes, indeed. Just a tiny drop too.'

I thought this man to be a fool. I stared at the golden egg in his outstretched palm. 'Can I feel it?' I asked.

'Certainly.' He handed me the egg. It was heavy and smooth and cool in my hand. It certainly felt heavy enough to be gold, though I'd never handled such an amount of gold before. 'It's really gold? I asked.

He nodded briskly.

'And you'll give me this in exchange for a drop of blood?'

'Yes.'

'But why do you want blood?'

'To make sure you return the egg. I want it back a year and a day from today.'

'So St Stephen's Day next year?'

'I don't like to call it that, but yes.'

I shrugged. I kept the egg in my right hand and extended my left arm. The sleeve of my coat rode up exposing my hairy forearm. 'Take your drop.'

His grin broadened. He took out a little crystal phial, fiddled with the stopper and, when he had removed the stopper, he went towards my forearm with the fingers of his left hand. For the first time I noticed his fingernails. They were long and sharp, each one extending from his finger-ends like the claws of a chicken and it struck me that there was something exceedingly birdlike about him.

He darted forward and pierced my arm with the pointed nail of his index finger. I drew my arm back with a yelp, but he said, 'Arm.'

A stream of blood ran from where he'd pricked me. It was

nothing really, so I extended my arm towards him again. He took his little crystal bottle and placed it under my arm to catch the drips.

'That's more than a drop,' said I.

'What's a drop or two between friends?' said he, grinning and showing me his sharp little teeth.

And then his crystal bottle was full. He pushed the stopper back in it.

'So that's it?' I asked.

'Absolutely,' said he.

'Give me the egg.'

'Of course.' He was still smiling. It was obvious I had the better part of the deal because all he had was blood and I had a golden egg. Even if it was brass, I'd still get a shilling or so for it in Carlisle. I had no intention of returning to this spot next St Stephen's Day. None whatsoever, despite what Mr Spindledrift Goodfellow might think.

'I can leave now?' I asked.

'You can. But be back next St Stephen's Day with my egg.'

I took the egg. Slipped it in my pocket. The weight was reassuringly heavy. It might even be gold. It might even be. I smiled.

As I turned Jenny to leave Mr Goodfellow, he said, 'Think of this as an act of philanthropy, Mr Armstrong, but remember this is merely a loan. Once it has given you a year of riches.'

'Yis, yis, aye,' said I as I trotted off on Jenny.

Soon, like a curtain falling, I was back in the snow and the golden glow was a memory. In fact, it felt like a dream. So much so, that I tapped the pocket of my overcoat but found the heavy egg reassuringly present.

I got home. Got my goose, drank my ale and fell asleep by the fire while Jane and the girls cleared up. The lads had gone courting to their fancy pieces. Christmas came and went. And New Year. I had a fine New Year, made even better when my uncle Joseph from Lanercost died and left me £5.

When I heard that, I took the egg from the hidey-hole I'd found for it in a hole in the byre wall and I swivelled it round in my fingers, talking to it like it was a child. 'So did you do this, oh egg?' said I, but the egg didn't reply, just glistened in the light of my lantern. 'Did you bring me £5? If so, I thank you.'

And in January, five cattle strayed onto my land. So I kept them. Andrew Hetherington from over Gillalees turned up at my gate saying they were his, but I saw him off at the tip of my sword. They maybe were, but he couldn't prove it. Silly fool hadn't marked them.

In February, my daughter Mary got a wedding arrangement and me a generous dowry from Tom Greenhow from Triermain's father for him to take her off my hands.

I had thought of taking the egg to Carlisle to sell it. It seemed hard to believe that my good fortune was tied to this thing. But I smiled when I held the egg, turning it over and over in my fingers. Maybe it really was magic.

In March, the weather still didn't improve, but my Jane took ill and died, which was a blow, for I had no one to cook and clean for me. The children were mortally upset at the death of their mother, but they were always soft.

So, I had to hire a maidservant to do the work that Jane had done for nothing, especially with Mary going soon. The cost of it grieved me, though I did drive down the price from the ridiculous sum the girl first asked.

She was a comely one, the new maid Sarah Morton. Very comely, dark-haired and young. With a few drinks taken, one night, I grabbed her firm arse, and that was that. She agreed for me to be her husband. I am an attractive man, if I say so myself. My animal deals were going well, and I prospered. Now, I had a lithe young thing in my bed at night, and because she was to marry me, I didn't have to pay her now for the housework. So, Jane's death worked out well. After I took Sarah Morton to my bed, the children refused to speak to me, and left. Another cost removed.

In April, the weather improved, and I decided to take my trip to Carlisle. I got Jenny out and took the egg to get it valued. It took me all day to get there, but I stayed in the Crown and Mitre. Then I walked round to see John Walker, who was a jeweller and silversmith who had a shop on English Street. Walker was a Scotchman, originally from Kirkcudbright, though I didn't hold that against him.

He knew his stuff and as he sat there with his eye-glass and the egg up close. 'Where did you get this?'

'Here and there.'

He snorted.

I asked, 'Is it gold?'

He nodded and said in his Scotch brogue, 'Aye, it is. Pure too. Honestly Mr Armstrong, this is a most uncommon thing. It's worth a fortune.'

He was foolish to tell me that. 'How much would you give me for it?'

'Well,' he began to mutter. I knew his brain would be calculating his profit. 'Really...' He mumbled on.

I grew tired with him. 'How much Mr Walker?'

He stuttered. 'I'll give you £200 pounds for it.'

'Scotch or English?'

'Scots.'

'Make it English.'

'Very well.'

'It's worth more than that,' said I and he remained tight-lipped. It might be worth more than that, but I'd have to travel to York or London to get more. £200 was a fortune indeed. So I agreed. '£200 pounds English then. When can I have the money?'

'Tuesday.'

It was Saturday. 'Too long.' I said. 'Make it Sunday.'

'I don't trade on the Lord's Day.'

I snorted. 'You trade any day.'

'No, sir; I do not.'

Idiot that he was. 'Monday then,' I said.

He looked pained. 'Monday it is.'

'Grand'. I shook his hand. I don't think he was too pleased with me from the limpness of the grip. He said, 'Can I keep the egg, to raise money against?'

I laughed, taking the egg back from his feeble paw. 'I think not, Walker. I think not. How do I know you're an honest man?'

He looked taken aback. 'I assure you, sir. I am. A good Christian too.'

'Aye, well, you'll have the egg when I have my money. I'll see you Monday, midday sharp.'

And that was that. I extended my stay at the Crown and Mitre and enjoyed myself with chops and ale. Monday came, Walker gave me the money, and I him the egg.

My journey home was uneventful, but when I got back, Sarah Morton was gone. And before we had officially married too. Never mind, thought I, I'd had the use of her. I hired a new maid at a less wage; she was not as handsome as Sarah, but she did. I had he use of her too, but didn't marry her.

I had no more strokes of luck or windfalls, but it didn't matter as I had my £200 and that did me well.

The year went by and winter came. I lived by myself, with yet another maid; it seemed they didn't tolerate me too well, or my roving hands, but there were always more. And I liked the variety.

Christmas found me at the King's Head in Bewcastle, sinking Christmas pints with Ned. The weather was bad; rain rather than snow, but sleety cold rain. I took rather too much ale in my leather tankard and stayed overlong. Ned's wife put me up in the rude hovel they call an inn-room, and it was St Stephen's Day by the time I'd had a hair of the dog that bit me, and was ready to saddle my Jenny and make my way home.

The rain swept across the moor as I rode. I got to the trees again and saw a familiar golden glow. Mr Spindledrift Goodfellow. I'd forgotten about him and his egg since I'd sold it in Carlisle. But I didn't intend to make his acquaintance again. No, sir, I did not.

I rode through the wood, head down. The glow persisted. It was to my right. I knew a rough track. It would be a bad in this weather, but my Jenny could manage it, so I took the reins and steered her up towards the fell.

The light shifted until it was right in front of me. That was odd. I steered right, back towards the main road. And the light shifted in front of me again.

The weirdness of this unnerved me. I decided I did not want to meet Mr Spindledrift Goodfellow at all that day, so I turned right round and headed back to Bewcastle. I'd spend another night at the King's Head and come back when it was no longer St Stephen's Day.

But the light grew in front of me, some yards ahead, and then suddenly a dome of light appeared above and on all sides. The rain vanished, and I sat on horseback on what to all appearances was a mild Spring day.

Mr Spindledrift Goodfellow stood there in a blue coat, brocaded in gold. His long white hair hung down his back. His bone white skin shone with a strange pallor. His violet eyes fixed me and he licked his lips showing his tongue and rows of sharp white teeth. I was no longer sure he was French.

'Good day, Mr Armstrong,' said he. 'I hope you weren't trying to avoid me?'

I coughed. 'No, of course not.'

'You didn't forget our appointment?'

I shook my head.

'Good,' said he. 'I trust my egg brought you fortune.'

I nodded.

'Then,' said he further. 'The year is done. One year and one day, just like in the old bargains. And now I'd like my egg back.'

'I don't have it,' said I, bold as brass. That's the way to face down these mountebanks and charlatans.

He cocked his head. 'You don't have it?'

'No. And what will you do about that?'

I thought him being so thin and spindly, what could he do against a man like me in the prime of health? Gone a little to corpulence I admit, but still strong in the arm, like my name. I thought, once I put my fists up, he would bluster and bluster, and fuss and fuss like a woman, then go.

'What will I do?' he smiled. He seemed amused.

He reached into his coat and pulled out the little crystal bottle. I saw it held a filament of red. He took off the top, turned the bottle upside down and dabbed it on his index finger. Then he licked it. He grinned. 'Very tasty, I think I'll have some more.'

Still with the bottle in hand, he said, 'And don't worry about the egg. Mr Walker sold it to me for £300. It's more your lack of honesty that is of interest to me.'

I swallowed hard. My throat was dry. 'Of interest to you?'

He laughed again; his tiny sharp teeth were wet with spit and stained with my blood. 'Of interest,' said he. 'Because I can't touch an honest man. Luckily, you're not.'

'I don't know what you're talking about.' I decided not to turn to fisticuffs. I'd just go home. I turned Jenny and began to trot off, but every way I went, the dome of golden light followed me, imprisoning me. And he was always there. He neither went further away, nor did he come closer.

I went this way and that and he followed me, laughing as if my panic was a jest. I had to get away and clicked and spurred Jenny, kicking her with my heels. But I couldn't get away from that infernal Mr Spindledrift Goodfellow.

After half an hour, my heart was in my throat. My blood pulsed in my ears, both Jenny and I were lathered with sweat.

He grinned. 'Try as you might, Mr Armstrong, you can't escape your fate.'

'My fate! My fate! I'll have nowt to do with you.' But I stopped. There must be some other way. He stood in front of me now.

And then I was on the soft tussocky turf, lying on my back. Jenny stood over me, then started grazing. It was as if she was glad to have me off her back, and didn't care I was laid low, the callous, faithless animal.

And Spindledrift Goodfellow had my head cradled on his lap, stroking my jugular vein with his sharp fingernail. I felt my artery bound under his firm touch. He tapped the blood vessel, as if testing its pressure.

'Who are you?' I said hoarsely.

'Mr Spindledrift Goodfellow.'

'But who is that?'

'They call me many names: The Light Bringer, the Prince of the Air.'

'You confuse me, sir. Indeed you do.'

He whispered more names. 'The Adversary, the Lord of the Flies and the Serpent.'

It's long since I've read the Bible or gone to church, but I was beginning to realise into whose arms I'd fallen.

And Spindlethrift Goodfellow continued in a sing-song voice, light as thistledown. 'Or Old Nick,' he laughed. 'They sometimes call me that.'

He gazed down with violet eyes, his needle-like nail on the pulse of my neck. 'But you can call me the Devil.'

The Holly King

The Empty Church by R. S. Thomas

They laid this stone trap
for him, enticing him with candles,
as though he would come like some huge moth
out of the darkness to beat there.
Ah, he had burned himself
before in the human flame
and escaped, leaving the reason
torn. He will not come any more
to our lure. Why, then, do I kneel still
striking my prayers on a stone
heart? Is it in hope one
of them will ignite yet and throw
on its illuminated walls the shadow
of someone greater than I can understand?

TRAVELLING IS ALWAYS MORE difficult at midwinter, at the time of the Solstice, with all the dark and the cold that comes at that time of year. But sometimes circumstances beyond our control dictate the timing of our journeys—fate's twists, the weather, unexpected discoveries, the uncertainties of birth and death.

This was no birth, though it did involve a death.

It was December, *y Mis Du*, the Black Month, as the old people called it in Pembrokeshire when Arthur Jones was young.

Born in Haverfordwest Hospital, Arthur was a retired Geography teacher. Trained at Carmarthen College, moved to London aged 22, lived in Ealing and never lived anywhere else since, married, childless through choice, (though they could not conceive) and now retired from Geography and enjoying his sixties as an amateur mythologist and host of the podcast: *Tales of King Arthur.*

He had 35,000 subscribers on YouTube.

Arthur Jones had always been a fan of stories of King Arthur, ever since he was a boy – perhaps because he himself had been named Arthur. He remembered the day his interest in the ancient king began. It was kindled by the surprise of being told by a student teacher that Arthur in reality was a Welshman, not an English knight. This somehow made the mythological figure more personal, creating a resonance between the Arthur of Myth and the Arthur of Cwm-yr-Eglwys, aged eleven.

Strictly speaking, Arthur was not Welsh — he was a Briton claimed by Wales, Brittany, Cornwall, Somerset, Southern Scotland and of course Cumbria, Arthur Jones's current destination.

20th December he was on the motorway, the bright lights of oncoming cars dazzling him as he drove, the dabs of wet snow falling on the windscreen being brushed away by the flicking wipers.

His rucksack was on the back seat. Arthur had packed very lightly for the trip, just his field recorder, a notebook, a camera, spare batteries, a change of clothes and a packed lunch Madelyne had made him.

At this time he was just south of Stoke, which felt halfway but probably wasn't. He was a fan of motorway services, where instead of consuming his wife's home-made sandwiches Arthur had chosen to eat unsatisfactory meals in that succession of in-between places, not quite somewhere, not quite nowhere, which made Arthur feel like a winter traveller, like one of Arthur's knights on a quest across the frozen land of Britain.

At the beginning of the week, Arthur felt something big was on the horizon for him. His Arthurian podcast had been steadily growing for the past two years and now, he had biggest scoop in Arthurian lore since the monks in Glastonbury dug up the late king's grave in 1191.

The particular podcast episode he was about to record up in Cumbria, was tentatively entitled, *The Search for the Green Knight*.

It had been sparked by a visit to the London Library off St James Square.

Three days previously, Arthur had been prowling the stacks of books. He was partly looking for material for the podcast, but at least half was simply because he liked being among the book-stacks. It was so peaceful with the old books and the other old duffers for company. The library was dotted with old wooden desks in cosy recesses where he could take his finds and flick through them, notebook and pencil in hand, as no ink pens were allowed.

He'd sat with a stack of three books to be read to the left hand side of the desk, one that had been perused to the right, and one in hand, in process.

This book was dated 1818, printed in Kendal by Hodgson and Tinnion entitled: *Legends of the Lake Counties*. The author was a man called Joseph Blackett.

Arthur first went to the book's index and, as with every book he perused, thumbed through it for mention of King Arthur. He found one on page 237.

"It is well-known that King Arthur held court at Carlisle. It is also known that Arthur in those days hunted in the great Forest of Inglewood that stretched from just south of Carlisle to Penrith and west to Hesket Newmarket."

"But," continued Blackett with Arthur Jones as his eager audience, "It is also true and well-known that The Forest of Inglewood was the scene for Sir Gawain's encounter with the hideous Dame Ragnall."

Gawain, Arthur's favourite knight!

"What is less known, is that Inglewood was also the location for the famous Green Chapel where the Holly Knight resided and where Gawain fatefully sought him out one Christmastide. Others erronously claim that the Chapel was in the Welsh county of Denbigh, near St Asaph, but I have evidence," continued Blackett, though, annoyingly, he did not evidence his evidence, "that the Green Chapel was in fact to be found on a hill called Lessonmark. My source," (Again infuriatingly not identified) "says that in 1586, the ruins of the Green Chapel were still to be seen at Lessonmark. However, the name Lessonmark is now lost and we do not now know where these ruins are."

Arthur Jones scratched his chin with his left thumb. 1586 was the year of the publication of Camden's Britannia. So was William Camden the mysterious source for the location of the Green Chapel? Arthur hurriedly searched the stacks for a copy of *Brittania*. The library had a copy of the 1600 edition, but it was reserved. Arthur found a facsimile copy dating from 1974. Eagerly, he reached it down.

A search through the index and a flick though the pages discovered no Lessonmark and no reference to the legend of the Green Chapel.

Perhaps Joseph Blackett had a fuller edition, or it was another author altogether, or he was making it up.

Arthur rooted around and found a copy of the Charters of Holme Cultram Abbey, the Wetheral Priory Charters and Victorian editions of cartularies of Lanercost and of Furness. No mention of Lessonmark in any of them.

The name was interesting: could it be a version of the British *llys an marchog*? If so, Lessonmark could mean <u>The Court of the Knight</u>. That would tie in. But the name was lost. Damnation.

And then, on a whim, he fetched *The Pipe Rolls of Cumberland and Westmorland from 1222-1260*, and, while browsing the index, found a reference to Lessonmark, from where hailed Gowan Strang who was fined for poaching deer on Wedholme Flow. The editor (Mr Parker) helpfully noted Lessonmark was now called Warnell, a hill near the hamlet of Sebergham.

Arthur sat back with a broad smile. Here was the solution to the puzzle! Arthur now knew something that no one had known for nearly a thousand years — the location of the Green Chapel, home of the Green Knight, or Holly King as he was otherwise known.

What a scoop this would be would be for his podcast!

After leaving the London Library, Arthur strolled down Pall Mall past the Reform Club, the Travellers Club and the Athaneum, none of which he had ever entered, and then to Trafalgar Square, catching the train home. The train from Charing Cross went to Plumstead and then he needed a 96 bus to East Wickham where he lived, not far from Kate Bush's childhood home, the area's only claim to fame.

Arthur had to run for the bus and the exertion brought a slight tugging pain in the centre of his chest. It was not the first time he'd noticed that niggling ache. Another time, he'd carried a heavy box of books upstairs to the attic and noticed it then too. He'd need to get it checked out, but not now.

When he got home, Madelyne, his wife, was cooking a stir fry with a jar of teriyaki sauce. Some was for him, which he would accept, though not enjoy.

"Have a good root round in the London Library?" Madelyne said absently as he entered the kitchen, all the while stirring the wok with a wooden spoon.

Arthur's enthusiam spilled over like that of an excited labrador. "It was fabulous!"

Madelyne's expression suggested incredulity that an afternon spent in The London Library could be fabulous.

Arthur grinned. "I'm really onto something, Lyne."

"That's nice," she replied

He wagged his finger. "I think I've found the location of the Green Chapel."

"Isn't that on the Bakerloo Line?" she said.

He frowned. "The Green Chapel of Arthurian legend, I mean."

"I was joking, Arthur."

He cocked his head. "You know about the Green Chapel?"

"Not as such."

"Its location has been lost for centuries. Even in the 17th Century they'd forgotten where it was."

"And you've found it?"

"By putting two and two together, I have!"

"That's amazing, Arthur," she said, still stirring the wok.

"It's in Cumbria, Lyne. I've got to go."

She stopped dead. "Cumbria? Now, hang on a minute, Arthur. It's nearly Christmas. You can't be haring up the country on a whim."

"It'll be the most stupendous podcast episode — really ground-breaking, not just regurgitating things already known, but uncovering the past — uncovering arcana."

She frowned. "But you can't go all that way before Christmas. We've got my mother coming round."

"I'll be back before Christmas Eve."

"Arthur, it's the 19th of December already and Cumbria is a very long way from London."

"I don't care, Lyne. I'm going."

Lyne knew better than to try and stop her husband when he was in the grip of one of his enthusiasms.

That night Arthur Jones dreamt of a beast. From within the dark folds of his dream, it came. The beast stood seven feet high, towering above him. They were somewhere outside, standing as the snow fell and the light faded, surrounded by a grove of yew trees.

The beast stunk of wet fur and blood. Like a man, it stood on two legs, but it was not a man. It towered seven feet high and, in its hands, it bore a huge, double-headed axe of copper and on its head it wore a crown of holly, with berries as red as blood, and leaves as green as life.

Arthur shook from fear of it. He called out to it, "What do you want of me?"

But the beast did not speak.

The beast was not the kind of thing that could speak.

The next day, Arthur booked his B&B in Cumbria. It was at a farm in a hamlet called Thethwaite. He was lucky to get it because most of the other local B&Bs were showing no vacancies.

That morning, Arthur inspected his car. He took it to the garage and filled up with screen-wash and made sure the tyres were at 2.27 pounds per square inch. He fuelled up at the super-market as the petrol was cheaper.

He saw the front tyres were getting bald, but still legal. That was a job for the new year before the icy days of January and February came.

Once home, he took his portable recorder and plenty of batteries and a dead-cat muffler for the twin mic heads.

That evening, sitting by the fire reading, he thought of his mother. She'd died on 21st December, the Solstice, so this was always a poignant time for him. He'd been fifteen when she died, when they'd lived at Cwm-yr-Eglwys where his father had been vicar. His mother was buried nearby where she'd been born.

Arthur remembered on the day of his mother's death he'd visited the old stone church at Nevern.

It was softly raining.

Arthur approached the church through the Victorian iron-work of the gate, walking up the avenue of famous bleeding yew trees. No one knew why they bled their red sap, though some said it was a sign from God.

He entered into the silence and cold of the church with its smell of old prayer books and sense of the centuries settled into the stone walls.

There was no one else there. Arthur knelt on the step before the altar and prayed.

His heart broke. Where had she gone? How could she have been there all his life and now when he called out to her, there was only silence. In a rage, Arthur moved aside the bright-crocheted kneeling cushion made by the local Mothers' Union to feel the hard stone under his knees, as if his discomfort would coax an answer from God.

Hands clasped in prayer, he called to Jesus and all the angels or to any creature who could bring him news of his lost mother. And he waited.

Was he waiting for a word, an act of speech? But the church did not speak, not the stones of the walls, nor the wood of the pews. And the glass did not cry and the Holy Book on the lectern did not turn.

Was it a feeling that he expected — some warmth in his solar plexus, some tender caress on his cheek as he knelt there, eyes-closed, no longer muttering prayers, but heavy-hearted and silent?

He felt nothing but the cold, hard stone under his knees.

God never spoke to Arthur Jones before this, he didn't speak then and Arthur knew now He never would.

The stone and wood and glass and slate and lead of the church, the wind, the rain, the air, the bleeding yew trees, did not speak to him.

They were not the kinds of things that used words.

On the morning of the 20th of December, Arthur took his car out of the garage and made ready to go. His wife Madelyne gave him the packed lunch and kissed his cheek and laid her hand on his arm.

"You are a silly old man, Arthur. Why can't you wait until the weather is better? It'll be dark long before you get there. Surely, you're not proposing to go digging round the woods for your Green Chapel tonight?"

Arthur smiled, and took the tupperware box. "No, Lyne, don't worry. I'll get to the B&B tonight, go to bed early and go looking for the chapel tomorrow. I've got a map. There's a track leading into the wood at Warnell."

"I wish you'd wait."

He glanced at his car. "I'd better be off. It's a long journey."

She said, "Just the worst time of the year

For a journey, and such a long journey:

The ways deep and the weather sharp,

The very dead of winter," she said.

"What?" he said, then grinned. "Ah, Eliot!"

Madelyne had been an English teacher. They'd met at his school when he was forty. Neither of them had been married before, but the'd been happy ever since. At least he'd been very happy, and he hoped she had been too. He'd never asked her.

She stroked his cheek. "But be back by Christmas, you old bugger!"

Arthur came off the M6 at Junction 41 and took the road northwest. It was an Old Roman road — a good sign. Nearly there, he thought.

A sleety snow was falling again. Occasional cars came towards him on this old straight track but there was no one behind.

Then a deer darted across the road, a huge stag, many-tined antlers appearing suddenly in his headlights. Most bizzarely it was white. Arthur stomped on the brakes and skidded forward, tyres burning despite the wet and cold. Damn those bald tyres. And then the car stopped.

Arthur Jones sat clutching the steering wheel of his car with numb fingers. His heart hammered and he spoke to himself, "That was a close one."

His hand moved to where he had that little tug in his chest again. The kind of little tug that doesn't speak, but still carries a meaning.

The white stag had disappeared into the darkness to the side of the lonely road. Had he hallucinated that fine-antlered, pure-white stag — a harbinger of his Arthurian discovery, a messenger from the Holly King?

Arthur arrived at the B&B around ten minutes later. The farmer's wife, Mrs Beck, greeted him.

Mrs Beck asked if he'd eaten and offered directions to the pub.

"The Sour Nook Inn does good food," she said, but Arthur didn't like the sound of it. In any case, he still had Madelyne's sandwiches.

His room was small but warm. The walls were uneven and a black-painted beam ran across the ceiling. A TV hung on the wall, mounted on a bracket and the remote was on the bedside table. Arthur lay on the bed, made himself a cup of tea and flicked through the channels, but he had had a long journey and he soon slept.

The next day was the Solstice. The morning was dark, and Mrs Beck gave him gammon and eggs in a downstairs room converted into the B&B breakfast room. As he waited for more toast, he saw there was a row of paperback books on the windowsill — Frederick Forsyth, David Baldacci and Karin Slaughter,*Outside the Circles of Time* by Kenneth Grant and next to that *English Calendar Customs* by Mary Kathleen Briggs. Odd reading material for a Cumbrian farmer, but perhaps they'd been left by a former guest.

Arthur reached for the book on calendar customs and leafed through it as he sipped his tea and ate his buttered toast. He turned through the dates until he reached the 21st.

The Winter Solstice: the day when the sun stands still. The darkest time of the year when winter reigns. In these bleak days of darkness, many creatures, both plants and animals, and of course our own ancestors, died .

It must have felt to our ancestors as if life had abandoned the earth, leaving it to darkness and death. They stood, staring at the sky, looking for a sign.

This kingdom of dark and cold and death is the realm of the Winter King, whom to our pagan forbears took the form of a great beast — unspeaking as is the dark itself. For you see, the Holly King is forbidden to tell us what awaits us on the day we go under the earth.

"Any plans today?" Mrs Beck said, clearing his plate.

Arthur stood. "Going to have a look at some archaeological remains."

"Carlisle?" she said, "The Roman Wall?"

"Maybe," he said.

She didn't seem much interested anyway.

It was a short drive to Warnell from Thethwaite. Arthur parked at the bottom of the conical knoll some 900 feet high, swathed in dark fir trees. He checked his OS map. He guessed the ruins would be at the top of the hill, up the muddy track marked through the spruce plantation. He slung the rucksack that held his recorder, camera and notebook on his shoulder . Being there on the actual Solstice would make this the best podcast episode he'd ever done.

A metal gate with a line of rusted barbed wire snaked around the top bar blocked entry.

A sign said: Private Wood: No Entry.

Arthur mounted the gate, careful not to catch himself on the barbed wire as he went over.

There was no sign of recent human footprints on the path. He knew enough to recognise deer prints, maybe badger, fox, the prints of birds, but no people.

As he climbed the hill, it started to snow a wet sleet that brought a bone-cold damp with it.

Halfway up, Arthur began to get that dull ache in the centre of his chest again.

He continued the ascent. The track turned so that he was out of sight of the gate behind him that led back into the ordinary world.

The oaks, the ashes, the elms had lost their leaves. The blackthorn and hawthorn, the musk rose and dogwood were bare, but the fir trees stood green still.

Out of breath now, almost gasping in billowing clouds, the spruce beside the track gave way to lines of dark yew trees. They led uphill as if it were a processional avenue.

The yews reminded him of Nevern churchyard, and he saw

these yews too were bleeding, a sticky red sap running down their gnarled trucks.

The snow got thicker and colder and started to cover the mud of the path with white.

Arthur was struggling. He stopped, catching his breath and tapped the centre of his chest as if he could press the ache away.

To take his mind off it, he imagined Sir Gawain coming to his tryst with the Green Knight, the knight whose head he had lopped off, and seen pick up his rolling head and walk away. It was hard to know what the story meant, but he'd always felt it meant something, as if there was meaning peeping out between the words, despite the words.

The Green Knight had once promised to meet Gawain in the heart of winter at the Green Chapel, on this dark hill: here.

This must have been the track Gawain climbed too. In all these centuries there would be no reason to move it.

Finally, he entered the circle of yew and holly at the hill's top.

Here the yews and spruce and holly clustered thickly, draped in ivy, prickly with gorse, evergreen. The snow lay like a blanket on the ground draping the trees in white, ice-lace, like the white shrouds of those who have just died. And the trees were his witnesses, knowing in their green way, that he was here.

Arthur saw with excitement, that stones lay among the briar and gorse. Not just any stones, but cut and dressed as if they'd been part of a wall. And most astonishingly, for local stone here was red sandstone, this stone was greenslate — a block of green slate to build a green chapel from.

Arthur put down his bag. That chest pain nagged at him, but he didn't care. Finding the Green Chapel was the culmination of his life. He'd be written about in history books for this.

He got out his recorder. He pushed the on switch with his thumb and the red light blinked on. He spoke, "Ladies and gentlemen, I've found it! I, Arthur Jones, host of the Arthurian Legends Podcast, have found the Green Chapel, famous in lore, lost for nearly a thousand years, buried deep in this Cumbrian wood. I am so excited to bring this discovery to you. It's the culmination of my whole life."

Something moved behind him.

He turned round; it was in the trees. Behind the yew and the holly, behind the screen of tangled ivy, behind the wall of green gorse; it moved now.

It was big. It wasn't human.

"Hello?" Arthur said, "Hello?" He used his thumb to switch the machine off.

No one answered.

"Is there anyone there?" he said. He was frightened now. He stooped to pick up his bag, preparing to run away, but he was disorientated. The pain in his chest was worse.

The trees seemed to encircle him. He couldn't see a way out through the thicket of evergreens.

The Holly King stepped into the clearing, as if it had been expecting him, axe in hand, unspeaking, smelling of blood and fur and fate.

It was monstrous, inhuman. Huge, tall, impassive.

Arthur had no words for it, because words are a trick to dazzle us from what is really happening, and this was real.

And he thought — The Holly King's crown bears berries as red as any blood. And the Holly King's crown bears prickles as sharp as any thorn.

Arthur yelled. "Who are you? What do you want from me?"

But the Holly King is not the kind of thing that uses words, but still he bears a message.

Arthur put his hand to his chest.

The Holly King raised his copper axe.

And Arthur knew finally, that God does not speak to you in churches.

That the The Holly King does not speak in woods and fields.

But without words they bear a message. The message of the falling rain and the drifting snow and the soughing wind.

Arthur fell to his knees, his recorder tumbling from his hand, and then he toppled, his head hitting a block of green slate.

Like a dying stag bleeding into the snow, Arthur lay there and the Holly King stood above him and brought down his axe.

We could give words of comfort that said when Arthur's blood ran on the cold earth, rising in clouds of steam, that his spilt blood would fructify the earth and life would begin again.

Perhaps with the sprouting of a holly sprig.

Such words would be a comfort for us all. They would trick us into thinking we understand.

Words would be a comfort indeed.

But neither God nor the Holly King will give them to us.

Uncle Lanty's Story

"I'M AN OLD MAN NOW, and old men are full of stories. So, if you have the time and the inclination to listen, may I tell you one?" The old man, his thin grey hair hardly covering his head, but wearing a fine linen shirt, woollen trousers and polished leather boots sits by the hearth, a peat fire burning beside him.

You say, "Why not?"

"There's no reason why you should know my name, but I shall tell you it. I am Arnold Weyland and I deal in corn. This story goes back to when I was a lad. Brampton then, in the 1650s wasn't the bustling town it is now. In those days we had no King; it was the Commonwealth, and there had been war upon war, with the Scots invading England and Cromwell invading Scotland and Ireland and crushing both, and then Robert Cromwell unable to keep the peace once his dad had died, and the new King invited back."

"They were terrible times for grown-ups, but as a boy, I knew nothing else. I was more interesting in fishing and climbing trees, and stealing birds' eggs, and listening to my uncle Lanty."

"You see, my own father and mother were dead and Uncle Lancelot brought me up. He'd been in London as a silversmith, but now, older, was back in Cumberland, which I think he preferred. Myself, I've never been to London. I've never seen the need."

"Uncle Lanty did well for himself and his work was known in Carlisle and Newcastle and as far away as York and Lancaster. But though he made forks and spoons and silver plates, my Uncle Lanty's chief love was clockwork

"Clockwork?"

"Yes. But Lanty, as I said was a well-travelled man, and when younger he had visited the castle at Heidelberg in the Palatinate with its *Hortus Palatinus* that was full of clockwork nightingales and cuckoos that sang from their metal throats, and a statue of Memnon that moved and would bow and gestured to passers' by. Fantastical things, he said! The sight of them made an impression on him, and as he was clever with both his hands and his brain, he took to studying until he could make such things himself, and create them, moving creatures, copying life itself."

You say, "That's not possible. Only the Lord himself can grant life."

The old man turns and points. " You see this?"

"That? What is it?"

Arnold gestures to the table. The fire in the heart shifts and crackles and its flames casts shadows and gleam on a silver item on the sideboard. It is in the shape of a boy, about a foot high, and made of silver struts and inside its chest, where its heart would be, were it real, are intricate and interlocking wheels.

Arnold reaches into his shirt and pulls out a leather pouch and from that pouch he takes as a silver key. and leans to the clockwork boy and turns the key and says, "Watch!"

And as you watch, the boy begins to move.

He smiles and shakes his head. "It's not alive, you know. As you say, only the Good Lord gives life and men can only counterfeit it. It just looks like it's alive, a thing made by a man, albeit a very clever man. But there is a difference between what men make from nature, and what nature grows from herself. It is my firm belief that we should be humble to that difference and not think ourselves the equal of she who is mother to all things But I ramble on. Let me tell you my story."

Arnold then returns to his story while behind him, the clockwork boy continues to dance and bow, its gears whirring and ticking with an unceasing rhythm, with the ticking of its clockwork heart.

Arnold continues. "It's often hard to pick a time when stories begin, but for this story, it is not hard. After weeks of work, Uncle Lanty had finished the clockwork boy you see here dancing. He was rightly proud of his creation. It was night by the time he'd and he brought it through into this room. Like tonight, the fire was on, and like tonight the boy danced, and me, just a lad of seven years old, I watched enchanted and I could not believe what I saw and I did not understand how he could make such a thing, that moved like I move. "Can he speak, Uncle Lanty?" I asked.

"No, lad," he said. "He's not alive. He's an automaton, just like those I saw in Heidelberg. He dances and he bows, but he knows not that he moves, and he cannot speak to us. There is no spark of life in him, he is but a machine."

"'But he moves and he's pretty.' And suddenly, I said (and I don't know where I got this idea) 'Is he like the fairies?'"

Lanty laughed at me, but good-natured, like. "No, lad. Because there are no fairies. All the things the country folk believe are silliness and superstition. This clockwork boy is but the first step in our journey to understanding. The great philosopher René Descartes has explained that animals are simply machines and all life can be accounted for by mechanical principles. One day men make machines that will be indistinguishable from those nature gives birth to. . For now, my clockwork boy is my contribution to that."

'You will see,' Arnold says, 'that mine and my uncle's views on this were different. Even then, I felt he was wrong, and I said, —

quiet like, for I loved my Uncle and was obedient to him, " I believe in the fairies."

And he shook his head and with a smile, "You are sentimental. You have seen my dancing boy, this sleepy boy, called Arnold, that stands before me now, is for bed."

"No, Uncle! It's early yet for bed."

"No, it is not, as you well know. I made a promise to your mother, my dear sister, before she died that I would bring you up as my own and bringing up good and civil children does not involve giving into their every whim."

I was sly, even then. I tried another tack. "But can I have a story when I'm in bed?"

He sighed. "Aye, oh, Arnold, you always chip away at my resolve. And so I will tell you a story, but not until you are under the bedclothes. Should I tell you a story of the great streets of London or of Paris?"

"No, Uncle, tell me a story of the fairies. Tell me of Queen Mab."

He sighed good-natured as always. "My rational words fall on deaf ears, and instead you relish the false-comfort of fable. But, aye. I will tell you of Queen Mab, though she is pure make-believe."

When he had tucked me into bed, Uncle Lanty began his story. It was a story I'd heard many times before, but I loved the tales of all the fairies but most of all, Queen Mab:

Uncle Lanty told his tale:

On the border of fairyland, where the veil between worlds is thin, two travellers named Mary and Thomas journeyed toward Edinburgh. Mary was a devout woman, (though of the Papist side) and she felt her faith a shield against the ungodliness that lurked beyond their campfire's light. For she believed in those creatures of the shadows: the boggles, the dobbies, the elves.

Thomas, on the other hand, was a man after my own heart, and thought all those things foolish superstition.

The weather, as it often is in the borderlands between England and Scotland, was bad. Mary and Thomas journeyed on, and the mist grew thicker, and the forest path twisted and turned, leading them astray. The wind whispered as if telling secrets, and strange creatures flitted in the shadows, beckoning them deeper into the woods.

Mary, clutched her rosary tightly, praying for deliverance, for they, unlike we who have received the true revelation, they were Catholics. Mary in truth, but Thomas only on the surface, for he, like me was a believer in Réne Descartes!

Suddenly, a figure appeared before them. She appeared a mortal woman, but, a stunning woman with fiery hair that shimmered with a strange lights, as if her hair was spun from red gold and copper, and her eyes were filled with a glow as if the Northern Lights and the Southern Stars had married and given pup.

This was Queen Mab, midwife to the fairies, and she had taken notice of the travellers. Mary suspected Mab was of fairy kind, but her husband Thomas, blinded by his belief in rational thought that such things could not be, was deceived by her.

He asked, "How com'st thou to such a desolate and fearful place as this at such a time of night, away from all paths and thoroughfares?"

And Mab laughed, her voice like the music of finger-bells, and she said, "But a better question is how come ye to this same desolate place at such a time in such weather?"

"We are lost," said Mary, though her husband would have wished her to keep silent.

"You are lost? Well, I will show you back to the road to Peebles and you can continue on for Edinburgh from there."

"How do you know we are bound for Edinburgh?" said Thomas, alarmed at this odd woman.

"I know much. And if you add all I know to all I guess, then we find I know most everything. But ask me no more questions. Take your luck as you find it and come my way."

"How can we repay you, my Lady?" said Mary.

"I will take payment in my own way at my own time."

With Queen Mab's guidance, Thomas and Mary soon found their way back onto the right path. They thanked her and continued their journey with renewed spirits. She did not mention the matter of her fee again, and they did not ask.

Mary gave birth to their daughter, Elizabeth at their house in the Grassmarket two months later when Thomas was settled as a bookbinder and their night of wandering was forgotten.

Their daughter Elizabeth was a strange, beautiful child and nothing like her father and mother.

They loved her as best they could, but it was hard, as she was so wilful and her tastes so strange, for she would eat nothing but apples and drink naught but buttermilk. She played the harp and sang songs that brought up their skin in gooseflesh and brought tears to their eyes though they knew not why for the language was strange: it was not Scots, nor French nor Erse. It was the tongue of Fairyland which is older than any of these.

She lived with them and would not marry, and neither would she take a trade, not dressmaker, nor maid, nor nurse. And she did not age, but remained in the guise of a beautiful fey girl of fifteen.

But one day, when Mary and Thomas were old and grey, another girl suddenly appeared before them. They were surprised and did not know her but she said that she was their own true daughter, but that she taken by the fairies and had been living with Queen Mab all these years, and now she had been returned to them as a young woman.

This girl was called White-Shoulder and she was their true kin and they knew her from her hair and her face and her little habits and gestures that we think are our own, but in truth are passed down by blood — for we are nothing but a mosaic of our kin, close and far from generation unto generation.

Mary went through to find the girl they had raised as their own daughter, never mind how strange she was, this Elizabeth. They went to where she spent the days eating apples and drinking buttermilk, singing and playing music, but Elizabeth was gone and never returned.

What profit she had of her time fostered among humans, they never learned, for the ways of the fairies are strange and we who are doomed to die can never fathom the ways of those who live forever.

But White-Shoulder was their own and they called her then Fiona, which is White-Shoulder in Erse, and though the respectable burghers of Edinburgh did not look favourably upon the Irish or the Highland folk, even a Gaelic name was better to them than one spun in a fashion that was not Protestant and respectable, for they are limited in their understanding and their sympathy.

And so the story ends happily,' said Uncle Lanty.

I was sleepy then, and I saw my Uncle's kind and concerned face bent over me.

"I wish I could see Queen Mab," I said through my sleep.

"Whisht, lad, you get to sleep. You shall never see her, for there is no such thing as fairies."

And that night, as I lay in my bed, the soft moonlight seeping through the gaps in the shutters and filling the room with a glow that made the wood and the stone seem alive, just as I was about to close my eyes, a figure emerged from the shadows.

This personage was unlike anyone I had ever seen before. Her skin was as of beaten silver, and her hair glowed with a fiery radiance that was composed of interweaving strands of copper and gold, and her eyes were alight with the purple glitter as of amethyst and the soft shining as of pearl.

As she drew closer, I saw that her clothing was not made of any earthly fabric, but rather of delicate spider silk that shimmered with fireflies. She grinned at me with a mischievous twinkle in her eyes, and then vanished.

I drifted into a deep sleep, filled with wondrous dreams of magical beings and far-off lands and wondered if I had dreamed her too.

When I awoke, the following day, the town was abuzz with rumours and speculation. It seemed that Elizabeth Shaw had vanished without a trace. Elizabeth was a friend of my uncle's not least because they were both considered eccentric by the inhabitants of Brampton. But while Uncle Lanty made clockwork figures, Elizabeth Shaw was a witch.

By that I do not mean, and I never thought, unlike many hereabouts, that she was in league with the Devil, but that she had older knowledge of which plants would heal and she told the future by reading people's palms and told girls when they would marry and how many children they would have and told young men whether they would make their fortune.

She had a hut on the way out of Brampton on the Lanercost road. I had visited her there with my uncle and seen the herbs strung up on the beams, and her salves, and potions and her pet rabbit

"She was a good woman, Arnold," Lanty said, his voice heavy with concern. "It's not right that she should disappear like this."

"Where do you think she's got to?"

He sighed. "The river has been in flood because of all the rain. She was given to wandering the banks of the Irthing looking for her herbs. I just hope she hasn't been swept away by the high waters."

I walked with my uncle to the marketplace to get our messages and see if there was any news.

As we walked, folk were chattering about Elizabeth's disappearance. Most were making noises as if they were concerned though whether they were concerned is hard to say for people's words often pretend at feeling when their true feeling says nothing.

But some were fond of Elizabeth and had benefited from her healing of old. There was only the occasional sour tone. One was William Hetherington, the butcher, a curmudgeon and a churl.

"She's nee loss," said the butcherd. "She was a witch. The town is best off without such as she. In my youth they would have burned her and be done with it, now the river's done the job for us, and good riddance say I."

"Hold your tongue William Hetheringon," said my uncle. And though they thought Lanty odd, the butcher respected his money and Hetherington was quiet, though his look was surly.

It was a week later, when I was at my books, forming my letters at the desk when there was a knock at our door. Uncle's housekeeper answered and came through, white-faced.

"It's Goodbody Shaw, Mr Weyland," said the lass.

My uncle raised his eyebrows. "Elizabeth Shaw? Is she found?" His voice was shaking and without waiting for the housekeeper to answer, he rushed to the door. I was at his heels and there, on the street stood Elizabeth Shaw, smiling.

"Elizabeth! Where have you been? I've been worried sick about you?"

"I've been nowhere."

"Well, you've not been at your house, for it was closed up. And you've not been in Brampton."

"I've been through the fields and in the woods and by the river, Lanty. You should not have worried about me, though it is sweet of you to do so, for I have been well. But may I come in, or will you keep me on the threshold?"

"Come in, come in, Elizabeth? Will you take meat and ale?"

"No, I have not long eaten and just now long supped. I will not your food, but I will take your hospitality."

"Come in, Bess, for I have missed you, Bess."

She stroked his cheek, and I did not know it then as I was but seven years, but have guessed it since that the reason my Uncle never married is because his heart belonged to Elizabeth Shaw and she, being of unequal standing and status, could never be his wife.

And they sat and the weather was grey outside, but Uncle Lanty positively glowed. I sat with them, an observer, unobserved, remarking but unremarked, noticing but unnoticed by these two adults in their joy at being reunited.

Lanty, though he seemed old to me, was barely forty years then, and I guess she younger and I guess they had feelings that seven-year-old boys do not know, and old men like me now, hardly remember.

And Elizabeth held out something in her hand. "I found this," she said.

I looked and something seemed to gleam and stir on her palm. It was a small thing, like a mechanism.

My uncle leaned forward, peering. "What is it?"

"Something I thought would appeal to your love of intricacy."

He took it. "It's warm," he said. "But metal. And what metal?"

He had an eyeglass which he went and fetched it

I could see his joy quickly turned to confusion as she presented him with a strange device. It was made of a combination of metal, wood, and organic matter. It seemed to be a poor copy of a clockwork device, as if made by someone with no mechanical understanding.

The strangest thing about this mechanism was that it seemed alive and moved of its own accord, like a clockwork centipede crawling across his palm, but it was not clockwork but rather something that had grown from an egg or a seed.

Lanty examined the device closely, turning it over in his hands and inspecting its various parts. "Where did you get this, Elizabeth?" he asked.

"I found it in the ruins of Lanercost Priory," Elizabeth replied, her eyes gleaming with excitement. "I believe there may be more there, waiting to be discovered."

Lanty frowned, unsure of what to make of the strange device. He had never seen anything like it before.

"Elizabeth, what is this thing?"

But before she could answer, Elizabeth's gaze flickered towards the window, and she suddenly rose to her feet. "I must go," she said, grabbing the device and clutching it to her chest. "But perhaps you would come with me to Lanercost?"

Puzzled at her abrupt leaving, Uncle Lanty saw her to the door but as she went out, the sun came from behind a cloud and bathed the house in a butter-yellow glow and in that light, I saw Elizabeth's hair just for a second have the hue of copper and gold and her eyes as she looked at me and smiled, were made of pearl and amethyst.

"I am to go to Lanercost," my Uncle announced. "And you are to stay here."

"Please may I come uncle. I promise to be good."

"No, I am going with Elizabeth Shaw."

"To see if you can find more things such as she brought?"

"What did you make of that thing?" he said.

"I know not but that I saw a strange creature that was as if a mind with no knowledge of clockwork had tried to grow a mechanism instead of making it."

"Aye. But how can that be? It was such a strange thing, as if nature wished to copy man, rather than is the usual way, that man copies nature."

"Was it made by the fairies?" I asked, my voice shaking with excitement at the idea and from shame for I knew he thought me childish to cherish such ideas."

He shrugged and I continued. "For they do say that Goodbody Mistress Elizabeth is in knowledge and communion with the Quiet Folk."

"Enough of that. Mistress Elizabeth is a herbalist and an antiquarian, a knowledgeable woman, though not formally schooled. She is in no communion with fairies or elves. You stay here, Arnold and work on your penmanship, which is in a sorry state and must be improved."

But I did not heed him for I was sorely curious about the thing I'd seen and convinced there was something eldritch about its origin (which is a Scotch word, though we here on the Border know it too). So, I sneaked into the yard behind the house and found the cart. It was a cart we used for everything. There was a seat up front and behind a space for carrying goods. There was a piece of sacking there which we used to cover provisions and give them some protection from the weather and under this I went and waited.

I heard my uncle hitch the horse, Dickon, talking to him and calling him a good horse and giving him a handful of oats. Then he got up to drive.

Lanercost is two and a half miles northeast of Brampton. It was a great priory founded by the Normans in the old days and dissolved by old King Henry a hundred years ago and now lies in ruins.

It is a place for treasure hunters and hill-diggers as such lowly people are drawn to ruins and barrows in the hope of making their fortune easily rather than through hard work. Such is the place, and to Lanercost we went.

Uncle Lanty stopped outside Elizabeth Shaw's hut as it was on the way, and I felt the cart stop and from my hiding place, I heard her climb up and then I could make out their chat.

"So you're sure there's more there?" says my Uncle Lancelot.

"Indeed. This was but the first. I reached it and brought it to show you for you are the man who knows most in England about automata and clockworks."

"You flatter me, Elizabeth. Not in England, in Cumberland perhaps. But this is not clockwork. This thing is living, not made."

"And what is the difference? You've told me many times about your fine Monsieur Descartes who considers all creatures to be mere machines. And you think that yourself, don't you, Lanty?"

I heard him pause. She questioned him further, almost taunting him.

"You think there is naught to life but mechanics and you believe that man can make life as well as nature, don't you?"

"Not yet, Bess."

"But soon?"

"One day man will make things as well as nature. There is nothing supernatural about life. It is mere mechanism that thus far we cannot penetrate, but one day, man's mind will rise so that he can create an automaton that moves and thinks for itself, and it will not be mysterious, it will be within our power and we shall be masters of life."

"Ah well, Lanty. Wait until you see what I have to show you. Then perhaps you will believe in mysteries once again."

And before long, we were at Lanercost. The cart stopped. Dickon neighed and, from the crunching noise, Uncle Lanty gave him a carrot. I felt my uncle and Bess Shaw leave the cart and heard their voices move away so I, with great efforts at stealth, slid from beneath the sacking

The light was poor and the day was grey and threatened rain. The red tumble-down stones of the old priory lay ahead. Some still stood where the body of the priory was now used as the parish church, others in heaps. Ahead, I saw my uncle and Elizabeth leading him, her hand on his elbow and him letting her pull him forward. They moved quickly as if he were curious and she urgent to help him.

They went out of sight behind a wall and I ran to catch up so I could hear what they were saying. From behind the wall where I crouched, I heard him say, "Where, Bess? Where did you find this thing?"

"Just here," she said, "Just up here. A little way."

"But what is that?"

"What?"

"That light."

And I came from my cover and went forward and I felt the fairies' presence all around me. I could not have spoken even if it were wise to have done so. I stood amazed. There was more than Queen Mab here. She had her whole Seelie Court with her. They were a multitude of the Quiet Folk, of no size and all sizes, pressing in, seen and unseen, grinning, watching, waiting.

The air was was heavy with the scent of musk rose and honeysuckle and a warmth rose as if it were a summer evening, but it was not summer in our world and the weather was not warm.

The air was full with the odour of the scent of flowers but there was something else, a sharp smell, a metallic smell, the sort of smell the air has when lightning has struck through it.

I could see my Uncle, holding hands with Elizabeth Shaw. Ahead, Bess stopped in front of a small, unremarkable door nestled among briars and twisted bindweed, unseasonably in flower.

Elizabeth opened the door, and as I remember, it was such an ordinary door, though on reflection perhaps smaller than most.

My uncle stopped at its threshold. I could see he was not at ease.

"Through that door, Elizabeth? I am not sure I've ever seen that door here in the ruins of the Priory. And these flowers? They should not be. It is November. There should be no flowers like these. What is this place?"

"It is the place where things are found," she said and her voice was like the hum of bees in a summer garden, or like the endless wash of the waves across the Solway sands.

And when I looked at her, her hair was of gold and copper and her skin was of beaten silver. Her eyes were of amethyst and pearl and her arms moved like the branches of the willow and her breath moved in her like the mixing of the clouds.

"Are you sure, Bess?" said my Uncle Lanty as he stood before the open door, the door through which I could not see.

And she said, "Yes, Lancelot, I am sure. But I am no longer Bess."

And all around, I heard tinkling laughs and chattering voices. I thought I heard their sighs and felt the brush of their wings. And as I looked, Goodwife Shaw, Mistress Bess changed from a woman to a thing of living metal, and she moved as living things moved, impelled by silent mystery, for one knows where we come from, nor what makes us move, unless it is the Good Lord himself, or perhaps the Queen of the Fairies, though to say that, I know is blasphemy, and I say it nevertheless.

What we are is a mystery to us and from mystery we are born and to mystery we return, and yet it is not true to say we return because in truth we never left.

The storyteller, Arnold Weyland paused. "But that is not the end of my story. My uncle never returned and I inherited his house and all his automata. I was never drawn to such things myself and my living was made from ordinary things that grow among ordinary people who grow old.

But," Arnold Weyland says, do you want to hear it?"

"Yes," you say.

He continues. "Very well. There is one last thing. Two days after my uncle disappeared a fisherman discovered a body lodged by the trunk of an old alder tree that grows on the banks of the River Irthing near the old stone bridge.

It was Elizabeth Shaw.

They brought her back to the town and everyone was chattering about it, as they will. And I asked a friend whose father found her. He told me she'd been dead a week, and I remembered that it was less than a week that she came calling at my Uncle Lanty's house.

Not that it was any surprise to me that it was not Elizabeth Shaw who had brought that living clockwork to my Uncle's house.

I knew who she was.

And why she'd done it."

The Mallerstang Boggle

I'M NEARING old age now and no longer live in Cumbria, but I remember the hot summer of 1976 with its drought and swarms of ladybirds. A funny thing happened to me that year.

Before that, I suppose I thought all spirits were ghosts, and that ghosts were the remnants of dead people, if I thought about it at all. But I'll get to that.

Let me begin at somewhere near the beginning. My name is Malcolm Ellwood. I now live in Newcastle upon Tyne, but I was born and brought up in Kendal, which at that time was in Westmorland. In 1974, just before this story they merged us with Cumberland and parts of Lancashire and Yorkshire to become the new county of Cumbria, named after the ancient kingdom.

My father and mother had a caravan in Mallerstang, and I hope I don't offend the (few) residents by describing Mallerstang as a bleak and remote valley that leads from Cumbria into the Yorkshire Dales. But my old mum and dad loved it, mainly my dad really — my mum wanted to go to Spain. But he never listened to her, and we went every year to that caravan which was parked on what was in essence a farmer's field with basic amenities. We stayed every summer for six weeks and if Easter wasn't bad, we'd go there for two weeks then as well..

I was about 12 then and still happy with fishing with nets in the becks and wandering over the fells and camping up there with the old tent my dad got from the Scouts. It was so hot that year; we swam a lot in the Eden too.

My friends were Alan Tremble from Penrith and John Mossop from Kirkby Stephen. Their parents had caravans there as well and the grown-ups spent the evenings drinking gin and tonic and playing card games while we went on our bikes and made dens.

Pendragon Castle lies in the valley. They say that it was the castle of Uther Pendragon, father of King Arthur, though the ruins of the existing castle only date from Norman times. Who knows, maybe King Arthur's dad lived there before that.

One night, we camped in the ruin because Alan thought it would be spooky. We pitched our four-man canvas tent with rope guys and wooden pegs that you had to hammer in with a mallet. I remember the ground was rock hard because of the drought and the mallet hurt my hand.

We set a fire and sat round sizzling pork sausages on forks tied to bamboo sticks with string. Often the string would burn through and the fork would drop with the sausage into the flaming wood and we'd have to pick it out with fingers or sticks. Gritty sausages caked in red-hot cinders never did me any harm.

Alan told ghost stories while me and John Mossop laughed at him. Then we grew tired and simply sat. The shadows grew long around the castle ruins. Cows grazed not far away among the reeds by the river and owls hooted from the trees. It was still warm.

I wasn't sure I believed in ghosts. If you'd asked me, I would have said I didn't, but that airless night, sitting by the dying fire, my actions might not have matched my words. I wasn't scared exactly, but I wasn't happy either. Alan had been telling a story about a drowned woman's spirit coming from the dead. I didn't believe him, but I kept looking towards the river.

Then we went to bed and crawled into our sleeping bags. They slept. I didn't. I just had that image of a woman coming out of the river. I heard Alan and John's breathing. The night was so hot; I climbed out of my sleeping bag. Owls called across the valley: kwik kwik went the males, and the females answered: hoo hoo.

But there was something else out there too. Something moved among the trees. At first I thought I was imagining it. I held my breath so I could hear better, but it didn't help that there were two people breathing loudly in the tent with me. Whatever it was, it was close. My heart started beating fast. I had images of this woman coming from the river for me — that she would snatch me from the tent, while the others slept. I was on the left-hand side, by the tent wall. She could just reach under the fly-sheet and drag me out. I shuffled closer in, but I couldn't get away because John was there. He muttered as I moved into him but didn't wake.

Something was moving around the ruins. It wasn't a bird in the trees; it was something on the ground. Something heavy footed.

I froze with fear. It was close now. Maybe it was a cow. Maybe it was a badger, but there was no snuffling noise, it was more like a pecking — like something pecking the ground. That was weird. More than weird, unnervingly scary. It came closer, pecking, pecking, pecking. What the heck pecked?

Then something took hold of the tent, like grabbed it. It ripped the canvas up, like a knife, waking Alan and John instantly who cried out in sleepy terror.

"Jesus, what the hell?" Alan said.

John rolled away. The tent was cut open and more than that, lifted up and thrown away. There was no moon, but the stars sparkled like thrown diamonds in the sky above. And against them was a huge black shape. It was no woman; it wasn't even human.

I jumped up and ran. I fled out of the ruins, across the fields. I crossed a fence. I don't even remember crossing it but I must have. I didn't look back for the others; I was so terrified. I got to the farm and the three caravans. There were no lights on anywhere, and only now, with no one after me and my heart finally slowing, I turned to look back for my friends.

"What the hell was that?" John said. He was first back. Alan appeared as a shadow before I answered. Not that I had an answer. "I don't know," I said.

I knocked sheepishly on the door of the caravan and my tousled mother answered. I gave some excuse about the tent ripping which she looked puzzled about but didn't question. My dad did though the next day. We salvaged the tent from the castle ruins and he ended up stitching it back together. He presumed we'd been messing about with knives because something had sliced the canvas open. He wouldn't have believed the true explanation, so I didn't tell him.

"It must have been a lunatic with a knife," John said.

"Or a sword, maybe?" Alan said.

"A machete,' John nodded. "That's it."

I shook my head. "Did you see the size of it?"

They both went quiet.

"What was it then?" John asked.

"I don't know," I said.

"I'm not camping there again," Alan said. "I'll stay in the caravan."

I said, "With a blade like that it could cut through the caravan, anyway."

News of us ripping the tent apparently spread because we were on our bikes up by The Thrang two days later when we came across Billy Boustead. Billy was a labourer on one of the farms by Shoregill. I have no idea how old he was then. He'll be long dead by now though. Billy was cutting down ragwort in the fields. He was simple and the farmers just gave him little jobs and paid him pocket money so he could buy beer and fags. He knew us well from all the summers we'd spent there. We stopped to drink some bottles of Coke we'd brought with us.

"Tent got cut, eh?"

Alan and John ignored him and kept drinking. I could never ignore him. He was a nice enough bloke. There was no harm in him.

"Aye," I said.

"In the middle of the night, down by the castle?"

"Aye, that's it." I thought he would say something about us messing round with knives again, but he didn't.

"That'll be the boggle," he said. "Did you see it?"

Alan and John looked round. "Let's go. He's an idiot," Alan said.

I was interested though. "What do you mean, the boggle?"

Billy laughed like it was us who was slow. "The boggle. The boggle that haunts the ruins."

John said, "I thought a boggle was something up your nose."

"What do you mean, a boggle?" I called to Billy.

He laughed again. "You don't know what a boggle is?"

I shrugged. "No."

"Well, it's a spirit."

"Like a ghost?" Alan said.

"No." Billy grimaced like Alan was really thick. "It's like a big thing. It's always been there."

"What are you talking about, Billy?" John said.

"The boggle that haunts the ruins," Billy said.

"You already said that," Alan said. "Come on, let's go." He got his bike ready to go, one foot up on the pedal ready to push off.

"It's a big black hen," Billy said.

"What?" Alan and John were laughing. "That's not scary!" John said.

But I remembered the pecking. A huge sharp beak could rip open a tent as easily as a knife. And the shape against the stars wasn't human at all. Just huge: huge and black.

I said, "A big black hen haunts the ruins? Why?"

Billy said, "It's not a hen, it's a boggle. It just takes on the shape of a hen. It could take on any shape it liked: a pig, or a column of sparks, or a big slithering blob."

"Come on, I've heard enough," Alan said, and started pedalling. John followed him, but I held back.

"What's it doing there, Billy?"

Billy tapped his nose. "You'd better get on after your friends."

"Tell me?" I said.

He narrowed his eyes, "It's guarding King Arthur's treasure. But don't tell anyone I said that. I don't want the Boggle coming after me."

"Will it come after you?" I said.

"Oh, aye. If the boggle thinks you're after the treasure, it'll come and kill you."

I gave him a long hard stare. He believed what he was saying, and I almost did too. Then he went quiet.

It didn't look like Billy was going to tell me any more. He probably didn't know any more to be fair, so I got on my bike and pedalled hard to catch up with Alan and John.

My dad had fixed the tent. He used to have a boat on Windermere and had to repair sails, so he liked to show off his canvas repairing skills. He'd pitched it on the farmer's field within sight of the parents' three caravans. "Just to keep an eye on you," he said.

The three of us lads were outside the tent. John and Alan sitting and me throwing my sheath knife into a stump of wood. I told them about the treasure.

"He must mean King Arthur's dad's treasure," I said. "It was Uther's castle, not Arthur's."

"He doesn't mean anything," Alan said. "He's daft."

"I mean a huge black hen!" John laughed. "Come on."

"But what if there is treasure there?" I asked. I had just got hold of a copy of the Dungeons & Dragons rules and had been dungeon mastering it with some friends in Kendal. I liked the idea of finding treasure in a ruined castle, as unrealistic as it was. And I was a twelve-year-old boy of course.

"There's no treasure there," John said. "Someone would have found it already."

"Would they really?" I said. "What it it's been undiscovered all these years? What if we found it?"

Alan pooh-poohed the idea. John looked more receptive. "Well, we'd have to give half to the British Museum, but we could keep half as treasure trove."

I wasn't sure about the law but it sounded reasonable.

"You can't just go digging in a farmer's field," Alan said.

"Besides," John said. "It's a scheduled ancient monument. If anybody saw you digging, you'd get the police on you."

"And then you wouldn't get to keep the treasure," Alan said.

I pointed a victorious finger. "So you admit there could be treasure."

"I admit no such thing."

But we were boys, and it was the summer holidays and we were in the business of adventures, whether it was wading in the beck among the duckweed looking for sticklebacks and frogs with our nets, or pretending we were Commandoes on a mountain warfare exercise.

I asked my dad for a spade.

"No," he said without thinking. Then he said, "Why do you want a spade?"

"Just do. For digging."

"Digging what?"

"Tunnels." It was the first thing I could think of.

My mother stuck her head round the caravan door from where she was cooking Chicken Fricassee. "You're not digging tunnels. They could collapse on you and you'd die."

"So, no," my dad said. "No spade."

But we didn't give up. "There's some in the farmer's barn," John said. "I saw them."

"We can't steal them," I said.

"We wouldn't be stealing them," John said. "We'd give them back when we were done with them."

Alan nodded. "Exactly!"

So we stole the spades. There were two and a trowel. I got the trowel.

We stowed them in our tent under the sleeping bags while we drew up detailed plans for the treasure hunt.

It was midafternoon, and the sun was hot. We had more coke and mum provided three choc ices from the fridge in the van. When she was gone, we got down to business.

"I'm not camping there again," John said.

I thought of the huge shape and the cutting of the tent.

Alan looked scornfully at him. "Scared of the big black hen?"

"No!" John stared back.

"There was no hen," Alan said. "Don't believe anything Billy Boustead tells you."

"Then what cut the tent?" I asked.

Alan shrugged. "A branch. A broken branch that caught it in the wind."

"There was no wind," I said.

John nodded. "No. There wasn't any wind."

"There wasn't a big bloody hen either," Alan snorted.

I grunted. Alan pointed at me. "He thinks it was a big hen!" John laughed too.

"No, I don't," I said, "But it wasn't a branch either."

We went by night. Worried about being caught digging for treasure in a scheduled ancient monument, either by the police or the farmer, we'd elected for darkness to cover our misdeeds. Mr Eilbeck who owned the land was a bad tempered old devil and if he caught us he'd beat us with his stick. Strangers could do that to kids then.

I was nervous.

"There's no hen," Alan said, as we set off, leaving the lights of the caravans behind and the grown ups playing Canasta and drinking gin.

I said nothing.

"There's no hen, Malcolm," he said again.

"Yeah, whatever you say."

He nudged me. "It was a stick. A sharp broken stick."

I said nothing but watched the shadows.

I had the foresight this time to fetch my father's big black rubber torch. I didn't switch on the beam yet. We were too close to the parents for comfort; them and farmers and policemen who might be lurking in the dark. Not to mention huge black hens.

We sidled our way closer to the broken walls of Pendragon Castle.

"Where do you think the treasure will be?" said John loudly.

"Whisht, man," Alan hissed. "Radio silence."

The walls loomed higher above us. The moon had come up which turned them white-grey and black. The shadows were thicker than India ink. The old limestone walls had a faint sparkle to them.

I gestured so we would walk round the wall. There was an entrance way still roofed that we could stoop down into and get through to the inner courtyard. The courtyard was grassed over now. I'd been many times before. But in daylight.

"Do you think it was a branch?" John asked.

"Of course it was a branch," Alan said. "What else could it be?"

We stood there hesitating before the dark mouth of the entranceway.

"Put the torch on, Malcolm" Alan said. "So we don't bang our heads."

"What about policemen?" John said.

"There's nobody here," Alan said.

And I listened. I could hear the River Eden gurgling by about fifty yards away. A slight breeze shifted the trees which rustled still in full summer leaf. Away to our right a sheep bleated, but that was that: no traffic noise, no aeroplanes, no sound of humanity at all.

I pressed the stiff button with my thumb and the torch light came on, its yellowy beam sickly and weak but good enough to illuminate the rough entrance to the tunnel that would take us to the inner courtyard of the castle.

"Needs new batteries," John said.

"I know," I said. And I hesitated.

After a minute of me just standing listening for I don't know what: pecking, maybe? John said, "What we waiting for?"

Alan said, "He's waiting for the big hen."

"No, I'm not," I said.

"Then go on."

"Why do I have to go first?"

"Because you've got the torch." Alan's logic was as impeccable as it was irritating.

"Okay," I said, but I didn't.

"Go on!" Alan hissed.

I sighed, gathered my courage and stepped forward. I had to stoop to avoid banging my head on the uneven stones that roofed the passage. I guess this had been some kind of kitchen passage when the castle was functioning. It was pretty tumbledown now though.

I emerged first into the courtyard. There was nothing there, just stone and grass. I disturbed roosting crows who flapped into the air scaring Alan and John as they stepped out behind me. That made me happy.

Sickly moonlight bathed the courtyard. I had a trowel; they had spades.

"Dig here?" John asked.

"Aye, I think so," I said. "Start in the middle?"

The truth be told, I had no real idea of where we should dig and we could dig all night and find nothing, our plan was so harebrained. But I felt a thrill of excitement as I watched John turn the first sod. After a few shovelfuls he was breathing heavily. Alan stood with his spade idle, but I wanted a go.

"My turn," I said.

John handed me the spade, and I handed him the trowel. The trowel would be for when we found the treasure, to do the fine work of excavation.

I was digging heartily, when John said, "What's that?"

I stopped instantly. The moon still shone. All I heard was a vixen barking way off. "What?" I said.

"No, I heard it too," Alan said. "You were digging."

I had my hand on the spade. I'd managed to shovel a lot of dry earth. I hadn't heard anything. I wanted to dig more. I started again.

The moon went behind a cloud and I went to pick up the rubber torch I'd put down when I started digging.

Alan put his hand on my arm. "Listen."

I listened. I said, "I still can't—" but then I heard it.

"It's outside," John said. He meant outside the courtyard, through the tunnel. But something big enough could come over the walls too.

It was the pecking sound, I'd heard in the tent.

"What the hell's that noise?" Alan said.

"Pecking," John said. "Like there's something pecking at the ground."

Then the moon appeared again from behind the cloud. By the light I saw something metallic in the hole, at the bottom, covered by dirt. I said, "There's something in there."

"Stop," Alan said, "We've got to get out of here."

"We're safer in here," John said.

"What if it can get through the tunnel?" Alan said.

I picked up the torch and shone it. Something gleamed gold in the hole I'd dug. I knelt down and touched warm smooth metal. There was a golden plate, half buried, and coins. "Uther Pendragon's treasure," I said.

Then the boggle leapt the walls and landed in front of us. John screamed, Alan bolted for the tunnel out. I stood there petrified and shining the torch on the apparition in front of me.

It was a huge black hen the height of a giraffe but much wider. It had black shiny feathers and a red cockscomb that fell over itself. It had bright beady eyes and a yellow beak — a beak sharp enough to slice canvas, or my skin.

The hen lunged at me with its beak, but I darted sideways and then stooped and ran at the tunnel. More by luck than judgement I didn't brain myself on the stones. Panting, and wheezing with effort and fright, I shot out of the far side of the tunnel and ran from the castle, avoiding a low wall and jumping to land on soft grass. I turned and saw the huge shape of the hen clucking after me. I sprinted across the grass, hoping I wouldn't trip and got away from the castle. The hen was after me, then I jumped the narrow beck, mostly dried up by the long summer's heat.

And I fell. I was sure it would kill me, butcher me with its knife-like beak. But it didn't. I lay there cowering, my head down, waiting for my death. But when I didn't die, I turned. I rolled and saw the black hen with its black eyes watching me from the other side of the beck. I remembered something from old wives stories that spirits couldn't cross running water. That must be it.

As the black hen watched me, I stood up, spun round and fled. I didn't look back until I got back to our tent in the farmer's field. John and Alan were both there already.

Alan said, "We left the spades."

"And the trowel," John said. "Unless you brought it, Malcolm?"

I shook my head. "Did you see that?" I asked.

Both John and Alan remained silent.

"The boggle. The black hen."

"I don't want to talk about it," Alan said.

Whether it was for fear of ridicule or pure terror that such a thing could exist, we never spoke about it again. I went in the daylight to get the spades and trowels. They wouldn't come with me. There was no black hen. There was a hole where I'd dug, but in the clear light of the sun, there was no gold or treasure at the bottom of it.

And that was that.

Alan went to Australia and John died young of a brain haemorrhage. I never really saw either of them after that, because I got interested in girls and rock music so I stopped going to the caravan and stayed in Kendal with my school friends. Then I grew up and moved away.

I've been back to Pendragon a few times over the intervening years, but I never saw the boggle again. I'm not sure I'll return there now. Why would I?

But Pendragon Castle; that's where we used to meet — me and John and Alan — going on our bikes and fishing with nets and roaming the fells when we were young, at Mallerstang in the long hot summer of 1976.

The Twisted Wood

IT HAD RAINED FOR DAYS, endless Biblical days of downpour that came relentlessly as the wind; the deluge that threatened to break all banks and rise all rivers had arrived, while I was at work, shuffling between meetings and managers from Newcastle to Barrow, all the time in my car, listening to Mahler and Sibelius and Iggy Pop. Driving, driving, driving, windscreen wet, drenched by torrents, becks in spate overflowing the road.

You may know the road; it runs straight through an extended cut of pines? Not far from Soulby? No matter if you don't. I hardly know it. The motorway had been flooded and foolish as I was, I thought maybe this was a way through, back home to Barrow, or Baradise as the wits have it. Actually, Urswick, Great...

There wasn't much traffic on the road that night as the darkness blossomed in from the east like a cancerous flower and gobbled up the day.

The water sheet shone in the headlights. It stretched right across the road, illuminated in my yellow beams as I slowed. I paused. Perhaps I could get through it? It looked like a stream had diverted with the heavy rain and now channelled its way from wood to wood across this narrow asphalt corridor, upon which my fate and my fortune, or at least my chances of getting home in good time, now hung.

The engine idled, I havered, and then took my chance. I wanted to be home with my wine and warm, not out here in the middle of a nowhere made yet more null by this wind, this wet, this wuthering. I gunned the pedal and plunged into water that was deeper than I thought. The wave surmounted the bonnet with a hiss and then a sudden stop as though the car were poleaxed and left dead in the wayward water.

"Bloody Hell!" I slumped over the wheel. What was I to do now? I couldn't wait here. I saw the headlines: Community Arts Manager Found Drowned.

No indeed, I couldn't wait in the car, even now the water seeped in, dark and frothy around the soles of my shoes, soon threatening my mid-foot, then my ankle. This would not do.

I grabbed my gaberdine and hat from the back seat, reaching over with a grunt, pulling it all to me. I snatched the strap of my black rucksack and checked it was closed and nothing spilt out. I have a habit of checking things more than once, so I opened the rucksack, making sure I had everything, my bag, my phone whose battery was long dead, and my Tupperware box of uneaten sandwiches: hummus and rocket.

I opened the door and saw the flood. I had no option but hopped into it, and it came up to the knees of my elegant trousers. They always say I'm dapper. No bother, the trousers would dry, and the car was leased. I waved it goodbye. I have heard you should stay by your vehicle and await rescue, but I couldn't wait here, the waters would overcome me, or I'd die of hypothermia.

My plan was to walk back down the road I'd just driven. There must be a farmhouse somewhere. I vaguely recalled seeing a field of wigwams on the west side, but that was a summer's day years ago, probably the last time I'd travelled this way. They were for tourists, and there were no tourists now.

I trudged along the cheerless highway, face into the driving rain, with a wind that lifted and fretted at me, so I kept my hand on my hat to prevent it from blowing away. I walked for a quarter of a mile, that felt like a hundred miles, until at last, gratefully, the rain went from pouring to drizzling then to merely dripping from the overhanging branches of larch trees. The wind lessened as well from a roaring to a moaning, and I could take my hand from my hat and look around. No moon sailed the sky, or if it did, it was entombed behind thick miles of black cloud.

The forest hissed and rustled on either side. On every side, the gurgle and rush of floodwater. After another ten minutes, I reached a broken bridge. In the dark, I didn't I hadn't seen it as I drove across before the car went into the flood, but now I saw the stones of the bridge were carried away in the torrent that flowed the height of a man and more, driving all in its way, from broken boughs to agricultural barrels to dead sheep.

There was no possibility I could cross that. I thought of walking back to the car and trying to wade through that flood, but I knew that was suicide. I was stuck, trapped between two torrents of water in the middle of a dark and trackless wood. I would have to await rescue.

And then it came to me that perhaps in the poor visibility when the rain hammered down, I had missed a turning into the wood. Maybe there was a lesser way that led to a farmhouse or a cabin. God knew, a cabin to wait out the night would do me. In the morning things would be better.

I shuffled my weary way back along the single-tracked road. It was still dark, but somehow a tenebrous glow gave vague illumination, and I wondered if it were some phosphorescence from a strange fungus or rotten wood. After ten or fifteen, minutes--I lose count—I stopped. I peered to my left; the shadows seemed somehow thinner there.

I listened to the dripping of water and the rush of unseen watercourses. No animal moved in the wood. I stepped closer, yes there was a track, probably a forestry track, but did foresters need shelter? I told myself they did. Maybe a little way into the forest I would find a cabin or even a lean-to. I told myself it was healthier than standing out on that damned road all night until dawn. Such a shelter might also be dry.

I walked along the rough forest track, damp trees leaning in on either side and crowding in overhead like gossiping hags. After four minutes or so, I came to a clearing. Here were piled cut logs, rows and rows of them, stacked on each other maybe three times my height. In the dismal wood, I also saw a building. My prayers were answered. It was a rough hovel, not what I expected foresters to use, it looked older and more idiosyncratic than anything they would build. It looked just the kind of house a witch might have buried in the wood. I laughed at my fears. What was worse, the irrational fear of midnight witchery, or the real risk of death from hypothermia?

I went to the door, rattled the handle and yelled, "Anybody home?"

The weird cottage was lightless, the windows blind and blank. It smelled abandoned. It sounded as if it were asleep. The door was unlocked. I pushed it open. With a deep breath, I stepped inside.

If anyone had ever lived here, it was a long time ago. The furniture was made of wood and could not be dated. Any primitive might have cobbled together this rough stuff at any time from the Dark Ages until today. The windows were glazed but fusted with spiders web. Huge mats of cobweb, looking like they were centuries old, and dust on the floor so thick that my feet left inch-deep impressions. The place smelled damp, but the rain was not in.

It was not somewhere I relished being, but as the rain began again outside, I pushed the door closed and made myself as comfortable as I could. I had only to wait until dawn, then everything would become normal.

When I awoke, it was already day, or at least that's what I thought. It's true, the light came in the mildewed window, but the quality was odd, like a neon grey, brighter than it should be but also less penetrating. The cottage door was still shut, though I could see light seeping through cracks in the boards. I went out to peer at the weird day. I was where I had been, in a clearing with logs piled up amongst the churned-up ground. The tyre marks of heavy vehicles were evident, and oil-stained water glimmered blue and gold and black in the ruts. The cottage was even more ramshackle than I had taken it for when I arrived last night, but at least it had afforded me shelter, and I would not curse it for its lowly look. It had been useful. Hail to thee, cottage, and thanks!

Standing there, at the door of the hovel, I looked up. There was no sun, neither was the sky full of clouds. In fact, it seemed that light suffused the sky, rather than emanating from any one spot. It was spotless as a summer's day, but instead of blue, the sky was spread with a self-luminating grey.

And another thing was the trees. They looked ordinary enough, spruce and larch and pine, but they were festooned with hanging threads and webs as if enormous spiders spun gossamer between their branches. And if the spiders were this big, I quailed to imagine how large were the flies.

I'd never seen anything like it, and I wondered whether it was a local phenomenon. Perhaps this forest here was struck by a strange blight? As I listened, I heard no birds. The familiar sounds of jackdaws and pigeons were absent. No blackbirds called alarms, no wrens clicked their displeasure at my presence. Instead, the air was filled with clicks and whirrs and other noises stranger to describe and unrecognisable to me. Where had I ended up?

It didn't matter, for I knew the main road wasn't far hence.

The rain had subsided, and so soon, I guessed would the floods. My car would stand high and dry and likely immovable in the middle of that straight road that cut through this mysterious wood. I would wander back and leave this weird woodland behind me with its diseased webs and odd ticking and snapping noises.

But first, by habit, I checked whether I'd left anything in the hovel. I'd lost a hundred hats that way and countless sets of gloves and now always reminded myself to look again before moving off.

I shoved the door and glanced around the grim downstairs of the cottage. Rickety stairs led aloft, but I had no inclination to explore. I wanted to get home and comfort myself with familiar surroundings.

None of my possessions was mislaid, but as I looked around the room, I saw a glistening object on the floor, under the hollow legs of a rude wooden bench, looking as if it had been deliberately stowed to be out of sight, but my stumbling around in the dark had budged the bench and disturbed it. What was it? It was multi-coloured with rainbow hues, an imperfect oval like an overlarge fruit, bigger than a coconut or pineapple slightly. I went down on one knee and with fingertips reached and scrabbled to bring it forward so I could snatch it. It was wonderfully smooth and warmer than I had expected.

It felt organic, perhaps wooden, but as I handled it and felt again its mysterious heat, its smooth material; it seemed living almost. The thought occurred to me it might be chitin, the fabric that makes up the skeleton of insects. And the heat seemed self-generated as if a strange process were going on inside, a composting, or an alchemical fermentation. Instinctively, I tapped it.

It sounded hollow, or at least not solid. And then, as I examined it, I saw a seam, a crack and getting the edge of my thumbnail into it, I worked it, and it came open.

Inside, the most wonderful glittering thing was revealed. It was a cocoon of diamonds that sparkled by their own inner fire.

They hinted red and yellow and blue sparks of light. I was amazed, what wonder was this? How valuable a thing to find in an abandoned house in the middle of a deserted wood in the heart of an empty county.

The colours were vibrant, vaguely eastern, though whether from the Hejaz, Samarkand or far-fabled Malabar, I did not know.

I wanted to take it more than I can express. Its iridescent beauty, as bright as a peacock feather, had captured my heart, and I coveted that rare thing even though I did not know what it was. But it was not mine. I placed it on the floor. I stood, went to the door, but then turned and stared at my lacquered container. It lay, glimmering in the gloomy surroundings, blue and yellow and red and gold. It must be lost. It must have been stashed here years ago when this place was inhabited and since long-forgotten, its true owner beneath the sod many a year. In truth, it belonged to no one. No one owned it, and so it could belong to me.

In a rush, I knelt down, picked it up and stuffed into my black canvas rucksack where it was hidden among the Tupperware and notebooks, a jewel amid trivia.

I hurried out of the door, not looking back, though I was careful to close the door firmly behind me. Who knew, perhaps another traveller would need shelter, and it would be better to leave the spot as dry as possible.

I strode down the forest trail back, as far as I could tell, in the direction I had come the night before. All the time, despite the inhospitable surroundings, despite my aches from a night on a wooden bench, despite the cold and damp and my broken car, I felt the fire of triumph kindle in me. I had found this wondrous thing, and I knew it indicated a change in my fortunes. I had laboured with my talent unrecognised, a minor director of a community arts project in Barrow of all places. I deserved better, and now I would get it! I would tell the story of the box's finding, but with details concealed that its true owner could never prove from whence I obtained it, if they lived, if it had an owner. I suppressed feelings of guilt and even began to whistle with happiness.

But the trees were not right. They were not healthy trees. I had taken them for those that grow in an ordinary forest plantation, but that was not so. These were the oddest trees I had ever seen, and though I am no arboriculturist, I knew they were wrong. They glistened and were bulbous, and where leaves and needles should be, they had growths. But the trees, even in that ghastly grey light, were not the most unnerving thing. It was the sounds. I didn't know if the trees themselves made those odd whirrings and whisperings, or the clickings and chatterings, or whether whatever lurked amid their twisted boughs did it, but I hurried my pace. Soon, I would be back at the main highway and normality.

But I found I had somehow lost my way. The wood was not as I remembered it. This path was twistier and stranger, and soon I stopped and looked and tried to orientate myself with growing panic.

It was a minute before I noticed him. He was, I would say, a tramp. His clothes of brown and green were old and stained and much mended. His boots were sturdy, but not new. He had wild hair and a beard of brown but twisted with grey. His eyes were brown too, and he watched me.

"Ah!" I said, starting, for he had surprised me in his silent watchfulness. "My car broke down, last night... The flood."

'The flood," he said. "The weather was bad."

And then something moved in the tree over his head. My glance darted up, and I saw a spider as large as a big bird, scurry across a thread of silk into a funnel of web. I jumped back. "My God!"

He raised an eyebrow. "The spiders?"

I felt my stomach lift. I imagined its spindly legs crawling over me, and its huge faceted eyes peering into mine. "I've never seen one so big. And these trees. What species are they?"

He studied me. "You don't know where you are, do you?"

I shrugged. "I've never been here before, but I presume—"

"Don't presume. You are lost, and you will never be found again if left to your own devices."

My brow creased. I accepted I needed help. "Do you know where we are?"

"I do indeed. I come here hunting."

"Hunting? What, foxes?"

"Stranger prey than foxes," he said. "But don't you bother about what I'm after. I can show you the way out of here."

"Would you? I'd be very grateful. I find myself most disorientated."

He laughed. "Many do. But most who come here, never leave."

"Never leave? Whatever do you mean?"

"I mean what I say."

I had to be practical. All this jibber-jabber wouldn't serve. I said, "I'd be grateful if you could show me the way out."

He nodded.

I offered, "Do you need payment? I have some cash..."

He shook his head. "I don't need payment, I'd be glad to help you as a good deed."

"That's very generous of you. Very Christian."

"I'm not that," he said, "but then again, neither are you."

Something fluttered across the clearing behind us. I swivelled my head around and saw to my amazement, a moth around six feet long with whirring wings much broader than that. This was the cause of the strange whirring I'd heard.

The thing flew with its huge goggle eyes and, feathery antennae and powder white fur.

"A day-flying moth."

"I've never seen one so big."

He nodded. "It's late in the season. Most are at the pupa stage now."

"Right," I agreed as if I knew what he was talking about.

He said, "You find the pupae lodged in safe places, inside a chrysalis, awaiting the change to turn from caterpillar to moth. They liquefy and reform in the most wonderful alchemical process."

"You're quite the naturalist," I said.

"I'm a hunter," he reminded me.

As we walked down the forest trail with the brown-clad man as my guide, the path was wholly unfamiliar, but I trusted him, mainly because I had no option. Also, why would he try to trick me? There was no advantage for him in doing so that I could see.

As we walked, I asked, "Is the road close? Just, I am anxious to be on my way home."

"Of course, everyone wants to get home."

"So, the road?"

"Ah, yes. Very close."

We walked on. There was still no sign of the highway. I said, "I don't recall walking this far last night."

He smiled. "This wood is very strange, as you have noticed. Its ways are not those of other woods, you know."

And I struggled to remember which woods I knew, precious few, but even those I had a passing acquaintance with, were nothing like this.

As if making conversation, my brown-clad guide said, "You slept in the cottage?"

"The abandoned cottage? Yes. It was the only place I could find shelter."

He nodded thoughtfully. "It's been abandoned many a long year."

"Did you know the people who lived there?"

He shook his head and without looking at me, said, "It's empty now."

I shrugged. "Yes."

"Nothing of value in there now," he said, but something in his voice suggested he was testing me. I pride myself that I can read people. I cleared my throat. "I didn't see anything of value, it was a poor, run-down place."

"Indeed." And he said nothing more for a while.

By this time we should have seen the highway, but there was nothing but twisted, misshapen trees in every direction, strung with webs woven by loathsome spiders with massive bloated bodies. I was only glad they didn't leave their trees. I had no idea that spiders so big lived in my own country.

Then a sizeable day-flying moth flitted in front of us drawing a gasp from me, a shudder and a step back.

"You don't like them?" He grinned.

"Do you?"

He said, "I'm used to them. They're harmless."

"They're huge."

A thought occurred to me. "You say you're a hunter. Is it the moths you hunt?"

"Oh, no," he said most definitely. "The moths are interesting, though."

"Really?" I was unconvinced.

"They're big as moths, but they come out of a much smaller chrysalis. It's only about the size of a coffee flask, but multi-coloured, very beautiful."

"Oh."

"Have you ever seen one?"

I shook my head vehemently, perhaps too emphatically I said, "How could I? I've only just ventured into this place."

"Of course, and you haven't been anywhere to see anything like that."

The moth still hovered around, and I saw it drinking from huge arum lilies with a long proboscis that curled at the end.

He saw me gaze at it in fear and said, "They have a curious life cycle, those moths."

"Oh," I said, though I wasn't really interested. I just wanted to escape that damned wood.

"Four stages, not three."

"Well, that's all very interesting, but I'm sure we must have got lost. None of this is familiar."

He wasn't listening. "Caterpillar, chrysalis, and moth are normal, of course." He laughed as if enthralled with his own story. "But there is a stage between the chrysalis and the moth."

I stopped. "I appreciate this is your special interest, and I'm most obliged for your kindness in showing me out of the wood, but actually you haven't shown me out of the wood. Perhaps I should find my own way."

He shrugged. "Suit yourself."

I had hoped he would just shut up and show me the way out, but if he wanted to play it like that, I didn't need him. Eventually, I would find a road or even a field. There would be some end to these damned twisted trees.

I paused waiting for him to relent and say he had been teasing me and he would now show me the road, but he didn't.

"Fine," I said. "Well, thank you for your company."

He nodded. I began to walk away. This track must lead somewhere eventually. The big tyre tracks were long gone, and the only marks were strange slithering shapes in the mud and tree mulch.

From over my shoulder, I heard him call. "Just one thing."

He was going to change his mind. I stopped, smiling, then cleared my smile before turning to face him so he wouldn't see my look of triumph. "Yes?"

"I was thinking that the reason you can't leave the wood is that you have something that belongs to it."

"What?" I blustered. What did this even mean? How could a wood own anything?

"Yes, local stories say you can't take anything from the wood. It won't let you. If you want to leave, you will have to give up what you found."

"But I haven't found anything."

"No, of course not."

"Really!" Like all liars, I protested my innocence long and loud.

He just smiled.

I turned on my heel and hurried off.

As I walked, I thought of the beautiful coloured thing in my canvas rucksack. So that's what it was, the chrysalis of one of those alien moths. Such a beautiful thing of buttercup yellow and poppy red and lapis lazuli blue-veined with gold, and when I had cracked it open, inside was a thing of living diamond that sparked red and blue and yellow with its own inner burning. It was just bluster. I wondered if he had been looking for the chrysalis. Maybe that's what he was hunting. I was sure they were worth a fortune, and I was only surprised I'd never heard of such things before.

He had led me a circuitous route to bewilder me. He must have suspected the chrysalis was in the house and was probably seeking it himself, but I got there first. That's what his questions were about. He suspected I had it, but of course, he couldn't know for sure. I laughed softly to myself. And this last desperate comment that the wood wouldn't let me take anything that belonged to it was undoubtedly intended to persuade me to surrender the chrysalis, and then he would point the main road, out a hundred yards away beyond the trees, beyond which he had led me such a merry dance.

I looked at the path. There were no boot marks here, and that proved the trail was little used. No foresters came here because it led nowhere.

I turned, and the brown-clad tramp was out of sight. I sucked my teeth; this path led nowhere, so I would strike cross country. I looked up at that infernally grey sky. It gave me no directions then I remembered that moss grew on the north side of a tree, but there was no moss, only damp wads of cobweb hanging down. I shuddered again, imagining the spiders that wove them.

I glanced left. The trees were not thickly clustering together. I could walk through that wood. There was nothing in these trees in England that could harm me. I gathered my courage, and stepped off the path, heading, as best as I could tell, for the road.

I walked, at first light-heartedly, then less so. I found no road. I found no further path. I saw no sign of mankind, just the scuttling of the spiders and the whirring of the moths and the clicking of God knows what else in the depths of the trees. I shuddered and hurried on.

And after an hour, I was weary and sat down.

I made sure I sat on a rock away from the trees, so no enormous spider could scuttle down behind me, unseen. I put the rucksack on my knees and fished in it for my useless possessions. Strangely, I was not hungry, and neither had I craved food since I first entered this weird woodland. But the real goal of my rummaging in the rucksack was the marvellous chrysalis. Even in the folded dark of my bag, it glowed with its fantastic array of gleaming colour. I took the chrysalis out and held it in my hands. So light, and still warm. Now, I knew it was organic; the lightness of the material made sense. Not wood, nor plastic, but a living insectile material, sturdy, durable and so wonderfully coloured.

There along the side of it was the crack I had already cracked open. That must be the larva of the moth. As I sat, I felt drowsy. I struggled to remember the life stages of a moth: larva, chrysalis, adult. But the tramp had said these giant moths had four steps. This was the chrysalis, and I had seen the adult, and the larva was the diamond thing inside, but I had no idea what the intermediate stage was: the stage between chrysalis and adult.

My head lolled. Dreams weaved around me. The forest clicked and whirred and whispered, and I slept.

When I woke, I was lying on my back on soft beds of cobweb. I must have fallen from my rock and with no tree to keep me up, was now lying flat. Something moved on my arm, something, glittering, glimmering, sparkling, as it shuffled along with little heaves of its diamond body.

The grub had emerged from the chrysalis, which lay cracked and discarded on the forest floor nearby. I peered to see the little thing that was busy eating its way through my jacket and shirt. I saw smears of blood and drool on its quartzite mouth. Its head was halfway into my flesh, but I felt no pain. I looked blear-eyed: I was anaesthetised by the secretions of its chomping, grub mouth.

Standing nearby, closely observing was the brown-clad tramp.

"You!" I said, but I could hardly lift my head, so drugged was I by the little diamond thing.

"Me," he replied.

"But what....?" I was making little sense, I could scarcely form the sentence.

"You asked me what I hunted in this twisted wood."

If he expected a response, I could give none. The moth larva ate into me. I felt it burrow into my chest cavity, its crystalline angles chewing through muscle, sinew and fat. But it didn't hurt.

The hunter continued. "I didn't answer, because if I'd answered, it would rather give the game away."

"I don't understand," I said.

The hunter smiled. "Well, the truth is, I hunt people." He pointed. "And I use those little things as bait. It's the glitter and the colour, I think." He grinned. "The glitter and the colour. They never fail to hook men like you. The hook catches the fish, and the fish feeds the fisherman."

I raised a dying eyebrow. "You're going to eat me?"

He winked. "I should say so. But I'll hang you up for a few days so you're nice and ripe. I like 'em ripe."

A Grizedale Forest Wedding

"IF YOU RUN off with Gowan Fell, you'll never be welcome back here," her mother said, stony-faced. Rebecca looked at both her mother and her father who stood there at the door of the slate-roofed cottage at Grizedale, the only home she'd ever known

"But I love him," she said.

Her mother twisted her face in a grimace. "You're a foolish, eighteen-year-old girl. What do you know about love?"

"I know what my heart tells me, mother," Rebecca said.

Her father sighed and her mother glowered. Rebecca set her own face as if she didn't care what they thought, turned and walked down the path that led to the forest. It was summer. She walked down the rows of her father's sweet peas and blue lupins, the heat of the sun beating on her bonnet. She had her few possessions in a pack on her back. She stole a glance to see her mother turn and step back into the house. She could feel the older woman's dark anger even from here. Her father stood at the door and looked like he would cry; he was always the soft one. Her mother had been the disciplinarian.

Rebecca walked on, pushing open the garden gate, which was stiff as if it didn't want her to go either. Then she was walking along the grass verged path that led to the forest. Around them the fells rose - high and craggy across the lake to the west where the mountain called The Old Man stood like a brooding god above the water and softer, heavily wooded hills to the east. She hadn't reached the forest when her father caught up with her. She heard him but didn't look round, for she too was angry and stubborn. Then she felt his hand on her shoulder. She let it lie but kept walking until it fell away.

"Rebecca," he said, coming after her, slightly out of breath.

She softened. She loved her father. Other fathers would have beaten such a wilful and disobedient daughter until they obeyed, but that was never father's way. He would usually persuade, cajole, and make her laugh until she came round. Usually, but not now because *love is the higher law*. She'd read that in a story of knights and ladies. Fate set who your true love would be and then you had to be with him, come hell or high water.

"Rebecca," her father said again, and she came to a stop and turned to face him. Her back was to the forest that closed in around the path like a secret.

Her father was in his mid-fifties, grey at the temples, his face tanned and lined by his lifetime of working outside. "Do you have to go, lass? Your mother thinks you'll soon regret it and be back."

"I have to go, father. You always taught me I should do what's right - what my conscience tells me to do." Her face was pained. She hated to upset him; her mother less so, but her father certainly. She took his hand.

He said, "But is it right? Have you thought of the shame it'll bring upon us?"

She scowled. "I care not for shame, father. Shame is the way the priests and lords keep us in our place. Shame shall not stop me."

He stroked her shoulder. "Then not shame, but think of me. It will break my heart to lose you."

She shook her head. "You'll not lose me, father. I shall visit."

She took his hand from her shoulder and held it. "Gowan is my true love, and one must follow where one's heart leads."

Her father's brow darkened, and he looked down at his big gnarled hand in her soft white fingers. "Gowan Fell is not a good man," he said.

She snorted. "And I've heard that one too. Because he lives a free life in the forest and pays no respect to the great and the self professed good, they call him a bad man." She shook her head. "They call him a bad man because he doesn't do what they say, not because he is one."

Her father fixed her with his brown eyes. "I see your mind is set. But if he hurts you..."

She squeezed his hand. In a soft tone she said, "He won't hurt me, father. He loves me. He is my true love and I am his; he told me so."

"Many men say such things, Rebecca."

She dropped his hand. "I thought you better than this, father. You shouldn't try to poison my mind against my love, just to get me to obey you."

He sighed. "I've never been one to force you to obey. Your mother calls me soft. Maybe I am. But I trust that your love for us, your parents, will remain and you will recognise how much we love you. Even your mother, because beneath her disapproval, she loves you too."

Tears filled his eyes. She did not like to see her father like this; he was soft and gentle, yet always strong. But her mind was made up. She wouldn't abandon her family. She wanted to come back and see her little sister and she knew that she could outlast her mother's disapproval. In the end, they would come round and see she was doing the right thing. Her sister had given her a keepsake, one of her dollies. It was a badly made thing and cheap, but little Kirsten loved it, and it had been given with tears in the small girl's eyes to 'keep you safe in the wood.'

"I must go now, father. The way is long and I want to be there before dark."

"Do you have enough food?"

She nodded. "Mother gave me bread and cheese and some apples." Rebecca smiled. "She hated doing it, but she did."

"She wouldn't see you go hungry, no matter what she thinks."

Rebecca stepped away, backwards.

"They say..." her father began.

"They say what?" She frowned - this was another ploy of his to keep her.

He shrugged. "I don't believe in such things but..."

"Spit it out, father. You've begun some wild story, best finish it. Some story about Gowan no doubt."

He didn't speak.

"They say he's a womaniser? Is that it?"

He shook his head.

"That he's a wife beater?"

"No. I've not heard that. It's what his father was."

"His father?" She was incredulous. "A story about his father to put me off Gowan?" She shook her head more in pity than anger. "Father, you have to let me grow up."

Then, seeing her mind was made to leave, he reached into his belt and gave her his knife. Good steel was rare in those days among ordinary folk and she knew he prized his knife.

"I couldn't, father."

He nodded. "You can. You'll need a knife for all sorts of things. I have another." He had but not as good.

She took it.

"Visit us soon, my lovely daughter," he said.

She smiled at him. "I shall. May the gods be with you, father."

"Remember to pray. Don't forget your faith in God."

She laughed. "I shall. But mine is the god of the woods and flowers, of the mountains and wild beasts."

"Shush girl, don't let the priests hear you say that."

And she turned and walked off, leaving her father standing on the track at the edge of the Old Forest.

And he never did tell her the worst thing he'd heard about Gowan Fell's father.

Gowan Fell's house was hard to find if you were uninvited, but for those he made welcome, the way was easy. And Rebecca was very welcome. She knew the route — walk down to the small stream where the brown trout lurk, then over the old packhorse bridge dressed in moss. After two hundred yards on the narrow path, look for the lightning split oak and then strike out through the deep wood following the deer path until you find it. The house itself was a pile of turf walls amid fern and brier and the roof was of rough slate. "I shall make a pretty garden here," she smiled to herself as she stepped into the clearing before the house.

Gowan Fell appeared from her right, silent as a beast of the wood. He put his hand to her blonde hair, and she jumped.

"You scared the wits out of me, Gowan," she said in a mock scolding voice, but her smile was wide as he enfolded her into his chest.

His arms were muscled from his work in the forest and his skin smelled of wood smoke and the wild wood. He held her tight, and she melted into an embrace she could not break free from, even should she have wanted. His kiss was fierce, his lips parted and his mouth was hungry and passionate. His hand was to the back of her head and then his teeth were at her neck, kissing and biting. She almost swooned from the pleasure of it, but she said, "No, Gowan," because that was seemly and even though she'd run away from her parents; they'd taught her what was right and what was wrong. She knew she shouldn't give herself so easily. But she wanted to.

He took her hand and led her towards his cottage. When she dallied, thinking that she would only give him her mouth and her breasts this time, he tugged her with him. She put her hand on the doorframe to pull back; he was going too fast. But impatiently he turned and looked at her with his dark eyes — like glowing islands amid his black hair and his black beard. "Come," he said, and she yielded and went with him into the dark cottage.

The cottage smelled of him; a musky odour that she did not find unpleasant. There were two rooms, the further one unused except for storage of his tools. She saw saws, axes, and other implements she didn't recognise. This one room had his bed, a low thing of bracken and sheepskin. She glanced around. There was a cooking pot, blackened above a dead fire. Then he took her chin in his fingers, and smiling, with his other hand, began to unbutton her bodice.

"No, Gowan," she said, putting no hand up to stop him.

He halted, as if listening to her objection. He raised a dark eyebrow and smiled to show his white teeth. "Very well," he said, dropping his hand to his side. She went over to the bed and dropped the dolly her sister Kirsten had given to her to keep her safe in the wood. The thing's cloth eyes stared at the ceiling and on an afterthought, Rebecca took off her cloak and placed it over the doll's face so it wouldn't see what was about to happen.

Gowan stood near the fire, the yellow light flickering on his handsome face. "Are you sure you don't need a lie down?" he smiled.

Then she felt a smile growing on her own face in return. "Well, perhaps a little one," she said.

The woodsman needed no further invitation. He undid her bodice and tugged at her blouse until her small breasts with their pale rose nipples were exposed. He took her to the ground, kissed her, kneaded her, suckled, and played with her breasts with the tips of his tongue. She was not a virgin; something her family did not know. For once, in the woods, he had come upon her while she picked bluebells and even then; she knew he was the one for her; her own true love, just like it said in the books.

Whenever she spoke of romance, her mother told her that love was for ladies, not ordinary folk, but Rebecca knew she was special. Not for her a life among the common people following their petty rules and hand-me-down beliefs, told what they could and could not do by priests and squires; she would choose freedom and to be her own woman.

And this was her choice. Gowan was her choice. It was her choice that he made love to her. Gowan began to remove her skirts and then her petticoats. She smelled him. She felt his weight. She sensed the strength in those arms. He was a real man — not like her father, kind as he was, but powerless. Gowan took what he wanted, and what he wanted was her.

The silken hair between her legs opened to his fingers, and she bit her lip and groaned involuntarily as he found her. And then in his impatience, he shifted on top of her. He took her by virtue of his strength and desire but it was her will to give in. Though truly she could not have resisted his strength.

Later, he dozed in her arms and she stroked his head. She felt his sweet breath on her chest. Gowan Fell, she thought; you are mine and I am yours. We shall be free here; we shall live a wild free life and the only laws we shall obey are those of nature and of love.

It was early summer when Rebecca moved in with Gowan Fell. He was charming and attentive. He brought her rabbits and pigeons to cook with wild garlic and the leaves of the forest. All summer long the bees buzzed, and the flies droned. Overhead, the doves cooed from the branches and the jackdaws argued as they went to roost on the warm nights. Rebecca and Gowan made love every night and in the day when Gowan was away working, Rebecca cooked and mended his clothes and set to work planting her little garden.

She went back to her parents' house to visit and her father was glad to see her. Her mother was glad too but hid her gladness behind a look of disapproval. "No good will come of this Gowan Fell," she said.

"I love him mother, and that's that."

Her father gave her seed potatoes, and she planted carrots and onions in her patch. He also gave her sweet peas and stocks to scent the evening air around the cottage.

Gowan made love to Rebecca fiercely and the animals and birds heard her cries of pleasure but paid no mind, because they knew well the sounds of love and death and could tell them apart. She liked to be taken as if she was a mare and he a stallion, or he a dog and she a bitch.

And so the weeks passed, and she was content with her life. She felt the spirits of the wildwood and when he was away burning charcoal in the deep forest, she would say her prayers to Brother Wolf and to Sister Moon. She washed his clothes in the beck to clean them of the grime and soot. Then one day she found blood on his shirt. She scrubbed it as best she could, but the stain was stubborn as guilt and could not be wholly cleansed.

She brought it to him as they sat around their rough table after they had finished rabbit stew, seasoned with her onions and thickened with potatoes and the barley her father gave her.

"Husband, (she had taken to calling him that because in the eyes of the Forest they were married, if not in the eyes of the Church) how did so much blood get on your shirt. I've tried to clean it but as you see—"

With a sudden snarl, he struck her with the back of his hand. She fell back, putting her hand to her lip and feeling the beading blood warm against her skin and tasting salt and iron in her mouth. He had never hit her before and she was dumbfounded.

"Gowan!" she said.

"Don't ask me my business, woman," he said, glowering at her, his dark brows a straight line and his brown eyes intense and full of fury.

"I only wondered if you'd been hurt," she said "It was a lot of blood and I was worried."

"My blood is my blood, not yours."

And later, Rebecca wondered whether it was his blood at all, because she had seen him naked and he had no cut nor injury. That night he was rough with her and she did not like it. She called out for him to be gentle but he took his pleasure and when he was finished, rolled over to sleep. Rebecca watched him as he slept, as thoughtless as a beast, and her heart felt as if it had been pierced by the black thorn of anguish, as when someone we love takes their affection away from us.

The next day she visited her mother. The older lady was softening and gave her cake and China tea that Rebecca knew was expensive and her mother's way of showing affection because she could never say "I love you" in words.

Rebecca considered sharing her heartbreak with her mother. Her brow furrowed, and she went silent. Her mother said, "What is it, child?" in as soft a voice as Rebecca ever remembered her using. In the end, Rebecca could not face the "I told you so" that would surely come, so she smiled and said, "This cake is delicious, mother. You must give me the recipe."

Her mother's face twisted, and she said, "And how will you bake a cake in the forest, daughter, with no proper kitchen and so far away from civilised folk?"

Rebecca frowned. Her mother would never change and Rebecca would never admit she was wrong, not to her mother. So she smiled thinly and said nothing.

At the end of the visit she kissed her mother dutifully and sent her love to her father. Then she made her way along the deep green roads of the Old Forest, back to Gowan Fell's cottage.

. . .

He did not come back that night. And when he returned the next day he hardly spoke. He sat eating roast pigeon and licking the grease from his fingers by the fire. She went to him for love, but he brushed her off and later snored as he lay beside her. It was then she noticed a smell on him; one she recognised - the smell of another woman's sex.

The next morning, he dressed in his fine fair clothes, though he said he was going to the forest as usual. When he set off to work at his charcoal burning, she decided to follow him. She crept a hundred yards behind him. She wore her brown dress with her cloak of forest green. If he had been paying attention, he could have noticed her because she was not skilled in the ways of hunting as he was, but his head was clearly full of something else and he whistled as he went.

When he came to a fork in the road, instead of going right to where his fires were, he turned left towards the hamlet of Hawkshead. She kept back and to the side of the path so she was close to the undergrowth of hazel and whitethorn and could duck in if he turned. Once he stopped to piss, the thick jet raising steam as he held his penis with the self-satisfied look of a man who is going to get what he wants.

Hawkshead was a poor place - near the great lake with the forest behind it. Rebecca wondered how she was going to observe him now he was in the village. She came to the outskirts, stepping tentatively. It filled her heart with anxiety at what she might see and she clutched the folds of her kirtle tightly in her right hand, the left to her throat as she watched him enter between the first houses.

She didn't have long to wait before her suspicions were proved correct. A bonny dark-haired girl of her own age ran to greet Gowan Fell, throwing her slim arms around him. Gowan pulled the girl to him and kissed her deeply there and then.

Rebecca's heart broke. Hot tears flooded down her cheeks as she turned and ran back into the forest. The ice of abandonment and the fire of jealousy chilled then scalded her chest. She wept as she ran. What was she to do now? She had cut herself off from her family, because of the faithless Gowan Fell. Her mother and father had been right all along. She could run all the way back to them, but how could she face her mother's crowing victory and her father's sad eyes? We told you so, her mother would say. Her father would hold her, and they would take her back, but her pride wouldn't let her go.

Instead, she decided to wait and see what solution the morning would bring.

She did not sleep until late in the night. She heard the badgers snuffling outside her cottage and the bark of the fox deep in the wood. A shaft of sunlight woke her, that and the sound of someone knocking on the rough wooden door. At first she thought it was Gowan returned and her heart hammered, but then she realised he would not knock. A woman's voice said, "Is there anyone home?"

It sounded like an old woman. Rebecca was in no mood to talk to anyone and she lay there while the woman knocked again. Irritation fuelled by heartbreak, made her finally sit up and shout, "What?"

"Ah, there is someone home," the voice said. "Do you want to buy ribbons? Lovely silk and satin ribbons in all colours."

Rebecca exhaled. Her natural demeanour began to surface, breaking the vinegar bitterness that had soaked through her. When she'd gone to bed, she had hated the world — men for their faithlessness and women for being their willing accomplices, betrayers of sisterhood.

"A minute," Rebecca said. She stood hurriedly and pulled on her green kirtle, covering her underslip. Then she went to the door and opened it.

The woman was black-haired with strands of grey. Her

face was lined and brown as if from years walking from town to town with her wares. She had a pack on her back and was already unloosening it and unpacking brightly coloured ribbons.

She took them in her hands and offered them to Rebecca. The girl shook her head and made to pull away, but she had never seen such fine ribbons. The colours were names she hardly knew.

The woman said, "Cerulean silk, and here carmine satin." She gave them to the girl who wound them round her fingers and in-between, feeling their silky texture. "And here viridian, and here amaranthine. This is smaragdine, and this one is heliotrope, while this is icterine and this one, fuliginous black."

Rebecca put her hand to her mouth and laughed. "Are these really words?"

The older woman laughed too. "Words made to charm a buyer."

Then Rebecca smiled sadly and said, "But lady, I am no buyer. I have no money."

"If not money, then food?"

"Poor fare that." Rebecca pointed at the small cauldron by the fire that had the remains of the last stew she made.

"But better than none for a hungry belly. May I come in?"

Rebecca nodded. "What is your name?"

"My name is Blodcuwedd," said the woman.

Rebecca said, "That is in the old tongue. What does it mean?"

The woman smiled. "I was Christened something else long ago. But long ago I began to follow the ways of the woods and changed my Christian name to something that was more mean-ingful. Blodeuwedd means flower face, and the owl was called that one time."

Rebecca nodded. My great-grandmother spoke some of the old language, but she is dead now and none of us learned it. "

Blodeuwedd said, "The old language grew here in this forest.

It made us what we are. When we lose it, we lose our essence. But your name, girl. What is it?"

Rebecca told her. "I believe mine is a Christian name, or Jewish."

She looked at her. "But I see nothing of that in you. I smell the woods on you. The deep woods and water call you more than any holy book."

Rebecca nodded. "Wait while I heat the stew. And would you like tea? Please sit." She gestured to the rough chair that belonged to Gowan Fell.

Blodeuwedd sat down. "This is a man's chair," she said. "A man lives here, but he is not here now?" The intonation of the words was as if they were a question.

Rebecca frowned and said nothing.

Blodeuwedd did not persist, but waited until Rebecca had warmed the meal.

She ate it with gusto. "What meat is this?" she asked.

Rebecca looked to her feet and said, "Crow. It's the best we have right now."

"No matter," Blodeuwedd said. "Black feathers like your heart made black with sadness."

Rebecca was taken aback. "How do you know I am sad?"

"I see it," Blodeuwedd said. "I know you. And I know the man who lives here."

"Gowan Fell?"

"Aye and I know his people. I know their kind."

Rebecca wanted to ask more, but she did not. Perhaps from fear of what she might find out.

Then Blodeuwedd rose and thanked the girl. "Here is a ribbon as thanks," she said at the door.

"What colour is it?" smiled Rebecca.

"It's only red."

"Not incarnadine?" she laughed.

The woman shook her head. "Merely red. Red as

blood." Blodeuwedd paused on her way out as if something weighed heavily on her mind. She made a noise as if to speak, but finally said nothing.

"Will you be back this way again?" Rebecca asked the older woman as she left.

"Perhaps." Blodeuwedd said, and then, as if an afterthought, she reached into her bag, took out a green ribbon, and gave it to Rebecca. "And this is green as life. There is a place in the forest you might find if you ever need to. At a join of the two streams, where the oaks give way to the ash and aspen, there is a white stone there that sparkles, half out of the water."

The girl nodded. "I know it. It is a pretty spot."

"It is my spot," the woman said. "Remember me there."

And with that, she turned and left.

Rebecca watched her until she disappeared into the trees of the Grizedale Forest and then closed the door and waited for the return of Gowan Fell.

When Gowan came back, he said little other than give a growl for his supper. He was not in his fair clothes but had changed to his normal working garb. He was covered with charcoal grime so Rebecca didn't doubt that he had been working as he said he had. Underneath the smell of burning, that animal smell of his had grown much less pleasant to her nose than it once had been when she desired him.

After supper, he took her. She told him no, but he took her anyway. And while Gowan Fell violated her, she hoped her father would come in with his woodman's axe and kill the beast, but no one came; she was too far away from those who loved her and so she suffered his vileness and prayed instead to her gods of the woods and the forest to send deliverance.

As they lay there, she said, "Gowan, do you love me still?"

He laughed a bitter, dry laugh. "I love your cleaning and cooking and mending my clothes."

"Nothing more?"

"And I love burying myself in you when I can not get better."

She felt quick tears, but they were drowned by shame. What a fool she was. But she would not let him hear her cry, so she clasped her hands tight so her nails almost pierced her palms, and she lay there until dawn.

Gowan was up early the next morning. She heard the small birds of the wood in full throat outside as they sang their morning chorus and orisons to the rising sun. She lay there while he pulled on his clothes, not his work clothes but the better ones that she had mended and stitched. She knew he was going hunting again. And she wondered from the blood on his clothes, whether he merely seduced the girls, or maybe did worse.

She had been charmed by the beast he was, as foolish girls will be, and as the pretty ones of the Hawkshead village would be. But a beast was a beast, and a girl was not a lover to Gowan Fell, but only prey.

And so once he was gone, she dressed quickly, and she followed him. In the pocket of her dress were the red and green ribbons given her by Blodeuwedd. She gripped them as she ran. She followed him to warn the girl he snared so she could avoid the grisly fate that Rebecca suspected Gowan would enact.

She ran quietly down the deer path that led away from their rough dwelling and to the main road through this part of the forest.

Instead of going to the village, Gowan took another path and went a way that Rebecca did not know. She watched him two hundred yards ahead, walking with an assured step, even whistling as he went, unconcerned and confident. After about two miles, the way grew broader and better trodden. Rebecca guessed they were approaching a village. Still Gowan did not suspect she was behind him. He had never looked behind at all, so secure was he.

Gowan went among the first low houses, thatched with sticks

from the forest and bracken, walls made of rough stone white-washed, flowers around their wooden shutters - lupins and red-hot pokers. The shutters were thrown open to let in the air of noon and Rebecca saw various good-men of the village greet Gowan warily, as if they knew him, but did not trust him.

She saw Gowan make his way to the tavern. And so, she thought, he had money, though he chose to give her none. Her use to him was housemaid and whore, no better than a slave.

How stupid she'd been to fall in love with him. She felt scalding tears on her cheek then she chided herself for a fool; tears would make nothing better, so she wiped them away and sat, near a cottage, within sight of the tavern door, so she would know when he came out. She pulled the hood of her cloak over her head. Gowan Fell would not suspect she was there, and even if he saw her, he would look past her hooded form.

And then after two hours, when the sun was still high, but flitting behind light clouds and not warm, he emerged. Again the village men nodded at him, but heads down, not meeting his eyes. And the girls and women, scattered out of his way like so many hens. All except one, a blonde girl who looked haughty and proud. She engaged Gowan Fell in talk and Rebecca felt a sting of jealousy in her breast. They tarried, and the flirting became more obvious. From where she stood half in the shadow of a wall, Rebecca saw a middle-aged village wife shake her head in reproach, but the girl was too taken up with the handsome Gowan Fell.

Rebecca saw Gowan reach inside his waistcoat and pull out a leather bottle. He offered it to the girl who with some little hesitation, as if pretending to obey the laws of propriety, eventually took it and swigged at it. Then grimaced and wiped the hot spirit from her lips. Rebecca saw the girl flush and laugh. Gowan laughed with her. He was a comely man, and Rebecca remembered the intoxication of his attention and how it brought a shiver to her breast and warmth to her loins, when she had first been enamoured of Gowan Fell.

And then, as surely as all such things are enkindled, the girl took his hand, and he led her down the path from the village. Again, Rebecca felt the sharp stab of jealousy. How she wanted to slap this girl and drive her away from Gowan Fell, but how now she also felt fear for the lass, foolish and vain as she surely was.

Rebecca followed them down through the beech woods as they went hand in hand, laughing and joking, towards the river. There they sat and Gowan Fell waited, as patient as a fisherman, for this blonde-haired fish to bite. It was she who moved in closer to him first, snuggling her side to his. And then, with the art of a master, Gowan Fell lifted his hand to caress the girl's shoulder. She leant her head into his and together they watched the silver water drift by. Rebecca remembered and recognised so well Gowan's artistry, his leisurely entrapping, so that a girl didn't know if it was love or lust he was after and persuaded herself that Gowan was set on love and it was her own lust that drove things to their disrobing.

And then, Gowan stood. Rebecca did not hear clearly but it was evident that he wanted to piss. Pretending to be a gentleman, he did not do it there, but rather stepped away.

They had been there long, and the light was turning golden as evening came. Up in the sky above hung the pale moon, barely lambent with the sun only just going. But Rebecca remembered how it had blazed white these past few nights as it made its way to the full moon it would achieve tonight.

And so Rebecca took her chance. While Gowan went, she ran lightly across the ground. The girl almost cried out but Rebecca signed for her to be quiet. If she'd been a man it would be different, but the girl saw no threat in another young woman.

Rebecca stood there before the girl and the girl stared back at her amazed until she said, "What do you want?"

"You must leave. Don't wait for Gowan Fell."

The girl scowled and said, "And who are you?"

"I am the wife who lives in the wildwood with Gowan Fell."

The girl shook her head. "Gowan has no wife for he has told me he is a single man, and besides neither he nor you wear a ring."

Rebecca frowned. "We are married by the ways of the forest, not the Church."

"Then," the girl said, "You are not married at all."

Rebecca reached out to touch the girl. "For your own sake, leave now."

The girl slapped her hand away. "I will not leave on the request of a jealous shrew. Gowan is with me now, so go."

The girl got up and her eyes were angry and Rebecca thought she might strike her.

"He will rape you," Rebecca said.

"It's only rape if I don't want him to. And that's what's bothering you." At this she reached down for a stone and went to throw it at Rebecca. Rebecca also saw the shape of Gowan Fell returning from further down the river.

Rebecca felt fear. If he found her here, he would surely hurt her. She turned to run. She broke through a screen of branches and crashed through the undergrowth as a rock came thudding after her. She heard Gowan Fell's voice scream, "Rebecca, I'll kill you for this!"

Darkness had fallen on the forest before Rebecca got back to the hut. She arrived at their rough cottage when the tawny owls were calling from tree to tree above her head. Her way was lit by bright mother Moon, but her breath was ragged as she ran then walked then ran. The briars and thorns cut her along the way and lines of red marked her legs and arms like the bloody striations of self-flagellation.

And when she was home, she lit a rush dipped in tallow and waited in the smoky yellow light for Gowan Fell.

But he did not return, at least not immediately. And as she waited, she shivered, not with cold but with fear. The smell of beast was heavy on their hovel. If she had not minded it before the odour now almost choked her. It was his smell. The smell of a man, but the smell of something else too.

When he did not return after many hours, she ventured outside, her fear now replaced by a sense of resentment and growing courage.

She would go back to her mother and father. They would tell her how foolish she'd been and that would hurt her young pride. How she'd seen herself as a spring flower, or a young fox finding its way in the woods and fields. But now she knew she'd been a fool, taken in by a lout and woman beater. And worse, a rapist. She wept bitter hot tears, gathered her few things, and stepped out of the hut.

The moon was bright outside as she walked down the deer track, her heart beating fast in case she ran into Gowan Fell. But he was not there. The nightjar called, and she heard beasts snuffling in the undergrowth, but they meant her no harm.

And then she came to the wider path. She walked down the rough way, avoiding the puddles from an earlier shower of rain, stepping on the lush grass that grew in a line down the centre. This path took her some way back towards the village she'd fled from earlier, before splitting and leading her back to her parent's house. She was lost in her thoughts of heartbreak and self-blame when she sensed someone up ahead.

She stopped. She listened and heard nothing. She listened harder, straining every fibre to catch what she'd hearkened to before, the subliminal warning that had made her halt. There was something on the breeze, but she couldn't comprehend it. And then she realised part of what had stopped her was the silence, the unnatural silence of the wood, where before there had been owls and the flitting of bats, now there was nothing, as if the whole wood was holding its breath.

There were shapes down the path. They were the size of men and walked on their hind legs, but they were not men. As the breeze shifted, she caught their scent. It was the scent of Gowan Fell, but this time mixed with something more animal — something doglike or worse. He was with another of the same kind. Rebecca stood frozen with fear. And then the breeze shifted. She saw one of them raise his snout to the air, blackness silhouetted against the dark violet of the sky behind. He appeared to be sniffing. He had scented her out.

Rebecca turned and ran. She fled in the direction of her father's house. She ran until her legs burned and her lungs were on fire and she didn't stop running until she crossed the stone bridge dressed in moss and was at the edge of the forest near to where her father and mother lived. And there she stood, hands on thighs, gasping for breath. Gasping for breath, but at the same time looking back into the forest in case she was pursued. In case, Gowan Fell had followed her to her parents' house.

She saw no sign of him, but when she had her breath back, she ran again. She stumbled and half fell through the pretty gate of her family house and along the path between the vegetables up to the door. It was deep night, and the moon rode high with her company of stars. Rebecca hammered at the door. It was her mother who answered. "Rebecca, what are you doing here? At this hour!"

Little Kirsten was beside her mother seeing who it was, then she rushed out and hugged her sister.

"Rebecca, answer me!" her mother said, tugging at Rebecca's sleeve.

Rebecca's face was wet with tears. Her chest heaved with sorrow and if felt like there was ice where her heart should be. She feared her mother would send her away again, back to Gowan Fell, that she would say, *"You've made your bed, now lie in it."*

But then her father came to the door. He kissed her cheek and said, "Welcome home, my daughter. Come in and I'll keep you safe."

"You're thin as a rake, girl," her mother said. "I'll get you some broth," and she scuttled through to the kitchen to get food for her daughter. Rebecca was crying tears of relief to be back in the safety of her family. Her father and little Kirsten crowded round as she sat by the fire. They were burning cherry wood that gave off a sweet smell. The interior walls of the cottage were whitewashed, and the furniture was made by her father, sturdy and carved with the spirals and knots beloved of the northern people. He had his hand on her shoulder.

"What happened?" he said.

At first, she couldn't speak. A mixture of shame and jealousy held her words back. Kirsten stroked her knee and gazed at her with concern. Then Rebecca looked up at the ceiling and without making eye contact she said, "Gowan went with another woman."

Her father sucked his teeth. Then he said, "Well, that's no surprise."

Kirsten looked bemused, she was about to ask a question. Their father said, "Kirsten, go to your bed."

"But father," the girl said, "it's only early!"

Just then, their mother returned, the broth steaming and with it a chunk of her homemade bread and butter from the family cow. She said, "Kirsten, do as your father says — bed!"

The little girl pouted and stomped her foot but she turned and did as she was bid. Not like me, thought Rebecca, watching her go. At the door of the living room, Kirsten turned and said, "Rebecca, did you bring my dolly?"

Rebecca's eyes widened. Her hand went to her throat. She had a flash of panic almost as if she had left a living thing to the mercies of Gowan Fell in that hovel in the woods.

Kirsten looked sad, but shook her head and smiled. "Don't worry; we can get it another time."

Rebecca reached into her pocket and pulled out the red and

green ribbons given to her by Blodeuwedd. "Here have these. A kind lady gave them to me."

The little girl's eyes widened. She ran over and took the ribbons. "These are lovely!" she said. She leaned up and gave her big sister a kiss on the cheek, then she turned and left.

Her mother's eyes narrowed. "You got those from the pedlar woman?"

Rebecca nodded. "She was kind."

Her mother said, "I hope you didn't invite her, or worse still, give her food and rest."

"I did, mother. It was only hospitable."

Her mother spat. "That one, that calls herself "Flower Face" is a witch. She was trying to grab your soul."

Rebecca shook her head. "No, she was just a kind old lady."

"Mary-Hannah," Rebecca's father said to her mother. "You demean yourself by repeating old wives' tales. There is no truth in witches."

Mary-Hannah said, "There are strange things in the forest."

Ignoring her mother, Rebecca turned to her father and said, "I left Kirsten's dolly! I must go back."

Her father's brow furrowed. "I think not. Let it be. I would rather you never saw Gowan Fell again."

"But it was Kirsten's favourite. She gave it to me. I can't leave it with him."

"You're talking silliness, girl. You're tired. It's only a rag-doll."

Then her mother spoke. "No, you should go and get it. He should have nothing of ours, that Gowan Fell." She spat his name.

"I will go and get it, father." Rebecca went to rise from her chair, but her father stopped her down with a gentle hand. "No, you won't!"

"Not tonight, anyway," her mother said. "Eat your broth. Then sleep. You can fetch it in the morning."

And her father rose. "Mary-Hannah, Rebecca will not go to

that cottage. She will never see Gowan Fell again. That is my word, and that's final."

Her mother was taken aback, for it was rare her husband spoke with such authority. "Then *you* will go," she finally said to her husband.

Rebecca's father nodded. "Yes, I will go. First thing in the morning."

Rebecca felt sudden fear. She remembered the wolf thing she had seen on the path in the moonlight. She remembered the blood on Gowan Fell's shirt. She reached out and clutched her father's hand. "Don't go, father. He is a wicked man, and younger and stronger than you."

Her father smiled and held her hand tight. "Don't worry, 'Becca. I will not get into a fight. Anyway, I don't believe the stories about the Fell family."

Her mother sat silent.

He said, "Pagan nonsense is all they are."

Rebecca looked at them both. "You never told me what you had heard about Gowan Fell's father."

Mary-Hannah frowned deeper, but Rebecca's father laughed. "That." He grinned at her. "They say he was one of the Folk."

"The Folk?"

"They don't exist. How could they?" He said.

"Who are the Folk, mother?" She turned to Mary-Hannah as her father wouldn't give her a sensible answer.

Her mother shrugged. "The Folk. Country people believe in them. Those that have no education and who have never been to Church."

"But what are they?"

Her mother said, "Man wolves. Men who turn into wolves at the full of the moon and who walk on their hind legs."

"Nonsense," said her father. "Go to bed, my darling. I'll get the doll tomorrow. You need never see that scoundrel again."

She gripped his arm tight. "Please, don't go, father. At least get some village men to go along with you."

He leaned over and kissed her forehead. "Don't worry, Rebecca. I'll be fine."

The birds were in the roof space, flitting and cheeping. Outside owls and bats flew. Rebecca shared a room with her sister who stirred and muttered in her sleep. As she lay, head on the goose down pillow, she smelled the night-scented stocks from her father's flower garden and she lay there thinking of Gowan Fell. Eventually, towards dawn, she fell into a heavy sleep. When she awoke, the sun was streaming in through the willow lattices in the window that served instead of the glass they couldn't afford.

She got up and went through in her night shift. Kirsten was outside in the garden playing with the dog. Her mother was in the kitchen, and when she saw Rebecca, she brought her a bowl of porridge. She handed the steaming bowl to her daughter and bade her sit at the wooden table.

Rebecca began to eat the porridge. She had forgotten how good normal food was, not the findings of the forest, but proper food farmed and grown by people. After she had finished the bowl and then run her finger around it out of her mother's sight, she said, "Where's father?"

Her mother said, without turning from where she was preparing a rabbit, "He went early to get your doll."

Kirsten had come in and was threading Rebecca's hair through her fingers. "It needs washed," she said. Then her thoughts flitting like a child's will, she said, "Daddy's gone to get my dolly." She gave Rebecca's hair a tug, "That you left!"

"Ow!" Rebecca said, grabbing her hair back. But her heart was full of fear. Gowan Fell was not a reasonable man and her father was old now. Her father might want to avoid a fight, but Gowan might not let him.

She stood. "I'm going back."

Her mother shook her head. "Your father said for you to wait here. He'll be back by afternoon."

"No, mother," she stood and went to the bedroom to dress.

She heard her mother say, "You never do what I say, anyway." Then she turned to Kirsten and said, "When you grow, be a good girl, Kirsten, and always obey your parents."

The little girl said solemnly, "I will, mammy."

But Rebecca had thrown on her clothes, her kirtle and cloak still dirty with mud and leaf mould from the forest. She ran out of the door, shouting, "I'll be back soon, don't worry. I just need to help father."

She entered the Old Forest, and went along the forest road through the ragged avenues of oaks and ash, beech and willow, until she came at last to the packhorse bridge. She crossed that and then within an hour was at the deer path that led to the hovel she had shared with Gowan Fell. She felt her stomach churn and anxiety danced its electric dance from her throat to her fingertips. She was breathing more quickly, not filling her lungs, but instead panting lightly as she came to the clearing. Smoke curled through the rough roof, telling her that Gowan was inside.

She did not knock. Gowan was lying on his bed, their bed as had been. His eyes flickered open. His bare chest was covered in scratches and smeared blood, now dry.

She grew afraid. "Is my father here?"

Gowan raised his head. "Ah Rebecca, you're home."

"Is my father here?" she said more stridently.

He shook his head. "Your father?"

"Don't pretend to be stupid, Gowan Fell. He came to get Kirsten's doll."

Gowan reached out his long, hairy leg and with the toes kicked the rag-doll from the bottom of the bed. "This?"

Rebecca ran over and snatched it. She held it to her chest as if she had rescued a living thing from him.

Gowan sat up. He was naked. She could see better now that

the blood that matted the dark hair on his chest came from scratch wounds, five of them, as if someone had drawn a claw across him. The claw of a woman's hand in anger it seemed to her. He stood, arrogant in his nakedness. His penis hung long from the dark curling hair of his loins.

He reached and picked up his shirt. He threw it at her. It was covered in dried blood. "I need my washing done, Rebecca. It's timely you are home."

"I'm not staying. Where's my father?"

Gowan Fell, picked at his teeth with his fingernail. Then he shook his head. "The old fool called before. I don't know what he wanted. I sent him away."

"What have you done with him!" she screamed. Her fear for her father rose in her chest and up to her throat. Her head buzzed with terror and anger.

Gowan Fell smiled and shrugged.

She ran at him, fists flailing, but he easily threw her down. He stood over her, still naked, then he squatted and brought his face near to hers, the curly dark hair of his beard near her soft face. She smelled meat on his breath. Then he kissed her softly. "I've missed you," he said, standing.

He turned and began to search for clothes from the heap by his bed. She scrabbled to her feet and looked around the hovel. Her eyes darted this way and that and then she saw it. On the poor wooden table they had used, was her father's knife, which he'd given her to bring here. She had used it for skinning squirrels and rabbit. She watched Gowan. He had fastened his shirt and was pulling on his deerskin trousers. He still had his back to her. She darted over to the table, grabbed the knife, gripped it facing him and said, "Gowan, what have you done to my father?"

Gowan Fell turned, apparently unconcerned. He saw the knife. Her hand was trembling. He smiled. "Put that down, Rebecca, you might hurt yourself."

"Not as much as you hurt that girl."

He raised an eyebrow. "What girl?" Then he laughed. "Ah, the girl from the village. I hadn't realised you were so jealous."

"The blood on the shirt. It's hers?" Rebecca's voice was shaking because she feared it might be her father's. But the blood was mostly dry and if it was her father's it would not be dry at all.

"Blood, blood. The world is full of blood. Things kill things, Rebecca. You eat the meat of things I've killed. Don't be so squeamish."

"The girl. Is she alive?"

He shook his head. "Try to free yourself from your jealous imaginings. Come, I will show you where your father is."

Her hand trembled as she gripped the knife.

"Come," he said, most reasonably. "Round the back."

Rebecca knew that whoever had lived there before Gowan had a pen at the back for dogs. But there had been no dogs there since Gowan moved in. Dogs would not tolerate him. They slunk off with their tail between their legs, whining whenever they saw him.

"You go first."

"I have the knife." She brandished it at him. Her voice shook.

He grinned. "You won't hurt me, Rebecca. You haven't the courage. And besides you love me too much."

A ball of fiery anger burst inside her chest and she almost ran at him, but he met her stare and his eyes were quiet and cold. He smiled again, but without warmth. "Go," he said.

She went first. Gowan was behind her. They walked out of the front door and round to the left. The bracken was broken down as if someone had been that way recently. Her heart hammered and there was cold sweat between her shoulder blades and on her throat.

She stopped. She didn't want to see. "What have you done with him?" she sobbed.

"Go and look," Gowan Fell said.

She shook her head.

"Go and look," he said again. But this time he prodded her back.

She gripped the knife harder. If he touched her again, she would stab him. She exhaled, then she stepped forward. She saw the pen made from stout wood and rope. It was dark in the shade of the hovel with the trees clustering round. She couldn't make anything out. The door stood half-open. She walked up to it. "Daddy?" she said.

There was no answer. She heard her breath. She stepped closer. "Daddy?" she said again.

Then Gowan Fell lunged forward and shoved her into the pen. Before she could react, he had pulled the door closed and fastened the rope lock.

Rebecca screamed. Her father was not there. She shook with rage and fear and took the knife and slashed at the wood and rope.

Gowan Fell said, "I need a maid, Rebecca, and you will be her, willingly or no."

"I have a knife. I will cut my way out."

Gowan Fell gave a low laugh. "You will stay here and work, or I will kill your entire family."

She looked in his evil wolf eyes and she dropped her father's knife. It fell to the earth with a thud.

Gowan let Rebecca out of her cage so that she could cook for him and clean his clothes when she had finished cooking. For the first few days he did not leave the hut, nor her. He watched her even when she was working and then on the second day he let her sleep on the floor of the hut. The pen at the back was becoming cold as summer fled.

At first Rebecca wondered whether he had some care for her still then she guessed it was because he did not want his servant to die of exposure.

Around four days after she first came back looking for her

father, he left her to go into the woods. She thought then of running home, but she knew if he missed her on his return that he would come looking for her and she did not doubt that he would kill all her family. She hoped that her father was back at home and she longed to see him. She imagined an argument with her father wisely realising that Gowan Fell was younger and stronger and so would win any fight, after all it was only over a dolly.

She sat outside the hovel in the sunshine. The birds still flitted around her feet, but the sun now had the colour of old gold and the first leaves lay on the woodland paths. She detected a turn from green to brown in the trees and knew they would soon be yellow and red. She knew of an apple tree, not the sour crab apples but good eating apples that must have been planted long ago. She guessed it was too soon for them to be ripe but she thought she would go and look to see how long before she could pick them.

So she set off away from the hovel, down the deer path and instead of striking on the main forest road, rough as it was, she turned left and followed the stream. The water ran over smooth round stones beside her, clear and cold, not long down from the mountains. As she went, she was possessed by a great despair. She did not know how she would ever be free of Gowan Fell.

And then she smelled the stink of death.

Something was lying dead nearby. Perhaps an old badger or a dead crow. Her nose wrinkled, and she put her sleeve to cover her mouth and walked on. But as she continued on the path, she was walking towards the smell. And then she saw that the hazel bushes to the right were disturbed as if a large creature had stumbled that way. Or perhaps two creatures quarrelling and this was the end result. She had heard of stags fighting to the death, but it was too early in the season for that.

Her curiosity getting the better of her distaste, she stepped to the side of the path, moved some branches and saw the source of the gagging smell. A decayed corpse lay face down. She recognised the clothes instantly. It was her father. His face was pushed in the muddy grass and his back was ripped open. She saw that he had been partly eaten, as if a creature had begun to consume him but got bored and slunk away. She turned and was violently sick. Then she wailed, spinning around, shrieking her distress to the woods and the sky. She fell to her knees, banging her head with her fists. Tears ran down her cheeks and she cried, "Daddy, oh my daddy." And she knew Gowan Fell had killed her father. Either as man or as beast, he had killed him.

She stood and immediately wanted to go and find a shovel to dig her father a grave. There was one at the hovel. She ran to get it, but soon, after only a few yards, her head whirling, she realised that she was lost. Her grief overcame her, and she fell to her knees and sobbed while above her, crows called and the wind shifted in the tall trees. She remained there, her knees damp as the wet sods of grass soaked her dress. All she knew was the pain in her heart, and all for a doll, and all because she had gone with Gowan Fell because she had wanted to be free. Grief ripped her heart.

A cold rage possessed her. She stood. She was lost in the wildwood. She did not care that she was lost or if she would ever be found, but she had two tasks to complete. First, she had to bury her father, then she had to kill Gowan Fell.

She wandered, disorientated, until she came to the stream. She followed it down as it ran carelessly on. She was still in the oak wood but soon the ground underfoot became damper and the oaks gave way to other trees. There were ash trees and willow and aspen. Green rushes interspersed the soft grass and her feet sunk deeper. Then she came to a place where her small stream ran into another bigger one. The rocks that stuck out of the ground were granite and the micro crystals shone as the sun struck them. The water glittered and fish moved in the deep places of the confluence. And there in the middle of the water, like a boat cresting an endless wave, a rock of quartz stood. It was fissured and cracked, cloudy in places but the sun illuminated it and it gave back light like some sacred, magic thing.

And Rebecca remembered the goodwife, the flower face pedlar who had come calling and tried to sell her ribbons. This was the place she had mentioned: *'At the join of two streams; where the oaks give way to the ash and the aspen.'*

Rebecca stood by the bank and watched the rock sparkle in the light, then, without knowing why she did so, she hitched up her skirt and waded through the water. The water was cold, even in summer, because it was mountain water. It came to her knees and the rocks underfoot were slippery with weed and moved as she put her feet on them. Nevertheless, she made it across to the shining stone. There she hugged it as if it were a person and a rescuer. She felt it smooth under her hands and warm to the touch from the sunlight. She peered into it and saw in a million fractures and imperfections, a whole other universe. Her eyes tricked her into thinking she saw the form of Flower Face deep inside. And she prayed to her: "Mother of the Forests, give me my revenge on Gowan Fell."

But nothing happened. The water rushed by. The breeze moved across her cheek. Above the clouds shifted, and the sun shone. Swallows swooped low across the water, catching flies. And she laughed bitterly. There were no gods of the wood, no brother wolf, no sister moon, just objects - a dead universe peopled by foolish imagination. How had she thought a stone could help her? It wasn't even that the stone didn't care, or the trees or the birds. They were just things without mind or soul. And so another of her dreams left her.

Rebecca swallowed. She felt the lump still in her throat and the pain of grief in her chest, but her blood ran hot. One thing she vowed; she would have her revenge on Gowan Fell whether there were gods or not.

She picked her way across the stream's bed onto the bank and she let her wet skirts drop. From here, she knew her way back to the hut she shared with Gowan Fell. She walked slowly and listened to the singing of the birds but knew it was without meaning. And on her way, she came across a bank where honeysuckle and musk rose grew among white thorn and black. She stopped the smell the roses; beautiful even though they were meaningless. She plucked them; the thorns pricking her fingers. And she grasped a twine of honeysuckle and inhaled the sweet heady scent. She took a sprig of that too. As she walked, she held the two flowers in her hand. She no longer believed in love nor in the benign gods of water and wood. There is no one as empty as an idealist who has lost her belief. But instead of belief she now had hate. And it was hate that drove her now.

When she came home Gowan Fell was at the door, wearing his good clothes. His collar was loose and his waistcoat unfastened. "I thought I was going to have to come after you," he said with a wicked smile.

Rebecca stood, the rose and honeysuckle drooping in her hands. She couldn't meet his eye lest he see the hate in there and guess what she planned.

"Come in. It's time for you to cook." He stood aside from the door, the bright wicked eyes in his dark, bearded face, watching her every move. She breathed heavily and said, "I'm going to plant these first."

"Those dead flowers? They won't grow."

She nodded. "I will plant them first." And then, she thought, I will kill you.

He took a step towards her and grabbed her round the wrist. He squeezed until her fingers went white. She gritted her teeth to stop the cry of pain, but he was too strong, and she dropped the flowers.

He heeled the rose and the honeysuckle into the dirt with his boot. "You cook when I tell you to cook." He let go of her hand and then, as if an afterthought, he struck her across her face. "You do what I tell you when I tell you, bitch."

Rebecca felt the pressure of tears, but she would not let them come. She put her hand to her cheek to feel the heat of his blow and the throbbing of the pain. She bowed her head. Then he lifted his foot and with it, shoved her into the hovel.

By the area she used for cooking was fresh meat. It didn't look like the usual crow or rabbit that he managed to catch.

"What's this?" she asked.

"Pork." He was grinning smugly.

"Where did you get the money for this?" she said.

"I didn't need money. I got it from the butcher's wife. Meat for meat." He threw back his head and laughed.

Rebecca felt her stomach turn. She saw her father's knife that she had brought back into the kitchen days before. She wouldn't make the same mistake this time. She would wait until he was sleeping.

She saw there were also fresh vegetables and a bottle of foreign wine. Gowan had brought them all back from the fair at Hawkshead.

"More gifts?" she said. Her voice was cold.

He guffawed. Then he said, "So many ladies. So many things they want to give me."

"And did you kill them?"

His eyes narrowed. "No, not kill them. Sent them back to their husbands bruised and torn, but I didn't kill them."

Her voice was icy. "How do you decide whether to rape or kill?"

"Rape is a nasty word, Rebecca," he whispered. He came closer. "But be honest, you always preferred it when I was rough."

She tasted bile in her mouth. He ran a finger across the cheek he had recently struck. He was smiling.

She turned. "I'll cook," she said.

He grunted. "Pour me wine." Then he went to sit on his chair outside, as the afternoon became evening.

She fried the pork with vegetables. She was tempted to over-salt it but he would notice that. Instead, she spat in it though it gave her no satisfaction. Revenge for her father would need deeper injury than that.

She brought him the food as he sat outside, boots kicked off, shirt open to the sun that filtered through the yellowing leaves. Crows called from the branches of the oak behind the hovel. The rooks prepared to go to roost.

"Sit with me, Rebecca," he said, motioning a tree stump near where he sat on the sheepskin-covered chair.

She shook her head.

"Sit," he snarled.

"I have work to do in the garden; I need to weed the onions and garlic."

He snorted. "Go, weed the onions. Wash the dishes and then get in my bed to make it warm for when I come to you."

Without answering, Rebecca turned and went towards the small vegetable plot that she had so lovingly tended for him. As she passed, she stooped and picked up the wilting honeysuckle and the broken rose in a quick movement so he should not tell her to drop them and throw them away. She went out of his sight to where the garden was. There with her hands she scooped two holes in the damp earth and placed the plants in them. She stood them so they propped each other up, but they were sad and drooping and she knew they would die. It was the act itself. She had not thought to do it, some unconscious impulse had caused her to pluck them and carry them and plant them here.

Somehow, it seemed like something she should do to give herself hope. And when she had scooped the soil back into the holes to support the plants as best it could, she bowed her head. She prayed, "Mother of the Forest, though I no longer even believe in you, help me in my need. If you are there, help me in the way you know best. Deliver me from the power of Gowan Fell."

And then she heard a sound, opened her eyes and turned and there he was standing behind her, a look of cruel mockery on his face. "Praying to your silly wood spirits are you? I will never release you from my power until you are dead. And when you die, it will be because I have a better maid, and I will kill you with my own hands."

He grabbed her long blonde hair, and he yanked her to her feet backwards, stumbling. Then he kicked her forward and when she fell, he grabbed her upper arm to drag her into the hovel. Once in the hovel he said, "Wash my plates. And when you're done, take off your clothes."

He went over to the bed and stood by it, pulling off his trousers. She washed his plate but kept an eye on him and when he pulled his shirt over his head and could not see; she took the knife and put it in the pocket in her woollen dress.

He stood there naked. "Done?" he said.

She nodded.

"Here," he said pointing to his feet. She walked towards him.

"Take off your dress," he ordered.

She quietly disrobed, but dropped the dress and the knife it concealed close enough to the bed so she could grab it without stretching.

She stood there bare in front of him. He looked her up and down. She moved to cover her breasts and her pubis but he pushed her arms away.

"You are mine to look at." Then he snorted. "Not bad. I can see why I chose you."

He gestured to the bed. "Get in."

She knelt and then got into the bed. Before he got in with her she said, "Gowan, did you ever love me?"

"I only love myself," he said.

"But you said that I was special, that I was the one." Her voice sounded weak.

He laughed and said, "Girls should never believe what men tell them."

Then he lay on her. Her forced her knees apart. She put her arm between her teeth and bit so she would not cry. She knew she would have to endure this. Then, when he slept, she would kill him.

When he had sated himself and was snoring, his arm drooping out of the bed, Rebecca lay awake. She monitored the sound of his breathing to make sure he slumbered. Then she inched her hand towards the dress and the knife within it. She moved it an inch, and he stirred. So she waited. Then when his breathing deepened, she moved again, her fingers crawling over the cool hard clay floor like a spider. She found the rough edge of the woollen dress and pulled it towards her with her finger ends. Then he turned and muttered. She stopped and his breathing grew heavy again. This time she dragged the dress and when it was close enough, she felt for the opening of the pocket. She reached in and felt the wooden handle of the kitchen knife. The wood was smooth. Her heart became electric with fear and hope. Her breathing grew more rapid.

She closed her finger ends on the knife haft, and then without warning he struck her heavily on the forehead. "Sleep bitch," he said. Her vision flashed yellow and blue from the blow. She withdrew her hand, bit her lip and waited.

Outside the sky was dark. No moon rode the clouds yet. Later it would rise, but no longer full. He breathed heavily. And she waited. He turned over and his arm flopped. She waited still. Then his chest rose in a regular rhythm and his snores came repeatedly. Her hand drifted towards the knife, and she clasped the hilt. She brought it to her chest and still she didn't move. She lay there with the knife in her hand staring at the dark ceiling. If any help was coming from the gods, then this was the time —

some miracle to stop her from having to kill. But she realised that was just cowardice.

She wanted him dead; she wanted revenge — she was just too scared to do it herself. She waited still as if divine intervention was on its way. She heard the wind in the trees outside. She held her breath and then turned on her left side; the knife clasped in her right hand. Her hand was sweaty on the grip. She held it so tight her fingers started to go numb and then quietly she raised it. She would stab him in the throat.

She saw his dark shape beside her. He was on his back. She could see his nose and beard silhouetted. She took the knife high and brought it down with all her strength. But before it struck, she held it back. She gasped. She was no killer. But he was. He woke out of sleep instantly and smashed her hand away, sending the blade spinning into the dark room.

Then he heaved her out of bed, lifting her with both hands and throwing her across the room. She smashed into the table and she knew she was injured. He covered the ground in an instant. He picked her up with both hands and raised her to slam her against the turf wall of the cottage. He held her there while he drew his head back and butted her - breaking her nose. The pain flashed through her and blood ran down the back of her mouth and from her nostrils, making it hard for her to breathe. She threshed her head this way and that but he had her by the throat.

"You whore," he snarled. "That's what I get for trusting you."

Then he dropped her. She fell heavily to the ground. "You're lucky I need someone to clean for me. But from now on you'll be wearing a rope round your ankle to stop you getting up to any mischief." He took her and bundled her naked out of the door, back to the dog pen. "And this is where you'll always sleep." He shook his head, as if in regret. "To think I let you share my bed," he said. He threw her into the pen and roped the door shut. "I'm just too good natured," he said. Then he spat. "You won't take advantage of me again that way," and he turned and walked away.

The pain in Rebecca's nose was like someone digging a hole in her face with an axe. She couldn't sleep because of it and she saw the dawn crawl up through the trees to the east. Inside, Gowan Fell slept on. She heard him snore. She gripped tight onto the wooden poles that made up her cage. Half-congealed clots of blood came out of her mouth and she gingerly wiped them away to avoid jolting the broken bone. Her own dried blood smeared her chest. She bowed her head against them. Gowan Fell had won and her father would lie their rotting in the wood with no one to revenge him.

He opened the door of her pen around mid-day. "Cook," he said.

"I have nothing to cook with." Her voice sounded strange because he had broken her nose.

Seeing the mess, he said, "Wash your hands before you touch my food." He prodded her to the door of the hut. Inside, there was a ewer of stream water that she herself had carried. She would have to fetch more for him later. While she washed her hands and tried to clean her face, he made a rough loop of rope and pulled it tight around her right ankle. He tied the other end to the cruck that held up the hovel, bedded deep in the ground. She couldn't move it.

He threw her a dead rabbit. "Skin that."

"The knife..." she said.

He stooped and picked it up from the floor where it had landed when he knocked it out of her hand. "You should know by now Rebecca, there is no weapon that will allow you to best me. If you try to misuse the knife again, I will break your fingers one by one and then I will snap your wrist. Do you understand?"

She nodded. Her nose was agony.

"Can I put my dress on?" She asked.

He shook his head. "It suits me to watch you naked."

So she skinned the rabbit. She said, "I need onions, from the garden."

He grunted, displeased, but then untied the rope. He watched her as she went into the garden and followed her as she went to the vegetable patch. There, to her amazement, the honeysuckle and the rose were growing. They had rooted overnight in some miracle and grew twisted around each other. She gasped.

"What?" he said.

"I stepped on a stone. It hurt."

"Weakling." He laughed, but he accepted the explanation. She gathered some onions from the dirt and brought them back to the hovel under his watchful eye. Just as she turned the corner, she glanced back at the rose and honeysuckle, unable to believe they were growing where she'd planted them.

She made him food, and he ate it greedily. He offered her none.

She asked, "What about me? I must eat if I am to work."

He shook his head. "Not yet. You're not hungry enough yet," and he sent her naked back to her pen.

The pain in her nose was still there but had lessened so she got some sleep. The next few days were the same until it was time for him to put on his fair clothes and go back to Hawkshead hunting for women. He made her cook him porridge for breakfast, sweetened with honey she had collected from a bees' nest in the tree near the little hill before he imprisoned her. He was there in his finery and she still naked, covered in dirt with the remains of her smeared blood on her face and chest. He let her scrape out the porridge bowl and sneered as she gobbled it hungrily.

It was then that there was a knock at the rough door of the cottage.

"Who's there?" snarled Gowan Fell.

A woman's voice answered. "I am looking for the charcoal

burner." Rebecca saw the interest in Gowan's face when he heard a female voice, though she knew he had no time for women he considered unattractive and would treat them badly.

"I am the charcoal burner, Gowan Fell," he said, and he opened the door.

A young woman with orange red hair and green eyes stood there. She was of medium height but slim. Rebecca saw Gowan's eyes measure up her figure. He smiled. He must like what he saw, she thought. The woman wore a white gown. Rebecca wondered how it was not covered with mud and moss from being in the wood. The woman looked first at Gowan and smiled. then she glanced around the room and met Rebecca's eyes. Rebecca put her hands to cover herself and she looked down. What must this beauty think of her standing, naked, dirty and bloodied, with black eyes and a livid purple bruise across her face? But the woman said nothing.

Gowan stepped outside and half closed the door. Rebecca couldn't see them now but she could hear. He said, "And what does a lady in her fine clothes want with a charcoal burner?"

"My father sent me with an errand. He owns a smokery in the village and has contracts with Lowthers to provide them smoked meat. But our usual supplier let us down so he sent me here to find you."

"He sent a pretty thing like you into the forest on her own?" Gowan flirted with her. "He was risking something valuable."

Rebecca heard the woman laugh. "I'm not frightened of the forest, Gowan Fell. I was born here. It cares for me."

"It's not the Forest, you should be frightened of," said Gowan Fell.

"Then what?"

"Me."

She laughed again. "And what harm would you do me, Gowan Fell?"

He said, "Only what you secretly want me to do."

The woman laughed again, but lower. "So you are interested in my father's contract?"

"I'm more interested in his daughter."

"You'll have to woo me," she said.

"I can do that. I have what all women want."

"We shall see about that. Can you sing me a song?"

He laughed. "I'm no bard. I'm a real man not a song maker."

"Can you make things with your hands from wood?"

"No, but I can break them easily enough."

"In the village they say you have a secret," she said.

"Oh?" Rebecca could hear the self-love in his voice. He would think it was a compliment.

"Yes," the woman said, "They say you are one of the Folk."

Gowan paused but did not deny it, then said, "And you would like that - to be taken by a wolf?"

She said, "Come for a walk with me."

"Where?"

"There is a place where the two streams meet, where the oak gives way to the ash. There is a stone shot with crystal that stands in the water."

"I know it. But I won't go there. That place is full of witchery."

"Walk some way into the woods with me then. There is a place before that one, where we can lie down."

"I like the sound of that. Let's go."

Rebecca heard the eagerness in his voice.

"But the girl," the woman said, "The one you keep naked in your hut. Will she be safe?"

"Safer without me than with me," he said. "Besides, she is just a maid. If anything happened to her, you could take her place."

Rebecca didn't hear the woman's reply, but she heard Gowan Fell's laughter as he followed her into the forest.

. . .

Even with them gone, Rebecca was still stuck - tied by her ankle. She couldn't untie the knot because he'd made it fast with his beast strength. But then she remembered her father's knife. In his eagerness to be with the woman, Gowan had forgotten it was there.

The rope was long enough to get to the table where the knife lay. She cut the rope with the knife, found her dress, and put it on. She took Kirsten's dolly from where it lay in the dirt and she stuffed it in her pocket. She gazed at her dead father's knife in her hand. She'd been a fool to trust her own strength and cleverness when she'd try to kill him. She knew now she couldn't beat him on her own. She thought of running home. There she would get men of the hamlet where her mother and sister were and she would tell them that Gowan Fell was a wolf and that he murdered women and he had killed her own dear father. Then they would return with fire and strong as he was, he couldn't beat all of them.

But then she thought of the poor woman. She might just be another foolish girl, but she was not safe in the woods with Gowan Fell, no matter how clever or strong she thought she was. He was a beast and his strength would overcome her. Rebecca couldn't leave her to suffer as he'd made her suffer. She began to run to her own hamlet to get help. But she had not gone far before she realised that she could not get to the hamlet and get back with help before Gowan would have done what he wanted to the woman. So when she got to where the paths split, instead of running home, she went into the woods. The knife was in her hand. Rebecca knew she had to try to save the girl, even if she died in the attempt.

So she ran as quietly as she could along the woodland path towards the crystal stone and the confluence of the two streams. And then she heard laughter, both a man's and a woman's. She slowed down and went quietly. She shifted the knife into a downward grip, the better to stab him with, but her hand was shaking and she doubted she could do it. She thought of just grabbing the girl and pulling her after her to safety. But he was fast. He ran with a wolf's speed. She feared he would catch them, but she could not let another innocent suffer at his hand.

She was close to them now. They were through a screen of brushwood; hazel and ground elder blocked the way, and the path went round to the right. If she went right, he would see her but if she didn't go right, she wouldn't be able to help the girl.

So she went right, slowly to the edge of the bush. She peered ahead. The girl was lying down. She had taken off her robe and was naked. Rebecca saw the copper red hair on her pubis and the milk white of her bare skin. Her orange mane lay around her head like a shower of fire. Gowan Fell was taking off his deerskin shirt.

The girl caught her eye. But she didn't cry out. There was a message in the look. A message not to approach. Rebecca stood stock-still.

Then Gowan turned and saw her.

He snarled. "Rebecca, and with her father's trusty knife too. You've tried twice before to kill me with that old blade. You won't succeed now and then, as I promised, I will break each finger and then snap your wrist. I will bend your neck round until you die, because I have a new maid now."

Rebecca said, "I'm not frightened of you, Gowan Fell," but her voice stammered. She held the knife in front of her but her hand shook.

He turned and picked up a rock. Then he advanced toward her. With a scream, she ran at him, slashing wildly. He easily grabbed her wrist with his left hand and then, with his right, he punched her stomach hard, knocking the wind out of her. He twisted her hand until she dropped the knife on the mossy floor. Then he put his powerful grip to her throat. She looked into his dark eyes as he began to choke the life out of her.

Over his shoulder, as her sight began to dim, she saw the woman stand. Gowan choked tighter and Rebecca heard her own breath gurgle. She feared she was dying.

But over Gowan's shoulder, Rebecca saw the woman's legs grow into roots and reached into the ground, anchoring her there. And then her arms became tendrils like the tendrils of honeysuckle, and her face became the bloom of a rose, surrounded by thorny briars. The tendrils spread across the floor, like a living forest and began to run and twine around Gowan Fell's legs. He turned, shouted and let go of Rebecca's throat. She fell back, gasping, stars bursting in her eyes.

Rebecca watched as the flower woman grew around Gowan Fell. He began to yell in terror as the tendrils ran up his legs past his knees. He struggled, but he was stuck fast now. And the briars covered with leaves and sweet roses reached around his shoulders and began to wrap around his neck and up to his face. He screamed.

And then the tendrils began to grow into him, puncturing his clothes and his body, running their plant life into the spaces of his bowels. The rose briar grew into his mouth and into his nose and the honeysuckle wrapped him round like a lover. The thorns ripped his skin and his blood ran red over the fresh green tendrils of the plant. And then the embrace of the flower woman trapped him, and she was kissing him with her honeysuckle and her fresh red roses, squeezing the life from his lungs.

And the flower faced woman kissed Gowan Fell to death, her green life entering into his skull and wrapping around his brain. Gowan Fell shrieked as the last life left him and he hung like a sacrifice in the arms of the flowers.

Rebecca saw his death. Saw the wolf slain by the rose. Revenge for her dead father, and the revenge of plant over animal.

Rebecca stood, afraid that the flower woman would take her too, for was she not an animal too? But the tree grew no more. The glade was filled with the scent of honeysuckle and roses and bees came to buzz around the flowers that took their nourishment from Gowan Fell.

Rebecca heard the voice of the flower woman. A voice she had prayed to hear but had thought was only silence, or a sound as meaningless as the noise of the river and the rain or the breeze through the trees. But these noises have their own meaning. The voice of the wildwood spoke to her on the rustle of the wind and in the drone of the bees and it seemed to say that strength was beaten not by strength, but by beauty.

And Rebecca left the glade and went to bury her father. Then she returned home to her mother and sister, and they lived at peace, because the evil of Gowan Fell was done for good.

The Tricking of Lord Thomas

LORD THOMAS WENT HUNTING. On his fine bay horse on that fine Autumn day, he rode from the great priory at Lanercost in the Vale of Irthing, on and down through Geltsdale, riding all the day long until he had reached as far as Castle Carrock and then, having lost the rest of his party, and his fine bay horse was weary and sweating, he came to a halt under the fell known as Tarnmonath.

He rested there and ate while he watched the eagles soar over the ridge to the south. And as he ate, he heard a man coming close.

Lord Thomas turned, hand ready on his sword, but then stood easy for it was only an elderly wanderer dressed in the habit of a brown friar. This one could be no threat to such a strong young man as Thomas Neville, youngest son of the Lord Warden of the West March, so Thomas's grip relaxed on the hilt of his fine sword, and he offered the stranger a greeting.

'Hail, father. Good day to you, doing God's work, praying as you walk in this wild country." Thomas talked, intending to put that man at his ease so he would not be afeard of the fine young lord with the long silver sword in its scabbard decorated with gold wire and shining stones. But the man only watched him, his long face peering from beneath the folds of his hood, his thin arms—strangely pale—visible within the cuffs of his simple, homespun habit.

Despite the feeble look of the man, Thomas's horse shied away and threw up its head. Thomas gripped its bridle and whispered comfort to it. The horse settled. There was something about this stranger, and Thomas thought of the tales of the elves and fairies who were said to walk this land in disguise. But Lord Thomas was a worldly man, and he didn't believe in such creatures.

Calming his horse's wildness and holding it tight, though it snorted and rolled its eyes still, Thomas offered the man bread, cheese and meat, and even a sup of Frankish wine.

The man shook his head. 'I want not bread nor cheese, nor yet wine from thee, Thomas Neville.'

Lord Thomas smiled. "You know me?' He was flattered by the stranger knowing his name, for he was a proud man, though that pride had nothing evil in it, only the joy of a young man, arising from his state in life and his high born blood.

The man said, "Truly I know thee, Thomas Neville, and I know what thou wilt, the most secret desires of thine heart. Perhaps I know it even more clearly than thou, thyself.'

'And what do I wish, father?' Lord Thomas grinned. 'Tell me my dearest desires, for you make me curious.'

'You wish to be greater in rank than your father, John Neville, Earl of Westmorland, even though he be Lord Warden of the West March of England, and as well as this, you wish to be greater in rank than your brother Ralph Neville who will be earl after him.'

Lord Thomas blushed. He had thought his ambitions were known only to himself though perhaps guessed at by his wife, Maud. He dearly loved both his father and his brother, but with them living, he would never succeed to high rank, being only the younger son. Because he loved them, he would never harm them, and so it seemed to him that his ambitions would come to nought, and so instead of seeking advancement, he spent his time in hunting and jousting and wishing for war, for on the field of battle he might show his mettle.

But this man had known what he had never told a living soul, and he said hastily, 'But what rank that I could attain would be greater than that of my father or my elder brother?'

'You know well what you want, Thomas.'

'Do I?'

The stranger laughed, and his eyes were dark and they unnerved Thomas with the sharpness of their stare. 'Yes, you do, Lord Thomas Neville. Because Lord Thomas Neville wishes to be king of England.'

Thomas glanced away back at the eagle that soared high above the mountain. But he said nothing, for the stranger had guessed true.

The man continued. 'And I alone can give this rank to thee.'

Lord Thomas snorted. 'And who art thou then but a poorly clad stranger, wandering the wilds of Cumberland as if he had no roof to shelter him. Who art thou who could give me the throne of England?" He added hurriedly, "Even if I wished it.'

The wanderer said, "If I give thee the crown of England, there will be a price to be paid.'

And Lord Thomas could not answer. His brow knitted, and his lips pursed as if to speak but he merely watched the brown-clad man as the stranger began to walk away down the path.

Thomas called after him. 'What about the crown of Scotland?" He said it in jest, but in truth it was only half jest.

Over his shoulder, the stranger called back. 'That too can be thine. But that too will cost thee a price dear to thy heart.'

Without halt or a backward glance, the stranger continued north along the fell path, and was going out of sight.

Just then, Lord Thomas's two men at arms caught up with

him. 'Lord, you should not have gone off at such a tilt. We lost you until now.'

This was John Marr who spoke. Thomas shook his head and gestured. 'The only danger I came across was that poor old friar.'

Another of the men at arms spoke, a dark-haired Cumbrian man called Mungo, 'That is no friar, my Lord.'

Thomas shook his head. 'No? I took him as such.'

John Marr looked down from his saddle. 'No, Lord, not a friar, nor even a Christian soul."

Lord Thomas frowned. 'Who then is it?'

'That is Michael Scot, a sorcerer.'

Barely a week later, outside Naworth Castle, Lady Maud pulled at her husband's gloved hand as he sat by her mounted on his fine bay stallion. 'Do you have to go?' She asked.

The September breeze was chill, the year was turning, and winter would soon follow a brief autumn in the north country.

Lord Thomas Neville shifted uneasily in his saddle. The men at arms with him watched blankly, ready to follow his every word whether that led them to life or to death.

Though the grey stone of Naworth Castle stood sombrely behind them to the south, Lord Neville's eyes always strayed to the north.

'I will be back as soon as I can, my love,' Thomas said.

'But how long will that be — weeks? Months?" Her face fell. "Don't say months, my love."

Thomas shrugged. 'As long as it takes me to find what I need.'

Maud brought the sleeve of her gown to her face. She whispered, 'But do you truly need it?'

His mouth straightened as if this was a subject they had discussed before, rehearsing the same arguments both of them for and against. Emboldened by Michael Scot's words, he had decided to unburden himself and share his desire for great rank with his wife.

'I will be king,' he said.

'I am happy for you to remain a baron.'

'The second son! I won't settle for that. I will never be earl while my brother lives, and I wish him long life. Natural means will never make me king, so I must seek out the less natural.'

His horse grew restless, perhaps sensing his mood, so Thomas said, 'The day is wasting. We have miles to travel, and we had best be gone.'

At his words, the two men at arms with their long spears and small shields stirred on their shaggy border ponies.

Lady Maud's eyes shone with tears. 'Come back soon,' she said. 'Your daughter and I will be waiting.'

Lord Thomas bent to kiss Maud. 'Give my love to Isabel.' And then the three men rode off, heading out from Naworth, north beside the beck called Pol Teyrnan until they crossed the River Irthing at Lanercost.

Lord Thomas and his companions journeyed north to Bewcastle and then over the wild moors as far as Hawick, and further to Jedburgh and Roxburgh and everywhere they went they asked the whereabouts of Michael Scot's tower, and everywhere they asked those they asked grew dark-faced, and some crossed themselves, and all left without speaking until it seemed Lord Thomas would never find the man who had promised him a crown.

The weather broke with flurries of snow across the vast, empty hills, and Lord Thomas and his two companions drew their cloaks around them, and their horses trudged on through sedge and heather over the bad, broken ground.

'My Lord, we should seek shelter for the night," Dark-haired Mungo said, pointing to the lowering clouds and the darkening horizon.

'Aye, sir, he's right,' said John Marr, sitting tall in his saddle, straining to see in the gathering gloom. 'What is that yonder? A building?'

Lord Thomas looked and saw a tower set up against the dark crest of a drear hill. "Without doubt, the lord of that place will give us shelter for the night.'

But the tower stood farther off than they thought, and as they rode, the mist rolled down from the higher ground as the clouds came to earth and bathed it in their melancholy grey.

'It's hard to see, Lord,' John Marr said.

Lord Thomas turned his head. 'Where is Mungo?'

Mungo was no longer with them. It seemed they had been separated in the murk, and they called out, but their voices were quietened by the rolling air and hushed by the acres of marsh and pools of dark water from which the bullrushes grew. And after some searching, they did not find Mungo but trusted he would make himself safe, for he was a resourceful man and no stranger to these wildernesses of the debated border.

'Which way was the lone tower?' Called Lord Thomas, and John Marr pointed. 'That way, I think. But I'm no longer sure.'

As they rode farther, the fog thickened, and the night fell, and they could see nothing, not even each other, and when Lord Thomas next turned, he found himself alone. Thomas stopped and cupped his hands to his mouth and called, but the only reply was the echo of his own voice from the empty wind ringing in the hollow mist.

And having no other choice, for there was no shelter near him there, and in that cold place a night without shelter was not something he relished, he took his reins in hand, gently urged his stallion with his heels, and rode on.

Of a sudden, the lone tower loomed up in front of him out of the darkness. And close-to he saw a broken building of lichen-clad limestone whose stones had fallen and whose windows were owl-haunted and blocked by grass and ivy.

He would not find the warmth and welcome of a lord's manor here. But some walls were better than none so he dismounted and led his horse through the door into the ruined hall so the stallion too would benefit from the shelter of its walls. Damp stood the walls, but they still held out some of the weather.

Lord Thomas had with him flint and iron, and he made sparks by striking them against wood shavings and dried leaves until there was a small blaze, and around that, he built a cage of the twigs that had fallen from crow's nests in that lonely place. His horse stamped in the corner, and he fed the fire with bigger sticks and he dried chunks of log fetched from a stand of trees outside, laying them around the uncertain blaze until that wood was dry enough to burn, and then he sat and smelled the smoke and hoped the light of the flame would be a beacon to his lost companions.

But they did not come. And then he rose and stood at the door and cupped his hands to his mouth and cried out, 'John! John! Oh, John Marr!' and 'Mungo! oh, Mungo Wallace! Where are ye both?' But no reply came, and he hoped they had got safe and at least found one another.

Thomas huddled in his cloak in the corner of the room, and as desolate a spot as this was, he dozed, and after dozing, slept deep, and while sleeping so deep, he dreamed. And as he dreamed, he was no longer in a broken tower in the moors of the Debatable Land but sat in a chair in a sumptuous room, tapestried with scenes of hunting and fair ladies, lords hawking and boats with coloured sails. And the floor was wood and strewn with fresh straw. And the tower had windows with diamonds of thick glass, and outside it was night. And furniture there was of oak and boards of yew, and a fire blazed in the great hearth.

And there was another chair and in this other chair sat a man with piercing eyes and Lord Thomas knew that man as Michael Scot and Michael Scot smiled, steepled his long fingers and said,

'Welcome to my home, Lord Thomas Neville. You have sought me long, and now your search is rewarded.'

'This is your home?' Lord Thomas said, locked in the dream but sitting as one awake. 'This broken tower?'

Michael Scot gestured. 'Look around thee, Lord Thomas Neville. Is it not a fine tower furnished from Italy and France?'

Thomas said, "But the tower I entered was broken and choked with weeds and damp and nothing but the abode of owls and mice.'

'That is the glamour I lay on it so that none should find me unless I wish them to.'

'So you wished me to find you?' Lord Thomas said.

Michael Scot nodded. 'Indeed, for we have a bargain to strike.'

'A bargain?'

Michael Scot gave a low laugh. 'Do not play the coy lad, Thomas. We both know what you want and why you came."

Thomas tilted his head, uneasy. "Are you sure you know my heart so well?"

'Aye, I do. You wish to be King of Scotland, and after that King of England too.'

Thomas bowed his head, and Scot continued. 'And I can give you these both.'

'And in return, you ask what?'

'I ask only for the dearest thing in your life. I think that is fair payment for my granting your ambitions.'

And as Scot named the dearest thing in Lord Thomas's life, his mind leapt to his daughter Isabel, and her picture sprang unbidden to his mind's eye.

As if the sorcerer could read Thomas's mind, though indeed he could not, Scot said, 'You have a daughter, do you not?'

Thomas nodded.

'How old is she?'

"Isabel is six years old.'

'And very dear to your heart? The most dear thing perhaps?"

Thomas sat silently in the oaken chair as the fire crackled and the wind moved outside the glass windows. And in his mind a picture of his wife, Maud, played, as beautiful as the sun rising on a spring morning.

Scot sat forward, 'But you have a wife also, the Lady Maud? Perhaps you love her more than your daughter?'

'I love them both equally,'

Scot licked his lips. 'Then perhaps both? For you wish to have two crowns, so I do not think that two souls is too dear a payment.'

Lord Thomas shook his head. 'I will settle for one crown, after all. Give me the crown of England alone.'

'One soul then? I am content.' Scot leaned forward and took out a gleaming silver needle. 'One drop of your blood is all I require to seal the bargain.'

Lord Thomas stared at Scot. He thought of withdrawing, but before he could speak, Scot darted forward and stuck him with the pin, and a bright bead of blood rose up like a garnet on his pale, freckled skin.

'I will make thee king of England, Lord Thomas, but thou wilt pay me with the soul and flesh of thy best beloved.'

'But how am I to decide which it is?" Lord Thomas said.

'That is a simple thing. You do not have to choose, for the one who loves you best will rush to you fastest, and so when you arrive home, the first living person that you see will fall dead by my magic, and as they die, I will drink in their soul, and they will rise no more between this place and the next.'

'And how will you make me King of England?'

"Once you have paid the price, I will teach you the words of the spell that Merlin gave to Uther Pendragon so that he took up the likeness of Lord Gorlois of Cornwall so that he could sleep with Gorlois's wife and she none the wiser. The same spell that

Arawn King of Hell wrapped around Pwyll Prince of Dyfed so that he could rule in his stead for a year and a day in the underworld, and neither Arawn's wife nor his courtiers any the wiser. So, you shall go in the guise of King Henry of England and take his place. Do with him as you wish, kill him if you want, but with my magic, none shall miss him, mistaking you for him at every turn.'

'So I shall be as King Henry?' Thomas thought of the position.

The old sorcerer looked hungrily at him, and Thomas watched as the hood-eyed man licked the drop of blood from the pin end and sucked it down and smacked his lips after.

Scot said, "The bargain is sealed. I will teach you the words of the spell, and in return, you will give me the soul of the first living thing you see as you return home to Naworth.'

And Lord Thomas fell into a deep slumber. And in his sleep, he heard the echoing voice of Michael Scot whispering the words of the promised spell of changing, whispering them so quiet he caught only a hint and he would not be given them in full until he had paid Scot what he loved best in all the world. And he saw the face of his wife Maud and the face of his daughter Isabel and both were in tears.

When he awoke, his neck was stiff, and his back was sore from the hard floor, and the fire had died out, and his fine bay horse was hungry. The mist had gone, and he led the stallion out onto the open moors where a fine day had dawned. And he looked south, mounted his horse and headed back to Naworth Castle.

When he got to Bewcastle, he found John Marr and Mungo Wallace, who had waited for him and were glad to see their lord.

'What ails you, Lord Thomas? You look grey."

'Find me a priest.'

And so they found the priest who was in charge of the lonely church at Bewcastle, and Lord Thomas dictated a message to be written on thick paper with black ink.

The priest frowned as he took down the message. 'Are you sure this is all, my lord? It seems such a trifle to send a message as this.'

Lord Thomas smiled and gave the priest a silver shilling. He took the note, sealed it with hot wax and handed it to Mungo Wallace and bid him to ride hard to Naworth Castle and give the message to Lady Maud.

'Aye, sir. I shall.'

Lord Thomas said, 'You must get there before we do.'

Mungo Wallace frowned. 'If you say so, my Lord.'

'And if Lady Maud questions what I have written on the note, you must tell her to do exactly what I have said and not deviate from it.'

Frowning, Mungo Wallace left the church, mounted his horse and rode hard from Bewcastle south towards Naworth.

'Come, John Marr. Let us follow after him at our own leisurely pace.'

And so they dawdled and took their way almost at their leisure over the fell roads, first to Lanercost and then to Birdoswald and then to Naworth.

And it was evening when they arrived at Naworth, and Lord Thomas drew up his horse and said to John Marr. 'Go ahead and ensure that Mungo Wallace has arrived and delivered my note and that Lady Maud has understood it and is willing to do what I say.'

And Lord Thomas sat and waited, and in due course, John Marr returned. He nodded and said, 'Lady Maud has the note, and though she asked me why you would want to do such a thing, she agreed to do it.'

'Good.'

'And what now, my Lord?'

'We wait further.'

And so they waited until there was a noise as if a wind woke behind them, and a hot breeze and a turmoil in the air as if the devil himself had arrived, and Lord Thomas turned and saw

Michael Scot dressed in brown. The sorcerer whispered, 'Why do you linger, Lord Thomas? Greatness awaits you. Greatness after you pay the price. Pay the price, and I will give you the words of the spell of change, and you shall have all you wish.'

John Marr gripped his reins as he saw the sorcerer and looked at his lord for guidance.

Lord Thomas said to John Marr, "Let us go forward.'

And Lord Thomas rode his fine bay stallion slowly — as slow as creeping death itself.

And Michael Scot said, "Do not think thou canst get out of this. I have taken thy blood, and thou canst not renege on that or I will take thee instead.'

Thomas ignored the sorcerer.

And as they came in sight of Naworth Castle, Lord Thomas spurred his horse and there propped up on the middle of the bridge that led to the castle, was a fine mirror.

'What nonsense is this!' Michael Scot yelled and followed Lord Thomas haltingly. There was no one outside the castle, not a child, not a servant, not a dog, nor a horse. But instead, the fine silver mirror brought from France stood on the bridge.

And the first living thing Lord Thomas saw as he came into the grounds of Naworth Castle was the form of Michael Scot captured in the mirror's silver face.

'What trickery is this?' Michael Scot yelled.

'You only said the first living thing I saw as I crossed into my castle would be what you took. You did not stipulate that I should not see it through a window or through glass or in the silver of a mirror. And you have sworn to take the first living thing I see, and the first living thing that I see is thee, Michael Scot."

And the sorcerer was consumed in smoke and blood and his soul dissolved by his own dark magic.

Lord Thomas stood by the blackened ring in the grass and the smoking brown rags that were all that remained of Michael Scot, the sorcerer.

'But why did he take his own soul?' John Marr asked his Lord.

'Because a bargain sealed in blood can never be broken, as he well knew. Not by all the devils in hell nor all the angels in heaven, but only by the power of the good Lord himself, and Michael Scot was far indeed from such grace as that.'

The Milk White Child of Ravenglass

I WANTED to get away from it all. I'd had it up to my back teeth with work, and the boss said to take some time, lower the stress levels and when I felt better, to come back. He gave me a month. That was generous of him, and I appreciated it, and I thought he must think something of me to cut me the slack.

Scrolling through Trip Advisor, I thought of the Scottish Highlands or Wales or Ireland, but in the end, while I had abandoned the computer and was flipping through a road atlas one night at home, the endless traffic on the North Circular buzzing outside my window, I saw Ravenglass. I liked the name, so I thought I'd go there. It had the added bonus of a railway station and I wouldn't have to drive. My nerves had been shredded that past few months, and I don't think I could have taken the motorways, heading round the M25, then feeding myself into the pasta maker at Spaghetti Junction in Birmingham. Ravenglass allowed me to escape all that. Ravenglass seemed to be calling me.

It took ages to get there on the train. After reading *The Guardian* and then *The Spectator* (I like to be contrary) and finishing both and flipping through them again to see if I'd missed anything, then eating two packets of crisps, gazing a long while out of the window, staring blankly down the carriage and finally heaving down my bag from the overhead rack, I alighted from the train at the empty railway platform and saw an adjoining miniature steam railway at the station over the line. That was the one that ran down the valley between the mountains.

Ravenglass is by the Irish Sea, in case you didn't know. The smell of salt and seaweed invaded my nose as I took the path from the station. I checked the directions to my B&B—'The Old Church House' it was called. My landlady was a Mrs Nelson. I found it quickly enough.

Ravenglass is basically two rows of houses that run along the seafront with a cobbled street between them. The street starts not far from the railway station and ends at the beach.

When I saw it I knew it was exactly what I wanted. The Old Church House was a prominent building that looked Victorian made of red sandstone. It had a shallow front garden where summer flowers bloomed madly: roses and geraniums and iris and lupins.

Mrs Nelson had a bird-feeder out front. My opening the green-painted wooden gate scared off the greenfinches and blue-tits that were feeding there.

There, amidst the blooms I stopped and breathed in, filling my lungs with a mixture of sea air and the sweet stocks. It was still light even at eight o'clock that night just slightly before Mid-Summer.

I rang the doorbell, and Mrs Nelson opened it. I had imagined an old lady in a frock wearing a pinafore, but a completely different woman opened the door. She was about forty with auburn hair and freckles and cool, blue and red-framed designer spectacles. She wore denim shorts with sparkly sandals and a loose summer blouse white with blue and yellow flowers printed on it.

She reached out a hand. 'Mr Jones?'

I smiled awkwardly. "Call me Owen.'

'I'm Sally. Want a brew?'

She boiled a kettle on her gas hob. She got out a blue teapot with a golden dragon design. It looked Chinese, I thought perhaps Jing Dezhen, though I'm not up to the mark these days on Chinese ceramics. Then Sally grabbed a silver spoon in her left hand, a 1920s-looking, gold and red decorated tin tea-caddy in her right and took out three heaped spoonfuls of black, aromatic tea, which she popped into the dragon teapot.

'One for you, one for me and one for the pot,' she said.

When the boiling kettle whistled, Sally poured the steaming water into the teapot and then, after giving it time to mash, as they say up here, made me a cup of tea in a Claris Cliff teacup that sat on its saucer in front of me.

'Milk?'

I nodded. Sally poured the milk from a Portmeirion milk jug. None of it matched, but in some way, that added to the charm. I felt suddenly strangely relaxed, almost serene. It was as if I was being treated to a special Cumbrian Tea Ceremony.

She tipped the jug, dropped several drops and a gulp of milk into my cup then lifted the milk jug's spout, holding it poised in case I said I wanted more. 'Enough?' she said.

I smiled. 'Thanks, Perfect.'

'Sugar?' She stood ready with silver sugar-tongs, about to lift an irregular lump of white sugar from a Portmeirion bowl. It was the Moss Agate design—never produced in large numbers but which received high critical acclaim when Susan Williams-Ellis designed it in 1961. It was very valuable, and here was my B&B landlady, Sally Nelson, using it every day.

'You're a collector?' I gestured to the jugs and bowls.

Sally smiled. 'I'm an art teacher, but my love is ceramics.'

'Weird.'

'What is?'

I sat back. "I'm a ceramics designer. I work in a commercial pottery in London. I design plates and jugs and things.' I grinned.

'Nothing as special as those you have here. These are valuable, yet you use them every day.'

Sally said, 'Their beauty comes from their function. If you don't use them, you rob them of their purpose.'

Movement in the hall outside caught my eye. I glanced and saw a child peering round the door—a girl, I think. It must be Sally's daughter. She was very pale and darted her head back when she realised I'd seen her.

I went back to studying the tea dishes. "We both love ceramics. What a coincidence that I ended up booking here.'

Sally smiled and finally sat. "There are no such things as coincidences, Mr Jones.'

Of course, she was a hippy. You could tell that from the clothes she wore and the Buddha on the window sill and the book on Mandalas, open face down on the sideboard near the yew-wood chopping board with its loaf of artisan bread and pat of yellow, organic Cumbrian butter.

I'm not a hippy. I'm more practical than that. I work with my hands—worked with my hands—mostly it's computers now. But I am a down to earth man. If I can't touch it or at best see it, I doubt its reality. A coincidence is exactly that; there's nothing mystical or meaningful to it.

The child in the hall flitted across the doorway again as if she were playing hide and seek.

'She can come in if she wants," I said. "No need to be scared of me."

Sally smiled again. 'Who can?" She saw I was looking into the hall. 'Oh, the cat? He's a tom: Marmaduke.'

'No, the girl.'

Sally frowned. 'Girl?'

I gestured. 'The little girl in the hall. I thought she was your daughter.'

She shook her head. "My kids are at school.'

I sat back. I was sure I'd seen a little pale girl. When I thought of her, she came more vividly to mind as if she flourished and grew in my imagination, becoming more present and luminous than the brief glimpse of her in the hall.

Sally stared at me.

I laughed. 'Now you're going to tell me the house is haunted. A big old ex-vicarage like this is bound to be haunted.' I didn't know why I'd said it. I didn't believe in such things, but I bet she did.

Sally said, 'You're pulling my leg." Her smile, at first hesitant, grew broader. "You are a wag, Owen.'

'So it's not haunted?'

She shook her head. 'I've never seen anything. No guests have ever reported anything, and the kids have never talked about ghosts. So much as I like the idea of it being haunted.' She put her hand over her heart. 'I can't honestly say it is. Sorry. Did you want it to be haunted?'

'God, no. That's the last thing. I don't believe in ghosts.'

'But you just saw one.'

My jaw tightened. 'I saw a girl.' I shrugged. No point getting annoyed. 'I thought I saw a girl.'

'I don't think so. The only living thing in the house except you right now and me is my big ginger tomcat, and he's very likely asleep on my bed.'

I slept and saw no ghosts, but that picture of the pale young girl with hair like silver and eyes huge and full of moonlight and cobwebs drifted through my dreams. The girl didn't speak, only stared, and I thought she wanted something. Then I awoke.

It was a beautiful morning. Sparrows chirped outside my window. I opened it so I could listen to them and the sound of the waves' murmur. A slight breeze shifted the gauzy curtain. I lay until I thought I'd better get a shower then breakfast. I had nothing to do that day, and I thought I would get up early and enjoy doing it.

There was another man in the breakfast room sitting on his

own table. He looked up and nodded to me, knife and fork in hand, knife lifted smeared with egg, fork raised ready to spear a piece of black pudding. 'How do?' he said.

'Good. Thanks.'

I sat. Sally bustled in. 'Full English?'

'I'm vegetarian. Should have said.'

She smiled. 'No problem. Ovo-lacto?'

I nodded. She brought me slices of farmhouse bread cut thick, toasted golden brown, with curls of organic butter and Cumbrian heather honey dribbled on and spread with the big silver butter knife. The coffee was organic, fair-trade—Guatemalan. The milk was local, organic, naturally. Then I had porridge with more local milk, a drib more honey swirled in. The oats were Scottish. That was fine—not too many air miles, especially if they came by boat across the Solway Firth.

The man at the other table wanted to talk. He was looking at me, waiting for me to meet his eye. Eventually, I did.

"I'm Taffy.'

'Owen.'

He sported big whiskers and watery blue eyes. He wore a brown tweed waistcoat with a broad check and a yellow tweed jacket that didn't match—nearly but not quite. His shirt was white, and I saw he had silver cufflinks, visible as he waved his knife and fork while talking. 'On holiday?' he asked.

' Taking a break.'

'I'm a storyteller.'

I'd met plenty in my time, but I guessed he meant that was his job, not merely his inclination.

'Nice," I said.

'Doing the schools roundabouts. Contracted by the County Council.'

I smiled and said, before biting my toast, 'Sounds interesting.' Then I bit. It was delicious—a mouthful of Paradise as the bread crunched with melting butter and gooey honey, and I chewed while listening to the Storyteller.

He said, "I do Cumbria mostly and festivals, and of course, North Lancs, North Yorks, the closer side of Northumberland, National Park centres, et cetera.'

I swallowed my toast and took a sip of coffee. 'What kind of stories do you tell?'

'Folk tales. Fairy tales. Embellishments on the truth. Twists of History. Unrealities and make-believe, all with a strong moral element.'

'A moral element?'

He looked serious. "It's important that the little buggers know how to behave.'

'The kids?'

He laughed out loud. 'That's a good one. Of course the kids! Who did you think I meant—the fairies?'

I sat quietly.

He jerked a thumb as if the wall was invisible. "I'm at Ravenglass school later. I know Sally. Knew her husband, poor lad.'

'Oh.'

'He died. Was drowned.' He pointed at the unseen sea through another wall. 'Out there. It's treacherous to walk on these sands. Three rivers come to the sea here: the Esk, the Mite and the Irt. This confluence creates a lot of channels and currents. Of course, this area is isolated. It sits on a promontory sticking out into the sea. Muncaster Castle at the high bit facing inland. The old Roman port was up there.' Again he pointed through a wall.

'Romans?' I said.

Taffy nodded vigorously. "Romans, Celts, Vikings, Anglo-Saxons, Irish pirates, Manx fishermen—lots of tales. I'm doing King Eveling today.'

I smiled in polite interest. 'Eveling? Never heard of him.'

'He was a Dark Age king of the Britons. They had lots of little kings, sub-reguli Gildas called them. He appears in the Arthurian stories as King Evelake of Sarras, most probably. I'm telling a story about him, anyway.'

'You seem to know your stuff.' I bit more toast.

'I have to, old boy. It's my living: stories.' He raised a finger. 'But the legend says Eveling was King of the Fairies —that Ravenglass was then part of fairyland, or at least fairyland broke through into the real world here. Its old name was Renglas, which may mean The Green Promontory: *Rhyn Glas* in old Cumbrian.

As if he suddenly remembered something, he got up. 'Sorry, old lad, time and tide and all that. Well, they don't wait for me. Don't know about you. Hah!' And he left in a great bluster of tweedy waves to Sally and brisk nods at me.

After he'd gone, I reflected that in Ravenglass, time, if not tide, would wait for me. I had all day to do nothing much, and I loved it. It was the freest I'd felt for years.

Sally stood drying knives with her tea towel by the kitchen sink, door open to the breakfast room. 'Off anywhere nice today?'

I shrugged. 'It all seems nice.'

'Yes, it is. You could go on the La'al Ratty.'

'The what?'

'The steam railway.'

'Ah yes, I saw that.'

'Or up to Muncaster Castle.'

'Yes, that sounds nice.'

'There's a footpath. Go over the footbridge over the railway line, past the Bee Garden on your right and strike up through the woods. It's a lovely day for it.'

So that's the way I went. I fetched my boots and knapsack from my room, put on my shorts, got onto the landing then remembered my sunglasses and cap. I went back and got them, but as I locked my room and stood there, I had a strange feeling that I was being watched. I spun round and saw nothing, but as I stepped down the stairs, I thought that with some inner ear, not the natural worldly one, but one more attuned to things mostly unheard and mainly unspoken, I heard a soft voice say, 'Past is in future, and future is in past. What you do for us today. We do for you tomorrow.'

I shivered like someone had run a peacock feather up my spine. It was the strangest sensation and, pleasant as it was, it made me quite anxious, but I stood there, hand on the polished bannister and told myself I didn't believe in such things. It was only the stress being lifted from me. It was simply a relief that I didn't have to face my life for a while.

The walk up to the castle through the cool woodland was a dream. I strolled along the long drive after buying my entry ticket. The rhododendrons were all out in their glory, and blackbirds warbled from the bushes. Muncaster Castle itself was ancient, massive and hewn from dark sandstone. With all due respect to the National Trust, who do a great job of preserving the nation's heritage, their places can feel samey and regimented: a sort of corporate version of heritage, but Muncaster was gloriously independent, and even a little eccentric. I enjoyed the human touches and the humour and the fact that the same family lived there who'd founded the castle in the 1200s.

And then I walked back.

Sally had offered to cook, and she made a vegetarian tagine, and she and Taffy and me drank organic wine—French, not Cumbrian. 'I get it from a bloke in Penrith. He has a company called Black Hand wine. He's an organic winemaker—no sulphites, so no hangover.'

Of course, that wasn't true, but the wine slipped down like fruit punch. Taffy went upstairs to his room to do some work, and that left me with Sally.

'Would you like to see my studio?'

I said I would. The wine added to the day added to my pleasant company made me feel agreeable indeed.

She was good at pottery. She had a kiln and a potter's wheel and all the other bits and bobs a ceramic artist needs in her brick shed in the long garden on the landward side of the house. It was simple, but I had become over-sophisticated and arrogant. When you live in London, you come to believe that nothing worthwhile can originate from anywhere else. Maybe New York or Paris — Berlin or Tokyo at a push, but everywhere else must be second rate because it's not London. Except Sally's work wasn't second rate. She wasn't world-shattering, but she was very competent and her work had real charm.

She hitched up and sat on a bench. She motioned for me to sit on her stool. I looked around me, taking in the range and quality of the items she'd made.

'You could sell this,' I said.

She shrugged. 'Not fussed.'

'You don't want to sell it? I've got contacts in galleries in London. I could get you an exhibition.'

'Why?'

'So more people would see your work. So people would buy your work. So you'd be properly rewarded for your talent.'

She grimaced and took a sip of her organic Tempranillo. 'I do it for me. Because I enjoy it.'

I nodded rapidly. "Yes, of course. But even so. You could make a name for yourself.'

'I have a name: Sally Nelson who lives in Ravenglass. Part-time art teacher, part-time B&B lady. You know her?'

I smiled. 'Yes. It's just....'

She cocked her head. 'Tell me, Owen. Do you like *your* job?'

"Like it?' I sighed. I stopped. I ran my hand through my thinning hair. 'I used to. I used to love making things.'

'But not now?'

I said, "Now, I don't make anything. I come up with designs. We put them through the team. We do market research and focus groups, and in the end, we come up with saleable items. We get them into the best stores.'

'But you don't make them yourself.'

'No, how could I? It's a multi-million-pound enterprise—worldwide. We ship tens of thousands of items. We have factories in China and Brazil.' I laughed. 'If I had to throw each bowl on the wheel", I gestured to her potter's wheel. 'I'd never finish.'

She said, "Would you like to make things again?'

I exhaled. 'I wouldn't like to make the shit we produce.' Then I corrected myself. 'No, that's not fair. Our products have very high production values.'

'Yes, but the production values aren't high enough to touch your soul,' Sally said. 'You should try making something that isn't designed to position it in the market. You should make something with your hands just because you want to.'

And she was right. That was why I was burned out. I'd sold my art to the machine, and the machine gobbled it all up and spat out the pips.

Sally nodded. 'Let's go back to the house. It's more comfortable.'

We sat down on the sofa, and Sally put on some Nick Drake and then some John Martyn, and we talked about colours and clay and what it felt like to form things and mould them with your fingers until something inside told you that you had the shape right and then you could stop.

That night I dreamed of the milk-white child again with her long wisps of hair and her eyes like mother of pearl and her lips the colour of chalk. I woke with the moonlight flooding my room. I'd left the curtain undrawn, and an illumination of ivory spilled in. It came over the carpet and up to the end of the bed, lighting up the chair in the room's corner. And there, sitting in the chair, was a child the colour of snowflakes and moonbeams, blinking at me with eyes like selenite through eyelashes fringed with crystal clear as quartz.

I watched, amazed, horrified, unable to believe what I saw was real, and the girl-child leaned forward and said, 'Your future is my past. I recall what you will do and I give you thanks. I will not remember to ask you in future, so what can I give you now in repayment?'

As I sat, trying to think of an answer, a dream answer, for surely I must be dreaming, the child was gone. She had slipped away like a story when the page is turned and the plot only half remembered. But the page can always be turned back if you know how to do it.

I lay awake until dawn which came early with birdsong and always the slow shushing of the waves on the sand out of sight behind walls. Then I slept.

I was late for breakfast. Taffy had left already. I walked alone again.

I found myself in the woods behind the village, climbing the hill through dense rows of trees. This was *Rhyn Glas* —the Green Promontory indeed. At times, I saw the sea behind me, the estuary with its sandbanks and bobbing yachts. But as I went further, there was no more sea, no more mountains to the east, only trees. The trees went on forever like an ocean, and the paths grew wilder and criss-crossed with briars, rosebay willow herb, mugwort and wild rose until I realised I was lost.

I heard the thin reedy notes of the pipes long before I saw the piper.

In my vision it was as if the curtains of a theatre were drawn back for the show to begin and behind the red velvet hangings, were painted scenes of far countries.

The wood rippled and then everything was more ornate, more vivid, more vibrant. The flowers were huge and alien. Incredible insects buzzed on iridescent wings from orchid to orchid, pollinating them. Strange, bobbing birds trilled and hooted from a canopy of unfamiliar foliage.

But it was the people that amazed me. A procession wove through this extraordinary English woodland, made so strange and new by their presence. At their head was a king with long white hair and a crown of pearls. He walked with his queen, a stately, tall woman, with a face as white as alabaster. Her gown was pale, but silver rings studded with gems—yellow and red as fire—sparkled on her fingers. Behind the King and Queen, a graceful troupe followed, laughing among themselves, pipers playing on fine fairy pipes, others clicking fingers to strike tiny cymbals that rang out sweet and clear through the glade. There were perhaps twenty adults and ten or so children, playing and frolicking behind as their elders walked on.

I thought that somehow I was seeing the Court of King Eveling and that I had been granted a vision of the other world where the fairy folk still walked abroad.

Instinctively, I had crouched when they appeared, but my stance was painful and needing to stretch my calf, I moved. That was all it took. My movement attracted the attention of twenty heads and all the milk-white eyes.

A cry of alarm went up, and the fairies disappeared, melting into the leaves, and within a second, they were gone. The children were less adept, but they too ran from me, though I meant them no harm. With shrieks of alarm, they vanished. And then a cry of pain went up. One of them was injured. I ran to where I'd heard the sound.

And there, sprawled among the undergrowth, was a fairy child, only four or five years old if it had been human. It was pale-skinned with pale hair and eyes lustrous and empty as pearls. A metal snare such as some leave out to catch rabbits was twisted round its ankle, and where the taut wire dug into its flesh was a ring of red. I saw that despite their pale skin, the blood of the fairies was as red as ours.

As I reached to help, the child backed away in terror from me, but with gestures, I tried to show I wanted to free it and tell it that the snare was nothing to do with me.

The child pulled away as far as it could, but that made the wire dig deeper and made it scream, and crystal tears ran hot down its cheeks. Eventually, it lay still and allowed me to release the snare. It seemed not to know how they worked and had been unable to release it itself, whether from ignorance or through pain, I did not know.

I was sure this was the child I had seen in Sally's house that said its past was my future. It had spoken to me then, but it did not talk now. It merely looked at me with its empty white eyes and blinked tears from its crystal eyelashes onto its lily-white cheeks.

And then I picked up the child and held it against me as it sobbed. It was light and limp, and I thought I would need to seek medical attention.

I carried the milk-white child slumped over my shoulder, my shirt and trousers smeared with blood from its cut leg. I got into Ravenglass, but there was no one close, and no one paid me attention, and I hurried to Sally's house.

I found her in the kitchen.

'Who's that?' Sally said, her eyes wide.

I put the child down on the wooden kitchen chair.

'A child. She had her leg caught in a rabbit snare in the woods when I found her.'

Sally stared at the pale child, and it looked back at her with pearly eyes that were devoid of any pupils.

'What's the matter with her?' Sally said. 'Is she an albino?'

At that moment, attracted by the commotion, Taffy, the storyteller, came into the kitchen. 'Oh my God!' he said.

We both turned around. The milk-white child stared at him impassively.

Sally said, 'Owen found the girl in the woods. Unfortunately, she had her leg caught in a trap.'

Taffy said, 'That is no human child.'

I said, 'How do you know?'

Taffy said, 'Because I know the stories of the White Folk. She is fairy kin.'

Sally said, 'You believe that? She's just an albino girl. Her leg's hurt." She stepped over. "Here, love, let me look.'

'We can't treat her. She needs to go back to her own kind,' Taffy said.

Sally shook her head. "She's not a fairy, Taffy. You've got confused with your own tales.'

But I nodded my head. 'I saw them,' I said.

Taffy turned his eyes on me. 'Who?'

I rubbed my forehead. 'I think I saw the Fairy King, Eveling, in the woods. It was like a door opened, and I saw another world.'

Sally stared bemused as if she thought both Taffy and I were drunk or drugged, but then she looked at the white-skinned girl. The girl was ethereal and strange. No human child had ever looked like this.

'If that's true, then you need to put her back,' Sally said.

'Where?'

'In the woods.'

'She'll die,' I said. 'We can't leave her there.'

'She's dying now,' Taffy said. 'She can't thrive in our world. The snare trapped her and brought her here with its iron. Iron and steel are poison to the fairies. She's sick.'

'Then what can we do?'

'We have to wait until they come to fetch her,' Taffy said.

I looked at the girl. Already she was languishing. She lay back, weak, with her breathing shallow. 'Can we feed her?'

Taffy said, 'Well, according to the stories, the White People can only eat white food.'

"White food? How strange. Like what?'

'Egg white and milk.'

Sally got a glass of milk from the fridge, and I held the beaker to the girl's mouth. At first, she pushed it away, but she was weak and getting weaker. Some drops of milk fell onto her lips and tentatively, she licked them. Taffy cheered. Then she started to drink though only sips, but enough so that half the glass was soon empty.

And so we spent the summer night, waiting with the fairy child on the sofa in the living room, feeding her milk while Taffy ate egg yolks.

The night stole on us unseen. One minute daylight lingered, and then the pale blue of the summer night fled the sky, stars appeared, and a great ivory moon rose. The moonlight came in through the window and bathed the child in its wash of light. She stirred as if revitalised by its cold white glow. But still, no King of the Fairies came.

And it grew very late, and first Taffy and then Sally went to bed, leaving me with the slumbering child. I nodded and dozed, my chin on my chest and then I opened my eyes to see her staring at me.

For the first time since I rescued her, she spoke, 'My father will come soon.'

The moon illuminated the room, and everything it touched grew mysterious. Though I had not left Sally's house, again, I entered an otherworld, and I heard the soft jingle of bells, and the child looked to the door, and the door opened and in stepped Eveling, King of the Fairies and with him his fairy wife, Vivienne, and Vivienne bent down, and the red and yellow gems in her silver rings gleamed in the pale moonlight, and she scooped up her daughter.

King Eveling turned to me and said, 'Thank you for saving my daughter. Trapped with iron in the day world, she would have wasted away and died if not for you.'

I said, 'It was the least I could do.'

He studied my face. 'What gift would you have of me?'

Beautiful as he was, I feared him. Stepping back, I shrugged. 'I don't need a reward.'

Eveling, King of the Fairies, said, 'But you shall have one nevertheless.'

He bent forward and whispered in my ear.

And I dreamed on and my dream twisted and changed and only when I woke did I realise that I had slept for several hours.

Sally came down in her dressing gown. 'She's gone,' she said.

But I had seen something on the seat where the girl had been. So I went over and saw it was a beaker made of porcelain, but porcelain so pale and silvered that it looked like mother of pearl and moonlight had been mixed into it.

'What's that?' Sally said.

'It's for me,' I said.

'It's beautiful,' Sally said, staring as I turned the beaker in my fingers.

I gazed at it in silence. I was so quiet that Sally studied me, frowning, but also faintly smiling.

Finally, I said, "I can make something like this."

Sally put her hand on mine. 'Then you should.'

ANTHONY WILL HAVE to set off driving early the next day if he wants to miss the traffic. It's a long way, but he and Amanda have decided that this is what they want: a complete change, and a new life.

Anthony knows his mother is unhappy with their decision. He goes to see her on his own, to make sure there isn't an argument with Amanda and his mother locking horns about their decision to move, which his mother sees as Amanda stealing her son and taking him to the far north.

In her small but elegant flat off the Cromwell Road, Anthony sips tea out of the bone China cups his mother insists on. It's winter, and the central heating is on, making the room stifling. In the square outside the window, rain-soaked trees huddle beneath the downpour.

'It's too far, Anthony. Just too far.' She holds the cup's narrow handle between finger and thumb and can't meet his eye.

'We've decided—'

'She's decided,' she mutters, looking at the floor.

'Not 'she' mum — Amanda, my wife.'

'Hmm.'

A long pause as the rain drizzles against the window, and he wonders if he's been there long enough for him to leave without causing too much offence. Then his mother blurts, 'You can't trust them, you know — those northerners.'

He sighs. 'Really, mum.'

But she continues her tirade. 'They're not like us. Barely civilised. And those ones where you're going. It's so remote — not civilised at all!' She looks up with her eyes like an old bird's. 'Where is it even that you're going?'

He's told her before, but he'll tell her again. 'Long Sleddale, mum. It's a lovely house we've bought. You must come up.'

'Never. I can't travel that far. I'm too old. You'll regret it once you're isolated somewhere like that. Then you'll long to be back in London, but it'll be too late then.'

'Come up on the train when the weather improves. I can pick you up from the station.'

But she's not listening, muttering instead, 'Mark my words, no good will come of this.'

Anthony puts down his teacup. 'We'll be fine, mum. Honestly, we will.'

The next morning, it's dark when Anthony and Amanda set out. It takes almost an hour before they're out of London and heading up the M40. They pass blue signs for Oxford within the next hour. He's doing well, streaming down the dark road, catching up with red tail lights and passing them like silk. Birmingham two hours after London and then north again. It gets light about Stafford and the rest of the journey, with a break at Charnock Richard motorway services, takes place in the grey overcast light of a January day.

Anthony pulls the car off the M6 at Junction 36 with the signs indicating "Kendal and the Lake District". He can feel Amanda's excitement. She dozed some of the journey. Earlier, she'd offered to drive a bit, but he didn't need her to. When she wakes, she reads her Kindle until she says it makes her feel sick and then they stream *Dead Can Dance* on the car sound system for fifty miles, then she starts to talk as if she can finally believe her dream is coming true.

From Kendal, they take the old road into the mountains. Anthony himself feels excited at the great grey bulks around them covered in greensward grazed short by bedraggled sheep and the stands of dark green trees and eruptions of craggy rocks. This is their new life. So different from London.

The road goes on, climbing and bending. There are few houses to be seen, the odd car, but no people, except once a farmer on a tractor distributing turnips for the sheep.

They turn down a minor road, and after that, an even smaller one signed for Long Sleddale. They're among the mountains now. Huge hills that loom high on either side. The Sleddale valley is like a snake, or a funnel, pointing them down to a dead-end where no car can drive further.

They've been here before, but the weather was better when they bought the house and its five acres of rough ground. That was July. He drives carefully. The road is lined by grey stone walls built without cement, laid stone upon stone, each fitted to the next by the skill of the men who made the wall centuries ago.

The mountain slopes soar up. Amanda begins to quote:

'But huge and mighty forms, that do not live
   Like living men, moved slowly through my mind
   By day, and were a trouble to my dreams.'

'Wordsworth,' she adds. 'From *The Prelude*.'
'I know,' he laughs. 'You've quoted it before.'
Then, glancing up from the driving wheel to the bulk of the mountains on all sides, he says, 'I hope the huge and mighty forms won't turn out to be a trouble to my dreams.'

She says, 'Of course not. They're beautiful.' She reaches and strokes his neck. 'I feel so free.'

He has to concentrate on the road. He's not used to such narrow lanes, and now he has to turn left onto a tighter lane with grass growing in the middle. He brakes and hits the indicator, and the light blinks and ticks, not that there is anyone behind or in front that needs a signal that he is turning.

They travel this small road about three miles until from afar, Amanda sees the house. It's grey—built of slate and stone, and it stands by a group of yew trees, surrounded by its own drystone walls whose moss drips in the downpour. He slows the car as he approaches.

'Elva House!' she says. 'Our new home.'

They park and stretch, only now realising how stiff the long drive has made them. Amanda turns and regards the narrow road they've driven down. 'Don't know how the removal van is going to get down there.'

Anthony smiles. He has the house key in his pocket posted by the Estate Agent. 'Don't worry,' he says. 'They'll be fine.'

The house is cold and empty and echoes until their furniture arrives, which happens the next day. With their things around them, even boxed, turned on their ends or piled one on another, the place begins to feel like home.

The removal man, a Cockney, says, 'Rather you than me, mate,' gesturing to the mountains and steep slopes around the house. 'There's more sheep than people here.'

Amanda smiles. 'That's what we want. There's such a sense of freedom here, away from the rat race, don't you agree?' She's teasing the Cockney removal man, who scowls and says, 'Give me the Old Kent Road, any day.'

But it is remote.

The nearest house is half a mile further down the narrow lane, about ten yards before the road transforms into a track of stones and rubble not fit for cars and barely fit for a horse.

When the removal men are long gone and the couch and chairs pulled into some sort of shape, Amanda and Anthony take a bottle of French wine and some fruit: sharon fruit and persimmons they got at Sainsbury's in Kensington and make themselves known to their neighbour.

After crunching down the road, lifting the rusty black-painted gate off its latch to open the way before them, they knock on the peeling green paint of the cottage door. It takes the inhabitants a long time to answer as if they aren't used to visitors. Eventually, a woman comes. 'Yes?' she says.

She's thin with a nylon housecoat showing faded flowers. The housecoat looks cheap. She looks poor. Her face is lined and grey. Anthony guess she's in her early fifties though she could pass for a much older woman.

Amanda is a similar age, but slim and toned from Pilates and Yoga. Amanda models a tight-fitting dark blue Rab puffer jacket, black yoga pants, a Jack Wolfskin hat and gloves and the best walking boots she could afford. Amanda's long blonde hair is pulled back into a ponytail. The neighbour woman's hangs lank. The two women are worlds apart, thinks Anthony. He prefers Amanda.

'We're Amanda and Anthony,' Amanda introduces them. 'We're your new neighbours.'

The woman isn't unfriendly. 'At Elva?'

'Yes,' Amanda smiles.

Anthony is curious; he asked the Estate Agent, but she didn't know. This woman is local. She looks like she's lived in this valley all her life. She'll know. 'An interesting name: 'Elva'. What does it mean?'

The woman says, 'It used to be Elf How in my grandmother's time, but they shortened it. They didn't like it spelled out.'

'Elf How?'

'A "how" is the local word for a small hill. You know what an elf is.'

Anthony smiles. He's thinking Tolkien, but he guesses the elfs that live here are altogether older and darker. Still, it's a nice reference. It makes him feel like he is involved in a place that's ancient and rooted.

'Sorry, I didn't catch your name,' Amanda says.

'I didn't give it,' the woman says, but there's a hint of a smile on her face. She's not too bad.

'Oh,' Amanda blushes, not knowing what to do now, but the woman saves her. 'Peggy Fawcett, that's me.'

'Do you live here alone?' Amanda asks, and Anthony winces because he thinks she's being too personal.

'I do now,' Peggy says. 'My husband left me, and my two lads live away.'

Just then, there's a clucking noise, and Anthony looks round to see a small flock of black hens. He hasn't noticed them before.

'That's my family now,' Peggy says, and she's smiling.

As they walk away, Amanda says, 'Well, she wasn't too friendly. I thought northerners were supposed to be warm and chatty.'

Anthony says, 'They're country folk — conservative.'

Amanda snorts, 'And from the way she looked at that persimmon, I don't think she knew it was edible.'

'Maybe never seen one before,' Anthony says and realises it's likely true.

'At least she'll be able to drink the wine,' Amanda says as they're within sight of Elva House.

'Maybe,' says Anthony. He glances at the hills—not much wine was ever produced round here.

It's the weekend, not that weekends make any difference to their working lives. On Saturday, they drive up to Grasmere and

Ambleside so that Amanda can put up her business cards advertising her services as a Reiki Master, offering healing. 'It'll take time to build the business, I know', she says. 'But I'm hopeful.'

Anthony works in social media marketing. He can operate from anywhere as long as there are good Internet connections, and thankfully, Cumbria benefited from European Money to extend broadband connections to remote areas like Long Sleddale. They managed to get it in before the Brexit vote.

Saturday was driving around. It rained, but it didn't matter because they were in the car. Sunday is a better day. Crisp and cold and icy. A good day to test out their new hiking gear. They head out with rucksacks, walking poles and picnics. They need their polarised sunglasses, it's so bright.

'Not too high a climb today,' Amanda says. She's fit from all her exercise classes, but there aren't many mountains to practice on in London, so all she lacks is confidence. Hand in hand, they trudge along the rocky path up the mountainside. It's steep in parts, so they drop hands, and Anthony's glad they have their walking poles.

Halfway up the slope, they stop, unstopper the flask and drink a lidfull of steaming tea while looking back over where they came from. The valley gleams in the sunlight.

'It's so beautiful,' Amanda says.

He studies her. 'No regrets?'

'None,' she beams. 'None at all.'

'Look how narrow it is!' Anthony says, pointing. From here, they can see down Sleddale. The valley bottom is narrow between steep slopes that go up about five hundred metres on either side. Amanda follows his finger down the long valley.

'Is that a hill-fort?' she asks, nodding to the valley end.

Anthony peers. It's hard to tell. There is a round eminence, quite considerable and ringed with trees at the valley's far end. 'Maybe,' he says. 'Looks defensible.'

'I saw a programme about the hill-forts. The Celts built a lot of them in the Iron Age.'

'Interesting.'

She continues, 'But some are older still. Or at least on older sites— Bronze or even Stone Age.'

Then it's time to continue the climb. They're not even halfway up the fell yet. It takes them more than an hour to reach the summit, but at last, they pull up onto the flatter top. It's a ridge that runs for miles. At times it's flattish, and here it becomes a narrow cockscomb of vertical rocks. It's wide enough to walk along.

'Careful,' Anthony says, 'It's icy up here. Watch your feet.'

The slopes on either side promise a tumble of hundreds of metres that would almost certainly be fatal. It's quite scary. He's prepared not to go if Amanda is frightened, but she appears now surprisingly confident. It must be the sunshine raising her spirits.

They pick their way along the ridge top, heading west. It isn't as hard as he'd feared. They stop for a sandwich on the ridge. Amanda indicates ahead, maybe fifty yards. 'That's the cairn. That must be the summit. We'll go there then look for a way down to the valley bottom.

They reach the cairn. Who knows how long these heaps of stone have been there. They could be modern inventions or placed there by the men who made stone hand-axes here three thousand years ago. Anthony has found a trail going down. It's steep but should be manageable.

Amanda blurts, 'Hey, look what I found.'

She brings it up to him. It's a figure roughly carved in local stone.

'Not much of a craftsman — whoever did this,' Anthony said. 'Looks like it was done by a kid.'

And it's true. There isn't much definition— crude legs, arms, a round belly and head with big lentil shaped eyes and mouth dug out of the grey stone. It's about six inches long.

'It's archaeology,' Amanda says. 'It could be ancient.'

'How would one know?' Anthony says. 'Could have been made last week.'

She shakes her head. 'No, Tony, it's much older than that. Look.' She thrusts the figure towards him, but he's not convinced.

'Put it back, Mand.'

She hugs it to her. 'Could be worth a fortune.'

'Probably not. Besides, it belongs here.'

She looks at him slyly. 'I'll take it to the museum in Kendal. Then, if it's not worth anything, I'll bring it back.'

He grimaces. 'We don't need the money, Amanda. I'd rather we left it here.'

She says pointedly, 'You don't need the money, Mr Successful, but I'm only building up. We moved from London where I had all my clients...'

'I thought you wanted to move here?'

'I did. I do. But let me keep little Harry.'

'Little Harry?' He laughs.

She smiles. She can always get around him. 'That's what I'm calling him.'

'Put it back, Mand. Please.'

'Okay.'

The next day, Amanda goes to get some eggs from Peggy Fawcett's black hens. When she comes back, Anthony is at his iMac, working on a campaign for a client in London.

'Get the eggs?' he asks over his shoulder.

'Yes, got a dozen. Dirt cheap. They'll be tasty too, eating all the shit she's got around her cottage. I think she throws her rubbish on the heap.'

He says, 'The midden. That's what they do.'

Amanda comes into the study with a cup of coffee: Guatemalan that she got from Booth's in Kendal. He takes it.

She sits down. 'She's a funny woman,' she says, sipping the coffee.

'Oh yes,' he says, turning back to the screen.

'You know Little Harry?'

'The effigy from the cairn?'

'Yes. She says it's called Mabbin.'

'What? She recognised it?'

Amanda nods. 'Apparently, you're supposed to leave them be.'

Still, without turning, he says, 'What's this Mabbin supposed to be then?'

'Some kind of local sprite. She took it very seriously. She said nobody should ever move it.'

He turns to her and says quietly, 'Good job we didn't then.'

A week later, they decide to take a walk as far as they can to the end of the valley. It's a flatter walk than their previous one, and they head for what they took to be the hill-fort at the far end. From afar, they see it rising above them with its ring of thorn trees like a broken crown. They're still a mile or so off, but it's distinct. It looks like a special place, whether built for defensive purposes or maybe ritual ones, they can't say.

The land rises, and they follow a stone path that sometimes gets lost in the grass. Finally, they come to a boggy area, and their boots squelch through the sedge. Then the weather threatens change, and clouds gather on the tops.

'I think it's going to rain', Amanda says, picking her way with her chromium walking poles. The brown mud is over her boots and has spattered her fancy leggings. She has a fake-fur headband to keep her warm. She takes off her sunglasses as the light gets worse and folds them into their case, which she puts in her rucksack.

Anthony looks up at the fell tops on either side. The cloud

creeps further down by the minute. 'At least we're not going up there,' he says.

She gazes and nods, and he sees her shiver. 'Looks scary,' she says.

'We do have to climb a little bit,' he says. The hill fort, or whatever it is, is about two to three hundred feet in elevation in front of them. 'We don't have to go today,' he says.

'No, no,' Amanda says. 'We're nearly there now.'

So they continue to climb. It is much lower than the fell tops they did last week, but it's still a hike to get up to the fort from the valley bottom. The path is hard, though it looks like it is walked because they see some old orange peel by the side of the trail, and a little later, there's a cigarette butt.

They climb higher. Their breath is steaming in the damp air. The light has failed now, and it's getting dark even though it's only 3 p.m.

The clouds reach halfway down the mountains now, and they see the top of the hill-fort has scraps of mist above it.

'Not far now,' Anthony says. 'Then we can have our picnic.'

'I don't want a picnic,' Amanda says, 'Not there.'

'We don't have to go at all,' he says. 'We can turn round.'

'No, no, don't be silly. I want to get there, then we can turn round.'

They struggle on in silence. The path here is set between raised banks on either side.

'This must have been the entrance to the fort,' Amanda puffs as the path spirals around the hill, promising to take them around the back before it delivers them to the gate.

'They could stand above and throw spears at invaders,' he says.

She shudders. 'I feel like we're the invaders.'

'We have every right to be here,' he says.

'Do we?' she answers but keeps on walking.

· · ·

The spiral path winds round the rocky green hill at the valley's end. They trudge up it until they find themselves above where they were between the high banks of the track, and the broken mouth of the hill-fort opens in front of them.

Rock piles stand on either side of what must have been the gateway, but they are tumbledown and ancient, covered by lichen and moss. The air here is almost silent; there are no sounds of mankind save their own ragged breathing. The high croaking of ravens haunts this place, and the soughing of the wind, and the soft drizzle of water dripping somewhere unseen.

'It's creepy here,' Amanda says.

'It's because it's remote,' Anthony answers. 'That and the closed-in weather,' and he points up to where the grey clouds have sunk down to less than a hundred feet above their heads.

In front of them, the middle of the hill-fort is raised up. Raised up so far that it catches wisps of mist. The centre waits and broods in front of them, obscuring the view.

'We can go back now,' Anthony says. 'We've made it.'

Amanda says, 'Let's get to the middle. Say we've been and turn round.'

'It's in the mist,' Anthony says.

'Yes, but it's not dangerous. We go up, touch the middle and turn round. We can't come all this way and not get to the middle.'

'Okay, if you want,' Anthony says, but his voice sounds uncertain.

Amanda strides forward abruptly, and he follows after her. She's walking fast, and he breaks into a run. Then she runs ahead, and as she climbs to the middle, the fog encompasses her.

Sudden panic catches at him, and he runs after her. He finds her standing in the middle of the hill-fort. It's a raised platform of rock and grass and around the centre stands a ring of standing stones. The stones are grey and of uneven height. Two or three of them have fallen.

'Someone's had a barbecue,' she says, grinning. Relief washes over him. Barbecues seem suddenly normal and comforting. What was that stupid panic about? The odd way she ran forward like she had something to do.

He looks at the giant heap of sodden ash and charcoal sticks.

'Just a fire,' he says.

She gestures. 'There are bones in it.' She pushes the wet ash with the toe of her boot.

He looks and sees the bones — long ones. He frowns. 'Sheep maybe?'

'It looks big for a sheep,' she says. 'Someone's cooked it.'

'Hog roast?' he volunteers. Maybe the remains of some midsummer party.

'I don't know.' Then she takes off her pack and rummages through it.

'Thought you didn't want a picnic here.'

'I don't. It's too foggy. It's cold.'

'Then what—'

But as he asks, he sees her take out the stone effigy from the mountain cairn. 'Little Harry,' she says.

'Mabbin. I thought I told you not to take it?'

She frowns. 'Sorry, I thought it might be worth something.'

'But you can't remove archaeological artefacts.'

'You said it was modern.'

'I said it could be modern.'

'Then it's not archaeology.'

He's about to argue further, but she says, 'Whatever you say, I'm putting it here.'

'But this isn't where it belongs. It belongs on the fell top.'

She indicates up where the fog is completely obscuring their view of the surrounding mountains. 'We can't go up there in that. And I didn't want this thing in the house. It started to give me the creeps.'

'But why put it here?'

She shrugs. 'It's kind of a sacred place. I didn't think they'd mind if I put it here. It's some kind of reverence, isn't it?'

He has nothing to stay. The breeze stirs the fog. It's almost as if there's somebody there with them. He looks around him.

She places Mabbin beside the remains of the fire. 'Let's go,' she says. She forces a smile, but he sees she's as unnerved as him. Something about this place makes them both feel unwelcome.

Back at Elva How, Anthony opens a bottle of wine. He's done with work for the day. They sit on their leather sofa in front of the log burning fire. The curtains are drawn. They could be anywhere. Outside, the wind is up and howls down the valley, getting into the chimney, fluttering the flames in the fire, moaning through the corners of the window and lifting the curtains like spectral fingers.

'Need to get that double glazed,' he says, sipping the wine.

'I hope you're not mad at me about Mabbin,' she says.

He frowns. 'No, of course, not. But you shouldn't—'

She puts her slender hand on his arm. 'But it's back now.'

He shakes his head. 'It's not back.'

'As good as back. If you want—tomorrow, or when the weather's better, we can drive as close as we can to the fort, get the statue and take it up the fell to put it back where we got it.'

He thinks of the weather outside and the clouds that sit heavy and low on the mountains. He doesn't say anything. Instead, he reaches for the remote when there's a knock at the door.

Amanda furrows her brow. 'Visitors? I don't think so.'

He shrugs. 'I'll go see.'

At the door, Peggy Fawcett stands. He steps back in surprise. Maybe she wants to borrow some food or something, but she stands without coming in, clutching herself against the wind. She says, 'You shouldn't have moved it.'

'Eh?' he says, but he knows.

'The stone man: Mabbin. You shouldn't have moved it. They saw you.'

Anthony furrows his brow. How could anyone see them? They were on a mountain top. There was no one around for miles.

'They came and asked me,' Peggy says. 'I couldn't lie to them. So I said she'd been here with it, asking, but I'd told her to put it back.'

'Who's 'they'?'

Peggy shakes her head. 'Never mind. But you've got to leave. I saw them moving.'

'Who?'

But Peggy continues. 'They only come at night. You need to go. Please. You're not bad people. You don't know our ways. You didn't mean anything by it. I told them that. But they don't listen. They don't listen to us.'

Anthony is riled by her. 'I don't know what you're talking about.'

She says, 'I've come to warn you. I didn't need to do this, but I thought you're not bad people. You didn't know.' She says sourly, 'They don't care you didn't know. You touched it. That's the thing.'

'Who are 'they'?' Anthony says again, but Peggy Fawcett has turned and vanished into the howling dark.

'Who was that?' Amanda says, wine glass to her lips. Her wine-wet lipstick has smeared the crystal like a bloody kiss.

'Our crazy neighbour.'

'What did she want?'

He sits and grunts.

'What?' Amanda says, more insistent. She looks worried.

He sighs, rubs his mouth.

'What, Tony?'

'That stupid statue thing. She says we shouldn't have moved it.'

'So what? We put it back.'

'Sort of. Anyway, she's gone now.'

'She came all that way to complain about us moving the Mabbin thing? Why didn't she say that when I first showed it to her?'

'No, she's not bothered. Or as bothered. She says mysteriously, 'they' saw us take it.'

'There was nobody there to see us.'

'Unless they were invisible,' Anthony says.

'More likely binoculars. But why would anyone be watching us?'

'Maybe they watch all strangers.'

'If they were watching us then, which I don't believe,' she says, 'they'll have been watching us today and seen us put it back.'

'You.'

She puts down her glass on the table.

'Me? So it's me only now, is it?' She sparks anger at him. He knows he deserved it. The word had slipped out. 'Sorry,' he says.

'So you should be.' She snorts, takes more wine. 'I don't believe Peggy Fawcett. She's cracked.'

They go to bed. It's not late, but it's so dark that it feels late. The wind drops. He looks out of the bedroom window to check the weather. The vanished wind allows the fog to gather. It's thick. There are no streetlights outside. The house lights hardly penetrate the mist. It doesn't matter. It's night.

Amanda is already in bed, her cheeks rosy from the wine. They'd had a second bottle. She has her black silk nightie on. That means she wants to make love. He feels the flush of desire rise in him. He climbs onto the bed. He kisses her, and she kisses him back.

Then a noise clunks from the back of the house. Amanda freezes, stops kissing. 'What's that?'

He pulls himself to his knees. 'Don't know. Sounded like something being knocked over.'

'Could be an animal. A fox maybe prowling around?'

'I don't know.' He is in two minds now, his ardour subsiding, but he turns back to her. Then the clunk comes again.

'Must be an animal,' she says.

'Not a fox,' he says. 'Something bigger.'

'A sheep come down from the fells?'

'I don't know,' he says and goes to the window. He's still wearing a t-shirt and underpants. He draws back the curtain that would show him the yard at the back of the house, except now it shows nothing but a shifting screen of fog.

'Did you lock the door?' she asks.

He nods. He'd said they wouldn't need to here, but it's an old London habit and hard to break.

'Well, no one can get in.' She pauses. 'Back door too?'

'Yes, yes.'

'Then come back to bed. I'm getting cold.'

But he can't settle. He goes to the front window. 'I think there's someone out there.'

She sits up, gathering the duvet to her knees and hugging it to her. 'How do you know? You can't see anything.'

'No. I just feel it.'

'Imagination.'

'But the sounds?'

'That's what's set the imagination off. A sheep has wandered down and knocked something over. That starts all sorts of thoughts off in the dark.'

He comes back to bed. 'You're right.'

He sits next to her. 'Sorry, I've gone off it.'

She strokes the back of his head. 'Don't worry. Lie down.'

He lies, and she switches off the light. It's totally black. Not city black. Not Bible black, worse than that—as black as the black before time began. He feels queasy, unsteady, lost—like nothing exists, nothing familiar to grasp onto. But he can feel the bed. He can hear Amanda breathing beside him. It's all real. It's all normal. He exhales. She stirs. She's not asleep either.

'Are you scared?' she asks. 'You sound scared.'

'Of what?'

'I don't know. The dark. This place.'

'No, of course not.' He wouldn't tell her if he was. He doesn't want to set her off. He knows what she's like. He's breathing quickly.

'What's that?' She sits bolt upright.

'What?' His heart is hammering.

'Something downstairs. The door. It sounded like it was opening.'

'It's locked.'

'Are you sure?'

'I think so. Yes. I think.' He pauses. 'Do you want me to go check?'

She reaches out and squeezes his hand. 'No. If you say it's locked. Just hold me. I'm spooked—not used to this country quiet.'

'Or the country dark.'

She whispers, 'No. It's so dark. We're not used to it being so dark.'

'No.'

He hears her breathing.

There's a scraping sound below.

'That was definitely downstairs,' she says.

'How can it be? It's a trick of the sound. The fog makes things sound different.'

'Okay.'

It's less than two minutes before another scrape—like something is being dragged.

Amanda moans. 'I'm scared now, Tony.'

'I'll go and check.'

'I don't want you to.'

'I'll be all right.'

She reaches out to squeeze his hand, but he's up already. The floor is cold under his bare feet. The temperature has dropped. He shivers. He can't see where his fleece dressing gown is. He reaches for his bedside lamp. The switch clicks, but the light doesn't go on. Everything in this place is unreliable.

He stands, reaches and feels for the wall switch in the dark. At first, he doesn't find it, but by sweeping his palm across the old, uneven wall, he touches the metal light switch. He flicks it down. That light doesn't go on either.

'Fuse must have gone,' he says.

'Where's the fuse box?' He hears the fear in her voice.

'Downstairs.'

'You'll fall.'

'I've got the light on my phone.'

He finds his phone on the bedside table and presses it on. Pale blue light floods the room, making it strange and cavernous. 'I'll go do the fuse.'

He steps over to the bedroom door, puts his left hand on the handle's cold metal, and turns it. He stands with the door ajar and listens. The scraping sound comes from downstairs, a scraping, dragging sound. Maybe they're being robbed? His computer? The sound system? But they wouldn't drag those.

Anthony strains to hear through the partly open door. It's hard to say, but there is more than one of them. Without doubt, they are downstairs. They must have broken in and killed the electricity. He switches off his phone screen. He doesn't want them to see the light. Maybe the burglars thought the house was empty.

But the car's outside. So they must know he and Amanda are in.

He takes a big inbreath. He's not built for fighting. 'Amanda, hide,' he says.

'What? she hisses.

'Hide. Please.'

He hears her move. He switches on the phone and steps down the stairs. Then he stops.

They're at the bottom. There are a lot of them. They have eyes, eyes that glitter in the light from his phone—lots of eyes and teeth. They're not men.

There is movement in the valley. The wind rises. By midnight, the fog is all blown away.

She sees the smoke and the flames at the Hill Fort all the way down the valley. She sees the fire clearly from her upstairs window. She checks her watch. It's near dawn now but still dark. Dark apart from that fire. Peggy Fawcett pulls her curtains closed.

PART THREE

Scotland

PART ONE

Dungarvan Castle

One

ON ARRIVING at the British Club in Udagamandalam, some sixth sense made Captain William Thorpe hesitate at the door. He stepped aside, took a cigarette from the silver cigarette case, lit it with a flare of his petrol lighter, and waited.

Two men walked out, and Thorpe retreated into the shadow of a large Nigilri rhododendron so they wouldn't see him.

When he recognised the first man as William Stables, he pushed back further and cupped the glowing end of the cigarette in his fingers. When the light from the Club's door lit up the second man leaving, Thorpe grimaced and held his breath. It was Andrew Morris, a tea planter.

Thorpe stood silently while the Indian servant brought the Crossley RFC. The other two Englishmen climbed into the car after tipping the man, and Thorpe saw Stables was driving. From snatches of conversation heard through the open passenger door until it clunked shut, Morris was upset and angry.

Thorpe waited until the motorcar crunched over the gravel and down the Club's long drive. When its tail-lights were out of sight, with five minutes more thrown in for luck, he stepped into the yellow electric glow light spilling from the door of the Club.

The Indian servant started as Thorpe emerged from the shadows. Thorpe recognised the servant as Sandip and nodded. Sandip, regaining his composure, greeted him. "Are you for dinner tonight, Captain Thorpe?"

Thorpe grunted, cigarette smoke curling up. "I'm meeting Mr Thomason."

Sandip said, "Mr Thomason is already here."

At the reception desk, Thorpe dragged off his overcoat and handed it to a boy. The boy scurried off to some cloakroom with the coat. He gave Sandip a few rupees, entered the Club and, as he walked down the corridors, scanned the hall for anyone he knew. Seeing no one he knew well, he exhaled, drew on his cigarette, and stepped forward.

The Club was one of the social hotspots locally. The other place to be seen in Udagamandalam, or Ooty as the British called it, was St Andrew's Church. It was cold in here. The British Club looked like a Scottish Manor House and tonight had the climate to match.

Fires blazed in hearths in the several rooms he passed. Despite Ooty being in south-west India, it was at a height. This was why the British came: to escape the oppressive heat of the lowlands.

The strains of HMS Pinafore playing on a gramophone came from somewhere out of sight. Second-rate paintings of Cumberland and the Scottish Highlands decorated the magnolia walls. Drab plants stood in pots here and there. Thorpe passed many people he knew, but they avoided his gaze. He shrugged. What did he care about the judgement of such bores as these?

Kit Thomason sat nursing a gin and tonic, reading a month-old copy of Punch and smiling to himself at the cartoons. He glanced up when he noticed Thorpe. "Well-timed!" From the look on his face, this was a joke.

Thorpe frowned. "Well-timed?"

"You just missed Morris and Stables."

Thorpe sat, ordered a Scotch and ginger from the attentive Indian servant and said, "I saw them."

Thomason raised an eyebrow. "Pistols at dawn is it?"

Thorpe glowered. "Don't be absurd." The whisky arrived. He sipped it. "You think this is very amusing, don't you?"

Thomason laughed. "Doesn't matter what I think. You still did it."

"You don't know what I did."

Thomason grinned. "But you do."

They lapsed into silence, Thorpe scowling over his whisky. The waiter came to take their order: Mulligatawny Soup, Fillet of Sole, Mutton Curry.

As the waiter left, Thomason said, "I hear he sent Vivienne to Mysore."

Thorpe pushed his hand through his fair hair. "Makes no difference to me."

"Suppose not, now the deed is done. They do say she was distraught. They say she was going to leave him for you."

"Do they?"

"They say he wants his revenge."

"He can try to get it. I wouldn't put money on him winning though."

Thomason laughed. "They say he's burned up with jealousy."

Thorpe drew on his cigarette. "I never bothered with jealousy. It seems a pointless emotion."

"You just never loved anyone enough to feel jealous."

Thorpe sighed. He studied the tablecloth.

Thomason said, "But I think you had a little something for Vivienne—"

"—Will you please leave it?"

Thomason shrugged. "Of course, old man."

Thorpe drained his whisky and ordered another. He lit a cigarette while waiting for the drink and said, "I'm heading back to England."

Thomason seemed surprised. "Really?"

"I'm done here. These narrow-minded fools will always look down their noses at me if I stay in India."

"But what'll you do in England?"

Thorpe snorted. "Old man's got me something lined up in the City, but I thought I'd take a month or two off and do some touring first."

* * *

Thorpe strolled through the crowded Bombay bazaar, not looking for anything special. He glanced at his watch. He had three hours to kill before he had to be on board and four before his ship departed.

He was perspiring and red-faced. This place was a maze. He stopped to get his bearings and looked around him. Today would be the last time he would see India, probably forever. Some impulse sprang into his mind that she should take home a souvenir. He hadn't come to the bazaar to buy gifts. He didn't believe anybody in England would want a gift from him. Maybe his mother, but why not buy one for himself as a memento of all he'd failed to do in India?

Thorpe wandered down the crowded bazaar alleys, but nothing caught his eye. He passed stalls piled high with spices: turmeric and coriander, cardamom and cloves. Then booths that displayed multi-coloured saris in silk and cotton.

As he walked, jostling and being jostled, the sweet scent of a flower stall replaced the aroma of spices. A dark-skinned man heaped garlands on the table in front of him. They lay like coloured snakes in piles on the counter. The stall-keeper was doing a roaring trade as men and women of all ages huddled round to buy garlands. When they'd purchased their bouquets, they pushed past Thorpe on their way to the myriad Hindu temples hereabouts. As well as offerings to the gods, young women bought sprigs of jasmine to twist in their dark hair. He smelled the jasmine as they walked by.

He walked on. The stalls repeated. They displayed spices, flowers, vegetables and fruits and then fruits, vegetables, flowers and spices, occasionally pans. He sighed and mopped his forehead with his handkerchief. The bazaar's smells and hubbub and kaleidoscopic colours disorientated him. The sudden alterations of sun and shadow were hypnotic.

Thorpe stopped to get his bearings. He was by a stall that sold small brass gods. Thorpe had been in India for five years but knew little of Hinduism. He paused to wipe his brow again.

A curl of incense floated up from a joss stick, and, in English, the bright-eyed woman behind the stall began her sales patter.

"Sir, perhaps Lord Ganesha? Lord Ganesha is very kind. He blesses beginnings and journeys." She offered him a small metal idol of the elephant god with a mouse at his feet. Thorpe didn't take the proffered icon.

"Perhaps you have a journey?"

Thorpe didn't reply.

She picked up another. "Or Lady Saraswati who brings prosperity?"

Thorpe shook his head. He started to move off, but his attention was drawn by a many-armed goddess riding a lion. She wielded swords in some of her hands, and others held severed human heads.

He smiled. "That's rather bloodthirsty."

The stall keeper gazed impassively. Maybe she didn't understand him. He pointed.

She said, "That is Kali Mata."

"Kali Mata?" Thorpe said. He looked at his watch. It was 10:30. The ship didn't sail until 3 pm, and he didn't have to be on board until 2 pm. He might buy this thing.

"You are interested in her?"

Thorpe shrugged. "I'm a soldier. It was the swords that attracted me. She looks warlike."

"Perhaps you have done wrong. Perhaps you have killed a man."

Thorpe exhaled. "I'm a soldier."

She smiled. "And a handsome man like you has broken many hearts."

He held the statuette, weighing it in his palm. "How much?"

The woman went on. "Mother Kali is very auspicious. She eats your karma."

Thorpe gave a wan smile. 'Karma, eh?"

"Your sins. Everything you have done shapes your life. That is your Karma. At death, all souls merge with Mahakali, and she purifies them, though there may be an ordeal."

Thorpe laughed. "I'm Church of England. We don't have that."

She was serious. "We all have karma, sir. We cannot outrun it, however far we flee."

Last night's whisky was making his stomach sour. He said, "I'll take it. How much?"

The woman named a tiny sum in rupees. It was such a small amount that he gave her a tip.

"Thank you, sir." She hesitated.

"What?"

"Nothing, sir."

"You were about to say something? Something about the idol?"

"No, sir. Not about the statue."

"About what then?"

"About you."

Thorpe frowned. "About me? What on earth would you want to say about me?"

"There is love and there is power. If you have one you can

never have the other, and even a soldier must one day sheathe the sword."

Thorpe frowned, and without speaking walked away, but something made him look back. The woman was watching him, and she wasn't smiling.

Thorpe tucked the statue of Kali Mata into his blazer pocket. He grunted and walked on. His mouth was dry. Once out of the noise and heat of the bazaar, Thorpe clicked his fingers for a Rickshaw.

"Taj Mahal Hotel," he told the boy. "'Please."

At least, at the Taj Mahal, he'd get some English food. He planned to eat an early lunch, then head over to the port.

The ship sailed on time. Like the other passengers, he stood at the rail on deck and watched Bombay disappear into the afternoon. By the time they were out of sight of land, it was evening.

The ship was the *ss Ranchi* owned by the P&O line. The journey went via the Suez Canal rather than round the Cape of Good Hope.

It took just short of two months before Thorpe set foot on dry land at Tilbury. He made no friends on the voyage home but read a lot of books. He spent a lot of time drinking gin on his own and staring over the bow rail at the memory of places and people he'd left behind.

When he got back to England, he bought a car. When he had his car, he went touring. He headed to Scotland. He didn't know why.

THE MAN in Glencoe that morning warned Thorpe not to take that road, but Thorpe smiled and pointed at his Aston Martin Sports. "She's a good car. She can handle anything these roads can throw at her."

The man shook his head and watched Thorpe head down the pass. At Ballachulish, when he stopped for water and told them his plans, folk repeated that the road was too dangerous for motor vehicles. Thorpe shrugged. "I'll be fine."

The woman in the hotel at Auchindarroch where he had his early lunch told him that he should keep the speed down if he insisted on taking the car on that road, but he just laughed. When he'd gone, she turned to her husband and said, "That young man has a death wish."

Captain Thorpe was confident in his driving, but he wasn't as skilled as he imagined, and he was also angry.

Coming round a sharp bend too fast he saw a woman standing in the middle of the narrow road. Thorpe yanked the Aston Martin's wheel left and then right, but lost control. Time slowed down as the car skidded and all he could do was jam his foot on the brake. He hit a rock. The sudden noise was so alien in that remote place, a blow of metal against stone. The shearing noise of the engine cowling coming off screeched like a ripped soul.

After the crash, the echo repeated against the mountain buttresses like a cannon, the sound rolling down the glen to the sea: a hundred gun salute announcing the accident.

Finally, the noise faded, leaving only the sound of steam hissing from the shattered radiator. In a curiously delayed reaction, ravens lifted in slow alarm from the crags. They circled above the stricken driver, but he wasn't yet dead. They wheeled in a leisurely circle; they were prepared to wait.

The open-topped Aston-Martin was on its side, wedged against the rock, buckled wheels still turning, and on his side in the soft moss at the side of the narrow Highland road, lay the ejected driver. The passenger seat was empty.

The July sun was not yet at its noon-day zenith but still hot. The clear water of the burn gurgled beside the road, washing over jagged rocks of grey and round stones of sparkling quartz, but he couldn't hear it. Bubbling on, the stream tumbled down the glen until it dropped in an abrupt waterfall.

The narrow road followed the burn as far as the waterfall, then it veered left to make a steep but safer descent toward the bottom of the glen and the sea loch that lay out of sight behind the mountain arm.

There was a dark stand of trees and a castle.

Captain William Thorpe lay in a dream between life and death. The sun sailed higher, and still he did not wake.

Thorpe didn't see the crofter and his son's horse and cart nor hear their rapid conversation in Gaelic as they jumped off the wagon and came running. They surveyed the crash, saw there was no one in sight but them and the stricken driver.

The Highlanders reached him, crouched over him and shook him and spoke what English they knew, but Thorpe did not move. He was somewhere far away.

The crofter got his son to unharness the horse from the cart because he knew Thorpe's condition was serious and beyond his ability to fix. He urged the lad to get on the big horse and ride it bareback, kicking its flanks into a gallop down the zig-zag road down towards Dungarvan Castle and help.

When Captain Thorpe awoke, the first thing he was aware of was his thumping head. The next thing he was aware of was that he lay in an old-fashioned bedroom in an old-fashioned bed. Standing around the bed was a small crowd of concerned faces. Thorpe's vision swam into focus. Bending over him, was a man in a three-piece tweed suit, with thin ginger hair.

To the right of this man stood a blonde woman of around forty-five. She was strikingly beautiful with wavy hair and blue-grey eyes. She had an air of great authority.

To her right was a younger woman, dark-haired, also lovely. Thorpe's gaze lingered on her. Her hazel eyes seemed to penetrate him. She had shining hair that fell in a wave to her shoulders, and she wore a cotton summer dress that emphasised her slim figure. She was just his type, and she reminded him of someone: a name just beyond memory for now.

Behind these three, a young red-headed maid peeked to see the drama between the shoulders of her betters. The blonde woman said something in Gaelic to the maid and the girl nodded and left.

"He's awake," the blonde lady said.

"At last!" the dark-haired woman said.

Thorpe got up on his elbows. "Where am I?"

"Take it easy, old chap," the doctor said.

The blonde lady smiled. "You're my guest in Dungarvan Castle."

Thorpe rubbed his eyes. His shoulder hurt. "What happened?"

"You had a car accident," the doctor said. "That road is hazardous. You shouldn't have been driving so fast."

Thorpe grunted. "And who are you?"

"I'm Dr McKinnon. I live here in the castle."

"Dr McKinnon is my husband's physician."

"Edinburgh trained," McKinnon said.

Thorpe looked at the blonde woman. "And you?"

She smiled indulgently. "I'm Gráinne McScaigh."

"Lady Gráinne McScaigh," Dr McKinnon added.

Thorpe turned to the beautiful dark-haired woman. She was so familiar, but he couldn't yet remember her name. "You?"

She stepped closer. "You silly! I'm your wife!" She reached and squeezed his hand. He shook his head. Something wasn't right.

"My wife?"

But she grinned. "I'm Mrs Vivienne Thorpe!" Then with a strange smile she said, "Who else's wife would I be?"

Dr McKinnon looked at Vivienne and said, "He's had a bang to the head. It will take a while for his memory to come back fully."

Thorpe struggled up in the bed, bedclothes tangled around him. "There's nothing wrong with me."

The doctor looked alarmed. "Steady on, they only pulled you out of a wrecked car two hours ago."

Thorpe exhaled. "How wrecked?"

Lady Gráinne said, "My mechanic says he can fix it, but it will take at least a week."

"I'm on a motoring tour of the Highlands," Thorpe said.

"We..." Vivienne said.

"For how long are you touring?" Lady Gráinne said.

"A couple more weeks."

"You see, you do remember." Vivienne stroked his arm.

Thorpe winced involuntarily. He shrugged Vivienne's hand off him, then kicked back the covers and said, "I'm fine."

They watched him as he limped a few steps and then looked down at himself. He was wearing tartan pyjamas.

"My husband's pyjamas," Lady Gráinne said.

Dr McKinnon said, "I really do think you should rest. Get back into bed, there's a good chap."

"Thank you, doctor, but I will decide what I do." Thorpe supported himself on the bedpost, but winced and sat again.

Vivienne looked at Dr McKinnon and Lady Gráinne. She grinned. "That's typical William—far too courageous and manly for his own good."

"Your husband has a private physician? I don't see your husband here, though the world and his wife seem to be present in my room. What—is he a crock?"

McKinnon frowned. He was about to say something, but Lady Gráinne silenced him with a glance. She said, "My husband has a war wound."

"A soldier?"

"He was."

"Like you." Vivienne smiled.

"Not sure what I am now." He rapped his knuckles against his forehead.

Lady Gráinne smiled. "Perhaps if you take a little nap, you'll start to remember better."

Thorpe looked around the room. Rich drapes hung all round his four-poster bed, held open by velvet ties. The floor under his bare feet was of polished wood covered with brightly-patterned Persian rugs. There was no electric light. Instead, silver candlesticks stood on the old oak dresser, and a crystal chandelier hung in the centre of the room. The candles in the chandelier were half burned, their wicks black, and fingers of wax on their flanks now solid and cold. A potpourri of dried Seville oranges, with sticks of cinnamon mixed in, lay in a China bowl on the dresser. By the China dish sat a ewer and bowl for washing.

Thorpe muttered, "Is this the twentieth century or the eighteenth?"

Lady Gráinne chuckled.

Vivienne said, "He doesn't mean to be rude."

McKinnon snorted. "Doesn't he?"

"Where are my clothes?" Thorpe said.

"I hung them in the wardrobe," said Vivienne

"We'll leave you," said Gráinne. "Dinner will be at seven pm. You will hear the gong. If you feel up to it, you can wander outside beforehand. It's still a lovely afternoon."

Dr McKinnon said, "But you'd be better off sleeping until dinner."

Thorpe watched them go to the door, the doctor, Lady Gráinne and the red-haired maid. The door clicked quietly behind them. Then he was alone with Vivienne. He looked at her as if seeing her for the first time. She stood there and smiled back. Then she turned and went to the window that looked out onto sunlit mountains. The way she walked was full of confidence, self-possessed and sinuous.

"Nice place they've got here," she said. "Very grand. Old-fashioned but splendid."

His brow furrowed. "You were in the car with me?"

She turned. "Me?"

He nodded.

Vivienne shrugged. "I'm your wife. Where else would I be if not in the car with you?"

He looked her up and down. "But you weren't hurt?"

"No, I'm fine."

He grunted. "I don't remember the crash. The last thing I remember is a woman in a hotel in some village."

"Ah, yes."

Vivienne came over, smiling. She draped her arms on his shoulders, and he let her. She stared into his eyes, and he looked away.

"You need to concentrate on getting better," she said. "But I'm really pleased we've got time to ourselves at last."

"What do you mean?"

She gestured with her slim, well-manicured hand. "Well, there were always the others to get in the way before. Now it's just we two."

"What about Gráinne and what's-his name, the doctor?"

"They don't count."

She was close. She smelled sweet and warm, like roses and sea salt. He couldn't meet her gaze. Memories crowded for attention, but they were ill-formed and faded before he could digest them. He remembered nothing. She said she was his wife: Vivienne. Thorpe rubbed his eyes.

She stepped away and went to the window. "Should we go for a walk outside?" said Vivienne. "I've hardly seen the place. It looks divine."

"I thought they wanted me to rest."

"You said you felt fine."

"Well. I'm a little sore."

"Of course, if you don't feel up to it..."

His voice was sharp. "Of course, I'm up to it"

"Well, then."

He still sat on the bed. "Where were we heading? Before the accident?" he said. "That knock on the head has done something to my memory."

"Not sure. You know I never bother about directions. I always leave it to you, darling. This trip was all your idea. I don't mind where you take me, as long as you take me with you."

He struggled to his feet and limped over to the heavy window, its mullioned glass held by diamonds of ancient-looking lead. It was open, and the air outside was warm. The scents of summer drifted in.

The stone around the window was grey and solid. Through the window, was a view of the castle terrace and then beyond the terrace, the vista led his eyes into the jaws of the glen. And on all sides stood massed ranks of mountains. The sun was still high. These were the long days of summer, and in the Highlands of Scotland, it would be light even after 11pm.

Then his eyes caught a little bronze statuette sitting on the dressing table. He pointed. "I remember that at least." It was a hideous thing—a woman with many arms, some holding swords, others severed heads.

"It's yours," Vivienne said.

"I got it in India."

"Of course."

He stared at her. "Were you with me in India?"

"You ask such silly questions." Then she said, "But it's the bang on the head. The doctor said it was to be expected."

He remembered something. "You were with me in India." He pushed his hand through his hair. "I remember."

"Do you?"

"Not all of it. But you were with me."

Vivienne smiled. "I'm your wife. I'll stay with you as long as you treat me with respect."

"Respect?"

"You must respect me. You made me promise to love, honour and obey." She laughed. "Though there won't be any obeying."

He said, "I'll settle for love and honour then."

* * *

Thorpe found his clothes hanging in the wardrobe, where Vivienne already told him she'd put them. He took off his pyjamas and put on his shirt then his trousers. He drew out his silk tie from the wardrobe and knotted and tightened it. Vivienne watched him but didn't speak. Then he pulled on his jacket and winced. A smile haunted Vivienne's red mouth.

"Does my pain amuse you?"

She said, "Of course not."

He snorted and shook his head.

"You're in a hurry," she said. "Do you have anywhere to be?"

Thorpe muttered. "I want to see the damage to the car."

"Of course," she said. "I'll come with you."

He shrugged. "You don't have to."

"I'd like to. I almost lost you, after all. I want to make the most of our remaining time together, darling."

"Our remaining time? What on earth do you mean?"

She went to tickle him under the chin, but he pulled back. She grinned. "What do you think I mean?"

"I have no idea."

Thorpe checked himself in the mirror. He pulled his jacket straight, buttoned it and turned to the door. Vivienne got the door for him.

"I'm not a bloody invalid."

"Of course not, darling." She laughed, took his hand and twined her fingers through his. At first, he pulled away, but she wouldn't let him go. By the time she closed the door behind them, he had let her fingers stay locked through his.

Their room was on the third floor of the castle. The walls were of grey stone panelled with dark wood. Pictures of local lakes and mountains adorned the short corridor that led to the top of the stairs.

A grand staircase descended in front of them. On the first step, Thorpe halted. The stairs were steep. He teetered and brought his free hand to his brow.

"Are you all right, darling?" Vivienne said, squeezing his fingers.

"Fine."

"You looked unsteady."

"I felt dizzy. Must be the accident."

She smiled at him. "Must be."

"What are you looking at me like that for?"

"Like what?"

"Like a moonstruck calf."

"I love you." She tilted her head. "I hope you still love me."

He sighed and shrugged.

With her free hand, Vivienne stroked his cheek. "I'm so happy to have you back. You're mine now. No one else's."

They looked down from the top of the oak staircase. Thorpe gripped the bannister. The polished treads descended to the castle's entrance hall.

Suits of armour stood in the hall, and stags' heads were mounted as trophies around the walls. Heraldic displays of tartans and coats of arms with Gaelic and Latin mottoes hung between the stag's heads.

Thorpe and Vivienne descended the staircase and, as they went down, Vivienne commented on a dark tartan. Thorpe glanced at it. The family name was McScaigh, and the motto was *De Umbris Venio*. Upon the tartan was superimposed the image of a spear.

"The lady of the place is a McScaigh. It must be the family tartan."

Taking care where he placed his feet on the wide treads, Thorpe went down, Vivienne stroking his arm.

"Don't do that."

"I thought you seemed like you might trip."

"I'm fine."

"As you like, darling."

The entrance hall was floored in tiles in red and black diamonds. A classical statue of the Roman goddess Diana and another of Venus flanked the stairs.

Leading outside was a heavy studded wooden door that looked as if it could withstand a siege. It was partly open. Thorpe felt the afternoon sun's warmth and smelled the heady scent of roses coming in from the garden.

Vivienne cast her gaze around the entrance hall and peered down the connecting passages. "No one about."

Thorpe held back, but Vivienne tugged him with her as she approached the door.

Vivienne shielded her eyes as she stepped out into the day. Thorpe scanned the rose garden for someone to ask directions from. He heard the sounds of someone working, then saw a young man. He shouted over, "You! My car, do you know where it is?"

The man, who was about twenty, stopped hoeing and looked over to Thorpe. The man spoke with an understandable accent, but whose vowels betrayed that English was not his first language.

"Yes, sir," he said. "If you take the path to the left and follow it round towards the stables, you will find Muirdeach who is fixing your car."

Thorpe saw Vivienne cast a lingering glance at the young man who had now returned to his work. He imagined her admiring his short brown hair and skin tanned by his work outside and felt an unfamiliar twinge of jealousy. "Like him, do you?" he said.

Vivienne laughed.

Thorpe sneered. "I'm going to find this Murdo, chap. You can stay with your gardener if you want."

Vivienne said, "I'm coming along with you. I told you, William. I'm going to stay with you always now."

But he set off without her.

Thorpe was walking past the stables when she caught up. He caught the familiar stink of horses. It reminded him of India and the Army. Walking past the horses with their stamping and whinnying, he found his car inside the far stable. A door sat open to let out the heat and let in the sun. Another young man with a shock of black hair was bent over the engine. He was tall, healthy, and well-muscled. He looked up as Thorpe blocked out his light.

"You're Murdo?" Thorpe said.

"Muirdeach."

"That's what I said."

Muirdeach stared back at him evenly.

Thorpe said, "You're the mechanic?"

Muirdeach opened his left hand to show the spanner he held, then the right to show the screwdriver. He grinned. "Aye, I'm the mechanic."

Thorpe scowled. "How long?"

"You mean before the car is fixed?"

Thorpe snapped. "Of course, that's what I mean. Is everyone here an idiot? Is it inbreeding or something racial?"

Vivienne stroked Thorpe's shoulder. Thorpe saw her smile at Muirdeach.

He snapped. "How long before the bloody car's fixed?"

Muirdeach was unfazed. "I am thinking it will be at least a week. I will have to send for parts to Glasgow."

"Pah". Thorpe snorted. "A week? I can't bear to be cooped up in this place that long."

"I can only do what is possible," Muirdeach said. His manner was mild, and his blue eyes unconcerned at Thorpe's abrupt manner.

Looking away from Thorpe, Muirdeach smiled at Vivienne. "I hope you are enjoying your stay here more than your husband."

Thorpe saw her smile back. Thorpe glared at her. Was she deliberately trying to humiliate him? The conversation was over. He stormed out of the stable by the open door. Vivienne lingered. He hesitated, waiting for her, but when she didn't come immediately he stalked off.

After a few yards, Vivienne caught him and took his hand.

"He's only doing what he can," she said. "These are remote parts."

Thorpe fumed. "Did you hear the way he talked to me? In the Indian army, we would have had the natives horsewhipped if they spoke like that to an officer."

She said gently, "He's not a native, William."

"Well, what is he then? He's not English. What is that bloody jabber they speak, anyway?"

Vivienne squeezed his fingers, not letting them go. "William, let's go for a walk along the terrace, then we can go back and relax before dinner."

Thorpe said coldly. "You can go where you want. I'm going back to the room."

He walked off without looking back. But as he got to the corner, about to enter a tunnel of trees, he turned. She was gazing at him, smiling. She waved and turned to walk away.

If she thought she could play him like this, she had another think coming. Thorpe's jaw tightened as he watched her stroll down the terrace. When she was out of sight, he continued back to the castle.

Three

THE SOUND of someone clipping hedges drifted in through the open window. Thorpe's shoulder ached, and his legs were sore. He'd taken his trousers off to inspect his bruises. They were many. Then he'd found a three-week-old London Times on the side table and was reading the sports pages as he sprawled on the four-poster bed. When Vivienne entered, he glanced up. She had caught the sun while out on her walk, and her face was flushed.

"Go back to see your boyfriend, did you?"

She shook her head. "William, please don't be silly."

He glanced back at his paper, but when she went to undress, he put the newspaper down and watched her. He followed the flicks of her fingers as she unfastened her buttons one by one.

"The terrace is lovely," she said. "What a view of the mountains! And the smell of musk rose and honeysuckle was so sweet it was almost overpowering."

He still didn't speak.

She continued talking, taking off her dress and standing now in her slip. "There's a strange cave at the end of the terrace, with a deep old hole in the floor. It looks ancient."

He shrugged. "Places like this always have things like that."

Her eyes flashed. "But I bet this castle is haunted!"

"I don't believe in ghosts."

"You wait until you see one."

He grunted. "I'll be waiting for a long time."

"You old sceptic. By the way, did you find out where the bathroom is?"

"No, but it won't be far. Down the corridor, I suppose."

His eyes devoured her curves as she stood there in her underwear.

"I'm going to bathe," she said and walked over to the pile of clean white towels. Stooping she picked one up and wrapped the bath sheet around her. She strolled to the door.

He snapped. "You can't go out of the room like that. It's not decent."

She chuckled. "For your eyes only am I, William?"

"You're my wife. Only I get to see you like this."

"I can do what I want, William, walk where I want, dressed as I want. Be who I want," she said.

He glared. "Of course you can't. Not if you're my wife; you'll do what I damn well tell you."

"Not if I'm your wife? What a strange thing to say: of course I'm your wife. But, remember, I do as I wish, not what a man tells me."

Vivienne cocked her head, grinned and turned. She opened the door and wandered half-naked down the corridor while he watched.

Thorpe crumpled the newspaper in two hands and hurled it against the wall.

As she walked away, he could even hear her humming. Anyone might hear her humming, and they might go find out who it was, and if they did, they'd see her. They'd see her like that.

As she turned out of sight, Thorpe stood up as if to go to the door. He should grab her, twist her arm and drag her back. But he stopped himself. He wouldn't give her the satisfaction of thinking he cared that much. He went to the window and stared out. There was the brown-haired boy still clipping the rose bushes. Thorpe gripped the sill hard, fingers whitening. He spat. "Bloody, peasant." Then more quietly: "Bitch."

Composing himself, he bent down to pick the crumpled newspaper and tried to pull the pages straight. Then he sat in the window seat to read them. His eyes followed the lines of print, but the words wouldn't go in and he had to re-visit every passage. His eyes kept flicking to the door. Finally, with a grunt, he threw down the paper and drummed his fingers on the windowsill. Listening to the click of the shears and the twittering of sparrows in the eaves, he clamped his hand to his eyes and swore. Then he looked at his watch again. After another minute, he got up and opened the room door to stare down the empty corridor. He slammed the door shut and threw himself on the four-poster bed.

The clicking of the shears outside stopped.

Lying on the bed, Thorpe stared at the plaster moulding of the ceiling. His eyes traced it all around the corners and the edges of the room. When that was done for the third time, he blew out air, swung his legs from the bed and jumped up. Landing on his sore foot, he winced.

Then a memory returned. It was of Ooty and a tea-planter named Morris. This Morris was connected to Vivienne. He chewed his thumb. Had Vivienne had an affair with Morris? He remembered that Morris had been scared of him, that was one thing. But Thorpe knew he intimidated other men. He relished the power his violent reputation gave him. That's how he'd managed his Company in the Army.

But that was in India. It all seemed like a dream now.

His eye caught the statue of Kali Mata where it sat on Vivienne's dresser. He snatched the statuette and thrust Kali Ma beneath the socks and shoved the drawer shut.

She still wasn't back. He checked his watch again. What was she doing? Who was she with? Perhaps she'd made an assignation to meet the mechanic. She'd liked him, that damned Scottish Murdo. He stared at himself in the mirror. He needed to get a grip. This was stupid. He balled his fists so tight that the fingernails dug into the palms. This was absurd. It was ridiculous. Thorpe stared at himself in Vivienne's mirror. No woman had made him feel like this before.

But he would not dignify her games by letting her know how agitated her teasing made him.

He started to get ready for dinner. He took off his tweeds and hung them in the wardrobe. Then he washed with the ewer and shaved in cold water with the cut-throat razor from his shaving kit. He had on his shirt and underwear but not his trousers.

Halfway through his shave, Vivienne returned, her dark hair wet and shining. She stood, still swathed in towels and nothing else. "I had a lovely bath," she said.

Scraping the lather from his cheek, he grunted.

Vivienne unwound the towels and dropped them in damp heaps on the floor. Thorpe watched her in the mirror as he shaved. He saw the dark triangle between her legs and the soft shake of her breasts. He moved slightly to see her better and nicked himself. A bead of bright blood rose up at the wound.

Vivienne went to her wardrobe and got her black-sequinned dress. She held it up by the window to admire it.

He stopped shaving. "Someone might see you." He said.

"I don't think so. We're too high up for them to see in."

She ambled across the room to her dressing table.

Thorpe put down his pearl-handled razor beside the bowl. He wiped the remaining soap suds from his face with the blue towel. Then he dabbed the blood away and put the towel down.

He reached for the matching pearl-backed hairbrush and brushed his blonde hair, still watching her.

Vivienne sat on the chair by her dressing table. She rolled on her stockings and clipped them to the suspender belt. Her skin was olive. He thought about how succulent and yielding it would be.

He turned to face her. He wanted her, and he wanted to punish her as well. He would teach her who her master was. He would teach her to respect him. He couldn't remember when they'd last made love. "Vivienne," he said.

She looked at the swollen state of him and raised an eyebrow. Then she smiled and kept on dressing.

"Vivienne," he repeated.

Her long elegant legs were now encased in silk. She pulled black French knickers up round her soft buttocks then stooped for the black brassiere. As she moved, he saw her swaying breasts: white and round, topped with the nipples like dark cherries.

He stepped over to her and snatched her elbow to jerk her towards him. "Don't tease me." He hissed.

She grinned.

His mouth twisted, and he yanked her up from her seat.

Vivienne tried to resist, but Thorpe was stronger. He pulled her to him and gripped her hips. He pressed himself against her and shoved her to the wall. With her back to the plaster, he pushed himself into her so she could feel him. His right hand was on her breasts, and his left tangled through her wet hair.

At first, she let him kiss her. He could feel the smile in her mouth as she played with his teeth and tongue. He wound his fist in her black hair, and she didn't prevent him. He cupped her full breasts, but then she said, "No."

Thorpe didn't stop; he couldn't stop.

She put her fingertips against his chest and pushed him away.

He staggered back, astounded. Then he moved forward again.

She took his shoulders forcibly and pushed him away. "I said —no." She was still smiling.

His mouth twisted in a snarl. "But you're my wife."

She met his stare with eyes as black as a snake's. Her mouth was half-open and amused, but she shook her head. "There's a lot you need to learn about women, William."

He spluttered. "I'm your husband. I have rights."

Vivienne touched the tip of her finger on his bottom lip. Her hazel eyes stared into him. "I am my own mistress. I decide when and who I want to fuck."

The Anglo-Saxon word stung him like a whip. He stepped back. "What did you say?"

"You heard. Get dressed," she said. "And put that away."

She reached down and playfully twisted the end of his hard penis. Then she let it go. "If I have a use for it later, I'll let you know."

He raised his hand.

She shook her head. "You wouldn't hit a woman, William. That's not in your code."

He lowered his hand but spat. "You bitch."

She moved away and picked up her slip. "Now hurry. They'll be ringing the gong soon, and I still have to dress."

* * *

Dinner was set out on the long table in the Baronial Hall. The room was huge, with a high ceiling and a gallery running around it. Someone standing on the gallery could look down on the diners unobserved, but, glancing up, Thorpe didn't see anyone this evening.

More heraldic designs adorned the walls. A crisp white linen cloth covered a long table of dark wood, and crystal glasses were set by each dinner place. Silver cutlery lay on three sides of each setting. Gleaming six-armed candelabras stood along the middle of the table, candles already burning. The thick walls and small windows of the Baronial Hall meant the room stayed dim, even though outside the summer still light lingered and the candle flames flickered in an unfelt draught.

Thorpe and Vivienne were not the first to arrive. As they entered, a handsome, patrician-looking man with clipped greying hair and beard that had once been fiery red sat at the head of the table. He wore a black dinner-suit with a white tie. At the opposite end of the long table, sat the blond-haired woman Thorpe recognised from when he woke. He remembered she called herself Gráinne.

The man rose and came to greet them as they came in. First, he greeted Vivienne by kissing her hand, saying. "Mrs Thorpe. You are as lovely as my wife led me to believe."

Then he extended his hand for Thorpe. Thorpe shook it. The man had a grip as firm as Thorpe's own.

"Captain Thorpe," he said, "How delightful to meet you. I'm only sorry about your car. I hope we can make up for the inconvenience."

Thorpe dropped the handshake. "This is your castle?"

Vivienne glared at Thorpe. "Darling, you shouldn't—"

The man nodded. "I am Eachann McScaigh. I have the honour of being Laird of Dungarvan and its estate."

His wife, Lady Gráinne, nodded at Vivienne as she took her seat. Thorpe sat down beside her.

Next to Lady Gráinne, Thorpe recognised the quack-doctor, McKinnon.

Lord Eachann said, "Captain Thorpe, this is Dr McKinnon—"

"—we've met," Thorpe said.

"And this," Lady Gráinne said, "is Mr Alastair McDonald."

She indicated a fresh-faced young man with blond hair. The young man's eyes darted between Thorpe and Vivienne. He clasped his hands on the table before him as if he didn't know where to put them. He didn't speak, he just blinked.

Lady Gráinne said," Alastair is our guest here while he does some academic research. He's a local boy but belongs now to the University of Edinburgh."

The young man stammered. "Pleased to meet you, Captain Thorpe, Mrs Thorpe. Lady Gráinne is a wonderful hostess. I'm sure you'll enjoy your stay here. Dungarvan has a marvellous library. Lord Eachann has collected many volumes on Highland and Gaelic myths and folk tales. That's my subject."

His speech frothed forth, jumping from subject to subject. Thorpe thought this Alastair McDonald wouldn't last long in the Army.

As McDonald prattled, Thorpe surveyed the room. Nothing he saw attracted his attention until his eyes rested on the maid. He recognised her as being in his room with the others when he woke. She stood in the corner of the hall. She was pretty. Noticing the direction of his gaze, Vivienne slipped her hand over to cover his. Thorpe let it stay. For a second he thought a secretive glance passed between the two women, but of course they didn't know each other. Women knew things anyway, some kind of sisterhood they shared, keeping men out.

Now everyone had sat down, the male waiter with dark hair and the pretty maid brought the soup. He looked familiar. Vivienne was very friendly with him, how she smiled.

When the soup was served, steaming before him, Thorpe stared at the dish. "Cock a' Leekie," he said. "At least we can never accuse the Scotch of breaking with tradition."

Lord Eachann beamed. "Tradition is everything here," he said. "I hope you enjoy your meal."

Thorpe realised that the waiters were the staff that he'd already seen. The rose clipper, the mechanic, and the red-haired maid all wore different clothes for their different roles..

Lady Gráinne watched as Thorpe's studied her servants. She said, "Yes, we are so remote here that we have such a small staff. You will recognise Muirdeach from the garage, and this is Calum, whom you may have seen among the roses."

Calum poured white wine into Thorpe's glass.

"You've forgotten the prettiest one," Thorpe said.

"You mean Màiri?"

Thorpe raised his glass at the maid. She blushed. Lady Gráinne nodded at them, and the staff withdrew.

"Very gallant, William," Vivienne said. "To salute the maid."

Lady Gráinne said, "She's taken, I'm afraid—promised already to Muirdeach."

"The mechanic?"

Eachann nodded. "He's a fine lad. He could have had his choice, but he and Màiri are to be married in the Autumn."

Thorpe laughed and took a gulp of wine.

Conversation was sporadic around the table as they drank their soup.

Dr McKinnon was engaging Lady Gráinne in conversation. She looked bored. A few minutes into the meal, Lady Gráinne said, "I hear you were decorated for gallantry in the War, Captain Thorpe?"

Thorpe nodded but didn't look up.

"He doesn't like to talk about it," Vivienne said, "But yes, he was fearless."

Thorpe muttered. "Any officer would have done what I did."

Lord Eachann said, "Few men win the Military Cross."

Thorpe glanced at the older man. "You looked me up?"

"I hope you don't mind. I peeked in Who's Who."

Lady Gráinne said, "Tell us the story, Captain Thorpe."

"It's not very interesting."

"I'm sure it is," Dr McKinnon said.

Vivienne squeezed Thorpe's hand. He pulled his fingers away.

"Please tell us," Lady Gráinne said.

Thorpe grunted. "The Boche were pinning down my men, picking them off. Someone had to go and clear out the machine gun nest. I was best placed. That's all there is to it."

Lady Gráinne said, "You are lucky to have such a courageous husband, Mrs Thorpe. And such a handsome one. I'll wager you had a fight on your hands to land the brave Captain."

"I certainly did. But please call me Vivienne."

"And please call me Gráinne."

Vivienne patted Thorpe's hand. "But yes, there was some stiff competition. Lots of the other girls had their eye on him. I was lucky enough to be the one he finally chose. Though I believe he did do some extensive research."

"I can see why you're together," said Lord Eachann. "You are a very handsome couple."

"Yes, he's mine now," smiled Vivienne, taking Thorpe's hand again. "Mine forever."

Thorpe frowned.

The servants came in to collect the dishes and returned shortly afterwards to bring the main course. The main course was roast venison with a red wine jus. Màiri went around the table, pouring red wine to accompany it. Thorpe shook himself free of Vivienne.

Spearing a piece of venison, Thorpe said, "The mechanic told me it would be a week or so before my car was fixed."

"The problem is," Dr McKinnon said, "that everything has to come from Fort William, or if it's more specialised, even from Glasgow."

Thorpe nodded. "I understand that. I'm not dense."

Vivienne said, "You're very gracious, Lord Eachann, for putting us up."

"It's my pleasure," said Eachann. "Is your father in the military, Captain Thorpe?"

Thorpe shook his head. "He's a merchant banker."

"But you didn't want to follow in his footsteps? I would imagine that it would be quite lucrative."

"He wanted me to, but I prefer a life with more action."

"Preferred," Vivienne said. "William will be going into the family firm when we return to London. I need him to be safe now."

At the end of the main course, Lady Gráinne said, "Captain Thorpe, did you enjoy the War?"

Thorpe dabbed his mouth. "I don't think 'enjoy' is the right word, but it gave me a sense of purpose. I suppose I was suited to it in a way I'm not suited to peace."

"You must have seen some dreadful things," Gráinne said.

"I think sometimes difficult situations cause us to make choices. And good choices can ultimately make us better people," Vivienne said.

Eachann said, "Ah, Mrs Thorpe. How wise! You remind me of my ancestor—the one after whom I'm named. Alastair can tell the story better than me. Go on, Alastair."

Alastair McDonald blushed. "Oh, I don't know..."

"Please Alastair, you're the expert," Gráinne said.

"Oh very well," he said. He sat back and cleared his throat, looking pleased but nervous to be performing his party piece. "Once upon a time, as they say—but probably back in the ninth century, or so—no one really knows, but from my research, I think that's about it."

Everyone listened in polite silence. Thorpe followed the maid round the room with his eyes, watching her top up glasses.

"Well, in those days, Eachann Dubh Mac Scathaich: they called him 'Black Eachann son of the Shadow,' as it could be rendered, was Lord of Dungarvan. It's said that one day when he was hunting, he saw a dark snake of a type he'd never seen before. He followed the snake to the entrance of a cave he'd never noticed before. He went into it hoping to catch the snake, skin it, and add it to his many hunting trophies."

Alastair glanced around the table. They were all listening.

"They say he was a man who knew no fear. But at the end of cave there was no snake, only a pool of water, but water so deep that he could not see the bottom. By the light of his torch, he gazed down into it, and then he realised he was not alone. He turned round, and he saw a beautiful dark-haired maiden wearing a cloak of silk."

Even though they'd heard it many times, Lady Gráinne and

Lord Eachann were gazing on with rapt attention. Dr McKinnon was smiling at the performance, and Vivienne seemed enthralled.

When the maid, Màiri, came close to Thorpe, she stood very close to him. He felt her thigh against the back of his hand. He was sure she pressed herself against him. He looked up at her but she was busy serving. Màiri stepped away and carried on with her work. Thorpe glanced at his wife who had not taken her eyes off Alastair.

Alastair continued, "So... the Lady of the Fountain, as she is called in the story, became Eachann's wife. But she had two sisters, each as beautiful as she was. She was dark but one sister was blonde and the other red-headed. Eachann was the kind of man who thought that anything he could take was his and he thought he could take his wife's two beautiful sisters. But his wife watched him with them, and she went to her sisters in secret. The women swore never to betray each other."

Alastair cleared his throat and went on. "It was clear to all that the Lady of the Fountain was of faery kind. She knew that Black Eachann was tempted by her beautiful sisters. She commanded him to be faithful to her, but he, like all men, took his own counsel on that."

Alastair blinked. "You will know that Celtic women were often powerful and rivalled their husbands in prestige. The Lady of the Fountain and Eachann Dubh were engaged in a war between the sheets."

"Go on," Lady Gráinne said.

Alastair continued. "At first he recognised that everything he had came from the magical success granted to him by his wife, and he was grateful. But he grew proud and thought he could fool her. She warned him that if he was unfaithful, she would punish him. He swore he was true, but she sent her sisters to tempt him..."

"Ah," said Eachann. "Here's the pudding!"

Black-haired Muirdeach served to the end of the table to Thorpe's right. He saw him talking to Vivienne as he put down the plate and thought Muirdeach lingered with Vivienne longer than he needed to. Thorpe watched him laugh and joke and saw Vivienne touch the young man's arm as she joked back. Then William saw Màiri standing by the door glaring at Muirdeach as he flirted with Vivienne. Her eyes were full of poison as she stared at her man.

The servants withdrew, and the guests ate.

Alastair said, "Well, to finish the story quickly—the Lady of the Fountain told Eachann if he was ever unfaithful to her she'd leave him."

"You told us that already." Thorpe said.

Alastair blinked. "Yes, but he was unfaithful with her red-headed sister. He denied it at first, but she knew. She gave him another chance and—"

"—and?" Thorpe asked.

"She said she'd kill him if he did it again."

Vivienne said, "And did he?"

"What?"

Thorpe rolled his eyes. "Did he go with another woman?"

"Yes."

"And?"

"The Lady punished him."

"How?"

"She cut off his..." Alastair's cheeks blushed beet red.

Thorpe snorted.

"Thingy." Alastair said.

"God give me strength," Thorpe muttered.

Vivienne laughed. "And that's it?"

Alastair frowned. "It was quite serious. He became an outcast and a wanderer for the rest of his life, which was short and brutal."

Vivienne turned to Thorpe. "So, you see, darling, the moral of the story is don't take your fairy wife for granted."

Thorpe raised an eyebrow. "Really?"

Vivienne said, "The Indians call it karma."

Lady Gráinne said, "And the Gaels call it geas."

"Superstitious peasants the lot of them," Thorpe said.

No one spoke. The silence grew strained, then Dr McKinnon said, "I hear young Calum's in trouble, eh?"

Lord and Lady McScaigh ate on in studied silence.

The doctor went on. "He is though isn't he? He's got the Fraser girl from the village in the family way. I hear he isn't going to stand by her and her father is gunning for him—literally, probably."

"We don't approve of what Calum did," said Gráinne, without looking up.

"I've spoken to him," said Eachann. "Told him to do his duty, but he has other ideas."

Gráinne's expression and her grave, grey eyes suggested the subject was now closed.

McKinnon went back to his pudding.

When he had finished his dessert, Thorpe put down his spoon said, "Is there a gymnasium here? I will need some exercise if I am to be here a week."

"There is no gymnasium," said Gráinne. "But you could walk the mountains?"

Thorpe said, "Walking's fine, but I will need something to get rid of my frustration." He looked at Vivienne, but she was talking to Dr McKinnon.

"We do have a fencing room," said Lord Eachann. "Though it hasn't been used for months."

Thorpe said, "That sounds perfect. I was a good swordsman in the Regiment." He looked over at Alastair, "But I'll need an opponent. You're the only one of roughly similar age. I fear Lord Eachann and Dr McKinnon are rather too old."

Alastair blustered. "I'm not really a fencer."

Thorpe said, "I'll show you. I won't take no for an answer. I'll see you down there after breakfast."

As Thorpe made his way out of the dining room after the meal, Vivienne walked a few paces behind. From ahead in the Entrance Hall, Thorpe heard the low voices of people arguing. They sounded angry but trying to keep their disagreement quiet.

As they got closer, Thorpe saw it was Muirdeach and the red-haired maid, Màiri. They looked over and saw William and Vivienne. They went quiet. Màiri looked at Thorpe and half-smiled. Vivienne saw the look and glanced at Thorpe, one eyebrow raised. Màiri glared at Vivienne, turned and went through the servants' door, slamming it after her.

Muirdeach looked over and grinned, but he was grinning at Vivienne, not William. Vivienne smiled back at him. "Good night, Muirdeach. Will you be serving us breakfast tomorrow?"

"I will, madam."

Vivienne said, "I will look forward to seeing you then. Good night."

Later, in their room, Vivienne said, "I think you frightened Alastair with your fencing challenge. He's not really a fighter."

Thorpe laughed. "No, he likes stories and reading. But I could see that you took to him."

"I love stories and legends. That's why you got me that statue of Kali Mata."

Thorpe frowned. He'd forgotten that he got it for her. He said, "Don't worry, I won't rough him up too much."

Vivienne said, "What did you think of his story?"

"Wasn't listening."

"No, you were too busy looking at the maid."

Thorpe gave a derisory snort. "Well, you weren't paying me much attention."

"Don't be a baby."

Thorpe bit his lip. "I'm going out for a smoke."

* * *

Thorpe strolled down the staircase and out through the main door. Was she trying to drive him crazy with jealousy and desire? He walked without knowing where he was going. It was now dark, and the air was heavy with night-scented stock. He looked back at the castle, silhouetted against a clear sky that was still red with the fingers of day. All around the dark bulk of the mountains towered. Thorpe lit his cigarette. He drew on it, and the ember flared in the dark.

As he stood by himself and smoked, the warm evening air calmed his anger. He was by the servant's entrance.

Màiri started as she came out of the door and saw Thorpe in the shadows.

"Don't be frightened," Thorpe said.

He saw her grin in the light from the small window. "I'm not frightened, not by a handsome gentleman like you who would never do a girl any harm."

"Wouldn't I?"

"No." She studied him. "You seem upset."

"It's nothing."

"Affairs of the heart?"

He shrugged. "I just don't understand feelings, really."

"I've been upset too," she said abruptly.

"Oh?"

"Muirdeach. He has a roving eye."

"He neglects you then?"

"Oh, yes. He runs after every pretty girl he hasn't had, then he comes back to me."

"That's a pity. But you are still going to marry him?"

"I love him."

"Yes, it's a bit of a rum do, love,' Thorpe said. "I've never been much good at it."

Màiri said, "I was just going home. You can walk with me a way if you like."

"Do you live far?"

"Just on a farm in the valley."

"Do you live alone there?"

She shook her head. "No, with my father and mother and brothers."

There was something very sweet about her. She was attractive too, and she knew she was, but beauty isn't a crime, he thought, nor is knowing you're beautiful. He smiled at her.

"What?" she grinned. She was flirting now.

"You're a lovely young woman, you know. He doesn't deserve you."

"No, he doesn't. But that is my fate."

He said, "You're Mary, aren't you?

"Màiri, sir."

They strolled together. "I've just come from India. In India, in wild places like this, there are tigers."

"We don't have tigers here."

He laughed.

"There are the wolves. But they don't come close to the castle unless they are hungry. They sometimes take lambs and the wild deer."

He raised an eyebrow. "Wolves? I thought they were extinct in Scotland."

She shook her head. "Not here, sir. We have lots of things at Dungarvan that have gone from other places."

Thorpe thought her mention of wolves was an encouragement, a way of giving him an excuse to walk with her. Then he walked close enough so he could smell her clean hair and feel the heat of her skin.

"Want a cigarette?" he said.

"I'll have one, sir." He gave her one from his cigarette case and leaned in to light it from his. Màiri laughed. She smelled of warmth and life and night flowers.

"Let's walk then," she said.

"This way?"

She nodded.

"Are you sure you want me to?"

"It would be rude of you not to," she said. "With the wolves, and all."

"Ah, yes, the wolves."

She smiled. "Maybe tigers too. You never know."

They walked down the main pathway from the castle with its high box hedges. Then they came to a stile.

"Will you help me over, sir?"

Thorpe said, "Don't you normally manage it yourself?"

She smiled. "I just thought it would be nice for you to help me since you're here."

At her direction, Thorpe put his hands on her waist and lifted her over. Then he stepped over himself. They walked in silence until they came to the shadow of a field barn.

Màiri said, "I feel a bit tired. Do you mind if we stop for a rest?"

"A rest? We've only just started walking."

She laughed softly and leaned back onto the wall of the barn. Thorpe put his hands on the stones which were still warm from the day's sun.

She took his hand, and he let her take it. She put it on her breast. He felt it firm and yielding. "I like that," she said.

Thorpe cleared his throat. He smelled her sweet skin. He could almost feel her laugh in the dark. She put her arm on his shoulders and pulled him in. He hesitated.

"What if we kissed?" she said.

"We probably shouldn't."

"But you want to."

He sighed heavily. She was intoxicating. His lips were dry.

She said, "I want to pay Muirdeach back. And you are very handsome."

His arms were still round her waist.

She said, "Why should't you?"

"Well, I'm married."

"Are you?"

"Of course."

"I didn't know."

He frowned.

She said, "Wherever she is, she need never know."

Instinct was taking Thorpe over.

Màiri leaned in close. He felt her warm breath on his cheek. She smelled of summer and salt and flowers. She said, "I don't think you're a stranger to this kind of thing. I know your type."

His hands dropped to her hips. She knew his type.

"I can feel you're enjoying yourself." She stroked his arm. "You really are a very handsome man. And very brave." Màiri pulled him in. "It'll be fun."

He knew she was doing it out of jealousy to get back at her flirtatious boyfriend. He knew he shouldn't but she was attractive and clever and Thorpe's resistance melted, and he bent to kiss her. She returned his kiss with a hunger that threatened to eat him up.

They grew more passionate. He unbuttoned her blouse, kneaded her breasts then stooped to shower them with kisses. His lust raged in his loins and his urgency to have her almost overwhelmed him. He hitched up her skirt and pushed her against the wall of the barn. Then he unbuttoned his trousers and when they were round his ankles, she took him in her hand and guided him into her.

Màiri wasn't a virgin. She moaned in rapture as they coupled and kissed him back, passionately. With his hands grasping her buttocks, it took minutes until he finished with a grunt. He brushed her damp hair from her face.

She kissed him tenderly. "That was nice. I don't regret doing it with you."

Thorpe sighed. He bit his bottom lip. He dressed while she lingered.

"What's sauce for the goose is sauce for the gander too," Màiri said. "Remember that."

She turned to go but stopped. "And remember, this is our little secret," she said. He thought he heard her laughing as she disappeared into the darkness.

* * *

When he got back to the room, Vivienne was in bed. The moon had now risen. He undressed by its light and put his clothes on the back of a chair.

Vivienne stirred and said, "Where've you been?"

He whispered. "I couldn't settle. I went for a walk. Go back to sleep."

He got in bed beside her. He was starting to doze when Vivienne sat up.

"What?" he said.

"Where have you been?"

He rolled over and muttered. "I just went for a walk."

Vivienne didn't speak again, and within minutes he was asleep. Much later, he woke from a dark dream of snakes in the depths and quiet of the night inside the grey stone castle.

Then he fell asleep again. Later, he was aware of his wife's smell, the feel of her damp hair and the firmness of her sinuous body pressed into his.

Just before dawn, she was gone.

Four

IN THE MORNING, when Thorpe woke, Vivienne was not in the room. The day was bright outside, and he heard the small birds cheeping in the ivy around the stone window. Thorpe presumed she'd got up early and gone for a walk in the garden. She might be hoping to bump into that gardener again.

Thorpe glanced over to the dressing table. The little bronze statue of Kali Mata sat in pride of place on the centre of the dressing table, grinning at him with arms full of swords and severed heads. He'd put it away. Vivienne must have got it back out. He got up, snatched it and stuffed it back in the drawer. There was no sign of Vivienne's things. He frowned. Neither was there any sight nor sound of Vivienne herself.

Breakfast was laid out down in the dining room, but there was no one else there. It seemed everyone had either eaten earlier or was still slumbering. Thorpe selected devilled kidneys with scrambled eggs and toast. There was one waiter there—the mechanic, Muirdeach. Thorpe felt momentarily uncomfortable and to cover it up made conversation. "On your own?"

"Calum has not turned in this morning."

Thorpe snorted. "Must be serious. I don't imagine you strong

Highland men ail for much." He turned around. "By the way, have you seen my wife?"

"No, sir," said Muirdeach.

Thorpe said nothing more, and when he had finished his breakfast, he made his way to the fencing room. The Fencing Room was past the Library and then through the Orangery. Lord Eachann had given him directions the previous night.

He walked through the Orangery and found Eachann tending the trees.

"Good morning, my Lord."

"Call me Eachann please."

Thorpe gave a small bow and said, "And please call me William."

Eachann said, "The sleep seems to have evened out your temper. But perhaps you were in pain. How are the aches and pains today?"

Thorpe moved his shoulders and his arms. "Seems fine."

"Must be the healing Highland air."

"I'm sure it is."

The Orangery was glazed over and hot already. Thorpe pulled at his collar.

Eachann pointed to the dark-leaved trees in their pots. "I love the citrus scent. It's very refreshing. We have apple trees outside of course, though you've missed the glory of the blossom. I take it you're on your way to fence Alastair?"

Thorpe nodded.

"He's been there for an hour," the older man smiled. "I think he's a little nervous."

"I won't humiliate him," Thorpe said.

"Of course not. He's a gentle soul."

"If you'd excuse me," Thorpe said.

Eachann looked at him as if trying to work out what kind of man he was. "Of course," he said.

As he was about to leave, Thorpe turned and said, "Have you seen my wife?"

Eachann frowned.

"Yes, Vivienne."

Eachann's frown grew deeper. "Erm, no, I haven't seen her."

"She won't be far," Thorpe said, and left to find Alastair.

When he arrived in the fencing room, Thorpe found Alastair already practising with the dummy. He was wearing his lamé and gloves, but not his mask. He held a rapier.

"Good morning," Thorpe said.

Alastair looked hot and sweaty. He studied his sword and muttered, "Morning." He didn't meet Thorpe's gaze.

Thorpe went over and began to dress in his protective lamé and took his gloves. He spent some time examining the swords in the rack.

Alastair went back to his practice with the dummy.

"Done much fencing?" called Thorpe over his shoulder as he hefted the sabre he had taken from the rack, testing it for balance.

"A little. I was in the Naval Cadets. We did a little then as one of the senior officers was keen on it."

"It's a damned fine sport," said Thorpe. "I don't believe in exercise for its own sake—dumbbells and the like. A man needs exercise that will remove his aggression."

"I'm not very aggressive," Alastair said.

Thorpe grunted. "Nature built men to fight."

"Yes, if you believe in Evolution and all that. But what purpose has fighting now?"

"You need to be able to take what you want in this world."

Alastair laughed. "Not sure the Law is too keen on that—the 'taking what you want' stuff."

Thorpe ran his thumb along the sabre's edge. "Ah, the Law. I bet you obey all the laws, don't you? Anyway, here."

He reached out the sabre to Alastair who looked at it but didn't take it. "It's a little too heavy for me. I've only ever fought with rapiers."

"The sabre is a manlier weapon," Thorpe said. "Don't worry; I won't hurt you."

Alastair's eyes darted to the proffered blade. Thorpe still held it out to him. Alastair hesitated but then went forward and took the heavier sword.

"You'd better put your mask on," Thorpe said.

Alastair fiddled with it, taking three attempts to close the catch.

Thorpe called "Ready?"

Alastair's voice was muffled behind the mesh of the mask. "I suppose."

Thorpe shouted, "*En garde!*"

They began to fence. Thorpe tested his opponent. Alastair's technique was poor, and his stamina was poorer. But Thorpe went easy on him, checking him now and again with a touch to the mask or lamé. He even allowed Alastair some advantage so that he wouldn't be too discouraged. They fought for fifteen minutes or so. Thorpe prided himself on his physical fitness. He wasn't tired, but he could hear Alastair's ragged breathing.

"Do much exercise?" Thorpe shouted. "It's important."

"I walk," said Alastair.

"I didn't mean walking. Old women can walk. What about boxing? I was a member of a gentleman's boxing club in Mysore, and of course, I fence ."

Alastair was out of breath. He couldn't talk and fence at the same time.

Thorpe decided to be merciful and end it. With a flurry of flicks from his sabre and a lunge, he had Alastair against the far wall. He went inside Alastair's guard and touched the tip of his blade on his chest. "Yield?"

Without a word, Alastair struck at Thorpe's sword and

knocked it away. Snarling behind his wire mask, Alastair slashed and swung. His attack was ill-timed and worse executed, but the speed and anger of his whirling blade set Thorpe back a step. Thorpe retreated, measured up his opponent, blocking slashes and cuts but then recovered his composure, and with deft use of his sword, cut left and right and came from underneath making Alastair recoil and stagger off balance. Thorpe pressed the advantage, jumped forward and pushed Alastair back further. With determined strokes, he drove the younger man to give ground until they were halfway down the hall, the only sounds now the grunting and the harsh clash of steel, then, after a weak slash from Alastair, Thorpe's lightning-fast riposte knocked the sabre from the young man's hand and sent it clattering across the wooden floor.

"Very plucky," Thorpe said, laughing.

Alastair went to retrieve the sword from where it had fallen, but Thorpe kicked it away.

Alastair lunged for the sword and would have come round to attack again.

"Enough," Thorpe said, removing his mask. "Bravo for your spirit," he said. "But remember not to lose your temper. That's how you lose the fight."

Alastair pulled off his mask. His face was sweaty and red, flushed and angry, and his eyes were raw with tears. Thorpe went up and offered his hand, but Alastair wouldn't take it.

"I meant it," said Thorpe. "Well played."

Alastair took off his fencing gear with his back to Thorpe.

"Suit yourself," Thorpe said.

Alastair turned, still breathing lightly. "Thank you."

"No problem. I enjoyed it. We'll have to do it again," said Thorpe. "You might win next time."

Alastair laughed. "I'll get the better of you eventually."

Thorpe clapped him on his shoulder. "Well said."

Alastair breathed out, nodded to no one in particular then

rubbed his face with the towel. "I'm off for a quick wash. Will you be coming to the Drawing Room for coffee with Lady Gráinne? That's the normal morning routine."

Thorpe shrugged. "Why not? There's damn all else to do around here."

"You're on the third floor?" said Alastair.

"Yes."

"I'll show you a short cut. This place is enormous, and it takes time to know your way around."

Thorpe followed Alastair out of the fencing room and up a back staircase panelled in dark wood. There was a Turkey pattern carpet with brass stair rods on the stairs. Busts of Roman Emperors glared from alcoves every few steps.

Alastair pointed. "You see that door?"

It was a nondescript door. "Yes."

"That's a quick way to the Rose Garden if you don't want to have to come in through the Entrance Hall."

As they mounted the stairs, Thorpe said, "Have you seen my wife by the way? Damned if I know where she's got to."

Alastair was a stair ahead of him. He said, "Your wife?"

"Vivienne."

"Is she here with you?"

Thorpe frowned. "Of course she is. You were talking to her at dinner last night."

"Oh," said Alastair. He appeared to be about to say something else but stopped. Then he said in a very considered way, "No, I haven't seen your wife."

Alastair pointed out Thorpe's room. "I'll see you in the Drawing Room for coffee in about twenty minutes. Can you find your way?"

"I'll manage," said Thorpe. "Thanks for showing me the short cut. Doubt I'll remember it again though."

When he got back to his room, there was still no sign of Vivienne, or that she'd ever been there.

* * *

When Thorpe went down, Lady Gráinne was already in the drawing-room with Dr McKinnon. Alastair came in behind him.

Muirdeach served the coffee from silver pots, and they took it in bone china cups with cream and sugar. Comfortable chairs and sofas furnished the drawing-room. A black and white cat wound itself round the legs of Lady Gráinne's chair. Wide French windows gave a view down through the castle gardens, and beyond the castle terrace stood the mountains and past them, a faint glitter of blue water.

"I haven't seen this side of the castle before," Thorpe said. "I didn't realise you were so close to the sea."

"Technically the Atlantic Ocean," said Dr McKinnon.

Thorpe smiled thinly. "The sea's the sea to me," he said.

"Ah, but you're an army man, not navy! I should say a navy man would not have the same view—eh, Alastair?"

"I'm not in the navy any more," Alastair said.

Dr McKinnon chuckled. "No, you're an academic now, and a very promising one too, if what Lady Gráinne says is true. I was quite respected too in my time at Edinburgh, you know. I could have had a career at the University. I'd be a professor by now. But the ocean it is though. You of all people should know the sea from the ocean!"

"Does it matter?" Thorpe said.

Gráinne gazed out of the window. "I was brought up by the Atlantic in my youth."

"Where was that? If you don't mind me asking."

"In the southwest of Ireland. A long time ago." She sipped her coffee. "So I'm used to the wild Atlantic."

"I visited County Kerry once," Thorpe said.

"Near there."

"Charming place, I thought. Nice people too."

Gráinne smiled. "Thank you. You do have a hidden grace, I see."

Thorpe grunted.

"It's a compliment!" said Dr McKinnon. "Accept it!"

"It's such a nice day," Gráinne said, "I think we should open these windows. Though I fear they're a little stiff. Would you, Captain Thorpe?"

"Of course." He put his coffee down on the occasional table and stood up. With a slight effort, he had the French Windows open, and the outside breeze blew in with a refreshing tang of salt.

"Would you care to walk with me a while, Captain Thorpe?" she said.

Thorpe frowned. "Are the others not coming?"

Lady Gráinne smiled. "Just we two, for now. Would you?"

He nodded. "Of course."

They stepped through the French Windows and into the garden. Lady Gráinne led him through an orchard where there were stands of trees: apples, cherries and espaliered pears against the walls.

Thorpe gestured to the apple trees. "I should think these are beautiful when they're in blossom."

She smiled. "Yes, they are. But you've missed them this year."

They turned and walked down a gravel path along a terrace above the gardens.

"Have you seen Vivienne by the way?" he said as they walked.

Gráinne pursed her lips. "Vivienne?"

"My wife."

"I didn't know she was here."

Thorpe furrowed his brow. He stared at Lady Gráinne as if trying to see whether she was playing a joke on him. Finally, he said, "This is damned strange. She was at dinner yesterday, and you all spoke to her, and now I can't find her, and everyone says they haven't seen her."

Lady Gráinne gave a slight shrug. "As far as I knew, Captain Thorpe, you were on your own."

"No," he said, starting to become angry. "I was with Vivienne. If this is some kind of practical joke that you and she have cooked to teach me a lesson or something, then I must say I don't find it funny."

Gráinne was serious. "You were alone when we found you after your car crash. There was no one with you."

"That's absurd. Vivienne ate with us all last night. She slept in the same bed as me."

Gráinne shook her head. "I don't think so. Perhaps you should see Dr McKinnon again. You did have rather a bang to your head."

"That old quack? I don't think so. There's nothing wrong with my head, I can assure you."

Gráinne looked sympathetic. "People can act out of character after a head injury."

"Out of character?"

She kept on walking. "Or it can change their character. Sometimes people feel they are given a second chance after a serious accident—an opportunity to change."

They continued to walk. There was a silence, and then Thorpe said, "From your tone of voice, I think there's an implication in what you've just said. But I can't tell you what it is."

"Can't you?"

He shook his head.

She said, "I spoke to Màiri this morning."

"Ah."

"The maid."

"Yes, I know her."

Gráinne said, "The women of this castle are not here for your amusement, Captain Thorpe."

"Of course not." Thorpe frowned. In fact it was Màiri who had created the opportunity rather than him, but to say so would be ungallant, so he kept quiet.

Gráinne said, "I understand Màiri fell out with Muirdeach. Muirdeach is a ladies' man. She probably wanted to make him jealous."

"It's not for me to say."

"In any case, this matter is now closed, but I would be very displeased to hear of you abusing my hospitality again."

Thorpe stopped, about to defend himself, but he couldn't without casting a poor light on Màiri. Lady Gráinne seemed to think she was an innocent, and Thorpe didn't want to be responsible for damaging Màiri's reputation.

Lady Gráinne turned. "You are going to say something?"

Thorpe shook his head. "Nothing. Point taken. That's the end of it."

They came to the end of the terrace and stopped a while to take in the view. Gráinne seemed entranced by the scenery and stood in silence, admiring the mighty hills.

Thorpe was quiet. His cheeks were red.

After five minutes, Gráinne turned and offered her arm. "Would you lead me back? I want us to be friends."

"I just want to get my car fixed and be on my way."

"Without your wife?"

He frowned and rubbed his eyes. "You admit she is here then?"

Lady Gráinne said, "I'm sorry. I was teasing you. I shouldn't have. I know no one here called Vivienne."

He exhaled. "I assure you I am married and that she is here with me."

Gráinne pursed her lips. "It's important for you to make the correct moral decision."

"About Vivienne?"

"About everything. About how you deal with people."

"Women?"

"If you like." She continued. "People will make allowances for you. But there are only so many allowances anyone will make. Do you understand me?"

He didn't meet her gaze.

She said, "I don't think you're a bad man, Captain Thorpe. But it's not good for a man to always get his way; because then he doesn't know how to make difficult choices."

Thorpe cleared his throat. "A man gets his way if he has the strength and determination. I had it drummed into me at school and then in the Army."

"But the true knight mixes fearlessness and strength with compassion and mercy."

He snorted. "It sounds like the tales of King Arthur. I used to read those when I was a boy. Pity they're not real."

Gráinne said, "Let's go back to the others."

WHEN THEY GOT to the Castle's front door, a young woman emerged who Thorpe had not seen before. She wore a long cream dress, and her blonde hair was up. She was pretty, but she was not smiling.

"Oh, mother," she said.

"What is it, Fiona?" Gráinne said.

"Something terrible has happened. They've found Calum on the Terrace, near the Well."

"What do you mean?" Gráinne said, taking her daughter's hands in hers.

"He's taken very ill. I don't know what's the matter, but he's hardly moving, just muttering nonsense."

"Goodness me."

"Muirdeach found him. He hadn't turned up for work and wasn't in their lodgings. Muirdeach went looking for him when he'd finished serving coffee. Dr McKinnon's gone over. Will you come?"

"Of course." Gráinne paused. "This is Captain Thorpe, Fiona."

"The automobile accident man?" she said, hardly looking at him.

"Pleased to meet you." He gave her his hand. She shook it briefly. Thorpe said. "I'm sorry it has to be in this situation."

Fiona nodded but looked to Lady Gráinne. "Come with me, mother. It's awful."

Gráinne was halfway toward the door with her daughter. She turned and said to Thorpe, "Are you coming with us?"

"No," he said. "I'm going to search for Vivienne."

Lady Gráinne looked at him for a minute then turned away and went after Fiona.

Thorpe went back to his bedroom. He checked in the wardrobe and found her clothes were gone. Her perfume was gone. Her shoes were gone. There were no effects by the washstand to indicate she'd ever been there.

He put his head against the pillow where she'd laid her head the night before, but instead of her perfume or the scent of her flesh, he smelled only fresh linen.

He yanked out each drawer with increasing violence and found nothing: no sign of Vivienne at all.

And then on the dresser—he didn't know how he hadn't seen it before—was a folded note. The bronze statuette of Kali Mata sat on it like a paperweight.

He recognised Vivienne's handwriting as he pushed the bronze figure away and grabbed the note. He flicked it open. It said simply:

I warned you not to be unfaithful to me, or I would leave. The next time you are unfaithful, you will have to pay a heavy price.

Pay a price? What the hell did that mean? He knew what had happened. Vivienne had stomped off in a jealous rage: somebody had told her about Màiri, and that someone was probably Gráinne. And that after denying Vivienne even existed. They were at some game, he knew it, but he couldn't fathom why.

But Vivienne was gone. A sudden agony wracked Thorpe and he was pierced by an unfamiliar emotion so strange that he didn't even recognise it at first. What was it: Remorse, regret, anger? He knew anger—but anger wasn't it all or even most of it.

He dashed around the room thinking of new places to look and then searching places he'd already searched. Between his frantic turning over every paper and opening every drawer just in the hope they might contain a clue to where she was, he kept looking at the door, as if Vivienne might push it open and walk in, smiling.

If she did, they would have a row, and then it would all be all right again. He would apologise and say he'd never do it again. She would be his again and not gone. He recognised finally that the feeling rushing through him was panic — panic that she might be gone forever.

Not having anywhere else to look, he stepped out of the room. He hurried down the short corridor to the top of the staircase they'd descended together the previous night. He took the stairs two at a time, getting to the bottom as fast as he could, then he half-ran through the whole castle. He rushed from the Drawing Room to the Dining Room, to the Library and to the Orangery.

Pulling open a heavy door, he found an unfamiliar room. It was a chapel. The room was quiet and cool with the air of damp and musty books. On the altar stood a strange symbol. He had presumed that the Lord and Lady were Roman Catholics, as many of the old Highland families were. But this was not a crucifix bearing the figure of Jesus. Instead, it was a slate slab with three women carved into it. The women were blank-faced with lentil-shaped eyes and lines for mouths. The carving looked ancient, and it looked primitive.

Thorpe stared at the image, then left, hurrying on in his search for Vivienne.

He stalked down the great hall flanked by classical statues, his feet echoing on the wooden floor. Despair flooded him. He could not see Vivienne; he could not hear her; he could not touch her; he could not smell her. She was gone.

Finally, Thorpe leaned on his arms against the wall and dropped his head. Whatever they said, he knew Vivienne had been with him. Then he'd done that stupid thing with the maid, and now she'd left him. When would he ever learn? When would he ever stop running after women? It wasn't love that made him do it, it wasn't even lust, it was always to prove he could, to collect women like beads on a string.

He stood upright and slowly walked on until, in a daze, he found himself back in the Drawing Room.

He slumped into one of the chairs and stared through the open French Windows. He felt the sea breeze on his cheeks. The sea tang mixed with that of honeysuckle and roses as the summer day drifted towards noon. He lost track of time. It was as if his grief had emptied him out.

He did not notice Lord Eachann enter and he started as Eachann put his hand on the top of his chair. "A wonderful view," Eachann said. "I never tire of it."

"No. It is lovely," Thorpe's mouth was dry.

Eachann walked over to the chair nearest to Thorpe's and turned it so that he too faced the open doors. Thorpe noticed Eachann walking with a limp. He remembered that Dr McKinnon was Lord Eachann's personal physician. The old man was either a hypochondriac or the injury was serious and long-standing.

They sat in silence for a while, Eachann gazing out. Thorpe saw him looking past the cultivated castle terrace, past the rocky green fields of sheep and cattle, until his eyes seemed to rest at last on the sparkling sliver of the sea.

Thorpe covered his eyes with his hand.

"You seem troubled," said Eachann finally, without turning his head.

"My wife."

"Ah."

Thorpe started. "You remember her?"

Eachann shook his head. "I haven't had the pleasure of meeting your wife. I'd presumed you'd left her in London. Though to be honest, in Who's Who, it doesn't mention you're married."

"Ah yes, you looked me up. Don't you remember her commenting on my war record when you raised it at dinner last night?"

Eachann said, "I'm sorry I don't. This is all probably the injury. Do you think perhaps you left your wife in London? We can send a telegram."

"No, she's not in London."

"You seem very certain of that."

Thorpe put his head in his hands. "Vivienne was at dinner last night here at Dungarvan Castle."

Eachann shook his head, still without looking at Thorpe. "No, I fear not. At dinner were myself, Lady Gráinne, Dr McKinnon, young Alastair and yourself. That is all. My daughter Fiona only came back from Edinburgh today."

Thorpe remembered suddenly. He patted his jacket pocket. "I have a note." He reached into the pocket where he'd put it.

"You have a note?" Eachann said.

"Yes." Thorpe rummaged through his pockets, but even though he turned them all out, there was no note.

Eachann looked sadly on.

Thorpe snapped. "She was here."

Eachann went back to staring out of the French Windows. "Perhaps you saw the ghost."

"She's no ghost. Vivienne is as real as you or me."

Eachann said, "But there is a ghost, you know. This castle is haunted by the spirit of a woman."

Thorpe said sharply. "I know my own wife."

Eachann said, "I'll ask Dr McKinnon to take a better look at you."

"She was here."

"I don't mean to offend you, but what do you remember about her?"

"What do I remember? Everything. Her smell, the way she walks, the colour of her eyes. Her voice. Her black hair. Everything."

Eachann ran a finger over his bottom lip. "Your black-haired wife?"

"Yes, black-hair with hazel eyes."

"She sounds pretty. Do you love her very much—this wife of yours?"

"Yes. I do love her." He paused. "I don't always show it, but I'm not demonstrative; that's not my way."

"Does she know you love her?"

"Of course she knows I love her."

Eachann said thoughtfully, "Perhaps it's lucky she didn't come with you. That accident was very serious. If she'd been with you in that car, she could have been killed. So could you in fact."

"I'm fine. I haven't come to any harm."

Eachann looked at him for a second, then said, "Would you care for a whisky? From the local distillery? I know it's early but what with poor Calum, I think I need one."

Thorpe rubbed his eyes. "Thank you. That's very kind."

Eachann stood, his limp evident. "The servants are all busy. I'll fetch it myself."

Eachann came back with a bottle and two crystal glasses. He

poured a good measure of the golden liquid for Thorpe who took a mouthful and felt the soft burn of the old whisky settle on his mouth and throat.

Whisky poured, Eachann sat. "Tell me, and I don't mean to be rude, but where were you married?"

"Where were we married?" asked Thorpe. He sat in silence as the grandfather clock ticked the minutes by. "Where were we married...?" He forced a laugh. "Mysore? Ooty? Surrey?" He took another sip of whisky. "Ask me another."

"Very well—where are her people from?"

Thorpe shrugged. "London, I think. Or Surrey. I don't think I've ever met them."

"You haven't met your father and mother-in-law?"

Thorpe smiled without any humour. "It seems odd when you put it like that, but I don't think I have."

"They can't have been at the wedding then."

"No, I suppose not." He sat forward. "It was in Ooty—in St Andrew's Church. They were in England. They couldn't make it."

"Couldn't you wait for them?"

"No, we couldn't."

"Do you remember why not?"

Thorpe rubbed his forehead. He took a sip of whisky. "No. I can't."

Eachann said, "Does she have brothers and sisters?"

Thorpe shook his head. "I don't think so."

"What's her favourite colour?"

Thorpe smiled. "Ah, I know that—gold. She loves gold: golden flecks in the gravel of a clear mountain stream."

Eachann pursed his lips.

"You ask a lot of questions," Thorpe said.

Eachann laughed.

The door opened, and the young blonde woman entered.

"Ah, Fiona. This is Captain Thorpe."

"I know, Daddy. We met earlier."

"Father," said Fiona. "Dr McKinnon is with Calum. He's still making no sense, but he seems to be out of danger. The doctor wants to see you about him."

Eachann rose stiffly from his seat. "Very well. I won't be long. Will you entertain Captain Thorpe in my absence?"

"Of course." She smiled. "Could I have a whisky too?"

"It's not really a lady's drink. Your mother wouldn't approve."

Fiona winked. "Don't tell her then, pop."

Eachann grinned. "Oh, Fiona, you are incorrigible." He waved at the bottle. "Help yourself."

Eachann walked out of the room, using his stick.

"Terrible about the boy," Thorpe said.

"Goodness, I know. I grew up with him. He is a bit of a philanderer, but he has a good heart really." Her eyes were red, and it was apparent she'd been upset. She had taken her father's whisky glass. Her hand trembled slightly.

Silence ensued. Then Thorpe said, "So, you've just come back from Edinburgh?"

"I was staying with friends. I need to get away from Dungarvan sometimes—beautiful as it is." She took a sip of whisky. "There's just something about the atmosphere that's too heady."

"Must be the ghost," Thorpe said.

Fiona raised her eyebrows. "You're a believer?"

"Not really."

"But you know the story."

"Only that there's supposed to be a ghost."

Fiona said, "Alastair has a theory that the ghost is an old Celtic mother goddess. There's a cave in the grounds with a well that's called *Tobar na Màthar*: the Well of the Mothers, not just any old mothers either—the divine feminine."

"Not really my thing, mythology."

After a silence, Fiona said, "I understand you've not been well either."

"No, I'm fine."

"Oh, I thought my mother said..."

"What?"

Fiona laughed. "You'd had some funny ideas—you'd been seeing things."

"My wife? Or as you all here would have it—my hallucination?"

Fiona gave an awkward grin. "Some of the best people are crazy."

"You're very forthright," Thorpe said.

"I didn't mean to be insensitive. It must seem terribly real. I've read about such things."

"Vivienne isn't a hallucination. She's real. I just don't know where she is. Perhaps the bang on my head did make me a little confused, but the woman I love is real."

"Of course. Sorry." Fiona stood up and knocked back her whisky. "I'm going to find my father and mother, but afterwards, do you fancy a little walk after lunch? Up Beinn a' Choire?"

"Up what?"

"The mountain behind the castle. Not the biggest. But it's a nice walk and a lovely view from the top."

"Yes, I'll come. I have nothing else to do."

* * *

After lunch, Thorpe met Fiona on the terrace. She had changed into clothes more suitable for hiking—a white shirt, trousers and sturdy boots. He had walking clothes amongst his things and had pulled them on to come down and meet her for the walk. Fiona had a backpack, and she handed him a stout walking stick. He took it and waved it around.

"It's not a sword!"

Thorpe laughed.

Fiona looked at the ridge line in the summer sun. "Not too hot—just pleasant."

They set off through the castle garden, and out by an almost hidden wooden gate. From then, it was a walk across the fields until the path started to rise. Ahead of them was the mountain called Beinn a' Choire. There were white clouds high up, and the sky was full of swallows, swooping and chattering as they flew.

She walked well.

"I noticed your father has a limp," said Thorpe as they started to climb.

Fiona called back over her shoulder. "Yes, he was wounded in the South African War at Mujaba Hill by a sniper."

"Lucky he wasn't killed. What outfit was he with?"

"The Gordon Highlanders."

They were climbing the first steep slopes of the mountain now, coming out of the bracken and into the heather. Next month he guessed the heather would bloom in a glorious sea of purple all over the mountain's flanks. It would be quite nice to see that.

Thorpe got into the lead so that he could help Fiona up the craggier parts, extending his hand. At first, she hesitated as if wary of him, and he wondered whether her mother had told her about Màiri. But then she took his hand, and he pulled her up.

"Nice view even though we're not at the top!" she said, shielding her eyes from the sun. Thorpe admired her shining blond hair, her smooth young skin and the curve of her bosom. He liked how she sucked her bottom lip while climbing as if she were concentrating on where to place her feet. She started going up again without waiting for him. She was a few steps ahead now, so he hurried to catch her and then, without it being too obvious, place himself in the lead once again.

"Not married then?" he said, out of breath.

She laughed, panting too. "Nearly. Lucky escape really."

"Oh?"

"He was an advocate. Very well connected. We almost got engaged, and then he broke it off."

"Foolish man," said Thorpe, now in front, helping her up a scramble of rock.

She grinned. "He said I was too opinionated. But he didn't really want someone like me. He wanted a maid and a mother for his beautiful children to be and someone to impress his friends."

"I'm sure you'd do that."

"How gallant you are Captain Thorpe." She flashed a smile at him. "Trouble is I can't keep quiet if someone says something foolish."

"That's a good quality, in my opinion. At least—"

" —'in a man', were you going to add?"

Thorpe shook his head. "I was going to say 'at least if you don't mind not being liked.'"

"No, I don't mind not being liked. I prefer to do the right thing rather than keep people happy all the time.

Thorpe said, "Did you bring some water? I'm parched."

"I have both water and whisky."

"Water, please. Whisky will dehydrate us."

"Goodness me, I thought you were the wild man, and you're worried about your health."

He blushed. Then he said, "Somewhere like this looks kind in the sunshine, but if the weather turns, it can turn nasty."

"These are my mountains," Fiona said. "I know them well. But you are right. Even so, when we get to the top, I am planning on a dram."

Thorpe looked around. The weather looked fixed to stay fair. "We'll probably be fine."

"Thanks for letting me know. Now, you've reassured me, I can relax."

Thorpe checked to see whether she was teasing him. She handed him the water bottle and took out a silver hip flask herself. "Think I'll have a nip now."

"You shouldn't, not yet anyway."

She uncorked the hip flask. "I told you I don't take advice well."

They both laughed.

Thorpe said, "Neither do I. I've been accused of being pig-headed, as well as self-centred."

She sipped the whisky, corked the flask again then took back the water bottle from Thorpe and put it in her pack. "I don't think you can be so very self-centred," she said.

"How's that then?"

"Well, what you did in the War—the medal—cleaning out the machine gun nest. My mother told me."

He looked at her, trying to work out whether she was flattering him. He couldn't gauge her so decided to take her at her word. He said, "People say I did it for the glory. But that's not true."

"You did it to save your men."

"I honestly didn't even think of what I was doing. It was just my duty. But as I say, some people don't take to me."

"They don't take to you?" she was smiling. Thorpe didn't know how to respond.

They continued up a craggy face of scree, picking their way through the broken rock.

"I hope Calum's going to be all right," she said.

"Any idea what happened yet?"

"The gossip is that it's punishment because he got a girl pregnant in the next village and wouldn't stand by her. They say the girl asked the wise woman to cast a spell on him."

"A wise woman? Like a witch?"

"A '*cailleach*' they call them in Gaelic."

Thorpe snorted. "But what really happened?"

"No one knows. He's gone back to his parents' croft to recuperate."

They were walking across the shoulder of the mountain now. From this high, they saw the ocean sparkling down to the west. Dungarvan Castle nestled below them between the arms of the mountain, cut off from the road by a dark wood.

"No one would know the castle was there," he said.

"We're very secluded. That's why it's nice to get visitors—even by accident."

"And what an accident!"

The grass opened, as a viper curled out of the heather and raised its head to strike Fiona's leg. Thorpe hurled his walking stick, and it hit the snake, which recoiled but then reared again. He grabbed Fiona's arm and yanked her out of the way of the serpent's strike. He snatched his stick and clubbed at the snake but missed it. The beast thought better of the fight and slithered away into the undergrowth.

Fiona was breathing heavily. Thorpe felt her pulse in the wrist he still gripped tight.

She clung onto him. "Oh my God," she said, shaking. "Thank you."

He let her go. "You're welcome. I wouldn't have liked to have had to carry you all the way down."

She laughed. "I'm not sure Dr McKinnon is such a whizz with snakebites either." Then her expression changed and softened.

"What is it?" he said frowning.

"Just that I'm enjoying your company."

"Are you surprised? Didn't you expect to?"

"Daddy told me to entertain you. He thought you were bored."

"He thinks I'm mad."

She said, "Not as such."

"Not as such? What then?"

"He thinks you're bewitched too."

"Bewitched? Seriously?"

She nodded. "He is a Highlander after all. And he's married to my mother."

"She's a formidable woman."

Fiona laughed. "Indeed, and I hope I take after her."

"I think you do. Anyway, I'm glad you took him up on his offer of entertaining me."

"So am I. But I felt wary."

"Why?"

She gave him a strange look. "Because you're a bad man."

"You just said I was a good man."

"I mean you are a heroic good man, but I think you're a bad man with women."

His mouth tightened. "Did your mother tell you that?"

"Yes, but I'd know anyway. I know your type."

"Ah," he said. "My type."

"There's no point being offended," she said. "You either like being like that, or you change the way you are."

"A leopard can't change its spots," he said.

"You're not a leopard."

They carried on climbing, and the path became steeper. The fresh mountain air cheered them both. In some places, they had to scramble up rock staircases. Then they waded or skipped over the clear mountain burns using rocks as stepping stones. The mountain was deceiving. They thought they saw the summit ahead, but when they crested each ridge, they saw another in front of them. They were sweating and out of breath as they finally reached the cairn on the top.

It was very high, and Thorpe stood there, enjoying the vast expanse of mountains and sea and islands. "What a place!" he said.

Fiona lay down on a large flat rock. "I need a rest," she said.

He looked around for somewhere to sit. He said, "You've got the best rock. The rest are all sharp."

She patted the rock beside her. "There's enough room here. Come on. I won't bite."

"Unlike the viper."

"Yes, thank you again for my rescue, Captain Thorpe."

"You're very welcome."

He regarded her, wondering what her invitation meant. She looked pretty sitting there, and it had never been in his nature to look a gift horse in the mouth. He went and sat down close to her. The stone was wide and flat, after a moment's hesitation, he lay. The stone was warm under Thorpe's back. He gazed at the blue sky overhead and then looked down to the mountains stretching on either side of the glen and all the way down to the glittering sea. There was a slight breeze that ruffled Fiona's hair as she sat gazing silently over the sea. Thorpe smelled the heather and the peat and heard the staccato call of a peregrine falcon as it made its way home to its nest in the crags that fell steeply away to the east.

"More water?" Fiona said.

"I'll try a whisky now," he said.

She reached and got the hip flask, which she handed to him. "You see—you did take my advice eventually."

He took a mouthful, got a mouthful of the burning spirit and handed the flask back to her. He turned and looked at her, propping his head on his arm. He was alone with a beautiful woman, and one who was giving him signals that she didn't mind being alone with him.

"I have more goodies," she said. "Here." She delved into her backpack and pulled out a loaf of bread." Fresh-baked at the castle this morning."

"Very nice!"

"And..." She rummaged further in the bag and came out with a lump of cheese. "Highland cheese from our home farm."

He laughed. "A veritable feast. No cutlery? Do we just rip lumps off them like savages?"

She flashed a smile and from her belt, pulled a black-handled knife. He hadn't noticed it before. "I have my *sgian dubh*!"

"Your skiing what?"

She prodded him with a finger. "You know so little about our Highland ways. All good Highlanders carry the 'black knife.'"

"Even the Highland women?"

"This Highland woman does. I can't speak for the others." She cut him a portion of bread and cheese. The meal was simple but good. He ate, staring at the sea. Then he watched her eat.

"What are you looking at?" she said.

"You."

"Oh?"

"I was thinking about how beautiful you are."

She grinned. "Lots of people tell me that, so it must be true."

"How immodest of you, though honest," he said but smiled. "I admire that."

"Anything could happen up here," she said.

"Could it?"

She shrugged.

"You hardly know me," he said. "Do you feel safe?"

"I feel as safe as I want to be."

She was lovely: bright and bold and beautiful.

She turned and looked at him; her eyes different hues of blue like a stained glass window. "I always seem to get involved with men who aren't good for me," she said.

He glanced away. "I'd like to be good for a woman. I got myself a bit of a reputation in India. It was too easy, all the bored wives. You can imagine."

"And none of them stole your heart."

He shook his head.

"Until your wife, Vivienne, of course."

He nodded. "Until Vivienne."

'So, despite you being that kind of man, I'm safe from your

advances?" She was lying on her side, head propped on her arm. She was looking at him, half-teasing, but half-serious.

He flushed. "But whatever they say I was, I would never force myself on a woman."

"Of course not," she said. Still, she looked at him. "And, in any case, there's Vivienne."

"Yes, there's Vivienne."

THAT NIGHT, at dinner, they talked about dogs and fishing and after they'd eaten, they retired to the Drawing Room. Thorpe sat in a leather chair drinking malt whisky. The room was warm from the blazing log fire.

The grand piano stood towards the window, and a gilt candelabra with four candles burned on top of it. Seated on the stool, Fiona prepared to play. As Thorpe listened, the gentle notes of Debussy's *Clair de Lune* arose and rolled through the room. Fiona played well.

Lady Gráinne watched her daughter. She drank red wine, and Lord Eachann sipped his whisky while he too gazed adoringly at his talented girl.

When Fiona finished Clair de Lune, the audience gave a ripple of applause. Then Alastair stood to give a rendition of the Highland Lament, *Cha Till Mac Cruimein.*

He glanced at Fiona, who sat ready to accompany him. Lord Eachann smiled indulgently at the two of them.

"This is a song about the famous piper Dòmhnall Bàn Mac Cruimein who was killed in the 1745 rebellion."

Alastair's voice was light but carried with it all the grief of the clansmen who lamented the death of their piper in that long-ago war.

Cha till, cha till, cha till Mac Cruimein
An cogadh no sìth cha till e tuille

It was a song of war and honour. Thorpe's eyes moistened with his own memories, and he took a gulp of whisky and blinked the grief away. He was embarrassed at his tears, and extinguished them with the heel of his hand.

After he finished singing, Alastair translated the song. "Basically, it says that MacCrimmon would not return ever to the mountains and farms of his people. Neither in war nor in peace, he would return nevermore."

"I'm sorry," said Thorpe, softened by the wine and whisky he'd drunk.

"What for?" said Alastair, genuinely puzzled.

"You know—for the wrongs my people did here."

Eachann said, "Not your people; it was all governments and politics. Not your fault, Captain Thorpe."

"In fact, MacCrimmon and his Lord MacLeod were fighting for the British government," Lady Gráinne said.

Thorpe laughed. "Really? Even more complicated then."

Lady Gráinne said, "Situations aren't always what you first think them to be, Captain Thorpe."

The absurd idea that he was here at Dungarvan to prove himself in some way came into his mind. Then he dismissed it. This strange feeling of guilt and unease arose from the whisky and the car accident. That was all. He would feel better soon.

Eachann came to sit in the leather chair beside Thorpe, a crystal decanter of whisky in his hand. "Would you like another dram?"

Thorpe said, "Why not?"

Eachann poured a generous measure. As they drank, Eachann

indicated with his glass. "They're a lovely couple, don't you think?"

Thorpe followed where he was pointing. "Those two?"

"Yes, Alastair and Fiona. They grew up together. His father was my solicitor, but he died young, and I took Alastair under my wing. In the past, Fiona's taken it into her head to run around with different kinds of men, but she needs a kinder soul—a man with a soft heart like Alastair's."

Thorpe shrugged. "Depends on what she wants."

"I think if she runs after a soldier, she'll regret it."

"You were a soldier, weren't you?" Thorpe said.

"I was."

"So you don't want her to have a man like you?"

Eachann laughed softly. "No. That's my point. They would quarrel all the time. She's too strong-willed to have a man equally as strong-willed."

Thorpe smiled. "So, she would dominate Alastair, tell him what to do all the time. Is that what you want for her?"

"Better that than he dominates her."

Thorpe drained his glass, then stood. "I'm tired. I think I'll retire to bed."

As he stood, Dr McKinnon said, "I hope you sleep well." He'd probably been eavesdropping.

"I hope you don't dream too much. This place is famous for making people dream," Lord Eachann said.

Thorpe nodded. "Thanks for the meal, Lady Gráinne." He bowed toward Fiona and Alastair. "And for the music."

"You're very welcome, Captain Thorpe," said Gráinne. "Sleep well."

As he went out past the piano, Fiona caught his fingers. "William," she said. "I enjoyed our walk today. Perhaps we could do another tomorrow. Or go down to the sea in the horse and trap?"

"Yes, I'd like that," he said.

She dropped his hand and smiled.

Thorpe saw Gráinne look at her husband and raise her eyebrows. Eachann took a puff of his pipe and shook his head.

As he left the room, the last thing Thorpe saw was Alastair gazing doe-eyed at Fiona.

Ah, that's it then, he thought.

* * *

Once in bed, Thorpe slipped into a deep sleep, but somewhere in the middle of the night, he stirred. He felt Vivienne come into the room. He knew it was her because he smelled her scent and heard her bare feet on the wooden floor. Thorpe sat up in bed and looked around the darkened room. The bed was warm beside him as if someone had been lying there. Vivienne wasn't in the room, but he still smelled her lingering scent.

Her laughter came from outside the door. He was so convinced it was her laughing that he swung his legs out of bed and pulled on the dressing gown he'd been lent. Moonlight pooled in through the window, but everything else was draped in deep shadow.

Thorpe fumbled for a match and from that lit the candle. By candlelight, he opened the door of the bedroom and went out onto the landing. No one was there either.

He saw from his wristwatch that it was 3 am. The house sat in profound silence. He walked to the top of the wooden staircase. There was still no one. He couldn't even hear the wind outside. The whole castle seemed asleep.

He was about to go back to bed, thinking he had indeed dreamt Vivienne's return when he heard voices. He stepped down the stairs, one tread at a time. Her laughter rose up the stairwell. It was her, he was sure of it. And she was with someone else.

He was stealthy so he would catch Vivienne and whoever was there with her. He heard them laughing. He heard Vivienne's voice again, and a low, lustful moan. He stopped. He thought his heart would burst with anger and grief. The sound made him nauseous. There was no doubt it was the sound of a woman in pleasure. There was a man's voice too. The man laughed softly, and Vivienne cried out again.

He hurried down the stairs and turned down the corridor. He didn't care about being quiet now. He wanted to confront them. She was his wife. Whoever this man was, he would fight him for Vivienne.

Thorpe came to the long corridor that led to the library. At the end of it, he saw a dark-haired woman, leaning back against the wall with her dress hem around her waist. Her pale thighs were wrapped around the legs of a man whose trousers were round his ankles. She looked when she saw Thorpe's candle, and Thorpe recognised her dark beauty.

"Vivienne!" he yelled and ran to them. The woman broke away from her lover and, hooting with laughter, opened the door into the library and ran through it. The man hitched up his trousers as he went. Thorpe saw only the back of the man's head, but he was sure it was Muirdeach.

By the time Thorpe reached the end of the corridor and followed them into the library, they were gone.

Nothing stirred. There was only the silence of the dark leather-bound books in their shelves. His candle fluttered and threw shadows that made it seem that people were hiding behind the shelves. He searched, but there was no one.

In despair, he shouted out. "Vivienne! Come back to me! I love you."

His voice died away. The shadows the candle cast danced and shifted. The place seemed to listen as if the castle was keen to know the next scene in this unfolding drama. It was like he was in a play, not in reality at all.

The atmosphere was so odd and dreamlike that Thorpe

wasn't sure whether he was fully awake. Was it really the blow to the head that made him think he saw Vivienne?

He walked back to his room. Vivienne had not returned there either. But what was there was the small statue of Kali Mata, sitting on Vivienne's dressing table. He knew he'd put it in the drawer and no servant would have taken it out. It was Vivienne who'd taken out the Indian goddess of karma. It was meant as a sign for him.

Thorpe didn't sleep. He watched just in case Vivienne returned. After long hours, the early dawn lightened the sky with grey. Then the sunrise slowly flooded the room with warm yellow. The growing light revealed the patina of the wooden floor. The warm rays highlighted the motes of dust swirling in the air. The yellow beams picked out the gold and blue of his borrowed dressing gown that hung over the back of the chair where he'd thrown it. Doves started cooing outside his window.

But Vivienne did not come back. He wondered whether he'd dreamed her completely. He even wondered whether he'd left her in India, whether she'd ever existed. All the details of his life swam together like goldfish in castle's pond and everything that happened before the accident was vague. He wasn't sure what he remembered anymore.

Seven

DR MCKINNON WAS ALREADY in the Dining Room at breakfast. "Good morning, Captain," he said as he bent over his kippers and the morning sun shone equally on his silver fish knife and his shiny forehead.

"Good morning, Doctor," Thorpe replied and then turned to Muirdeach to ask for bacon and eggs.

How smug Muirdeach looked standing there. Thorpe scowled and went to sit. Around ten minutes later, Màiri brought his breakfast, though she avoided his eye and gave a brief nod to his greeting.

"How's your patient?" Thorpe asked McKinnon sitting opposite.

"Calum? Back home with his parents. He's somewhat better but has not recovered his senses. He's quite delirious; keeps talking about a woman with eyes like a snake."

"Poor man," said Thorpe. "I hope he gets better soon." He poured himself tea from the antique silver teapot. After a minute, he said, "I saw my wife last night."

"Oh," said McKinnon, obviously embarrassed.

"It's all right. I know you don't believe me."

"It's not that..." blustered the doctor, still not meeting Thorpe's eye. "There are just other explanations for what we sometimes think we see."

Thorpe nodded, accepting but not agreeing what McKinnon said. He bit some bacon. "Lord Eachann said he was going to ask you to examine my head."

McKinnon nodded wisely. "He did mention something of the sort to me. But really, there's very little I can do. You have no obvious injuries, and I think if you had a contusion on your brain, you would be a lot more ill than you are. For example, I would expect your balance to be off and your cognitions disturbed."

"My cognitions disturbed?"

"Yes, you would have lost contact with reality."

Thorpe met McKinnon's eyes. "So you don't think I'm crazy?"

McKinnon looked embarrassed and took a fishbone from his mouth with the flat of his knife. "Psychiatry is not my field."

"She was with Muirdeach."

McKinnon raised his eyebrows. "Who was?"

"They were outside the library."

"Who? Your wife?"

"He was making love to her."

"Come now. You shouldn't be slandering the poor man."

"I'm sure it was him with Vivienne."

"And when was this?"

"In the middle of the night."

"Are you sure? It seems unlikely."

"I'm sure."

They didn't speak any more about it. Thorpe waited until McKinnon had gone and he was alone with Muirdeach. He stood and went over to the servant.

"You don't have the guilty air of an adulterer, I'll give you that," said Thorpe.

"I'm sorry, sir?"

"Do you know my wife?"

Muirdeach looked puzzled. "I didn't know you had a wife, sir."

"You met her the other night when she came with me to look at the car. You said it would take a week to get fixed."

Muirdeach shook his head. "No, sir. You were on your own."

"You damned-well smiled at her. Then you flirted with her at dinner. That's why Màiri was angry with you."

Muirdeach held his tongue.

"I tell you, I saw you last night - with my wife."

Muirdeach stared down the breakfast room, ignoring Thorpe. He looked as if he wanted to leave, but couldn't.

"Outside the Library at about 3 am," continued Thorpe.

"Not me. I was fast asleep."

"I saw you. At least I saw the back of your head."

"I'm afraid you must be mistaken, sir."

Thorpe went and perched on the edge of a heavy wooden table, still between Muirdeach and the door. He pushed a Chinese jade elephant out of the way so he could sit. "Well if it wasn't you; who was it? It looked like you."

Muirdeach said, "I've never met your wife."

"Vivienne. I saw how you looked at her the first night. The way all men look at her."

"I'm sorry, sir, but I've never met your wife."

Thorpe raised a warning finger. "If I catch you with her; I swear I'll kill you. She would eat a man like you for breakfast. She's clever as a snake—you wouldn't stand a chance against her, you Highland peasant."

Muirdeach's jaw clenched.

Thorpe turned and walked out of the breakfast room. He stalked the long corridor towards the Baronial Hall, marching as if he had somewhere to be. Or, as if he was looking for someone, but now he didn't expect to find Vivienne. She had retreated from him. He found himself outside and went and sat on one of the stone benches in the Rose Garden.

He lit a cigarette, taking three attempts because he couldn't hold his lighter steady. And then he breathed out smoke as the bees and hover-flies went around their business with the roses. Ants crawled over the stone flagstones in a line carrying the body of a bumblebee back to their nest. He lost track of time. He was there almost an hour, maybe more.

Not knowing what do to with Vivienne gone, not knowing what to believe and why they would lie to him, he decided to check on his car. The sun was still not at its zenith, but it was hot. He stood in the shadow of the high box hedge and wiped the sweat from his brow with the back of his left hand. He had a cigarette held in his right.

He smelled the horses and heard them stamp and turn in their dark stalls. The converted stable that Muirdeach used as his makeshift mechanic's shop was past these stables. Thorpe heard Muirdeach's voice before he saw him. It was nearly an hour since breakfast finished and the mechanic was back at his other job. Muirdeach was telling someone an amusing story, and a woman was laughing. At first, Thorpe thought Màiri had gone back to him. That's what happened, lovers tiffs were soon mended. Poor Màiri. She had spirit. What was she doing making up with this faithless lout?

But then he slowed. He heard the woman's voice clearly. They were speaking English, not Gaelic. And the woman had a well-spoken English accent. It wasn't Màiri—it was Vivienne. He balled his fists and stepped out of the shadow into the stable. But only Muirdeach was there. He wasn't bent over the car. Instead, the mechanic was standing by the door as if he'd just said goodbye to someone.

He looked at Thorpe. "You again. Why don't you leave me alone? I have work to do."

Muirdeach looked pleased with himself. He must think he had the better of Thorpe, that he'd cuckolded him. Thorpe had forced many husbands to wear the horns of the cuckold, but he'd never felt that raw betrayal himself.

Thorpe gripped the wooden post by the stable door to steady himself—damn Vivienne for making him feel so weak.

Muirdeach looked at him with his steady, confident gaze. "Are you well?" the mechanic said.

Thorpe tried to steady himself. "I've come about the car." No, it was Vivienne. He heard her. She was real.

Muirdeach nodded. "I guessed."

"How long now?" Thorpe asked. He struggled to focus. He kept imagining Vivienne was outside the stable, peering in, mocking him. His forehead broke out in a rash of sweat.

Oblivious to Thorpe's inner turmoil, Muirdeach nodded. "As I said before—it will be a week."

Thorpe stammered, "Was Màiri here just now?"

Muirdeach shook his head.

"Who was the woman you were talking to?"

"A woman? No woman here."

"Don't lie to me. I heard you as I was walking up."

"I was talking to one of the horses earlier. Maybe that's what you heard."

Thorpe's mouth twisted. "I'm not a fool. I know she was here."

"I don't know what you're talking about, sir." He said the last word with an emphasis to make it sound like a sneer.

"I know your type," said Thorpe.

"And what type is that?" said Muirdeach, putting down his spanner and wiping his hand with the oily cloth.

Thorpe said, "I know your every trick. I know your every little insincere compliment and every little way you wheedle your way into a woman's affections."

Muirdeach laughed. "I think you're losing your mind, sir."

Thorpe turned. The world span round. He felt off-balance, and his mouth was dry. He loosened his tie and stepped out of the stable into the cooler air.

Muirdeach watched him as he walked away. When he'd got about ten yards, Thorpe stopped and said, "You treat Màiri well. She deserves better than you."

Muirdeach said, "Màiri knows what I'm like, and she doesn't mind."

Thorpe stood, supporting himself on a stone wall. After ten minutes, he was steady enough to go back to the castle. Though when he got there, he had no idea what he would do.

Thorpe was walking by the high grey walls of the west side, when Fiona and Gráinne appeared, walking down the gravel path from the vegetable garden back to the castle.

"Hello you," said Fiona. "I was wondering where you got to."

"Nowhere much," said Thorpe.

"Are you all right, William?" Fiona said.

"You sound glum," Gráinne said.

"Been to see the car. It's a long way off being fixed."

"That's good—it means you'll be our guest for longer," Fiona said.

Thorpe looked at her, squinting in the sun. She looked radiant, her tanned skin brought out the blue of her eyes.

"Captain Thorpe looks bored," said Gráinne. "You should entertain him, Fiona."

"Everyone thinks I'm bored."

Fiona said, "Well, we could play tennis. Do you play?"

"A little," he said.

"Let's have a match before lunch."

"I have no suitable kit."

"You can borrow some shorts from Alastair, I'm sure."

"Ah, Alastair," said Thorpe.

"He won't mind lending you something. He's a lovely chap. Very kind. Well-meaning." said Fiona.

Gráinne just looked at them both and said nothing.

"I'll ask someone to bring them up to your room," said Fiona.

"Not Murdo."

"Oh. You don't like Muirdeach? Someone else then. How about an hour? After tennis, we can have lunch."

"I will just be a minute here. I'll make my way back shortly," said Thorpe.

Lady Gráinne studied him. "You don't look well, William. Are you quite yourself?"

Thorpe nodded. "I'm fine. Not used to your whisky." He forced a grin.

Fiona said, "Fine. See you later. You know where the tennis court is?"

"I'll find it."

"It's easy," said Fiona.

Lady Gráinne said," Come on, Fiona. I want to get some flowers for the Drawing Room."

The two women walked off. Thorpe watched them go. Before they turned the corner and went out of sight, Fiona looked back over her shoulder. She smiled, and he smiled back. When she'd gone, he shook his head and sighed.

Thorpe went up to his bedroom. He found the tennis shirt and shorts laid out on the bed for him. He dressed in them, and as he opened his door, he saw Màiri coming along the landing. She looked down. He felt himself redden but said, "Hello."

She didn't speak at first. As they passed, he said, "I know it was jealousy and rather hot-headed of me, but..."

She said, "You didn't force me."

"I was just enraged about Vivienne and Muirdeach flirting."

Màiri looked concerned. "Who is Vivienne?"

"My wife. We spoke of her last night. You were angry with Muirdeach because he paid her too much attention when he was serving her at dinner."

Màiri shook her head. "No, I was angry because of him going with that Cameron lass."

"No, it was Vivienne; we spoke about her. You served her soup at dinner last night."

Màiri said, "You were not with your wife at dinner last night. You were on your own. You have no wife here."

Thorpe sat heavily on the bed, crumpling the tennis shirt. He had his head in his hands. 'What on earth is going on here? What trick are you all trying to play on me?"

Màiri came over. "I am sorry for you, Captain Thorpe. I think you are under the spell of the *bean sìth*."

Then he saw that she was carrying white flowers. The flowers had long shiny leaves of dark green with white flower heads in bunches. They were pungent.

"What are those?" he said.

"Garlic."

"Oh. Bit smelly."

"I was going to put them up at your window."

He frowned. "Why?"

"For protection."

He raised an eyebrow. "Protection? From whom?"

Màiri didn't meet his eye. "The spirit of a woman haunts the castle. Something has woken her. All men are at risk from her. She's taken Calum. Garlic and iron will keep her away."

"Is this the woman of the story that Alastair told—the so-called Lady of the Fountain?"

Màiri said, "She ha other names."

Thorpe said, "So you really believe in these legends?"

"I do. We all do. They come again and again. Dungarvan is a place where the story must repeat itself time and again."

Thorpe glanced over at the statuette of Kali Mata. Like a bad joke, she sat again on the dresser.

Thorpe said, "So, this Lady of the Fountain doesn't like men."

Màiri shook her head. "The *bean sìth* likes men well enough. But she also punishes them. She told her husband Eachann Dubh never to be unfaithful to her. If he did, he would pay a heavy price."

"If that means what I think it does, it sounds unpleasant."

She gave a laugh. "I think it was meant to be."

"So if he knew he would be punished like that, why did he do it?"

"He was a man, and men can't help themselves."

Thorpe remembered himself and Màiri and how he'd been overcome by his own passions, lust certainly, but anger at Vivienne too for her flirting, and resentment that she went against his wishes. He regretted all of that now. He had been no better than an animal in his behaviour, no better than a fool in his emotions.

"Keep the garlic in the window," Màiri said.

As she stepped into the light of the window, Thorpe saw a bruise on her cheek. He stopped and almost reached out to touch it. "How did you get that?" He asked.

"I walked into a door."

"A door? It looks like someone hit you."

Mairi shook her head quickly. "No. I walked into a door."

"Did he hit you?"

"No."

She put the garlic around the window and hurried out. "I'm sorry. I must get on."

Thorpe nodded, but his mouth tightened. He disliked the man even more now.

* * *

Thorpe went out via the short cut Alastair had shown him, pleased he remembered it because it saved him walking all the way to the front entrance when the tennis court was by the rose garden.

Fiona seemed pleased to see him. She commented on his tennis gear. "Very fetching. Sad to say for poor Alastair, but you look better in his tennis kit than he does."

Thorpe shrugged. "Come on then, let the thrashing begin."

Fiona winked. "Yes, I hope you aren't a bad loser."

They began to play on the hard court surrounded by high box hedges. Fiona wasn't going to let him win easily, but still, he pulled ahead. The tennis took his mind off Vivienne. Playing tennis was a return to normality after the strangeness of the dream he'd felt immersed in lately.

After he won the first two sets, he said, "30 - Love."

He waited while she wiped her brow with a towel. "Phew, it's hot. I thought you said you only played a little."

Thorpe grinned. "I may have downplayed that. There's not much to do in the Army other than shoot people and play sports. You're good, though."

Fiona smiled back. "I was champion at my school. I'm ready. Do your worst Captain Thorpe."

Soon the court resounded again to the sound of the tennis ball hitting the strung rackets. There was a rally. Then Fiona suddenly volleyed, wrong-footing Thorpe who lost the point. "30 -15," he said.

Fiona grinned. "Your serve."

He served, but she hit it back once and then again. The ball shot across the net, and she scored another point. "30 all," she shouted, waving her racket triumphantly.

He smiled back at her. "You haven't won yet."

"It's only a matter of time." She laughed.

Then they began again. Thorpe served strongly, but Fiona deftly caught it in mid-air and whacked it back. The ball ricocheted between them back and forth. Then Thorpe stumbled and let the ball through.

"Match!" she yelled. "Match! I beat the great Captain Thorpe!"

He grinned back at her. "Yes, you did. Well played."

Fiona danced with joy. She came up to him and hugged him. He stiffened but didn't pull away.

"I'm so happy!" Then she frowned and looked up at him, still in a half embrace. "Hey, did you let me win?"

He cocked his head to one side. "Would I do that? Don't you know my reputation? I never let anyone beat me."

Fiona was still teasing Thorpe about her beating him at tennis when Gráinne appeared from the direction of the house. She was walking fast, and her face looked troubled.

"Mother?" said Fiona, stepping back from Thorpe and walking towards Gráinne. "What's wrong?"

"It's Muirdeach," she said. "He's dead."

Fiona's face drained of blood, and she dropped her racket. "Oh my God," she said. "What is happening in this place?"

Gráinne said, "He's over by the terrace. We need to move the body into the house. Will you help, William?"

"Of course," Thorpe said. Even he felt stunned and guilty—as if his dislike for the man had killed him.

They laid down their rackets and went at a half-run over to the Long Terrace. They still wore their tennis whites. The sun blazed overhead; it was a perfect summer day. Birds sang from the hedges, bees buzzed around the flowers, but someone was dead. They hurried along in silence. Gráinne strode ahead, lost in her own thoughts, Fiona lingered beside Thorpe. "He was only twenty-three."

Gráinne said in a soft voice. "Please. Hurry."

They found Muirdeach lying by the entrance to the cave Vivienne had spoken of. He was on his back, his eyes open—staring at something. He was soaking wet—his shirt was open and drenched. His trousers and shoes were wringing.

Dr McKinnon was kneeling by him.

"Looks like he drowned," Thorpe said.

McKinnon said, "If he did, how did he get back out here?" He bent down and touched Muirdeach's shirt then he tasted his fingers. "It's seawater."

"How on earth does that happen?" Thorpe said.

Lady Gráinne said, "The old well in the cave–*Tobar Na Màthar*; it goes down to some tunnels that eventually connect to the sea. When the tide is high, it comes up the well and floods over the cave."

Thorpe walked forward towards the cave. "A saltwater well?"

"Careful," said Fiona, grabbing his arm.

"What's there to be frightened of?" Thorpe said.

"Whatever killed Muirdeach."

Thorpe said, "Nothing killed him. It was most likely an accident. That's the way it looks. Maybe he fell into the water, managed to drag himself out, but died of shock or inhalation or something."

"I don't think that's possible," said Dr McKinnon.

Just then, Alastair arrived. He had run down the Terrace and was sweating, his blonde hair plastered over his forehead.

Alastair stared at the corpse. "That's horrible. Poor Muirdeach."

"Yes, poor Muirdeach," Fiona said.

Behind them loomed the vast mountains. Swallows and swifts darted through the air above them. Thorpe stepped into the cave.

"No, William!" shouted Fiona. Thorpe turned and raised a hand to reassure her. The cave was cool, dark, and damp. It wasn't deep, and he could see a hole that led down to unknown depths. From it, he could smell the sea and see the froth of the waves.

The women entered in after him. Alastair stayed outside.

"The tide's coming in," Gráinne said. "Be careful. If you fall down there, the tunnels will fill with water, and you'll be stuck."

The cave floor was wet. There were wet footmarks, but Thorpe couldn't tell whether they were Muirdeach's.

Fiona said, "It's cold in here," She held his arm.

Thorpe indicated a trail of water. "Someone's dragged him out of the pool."

"Dragged? Who?"

"I don't know. We'd better get the police."

The three of them stepped back out into the sunshine. Gráinne said she would arrange for the police. "They'll have to come from Fort William so they won't arrive until tomorrow at the earliest."

"Let's carry him," Thorpe said. Alastair and Dr McKinnon helped him, and they bore Muirdeach's body back to the castle.

Eight

LATER, after he had washed and changed, Màiri came with a message. She said Lady Gráinne wanted to see him in the Drawing Room for coffee. Before she left, he told Màiri he was sorry about Muirdeach. Màiri began to weep but stopped herself as if she would not let him see her crying, brushed the tears away and turned and hurried down the corridor.

When Thorpe arrived at the Drawing Room, Lady Gráinne sat with her black and white cat on her knee. It purred as she stroked it, looking up warily as Thorpe came in.

Lady Gráinne said, "Coffee, William?"

He nodded. There were no servants, so he poured himself coffee and cream. He took two cubes of brown sugar with the sugar tongs and sat where she indicated. He felt he had come for an interview with the headmistress. She watched him while he drank his coffee, all the while stroking the cat.

"It's all very distressing," Gráinne said.

"I didn't like him. But any death is to be regretted."

She raised an eyebrow. "Why didn't you like him? I'm surprised you even knew him."

"I don't like his type."

Gráinne evidently decided not to pursue the subject. "You're getting on well with Fiona," she said. It was a statement, not a question.

"We seem to be."

"I think she's taken a shine to you."

He shrugged. "She's a beautiful young woman — intelligent and spirited too. She'll make someone a good wife."

Lady Gráinne laughed. "I think she may be a little spirited for most men. They prefer a wife to be more pliable, and she'll never be that."

"More fool them," Thorpe said.

Gráinne took a genteel sip of coffee from her fine porcelain cup. "What are your feelings towards her? I only ask because I don't want my daughter to be hurt. She's been hurt enough already by thoughtless men. And we've spoken before about—"

"—about my taking liberties with your women?"

"I wouldn't put it so crudely."

"I wouldn't hurt Fiona for the world. Anyway, I'm not in the market for weddings. I'm married already."

Gráinne nodded slightly. "You know we disagree on that. But when you come to yourself and realise you aren't married, what then? Is Fiona safe?"

"Safe? That's an extraordinary thing to say. And, whatever you think, Vivienne is not a figment of my imagination. She's real."

"Real? I wonder."

"I know you all think I'm insane. Either that, or somehow Vivienne planned all this with you and that I'm somehow the victim of some monstrous practical joke.

"The victim of something maybe. Possibly yourself."

Thorpe sat back. He felt her scrutinising gaze on him.

She said, "You know they say power is the opposite of love?"

"Do they?"

"If you love someone, you submit to them and give them all your power. You make yourself vulnerable."

Thorpe shrugged. "Perhaps."

She sipped her coffee. "But you've never had the experience?"

He looked at his cup. It was white porcelain with blue Chinese willow pattern. After a while he said. "It sounds an unpleasant experience—to make yourself vulnerable to someone."

"Of course the opposite is true too. If you want power, you have no room left inside you for love."

"You're quite a philosopher, Lady Gráinne."

"And I'm your friend, though you don't realise it."

He changed the subject. "Tell me, what's all this nonsense with the maid Màiri putting garlic flowers around the place?"

Gráinne said, "We are very superstitious in the Highlands. The old beliefs remain. Things like garlic preserve things from rotting. It's because of this that they have authority against the powers of corruption like evil spirits or ghosts. Garlic is powerful against the *bean sìth*: the female spirit feared all over the Gaelic world."

"Banshees? I've heard of them of course. I thought they were in Ireland."

"We have them in Ireland, but here too."

Conversation lapsed.

He surveyed the view. "You've been very kind to me here, but I'll be glad when I leave."

"I wonder when that will be."

"Longer now with Muirdeach gone."

Lady Gráinne said, "I don't think your coming here was a coincidence. Not for you, nor for us." The cat stretched and jumped from her lap onto the floor. It sat there, staring at Thorpe with amber eyes.

He said, "Of course that's exactly what it was: a coincidence."

"I think what was waiting here, was waiting for you. Some old story is being retold, and it needs you to take the main part."

"You can't really believe that."

"I think I do."

"If I'm involved in some kind of play, I suspect you also take a lead part."

Lady Gráinne chuckled. "I played Queen Titania at our outdoor Shakespeare a few years ago."

Thorpe said, "She played tricks on her husband too. Women always want to punish men because they don't imagine their men care enough about them. It's like the story Alastair told."

"I thought you weren't listening?"

"I listened enough."

"'A war between the sheets', he said. Sometimes it seems that men and women always vie for power over the other. But it needn't be that way."

"No?"

Gráinne said, "Men and women can be equals."

"I don't know. I sometimes imagine that women think men have had it too good for too long. They don't want to be the equals of men, they want their turn on top."

"Then the power struggle would reverse, not resolve."

Thorpe said. "In your story, Lord Eachann's ancestor had his manhood removed. That's pretty sour."

"For the man."

He tutted.

She said, "In all of the versions of the story I know, he did. But maybe there's another version where he manages not to betray her trust?"

At that point, the cook entered. "Milady, I was wondering about tonight's menu. Could I have a word with you?"

Gráinne rose. "If you'll excuse me. So nice to have the chance to talk to you, William."

The cat followed her out of the room, and Thorpe was left alone.

* * *

Thorpe left the castle and went to the stable. Muirdeach was dead, but his car still lingered there, broken, but Thorpe was desperate to be gone. He felt with Calum's illness, and Muirdeach's death things were closing in on him. Màiri had said that all men were at risk here.

He saw his car sitting there. Muirdeach had done some of the work, and now Thorpe had half an idea that he might be able to fix the rest himself. He lifted the bonnet, stared at the engine for ten minutes. He fiddled with hoses and poked around the cylinders, but in the end, shook his head. He slammed the bonnet shut and stalked out.

He had nowhere to go: it seemed he was imprisoned in this place. Thorpe walked through the Castle's park, head down, taking little notice of where he went.

He reached the river and walked along its banks, wandering some miles beside the willows and wild yellow flag iris. Clouds covered the sky above. Curlews called their bubbling cry from the damp meadows. He saw a heron standing stock still as a prehistoric creature by the river bank. Eventually, he looked back and saw Dungarvan a distant dot behind him. He could walk away, but ahead were the mountains and wilder country. This country could kill a man. There was no escape on foot. No escape by car. Perhaps he could borrow a pony and trap? But then he was never one for running away. He would stay and play out the fate Dungarvan offered him.

With a sigh, Thorpe turned and retraced his steps. When he got back to the castle, he didn't see any of the inhabitants, which suited him fine. He went in by the main door. There was no one about. He trotted up the staircase and opened his room where he threw himself on the bed and slept within minutes.

* * *

Night fell. He missed dinner. Someone knocked to call him down, but he didn't answer. Eventually, they left. He didn't know how many hours had passed before something made him waken. Thorpe knew she was in the room, even with his eyes closed. Hardly daring to breathe, he opened his eyes. She stood in the corner. He sat up on the bed, and she didn't vanish. She was there, clothed only in shadows. He saw her white flesh, her round thighs and flaring hips. His gaze travelled over her soft belly and the swelling of her breasts. He took in the dark hair between her legs, and like every time he saw Vivienne, he wanted her.

"William," she said. Her face was half-hidden, but he saw her long black hair, rose-red lips, white teeth that glistened as she smiled. Her eyes seemed to have their own luminescence, gold and black like those of a serpent.

His throat was dry. "Vivienne. I love you."

She whispered, "I know you do."

He wanted her. His grief that he'd lost her and his anger that she'd left him both threatened his self-control. He stood up from the bed and walked to her. She welcomed him, took him in her arms and folded him to her. He caressed her full breasts. He bent his mouth to hers, and as she kissed him, the boundaries between them blurred and blended. He felt the heat of her sex and smelled the perfume of her lust. He ran his hand in her long hair, twisting it and pulling her to him. He felt her hands rake his back, but then she stopped. He was befuddled by his desire. He couldn't think straight, but she whispered, "No."

He gripped her tightly. "Vivienne, I love you. I want only you. From the first minute I saw you in India, I only wanted you."

"William, how many hearts have you broken without a thought? I will give you one more chance to show you can be truly faithful to me."

* * *

He woke again on his bed. Day shone through a gap in the curtains he hadn't drawn properly the night before. He looked frantically around him, but Vivienne wasn't there. If it was all a dream, it was a dream of what he wanted most.

He went down for breakfast which was served by a servant he didn't recognise. He ate in silence, then went back to his room where he stayed all day. He smoked too much and sat in the chair by the window staring at the clouds and mountains. He picked up one of the books left in the room for guests. He sat slumped in his seat and turned over pages one by one, reading but not remembering a word. He flicked thumbfuls of pages, then riffled pages a hundred at a time, picking up book after book. But he found nothing to take his mind off Vivienne.

Trying to shake off the bleakness that weighed him down, he decided he would join the life of the castle. Another day had gone by. He dressed for dinner and went down before the gong was sounded. Màiri was acting as a waitress, and there was a young servant man he didn't recognise. The mood was sombre. He was surprised that Màiri was at work after Muirdeach's death. Candles were lit on the table, the wine was poured, but the conversation was sparse. Fiona was staring at him. He knew it, but he was wary of returning her gaze in light of what her mother had told him.

In avoiding Fiona, he looked too much at the others. He saw Alastair gazing at Fiona. His eyes were dreamy like those of young men who read too much poetry. Fiona was why Alastair spent so much time at Dungarvan, but Alastair was in no way good enough for Fiona. He had no courage, and she needed a man with sufficient bravery to match her own.

The meal continued with stilted conversation about the weather. Then Fiona chipped in about an exhibition she'd seen at the National Gallery in Edinburgh. Thorpe pretended to be interested. He picked at his food. The pheasant was well cooked, but the sauce was too creamy for his palate. More wine was poured.

"It's a Claret," said Lord Eachann. "I'm not a wine expert, I'm afraid; I take my instructions on what to buy from Gráinne."

"And I submit to your superior knowledge about dogs, horses and shooting," said Gráinne.

Eachann reached out and put his hand on hers. Those two were the perfect symbol of enduring love—from youth to age and still devoted to each other. Thorpe didn't know if he believed in things like that. Could two people love each other all their lives? It was just another myth. They were smiling liars. This whole place was full of myths and stories and things that couldn't really be true.

Eachann said, "It's been a long and unpleasant day, I hope no one will mind if I retire to do a bit of reading."

Gráinne got up with him, leaving the doctor and the three younger people. The doctor then excused himself. He was an old fool. Good riddance. That left Thorpe with Alastair and Fiona. She was wearing a blue gown that matched her eyes and pearls that looked old and valuable.

"I'll go up too, I think," Thorpe said.

"No—stay. Please?" Fiona said. "We're going to retire to the Baronial Hall and put some records on the gramophone. I'd like to dance."

"I'm quite tired," Thorpe said. "I'm not much of a dancer, and I know little about music."

"Stay for me?" She said.

Thorpe sighed but said, "Who could resist such a gracious request?"

"Good!" Fiona said, clapping her hands.

She was thoughtful and kind. She had ideas and opinions, but it was easy to delight her, and when she was pleased, she had all the wonder and charm of a child.

"Let's go through," she said. She came over and took his hand, pulling him after her. Over her shoulder, she called, "Hurry up, Alastair!"

Alastair came through behind them without speaking. He just watched them as Fiona chatted away to Thorpe.

"Just before I went to Edinburgh, a lot of records I'd ordered from New York arrived, but I had to leave, so I haven't had the opportunity to listen to them. Do you want me to put a few on now?"

Thorpe shrugged. "I wouldn't know the good from the bad."

In the Baronial Hall, Thorpe glanced up the balcony above. Fiona told the two men to move the chairs to clear a space for dancing. Alastair set up the gramophone, and Fiona stood there, lost in thought reading the sleeve notes to herself, her finger tracing the words as she did so. He smiled. She really was a delight.

Alastair stood in the shadow saying nothing. Thorpe looked at Fiona and smiled. She would indeed make someone a good wife.

"This one is good," she said finally. Putting a record on the turntable and placing the needle on the groove as it spun around, she said, "This is 'A Cup of Coffee, a Sandwich and You,' by Billy Rose."

Thorpe shook his head. "Never heard of any of them."

"Dance?" she said, extending her hands.

He shook his head. "Alastair will make a better companion than me."

Alastair's face blossomed into a smile when Fiona's attention turned to him. He blustered something about not being very good at this, but she grabbed him anyway.

Thorpe watched as she had to teach him some of the steps. He was not a good pupil, as graceless at dancing as he had been at fencing. Then the music stopped, and he stopped, standing awkwardly in the middle of the floor.

Fiona went over to the gramophone again. "And this," she said, "is 'Brown Eyes, Why Are You Blue?'"

She smiled at Thorpe. "Dance now?"

He shook his head. "I'll sit this one out."

"Lucky Alastair then," she said, smiling, but she was looking at Thorpe.

"Indeed," he said.

Alastair watched her every move. He was smiling now, a soft-mouthed smile like he'd never learned how to do that properly either. He stepped forward and snatched at her hands. Then, as the music started, he was an ungainly jig of gangly arms and swinging knees as they did some American-style dance.

After that song finished, Fiona said, "I want a rest now." She came and sat on the chair close to Thorpe's. She cocked her head and said, "You seem blue. Are you?"

He frowned. "Blue?"

"Melancholy."

He laughed. "A little."

She put a hand on his where it rested on the arm of the chair. She stroked it, playing the part of a concerned friend. Thorpe squeezed her hand, then dropped it.

Alastair stood by the gramophone watching them. "Do you want to dance again, Fiona?"

She waved him down, "Not yet, Ally."

She turned back to Thorpe. He felt uncomfortable with Fiona. He didn't want to lead her on. Alastair had probably loved her secretly since they were children, and he was Eachann's choice, as misplaced an idea as that almost certainly was. Fiona wouldn't settle for someone like Alastair. Alastair was going to get his heart broken, but that was none of Thorpe's business.

Thorpe stood. "Listen, I'll be off now. I'm not very good company tonight."

It was dark now, and a ring of gas mantles illuminated the hall. The door to the Entrance Hall was half open.

She got up from her seat and snatched at his hand. "No, William, you spoilsport. I insist you stay!" She had the look of a little girl used to getting her own way. Then with a beatific smile said, "At least for one dance."

Alastair still hadn't sat down. He had a record in his hand. "What about this one, Fiona?" He showed her the sleeve. "I think it's one you like."

"Just a second, Alastair," she said, not looking at him.

"I really must go," Thorpe said.

"I want you to stay," she said.

Alastair threw down the record. It smashed as it hit the wooden floor. Without a word, he turned and stalked out of the hall.

"Oh dear," Fiona said, raising her eyebrows.

After he was sure Alastair was out of earshot, Thorpe said, "You realise he loves you?"

"I suppose."

"You should go after him."

"I don't want to. It'll give him the wrong idea. I'd rather stay here with you."

She took his hands again. He didn't want to pull them away, but he was uncomfortable. "I'm not right for you," he said.

She whispered, "I'll decide that."

She moved in closer so that her knees pressed against his.

"Do you still think you're married?" she asked.

He shook his head. "No. I don't know. Maybe I dreamed Vivienne. There was a real Vivienne. In India. She wasn't mine though I wanted her to be."

"Do you want to tell me about it?"

"Not really." He rubbed his forehead. "I don't think I'm very well."

"No, you're not." She stroked his hair. "But you will be well."

He put his hand over his eyes. "You're very lovely," he said. "But how can this work out between us?"

"Why don't you kiss me?"

"For all sorts of reasons—" Some prescient impulse made Thorpe look around.

At the door of the Baronial Hall, standing half in shadow was a figure. Thorpe snapped his head round to see who it was. She wore a black dress and had long dark hair. It was Vivienne.

He started up and went towards the door.

"Don't follow her!" yelled Fiona.

He turned. "I have to know who she really is. I have to break her hold on me."

Fiona called after him, "If you go, she will prove you are her slave."

Nine

VIVIENNE FLED from the hall door back into the passage, and without waiting for Fiona, Thorpe rushed after her. Her footsteps echoed through the castle in front of him and he chased her. He hunted her along the corridors and through room after room, seeing only her back, hearing only her laughter as she drew him on.

He realised she was heading outside. Panting, he reached the entrance hall and stood to catch his breath, hands on thighs, still without catching another glimpse of her. He hadn't seen her since that first glimpse, but he'd heard her footsteps. This was the way she must have come.

The oak entrance door swung open, and from the widening gap, summer fog seeped inside. Vivienne must have left it unlatched to show him she'd come this way and to tempt him to follow her. Aerial and tenuous, like the fronds of ghostly ferns, the fog's tendrils felt their way into the room. Thorpe put his hand to the door handle, damp with condensation, and looked. It was dark out there. The warm air had condensed on the ocean's edge and drifted inland to surround the castle, so Dungarvan was now an illuminated island cocooned in mist. Thorpe stepped out.

Where was she? The damp air wrapped him, cutting him off from the castle door behind and making the world dreamlike. It made sounds muffled, and the cries of birds echoed eerie and strange.

Thorpe's footprints crunched on gravel, but he could see nothing. Vivienne wasn't there. How could he find her in this fog?

"Vivienne!" He called, but only the dull echo of his own voice came back from the castle walls. Why had she summoned him if only to disappear? She must mean him to follow her and perhaps now he would be reunited with her, whoever she was.

As he stood, looking every way around him, Fiona stepped from the castle door behind. She wore a jacket and had an old tweed overcoat in her hands. "Here, put this on," she said.

Thorpe shivered and let her help him with it. Fiona leaned close to fasten the buttons and turned up his collar. "That's better. If you must go on a fool's errand, you might as well be warm."

She switched on the electric torch she held and waved it around, but the beam hardly cut the fog.

Thorpe had still not spoken.

She said, "So you still want to follow your dream?"

Thorpe said, "Where can she have gone?"

Fiona said, "You shouldn't go after her, you know."

He stared at Fiona. "So, you saw her?"

Fiona said, "I saw something."

"It was Vivienne."

Fiona said, "She isn't what you think she is."

Thorpe rubbed his mouth. "She says she's my wife."

She said, "Maybe finding her will help you shake off this obsession: get rid of this spell before it destroys you. I only hope that is possible."

"So what is she if she isn't my wife?"

"Do you even have a wife?"

He threw his head back and stared at the fog-bound sky. "I don't know what's real anymore, Fiona."

"I just hope you realise that you can never have her. If anything, it will be her that has you."

He faltered. "What is she?"

"A spirit. Maybe a woman. Their names change. Their faces change."

"So I'm not mad?"

Fiona gestured. "It's this place. It's my father's story, and now it's your story too. It seems men like you are fated to replay it time after time until finally, maybe one of them gets the ending right, and then it can stop. I wish I could stop it myself, but she's not interested in me. I'm not the hero. I'm only a supporting actor in this troupe of players."

"What is happening here?"

"Dungarvan isn't an ordinary place. Myth soaks the ground and we sink deeper with every step. I hoped you wouldn't be caught up in it. You are the first one I've liked. But it seems you'll have to play it to the end."

"Whatever she is, do you know where she has gone?"

Fiona said, "Do you have a cigarette?"

Thorpe reached inside his jacket and pulled out a pack of Egyptian cigarettes. He took out one for her and one for him.

"Does your father know you smoke?" he said.

She laughed. "Of course not. There are lots of things about me that my father doesn't know."

The lighter flared, first once then twice. They each lit a cigarette and then they were serious again, suddenly quiet.

"So what happens in this story to men like me?"

"We'll have to see," she said. "Maybe it won't end so badly."

And then they heard a sound. It was someone's feet in the gravel coming from about ten yards away.

Thorpe spun round. "She's over there." He went to go towards the noise.

Fiona grabbed at his hand and gripped it tight. "You'll get lost. You don't know the place like me."

"Let me go to her, Fiona. I need to know what she wants from me."

"Let me come with you."

He sighed and nodded. As they stepped down the stone steps, away from the light of the door, it was as if they descended into a dark sea. They dropped fathoms deep, wrapped in a garment made of mist and night.

More footsteps.

"Over there," Fiona said.

It was someone walking, but the sound was both magnified and muffled by the fog. Fiona pointed the torch. The beam cut a small way into the mist, but not far enough to be useful.

"We'll only to see someone if we actually walk into them in this," Thorpe said.

The footsteps sounded again. Whoever was walking had speeded up.

"They must have heard us," Thorpe said.

"Whoever it is is walking away. Must be going into the rose garden."

They went after the footsteps, Thorpe leading, Fiona hanging back. They entered the rose garden, and in his haste, Thorpe tripped over some stonework. "Ouch."

She shone the torch. "You've cut your hand."

The footsteps hurried away. "Quick, she's getting away," he said.

"Let me clean the wound."

"It's nothing. Go back to the castle. This is something for me to fix. I don't expect you to come with me."

"I want to."

"You're very brave—"

—For a woman?" she said.

"For anyone!"

She chuckled. "I suppose that's a compliment coming from you."

"Fiona, I know you think I'm crazy, but you're a good friend to me."

"A chum? Like you had in the Army?"

"I didn't have any chums in the Army. I never had any really."

Fiona said, "I think she's going towards the Terrace, but once she's off the gravel, we won't hear her footsteps. Let's hurry."

They hurried. The sound of their own steps drowned out the sound of anyone else's. Now and again, they stopped. They strained to hear and only moved when they heard the footsteps walking away.

"The Terrace is a straight walk from here, though?" he asked.

"More or less."

"Where's she heading?" He said.

Fiona laughed. "Where she always goes in the story."

"The Well?"

"The Well of the Mothers."

"Then we'll go there."

Fiona said, "I only wish you didn't want to."

They walked on. All went quiet.

"We've lost her," he said.

"Keep on to the Well."

A sound came from nearby. Thorpe halted, turning his head to catch it. "That sounded like a person."

"Vivienne?"

"No, she was ahead. This noise is to the right."

They heard footsteps on gravel, then on stone, then on gravel again. Whoever was walking was in the rose garden.

"That's definitely someone—just to the right of us."

"But—someone else?"

He frowned. "Must be. But who?"

Fiona shone the torch into the wet grey mist. "Who's that?" She yelled.

No answer came.

"It might be her," Thorpe said.

"I thought you said it was someone else."

"I don't know. I'll go and see."

"Wait!"

Thorpe ran into the fog. His feet echoed in the damp air. He went right then ahead. Then he stopped. He wasn't even sure he heard anything any more. He had no torch. The fog surrounded him. He could see nothing.

Behind him, he heard Fiona calling that she didn't know where he was.

"Vivienne?" he shouted.

He remembered Fiona was on her own in the mist. He shouted back to her that he would come and find her, and then something smashed into his head, and he stumbled.

Thorpe fell to his knees, the darkness around him illuminated by the bright stars of concussion. He staggered to get up and touched his head to feel blood seeping from the wound. He half-rose then was hit again. A heavy log smacked him on the shoulder, sending him reeling into the hedge. He tumbled into the rose bush's spiky fingers that scratched his face but stopped him tumbling over completely. Thorpe pushed back out of the bush and spun round to face his attacker.

"Vivienne, is that you?" he hissed.

But it wasn't Vivienne's voice that answered; it was Alastair's.

Alastair said, "You bastard."

Thorpe made out a shadow in front of him, darker than the surrounding grey. "What are you doing? Why did you hit me?"

Alastair sneered. "You think you can take her from me. She's mine; she's promised to me."

"What are you talking about?"

"You took Fiona from me."

"I didn't take Fiona from anyone."

Alastair brandished the heavy piece of wood. "Men like you think they can take what they want without giving a damn for anyone else, but her father has given her to me."

Thorpe's palm was sticky with blood. He backed off. "Her father can't give her to you. Fiona will choose who she wants."

"She will choose me!"

Thorpe laughed. "I actually don't think so."

"You pig!" Alastair held the log ready, ready to swing it again, but he held back.

Thorpe heard Fiona's voice calling from somewhere in the fog. "William, what's going on? Are you all right?"

Thorpe looked over his shoulder and shouted, "Fiona, go back to the castle."

Alastair swung the branch at Thorpe's head. Thorpe dodged, but the branch caught him a glancing blow on his left shoulder. Thorpe leapt at Alastair and swung a punch into his face with his right fist. As Alastair recoiled, Thorpe followed with a left then another right to the stomach.

Alastair went down, gasping in pain and dropped the heavy log.

Thorpe snarled, lurched forward and snatched Alastair by his hair. He yanked Alastair's head forward and pulled him close to bring up his knee and smash Alastair's nose. Then Thorpe stopped. He breathed heavily, and let go of the fistful of hair. Alastair was on his knees gasping in the grassy mud, and Thorpe grabbed his opponent's left lapel and stood with his right first clenched, ready to hit Alastair if he kept fighting.

Alastair pulled himself free, and Thorpe let him go.

Alastair said, "I only ever wanted Fiona. But you had to take her from me."

"I've not taken Fiona from you. Don't be stupid."

"Of course you have. Don't you see the way she looks at you? She has no time for me."

"She doesn't love you."

"She did."

"No, she didn't. You've been fooling yourself all these years. You've been a victim of your own imagination."

"You liar!"

Thorpe said, "Fiona's only fault was that she should have told you straight she had no interest in you and put you out of your puppy-dog misery. But she was too soft-hearted to do it."

Alastair backed away from him. "I'll make all of you sorry. You'll all regret underestimating me." Alastair wiped his face with a muddy hand, blood streaming from his nose. Then he turned and ran into the fog.

Thorpe stood alone, touching his head. When he concluded he wouldn't die of the wound, he let it be. He called out for Fiona, but no answer came. He hoped she was all right. She was a sensible girl, she'd have gone back to the castle, of that he had no doubt. He had no idea where Alastair had gone, and he didn't care.

Any idea of finding Vivienne had ebbed away. Whatever this apparition was, she wasn't his wife. She had convinced him they were married, but he remembered nothing of their life together. He did remember a Vivienne, but that was thousands of miles away. A day in Ooty Botanical Gardens came back to him. He remembered her telling him that she wouldn't leave her husband. He remembered begging her, imploring to go with him, telling her they would make a new life together in Australia. But she had turned and walked away. This thing at Dungarvan, this banshee had used his feelings for the real Vivienne and twisted them against him.

He started to walk back to the Castle. The fog was still thick, but he found his way. As he stepped through the massive door, he saw himself in the glass of a painting. He was wet from falling against the hedge, and his head was plastered in blood. His hand was smeared with red, and his nose was bruised and cut. He was a mess.

As he came into the Baronial Hall. Eachann was standing there, leaning on his stick and looking as if he had been waiting. He saw the state Thorpe was in and his face twisted in rage. "What have you done? Where's Alastair?"

Thorpe shrugged. "It was a misunderstanding."

"Look at the state of you! You've been fighting. You come to my house, and you fight like a thug."

"Alastair attacked me."

"And where is he now? Have you left him for dead?"

Thorpe sighed wearily. "No, he went off into the dark. Where's Fiona? Did she come in?"

Eachann exploded. He pointed his stick at Thorpe. "What? You tell me that my daughter has been out there with you, watching you brawl?"

"She came back to the Castle. I've come to find her. I need to apologise for running off."

"What have you done to her?" said Eachann, his voice shaking.

Thorpe frowned. "I haven't done anything to her."

"I know what kind of a man you are. I know about Màiri."

"Màiri wasn't what you think, and I assure you I've never touched Fiona."

Eachann was still shaking. "Keep away from my daughter."

"I assure you I only want to make sure she's safe."

Eachann shook his head. "I want you to go. Leave in the morning."

"What about my car?"

"Take it with you. Or walk. I don't care. I want you gone. You've done enough damage here. You woke the *Bean Sìth*. I put it to sleep, but you woke it again."

Eachann turned and began to walk away. Thorpe gripped his elbow and pulled the older man back. "It's time you told me what's going on here."

Eachann glared.

Thorpe said, "Fiona said something about this being like your story. What did she mean?"

Eachann was cold-eyed. "It means that you have woken her, as I woke her long ago. And I paid the price to quiet her again. She's feeds on the energy of men: men like I was; men like you are. She felt you coming along the road and knew what you were, so she caused the accident and brought you here."

"So what about Vivienne? Who is she?"

"Whoever the real Vivienne was, this creature is not her. Vivienne is your dream, and the Bean Sìth used the shape you provided."

"But why me? Why you?"

"Because I was like you, a soldier, a womaniser. We made a fetish of our masculinity. You, Captain Thorpe, you fight, you win, and you take. You have no care for others. You treat women as if they were objects for your pleasure. The Bean Sìth will punish you for the way you mistreat women. As strong and cruel as you are, she is stronger."

"But you beat her."

"I did not."

"But you said you put her back to sleep."

Eachann exhaled. "She came to me. She haunted me. I was married to Gráinne, but I was a terrible rake. My mistreatment of women woke the woman spirit of this place. Only I could see her, and I couldn't beat her. In the end, I gave in and paid her price."

"How?"

"I sacrificed myself to her."

Thorpe's brow furrowed. "What do you mean?"

"You're familiar with the Classical Goddess Cybele? Whom the Romans called Magna Mater—the Great Mother?"

"No."

"The pagan Gaels had a similar goddess: a terrible, devouring mother. They pictured her as three women in one: *Na Math-aireachan*: The Mothers."

"That well's called The Well of the Mothers."

Eachann said, "Yes. *Tobair na Màthar*. Sometimes they call these wells *Tobair Maire*: Mary's Well, but Mary too is a version of the mother goddess. She gives birth and takes back at death. She creates us and destroys us."

"Like the Indian Kali?"

Eachann laughed. "Yes, like Mother Kali, the little statue you have in your room."

"But how did you stop her?"

Eachann looked to the floor. "Cybele's priests were castrated. They offered their masculinity as a tribute to her."

"Good God," Thorpe said, stepping back. "No man should have to do that to himself."

Eachann lifted his eyes and met Thorpe's gaze. "And no woman should have to submit to a man's violence."

Thorpe felt sick. "Surely we're not doomed to an endless war between men and women, each vying for power over the other. Surely there is a middle ground."

"I never found it."

Thorpe shook his head. "I won't do what you did."

"It is the only way you can stop her. You will have to pay the *Bean Sìth*'s price. Offer yourself to her as her eunuch servant, or she will destroy you."

"I need to check on Fiona," Thorpe said. He turned and left Eachann in the Great Hall and ran up the stairs and along the passage. As he knocked on Fiona's door, he felt guilty for knocking when she'd gone to bed, but he wanted to make sure she was safe. The rapping echoed down the passage. No reply came. Thorpe knocked again, and then he listened at the door for sounds of movement inside. All was silent. Perhaps it was that she had just fallen asleep.

"Fiona," he whispered, then louder: "Fiona, it's me—William.

I just came to say I'm sorry for running off and make sure you got back safely." His voice died away without an answer. He steeled himself for her righteous anger and turned the handle of the door. It was locked.

He heard Dr McKinnon's door open from down the corridor, and the shiny forehead with its strands of ginger hair poked out. "What the hell are you doing, Thorpe?"

"I'm just making sure Fiona got back safely."

"Do you realise how late it is?"

"Oh, go and hang yourself you boring little man," snapped Thorpe and knocked on the door, again "Fiona! Are you all right?"

McKinnon hissed. "She's not there."

"What? Where is she?"

"She's gone with Alastair."

"Gone with Alastair? When?"

"About five minutes ago. I heard him coming up the back way, so I looked out. I don't think they saw me."

No, I bet they didn't, you little spy, Thorpe thought.

McKinnon continued, "No, and he seemed very serious, but she followed him out. She was always too soft-hearted, that girl, but I can't see her settling for Alastair. He's too weak."

Ten

THORPE MADE his way down the stairs. He did a quick tour of the castle's room on the ground floor and saw one of the maids. He asked her if she'd seen Alastair and Fiona.

"Yes, sir. They went outside."

"They went outside into the fog at this time of night. Didn't you think that was strange?"

She looked blankly at him. It wasn't her place to question the decisions of her betters, no matter how ill-advised they seemed.

Eachann was nowhere to be seen, and Thorpe guessed he had gone to bed. He couldn't remember which was the door that was the short cut to the Rose Garden though that must be the way Alastair got in without coming past Eachann and himself talking. Thorpe went to the Entrance Hall and hesitated by the castle's door. There was a rack of electric torches there. He took one and clicked the on button. It stuck, and it didn't work at first. But then he hit it, and it did. He stepped out into the fog, as impenetrable now as it had been before.

Alastair had told him he was going to make them all sorry. What the hell did he mean by that? Thorpe's mouth went dry with anxiety for Fiona. As he got further into the gardens, he heard someone. He gripped the metal torch tight. The grass was bent here as if something had been dragged through it. He dipped the beam and saw the grass was stained red. He leaned down and touched the red liquid, examining it in the yellow light, and saw it was blood.

Thorpe's heart beat faster. Whose blood was this? He followed the tracks in the grass. Though he could hardly see his way, he knew where he was going. He hurried past the rose bushes dripping in the night's dew, and broke into a run on the gravel path, jogging along the box hedge walk until he arrived on the Terrace.

His shoes were soaked from the wet grass, and his ragged breath issued forth in billows. He took a moment then went on, the torch beam swaying and conjuring demonic faces from the fog. It took longer to walk the terrace in the dark than he remembered from journeys during daylight. In this murky weather, he couldn't smell the honeysuckle or musk rose. The fog had drowned them.

He went along the terrace, down the dip he remembered, his feet slipping on the muddy grass. There was still a trail of blood. He was near the end of the Terrace now, and the cave was ahead. He paused outside. His throat was dry, and his voice nearly failed him. Clearing his throat, he shouted, "Fiona."

No answer came. Thorpe went closer to the cave mouth and called, "Fiona?"

His heart was hammering. What if she was hurt?

In response to his call, he heard a weak, gasping voice. He had heard enough wounded men to know that someone was in terrible pain. But it was a man's voice, not Fiona's. "Alastair, if that's you, come out."

From the cave entrance, Thorpe flicked the torch beam in front of him like a probe. Walls of fog reflected it back, but he could see the walls of the cave. They were slick, and the smell of the sea rose up.

He knew where the hole in the ground was where the well had been, but it took him a second to locate it with the torch.

By the gaping hole of the well, lay Alastair. His shirt and trousers were soaked in blood.

Thorpe said, "Where's Fiona?"

"Help me, Thorpe. I'm wounded."

"What did you do to Fiona?"

Alastair shook his head. "I just wanted to talk to her to apologise for running out. I needed to tell her I loved her."

Thorpe narrowed his eyes. "Why didn't you talk inside the castle? Why bring her outside?"

"Please, help me. I'm bleeding to death here."

Thorpe flicked the torch beam around. Blood pooled on the cave floor. Alastair was wounded, but how? A thought occurred to him. "Did Vivienne do this?"

"Vivienne?" Alastair frowned then nodded. "Yes, It was Vivienne."

Alastair turned to look where Thorpe gestured at the well. The tide was out and at the cavern below was empty of water. "I don't know Thorpe. But please, you need to help me. I'm bleeding."

"And you need to be honest with me—for the first time, you all need to be straight with me. I don't know whether I'm coming or going. Where is Fiona?"

"I don't know. When I told her I loved her, she left me."

Thorpe went silent. "But you think she's safe?"

"She must have gone back to the castle after our argument."

"How come I didn't see her?"

"You must have missed her in the fog."

"And then you ran into Vivienne—or the banshee or whatever she is."

Alastair nodded. He was very pale. Sweat beaded on his upper lip and forehead. Thorpe felt sorry for him. It was possible that Fiona had left Alastair and made her way back to the castle and he'd missed her in the fog. The banshee might have hurt Alastair. After all, she'd hurt Calum and killed Muirdeach for their crimes against women.

"Please take me back to the castle," Alastair said. He was crying.

Thorpe looked at the hole in the cave. In the light of his torch, he could see blood, but it was Alastair's. The cave was dank and dangerous. No one would go there of their own free will.

Alastair moaned. "Please help me. I'll die here if you leave me."

Up until now, they had all denied seeing Vivienne. But perhaps now they could see her. Thorpe closed his eyes. Then he decided. He reached down and took Alastair's hand. Alastair's bloody fingers slipped through his, but he grabbed again and got a solid grip around the wrist. Thorpe helped him up then Alastair was on his feet with his hand nursing his wounded groin. Blood was only seeping from the wound, but Thorpe didn't have a bandage. He hoped there would be something to clean up the injury in the castle. He guessed it would need sutures. He'd stitched men up when necessary in the War. The main thing was to get Alastair somewhere dry and warm and light so he could treat him.

Thorpe retreated, pulling Alastair with him and they made their way out of the cave back into the fog-bound night. When they were clear of the cave, Thorpe supporting Alastair as he limped along, Thorpe said, "How badly are you wounded?"

Alastair said, "The bleeding has stopped. But it hurts so much."

"All right, let's take you back to the castle. You'll have to bear the pain."

It took more time than he wanted for Thorpe to help the limping Alastair back to the castle door.

* * *

Eachann was back in the Baronial Hall when they entered. The clock's hands showed it was 3 a.m.

"What have you done to him?" said Eachann, coming over, leaning on his stick, his face melting in concern for Alastair, then a quick look of anger at Thorpe.

"It wasn't me," Thorpe said.

Alastair said nothing.

"But you're hurt," Eachann said, staring at Alastair's ripped groin. "My God."

Alastair grimaced.

"Do you have a bandage?" Thorpe said. "We need to clean the wound."

"I'll get Màiri," said Eachann. "She can help."

Alastair stood, blood dripping onto the floor from where it seeped through his trousers. There was a clean slash mark in the groin. It looked like it had been made by a sharp knife.

"Don't worry," Thorpe said. "We'll get you cleaned up. I've done lots of field dressings."

Màiri came. She saw the blood and where the wound was and her eyes filled with horror.

Thorpe told her, "I need you to clean as best you can. Use warm water. But first, can you get me a needle and thread?"

Màiri nodded and went off. When she returned, she had what was needed. She had brought a bowl of warm, clear water and the thread and needle. She cleaned Alastair's wound while he shuddered and moaned with the pain. When she had mopped away the congealing blood, Thorpe could see what he was working with. He began to suture it closed. Alastair put one hand on Thorpe's shoulder, and Màiri took his other as Thorpe worked. He didn't bear the pain well. And then Thorpe put down the needle and bloodied thread.

He said, "I've done what I can to repair it."

"Thank you," Alastair whispered. "I don't deserve your help."

"You're damned right, you don't. You're lucky I've got this sense of honour that won't let me leave a wounded man behind."

"Who did this?" Eachann said.

Alastair's eyes closed. He didn't speak.

Thorpe offered. "He said Vivienne did it."

Eachann's eyes widened. "Your imaginary wife? I doubt that."

Thorpe said, "You told me about the banshee. You know it's true. You know what she did to you."

"I think there is a less supernatural explanation. I think you did this."

Thorpe looked from Alastair to Eachann. "You think this is my fault?"

Eachann's eyes were cold. "Who else's?"

Thorpe said, "Alastair says that Fiona came back to the castle after she left him. Did you see her?"

Eachann shook his head. He looked at Màiri. He spoke in Gaelic, and Màiri turned to go.

Alastair was very quiet. Tears seeped from the corners of his eyes.

Thorpe said, "Why are you crying?"

Alastair brought his bloodied hand to his face.

Thorpe said, "Alastair, where's Fiona?"

Alastair shook his head. "I'm sorry."

"Sorry? What for?"

"I think she's out in the garden still," Alastair said.

Thorpe shook his head, puzzled. "What? But you said she came back here."

"No," repeated Alastair. "She's in the garden."

He was horrified. "She's out there? Why did you lie to me?"

Alastair said, "I just ran. When I couldn't run anymore because of the wound, I crawled. I didn't know where I was going, but I ended up at the cave."

"So Fiona's still out there?"

"Yes."

Eachann said, "Out there? In this weather, after this monster has terrified her to death." He pointed at Thorpe.

Alastair grimaced.

Thorpe said, "I'll go and find her. I'll bring her back safely."

Eachann said, "She doesn't need your help. I will find her. She's my daughter."

Thorpe sighed. "With all due respect."

"What? You think I'm a cripple? You think I can't protect my own daughter?"

Thorpe shrugged. "At least let me help you."

Eachann scowled at him then said, "Very well."

Thorpe nodded then went back out of the door. Eachann followed him, limping. He slowed Thorpe up, but he couldn't leave him, so they went slowly, Thorpe having to remember, stopping and waiting for Lord Eachann. All the time, tension grew, nearly choking him. Fiona was out here with the banshee. Though she'd never harmed a woman before, perhaps she might now. If only because Thorpe cared for her.

He and Eachann walked through the garden, searching. The fog was still as thick as it had been. The night lay so heavy on the place that he doubted it would ever be dawn. It was cold.

"Anything?" said Eachann from over his shoulder. "Is Fiona there?"

"No," Thorpe said.

Then Eachann said, "Shine the torch over there."

Eachann gripped Thorpe's hand and yanked it so the beam shone on a stone bench that would provide a private little spot for a summer's day. Tonight it was sinister.

"What's that?" Thorpe said. He stepped closer, bent down, touching it to make sure.

It was a woman's dress.

Eachann said, "It's hers."

The dress was ripped as if it had been torn off her. Something had made so great a rent in it that it would have fallen off her. It was stained in blood.

"Oh my God," said Eachann. His hand went to his throat. "My Fiona"

"We need more people," Thorpe said. "The banshee might have her. The thing that is playing the role of Vivienne."

Eachann stared at him then said, "Let me go back to the Castle. We need to have weapons."

"Will weapons hurt her? Is she human?" Thorpe said.

But Eachann was already walking off. Hurrying and stumbling, Eachann hastened to the castle. Thorpe followed behind.

* * *

Back at the castle, Alastair and Màiri were sitting where they had been before Thorpe went out. The gas lamps were still burning, hissing faintly. They both looked up when Eachann and Thorpe entered.

Eachann had Fiona's ripped dress in his arms as he entered. Màiri wailed. Alastair's mouth tightened.

"Oh my Lord," said Màiri. "Where is Miss Fiona?"

"We think Vivienne has her," Thorpe said.

"The *bean sìth*?"

Thorpe nodded.

"Oh, no."

Eachann said, "Màiri, do you know where the key to the gun case is?"

She nodded.

"Go and fetch my shotgun from the gun room and cartridges. Hurry Màiri please."

When she'd left, Eachann turned to Alastair. His strained face gave a kind smile. "How are you now?"

Alastair closed his eyes. He said nothing.

"I know how much Fiona means to you. Nearly as much as

she means to me. I know you probably blame yourself for letting her leave, but she's a wilful girl; you couldn't have stopped her. You weren't to know."

Alastair gave a weak smile.

"He's very quiet," Thorpe said. His jaw was set, and his voice grim. He fished Alastair's bloody and slashed trousers from where they'd been thrown on the back of a chair when they were cleaning his wound. Even at arm's length, he confirmed what he'd seen before. The cut that had caused the injury was straight and clean.

Did a banshee use a knife? He remembered climbing the mountain with Fiona when she'd produced her Highland dagger, her *sgian dubh*.

Eachann nodded. "He's been through a lot."

Thorpe shook his head. "But did he deserve it?"

Eachann's eyes blazed with anger. "What do you mean? You wait here."

He turned and yelled into the castle, "Màiri!"

Thorpe said, "And the banshee ripped her dress?"

"Hmm."

Thorpe prodded Alastair with his foot. "Don't pretend to be asleep."

Eachann glared at him. "Leave him alone."

Thorpe said, "He knows something about this."

Alastair's eyes flicked open. "What?" he muttered. He stared at Thorpe and when Thorpe met his gaze, glanced away.

Thorpe said, "I think it's time you told the truth."

Alastair licked his lips. It was as if he was about to say something, but he stopped. He stared at the ceiling.

Thorpe said, "You've never seen Vivienne, have you? You were just humouring me."

Alastair gave a bitter laugh. "I just needed you to bring me back here. If I had to go along with your madness, then that's what it took. There is no Vivienne. There never was."

"So who hurt you, and who ripped Fiona's dress?"

Alastair closed his eyes again.

Thorpe snarled. "If you don't tell me where you put her, I will break every bone on your body."

Eachann lifted a warning finger. "Do not speak to Alastair like that. He knows nothing about what happened to Fiona." He turned. "Màiri, hurry!"

Thorpe said, "Because Alastair sings and tells stories, because he prefers music to fighting, you think he's not capable of behaving as the worst men do."

Eachann said, "He's not the same kind of man as you."

"We're all the same kind of man—all of us. Unless we choose differently."

Eachann shook his head. "He's not like you."

Thorpe turned back to Alastair. "Where's Fiona? I'm warning you. Speak!"

Eachann's face twisted. "What are you accusing him of? How dare you? He adored Fiona. They were children together."

Thorpe said, "And after all these years, he finally decided to take what she wouldn't give."

Eachann screamed. "Get out while you still can!"

Thorpe said, "You need to think straight."

Eachann raised his stick and brought it down, aiming for Thorpe's head. With a twist of his shoulder, Thorpe avoided the blow, then he grabbed the stick, yanked it and threw it away. It landed with a clatter on the wooden floor.

When Thorpe's back was turned, Alastair raised himself and stumbled over to the fire. Thorpe tried to reason with Eachann, while behind his back, Alastair picked up the heavy iron poker. He covered the yards between them while Thorpe was still turned the other way, then he brought the poker down across Thorpe's back.

The pain ripped through Thorpe like a jolt of electricity and he fell forward, gasping. He shouted out, turned, jumped at Alastair and pounded his fist into Alastair's face.

Alastair's nose exploded, and he screamed, falling back to put his a hand up to his nose, blood streaming through his fingers.

Màiri entered carrying a shotgun.

Thorpe saw the gun. He yelled at Eachann. "You old fool, I would never hurt Fiona,"

Eachann hobbled towards her and reached out for the gun. "Give it to me! Hurry, Màiri!"

The girl looked terrified and confused.

"Give it to me!" commanded Eachann and Màiri handed the gun to him, her eyes darting to Thorpe then back to her master as if trying to work out what had happened.

"Cartridges!" he snapped.

Thorpe turned to Alastair who stood, one hand to his face, the other still holding the poker. Alastair stared over Thorpe's shoulder, watching Eachann scrabbling to load the gun. Thorpe had only seconds to get the truth.

"Tell me!" he snapped. "Where is she?"

Alastair screamed like an animal and brandished the poker but had no intent and no courage. He was like a cornered cur dog: he would bite if pushed, but Alastair was counting on Eachann to shoot Thorpe.

There was a click, then another click as Eachann pushed the cartridges into the shotgun.

"Lord Eachann," Thorpe shouted. "He knows where Fiona is. He put her there."

As Thorpe turned to face Eachann, Alastair lunged with the poker.

Thorpe spun round, sidestepped and swung. His fists met only air, but Alastair fell back, and Thorpe advanced. He ducked under the waving poker and came up to punch Alastair once then twice in rapid succession. Alastair stumbled. Thorpe snarled and went for him, losing his head in a red mist. Then out of the corner of his eye, he saw Eachann level the shotgun and jumped out of the way of the deafening double blast.

His ears rang, and a jolt of pain came from his left shoulder. But the bulk of the shot had gone past, embedding itself in the wood panelling. Màiri put her hands to her cheeks and screamed.

Eachann yelled. "Give me more cartridges!"

Alastair was weeping, his face smeared with blood, tears and snot. His mouth twisted in a snarl. "Fiona threw herself at you, but you didn't want her. So I tried to take her. How dare she scorn me all these years? "

Thorpe's hand was on his wound. He felt the sticky warm blood soaking through the tweed. But in his rage, he felt no pain. "You little shit," he said.

"After you hurt me, she was on my side. She tried to be nice to me, so I asked her who she wanted most. And she cried and said she wanted to be my friend, but she didn't love me. She said she loved you. How could she love you? She hardly knows you."

"So you raped her."

"I would have. If she hadn't done this." He pointed to his wound. "But either way, I beat you."

"You beat me? You vile beast, you misunderstand everything." Thorpe grabbed Alastair's jacket with both hands and head-butted him, breaking his nose. He heard and felt the crunch of the bone, and Alastair's blood ran down his face. Thorpe dropped him onto the floor and turned back.

Behind him, even with his fumbling fingers, Eachann had succeeded in reloading the shotgun. He pointed it at Thorpe. He hadn't heard Alastair's confession. From the other side of the Baronial Hall, he yelled at Thorpe, "Men like you should be locked up."

Thorpe turned, "He tried to rape your daughter. It's she who stabbed him in self-defence."

Eachann faltered. He went white. But he firmed his mouth

and shook his head. "I don't believe you. He's a good man. I've known him since he was a boy. If anyone hurt Fiona, it was you."

Eachann's fingers curled around the double triggers. He was about to fire both barrels.

Màiri said, "Don't shoot the Captain. You all need to go for Miss Fiona. She's not safe."

Thorpe looked at her. She seemed to be taking his side. He frowned.

Màiri said, "Fiona is not safe out there. You're the only one who is fit and able. You must go and find her."

But Eachann had already made his mind up who the villain was. He'd fired the first shot in anger. The second would be with unshakable determination.

When he saw Eachann's eye narrow, Thorpe ducked right and rolled on the floor towards the door.

There was a roar and a flash. With his ears ringing and heart thumping, Thorpe thought he had received his death-wound.

He looked back at Eachann, and he saw Màiri's face screaming "Go!" From Eachann's rage, it appeared Màiri had pushed him, causing him to miss.

Thorpe took Màiri's advice and ran.

Thorpe fled from the Castle, blood drying and matting through his jacket and shirt. Outside, the fog had thinned, and points of starlight littered the sky between high ragged clouds. The moon was up, pale and sick, and over in the east behind the mountains was a hint of grey. Dawn would be here soon.

He guessed Eachann was reloading and would be out after him before long. He had to find Fiona. Just because her dress was in the Rose Garden didn't mean that's where Alastair had finished his attack. Thorpe guessed he'd taken her to the cave because he thought that would be away from any chance of discovery while he assaulted her. His nose had been bleeding from Thorpe hitting him earlier, hence the trail of blood on the grass.

He hadn't seen her around the cave entrance or down the drop into the Well of the Mothers. Even though she'd stabbed Alastair he could have hurt her. She could still be somewhere round there. Thorpe started to jog in the direction of the Terrace. Where the poker had hit him was throbbing agony. It bent all his mind towards it, and he found it hard to think of anything else, but he had to focus. The few shotgun pellets that had penetrated his coat were nothing—like a stinging of nettles. Madness infected the castle. Lust and rage, rape and violence, filled the place, and it came from Vivienne.

He ran on until running hurt too much, and he had to slow. He walked through the garden, in pain and bleeding still heading for the Well.

In the dark, he heard someone call his name. It was a woman's voice. He looked through the dawn light and, coming through the garden, saw Màiri and her mistress, Lady Gráinne. He stopped, stood his ground and was ready for more hatred from them. But when Gráinne called his name, her voice was kind. "William, you must help us. You must save Fiona."

"Have you seen her?"

Gráinne shook her head. "Alastair took her down into the cave."

He nodded. "That's what I think too."

Gráinne said, "You must save her."

"She could die down there," Màiri said.

Gráinne took his hand and gripped it. "No one else here is strong enough to help her." Then as she got closer, she put her hand to her mouth. "You're covered in blood."

"Where's Lord Eachann?" he said. "Is he following me?"

They both looked blankly at him.

"He shot me. Màiri, you were there. You made him miss."

Màiri smiled gently. "I did it for you."

"Thank you. He thinks I attacked Fiona and that Alastair is innocent."

Gráinne said, "Alastair got what he deserved. But you must prove your courage, sir knight."

Màiri nodded. "You must risk your life to save Fiona."

"You're our only hope now," Gráinne said. "We brought you something." She nodded at Màiri, who was carrying a bundle wrapped in a blanket. She offered it to him.

"What is it?" he said, not taking it.

"Look," Gráinne said.

He hesitated then took it from Màiri's arms. He knew what it was through the blanket. He unwrapped it and there in the faint dawn light was a great Highland claymore.

"We took it off the wall," offered Gráinne.

"We covered it," Màiri said. "It's steel. Iron and steel are poisonous to the *Sìth*. They can't touch them."

He took the great basket hilt of the claymore. With his left hand, he gave Màiri back the blanket and then wrapped both of his hands around the claymore's hilt.

"Do you think I will meet the banshee down there?"

Màiri said, "Certainly you will. This is her test for you."

Thorpe held the claymore in front of him. "I'm not so confident this will work," he said. "I'm not sure Vivienne is made of flesh and blood."

"Don't lose your nerve," Màiri said. "You must go into the cave. You must keep your courage. Rescue Fiona."

"I will. I won't let her down."

"We like you," Gráinne said.

"We admire your courage and strength," Màiri said.

"We have some other things to help," Gráinne said. She showed him a rope and an oil lamp.

"Thank you," he said.

Màiri said, "Let us walk with you to the cave entrance."

"Are the caves explored?"

"Only partly. They go down to the sea, but they flood. Once you're in, you must keep going forward. You have to be careful the tide doesn't catch you, or you will drown," Gráinne said.

They started to walk in silence. After a few minutes, they arrived at the entrance to the cave. In the pale dawn light, he could see into it. He saw the rocky hole in the floor that led down to the sea caves. The water had receded; the tide must be out. There was no sign of Fiona, but there was a smear of blood on the rock. Previously, he'd thought it was Alastair's, but it could easily be Fiona's.

"Do you think that Alastair took her down there?" He said.

Gráinne and Màiri said together, "She is down there. So is danger. Hurry now."

Thorpe touched the blood. It came up wet on his fingertips. Alastair could have hurt her before she stabbed him. She may be grievously wounded. Who knew what he would do to her in his feeble rage?

"Is this the only way down?" he said to Gráinne.

She nodded.

"Be bold. Let not your courage fail you," Màiri said.

Gráinne said, "We are counting on your bravery and your will.".

Thorpe smiled grimly. "I hope I prove worthy of your trust."

He went to the edge of the hole. He knelt, then turned and lowered his feet down, then his belly until he was hanging by his fingertips. Unsure of the depth, but guessing it wasn't more than eight feet, he lowered himself as far as he could, then he released his fingertips and he dropped into the dark. He landed on the rock floor and shouted back up. "I'm down."

He saw the women's faces appear above him, orange in the lamplight. Màiri tied the lamp to the rope and lowered it down. When he had the light in his hands, she drew the rope up again and retied it to the claymore. She let that down too. When he had the sword, she released the rope that slithered down and fell in a coil on the damp rock floor. He couldn't get back up now even if he wanted to.

He put the lantern down on the floor while he wrapped the rope around his middle like a belt. Then he picked the lamp up in his left, and in his right hand he held the heavy sword.

Gráinne shouted down. "Please take care."

He looked up at their worried faces. "I will."

"Hurry to save Fiona," Gráinne said. "Be brave."

"Choose well," Màiri said. Then they were out of sight.

Eleven

THORPE MADE his way into the cave like a blind worm tunnelling into the earth. The light of the day world was lost far behind. Faint as it had been, that light had anchored him. Now the anchor was gone, and he wandered a netherworld of spirits and dreams.

As he went into the earth, it was as if he had entered an ancient and primitive realm of rock and water. Things moved out of sight. Imagination rose up to disorientate him. Dreams were more potent than in the daylight here. Things emerged from the depths of the earth and from nightmare in these nether caves. He smelled salt water, and he remembered Gráinne's warning about the tide. He wondered when it would be at its fullest and hurried to find Fiona before it rose.

Deeper and deeper he went, stumbling and almost losing his footing on the slippery rocks. At times, the path was level but tended always down. He came across a place that was frothing and boiling with seawater and jumped from one rock to another to avoid falling in.

Another time, slipping on weed, he teetered, unable to use his hands. He lurched backwards, balancing the steel claymore in one hand and his lantern in the other. Then, throwing himself forward, he lumbered one step after another onto a bank of sand. Oil sloshed in the bottom of the lantern as he stumbled. He shook it to work out how much was left and hoped he had enough to light his way down and light their way back.

It was cold in the cave. He seemed to go deeper and deeper. It was hard to believe that ordinary caves could be so labyrinthine. He had lost all sense of time. It must have been more than an hour, but it could have been minutes.

In the distance, he heard the primordial swelling of the ocean, a deep rhythmic beat of waves. The rock path led beside a flooded cavern, a finger of the sea. Thorpe looked down into the green water, and in the weak yellow light of the hissing lamp, saw creatures beneath the waves. Colossal fish flicked too and fro, agitated by his presence. There were white eels there also and things worse than those moving in the lightless deep.

Turning a corner, he nearly slipped and flung his arm around a stalactite to save himself. Breathing raggedly, he imagined falling into the water. Mind racing, he thought about going under and churning among the slithering things that lived there.

After that, he walked more carefully, choosing his footholds in the dim light of the lamp. He would be no use to Fiona if haste drowned him, but as he slowed, he cursed himself. He listened to the water and did not know how far yet he had to go. Then he saw blood against a rock. Examining it in the lamplight, he saw it was still wet.

He went on. He thought the flame burned lower and fainter. He grew frightened the light would die, and he would be left in the dark down here. Without light, he knew he would never leave. He would never leave and never find Fiona, and neither of them would ever see daylight again. He could have cursed Alastair, but what use was cursing now?

There were noises down here. Strange noises made by things that had never seen the sun. His heart skipped and his eyes darted to every shadow.

"Get a grip on yourself, man," he muttered.

The rock galleries flickered in the lamplight, and a thousand shadows fluttered suggesting someone was there. He felt people watching him, and things other than people. He imagined them breathing. Sometimes he thought he heard the chuckling of their old voices. He saw shapes out of the corner of his eyes, ahead, below and in front. The sea was rising. He had to hurry, so he put safety to one side and went at a jolting pace, until he slipped, almost fell in the water, and stopped to catch his breath and calm his jumping nerves.

To keep up courage, Thorpe began to mutter to himself. He told himself to be strong; he told himself to be brave. At one point he even sang snatches of the nursery rhyme his nanny used to sing him when he was small.

The sword was a terrible burden in his hand. The lamp heavy as lead.

Down in the sea caves, he heard a noise. It was definitely someone, not something. The noise came out of the darkness ahead. Thorpe stopped to listen. The waves slapped, the water dripped and the gusting air moaned in the deeps and whistled through dark holes in unseen walls.

But the noise he'd heard was not those. He listened harder until it came again. Yes, somebody was there.

Thorpe cleared his throat. "Who is that?" he said.

At first, there was no reply. He peered, lifting the lamp to see better. There was a thicker shadow ahead. It was different from the shadows around it. He couldn't make it out clearly.

A voice called: "William."

He stammered, "Who's that?"

A laugh.

His mouth was dry. "Don't play games. Who is that?"

"Màiri."

"Màiri?" The light was so poor. He couldn't see. But how could Màiri have got ahead of him? Unless there was another way down, and they had all played a trick on him. Unless they were all in it together

"It's Màiri; it's me," she said again.

"But how?"

She didn't reply.

"Come out," he said. "Step into the light."

He put down the lantern on the rock by his feet and held the claymore with both hands in front of him.

"Do you like me, William?" The voice came from behind now. The same voice. But how the hell could she have got behind him?

He spun around, sword pointed forward. "Màiri, what are you doing?" He felt the hilt of the claymore. Sweat made his fingers sticky. He closed his left hand over his right to get a more secure grip.

Màiri appeared from the shadows, coming out behind him. Her face flickered in the lamplight, but it was Màiri's face. And how young and fresh and beautiful she was; her red hair and her moss green eyes. But she wasn't wearing the same dress he'd seen her in when she'd knocked Eachann's shotgun. Instead, she wore a kirtle of green silk, far grander than a maid ever owned.

As he watched, she unfastened it and let it drop. She stood there in her underwear: pearl white against her pale skin.

"Màiri, I don't understand how you got here."

She unclipped her bra and took it off. Her white breasts swung free, and she stared at him with lustful eyes. "We can do it here," she said. "I know you want to do it with me. You liked it last time, didn't you?"

"I have to find Fiona."

Màiri stepped out of her knickers and stood there naked. The downy hair on her pubis was pale red. "I'm ready," she said. "Come and feel how wet I am for you."

He shook. He felt like he used to feel when he wanted a woman. He remembered the pleasure he'd taken in making a girl want him, holding her down and making her moan. It had all been about power over women, all about being their master. Now he shook his head.

"Do you think I'm beautiful?" She whispered in his ear.

"Yes, but please put your clothes on."

She laughed. "Come and be a man. Where's your courage, little boy?"

"Put your clothes on, please."

She came close until she stood only a breath away. He felt her warmth in that cold place. Her nipples puckered pink like rosebuds, and she pushed herself into him, grinding her pubis onto his thigh. Then she reached down and squeezed his crotch.

"See," she said. "I knew you wanted me."

"It's not right," he said. "I need to find Fiona."

She walked her fingers up his back and into his hair.

Thorpe stood there, the sword still in his right hand, but trailing now, almost touching the floor.

He balled his left hand into a fist to stop himself from grabbing her flesh.

She kissed him. She was like spring sunshine. He felt her naked body against him. He smelled her musk. His resistance to her was failing. He wanted to throw her down on the ground and push her knees apart with his so he could have her.

Through gritted teeth, he said, "No."

"A real man would take me here and now."

He shook his head. His hands ached with tension as he kept them away from her.

"I don't love you," he said.

She said, "What's love got to do with it?" But it wasn't her voice, it was Vivienne's.

He recoiled. And instead of Màiri's red hair and pale skin, it was Vivienne. She stood, dark-haired and olive-skinned as a Greek priestess. The hair between her legs was sable and perfumed with her lust. Her nipples were dark red as wine where Màiri's had been rose pink.

His hand tightened on the sword. She sensed his thoughts. "You'd never hurt me, William. I am your Queen. I'm the only one you ever loved. Of all the women you took, it was only me you loved. You will never be free. Nor do you ever want to be."

And then she melted like a black mist.

Vivienne was gone. Màiri was gone. But he was still there. Water lapped around his shoes. The tide was coming in.

He stood there, dazed. The lantern still burned. He gripped the sword tighter to give him confidence and he then he picked up the lantern and went on. He wouldn't be able to get back this way. He would have to find another way out.

He walked with greater urgency. Vivienne filled his mind. It was true the real Vivienne, of all the women he had seduced, was the only one he had feelings for. With her, he was the biter, bit: the seducer, seduced. And ultimately, she wouldn't have him.

His head was down. He was sloshing through water. He tried to tell himself this wasn't the real Vivienne. The real Vivienne was thousands of miles away in Mysore, back with her husband and lost to him.

But he hurried. Perhaps he hurried because he wanted to find Fiona before the tide rose. But maybe it was because his dream of Vivienne drew him on like a compass.

The water was around his ankles now. He splashed through it as he went deeper. The tunnels went deeper. Soon it would be too deep for him to progress. It would be too deep for him to get back. He broke into a run.

But he ran into the rising tide. It was round his thighs, then his waist. He held the lamp up high so the water wouldn't douse it. The heavy claymore was an unbearable weight. The wound in his shoulder burned like fire.

The water was below his breast as he forced himself forward. He had a plan that he would find a higher rock and stand there, wait the tide out. But he saw wet seaweed hanging from the ceiling of the cave.

They'd lured him to his death.

Thorpe heard a voice. He had heard so many voices here but they had never belonged to a human. But this one was the voice of someone in need and pain.

"Fiona?" He yelled.

"William?"

He gritted his teeth, this could be another mirage, another test, but he shouted, "Fiona, I'm coming."

He came to a low archway in the rock. It was the entrance to a tunnel. The water was waist high here. In the gloom, he could trip and fall in an unseen hole and go under the water.

"William," Fiona's voice called again.

He had to go to her. He ducked and went through the rock archway. The walls here were veined in quartz and amethyst, glinting white and purple in the light of his dying lamp. He shook it to see how much oil was left; not so much. He had hoped that this low rock arch signalled an end to his journey, but it was not so. Ahead, the darkness stretched. He glanced up at the ceiling with its sparkling quartz. It was still damp from the last tide. Seaweed hung down. This was a place for drowning.

How could Fiona be down here? It was too far—too deep

under the earth. This was the banshee again, and all the banshee wanted was his death.

His shirt and jacket were soaked and the brine stung his wound. He had lifted the lamp clear, but it was only inches above the tide now. If it got swamped, then he would have no hope, because it was as black as pitch down there. All the time the sea flooded higher into the cave system. The lamp flame flickered low.

If the tunnel was climbing, it didn't seem to make much difference to the water level, which still rose. His arms ached from holding up the claymore and the lamp. He was struggling to keep going. Each step was an ordeal. He held the lamp as high as he could, keeping it out of the water. He was going so slow, inch by inch. The tide was now at the level of his heart. But still, he laboured on, his breath coming in gasps. He thought of his own death. To come to this—to have faced the guns and anger of the enemy and live, to be saved only to drown like a rat in a hole.

He listened to the swishing water as in rushed in behind him. And then the lamp died. He held it, useless, for a minute and then he dropped into the sea water. The hot metal hissed as it disappeared. The darkness was now perfect. The blackness was so complete that it was as if nothing really existed. He hoped he would not lose his dignity in those last moments. He hoped he would die like a man.

And then, a soft white light bathed the cave. He saw his hands again—swimming out before him, one empty, the other grasping the sword. He felt his body buoyed up by the salt tide. The light was diffuse, and it was difficult to tell where it came from.

Ahead of him, on a bank of sand, Fiona lay. He waded out of the water, splashing his way towards her. He still held the claymore. The illumination came from somewhere past Fiona. He rushed up to her, knelt on the sand and she reached and took his hand.

"Alastair tried to rape me. He hit me and ripped off my dress."

He squeezed her hand. "I know."

"I ran. I didn't know where I was going. I was bleeding but he didn't catch me. I was so scared."

He saw her face was bruised. There were smears of blood beneath her nose and she had mottled thumb marks at her neck as if Alastair had tried to throttle her before she got to her knife.

"I'm so sorry, Fiona."

"And I got to the cave and he caught me, but I had my knife and I stabbed him. I meant to hurt him. I think I did."

"You did."

"Good. Then, in my panic I went down the hole. I thought he would come after me."

"No, he was too badly wounded."

She looked away, but muttered, "I said good, but I'm sorry I hurt him."

"He deserved it."

"I knew there was a way out of the caves the far end. I just hoped I'd find that. I didn't know how vast they were."

"There's light up there," Thorpe said.

All the time, Thorpe waited for her to change into another face of the banshee: another temptress, another dream. But she stayed human, her hair plastered, dark-blonde over her forehead. The light was brighter ahead. "Wait here a second," he muttered.

"I don't think I've got anywhere to go, really," Fiona said, forcing a smile.

Thorpe went forward to see where the light was coming from. He stepped a few yards past Fiona, then he looked up. There was a hole, surrounded by glittering amethyst. And through the hole, he saw Gráinne reaching down.

"Take my hand William," she said.

He looked at her, amazed.

"Don't drop the sword." She was wearing a white dress; the same one he'd seen her in the first time they met in the Castle.

"Fiona's back there."

"Go and get her, but then come back here."

He helped Fiona up. He shook his head, frowning deeply. "Your mother's there," he said.

Fiona said, "It may look like her, but it's not my mother."

Thorpe got to the hole and lifted and pushed Fiona until she could get out of the caves. When she'd disappeared from view, Gráinne said, "Take my hand."

"Do I still need the sword?" he said.

She said, "Yes, bring the sword. There is a use for it."

He held back. Fiona had gone up into the place above.

Gráinne smiled. "Don't let your courage fail you here, right at the end."

He reached up with his free hand. She grabbed him with both hands on his left wrist. She pulled. The water helped him up. His foot caught on a rock, and he used that as leverage. He pushed himself and grabbed the stone on the edge of the hole. He managed to pull and then reached and held with his left hand. He dragged himself up, and he was there with her in the cavern. It looked drier—as if the sea never or rarely reached this high.

He couldn't see Fiona.

"Lady Gráinne," he said, but couldn't continue, the words stopped, and he stared. "How are you down here? Where is Fiona?"

Gráinne stroked his cheek. "She's gone ahead. You have done well so far. Only the last test now."

He said, "I don't understand. What's going on?"

She nodded. "The price must now be paid—a price of submission or a price of wisdom."

"How do we get out of here?"

"Not down there," she pointed down the hole to the broiling sea which had by now almost filled the tunnel.

"Is there another way?"

She nodded. "Come with me."

He followed her then halted. "What about Vivienne?"

"Your wife?"

He rubbed his eyes. "I don't know. I don't think so. I think she's the spirit."

"Don't you know what she wants yet?"

"She wants power over me."

Gráinne said, "You think so? You still haven't learned?" She held out her hand, and he took it. They walked on. The tunnel looked man-made. The floor was beaten clay, packed down over the years as if by many feet.

"What is this place?"

"It's an old smugglers' tunnel."

"Where does it go?"

"To the crypts beneath the church. It's how the smugglers brought in their rum and tea once they'd landed it on the beach in the cove."

His heart filled with hope. He thought that they would get to the church crypt then come up into the daylight again. Then all would be well. Fiona must be already out.

He trudged his way up the steps behind Gráinne until they emerged into a stone-clad crypt. The boxes of the dead were all around. He smelled the dust and the dry decay of centuries, but they walked on. Gráinne led him up some steps until finally she lifted open a wooden hatch, more like a lid, and he smelled the musty book smell of church. They stepped up. Thorpe recognised the chapel in the Castle. There on the altar was the ancient carving of the Three Mothers.

Thorpe was in the old chapel. He saw watery footmarks leading out and guessed that's where Fiona must have gone, back into the castle

Gráinne pushed the door closed. She turned the key, and locked them in with a click.

Thorpe looked around the room. There was the strange stone altarpiece. He looked to the east, and beyond the altar was a throne. He saw that clearly now. It was a throne made for three. Sitting in the centre seat of the throne, wearing a robe the colours of a peacock's feather was Vivienne. She was young and beautiful; dark-skinned with eyes like a snake. He saw her bare feet and her slender ankles, and he knew that under the robe she was naked. Round her neck was a necklace and at her throat as its centrepiece was a silver moon.

To Vivienne's left, red-haired Màiri sat. Màiri wore a necklace of iron shaped like a star. Golden-haired Gráinne took her place to the right. She wore a necklace of gold shaped like the sun.

"You've come," said Vivienne. Hers was the voice that whispered in his ears before he woke all the mornings of his life. Hers was the voice of the woman who lives in men. She was the divine dream of woman that flowers like a white rose in the hidden garden.

Vivienne stood, and the robe dropped from her. The tan of her skin, her breasts, her throat, her waist and soft belly and the flaring of her woman's hips all drew his eyes. Between her legs, was her sable hair. Lust rose in him and with it fear. He reached for something to hold onto, to keep him steady. "Vivienne," he said, voice trembling. "Is it really you?"

He held the claymore in his right hand.

Vivienne walked towards him. She put her left hand on his shoulder. As she spoke, he saw blood-red lips and teeth white as sharpened bone.

"Do you want me?" she said and her serpent's eyes glittered gold and black. He shook his head, trying to clear his mind of the heaviness that had come upon him.

"Hmm," she said, her eyes gone smoky between dark lashes. She reached down between his legs. "You want me," she said. "You always want me."

Gráinne stood and descended toward him. She too was naked

now, her white robe dropped at her feet. Her skin was golden where Vivienne's was dark.

"The sword," Gráinne said.

He held it tight.

"You know what you must do," Vivienne said. "It is the price you pay for us."

Vivienne unbuttoned his shirt, beginning at his throat. She opened the shirt to his collar bone and leaned to kiss his neck. He smelled her hair—the perfume of jasmine and bitter nightshade. Her mouth brushed his throat, her teeth raked his carotid artery, her lips lingered like leeches. Her other hand held him harder between his legs.

"Give it up to us," Gráinne, standing in front of him. "It will be quick. The sword is sharp."

From his left side Màiri said, "Sacrifice or wisdom, which is it to be?"

He tried to pull away from Vivienne. He stretched back and took the sword in his right hand. Vivienne said, "You wanted to take me once against my will," she said. "Now I will allow you. For a price."

He looked around and saw Gráinne's eyes fierce and bright. "Give us the sacrifice," she hissed. "Be a man."

He stepped back, his lust for Vivienne, for all of them, almost overwhelming him.

To his left, Màiri had cast off her fairy-green gown. She stroked his arm and came to kiss his neck. Her small teeth brushed his skin.

Vivienne stood to his right, Màiri to his left and Gráinne in front of him. They undressed him. He ached for them.

Vivienne looked amused. She pushed her hands beneath her breasts and cupped them to him in offering, their dark tips red and hard. "Do you know what we want yet?" she said.

He still held the sword. He knew the price he would pay if he gave the wrong answer—the price Eachann had paid.

"So?" said Vivienne.

"What do you want most?" he said.

She nodded. The women watched, waiting for him to answer.

"I thought it was power over men," he said. He could feel their eyes on him. "But now I know it's not that."

"So what is it?" said Vivienne.

"You want to be free to choose."

Vivienne looked at him, and her eyes were tender. And then all three of them were gone.

* * *

Lady Gráinne found him collapsed in the old Chapel.

"Is Fiona all right?" He asked.

"Yes, it's been terrible, but are you unhurt? She collapsed but told me you'd be here."

He nodded. "Why did you send me into the sea caves?"

Gráinne looked concerned. "Do you know where you are?"

"Yes, at Dungarvan Castle, in the chapel. But you and Màiri sent me into the Sea Caves."

Gráinne shook her head. "I think you must have imagined that. Màiri and I have been looking for you."

"Where's Fiona now?"

"She's safe now. She's back in the castle with her father and Dr McKinnon. The police are on their way for Alastair. She stabbed him, it was in self-defence. Heaven knows what he'd have done to her if she hadn't had her knife."

"Thank God for her little *sgian dubh*."

"I carry one too."

Thorpe smiled. "I thought you might."

"Eachann thought it was you who'd attacked Fiona."

"I know."

"But after you'd gone, it became obvious. He wants to apologise. We went looking for you in the grounds. "

"Did you go to the Well?"

"Yes, but the tide was full and the well overflowing. We couldn't get down. I didn't even think you would go down there."

"It was some kind of test."

"Just like in the old stories. And it seems you have proved yourself a true and honest knight."

Twelve

THE GREAT HILLS around Dungarvan were covered in snow, and the pine trees swayed darkly in the breeze from the sea. The waters of the burn were locked by ice, and the great boulder against which William's car struck, still bore the scar of their fateful meeting.

But Dungarvan Castle overflowed with light and joy. It was decked for Christmas and for a wedding.

William married Fiona McScaigh on Christmas Eve. Her father gave her away. Kit Thomason came from India to be Best Man. Alastair went to prison and then emigrated and was never seen in Scotland again.

After the wedding ceremony, William's father stood with Lord Eachann enjoying a malt whisky by the blazing log fire in the Library.

William's father said, "Lovely service."

"Yes, it was nice."

"Bride looked beautiful."

"And the groom very handsome."

William's father hesitated. "By the way, that was a strange altar piece."

Eachann sipped his whisky. "It's very old. It belongs in the family."

"Is it a lucky charm?'

Eachann smiled. "Not exactly, but it reminds us of our obligations."

Mr Thorpe said, "Oh, and what obligations are those?"

"To love, to loyalty and to the land we spring from."

"Ah, well, can't say fairer than that," Thorpe's father said. "I think my William has met his match."

Eachann studied his glass. "Your William is a better man than I ever was–braver, more honest."

Mr Thorpe said, "That's jolly nice of you to say, but he wasn't always that way. For a long time he was a bit of a beast."

Eachann said, "But now he's a man you can be proud of."

"Yes, indeed, Lord Eachann. I think you're right."

Shadowkin

"MAY a raven of night consume his heart, and may he drown in the deepest shadows!"

These were the words, spoken to herself in her own empty room, that Lilith Smith spat out, as she brooded over the man who had dismissed her art. Thomas McKinnon of Kinmont Gallery, George Street, Edinburgh was the object of her ire; a man whose dismissal was rooted in his snobbery and adherence to the fashionable, rather than an appreciation for the soulful. But Lilith wanted to be authentic and he was one of the few Scottish gallery owners still left in the city.

Lilith identified an artist, in her heart and mind, and it was this which gave her the right to claim the title. Others didn't possess this right, for they were not artists. Their aspirations could be trampled upon and dismissed, much like the way she felt Thomas McKinnon had trampled on her identity and indeed her soul right now.

Lilith was not a friendly person, and she didn't care tuppence to be one either. She was an artist and her job was to channel ethereal forces into this mundane world. The struggle of being a struggling artist was her life.

Lilith was her chosen name, a significant change from her given name, Deborah. The transformation felt right.

After her education at Leeds Art College and three years at Liverpool John Lennon, she had attempted to sell her work in London's art districts. The reactions of the gallery owners had been bourgeois and narrow minded as they shrank back from her deliberately shocking works. It was the lack of vision and profit-driven blindness of the London galleries that had driven her to the north, to Edinburgh, where she found herself living in a rather unsavoury 'scheme' in Livingstone.

Livingstone wasn't an ideal place for an artist like Lilith. It was ugly and the locals didn't appreciate art, and she had found herself at odds with them more than once with her public performance pieces, which she had put on for herself and her daemon, not for them, the plebs. However, the biggest hindrance in living in Livingstone was the difficulty of obtaining absinthe, the Green Fairy, her chosen muse.

Religion was not a topic Lilith often discussed with her neighbours either, but her belief in Lucifer, the Light Bringer, was deep-rooted. She saw him as a figure of liberty, far different from the figure demonised in the holy books of the Xians. No, she did not commune with such shallow spirituality. She found her true will aligning with the views of Blake, Milton, Goethe and Aleister Crowley.

And her art was a direct reflection of her beliefs; infernal and distinct. Using an impasto technique with oils, she painted what her soul prompted, often ending with what the weak-minded found disturbing pieces. And as she sipped absinthe (she'd ordered it via Amazon) in her room on the fifteenth floor of her high-rise, gazing at the urban desolation that was her current life, she knew one thing: things had to get better.

. . .

Deciding it was time to give the universe a nudge in her favour, Lilith took out her chalks and drew a magic circle on the floor. Inscribing it in the Witches' Alphabet with protective words circled its edge, and she then fetched her stash of black and red candles (from Temu in fact. They'd taken a while to arrive) from her personal treasure chest. Placing the candles in the resin candlesticks, fashioned like screaming souls, (Etsy) she set the eerie scene in place.

Inside the magic circle, she sat with her goblet and athame. Pouring wine into the silver goblet, she sliced her thumb with the ritual knife, letting the blood drip into the wine. With the addition of wormwood and vervain, she consumed the concoction in her own little ritual.

She whispered a prayer to her spiritual guide, Lucifer. Her request was simple, yet significant. A plea for financial stability, a life away from the neo-liberal hell-hole of late surveillance capitalism, and a personal anathema for Thomas McKinnon of Kinmont Gallery for his poor taste in art.

As she finished the prayer, the room seemed to respond to her plea. The candles flickered in an absent breeze, and a low growl echoed through the silent room. The Demon had heard her! Thought it might just be the neighbour's dog, she mused.

Out of the magic circle, after another glass of absinthe and a few strokes on an oil painting of The Great Leviathan, Lilith turned in for the night. But not before indulging in an episode of *The Crown*, a show she detested for its display of privilege and authority, streamed through the despised colonialist medium of Netflix.

The next day, walking the city for infernal inspiration, idly watching the Scavvies emptying bins, she wandered past Greyfriars Boby, thought of dipping into Greyfriars Kirkyard to visit the Black Mausoleum to commune with the McKenzie Poltergeist, but instead visited the Occult Shop at the top of Candlemaker Row, where she spotted an advertisement on the community noticeboard. Among the tarot readers and past-life regression shamans, the note was simple: lodger wanted. The address was near here.

Lodger was an antiquated term, she thought, and 'tenant' seemed a better fit. Regardless, the location — Candlemaker Row, right in the heart of town, close to the Frankenstein Bar and the Occult Shop, was ideal. Taking out her mobile phone from her knapsack, she decided to act. It seemed her ritual might just have begun to bear fruit.

Lilith dialled the number, hoping for the best. The woman who answered had a voice as quiet as a whisper carried on a midnight breeze, and introduced herself as Martha Gray. Upon confirming the availability of the room, Lilith was taken aback by the affordability of the rent. Without a moment's hesitation, she agreed to visit the house. Her future landlady (though perhaps they could be friends?) opened the door to her knock.

Martha Gray was a monochrome figure, wrapped in a shawl of deepest black, her hair a mix of black and silver. She wore grey blouse, black slacks, and her bare feet were noticeably bony. Her thin frame suggested she needed more porridge. But what truly stood out was the peculiar birthmark on her neck. It was an odd, abstract shape, as if painted by shadow fingers in soot and ink.

"Are you hear for my muses?" Martha said. "They have called you, I think."

Lilith didn't know what the woman was talking about, but she never liked to be wrong-footed so she laughed and pretended she understood. Martha changed the subject. "I hope you like it."

The house Martha showed Lilith was a maze of stairways and

rooms. Martha lived upstairs, with another tenant named Jamie residing on the ground floor. The room she offered to Lilith was downstairs in the basement.

As they descended the narrow, wooden staircase, Martha inquired about Lilith's unusual name, to which Lilith provided a brief account of her identity as the first wife of Adam, mother of demons. Martha took all this in her stride and smiled, though whether with understand or in indifference, it was hard to tell.

Upon entering the basement room, Lilith noticed the dimness. Only two small windows near the ceiling allowed the natural light in, but Lilith had always preferred the dark anyway, so that wasn't a deal-breaker. The bedsit room was sparsely furnished, with a bed, sofa, and a table that held an antiquated television. But the thing that truly caught her attention was the artwork adorning the walls.

Lilith stood back and said, "Wow!"

Martha smiled, apparently gratified by Lilith's exclamation of approval.

Lilith stepped forward and studied the paintings closely. They seemed to depict a world on the edge of reality, of places visited in dreams but never in life. And the weirdest thing was that the daubs and trails of ink on the walls bore an eerie resemblance to the mark on Martha's neck. Perhaps the mark was a tattoo?

Lilith asked who'd painting such otherworldly and abysmal (in the true meaning of that word) wonders?

Martha's eyes took on a glassy look, and her thin lips parted slightly as if admitting this had an emotional cost. "They were painted by 'The Small Ones,' she said, during the night, and painted them in her dreams."

"What do you mean painted them in your dreams?"

"I dream they are painting them and when I wake up and come down there, the images I dreamt are on the walls in these marks of shadow and soot."

"Is it soot?" Lilith said, going forward to touch.

"No! Don't touch!" said Martha. "You'll spoil them, and besides, they told me never to touch them for the good of my own health."

"They told you in your dreams?" Lilith said, squinting at Martha to discern whether she was full of shit.

"And elsewhere."

"They certainly are haunting."

"They have haunted me," Martha said.

Lilith merely gave a hollow smile such as she imagined someone in a Huysman's novel would smile . She said, "I know they paint, but do the The Small Ones identify as artists?"

Marth said, "Judge for yourself. Only an artist knows another artist. All I know is that they come when I whisper for them to come, and sometimes they come anyway: *Vocatus atque non vocatus, parvi aderunt.*"

"Quite."

Leaving the house, Lilith said to herself, "Right". As she walked to the bus stop, she carefully repeated the rent amount to herself. It was so laughably low that she couldn't help but suspect something was amiss. Perhaps it was the dim, basement room itself. Or maybe it was the eccentric landlady, Martha, whose peculiar gleam in her eyes and odd birthmark on her neck did little to ease her concerns.

Nonetheless, Lilith found herself strangely drawn to the ink and soot paintings that adorned the walls. They called like siren songs that pulled her in, making her wonder if this small basement bedsit would serve as a muse for her own art. Perhaps the Dark Lord was delivering as she'd asked. She accepted the offer.

. . .

On moving day, she enlisted the help of Adam, a friend with a car, to transport her few possessions. They found the front door wide open and despite calling for Martha, received no response. There was an eerie stillness to the house, punctuated only by the distant chatter of tourists and the ticking of a clock in the hallway.

Upon reaching the basement room, Lilith noticed a key in the door, and with a turn, it unlocked with a circular click. "Seems you're expected," said Adam in his barbarous Scottish accent, teasingly called her 'Lil,' which she promptly rebuffed. As they descended the wooden stairs, and entered the bedsit, whose door was open, Adam caught sight of the wall paintings. His immediate reaction was one of disturbed awe.

"They're something, Lil. Not something nice thought."

Lilith explained that they were the work of 'The Small Ones,' a response that left Adam frowning. "Your landlady maybe painted them herself. Maybe she's a sleep painter rather than a sleep walker. I had a friend who claimed he planted potatoes in his sleep, dug them in and all."

"The Small Ones painted them. They are spirits." Lilith said.

"Righty-oh," said Adam. "Looks like they painted them in soot and cobwebs."

"You're not an artist, Adam. You are a barista. Please don't embarrass yourself by having an opinion on art, when you have no right to have one due to you not being an artist."

"Okay, but only if you stop having an opinion about coffee." He studied the walls. "Looks like a castle, a wood, and peculiar little figures that might have be bats."

Feigning concern about a possible parking ticket, Lilith sent Adam back to fetch the remaining cases from his car. He was reluctant, but eventually relented, leaving Lilith alone in the room.

Once alone, she sank down in the space she would call home, lost in her thoughts, revelling in the gloom, surrounded by the hauntingly beautiful soot and ink paintings, and the peculiar eldritch energy of the room.

Adam took longer to return than Lilith had anticipated, leaving her below street level, observing the feet of tourists passing the little windows at the top of the room. She could feel the old earth around her; Greyfriars Kirkyard was located right behind the house. She was deep beneath the surface, the environment cool and tranquil — chthonic even.

A soft, scurrying caught her attenton. She initially thought it was Adam returning with the bags, but the sound was more delicate, oscillating between low and high frequencies. It was a strange, eerie melody that seemed to throb in her chest and scrape against her throat.

Then, as she watched, something, or rather multiple somethings, entered the room. Not through the door or the windows, but through the floor itself. All around her, unseen presences flooded the room, and before her very eyes, they began to paint. Images appeared and changed, were erased, and painted over again. All the while, she saw no hands or bodies, only heard that strange, bi-tonal sound and a fluttering as of bats' wings.

The paintings depicted scenes of ancient warriors, distressed ladies, dragons, and demons, the creatures of darkness when the moon was absent. As she observed them, Lilith felt an odd sense of connection, a message being conveyed through the paintings. She stood on the bed beside the wall and reached out to touch the bricks. The sensation of feather-light fingers brushing over her hand startled her, and as they painted, the images emerged beneath her palms.

The realisation struck her that she herself was meant to paint like this, to allow these unseen entities to guide her hands and create work beyond the realm of human comprehension —the work of her lifetime.

A soft knock broke her trance. "Hello?" She called out, her voice sounding distant to her own ears. "Hello?"

"Just me, Lilith, my dear," came the response.

Lilith turned her head. Martha Gray stood at the bottom of the stairs, two cases beside her.

She apologised for letting herself in and explained that she had found the cases in the hall with the front door ajar. "I thought you were coming back for them so I brought them down to help you out."

"Did you see Adam?" Lilith asked.

Martha shook her head. "I saw no one. These cases were in the hall. There was no one there."

Lilith felt a surge of frustration towards Adam for leaving her belongings unattended in the open hall. She made a mental note to block him on social media.

Martha's gaze was fixed on the wall. "I see they have visited you," she said.

Lilith replied, "How do you know?"

Martha gestured toward the new colours appearing on the painting. "The addition of brown and russet is new to the mural. It is clear that your personality is coming through and influencing the images that the Small Ones are producing."

"I feel they want me to paint for them," Lilith admitted.

Martha nodded thoughtfully. "I understand. I once danced for these spirits myself. I was a ballerina, but my aging body no longer allows me to perform."

She paused, her eyes drifting to the mural. "The images the Small Ones created for me often depicted scenes of dancers and dance. Now, it seems they are turning to you, hoping you will take your memories and transform them into something new."

Lilith leaned in. "What exactly are they, Martha?"

"They are the Small Ones. We share our world with many different kinds of spirits. There are as many different kinds of them as there are fish in the ocean. These ones love to paint," Martha explained.

Asking whether these spirits were providing her with inspiration simply for the joy of creation, Martha replied, "Not exactly."

Before Lilith could probe further into Martha's cryptic response, she found herself drawn back to the images on the walls. By the time she emerged from her reverie, ready to ask for clarification, Martha had disappeared, leaving only the two suitcases behind.

"Damn Adam," Lilith muttered

As Lilith found herself drawn back to the haunting artwork on the walls, the dim light from the cellar windows accentuated its eerie quality. Gritty strokes of soot and intricate cobweb designs sprawled across the brick, each image imbued with an otherworldly essence that sent shivers down her spine. The artwork was an unsettling harmony of grace and horror, it would repel lesser minds she knew, but it attracted her.

As she studied them, she saw the scenes portrayed were less painted and more imprinted, as if each figure was an echo from beyond the walls of our world. She saw depictions of grotesque figures, twisted and contorted, yet imbued with an odd kind of beauty, a sublime horror that sent tremors down her spine. The lines were rough, yet purposeful, each stroke etched in soot and cobwebs revealing an unsettling symphony of silent screams and unheard cries. The use of browns and russets lent a haunting depth, enhancing the disturbing elements.

Juxtaposed were tranquil scenes — quiet, starlit nights, pristine forests, serene lakes — but even these were tinged with a sense of dread. The stars in the sky appeared as watchful eyes, the forest seemed filled with lurking shadows, the surface of the lake held hidden menace.

Suddenly, a low-frequency hum filled the room, vibrating

through the walls and floors. They were coming. Simultaneously, a higher-pitched sound resonated within the narrow space, a scratching akin to fingernails on a chalkboard. The bi-tonal sound grew in intensity, as if bouncing off the cellar walls and converging towards her, enveloping her in an sound. Then came the sound of fluttering winds.

The unseen entities, the Small Ones, seeped in through the floor, a current of unseen energy that caused the hair on Lilith's arms to stand up. As the Small Ones entered, the air turned cold, Lilith felt her heart beat fast, and a peculiar electric charge permeated the room. She felt their presence not as individual entities but as a collective force, a weaving of spectral threads liked daemonic bees merging and coursing through her body.

It was as though the Small Ones were a river and she, a willing vessel, letting them flow through her veins, into her very core. An unspeakable energy sparked in her fingers and filled her with an inexplicable urge to create. It wasn't possession — it was a communion, a merging of souls and a shared understanding that flowed like an undercurrent between her and the Small Ones.

She felt them guide her hands, their ghostly touch, featherlike of bat-wing and cobweb pushing her to draw lines and curves that mirrored their unfathomable aims. Each stroke felt fluid and natural, yet alien, as her hands moved not by her will but by theirs.

Adam stood at Lilith's front door, his fist clenched and ready to knock. His stomach churned with nerves, a mix of worry for her and the crush he'd been hiding forever. He hadn't seen her since she'd moved in. She'd become a recluse. Normally, she came into his coffee shop at least once a day, but he hadn't seen her since she moved into this new flat. Neither had anyone else; she'd become a recluse. He took a deep breath and still hesitated. His palms were sweaty as he thought about Lilith - she was just so real, so talented, so... her.

Before he actually knocked, the door creaked open and there stood Martha Gray, a small wisp of a woman with bony bear feet and a cardigan that looked like she'd crocheted it herself. Her long silver hair cascaded over her shoulders. She gave off a kind of eerie tranquility. She made him nervous.

"Lilith is in the basement," she announced without preamble. She motioned towards the narrow staircase leading downwards.

"It's just I haven't seen her."

"She hasn't been out for days, I'm afraid. The Small Ones have taken quite a liking to her. I took down the cases you gave me by the way."

"Ah good. Thanks." As he said it, he felt anxious for Lilith. This woman was odd.

"I was just collecting her lunch plates," Martha said.

The dark hallway sent a chill down Adam's spine. His gut twisted as Martha waved her hand toward the creepy basement door. He squinted, trying to see better in the dim light. The old house suddenly felt way spookier than before.

He saw that Martha was holding a plate with a few white breadcrumbs on it in her left hand and a glass with a few undrunk drops of milk in it in her right..

"She eats only bread and milk," Martha continued, her voice dropping to a whisper. "I've been bringing it to her myself. She needs to keep her strength while she creates."

Something about the way Martha said 'creates' sent a chill down Adam's spine, He knew Lilith was an artist, yes, because she'd told him, but wasn't this even a weird life for an artist, with the seclusion, the very odd landlady and the less than optimum diet?

Martha moved aside and stood watching him.

Adam's heart hammered in his chest as he eyed the dark staircase. The musty smell of the old house made his nose wrinkle, and a chill ran down his spine. He'd never been in a place that felt so... off.

For a moment, he thought about legging it out the front door. But then Lilith's face flashed in his mind - her pale skin, those dark eyes that seemed to look right through him. Aye, she scared him a bit, if he was being honest. But that didn't matter now.

Taking a deep breath, Adam clenched his fists and took the first step down. The stairs creaked under his weight, each sound making him wince. But he kept going, one foot after the other, driven by a mix of fear and something stronger - a need to make sure Lilith was alright.

"I'm coming, Lilith," he whispered, more to steady himself than anything else, as he descended into the darkness below.

As Adam reached the foot of the stairs, his eyes took a moment to adjust to the dim light of the basement. The sight that greeted him left him breathless — and not in a good way. Lilith's artwork was strewn about the space, but these were unlike any works he'd seen her create before. Each piece was an eruption of dark chaos, a grotesque dance of shadows and form. The paintings were disturbingly detailed, an unsettling mix of twisted figures, monstrous creatures, and nightmarish landscapes. Figures with hollow eyes and agonised expressions, beasts with gnashing teeth and curling tendrils, forests with trees that seemed to bleed darkness — each work was more horrifying than the last. It was a vivid expression of a terrifying world, a glimpse into a distorted realm that was even odder than most of the stuff she painted. These paintings were horrifying, filled with a chilling despair that made his skin crawl. But even as his stomach churned at the sight of the art, it was the sight of Lilith herself that concerned him the most.

She was seated on a stool, her hair wild, her eyes sunken, and her face pallid. She seemed almost to glow in the dim light, her skin stark against the horrific scenes she had created. As he watched her, she lifted a brush, her hands guided by an unseen force, adding more grotesque detail to the canvas before her.

"Lil, love," he said, his voice trembling. "Are you okay?"

She turned to look at him then, her eyes cold and detached. "You wouldn't understand, Adam," she said, her voice remote . "You're not an artist." She gestured around. "I know what this looks like to ordinary folk, but you can't see what I see."

Her words were a cold dagger, cutting deep. She always said things like this, but he'd come here to rescue her. He knew she wasn't going to be the typical grateful Snow White, but he hoped she'd show some warmer response to his playing Prince Charming.

He thought he loved her, and it pained him to see her this way, to see the darkness that had consumed her art.

Adam's mouth went dry as he stood there, gawking at the bizarre paintings around him. His head was spinning, trying to make sense of the twisted images Lilith had created. It was like nothing he'd ever seen before - beautiful, but in a way that made his skin crawl.

He felt proper useless, standing there like a lemon while Lilith was... what? Lost in this mad world she was painting? He couldn't wrap his head around it, but one thing was crystal clear: he was head over heels for her, and scared out of his wits about what was happening.

Even though she'd pretty much just told him to sod off, Adam set his jaw. He wasn't about to leg it now, not when she might need help. No matter how mental things got down here, he was going to stick around. For her.

"I'm here for you, Lil," he muttered under his breath.

Lilith didn't hear him.

. . .

Adam's footsteps echoed ominously as he stepped into the grand entrance of the Kinmont Gallery, the crisp invitation embossed card clenched in his hand. Posh art galleries had always been foreign territory for him, the pristine white walls and polished marble floors felt cold and alienating.

Roderick McKinnon, gallery owner and renowned art critic, was holding court near the largest painting — a nightmare concoction of skeletal trees and leering beasts that bore Lilith's new, unmistakable signature. McKinnon was gesturing, praising Lilith's work with effusive adjectives, his words dripping with admiration. Lilith was standing next to him, a glass of champagne in her hand, her dark eyes dancing with arrogant delight.

The air in the gallery was dense with expensive perfume and the murmur of elite chatter. The guests were a collection of the city's rich and fashionable, dripping with diamonds and self-importance. Their laughter rang loud and hollow in the grand space, their conversations dripping with faux camaraderie and art-speak that made Adam's skin crawl.

The paintings hung like dark omens on the walls, their discordant beauty sending waves of anxiety rippling through him. The imagery was decadent in its terror, forms twisted and contorted in unsettling detail, each piece an exploration of the grotesque and the sinister. The haunted faces, the sprawling limbs, the creeping shadows — they all bore down on him, their malice palpable, echoing the dread that had first gripped him in Lilith's basement.

Adam watched as Lilith basked in the adulation, her head tilted back in laughter, her gaze never once seeking him out in the crowd. Her voice floated over to him, in a symphony of self-praise and vanity as she claimed the nightmarish creations as wholly her own. The Small Ones — her silent co-creators — were conspicuously absent from her tale, their role in the disturbing beauty of her work dismissed and forgotten.

Each boast, each grandiose utterance sent a new wave of discomfort crashing through him. He ran his finger round his shirt collar to loosen it. The air grew heavier, the lights seemed harsher, the murmur of the crowd grew louder in his ears. The boundaries of the room seemed to shift and undulate, the artworks appearing to leech into his senses, the terrible scenes they portrayed worming their way into his mind. He felt ill. He could feel his heart pounding in his chest, his pulse thudding in his ears. He had come here out of love for Lilith, but with each passing moment, he felt himself drowning in the discordant symphony of the gallery — the arrogant chatter, the cloying perfume, the decadent terror of the paintings, and Lilith's unending hubris.

An abrupt gasp tore through the grandeur of the Kinmont Gallery. A single interruption that sent a ripple of unrest amongst the gathered elite. Adam looked. Lilith's artwork, previously fixed and inert on the walls, had started to move, each piece rippling and shimmering as if under an invisible breeze. A spectral spectacle, every shadow and stroke of paint seeming to come alive, their sinister figures taking on a life of their own, was unfolding before their incredulous eyes.

A woman screamed, clutching her pearls.

On the paintings, twisted faces scowled, tortured bodies tried to shake off the containment of pigments and become real. The eerie landscapes, which before held an unsettling yet immobile beauty, now swirled and pulsed, drawing the viewers into their ominous depths. It was as if the very essence of the painted terror was seeping out, reaching for the souls of those watching.

Even the most unobservant guests, previously lost in pompous discussions about St Moritz and friends in the Hamptons, stopped sipping their Bollinger and stood rooted to their spots, eyes wide and faces drained of colour. The tangible malice emanating from the paintings was overwhelming, the movement within them impossible to ignore, the oppressive sensation sending whispers of panic echoing through the gallery.

In the midst of this chaos, Lilith, her face pale and eyes wide with horror, turned on her heel and bolted towards the entrance.

Her black dress billowed behind her as she weaved through the frozen crowd, her panicked cries merging with the rising clamour of terrified guests.

Simultaneously, the gallery's lights began to flicker. An electrical hum permeated the air, the scent of burning wire quickly following. Flames ignited spontaneously, licking the edges of paintings and scorching the pristine white walls. The panicked cries of the spectators rose to a fevered pitch as chaos unfurled in the once tranquil gallery.

The spreading flames pulled Adam out of his trance. His heart hammered in his chest as he began to search for Lilith amidst the swirling, chaotic crowd. But in the flickering light and churning sea of terrified guests, Lilith was nowhere to be found. She had disappeared, swallowed by the cataclysm that her art — or rather, the art of the Small Ones — had instigated.

Three weeks later, Adam found himself standing outside the house once again. As he lifted his hand to knock, but before his knuckles had touched the wood, the door swung open to reveal Lilith. The sight of her should have brought relief after so many weeks searching for her, but instead, a knot of anxiety formed in his stomach. She was not the same. Her eyes held the same odd glint that Martha's used to, and her words mirrored the previous landlady's peculiar phrases. She was standing there in Martha's usual spot, at the base of the stairs, a ghost of her former self.

"Are you here for my muses?" she asked him.

"I'm sorry, I don't know what you mean," Adam said.

It was then that he noticed a birthmark on her neck, previously hidden beneath the high collars she liked to wear. The mark bore an eerie resemblance to the distinctive daubs on the walls of the basement.

"Are you looking for a room to rent?" she continued, like they'd never met.

"Lil, it's me, Adam."

But she didn't seem to know him. She said, "the rent is very reasonable, perfect for struggling artists."

He stared at her and the delusion that he'd called love, dropped from him all at once. There she was a pale-faced girl with too much make-up who'd got lost. He felt sorry for her but he didn't love her anymore.

He shook his head. "I must have come to the wrong place. I'm not an artist. I work in a coffee shop."

PART FOUR

London

The Silent People

ALFRED GREY AWOKE from sleep with a choking gasp. He had dreamt he was drowning in a river—an old, brown river where his feet couldn't find the bottom. He burst to the surface. He'd known where he'd been, but on waking, the name of the river dropped out of his memory, sinking like a stone.

By the time he rolled out of bed, the dream was hazy. By the time he made his cup of tea, it was gone. That is to say, the details were gone, but the feeling remained: damp, and dreamlike, and full of old, brown water. He shuddered as he fished out the tea bag from his mug with a tarnished silver spoon. By this time, he didn't remember why he was shuddering.

By ten o'clock, the light in the study had settled into that of a late English summer morning—damp and mild, overcast and intermittently raining. Outside, a steady drizzle on the window now blurred the view of the park below.

By ten thirty, Alfred Grey—a middle-aged man with an old man's name—sat at his desk. He was working, writing an article he hoped to sell to an American website. On the laptop screen, a document was open, dense with his text and footnotes: *Post-Revo-*

lutionary Energy Leverage and Strategic Denial in the Strait of Hormuz: 1979–2024.

He was bored with it himself. Time for a another cup of tea. He stood, stretched his back, and wandered through to the kitchen. It was narrow, galley-style, with a streaked linoleum floor and the smell of old toaster crumbs. The fluorescent tube above the sink flickered once before settling. He filled the kettle, placed it back on its base, and reached for the chipped mug on the windowsill.

As the water began to heat, there was a noise behind him. Something slipped through the letterbox with a soft *thack*. The kettle rose to a shuddering boil. He made the tea, and wandered through.

On top of one red demand letter from London Electricity and another marked 'Please Do Not Ignore' that he'd seen that morning but not picked up, lay a hand-written envelope.

Grey ignored the threatening letters, and picked up the one with the cream vellum envelope.

The envelope was thick, good stock, with a slightly ribbed texture. His name — **Mr Grey** — was written in an elegant, looping hand, not quite copperplate, and in green ink. Not biro. Not felt-tip = Something closer to a fountain pen. Or even, absurdly, a quill

He held it for a moment.

Then he lifted it to his nose, almost involuntarily. It smelled of roses. Not the synthetic air-freshener kind, but old-fashioned rose water — the kind Georgian ladies used. Underneath that: something drier. Chalk, perhaps. Or crushed leaves?

The scent stirred a memory he couldn't quite place.

He turned the envelope over. No stamp. No postmark. No return address.

He took the envelope back to his desk and sat down. He looked at it for a minute. It was a work of art in its own way.

The card was thick, expensive stock—cream-coloured, faintly

ridged, with a pressed floral grain almost imperceptible to the eye but obvious to the fingers. On the front, embossed in gold, were the words: *You Are Invited to Tea.*

He turned it over. On the back, in green ink, an elegant hand had written:

Hampstead Station. Wednesday. One o'clock. Come formally dressed. – Queen Mab

Outside, below, in the park, a child's shout rose faintly, then fell away. He looked down between the rivulets. Two teens in hoodies stood by the swings. A woman wearing a plastic mac with a Labrador on an extendable lead hurried down the tarmac path, a darker smudge between dripping privet hedges. He took a sip from his mug, Queen Mab! For God's sake! Still, he pulled a yellow legal pad toward him, and wrote:

Possible story – Hampstead avant-garde nonsense. The Spectator even?

He underlined it. Then underlined it again, more heavily. This was something different: stupid, artsy Hampstead pseudo-artist fops, possibly full-on posh girl cosplay. But someone might pay him for a piece on it.

How had they found him? It had probably come in response to a post he'd made on HARO, advertising himself as a freelance journalist looking out for leads. But he didn't remember leaving his address, just his phone number, name and email. Still, people have ways these days — people with advanced internet skills. He'd probably been doxxed somewhere online. That made him laugh. Who'd bother doxxing old Alfred Grey? Maybe they remembered him from his column in the FT. Maybe not.

And despite his contempt for the rentier capitalist company that plagued him with their persistent letters, the rent was indeed due or he wouldn't live in Tufnell Park anymore, and if he didn't live here, where would he live?

Heaven knows, the room was modest, the furniture aged but reasonably well-kept. His study cum living room had two of the walls given over to bookshelves packed with titles on energy policy, international law, Middle Eastern history. But half a shelf was poetry: Rilke. Heaney. Plath. A copy of Yeats's 'The Wanderings of Oisin' — the 1889 first edition —— lay splayed open on the arm of an old brown armchair, the edges of the pages well-thumbed. It was open to his favourite poem.

On the wall above the desk, a black-and-white photograph in a cheap wooden frame. A woman in her twenties, seated cross-legged at a campsite, caught mid-bite on a piece of toast. A gas stove behind her, and a tent's edge just visible in the background. The photograph had been taken without warning. Her mouth curled slightly, not into a smile exactly—something more ambiguous. Amused, perhaps.

Then a notification pinged on his rather old Hewlett-Packard laptop. He'd got the laptop when he worked for the Financial Times years ago, and they'd forgotten he had it when he left, so he kept it. Good job, as he couldn't afford a new one.

The notification blinked in the corner of the screen. A message. A profile photo.

He stood motionless, letting it register. Then he placed the card on his desk beside the laptop, next to his notes on oil concessions in the Gulf and a discarded printout of an article on OPEC's role in the 2024 energy market.

He didn't click the message straight away. When he did he saw it was purportedly from a very pretty girl, looking to be mid-twenties. But the text in the profile had grammatical errors. The photograph was obviously stolen. Luiza (apparently) wrote, "Hey, I saw your profile. You seem kind of interesting..."

He snorted. "As if a young woman like that would be interested in me," and deleted it. He got three of these a day —

Columbians, Ukrainians, all young, all beautiful, every one a lie. Catfishing they called it.

He sighed. He should get on with his article, but instead, he picked up the expensive, gold-embossed card again and laughed. 'Queen Mab! How ridiculous!' then put the card to his nose and smelled its scent of old roses.

The following morning broke damp and grey. A light drizzle slicked the pavements, but the rain had stopped and the sky was opening promising sun. He wasn't due at Hampstead until 1 pm so had time to finish something. He'd decided to go. Editors weren't buying his stock-in-trade geo-economical insights any more. This could be a new opening for him — quirky interest features to sell to Time Out or The Idler or even the back pages of The Spectator.

Grey sat, his latest draft article open before him—an examination of the growth of informal settlements east of Nablus, thick with citations and cautious adjectives. He read the first paragraph three times and failed to move past it.

His fingers hovered above the keyboard. He frowned, leaned back, then sat forward again, still unable to begin. The cursor blinked, patient and unmoved.

He got up.

On the back of the door hung a garment bag that had not been disturbed in months. He unzipped it. Inside was a dark three-piece suit, slightly out of fashion now, but well-cut and made in London. *Kilgour French & Stanbury*—he had found it years ago in a Knightsbridge charity shop, and though the lining was fraying in the cuffs, the cut still held its dignity. The shoulders fit. The trousers didn't bag. He had never known who it had belonged to before him, but the tailoring suggested someone who had a bob or two.

He dressed slowly, shirt first, then the waistcoat. At the back of the drawer he located a Liberty tie, navy with a faded art deco pattern, and began the slow, precise process of tying it. The knot had to be centred. The blade must rest just at the belt. Once it was done, he tugged the knot firm and stepped back.

In the mirror above the fireplace, his reflection regarded him. The tie was a little too bright against the worn suit, and the collar of the shirt had softened with age. His hair was thinning at the temples. His eyes looked tired—more than tired, older than he remembered. But he smiled anyway, caught himself doing so, and looked away. Stupid bugger.

He ran a hand down each sleeve, as though brushing off dust. Then he reached for the invitation card, still lying on the desk where he had placed it two days earlier and he slipped it into the inside pocket of the jacket. They might require it for entry.

The Northern Line train rattled and jolted as it sped through the darkness beneath London. Mr. Grey sat quietly in his faded Savile Row suit. Around him, a gaggle of commuters filled the carriage —students with backpacks, professionals in suits, tourists clutching maps. He felt a flutter of self-consciousness, acutely aware of his attire amidst the casual disarray of the morning crowd.

As the train approached Camden Town, the carriage lurched more violently, the metal frame creaking as though it might come apart at the seams. The overhead lights flickered for a brief moment, casting an eerie glow on the faces around him. Grey grabbed for the metal pole beside him as the seat bounced under him.

He hated the Tube. It was hot and clammy. God, this was a descent into the Underworld.

The journey continued, and as the train neared Hampstead, the deepest station on the Northern Line, he prepared himself. When the train finally came to a halt, he disembarked and made his way through the narrow, tiled corridors to the lift. He was always worried the lift would jam and he'd be stuck inside it with all these strangers. But it didn't stick, it slowly ascended, the hum accompanied by the occasional cough or shuffle of feet.

When the doors finally opened, Grey stepped out into a transformed world. Tufnell Park had been overcast. Hampstead was brilliant. As Mr. Grey stepped out of Hampstead Tube Station and into the bright afternoon sunlight, he took a moment to adjust to the transformation of the weather. Gone was the dim, enclosed world of the Underground, and in its place was a clear, azure sky and a gentle breeze that carried the scent of summer. He glanced to his right and was immediately struck by the sight of an extraordinary figure waiting for him.

The man stood out against the modern London backdrop like a character from Regency Farce. Tall and slender, his white hair was as fine and crisp as spun sugar, and his skin was bone-white, setting off the deep violet of his eyes—eyes that seemed to have no pupils, just large irises that dominated his gaze. His lips were a stark black, adding to his otherworldly appearance.

He was dressed in a long, gold-brocaded coat of blue satin, reminiscent of a French nobleman from the court of Louis XIV. The outfit seemed completely at odds with the contemporary scene, yet somehow perfectly suited this odd-look ing man. And he was odd-looking.

For a brief second, Grey was taken aback by the sight, but then a smile tugged at the corners of his mouth. Of course, this was all part of the performance, the theatrical experience he had anticipated. He imagined how he would describe this encounter in his article—the surreal moment of emerging from the depths of the Underground to meet such an eccentric figure. He thought of the Latin phrase from the Aeneid, *"Facilis descensus Averno,"* and chuckled quietly to himself—indeed, the descent to the underworld had been easy, and now here he was, greeted by his psychopomp — a costumed Mercurius leading him to his assignation with the Fairy Queen.

As Mr. Grey approached, the strange figure in the gold-brocaded coat extended a hand in greeting, his voice as smooth as silk. "Mr. Grey, I presume? Welcome to Hampstead."

Grey nodded and offered his own hand, the corners of his mouth still curved in that bemused smile. "And you are?"

"They call me, Spindledrift Goodfellow," the man said.

"I bet," said Grey, but then, deciding to go along with the role-play, gave a deep bow. "Enchanté, Monsieur Goodfellow."

Goodfellow said, "I'm not French."

"Oh, well — how do you do?"

Goodfellow smiled. "I'm not English, either."

"Oh, well," said Grey. "I give up. What nationality is the name 'Spindledrift'?"

"Its own. Just as I am my own."

Grey raised an eyebrow. "Well, it's certainly memorable,"

Goodfellow winked. "Unlike yours." He deliberately looked Grey over from head to foot. Despite himself, Grey blushed. Goodfellow said, "Yours is, ordinary but fitting. Grey by name, Grey by nature, eh, Mr Grey?"

"No need to be rude," Grey said.

"I read some of your work on the Internet. You used to have a bit of a name."

"Yes — used to have." Grey shrugged and smiled. This self-deprecation was a trick he used. It generally made people think he was a nice bloke. In England, no one likes a bragger.

Goodfellow snorted. "Let us go and see the Queen," and began walking. Grey lagged behind, as if unsure he wanted to follow. "Come on," Goodfellow said. "She doesn't like to be kept waiting. She might forget you're coming and go and do something else."

· · ·

As they began their ascent up Holly Hill, Mr. Grey took in the surroundings with a mixture of curiosity and envious admiration. Hampstead's streets were lined with stately Georgian and Victorian houses, their facades covered in wisteria and climbing roses. The early summer air was filled with the sweet fragrance of lilac and laburnum, and the gardens they passed seemed to burst with colour and life. Butterflies flitted from bloom to bloom, and the trill of birdsong filled the air.

He wished he could afford to live here.

The people they passed were equally refined, dressed in tailored suits and designer dresses, driving polished cars that gleamed in the sunlight. Even their casual clothes were pristine, not frayed or crumpled.

As Grey and Goodfellow reached the top of the hill, Goodfellow stopped as he came upon an old-fashioned gate in a high stone wall, its ironwork painted a shimmering silver. It was a rather posh gate and the metal, the wood and even the screws were the best of the best.

Goodfellow reached into the pocket of his brocaded coat and produced a delicate silver key. He grinned at Grey. With a deft twist, Goodfellow turned the key, he unlocked the gate and with a push of its hand, sent it yawning open. Beyond the gate was a garden more perfect and well-ordered than any Grey had seen before. It was so perfect it might even belong to another world, a better world, a world where dreams came true. Grey shook himself to clear away such saccharine imaginings.

But the garden even smelled like another world. The air was steeped in a perfume so sweet, so unearthly, it might have been drawn from the dreams of bees. The scent drifted around him—lush and intoxicating—its notes of honeysuckle, sweet peas, old roses, and phlox rising like a spell, permeating his thoughts as dust motes float in golden air. Even the birds sang differently here—sweeter, wilder.

"Wow!" Grey said. "How lovely!"

"And she is lovelier," said Goodfellow. He offered a hand. "Come and meet her. But guard your heart—she has a fondness for borrowing what doesn't belong to her."

Grey's hesitated at the threshold.

"Are you coming, or not?" Goodfellow said.

Once again, Grey was irritated by this actor in a Camden Market coat. "Yes, yes." and he stepped through the gate. Once inside he looked around. Tea roses unfurled in pale blush and creamy honeysuckle tones, their petals wet with dew and tremulous in the light. Hover-flies—striped gold and black—hovered like living jewels, drifting from flower to bloom in lazy circuits. Laburnum dripped golden wands overhead, forming a glowing canopy; their scent mingled with the lime-heavy fragrance of blooming linden, lending the air a deep sweetness. Hidden winding paths branched under dappled shade—one could easily lose direction among the shrubs and arches, the layout suggested a maze woven by a designer who was either drunk or dreaming, or maybe both. There were glades of grass between the flowers. Here the turf was immaculate, yet gentle disturbances betrayed life: a song thrush darted across it with quick grace, suddenly stopping, grabbing and pulling out a worm.

As they walked into it, Grey thought this was the most beautiful garden he had ever seen and no ordinary pleb walking outside would ever know it existed.

Goodfellow stood behind him, watching him. Grey turned. The garden gate was still open. "On you go," Goodfellow said, gesturing for Grey to walk deeper in. "But don't go too far ahead. I wouldn't want you to get lost." Grey hesitated for just a moment, a flutter of trepidation in his chest, but curiosity won out, and he stepped onto the path As he did so, Goodfellow closed the gate behind them with a soft click, and locked it with his silver key.

. . .

As Grey ventured deeper into the garden, he was enveloped by an atmosphere of surreal perfection. And beneath it all, the bees droned—not just a buzz, but a golden C-sharp that shimmered in the air like a tuning fork struck in sunlight. It was a sound he felt in his bones, a vibration he breathed in. The perfume of the flowers wove itself around that hum, scent and sound inseparable —each note of fragrance seeming to brush against his skin.

He felt almost intoxicated, as if honey-gold music were seeping into him, softening him from within. The world outside the garden began to blur, like the name of someone you once worked with and can no longer remember.

The gravel path crunched gently beneath Grey's shoes, a soft, regular sound that seemed to echo within the warm hush of the garden. To one side, lawns stretched like silk—lush, emerald green, each blade of grass impossibly perfect, as though combed and coaxed into place. To the other, the borders swelled with roses, peonies, and foxgloves, their colours thick and luminous in the sunlight.

The path wound gently on and round and then back and round again, dipping in and out of the shade. Sheltering lindens arched above, their broad leaves stirring in the breeze with a dry, whispering rustle. The alternating flicker of sun and shadow made the world ripple around him—strobing like light through half-closed eyes, hypnotic and dreamlike.

Grey went forward without quite meaning to, his feet moving with the path's curve, his thoughts floating. There was a strange peace in the stillness, and a quiet promise in the air—as though something important waited just ahead, wrapped in flowers and heat and light. It was as if he no longer knew why he was walking, only that the garden wanted him to go deeper.

Occasionally, Goodfellow murmured something behind him, or placed a hand lightly on his elbow to guide him forward. Grey responded without speaking, too dazed to answer, not resisting.

The path twisted again, now narrowing between walls of

green. Sunlight speared down through the canopy in columns, gilding motes of pollen and dust that swirled like gold leaf. It was like entering a maze, but one not built to confuse but to lure. He felt the garden folding inward, its silence deepening. A hush before revelation.

Then the green fell away, and the path opened onto a lawn.

Beyond a box hedge and beneath a white lilac in bloom, a table had been set on the lawn. It was the sort of wooden picnic table you might find in an old country rectory garden, weathered silver-grey by time, but here it was immaculate. On it: a linen cloth, pressed and snow-white. A teapot steamed gently beside a matching milk jug and sugar bowl, all of delicate bone china with a faded rose pattern. Two teacups, their handles as fine as porcelain could bear, stood waiting. A silver cake stand held cucumber sandwiches, their crusts precisely trimmed, and a dozen small, exquisite cakes—fondant fancies, macaroons, lemon tarts the size of a crown piece.

She was already seated.

Her beauty stopped him like a blow. The sort that stuns you on sight, that blinds you like sudden sunlight. He faltered. He blushed. His breath caught. A small, involuntary "oh" rose in his throat. Desperately, Grey composed his features, involuntarily tugged his suit sleeves straight and summoned what was left of his dignity.

This actress — this Queen Mab looked no more than twenty-eight. Auburn hair in soft waves to her shoulders. A summer dress in cornflower blue, modest but exact, its vintage cut—somewhere between 1930 and 1950—only deepening her impact. The fabric caught the light just enough. She was certainly well cast. Her photograph would have to accompany the piece when he submitted it for consideration. Her face might actually persuade them to buy the story.

Mab didn't rise. Didn't extend a hand. She sat with perfect stillness, one hand resting on the tablecloth, her head tilted slightly, as if listening to something just beyond hearing. Her gaze met his—calm, knowing, faintly amused.

"Hullo," she said.

"Hello," he replied, and hoped she hadn't seen the reaction she'd had on him.

Goodness me, he thought, I'm such an old fool.

Spindledrift Goodfellow stopped a pace short of the table. "Your Majesty," he said smoothly, "may I present Mr. Grey."

She gave no reply. Her gaze remained on Grey.

"Mr Grey," he said with a little flourish, "this is Her Majesty, Queen Mab."

Grey, uncertain, gave a shallow nod, then—realising that would not quite do—gave an awkward bow. The moment passed without comment. She neither acknowledged nor rebuked the gesture. She only watched.

As he straightened, the thought crossed his mind that the whole thing was absurd. The costumes, the garden, the script—delightfully arch, theatrical.It would make for a marvellous piece: a sly column on metropolitan performance art, the irony of enchantment in Hampstead. Yes, that must be it—a concept garden, a curated dream. Beauty arranged like props on a stage.

It was very well done, he thought—but who was behind it all?

Goodfellow nodded at the empty chair. Grey sat down somewhat awkwardly at the table, feeling the curious weight of Queen Mab's gaze upon him. Without missing a beat, Spindledrift Goodfellow lifted the elegant silver teapot and poured the tea into Grey's cup. The steam curled up gently, mingling with the soft scent of roses that lingered in the air.

"Milk?" Goodfellow asked, already reaching for the jug. Grey nodded, and a splash of milk turned the tea a warm caramel colour. "Sugar?" Goodfellow inquired, holding up a pair of delicate silver tongs. Before Grey could refuse, a single sugar cube dropped into the cup, dissolving with a quiet plink. Grey smiled politely and stirred, deciding to drink it anyway, despite his usual preference for unsweetened tea.

Queen Mab gazed at him. She was smiling but the smile looked practised. And she still hadn't really said anything. Breaking the awkward silence, Grey spoke, " What kind of tea is this?" he asked. "Lapsang Souchong?"

"Not sure," she said absent-mindedly. "I think it's the water we make it with that makes the difference. We have it shipped in from Greece. A little-known spring near a forgotten river. Absolutely the best for forgetting your troubles."

"So," said Grey, trying to take back control. "Thank you for the invitation to tea. I am presuming you have some reason for asking me."

"Oh, yes," said Mab, picking up a fondant fancy, then frowning and putting it back on the white china plate.

Grey waited.

Then she said, "Do you ride?"her tone light but curious.

Grey blinked. "What?"

She fluttered her eyelids and smiled. "I'm not particularly hungry, but you eat — please do."

He was momentarily thrown off. "Do I ride? What do you mean — horses? Bicycles?"

"Horses, of course," she replied, with a hint of amusement. "Do you hunt?"

He shook his head. "No, I'm afraid not. I've never been on a horse in my life."

"Oh, pity. It's such fun. But then I mainly ride swallows. " She winked.

He sighed. It was all so 'meta'. Then he said, "I'm a journalist. But of course you know that."

She shook her head, prettily puzzled. "Do I? Do we know he's a journalist, Goodfellow?" she called.

The retainer nodded. "We do, your Majesty."

"Ah good."

"So, I was wondering if you'd invited me about a story."

She nodded absent-mindedly, sipping tea. "Oh, yes. I suppose. By the way," she said. "Do you dream in colour. Some people don't you know, and I wondered, what with your name." She looked at Goodfellow, "It was Grey wasn't it? That's the one I told you to get."

Goodfellow smiled knowingly. "Yes, ma'am. It's Grey."

Grey wasn't sure how to respond. Was he being filmed? Would this end up on the Internet? Finally, he shrugged. "I suppose I do. Yes."

"Good," she said. "Then there's still hope for you."

"I don't know what you mean."

She sipped her tea, then looked up suddenly. "Do you like cricket?"

This time, Grey brightened. "Actually, I do. I'm quite a fan of Surrey, and I was at the Oval not too long ago..." He began to share a bit of his enthusiasm, only to notice that her expression remained politely blank. It became clear that while she had introduced the topic, she had little knowledge or interest in it.

He shut up.

Then, without warning, she leaned forward and said, quite lightly, "There is something I would like you to do for me, Mr Grey."

He blinked. "Of course. If I can," and then he thought: why did I just agree to help her? And realised it was because she was looking at him with her deep green eyes.

"There is a man in Kew Gardens," she said. "He is... obstinate. A philosopher, of sorts. He remembers things. I find that troublesome."

"Troublesome?"

"Memories are weights," she said. "Like stones in the pocket. You cannot swim if you are filled with stones."

"And what would you like me to do?"

"There is a stone he keeps. He thinks it is his memory. You are to take it from him and drop it into the river. We will pay you. We will won't we, Goodfellow?"

"Yes, ma'am. Generously, for such a small request."

"Yes, it is a small request, isn't it, Goodfellow?" She turned to Grey. "You see it's not much to ask and we can give you a hundred pounds for it. Goodfellow tells me you're struggling at the moment to find your rent."

Grey blinked. How the hell did they know so much about him? Into the air of the perfect garden, seeped something sinister. Had they been watching him? Intercepting his mail?

Mab reached out and tapped her fingers on the top of his hand. He felt her nails. They were healthy and perfectly manicured — no nail varnish.

He wondered again if he was being filmed and pulled his hand away.

"So shy!" she said and laughed.

"This task? Couldn't Mr Goodfellow do it? He seems most able" Grey asked, glancing towards the tree where Goodfellow now lounged with one boot against the trunk, hands folded, looking vaguely amused.

Goodfellow shook his head once, slowly.

Queen Mab's smile did not falter, but her tone sharpened, almost imperceptibly. "I am not asking Mr Goodfellow. I am asking you, Mr Grey. Will you do it? It would please me."

He met her eyes. They were brilliant, unsettling—clear as stained glass. Her beauty was undeniable, but it went beyond that. She had the kind of beauty that dissolved thought, that bent reason. It was beauty like a quick blade — sudden and breath-stealing.

She was looking at him in a way women no longer did. In a way few of them ever had to be honest. He mistrusted that gaze, those eyes, but he couldn't shut out the warm coiling fluttering feeling that blossomed inside him as a response.

He knew what he was and how attractive he was to women. And it wasn't very. He was fifty-one, and looked older. He'd only ever been average-looking, at best. The kind of man who passed unnoticed in public places.

He whispered a line of poetry—not for her, but for himself. A charm. A spell of smallness to ward off her gaze, which threatened to melt his resistance and lift him too high.

"I am not Prince Hamlet..."

She blocked it with a smile. "Well, Mr Grey, I think you're being a bit hard on yourself. That might be true for Eliot's *Prufrock*, but you — you're just what I need to do this teensy little task for me, and save a poor old man, and let's face it — the world at large — from the pain of his silly memories."

He knew it was foolish. Impossible. This was theatre, myth, delusion—he wasn't even sure which. But something stirred beneath the protective layers he'd built. Yes, he was ordinary, insignificant, a washed-up journalist who'd once thought he had a career and had sacrificed things for that career. He'd been stupid, selfish, self-obsessed, and now he saw through all that self-aggrandising deceit. But still.

But, under it all even now , he was still alive and he still needed to be wanted by someone, someone beautiful.

He gave a small, embarrassed nod. "So he lives near Kew Gardens?"

She nodded. "Yes. I don't like Kew Gardens. It has too much growing there. It all grows and never stops."

"Does he live actually inside Kew Gardens?"

She frowned and looked to Goodfellow. "Does the Philosopher live in Kew Gardens?"

Goodfellow shook his head. "No, not inside, your Majesty. Nearby."

Mab turned back to Grey. "No, it's not in Kew Gardens, just nearby. But it's the same idea. Too much grows there — the plants have too much future, in the same way the Philosopher has too much past. You see what I mean?"

"No, not really."

"No, but when you've been working for me a while, you will."

Working for me a while? thought Grey. A regular pay-cheque? That would be nice. Maybe this place really was hers. But the task she was asking him to do was absurd. It had to be theatre — or an art installation or something.

"So you'll do it for me?"

He shrugged. "Yes, of course. It's an odd thing to do, but yes, I suppose. I mean it's all part of the play, I suppose."

She reached and took his hand and stroked it. This time he let her. "Oh, Mr Grey — you're my hero!"

His eye caught the shining silver teapot, its surface perfectly mirroring the lawn and the white lilac behind it. And then, he noticed it: where Queen Mab should have been reflected, there was nothing but the garden. A slight frown creased his brow.

It was all theatre. Just roll with it, he said to himself. Think of the cash. And he looked at her. She was watching the clouds.

To fill the silence, he reached for one of the delicate sandwiches on the table. It was exquisite, each bite a perfect blend of flavours.

As he savoured the sandwich, a flash of vibrant colour caught his eye. A beautiful red butterfly, its wings shimmering in the dappled sunlight, fluttered gently and landed on Queen Mab's outstretched hand. She regarded it for a moment, a smile playing on her lips.

"Oh, how beautiful," she murmured, her voice soft and melodic.

For a brief second, Grey allowed himself to be drawn into the enchantment of the moment.Without warning, the Queen's fingers closed around the fragile creature, crushing it effortlessly.

Grey felt a jolt of shock, his eyes widening as he watched the powdered wings crumble. She brushed the remnants aside as if they were nothing more than dust, her smile unfazed.

"Beauty that clings to its moment must die. It should have stayed in the air, not landed," she said.

She sat, gazing around her. It seemed the audience had come to a close.

"I suppose I'll go now," he said.

As Grey stood up, Queen Mab's voice floated back to him, halting his departure. "By the way, Mr. Grey," she said, her tone light and curious, "May I borrow your name?"

He turned back, puzzled. "My name?" he echoed, not quite sure he'd heard her correctly.

"Yes," she continued with a gentle smile, "You don't use it much any more, do you?"

Grey blinked, still baffled. "I'm not sure I understand. How does one... lend a name?"

She laughed softly, a sound like chimes in a breeze. "Oh, it's quite simple. I'll just carry it with me for a bit, to try and brighten it up for you."

He scratched his cheek. "Erm, well, I'm not sure how you'll manage that, but," he laughed. "Of course, if it makes you happy."

She grinned. She had little white sharp teeth, he thought. They were perfect too. "Please, believe me, Mr Grey," she said, "after all this, you too will be much, much happier — completely unburdened and living in colour."

She gave a little wave and smiled beatifically. Spindledrift Goodfellow led him to the now familiar garden gate. Grey noticed that the path back seemed somehow altered, as if he were walking a different way . When he got there, the wood of the gate looked richer, the silver-work more lustrous, as if it truly were precious metal. With a theatrical flourish, Goodfellow produced the silver key and unlocked the gate, swinging it open to reveal the Hampstead street beyond.

Grey hesitated, taking in the ordinary world outside. He didn't want to leave. The smell of petrol and tar, the sound of construction on a nearby house jarred and made him feel positively ill.

"Time for you to leave now, Mr. Grey," Goodfellow said gently, though firmly.

Grey lingered stild , not quite crossing the boundary. With a knowing smile, Goodfellow placed a hand on his back and gently but firmly pushed him through the gate and locked it behind him.

Three Days later, Grey sat at his desk, blinking at the open document. Words blinked back—oil markets, diplomatic blunders, parliamentary noise. He remembered when he'd been excited by such stuff, but it no longer meant anything. He rubbed his eyes and sighed. Then sighed again, as if to confirm how shit he felt, how absolutely used up and colourless. He closed the laptop without saving.

In the kitchen, the kettle took its time. He tapped his hand on the counter impatiently and then wondered what he was impatient for. There it stood taking its time, the bloody kettle. He stood beside it, arms folded, listening to its rising breath. Jesus, the flat was too quiet.

Outside, rain whispered faintly on the window panes, though the forecast had said sun. He spooned in two sugars automatically — a new thing for him , added a dash of milk, then stood holding the cup for a moment as if unsure whether he wanted it after all.

Back at the desk, he set the mug down and hovered over the chair. Sat, sighed again, sipped, and stood.

He walked to the armchair and picked up the familiar volume from where it lay, broken backed liked a floundering butterfly — Yeats, well-thumbed and marginally annotated, with a cover faded to the colour of old bone. His fingers found the poem before his eyes did. And inside him something settled.

The host is riding from Knocknarea
  And over the grave of Clooth-na-Bare;
  Caoilte tossing his burning hair,
  And Niamh calling Away, come away:
  Empty your heart of its mortal dream...
  And if any gaze on our rushing band,
  We come between him and the deed of his hand,
  We come between him and the hope of his heart.

He smiled faintly. His smile was weak, sad really, but not without fondness. They knew what they were doing, those fair folk. He wished he'd taken him away with them. And then he sighed again.

He looked up.

The clouds had rolled away without ceremony. Below, in the washed light of the park, the grass shone pale green and slick. A dog chased something invisible near the railings. A child rode a scooter in tight circles.

And then—stillness. And for the first time that day, the quiet didn't annoy him, it didn't rake his nerves like a street dog howling. The quiet just sat there and for a second made him forgot he wasn't the man he'd never wanted to be.

Then, as if the whole thing were a play, and the next scene was announced, he saw a man sauntering along the asphalt path through the park. He wore a theatrically blue brocade coat. He was tall, bone-featured, white, utterly still. Not watching the children, nor the dog, nor the birds overhead. Watching Grey.

Catching Grey watching him, Spindledrift Goodfellow inclined his head, just once and lifted his stick.

Grey was still holding the Yeats.

Goodfellow smiled, raised a hand and gave a casual wave.

Grey blinked. The memory of the Hampstead garden felt like yester-night's dream—lucid but disjointed. But even so, there he was. Spindledrift Goodfellow.

What a name. They had no irony, no subtlety, these people. Did they even believe they were the characters, or did they archly take it all off when out of sight. Goodfellow came across towards the building where Grey lived. Soon he would be at the front door.

Grey could ignore him, extract himself from this whole ridiculous thing. But he found himself moving before he'd made a decision, like there was someone else inside him who knew what he was going to do before he did himself. He opened his flat door, descended the communal stairs, opened the main door—and there stood Goodfellow, waiting. He hadn't even rung the bell.

"The Queen reminds you of your errand," Goodfellow said.

"Errand?"

Goodfellow coughed to let Grey know the pretence was boring. "Yes, to go to Kew. She has provided the address. She had thought you were resourceful enough to find it yourself—but clearly not."

He handed over a scrap of notepaper, scented with roses and that same dry powder. Grey almost raised it to his nose, but stopped short as he saw Goodfellow watching him with sardonic amusement.

"Yes, she does get into your thoughts, and, I may say, for some, their affections."

Grey laughed. "She's very pretty, but she's not my my type and far too young, anyway."

"Well, she's older than she looks."

Grey laughed. "Oh, yes! Of course."

"So?" said Goodfellow.

"What?"

"Your errand."

"I'll go at once. It's just—I've been busy."

"Not as busy as you should have been, " said Goodfellow.

Grey blushed, annoyed with himself at letting this clownish man get on his nerves so. Recovering, he drew himself up.

"So tell me," he said, with arched irony, "what exactly is she Queen of?"

Spindledrift smiled. "Queen Mab? Why, she is the Queen of Forgetting."

There was a pause. He should have expected such meaningless theatricality. He was a journalist, his words had to be exact and mean something, theirs were merely performance.

"Will you find your own way to Kew, or shall I take you?" Goodfellow said

"I can find my own way to Kew, for heaven's sake."

"See that you do, old man. See that you do! The Queen is not used to being kept waiting. Most men rush to do what she wants." Goodfellow smiled, but it was a smile without warmth. "But not you, eh? You're special."

"I'm not special," Grey said. "I'm just me. But, I told her I'll go and so I will."

Goodfellow pointed at the letters on the mat that, Grey hadn't picked up. "And you need the money."

Grey stepped off the train at Kew Gardens. The platform was quiet, the late afternoon sun slanting low through the trees. A few other passengers wandered off towards the park gates, but Grey turned the other way, heading down a residential street where the light shifted, greener and more uncertain.

He reached into his coat pocket and pulled out a scrap of paper.

Ranelagh Drive. Third on left. Iron gate. No name.

This must be it.

The house stood before him, a looming Victorian relic. Its windows were shuttered, barely visible behind a thick curtain of ivy that crept varnish and weather. A tarnished knocker hung slack. The letterbox had been taped shut from the inside.

For a moment, Grey hesitated, hand poised to knock, as if crossing this threshold might seal his involvement in something he couldn't quite define. Then, with a deep breath, he let the knocker fall.

A long pause, muffled footsteps, then, the grumble of bolts, and the door opened just a crack.

The man who appeared behind it was not what Grey had expected. No eyeliner, no theatrical velvet. He wore a threadbare wool waistcoat, a dark cravat, and pince-nez glasses perched on a narrow, intelligent face lined by years. His hair, long since turned white, was combed neatly back. His skin was pale with the transparency of long indoor years. He blinked at Grey as though seeing something implausible.

"Yes?" he said, guarded.

Grey floundered. "I... I may have the wrong house," he began. "I was sent—well, given an address. I—"

"You're not from the council," the man interrupted.

"No. Not at all." Grey flushed slightly, already regretting everything. "I was sent by—" he paused, stumbling over how absurd it all sounded now—"by someone who thought you might need... assistance."

The man looked at him flatly.

"I was given this by—someone," Grey went on, fumbling the card out of his pocket. "A woman. She said I should speak to—someone here."

The man's eyes flicked to the card. Then back to Grey.

"Oh," he said at last, his tone dry as old stone. "She's sent you, has she?"

Grey cleared his throat. "That is, yes. I think so."

The door opened fully. The man stepped aside. "Come in then. If you must."

The house smelt of old books, lavender water, and dust. The

hallway was narrow, the walls lined with framed diagrams and brittle maps. Books overflowed every flat surface, stacked in Dickensian towers around furniture that looked ancient but recently unused.

"She usually sends someone prettier," the man remarked. "A girl once. Hair like wheat. Had no idea what she was asking for."

"I'm not entirely sure I know what I'm asking for either," said Grey.

"Then later, a young man. Didn't stay long. Nervous sort. Asked too many questions."

"I hope I'm less trouble".

The philosopher shrugged. "Sad ending, though. I believe he ended his life in the river at Richmond. Don't you do that."

Grey gave a short laugh. "I'm not the type."

"Come in, then," said the philosopher, turning inside.

"But," said Grey, closing the door behind him, "if I'm honest, she's paying me—and I need the money."

"Good," the man said. "Honesty's rare in her orbit."

The study was dim but strangely warm. On the mantelpiece, beside a dead rose encased under glass, sat a smooth, palm-sized stone—unremarkable in colour, but placed with care.

"Sit?" the man shrugged. "Or stand."

Grey cleared his throat.

"You should get to the point," the Philosopher said. "I'm interested to hear her latest offer. She's paying you, you said?"

"Yes, I think so."

The old man tilted his head and smiled, not unkindly. "But you'd do it for nothing just to please her? She has that effect on men like you."

"On men like me?" said Grey, becoming affronted.

The Philosopher sat on the threadbare green armchair. "Do sit. No, of course, I don't know you. You may not be like the rest. Perhaps you are not as dazzled by her—" he paused as if seeking the word. "Her primacy. Yes that's it. She's primal, if nothing else.

Goodness, when I was young I would have fallen for her too. Who wouldn't? But be careful of her."

"You're going to say she's not what she seems."

The Philosopher shook his head. "No, quite the contrary—she is *exactly* what she seems. That's the danger. She wears no mask. And to gaze at her true face blinds." The Philosopher grinned and tilted his head. "But maybe not you, eh? Maybe you're stronger than the average chap."

Grey, who had steadfastly remained standing, said, "Honestly, you don't know me. You know nothing about me or what I'm like."

"Just so. Touché. You're right. Perhaps you have more mettle." He paused, then added, more gently, "But it's not just her glamour, is it? It's the feeling that she picked you. That you're the exception. That you please her."

Grey laughed. "Of course not! I'm not a teenager."

"No, of course."

Grey scratched his cheek. "She said you're holding onto something."

"Oh," the Philosopher said, as if he had heard this before.

"She says it's hurting you."

"Something from the past? She always says that," the Philosopher settled himself into his armchair.

"Well, are you?"

"I am."

"Oh."

The Philosopher pointed. "It's that stone."

Grey looked again at the stone on the mantelpiece. "It just looks like a stone."

"Well, it is. But it's also a symbol."

"Of what?"

"Of memory."

Grey frowned. "The stone's your memory?"

"Have you ever thought about how old stones are?"

Grey shrugged. "It has crossed my mind. Once on the beach at Brighton…"

The Philosopher smiled. "See, you have memories too."

Grey said, "It must be more than that. Why would she be bothered about you having a stone. Is it what you remember, is that it?"

"No, no. It's all memories. But she hates the ones that make you what you are."

"I'm afraid I don't follow."

"You see, Mab is like a butterfly — all flutters and colours . She doesn't like the grey things we keep and that anchor us and make us regret."

"I mean, I can see her point. In her own way, she wants you to be happy."

"But perhaps just being happy isn't enough."

"It'd do for me."

"But Mab believes memory is an affliction. That the past is a weight. That suffering is a fault in the system." He adjusted his glasses. "But memory is what makes us human. Not breath, not body, not blood. Memory. Without memory we aren't ourselves, we're just a flow of sensations and ideas."

"This is too deep for me."

The Philosopher gestured to the stone with a thin hand. "That contains the last of mine. At least, the last I chose to preserve."

Grey stared at the stone. "And that's what she says is holding you back."

"She wants a world without grief, or guilt, or conscience. No decay. No disappointment. Just surface. Just now" He paused. "But there's a dignity in memory, even when it hurts."

"You think so?" Grey finally sat down.

"Are you all right?" the Philosopher said.

"Yes. I'm just tired. I've not been sleeping recently. Money worries and all that."

"I'm sorry to hear that."

Grey pointed at the stone. "So that stone reminds you of something? It's like a memento?"

"It's a memory, not a souvenir."

"Have it your way. Do you know what memory it is?"

"As I said, I did. Once. A face. A voice. A bright blue scarf, I think. But now it's reduced to ache. Still—I'll keep the ache. It's mine."

Grey nodded slowly. He had his own ache. The beach at Brighton when Anna made him have his fortune told by... who was it? Professor Mirza! He smiled. Picnics at Hever Castle in the sunshine.

The Philosopher was gazing at him.

Grey said, "She asked me take it away from you."

The man looked at him—not hostile, not afraid. Just sad. "Then you'll have to disappoint her."

A silence passed. Then, politely: "Would you like a glass of water? You do look pale."

Grey blinked. "Yes. Thank you."

The man rose stiffly and shuffled into the back of the house.

Grey stood in the silence. His eyes returned to the stone.

The old man was sad. He was kind. He reminded Grey of his English teacher at Charterhouse. The one who'd said he had promise.

Grey stood.

He stepped forward, reached out, and took it. It weighed heavy in his hand, heavier than it should. And it was warm.

Footsteps.

He turned, crossed the hallway in three long strides, opened the door, and stole away before the Philosopher returned.

As Grey slipped away from the Philosopher's house, the day had begun to darken. The ordinary London streets—lined with bus stops, takeaway shops, and taxi offices—felt almost unreal. Children on electric scooters zipped past, and early commuters trudged home from work. Everything felt thin, provisional, like scenery that might blow away if the wind turned. He walked and walked. Eventually, he found himself by the Thames right by Richmond Bridge, the river's surface reflecting the dimming light of evening. Grey reached into his pocket and withdrew the stone. It was heavier than he remembered. It felt electric in his hand.

It vanished with a soft splash, barely disturbing the surface—then gone, as if swallowed up by something vast beneath. A huge fish, maybe. Come up to drown a fly.

Grey stood there, hands in his coat pockets.

The old man had been cracked. A stone can't contain memories. And what use were memories at the end of the day — they just reminded you of your stupid mistakes . Best let them go.

Behind him, traffic buzzed and fretted, argued and honked.

The river moved on—an old brown god, dissolving all it was given.

Three days had passed since he'd drowned the old man's memories in the River Thames. Grey had finished his article on Middle Eastern politics and, to his mild surprise, felt a rare sense of satisfaction. Unusually, he'd forgotten the name of editor he was to send it to, even though he'd sent countless submissions the woman's way before. In the end he found it in a notebook, and emailed the piece. Sitting at his desk, he allowed himself a moment of contentment.

Then his mobile phone rang, the display reading "Call Withheld." Normally, he would have let it go to voicemail, but buoyed by his good mood, he answered.

"Alfred Grey speaking."

The voice was unmistakable — smooth and sardonic.

"Mr Grey. Congratulations. The Queen is most pleased with your efforts."

Grey said nothing at first but a flush rose in his neck. He felt uncomfortably warm.

He hated Goodfellow's tone — so confiding, as if they were friends! Still, he found himself nodding, as if to someone in the room.

"You'll have your fee," Goodfellow added lightly. "In used notes, too, if you'd prefer."

You wanker, Grey thought. Then he ran a hand through his hair. "Oh. Thank you. I—well. I'm glad she's pleased."

"She would like to invite you for tea once again. Same arrangement—Wednesday, 1 p.m., Hampstead Tube station. I shall be there to meet you."

Grey hesitated, then ventured, "I appreciate the invitation, but if you could just give me the address, I'm sure I can find my own way."

There was a brief silence, then Goodfellow chuckled softly. "Oh, I'm sure you can't. I will meet you outside the station as before."

The call ended. Grey sat. Then he got up, crossed to the wardrobe, and opened it. He only had a few clothes. He didn't see the point in having more than was practical.

Then he went back to his phone. He was frowning, then he forced himself to laugh. "They must think I'm an easy mark. But they've given themselves away — a fairy with a burner phone," he muttered. "What next, elves on WhatsApp? If they use modern technology, I can find them."

This would all feed into the proposed piece. It was even turning into a detective yarn.

He opened his laptop. He'd find them if they were to be found.

First, he typed:

"Queen Mab garden invitation".

Nothing. A few Pagan blogs, some theatre companies, a smattering of academic articles about Shakespeare and *Romeo and*

Juliet.

Then:

"Queen Mab Hampstead"

A yoga studio. A florist. A Tumblr page for "fairycore aesthetics" run by a teenager in Minnesota.

He tried:

"Queen Mab fairy Hampstead butterfly"

An Instagram account appeared: women in flower crowns posing in bluebell woods. He clicked, scrolled. Not her. She didn't have Mab's eyes. None of them did.

He rubbed his face, sighed, and leaned back.

And it didn't make sense — all this for his benefit? He felt like Patrick McGoohan in *The Prisoner*. But someone must be behind it. Someone with resources.

Who funds immersive theatre with real silver teapots and butterflies that crush like ash? Who sends scented cards written in viridian ink, with no postmark?

And Mab, she had to be an actress, selected for her beauty. She was just the kind of girl you'd find in drama school. Posh, entitled, so unaware of the realities of rent and weekly shops because of the allowance from Daddy, that she sailed through the world as if all belonged to her.

God, he thought. I hadn't realised how bitter I'd become.

His search was going nowhere. He stared at the screen, then shut the lid. The light in the room felt cold. Somewhere outside, a car alarm wailed and was ignored.

He had found nothing.

No trace. No name. No handle. No photograph. It was as if she existed only in that garden.

The slice of toast had gone cold. Thick-cut Frank Cooper Oxford marmalade clung to one edge like amber resin. Grey had taken two bites, maybe three. He pushed it aside and sat back. His waistband felt loose again. He'd lost weight without trying. Not from exercise or resolve—just absence.

Then his phone rang.

He glanced at the screen.

Simon

He didn't pick it up. Not at once.

He hadn't spoken to Simon in over a year. Maybe more. Not since... No, he couldn't remember when.

They had been boys together at Charterhouse. Men, in London in the mid 1990s. Double dates. Shared taxis. Four glasses of wine, two relationships, the promise of adult life still wet behind the ears.

But Simon had risen—*The Economist*, regular income, tasteful mortgage, child, dog, wife still in the picture. Grey had faltered. Fallen sideways. Drifted to where he found himself now like a lost dandelion clock.

The phone kept ringing.

He picked up.

"Simon?"

Simon's voice came down the line, bright and effortless.

"Alf, you slippery bastard! I thought you'd joined a monastery or died in a library."

Grey gave a tired smile. "Not quite. Though the silence has its appeal."

"Mate—what happened to you? Loved that piece you did on Hebron. Proper stuff. When was that—March?"

"January," said Grey.

"Bloody hell. Sorry. Life's a blur—kid's teething, the dog had gastroenteritis—don't ask—and Emma's been juggling God knows what. Honestly, I'm just about keeping my head above water."

Grey said nothing.

"Anyway—Anna was asking after you."

A pause. Grey blinked. "She was?"

"Yeah—Emma sees her at yoga. Some intense hot yoga place in Fulham. Vinyasa or Ashtanga or... something. They're both scarily bendy, apparently. Anna asked if we still talked."

Grey looked out of the window down at the park.

"I didn't realise they kept in touch."

"Oh yeah—Emma always liked her. Still does. She said you'd dropped off the radar. I said you were probably holed up with an old typewriter and a world-weary sigh."

Grey smiled. "Close enough."

"Look," Simon said. "We should catch up. Pint? My treat. I could come up your way—what's that pub? The Royal Haddock?"

"The Prince of Wales."

"That's it. Thursday evening?"

Grey hesitated. The thought of sitting across from Simon, all fresh-pressed and prosperous, filled him with vague nausea. But something in him nodded. "All right. Thursday."

"Excellent. It'll be good to see you, Alf. Really."

Grey let the call end before replying.

He set the phone down beside the plate and looked at the toast. It had hardened at the edges.

Outside, the wind stirred the trees in the park.

Somewhere in Fulham, Anna had asked after him.

The Prince of Wales had once tried to be a gastro pub. Now it had the tired look of a place that had given up. The floor was sticky. The beer smelt a day past drinkable. A fruit machine blinked to itself in one corner, unloved.

Grey arrived early, of course. He'd claimed a corner table near the back and sat nursing a pint of Guinness he didn't particularly want. The condensation gathered around the base of the glass, untouched. He fiddled with a paper napkin, folding it.

Simon arrived ten minutes late, as expected, in a well-cut navy overcoat and a soft grey jumper that looked expensive without shouting about it. He scanned the room, winced almost imperceptibly, and smiled when he saw Grey.

"Christ," he said, sinking into the chair opposite, "This place looks like the set of a Ken Loach film." He glanced at the taps. "God, do they even do wine?"

Grey raised his glass. "It's very Tufnell Park."

Simon laughed. "It's good to see you, Alf."

"You too, Simon."

Simon nodded. "You look... thinner."

"Stress diet. Highly effective."

Simon looked around. "I thought the chairs might be bolted down. The last time I was in a place like this I was twenty and too drunk to care."

"Atmosphere's cheap," said Grey.

Simon looked at the Guinness, then the pumps, then back at Grey. "They do wine?"

"Only red. And it comes warm, in a mug."

"Delightful. I'll risk the lager."

Simon got up, returned with two pints, and sat. He took a cautious sip, then shuddered. "That's horrific. What have you been doing to yourself?"

Grey shrugged. "Changed tack a bit. Journalism's gone soft. No one's paying for serious analysis anymore."

Simon raised an eyebrow. "You? Gone soft? Even at school you thought too hard."

"I'm trying my hand at arts features. You know. Local colour. Theatrical oddities. Avant-garde bits."

"Oh?"

Grey took a slow sip of his drink, then said, almost offhandedly, "I'm following on this weird thing that happened. They must have got my address from somwhere and wanted coverage. Got invited to Hampstead by someone calling herself Queen Mab."

Simon raised an eyebrow. "Queen Mab?"

Grey nodded. "Handwritten card. No return address. Turned up out of nowhere. I went—just to see what it was. Whole thing was... you know, theatrical. Honestly it was full-on garden party surrealism. Thought it might be a story. Still might." He shrugged and sipped his beer.

Simon tilted his head, amused. "Christ. That's very you. Everything was always a story."

Grey gave a small shrug. "She had a butler called Spindledrift."

Simon grinned. "Of course she did."

He took a sip, then shook his head.

"I blame the internet. That's all kids want to do these days. No one wants a real job. They just want to be influencers. It's probably an Instagram project with a Kickstarter and merch."

Grey managed a smile. "Probably."

Simon leaned back. "Still—beats writing about Turkish pipeline disputes, eh?"

Grey said, "Someone has to document the decline."

Simon sipped again, still grimacing. "This beer is really rank. But yes, that's the stuff that sells now. Colour supplements, lifestyle blogs. Emma follows this Russian photographer—Margarita Kareva. Does fantasy shoots for Vogue or somewhere. Fairies in fur cloaks with reindeer."

Grey blinked. "I've seen those. A bit..."

"...overdone? Totally. But they've got millions of followers. Emma loves them. So," Simon grinned, "So you're fixing to be an influencer now? Selling VPNs and flashlights in between shots of your kitchen and your latest meal?"

For a moment, Grey hesitated then he saw Simon's grin, saw the glint of teasing love behind it, and laughed.

"Christ, imagine. Me. Hashtagging my life in Tufnell Park. 'Here's me in the laundrette, thinking about Iran.'"

Simon chuckled. "You'd be brilliant. Utterly bleak. But there's this guy who posts nostalgia reels about Communist housing projects in Eastern Europe. People love it."

Grey said, without humour. "What has the world come to?"

"Braudillard predicted it," Simon said.

"Shut up! You know I hast post-modernism."

There was a pause. They both drank.

Simon cleared his throat. "You should come round sometime. Emma'd love to see you. We could do a proper meal. Bring a bottle. Real wine though, promise."

"I'll see what Lidl has."

They ordered a second round. The barmaid looked bored. The lager didn't improve.

Simon looked around again. "Remember that place in Soho we used to go to? With the basement jazz and the cheese board?"

"The French girl behind the bar who fancied you," Grey said.

"Ah yes. Juliette. God. That was a different life."

Grey nodded, then said nothing.

Simon cleared his throat. "But really, you should come round. Sunday roast. We've even got a decent garden now. Finally tamed the leylandii. Don't mind the midget or the hound."

Grey smiled politely. "That'd be nice."

Simon hesitated. "I'd invite Anna too, but... her husband might mind. South African. Something in finance. Tightly wound. The sort who thinks eye contact is a challenge."

Grey looked at Simon. Was he joking?

Simon seemed to realise he'd gone too far. He finished his drink. "Listen, mate. Lovely to see you. I really mean about you coming round. Don't lock yourself away."

"Yeah, of course, I will."

"You're still the best writer I know. Even if you are slumming it with performance art and mad women in the woods."

Grey smiled, crookedly. "What makes you think I'm not happy?"

Simon didn't reply. He just watched him, gently.

Eventually, Simon stood. "Right. I'd better go. Domestic life beckons. Story time, baths, the nightly siege."

Grey rose too. They went to the pub door. Outside, they hovered awkwardly. Simon opened his arms. "Come on, you miserable old sod."

As they pulled apart, Simon said quietly: "Love you, mate."

"Yeah, yeah. Mutual, I'm sure."

Simon hesitated. "Don't disappear again."

"I'll try not to."

"Hey, and good luck with Queen Titania."

"Queen Mab."

"Even better. Bring her round for lunch."

"Oh, yeah."

The day of his second meeting with Mab, Grey emerged from Hampstead Tube station into a day that matched his mood: grey-skied, wind-stirred, faintly leaden. The clouds pressed low, threatening rain without commitment. For a moment he stood still on the pavement, his coat collar turned up, blinking against the sharp breeze. He looked around.

Spindledrift Goodfellow was waiting, exactly as promised, leaning casually against a black iron railing just beyond the taxi rank. His outfit had changed: today he wore a dark green velvet coat with a high collar and silver frogs, tight russet trousers, and soft black boots that looked neither new nor old. A walking stick, too slender to be functional, rested in his gloved hand. His hair was the same spun-sugar white, and his eyes, as always, unreadable.

Goodfellow, seeing Grey, raised his stick in greeting but said nothing. Instead, with a theatrical sweep of one hand, he gestured up the hill.

Grey felt a strange relief—stronger than he'd expected — the appointment had been kept.

They began the climb up Holly Hill in silence. The pavement was uneven and last year's leaves lay tucked against the railings. The houses here leaned in on themselves, all high chimneys and iron balconies. Somewhere a piano was playing behind frosted glass.

"I could have found my own way to the garden gate, you know," said Grey.

Goodfellow smiled without turning his head. "Well, perhaps you could," he said lightly. "But my role is to guide you—should you become lost."

"Become lost?" Grey frowned.

"It's easier than you think, especially for a man in your state of life," said Goodfellow, glancing sideways now with the trace of a smirk.

"My state of life?" Grey shook his head. "You don't know anything about me."

"Oh, I do, Mr Grey. I know all about you," said Goodfellow. "But, in any case, the Queen doesn't like unannounced visitors. No, not at all."

Grey stopped. "Listen, Mr Goodfellow. Who are you really?"

"Hmm?"

"I mean, you must have a page in Spotlight."

"I like to keep out of the spotlight."

"Oh, very drole. But, I mean you must do other jobs."

"The Queen keeps me occupied, it's true, but I do have time for some freelance work. Keep walking. Let's not be late."

Grey set off alongside him. "So let's say, I wanted to hire you."

"You? Whatever for?"

"No, not me. I mean, that's not my business, I'm a journalist, but if a director wanted to cast you."

"Ah," Goodfellow said and chuckled. "You think I'm an actor?"

"Of course."

"And you think this," he gestured to his face, "is done with makeup and coloured contact lenses?"

"What else would it be?"

Goodfellow shrugged. "I'm not an actor."

Grey sighed. "So what is this I'm engaged in — doing weird, pointless theatrical stunts with rocks. And you're even paying me."

"We like bargains. And you need the money."

Grey blushed but went on. "Very funny. But what's it all about? If it's not theatre, then what are you doing it for?"

"It amuses us."

"Us?"

"Us means we," said Goodfellow.

Grey groaned. "This silly word play is boring. Who are you and why are you doing this to me?"

"With you, really. Not to you. Though you're not really as free to leave as you think."

"Whatever. Answer my questions."

"Well, some people call us the Good Folk. I've even heard it said we are known as the People of Peace. Ha! And as for why we're doing it, it's just because it's in our nature. Oaks grow acorns, dogs chase cats, we play with people like you."

"But your queen seemed to really want me to do that job for her, that throwing away the stone thing."

"Well, between you and I, the Queen is something of a philanthropist. She likes to help people."

"The Philosopher? He didn't want to be helped."

"No, not him —you."

"Me?"

"Ssshh! We're nearly there. Compose yourself."

As they reached the top of Holly Hill, Goodfellow veered off the road without announcement, turning into a narrow, overgrown passage between two Georgian houses. Grey didn't really remember it, but he followed the fop along the garden wall. The hedges scraped his sleeves. The sound of the city was thinning, as if they were leaving it behind.

And in the garden wall there was a gate. The same gate as before, looking nearly the same as it had the last time, but now the scrollwork was gilded, every leaf and curlicue painted fresh in gold. The plaque—he remembered it being blue and about Edmund Spencer —was now a deep red, inset with small ivory letters: "No Admittance Without Invitation."

The thought came to him that they had changed the wording on the sign because of his conversation with Goodfellow about him dropping in unannounced but that was only minutes ago. Still, if they had some kind of microphone on Goodfellow, they could have heard and they might have a 3D printing machine to churn out the new sign in minutes, all designed to keep him off balance. Or, he could be losing his mind. There was that.

Goodfellow drew a key from his coat. It was a different key from last time. It wasn't silver, it was gold like gate's ironwork, and unusually long, with a handle shaped like a crescent moon.

> *"The silver apples of the moon,*
> *The golden apples of the sun"*

The line just popped into his head. Then, with a stage magician's flourish, Goodfellow turned the lock and swung the gate wide. "After you," he said.

Grey stepped through.

"Remember, be on your best behaviour," Goodfellow whispered.

As Grey stepped fully into the garden, the air changed. It became thicker, sweeter, like a Midsummer Night's dream of night scented stocks. And the light faded.

It was warmer inside the garden—much warmer. The damp chill of London vanished, replaced by a heavy, perfumed tropical humidity that clung to the skin. He blinked. It was now dusk, a deep blue evening flecked with gold. Stars twinkled high above, multicoloured spangles of light, far off, set in blue enamel. Somewhere nearby from the formal garden, water murmured. The path beneath his feet was no longer gravel but crushed white marble.

He had to admit. It was clever how they did this.

The garden was vast—far larger than a Hampstead house could possibly hold. It was a Mughal paradise: formal, with geometric lawns edged in box, shallow pools set with lilies, white pavilions half-hidden among date palms and flowering hibiscus. In the warm dimness of the evening, soft yellow lanterns flickered from carved arches. Fireflies drifted like living embers. The scent of jasmine was overwhelming.

It looked like India. Not the real India—but the idea of it. A dream of India. Everything was artificial in this garden. This wasn't the world as it ever was, but the world as people wanted it to be.

He moved forward slowly, the sound of cicadas hidden in the bushes a rhythmic background track. Was it recorded? From somewhere came the faint, plucked notes of a sitar, drifting and uncertain. He almost laughed — what a production.

One of the fireflies floated sideways, circling back against the air, then like a flashcube popping on an Instamatic camera, it flashed, burned, and melted.

Then following Goodfellow, he saw her again. No longer the English Rose, instead she was an Englishman's dream of an Indian princess. All of it so unreal.

Queen Mab reclined on a peacock throne at the centre of a wide stone platform beneath a filigree awning of gold and green paint. Her dress shimmered like beetle wings—iridescent, clinging, embroidered with tiny mirrors. She was barefoot, one leg tucked beneath her, the other resting on a silk cushion. In her lap was a glossy copy of *Vogue*—a summer issue, he noted. She appeared to be reading it.

A silver hookah gurgled quietly at her side. A bowl of pomegranate seeds glowed red on the table beside her. The fireflies drifted lazily through the perfumed air.

She smiled—a slow, delicate curve of her sweet lips, breaking into a greeting—and something in him weakened and melted. He felt a rush of gratitude that she was pleased to see him. Then he looked up, and her green eyes were cool, steady, almost bored—as if the smile had never taken place.

"You're late," she said mildly, but without irritation.

"I wasn't given a time."

She tilted her head, examining him as one might an experiment left too long on the burner.

"No," she said at last. "I suppose you weren't."

She closed the magazine, tossed it carelessly onto the silk beside her, and fixed him with a smile that looked genuine. Or perhaps he just wanted it to be.

"Well, come along then," she said. "Let's not waste this heatwave. They're so rare in England, even imaginary ones."

"It doesn't look like England," Grey said. "I thought this was Scene 2: Inside A Mughal Palace."

Mab grinned. "Very good." She turned. "He's very good, isn't he, Goodfellow."

Goodfellow cocked his head. "I wouldn't say 'good', more 'too clever by half'".

Goodfellow pointed to a low cushioned stool beside Mab's throne, and when Grey sat, offered him a small brass cup of cardamom coffee—thick, dark, and lightly spiced. Grey sipped. It was startlingly good. He hadn't seen anyone pour it. It had been standing there ready, not too hot, not too cold, as if they'd known the time of his arrival to the minute.

Grey looked about. The fireflies drifted, undisturbed, in the still, perfumed air. A shallow channel of running water ran through the garden, filled with rose petals and floating lamps. The air was hot and languid. Somewhere, the sitar was still playing out of sight, a wandering melody, slow and plaintive. He glanced around for a speaker but found none. Maybe it was a real musician

"How is it night here?" he asked. "It was early afternoon outside."

Mab turned her head slightly, as if the question had arrived from an unexpected direction.

"Was it?" she said. "I lose track."

He looked up. The stars above were unfamiliar stars, glimpsed through the fronds of exotic trees, constellations he'd never seen. This didn't look like a technical fix, like some super CGI projection. It was more as if his mind was altered. He looked at the coffee. Perhaps they were drugging him?

"You always were literal," Mab said. She reached out idly, one finger hovering above a firefly that had landed on the rim of her goblet. Grey had a sudden, visceral memory of the butterfly in the English garden. He tensed, expecting her to crush it.

She winked at him andlet the insect rest there, glowing gently. After a moment, it lifted off and vanished into the air.

"I like these," she said. "So soft. Not like butterflies. Butterflies are vain."

She wasn't drinking coffee. She took a sip of something green from a cut-glass cup. It might be absinthe. Then she said, "Did you enjoy the hothouse at Kew?"

"I didn't go to the hothouse."

"No," she said, not at all abashed. "Of course. That was someone else. Or perhaps that's later." She waved the contradiction away. "And how did you find him?"

"I went to the address you gave me."

"No, no. Not 'how did you find him?' but 'how did you find him?'"

"That's the same thing," Grey said.

"Well, the words are the same, but anyone knows they mean something different. How was he? Did he mention me?"

The philosopher?" said Grey. "Yes, he mentioned you."

She grinned.

Grey continued, "I thought he was... nice. But sad."

"I think we're related," said Mab. "Or is he related to you, Goodfellow?"

"To me, Your Majesty. He's my father's brother's son," said Goodfellow from behind them, where he now lounged against a marble pillar, one leg tucked over the other, polishing an apple on his sleeve.

She said, "Your father's brother's son is you."

Good fellow replied, "Or someone else."

Mab rolled her eyes. "Men! Grey is too literal and Goodfellow not literal enough."

Mab tilted her head, smiled, then shrugged. "Anyway." She looked back at Grey. "You did it." She clapped. "Good, fellow!" She smiled at Goodfellow. "He's a good fellow! You're Goodfellow! Ha ha!"

Goodfellow sighed.

Mab turned back to Grey, "I have another task for you."

Grey felt unaccountably anxious.

"This one's better," she added. "More literary. More your thing."

"I'm not sure—" he began.

"I can pay again," she interrupted.

Grey blinked.

"Would £1,000 be enough?" she asked.

Grey opened his mouth but didn't answer.

"Or £5,000? Is that a lot?"

Grey hesitated. "I... can't really take that much."

Mab narrowed her eyes, not unkindly, but with a kind of disappointed amusement.

"Oh? Well then. £500?"

Grey, already regretting his own diffidence, nodded. "Yes. Thank you."

"Give him £500, Goodfellow."

"Very well, Your Majesty," said Goodfellow, who reached into his waistcoat and began counting out new notes. They were crisp, pristine—oddly so. The paper looked too smooth. The Queen's portrait on them, Elizabeth not Mab, seemed too luminous, her eyes somewhat sly.

Grey took the money almost furtively and slid it into his wallet.

Mab continued, "There's a bookshop. Bloomsbury. Not one of the famous ones, but a good one. I'm going to give you the title of a book. It's one I particularly hate. They have a lot of books but they'll know the one you mean."

"A book?"

"That's what I said, didn't I?"

"I'm a bit of a bibliophile."

She gave a mock-yawn. "That means 'bore'."

Grey tried to ignore her, but she was like a black hole, she pulled at his attention. He couldn't get his mind away from her. He said, "And what book am I looking for?"

"*Memoirs of My First Love*, it's called" she said. "By a man called Joseph Hector Sutherland. Privately printed. Mid-Victorian. Terrible prose, but very... alive. I believe that no one's ever written an account of a love affair so plainly. You know, I don't mind them being in love, not at all, in fact I quite applaud it. But what's the point going over it all again?"

Grey shrugged. "People like feeling nostalgic."

"Oh, you don't have to tell me that. Anyway, just get rid of it. Burn it," she said. "I want it gone." Her distaste appeared genuine.

"Why?" he asked.

"Memories," she said, her nose wrinkling. "I hate them. They're sticky. They trap people. In times, in feelings. You think they belong to you, but really, and if you understand this, Mr Grey, you'll have got it, you'll have exactly got it. If you have memories, you belong to them — horrid little anchors."

She reached again for her green drink with her left hand, the fingers of her right trailing through the firefly-laced air.

"That sort of thing, that blasted book," she added, "It's full of memories. It should not be allowed to survive. It's for everybody's good."

"All books are full of memories," Grey said.

"Yes, and I hate them all, but I hate that one most because it's full of very convincing memories, the sort that might convince people the past is real. And it isn't!"

Grey looked at her for a long moment. He suddenly thought that for all that she looked like a beautiful young woman she wasn't human at all. She was something pretending to be human.

He glanced down at the cardamom coffee in his hand because her beauty was eating him up.

The way she talked with her hands, her face, the way her mouth shaped the sentences of a story he could no longer follow. She'd finished talking about the book. It was something about a festival, or a coronation, or a crocodile hunt. It made no difference. The flickering light of the spirit lamps caught in her hair like flame behind glass. Her irises were a green so saturated they looked inhumanly green, like old emeralds, like stinging nettles.

She sat sideways on the throne now, barefoot, utterly without self-consciousness. He couldn't look away for her.

Until he felt it—that prickle at the back of his neck. The sense of being stared at. Spindledrift Goodfellow was watching him from the shadow of a colonnade, eating an apple. He bit slowly, eyes fixed on Grey with what looked like amusement mixed with pity.

Grey flushed and looked away from them both.

Mab had been speaking about something—a place near Dollis Hill, he thought—but now she was looking at him directly. "You've forgotten where that is, haven't you?" she said.

He hesitated, frowned then nodded. He'd always prided himself on a precise knowledge of London. "Yes."

She smiled. "That's good. It's working then—my influence on you. You'll feel much better once you've forgotten everything except the here and now."

There was a soft clink as she set down her glass.

She said lightly. "You may go." She looked away before he had the chance to respond and picked up her copy of Vogue. It was an old one, he now saw. Decades old.

Goodfellow appeared at his side. Without speaking, he gestured.

They walked back through the perfumed dark, through garden paths now faintly misted, fireflies still drifting like falling embers, like sparking cinders. At the gate, Goodfellow used the gold key again with a theatrical flourish.

Beyond the gate, it was Hampstead again, but it was night. The air was damp. The pavements gleamed from recent rain.. The day had been consumed during the short hour he'd spent in the garden.

That night, after he'd come home and had a single malt whisky, he fell asleep. He dreamt of Mab. In the dream, she undressed without ceremony. Not seductively—ritually, almost, as if the act had nothing to do with him at all. She stepped free of her gown like a snake slipping its skin, and stood calmly in the warm half-dark, surrounded by shadows and the scent of jasmine.

Her body was flawless in a way that unsettled him. Not idealised—inhuman. Her skin, pale as milk-glass, shimmered faintly, lit as though from within. Her limbs were long, poised, her waist impossibly slight. She moved without hesitation, as if unaware that she was being watched—or as if it didn't matter.

Her breasts stood small, high and perfect. Her hips curved like sculpture. Her hair in auburn waves tumbled down her back. He wanted to touch her.

Then her eyes found him.

They were Mab's own eyes and they were glittering, emerald, ancient, inhuman and indifferent.

And suddenly, she changed.

Her woman's body folded inward, seamlessly, fluidly. Skin gave way to scales, limbs coiled into a single undulating line. She became a serpent—a smooth, golden, muscular snake. It raised its head and fixed Grey with that same emerald gaze.

He woke sweating, heart racing, the image still vivid: the snake watching him without malice, without curiosity. Just presence. As if it had seen him before.

The light was changing, that uncertain grey before dawn that promises merely more of the same. He lay there a while, staring at the ceiling.

Then he got up and made tea.

At his desk, still in his dressing gown, he rolled a fresh sheet into the typewriter and began to write.

> A funny thing happened to me on the way to the theatre.
>
> The theatre was a garden in Hampstead.
>
> A very lovely garden, and my hostess was a very lovely queen…

He paused.

The keys rested under his fingers but he had no idea what to write next.

Grey took the Tube from Tufnell Park to Russell Square. The journey was short and uneventful. The train's windows showed him the tunnel, with its wires and sudden platforms, and his own reflection. He turned away from that.

He guessed he'd have to buy the book, using some of the money Goodfellow had given him and then destroy it. Though perhaps he could just say he'd destroyed it. Intuitively, he knew that wouldn't work. She'd know. Goodfellow would know. He sighed.

Emerging into the soft daylight of Bloomsbury, he found himself among university buildings and Georgian terraces, the air tinged with diesel and the cool of plane trees. He walked slowly past the buildings of University College London, through Gordon Square, and into the quieter backstreets near Tavistock Square.

He found the shop quite easily. The shopfront was narrow, Victorian, and slightly bowed. The hand-painted sign read: **Walworth and Daughters: Antiquarian Booksellers**. The brass handle was warm to the touch. A bell rang faintly as he entered.

Inside, the air was thick with the scent of paper, glue, and polished wood. Shelves reached the ceiling. Leather-bound volumes leaned gently on one another. Dust motes turned in the filtered light.

Grey held a slip of paper with the title Mab had given him. *Memoirs of My First Love* by Joseph Hector . He began to search on his own.

Someone came up behind him as he perused the shelves. A voice, crisp and RP, interrupted "May I assist?"

A young man in horn-rimmed glasses stood nearby, straight-backed, dressed in a cardigan and tie. Grey shook his head. "No, thank you. I'm just browsing."

But Grey couldn't find the book, so reluctantly, he sought the man out at the desk. "Actually... I wonder if you might have this? I can't seem to find it. I assume the books are sorted alphabetically? Anyway... " He handed the slip across.

The assistant read it, one brow raised and smiled. "Ah. That would be in the Rare Books Room."

Rare books. Yes, that made sense. Mab had said there was only one copy left. There was a pause. Grey could sense judgement—polite, but unmistakable: you can't afford a book like this.

Grey was quietly affronted. Why did people assume things about him? He said, "I'm acting on behalf of... a member of a foreign royal house." He forced a smile. "I'm afraid I can't say which."

That changed things. He wasn't sure if the man believed him but he said, without a smile, "Of course. If you'll follow me."

He was led through a narrow corridor and into a chamber panelled in walnut. It smelled faintly of camphor and leather and paper. The assistant crossed to a cabinet and removed a slim volume, bound in faded green leather, gold lettering barely legible.

Grey took it in his hands. It was beautiful. Fragile. He opened it. The story of a hidden love: passionate, confused, ashamed and proud. The prose wasn't half-bad. But then one probably couldn't take Mab's literary judgement seriously. She was probably more at home scrolling through Instagram.

He sighed. The poor chap. The preface said the author, Sutherland, had killed himself. Romantic. Just reading it, you could see how sensitive he'd been. It was Proustian, definitely that quality but undiscovered. Well, undiscovered by the masses, anyway. The bookseller obviously knew its worth. Grey knew that without asking the price. It would be worth a fortune if it was in this room in this particular shop. Far more money that Goodfellow had doled out to him.

He read on. It really was beautiful. Grey felt his eyes moisten. It was the same tragic story of love lost, but told in such a lyrical and sensitive way. It wasn't mawkish. The lad had recognised his mistake. Basically, he'd been betrothed to a local girl. She wasn't special, she wasn't beautiful, but they seemed genuinely to love one another. Then Sutherland had the idea he had to make his way in the world, so his father got himself a position in the East India company. And there he'd frittered away his life in trade and money, and all the while thinking of the ordinary lass he'd left behind. And something happened in India and he was ruined. So he came home, but by the time he'd come back to England with his much reduced career, she of course had married and was living happily with someone else and had the children and the dog and all that. Sutherland had seen her by the Serpentine one day, but she hadn't seen him. Or had pretended she hadn't. And that was the end of the book. It seemed he'd written it in full knowledge of what he was going to do on the day when he got to the last page.

Grey had become quite lost in the story.

The assistant lingered, watching him. Then the shop's telephone rang, shrill and officious. "Excuse me a moment. I'll only be a second."

Grey was alone.

He stood there for some time, holding the book. He thought of the only other book he'd ever stolen—he was sixteen, penniless, and obsessed with Michael Moorcock. He had slipped *The Fortress of the Pearl* into his coat and run, heart thudding. He hadn't stolen anything since.

Until now, of course.

In a moment of controlled panic, he tucked the book into his coat, turned, and walked quickly down the corridor. He got to the door, pushed it, and walked out into the street. Then he began to run.

The assistant's voice shouted behind him. "Hey, you! Stop!"

Of course there had been cameras.

Grey was still running.

The bell over the door jangled furiously way behind but he was off into the street. The assistant followed, calling after him—but Grey lost him among buses and bemused pedestrians. London, as always, looked the other way.

Panting, Grey slowed. His coat flapped open. He was shaking.

His hand gripped the book he had stolen. Then he remembered. He had to destroy it. How could he destroy it? The writing was beautiful, heart-rending, and irreplaceable because the man who'd written it was dead. He looked at it. This is what Mab wanted. She wanted him to feel the pain.

He could rip the book up page by page—but he realised he couldn't do it. It was too personal. It would be like tearing apart the man himself. He wasn't strong enough to do that.

If he threw it in the river, the river would take care of its destruction. But he wasn't near the river.

She had said, "Burn it."

A tobacconist stood on the corner of Marchmont Street.

He could burn it. He entered, bought lighter fluid and a cheap disposable lighter. The man behind the counter didn't look up from his phone, while Grey paid.

Then, in an empty square behind the Brunswick Centre, Grey knelt. The book lay on the paving, open to a page where Joseph Sutherland had written of his wasted life and his wasted love. Grey flicked the lighter. He ran the leaping flame against the page edges, holding it close.

The flames caught quickly. The pages curled and blackened. The book was old and dry. It burned quickly. The scent was acrid —burning leather and paper and the taste of something bitter at the back of his throat.

He watched until the words were gone. Two lives now reduced to smoke and blackened ashes. Mab had planned for him to feel like this. And he hated her. He hated her all the more because he still wanted her to think well of him.

Grey let himself into the flat and shut the door quietly, as if afraid to wake something. He'd stuffed the lighter and the empty can of fluid into his pocked. He put them now into the kitchen bin, then went straight to his desk. The adrenaline had faded but the dull ache of ruin hadn't. He'd destroyed something beautiful. He'd erased a piece of time. What had been merely lost time was now gone forever.

Grey sat down, opened his laptop, and reached for the card

again—the one from Mab, with the looping green handwriting. He was desperate to know who she really was.

He flattened the card on the desk, stared at it. Then took out his phone.

He opened a handwriting OCR app—something he'd used once to transcribe a handwritten interview with an Iranian exile. He held the phone steady and scanned. Then there was a site on the internet that could recognise handwriting. It took about ten minutes. Then it came up with a match:

CAROLINE LAMB

The name made him blink. He opened a new tab, searched.

Lady Caroline Lamb: aristocrat, scandal, Byron's lover, "mad, bad, and dangerous to know." Died 1828.

Was this a joke?

He cross-referenced the card's handwriting with a manuscript of Lamb's he found in an online archive. The loops were similar. The ink... well, impossible to compare. But for a moment, he felt the eerie thrill of plausibility.

"Or a good forger," he muttered.

He stared at the screen. Caroline Lamb had written one novel —*Glenarvon*, a thinly veiled attack on Byron. Not the Queen of Dreams, the Queen of Forgetting. Not this... creature.

Still, the name had surfaced from somewhere.

He turned back to the screen and typed **"Spindledrift Goodfellow."**

He got just one valid result. It was a podcast. *The Classic Ghost Stories Podcast*. The episode was titled *The Bewcastle Fairies*, by someone called Tony Walker.

He clicked play. The voice was calm, Northern. Grey listened. The story was about a man who meets a tall, strange figure in a blue coat, with white hair and violet eyes. "Spindledrift Goodfel-low," the narrator said. "An a gent of mischief, a tempter. Perhaps the Devil himself."

Grey paused the audio. The description was exact. It was him.

He sat very still.

Thinking it through. They would know he would try to find out who they really were, and that meant these days he would search the internet. And if he did that then they would know he would find this one reference to Spindledrift Goodfellow — a fairy, or perhaps the Devil himself. Once again, he thought it was so 'meta' so self-consciously breaking the Fourth Wall, as if to make him think he was in some kind of theatrical production himself. As if it were all staged like some kind of Truman Show.

Was he being played? Hunted? Enlisted? He didn't know, and there was no comfort in the not knowing.

Grey closed the laptop, but the screen's glow lingered in his eyes. In the darkened window, he caught his reflection—and behind it, just faintly, a flicker of green.

He snapped his head round to see who was watching him, but the room was empty.

The morning after burning the book, Grey rose early. He opened his wardrobe and stood for a moment, looking in. Once, long ago, he might have dressed with some idea of making an impression, but that had ebbed. What remained were clothes chosen not for style or statement, just clothes that wouldn't draw comment, wouldn't catch the light. Nothing flamboyant, nothing careless. Just the kind of garments a man wears when he pretends to himself he no longer cares much about being seen.

He pulled out a pale blue shirt—it had been ironed at some point, and looked good enough. The navy jumper was a bit bobbled at the elbows, but warm. He found his usual pair of grey chinos. They'd gone a bit shapeless but still did the job. His shoes were by the door: scuffed lace-ups he wore most days. *How to be Invisible,* a song by Kate Bush.

He took the Tube north to Hampstead, and he felt anxiety gnaw at him. So what if they saw him? So what if they were upset that he'd caught them un-rehearsed. They'd challenged him and he would challenge them back.

The sky was overcast, a pewter lid pressing down on the rooftops. He bought a coffee from a kiosk on Flask Walk and nursed it as he climbed towards the street he remembered—past Georgian terraces, clipped hedges, the faint hum of affluence.

When he came in sight of the garden gate—which was her gate—he saw the ironwork had changed again. It was now painted bronze. The pattern had shifted too, more intricate this time, like calligraphy glimpsed through fog. The enamel plaque was now green and said *¡Cuidado! Perro!*

More lies. There wasn't a bloody dog. He waited.

Dog-walkers passed him with narrowed eyes. A man with a whippet gave him a professional glance and walked on. A woman in gym-wear made a deliberate arc around him, talking loudly into her phone. A pair of sleek electric cars purred by in silence. Hampstead, for all its gestures toward progressivism, had little appetite for men loitering near private gates with yesterday's stubble and no visible purpose. Solidarity with the marginalised was admirable, as long as they stayed elsewhere.

Eventually, a police car crept to a stop beside him. The passenger window buzzed down.

"Excuse me, sir. Can we ask your business here?"

"I'm waiting for someone."

"You'll need to wait somewhere else, I'm afraid. Residents have raised concerns."

Grey opened his mouth, half-ready to mutter something vague about public space, about liberty. But then the gate clicked open behind him.

And Mab stepped through.

She was dressed as though en route to a party in 1974, looking like a friend of Bowie's, perhaps. Crushed velvet trousers, thigh-high boots, mirrored sunglasses, auburn hair bouncing in soft curls. She walked past the police car without looking at him, without seeming to see the officers at all. They saw her. They were men after all.

"All good, officers. I was just leaving," said Grey, with sudden eagerness.

The police glanced back at him, and said, "Okay, sir. But don't hang round these streets again. The residents don't like it."

Grey waited until the police car turned the corner before following Mab at a careful distance.

She wasn't hurrying. Mab moved down Flask Walk with an easy grace. She paused to crouch and stroke a white poodle, exchanging pleasantries with its owner. Grey watched her from about fifty yards behind. She would have seen him if she'd turned round, but then again perhaps he'd made so slight an impression she wouldn't even recognise him. There was something unearthly about her. Her figure shimmered faintly in the grey light, like something seen through heat-haze.

He followed her down Well Walk and then over the road and onto the Heath.

She made no effort to hide. Her presence was conspicuous: glittering, radiant, impossible to miss. And yet, he began to feel sick with doubt. What was he doing? Following a woman into woodland—what would anyone think? What did he think? Was this curiosity, desire, delusion? He needed to get a grip. And yet he had to find out if she was real.

He was anxious. Was he anxious in case she saw him, or was he anxious in case she never noticed him at all?

Mab turned, briefly, and a sudden break of sunlight caught her—turning her outline to gold. Whatever he wanted, it was impossible to look away from her. She walked on.

He followed.

Among the trees, about thirty yards ahead, she paused.

She didn't turn.

She simply... lifted.

Rising from the ground as though weightless, her arms by her side, her body elongating. She spun slowly, once, then twice, then again—like a sycamore seed caught in an invisible updraft. Her form blurred, became translucent, filamented, a dandelion seed almost. Her sunglasses fell, or seemed to fall, though they never touched the ground.

And then she was gone.

No flash. No puff of smoke. And he heard her laughter as if through a wall, from another room. Her form was gone but yes, her laughter remained—high, silver, trailing between the trees.

Grey stood rooted to the spot. The wind passed cold over his skin.

He knew for the first time, they were exactly what they said they were.

The letter arrived the following morning. There was no stamp, no postmark. It lay on the doormat as if it had simply appeared. The envelope was cream, thick as card, scented faintly with sandalwood. His name was written in her elegant copperplate—*Mr Grey*—in deep red ink. it was sealed with wax.

He carried it to the kitchen table, broke the wax seal, and unfolded the page inside.

The same precise, theatrical script as before, though this time written in rd

My dearest Mr Grey,

One final thing. (I do hope you're not bored.)

You are invited to attend a private performance of A Midsummer Night's Dream *at the Theatre of Memory, Soho. As before: Wednesday. One o'clock. You will be met outside Piccadilly Circus Underground Station by Mr Spindledrift Goodfellow.*

Dress as you would for a matinee. Not too modern. Not too dull. (Please — not too dull.)

Fondly (but not too fondly),

Mab

That was all. No address. No explanation. What did Queen Mab want now?

He turned the envelope over again, as though something might reveal itself under the light. But there was nothing. Only that persistent fragrance—faint, musky, hard to place—and a sense that things were accelerating.

Had she seen him when he followed her onto Hampstead Heath? He felt sure she must have. He even felt that her Mary Poppins ascent into the skies was meant just for him. It was all staged for him. They knew everything about him. All the theatricality, all the illusions and double-entendres, were meant solely for him.

He was being played and he hated it. He hated it, but he would still go to meet her. He didn't even tell himself it was for his story now — the story he'd hardly begun to write. At least he was self-aware enough now to admit he was going to see her because of her alone.

Grey emerged from the ticket hall into the glare of Piccadilly Circus. The usual chaos unfolded around him—tourists with phones, street hawkers selling balloons and phone cases, the flash and repetition of advertisement screens. And there, standing just apart from it all, was Goodfellow.

Goodfellow, in a pale-blue brocade frock coat with brass buttons and a high cravat, inclined his head, and raised his thin stick. "Mr Grey. Right on time. The Queen awaits."

They walked.

He was led through side-streets, arcades, and crooked lanes, past sushi bars and Szechuan parlours, vape shops and fetish-wear boutiques, the red signs of sex cinemas and the bright-cleaned glass of gay bars. Soho was still Soho. A place that wore its masks boldly.

They passed a row of theatres—some boarded, some blazing with LED banners—and turned down an alley Grey had never noticed before. There, tucked in beside a Vietnamese café and a dry-cleaners, was a narrow black door marked *Stage Door*. Good-fellow knocked once, twice, and someone opened it.

A woman opened the door and let them through without a word.

Inside the theatre there was velvet and wood and the warm lingering smell of greasepaint and last night's audience's perfumes. Grey looked around. It felt like falling into a painting from the 1880s: gaslight, footlights, ropes, and fly-rigs. He glimpsed high-ceilinged rafters, faded gold cornices, and stage curtains that hung red as dried roses pressed in a book.

The stage showed itself off in limelight and shadow, like a doorway left ajar between the real and the imagined.. It was smaller than he expected, but perfectly proportioned—like something out of a Dan Leno show: Victorian music-hall, down to the bones. The seats were red velvet. The ceiling fresco was a riot of cherubs and clouds, faded slightly at the edges.

On stage, a rehearsal was underway.

A thin young man in tights declaimed from centre stage. He was playing Oberon. Another actor—bare-armed, delicate-featured—rehearsed a scene as Puck. The atmosphere was not frivolous, but reverent. Everyone worked hard. And all the while, Queen Mab sat in a centre seat five rows back in the stalls.

Today, she was dressed like Dick Turpin. Or perhaps a roman-ticised version of a lady highwayman: a dark red velvet coat, cinched tight at the waist, black knee boots polished to a mirror shine, a tricorn hat tipped rakishly back. Her auburn curls spilled out beneath it, gleaming like spun fire.

She was watching the rehearsal and clapped at moments. It

seemed that her praise mattered. The actors kept glancing towards her, attentive to her attention to them.

Goodfellow led Grey down the aisle and along the row of seats towards her. Grey was trying to look composed, trying not to feel again the curious pull of her presence.

She turned and smiled.

"Oh, hello Mr Grey. It *is* Grey, isn't it?"

For a moment, he had a flash of panic. His name —he couldn't recall himself. His name d name slipped, hung just out of reach. He nodded and shrugged.

"In any case," she said, "It doesn't matter what you're called. But I do have one last little thing for you." Then there was a flourish on stage and she turned her eyes back to the actors and applauded. She called out, "Bravo! Well, done Lisa. Excellent!"

Lisa, on stage turned and bowed. "Thank you, Mab."

Mab blinked and turned back to Grey. "So, tomorrow night. Not tonight. Don't do it when I'm here! Don't do it when there's even a memory of me being here. But, tomorrow, I want you to come back here. Quietly. Through the same door. The Stage Door. I'll leave it open. Well, Goodfellow will leave it open."

He swallowed. "What for? What do you want me to do?"

She nodded towards the actor playing Oberon. "Him. He's called, erm, Christopher, I think. In any case, go to his dressing room. Find his wallet. It'll be in his trousers, hanging up. You'll see a tatty old photograph inside. Nothing special. But it must be taken and buried. In a hole. One of those municipal ones, you know—where they dig to lay wires or drains. It must be buried under clay. Clay is important. You do understand the symbolism of what we're doing, don't you?"

"No," he said.

She smiled. "In case it helps you follow along: water to dissolve, fire to erase, earth to contain, air to lift. This is earth."

She turned her eyes back to the stage, then added, almost to herself, "Of course, I myself am air." She was telling him she'd seen him. "And you, Mr Grey... are water. Do you remember?"

"Do I remember water?"

"Yes. Do you remember?"

Grey had no idea what she was talking about.

Beside him, Goodfellow said, with polite regret, "He doesn't remember, Majesty."

Mab nodded. "Of course. Of course not. Silly of me." She smiled faintly. "And it's for the best."

Grey said. "You want me to steal the photograph?"

She smiled indulgently. "Steal it and destroy it. Actually, I don't mind if you destroy it before you steal it. Oh, don't look so hang-dog! You've done worse. And I'll pay. Seven hundred and fifty pounds and seventy-five pence."

The specificity was absurd. Grey said, "Why the seventy-five pence?"

"I am just being precise today. Anyway, it's more than I paid for that silly little book, isn't it?"

"I can't just go through someone's wallet," he said, weakly.

She turned to face him fully. Her green eyes caught the lime-light and gleamed like malachite dug out of the earth for the first time since its creation. "Oh, Grey, come down off your high horse. It's a photograph. It's not money. It's not worth anything It's just a picture. A memory. He doesn't need it. It weighs him down. Honestly, I'm trying to help him."

Goodfellow remained silent beside him, watching.

"And besides," she said softly, laying her hand on Grey's knee. Her touch was deliberate and provocative. He felt it was like an electric circuit. She smiled, her fingers warm and firm. "You want to do this." She paused in case he'd forgotten. "For me."

Her sharp, plain nails dug lightly into his leg. Her perfectly shaped mouth curved slightly. She cocked her head. "You do want to please me, don't you?"

His throat was dry. "I..."

"You see you do!" She let go of his leg and sat back. "Help me free him from his memories, Mr Grey."

"All right, all right." He nodded. "All right."

Beside him Goodfellow was laughing.

The following night, Grey returned to the theatre alone. Soho was loud and alive—bright signs, late drinkers, the high chatter of crowds spilling from bars. Music pulsed from open doorways. A man shouted across the street to someone who didn't hear. The air was thick with heat, noise, and the smell of spilt beer and stale perfume.

Grey walked through it all unremarked and unnoticed. He wished someone would stop him, become aggressive, start a fight, just so he would have an excuse not to do what he was going to do.

He turned into the side alley beside the Vietnamese café, and the sound fell away.

It was darker here and quieter. The alley was faintly sour with wet brick and the smell of old cooking oil. The black door marked *Stage Door* stood waiting. Unlocked, as promised. Goodfellow had been here.

The small theatre was different now. A performance was underway. The façade was lit up—modern posters now, digital displays—but the alley and the *Stage Door* looked unchanged. He went in with a pounding heart.

The smell of the place hit him first: hot dust, makeup, old costumes, hairspray, something almost chalky from the backstage walls. He moved quietly, furtively. There were voices—soft, close. Someone laughed.

He passed a painted sign that read *No Entry – Cast & Crew Only*. He ignored it.

He took the stairs up, the wood worn smooth underfoot, past

posters for plays long gone. A stage manager came around a corner and stopped abruptly. She looked at him suspiciously.

"I'm here for Queen Mab," he said, forcing himself to sound casual.

"Oh," she said, uncertain. "Well..."

"She asked me to speak to the actor playing Oberon," he added. "Could you tell me where his dressing room is?"

The woman blinked. "Chris? Along there. Second from the end."

He thanked her, trying not to rush, trying to look like he belonged here.

At the corridor's end, he heard voices—Chris and a woman. They were laughing softly. Then the door opened, and the two of them stepped out into the corridor. Both were in costume. He recognised the woman as Lisa, the one playing Titania. Chris wore a crown of branches, gold-threaded robes. The woman wore a gossamer gown and wings that caught the light.

Before they saw him, Grey turned into a dark alcove. These old theatres were full of them—niches with forgotten furniture, iron-work, crumbling plaster roses. He pressed himself back into shadow. He wished he would go through the wall and not be here at all.

They passed, oblivious. He waited till they were out of sight. Then, with heart hammering, he opened the door and stepped into the dressing room.

It was small, cluttered and personal. A row of lightbulbs surrounded the mirror. There were mugs with teabags still inside them, scripts, half a sandwich. Chris's normal trousers hung neatly from a peg.

Grey groped in the pocket and pulled out the wallet.

Inside, among cards and receipts, was a photograph.

A colour print with a white border. The tones were just slightly off—the yellow too warm, the blue too pale. It was a seaside scene. A young woman knelt on the sand beside a small boy who was building a sandcastle. The boy's face was serious and focused. The woman looked at him with open adoration.

Grey turned it over.

In biro, in a neat but informal hand: *Me and Mum, Blackpool, about 1978.*

Me and mum. He thought about his own mother. He stared at it for a long time.

Then, quietly, he took the photo and returned the wallet to the pocket. He stepped out of the dressing room and made for the stairs.

As he turned a corner, he collided with Chris. They both reeled back from the impact, both apologising.

"I'm so sorry," Chris said.

"No, no. It was my fault," Grey said.

"Well, don't worry. It's a bloody cramped place this. I'm always walking into people." The actor was about to walk on.

Grey could have got out. He could have nodded, hurried out and disappeared into the night with this man's precious photograph. He could have got away with it, instead he called back, "Great performance."

"Oh?" Chris stopped then beamed. "Thank you!"

Grey reached into his coat pocket, surreptitiously took out the photograph and stooped, pretending to find it on the floor. "I think you dropped this," he said.

Chris's brow furrowed. Then he took the photo and gasped. "What—? Oh, God. How did I drop that? I always keep it in my wallet. How on earth is it here? But, anyway, thank you from the bottom of my heart. I didn't even realise it was missing."

"No problem," Grey said. "It looked important."

Chris smiled. His face changed. No longer the fairy king, but just a man, very human under his makeup. He shook his head. "It is. It's the only picture I have of my mum and me. She was diagnosed with cancer not long after this was taken. She died six months later."

Grey looked away. "I'm really sorry."

"That's very sweet of you," Chris said quietly. "There aren't many lives that don't have their own tragedies. But it was a long time ago. Still it's kind of you."

Grey said. "It's not the sort of thing you forget."

Chris looked at the picture again, and his eyes grew glassy. "No. The photo helps. Helps me remember her face. I was only little. Without it—I might've forgotten what she looked like.."

Grey nodded. "I'm glad you got it back," and he turned to go.

But Chris called after him. "Hey—wait. Are you the guy Alex said was looking for me earlier?"

Grey hesitated. "No, not me."

Chris frowned. "So you don't work for Queen Mab?"

Grey gave a forced smile. "Queen Mab? Who's she?"

Chris looked surprised. "Queen Mab! You work in the biz and you've never heard of her?"

"I don't work in the biz," Grey said quietly.

"Oh." Chris seemed disappointed. He scratched his head. "Well, if you do know her... let her know I'm looking for work. Anything going, really."

Grey paused. "I'd be careful with her."

Chris interrupted, half-laughing. "Thought you didn't know her."

"I don't like to admit it."

Chris said, "Oh, I'm used to fairy queens."

Grey didn't smile.

Chris explained, "That's a joke. Titania and all."

Grey looked at him for a long moment. "Yes. I'd steer clear of all them, " he said

Chris waved. "Anyway, thanks for finding the photo. You're a nice, sweet man. Thank you again."

Grey gave a crooked smile and waved. "Take care."

Then he left. The theatre door closed behind him with a soft clunk.

. . .

Outside, the lights of London were too bright, the humid air seemed to lack oxygen. Grey walked down the alley, hollow and ashamed. He walked quickly, without purpose, down the alley past the bins and the wet brick walls, past the heat-shimmer of kitchen vents and the rust-streaked fire escape.

He'd almost done what she'd asked. The first two times felt less real, the old man had almost forgotten himself, the author of the book was long dead, but Chris, this painted-Oberon, this decent, honest bloke had lost his mother and Grey had almost extinguished the memory of his mother's face.

But feeling tears rise to his eyes — tears of shame at what he'd nearly done, and a flush of struggling pride that he'd finally stood up to her, he knew that what really killed him was, now he'd defied her, he was afraid that she would not call for him again

The flat was quiet when Grey returned home. He did not switch on the main light. Instead, he moved by instinct through the shadows to the bookshelf, where a blue cardboard envelope sat wedged between volumes. *Boots Photo Centre*—yellow lettering now faded.

He brought it to the desk and turned on the lamp. Amber light pooled across the wood. He opened the envelope and drew out the prints.

The first showed Anna in front of a castellated red-brick manor, sunlight glancing off the moat behind her. She wore a denim jacket and a slightly awkward smile, as though unsure how seriously to take the photo. Her hair was tied up. Her hand rested on the stone wall.

He turned it over. *Me and Anna, Hever Castle.*

The next showed the two of them on a pebbled beach. A cloudy day. He was in profile, talking; she was looking directly at the camera with a faint smirk, as if in on a private joke. Their shoes sat behind them on a tartan blanket. The sea was grey and calm.

He turned it over. *Brighton 1998.*

The third was louder: three people on football day. Grey in a scarf, flushed and laughing. Anna in a wool coat, half-turned toward him. Between them, a woman with curly hair held a take-away coffee and grinned at the camera. They stood outside the stadium's brick façade, the crowd blurred around them.

He turned it over. *Anna, me and Julie – Highbury about 1999.*

He leafed through the others slowly. No words. No commentary. Just the slick shuffle of gloss prints against one another, the weight of photographic paper in the hand.

Then, gently, he gathered them, slid them back into the envelope, smoothed the flap closed, and replaced it on the shelf.

He switched off the lamp. The room darkened. London murmured on beyond the window, never quiet. Like the River Thames that ran through it.

Grey was barely awake when the knock came. The knock was on the door of his flat. Whoever it was was already inside the building, though he hadn't let them in.

The flat was cold, and his mouth tasted stale. The knock came again—sharp, rhythmic and unambiguous. Grey sat up, rubbed his face, and waited to see if it had been his imagination. It hadn't.

He opened the door in his dressing gown.

Spindledrift Goodfellow stood there. Today his coat was brocaded peacock-blue, patterned with gold thread that caught the dull light. His bone-white gloves were immaculate, and his violet eyes—pupil-less and flat—watched Grey with an expression that might have passed for fondness, or pity, or neither.

"The Queen wishes to see you," he said. "She'd like to know

how you got on. With the actor," he added in case Grey had forgotten.

Grey scratched his chin. "I haven't eaten breakfast yet."

"You know she doesn't liked to be refused."

"I'm not dressed."

"No need to make a fuss," said Goodfellow, already turning. "Something vaguely clean will suffice. I can pick."

"No, no." Grey went to his room and while Goodfellow waited, dressed in yesterday's trousers and a jumper that had lost its shape. His socks didn't match. It didn't matter.

"Hurry now," Goodfellow called round the door.

Outside, they walked to the main road. Here traffic was building. Goodfellow whistled once, and a black cab slid to the kerb as if it had been waiting all morning.

Grey climbed into the back seat beside him.

The cab was warm, a bit sweaty, covered by the smell of vinyl seats and the driver's cologne. Goodfellow sat next to him in the back. On Goodfellow's lap lay a thick cream envelope, visibly stuffed with cash. Grey saw it.

Goodfellow caught his glance and winked.

Grey said, "Where are we going?" he asked, pulling the door shut behind him.

"Richmond again. To the river," said Goodfellow.

"Where I threw the stone in?"

Goodfellow winked. "You're getting it."

The driver stared ahead and steered the car towards Richmond.

The streets rolled past in dreary succession as they travelled on. Grey watched puddles glint between parked cars and pigeons pecking at a torn bin bag. A man with a takeaway coffee passed by holding an umbrella, talking to someone on his phone.

Grey looked up at the rearview mirror. He could see the driver's eyes. The man's eyes were like a cat's —amber, slitted, and glossy-black where the whites should be. They held his gaze for just a second before turning back to the road.

None of this really mattered any more. Grey said nothing. He was thinking of Mab.

Goodfellow broke the silence. "You've done well, really."

"Done well? At what?"

"All this." He waved vaguely. "Shame, really. You always get this far. More or less. And then—well."

He didn't finish the sentence. He just grinned, shrugged, and turned his face to the glass.

They were getting closer to Richmond, but still on the north side of the river. They passed a boarded-up pub with faded signage, a skeletal playpark, a flooded gutter. The houses dropped away, and the horizon opened. They crossed Richmond Bridge. The Thames flowed grey and wide beneath the bridge. The water looked cold.

The driver pulled in by Cambridge Gardens, a small park by the river.

Goodfellow stepped out first. He held the door for Grey like a footman.

"She's just ahead," he said.

Grey climbed out. He adjusted his collar and walked towards the river path. And there was Mab perched on a bench. Today, for some reason, she was dressed like Marie Antoinette—powdered hair piled high in elaborate coils, a fitted gown of peacock-blue silk embroidered with silver thread, long white gloves, and a tiny, heart-shaped patch of velvet just below one eye. The wind caught the hem of her dress, but she sat quite still.

Behind her bench, the river rolled past, slow and wide, the colour of tea and old pennies. It carried with it the smell of mud and iron, sodden wood, and the faintest trace of the sea. Father Thames. The old brown god, flowing on and on forever more. You can't step in the same river twice, Grey thought.

Grey stood near the river's edge, coat collar up against the chill. He had a sense of vertigo looking into the water. The damp lingered—on his skin, in his lungs, deep in his bones. A crow called from a tree behind him and fell silent.

Goodfellow stood there watching Grey. The gold thread of his coat caught the light, and his bone-white gloves were immaculate. His skin looked glazed, as if it had been fired in a kiln. His violet eyes watched Grey.

Mab was tetchy. "You didn't complete the task," she said. "I know you didn't. I know you from top to bottom. I know everything."

"No," said Grey. "I didn't do it. I refused."

She stared and sneered. "Oh, *honestly*," she cried, spinning away with a flick of her hands. "What *is* the point of you, Grey? You never get it right."

She turned back, eyes flashing, skirts flaring as if she were about to stamp her foot or demand a pony from her fairy godmother. "Small and selfish and *dull*—Grey, Grey, *Grey!* Don't you care about saving people from their memories?"

Each name was a slap, flung like jewellery across a hotel room.

"I give you a moment, a mood, a *myth*—and once again you bring me back a sulk and a sob story."

Grey cleared his throat. He stood taller. "I've decided to be my own person," he said.

"Do you think this virtuous refusal will buy you Anna back?" she said, voice low now, but sharp with contempt. "Well, it won't. She's forgotten you. You are *nothing* to her. You put your ambition and your clever little columns—your half-baked, *mediocre* little career—before her. It was so transparent. She saw through it. Simon saw through it. Only *you* ever believed in you. God, even your mother never read a word you wrote."

The moment in the garden returned—the butterfly crushed between her fingers. He saw her now. He'd been dazzled by her, but she was nothing but a bitch. But. Because she was beautiful.

Because he wanted her to think him special, he'd almost sold his soul.

Grey cleared his throat. "Memories? Memories are important. So, according to you, I was supposed to destroy the man's photograph of his mother to save him? The photograph. Just a trivial thing you said. But it was a scrap of the past. It mattered to him to have a memory of his mother." He sneered. "I don't know what you are, but we humans have our own dignity. You think we're nothing, but at least we care for each other. At least we remember. People are memories, when you lose your memories you aren't you anymore. But you don't care about that."

He looked over at the river, and then back at her. She was watching him but he couldn't read her expression.

Grey continued. "You know, The man in Kew—the philosopher—he called memory an ache. Said it was all he had left. And I think... he was right. The ache is what binds humans — people— to time. To others. To ourselves."

He looked up again, voice firm now.

"It's pain that makes memory precious. It's time that gives shape to love and grief. Meaning doesn't come from your never-ending theatre of illusions. It comes from remembering. Even the things that hurt." He paused, "Especially those."

The wind tugged at his coat. She didn't say anything so he continued. "So, thank you, yes, I'd rather suffer in time than be like you and float outside it."

Mab listened. She did not blink. Her hands rested in her lap, perfectly still. The river, behind her, moved on.

He had nothing more to say.

She was quiet then her lips parted in a slow smile. Not warm or even cruel, more inevitable. She clapped her pretty little hands together. A dainty, well-bred applause, as if he were a courtier who'd just finished a pleasing recitation at Hampton Court.

"Very good, Mr Grey. Very good indeed. I do believe you're getting better at talking."

She turned to Goodfellow.

"He *is* getting better, isn't he, Goodfellow — at talking?"

Goodfellow bowed, low and mocking. "Oh yes, Your Majesty. Much better. Even brought a tear to my eye." He was grinning.

Mab stood and smoothed her coat. When she turned to Grey, something had shifted.

She stood before him, luminous—not with light, but with a presence that pushed through her skin. Her hair was iron-red, like blood rusted onto stone. Her eyes, no longer merely green, had deepened into something inhuman like the moss-dark hollows of the ancient hills, or the gleam of flint beneath water.

The scent that rose up around her now was thick with roses, and ivy but beneath it coiled a darker note: the ash of barrow mounds, of dead things, of old bone, of things left out too long to rot.

A word came into his head, from Yeats, from somewhere like that. He finally knew what she was. She was not a goddess. She was older than gods, and less forgiving. She was the banshee—one of the still people who watch from the fairy forts and the hollow hills. They come not to kill, but to remind us that, unlike them, we will die.

"Anyway, Mr Grey," she said brightly. "Time for tea."

From nowhere, Goodfellow produced a silver teapot, gleaming and ornate. A porcelain cup already sat on a tray, its rim traced with gold.

"We still ship the water in from Greece," Mab said. "You remember: 'A little-known spring near a forgotten river.' Absolutely the best for forgetting your troubles."

Grey stepped back.

Mab raised an eyebrow. "What?"

"I'm leaving," he said.

"Well," said Goodfellow, with a shrug, "in a sense—yes."

Mab's voice didn't rise. "No, Mr Grey. You're not leaving. You're going to do it all again."

"What?"

Goodfellow approached, silver tray in hand. He said, "Drink. Forget. And do it again."

Grey's mouth was dry. "I don't understand."

Goodfellow said, "You once asked what we are. The Celts gave us poetry—called us the *sidhe*, the people of the mounds. Pretty. Tragic. Wrong.

The Greeks—they were closer. Their *Lethe* is our river too. But always so dramatic.

The Germans, though. They got it exactly right." He smiled faintly. *"Die Stillen Leute."*

Mab nodded, almost fondly. "The Silent Folk. Not because we never speak—but because the only true things we tell are never heard by the living."

"And we have spoken true," Goodfellow said.

Mab nodded. "Yes, oh yes."

She stepped closer to Grey, cup of tea in hand. "You see, Mr Grey, you've been dead for quite some time," she murmured. "Ever since before you sat down to tea with us." She turned to Goodfellow. "Fifth time?"

"Sixth, Your Majesty."

"Ah. Thank you." She leaned close—her breath warm and, honeyed. Her smile that of a kind nurse. "So drink your tea. Close your eyes. Let the waters of Lethe take you." She shrugged. "And maybe, Perhaps one day you'll escape."

"Perhaps," said Goodfellow, raising his eyebrows.

Mab gave a loud, excited laugh. She put her pretty hand over her pretty mouth to stifle it. "Go on!" she said. "Drink!"

"Go on!" said Goodfellow. He pointed behind them. "And there's the river."

As if it were all ordained, Mr Grey picked up the fine china cup, and drank and dreamt and drowned.

Thames Dark Halloween Ale

I'M a northern boy in the Big Smoke. Though for me it's not so much where you're from as where you end up that matters. And if you end up by the Thames, sooner or later you learn that the river has moods. It drags things up in us, not only the dead but the parts of the living we thought we'd buried: our greed, our cowardice, our corruption — the small betrayals London runs on. Betrayals, yes, that's the word.

I came down in '87, when the docks still smelled of tar and diesel and you could rent a room above a pub without references or questions. None of this 'identification' they're so keen on now. Then if you said you were called Tony, that was what you were called. They didn't need you to produce five pieces of official identification that showed you'd been Christened 'John Anthony' and then claim you were lying when you said you were 'Tony.'

Forgive me, I'm a bit grumpy these days. My knees and back give me gyp. Probably from hauling all those barrels over the years since this all began.

Anyway, like I say, I just kind of drifted into town. I'd been working on a local newspaper up North, as a sort of cub reporter, but I had ideas of grandeur, well above my station as they say and I thought I'd do well as a freelance in London. That wasn't to be.

How I ended up in Wapping was that I had a mate called Martin. Haven't seen him in years now. He's probably dead to be fair, the amount he drank and smoked. Anyway, he lived nearby and he told me there was a cheap room above an old pub right by the Thames called *The Water Witch*

Now, the pub isn't really called that. But I changed the name because we don't really want to get sued, do we? Cause they'll say that what I'm about to tell you, didn't happen — couldn't happen. Couldn't possibly be true. Anyway, you'll have to judge for yourself.

So, I was a freelance journalist who didn't do any journalism, (probably cause I was a crap writer) and I needed some dosh, so one day I asked the pub manager, who lived there too, Harry Blane he was called, if he had any work. And he did.

I think Harry liked me. Truth be told, it wasn't me he liked, it was the fact I was a northerner and ,though he was London born and bred himself, his dad was from Doncaster, which is about 200 miles from where I'm from — but in the mind of the Londoner all the North gets squashed together. By all accounts, he liked his dad and that got transferred by the Grace of God, to me. He used to say to me, "Me and you, son. We're just the same. " I'd look skeptical and he put this pleading tone on. "We are, aren't we?" So I'd just grin and say, "Sure, Harry. Of course."

But inside, I'd think: no way are we the same. You're a washed up publican with questionable morals, and I'm a journalist. We couldn't be more different. See me? I'm going places.

Anyway, I thought I'd be there for the winter, then the journalism would explode and I'd get snapped up by *The Times* or *The Observer* as foreign correspondent or something. Maybe *The New Musical Express*. I wasn't fussy.

So I took a part-time bar job. Harry sized me up the way men do when they have spent their lives adding and subtracting.

"You any good at not breaking glasses?" he said.

"If it comes out of my wages, yes," I said, which he liked. He had that careful smile. Though what he was being careful about, I didn't then know.

He started me on glasses and ashtrays, then the till. "Trade," he called it. "Not art. The basics are not mystical. Keep the bar wiped and the floor dry. Keep your smile polished as if it's for sale, which it is."

"Pull a clean pint and remember that Northerners, Scots and Irish will complain if there's no head, and Londoners will complain if there is. If the beer looks cloudy, it is. Don't argue with them, just change it. The customer isn't always right, but it's easier if we pretend they are. Spirits come off the optics in a neat click but with them you do not argue with the measure, and neither do they."

"Count the change out loud. Do not get short-changed and do not short-change. Know who is next without being told. Calm a loud table before it becomes a problem. "

"Say 'please' to the drunks and 'sir' to the police. Pretend to believe the stag-night stories and pretend to care when they come in broken hearted. That's about it."

Second day, he took me down to the cellar and rattled the handle. It was locked.

"Why is that?" I said.

"My valuable beer is there," he said. "Don't want things to go awry. I keep the key. Don't go in on your own. Always ask me first if you need to go in."

"All right, guv'nor," I said. He liked me calling him that. "Do you get deliveries from the river then?" I asked.

He laughed. "That goes back a bit. The drinks come on the brewery lorries, but the special beer gets delivered by river. There's a loading door that opens straight out onto the Thames. Steps down to the water."

"Here have a look. Won't do no harm now." He took the key

out and showed me, just to be friendly. A small iron thing on a ring. He turned it and the door gave a little sigh, as if the room had been holding its breath. The air coming up had a taste to it. Rope and cold. I felt it on my teeth. It felt, what? Organic? I don't know."

"Quick look," he said. "Then out."

It looked old, but normal.

The cellar had that London river damp that never quite dries up even in long stretches of summer weather. The casks sat like sleeping dogs. There were normal metal casks and CO2 pumps and stuff but also some very old looking barrels that looked Victorian, or even earlier.

On the far wall a second door, lower, with a bolt at waist height and a rust mark along the sill where the tide had been busy. He didn't touch it. He didn't mention it. I wondered what was in there.

"Does it still flood down here?" I said.

"Yeah, on big tides," he said. "Slack water it mostly behaves. Mostly. All right?" he said.

I shrugged. "Sure."

He turned the key again and we went back up, and he put the keyring in his pocket as if it were nothing. But that door stuck in my mind.

We had a tourist party in. After they went, I said, "You know your special ales. Do you brew them yourself?"

"Nah, they gets supplied. Specialist brewer."

"So not the big guys: Youngs, or Fullers?"

"Nah, nah." He tapped his nose. "My little secret. That's what pulls them in, mate. Same beer, different hats. They're all the same rebranded: Winter Warmer, Spring Ale, Dark Summer--then the one that pays the bills: Thames Halloween Dark Ale."

"The punters don't notice?"

"No, the tourists never come back. Regulars don't care. They don't drink it cause it's dear."

I took to the work. I liked my colleagues. My mentor in the ways of *The Water Witch* was Ally.

She was Alison on payslips, Ally at the bar. Hair up with a pencil through it, cigarette parked behind her ear for when she had a minute. She moved the way good bar staff do, half a second ahead of everyone else. Chipped red on the nails. Quick at mental arithmetic. Quicker at reading a face.

"Northern Monkey, are you?" Was the first thing she said to me, but she was smiling.

"Better than being a soft Southerner," I said.

She laughed at that.

Ally showed me where to stand for a breather out of sight of the customers and of Harry. She showed me how to get the glass washing machine to work when it stopped, where she kept her dry cloths, where the spare float was and that if we needed it tell Harry or if he wasn't there leave him a note.

"He's particular about money," she said.

"Aren't we all," I replied.

She had her small commandments, straight off: "Don't pour Guinness fast, don't argue with a hen party, don't let the optics run dry, don't give advice on wine, this isn't France. You'll find it's mostly Americans who want tasting notes. Them and the Japanese 'cept the Japanese don't speak enough English to ask you. Also, wipe the tables as you go round — don't leave it to me because I'm a woman. If you break a glass, you might as well join in the cheer, and sweep up the broken bits before anybody walks into it and sues Harry."

Our clientele was mainly tourists. Mostly they came in groups. Sometimes in ones or twos. It was true; we never saw them again. Then there were the misfits and drifters. They might come in for a while and then move on. At least I supposed they'd move on. Leastways, then never turned up again in the *Water Witch.*

But I liked it. The place had atmosphere. The building must have been about four hundred years old. Maybe older.

I was there a while. It was getting to the end of October. Ally was up on a chair with a box of tat, dressing the place for Halloween. Paper bats, a string of plastic pumpkins with little bulbs in, a bit of fake cobweb round the mirror, and a fat candle in a jam jar for each table. Harry handed me the string for the beam and a handful of pins. "It's good for business. Sells the beer," he said. I held the chair while Ally leaned to fix a bat and the candle flames fluttered for a second, like the place was breathing. "Looks all right," she said. "This old place looks spooky enough without trying."

When Harry had gone, I asked her, "What's Harry like? He seems all right to me."

She grinned. "He's a tight-arsed bastard when it comes to money. But he's alright really. He has a weakness for women. Not me though. He likes blondes, brunettes, red-heads, greys and bald ones, like that woman in Alien II."

"Sigourney Weaver."

"Whatever."

She straightened a pump clip. "And keeps his stories."

"What?"

"Never mind."

"Why does he always keep the cellar locked?"

"He's very protective of his beer!" She laughed. "But don't be tempted to go down there yourself. Even he left the key. Just don't. All right, lovely?"

I shrugged.

Ally's eyes suddenly went to the pub door. "Here she comes," she said. She had a kind of knowing look on her face.

A blonde woman came in. It was misty outside and I could

smell the river. Tendrils of fog dissipated as she turned and closed the pub door.

Mid-thirties, I'd say. Tallish, five seven or so. Slim. Her coat the colour of wet slate, nicely cut. She was wearing red high heels that did not slip on the wooden floor and carried a hand bag that said Harvey Nics or somewhere else out Knightsbridge. She had the sort of face that stares out at you from a poster in a Bond Street shop. I mean, she was beautiful.

Ally said, out of the side of her mouth, "She used to be famous." Then, "She doesn't look famous to me. Never has."

The woman took a seat on a table in the corner.

"Oh, here he is," Ally said. "Like clockwork."

Harry came down from upstairs, waved us out of the way, popped a bottle of his good champagne and poured two glasses. Without a word to us he carried them over.

Ally rolled her eyes.

Harry put one glass in front of this newcomer and sat down without being asked. "Lovely to see you again, " I heard him say.

Then a French tourist came to the bar and interrupted us.

For some reason, before serving him, I glanced over to the fawning Harry and his mysterious blonde.

She saw me and gave me a quick look, bright as a click. I looked away.

Ally hissed. "You be bloody careful," she said. "You don't want to lose your job before you've properly started."

"What do you want?" I asked the tourist.

"I think — this?"

"Halloween Dark Ale?" I frowned. "It's strong."

He shrugged. "I'll try it. And a glass of red wine."

"Australian?" I asked.

He winced. "No, no. French, if you have."

"We've got some Côtes du Rhône."

"Very good."

Then the tourist said, "What is the story of the Water Witch?"

I shrugged. "I'm sorry, I don't know."

Ally stepped in. She tucked a strand of hair behind her ear and leaned on the bar like a storyteller who knew her craft.

"Oh, it's a good old story," she said to the Frenchman, "See, back when Shakespeare was scratching away over the river, there was a woman round here they called Old Meg. Some said she was a witch, and some said nothing at all because they were frightened of what she'd do if they upset her. Lived near Ratcliffe Stairs, so the watermen told it. The river was her son or her husband, or her father."

The tourist nodded.

"Yeah, they said she came out of the Thames itself," Ally went on, obviously enjoying herself, "born from its dregs and the dead things it keeps down there. On foggy nights she walked the steps with a lantern and a book of accounts. Still does, if you believe them. And it's often foggy round here at this time of year. If you were drunk, she'd guide you home. If you were guilty, she'd guide you elsewhere. She'd always make a bargain with you: Plague years, the Little Ice Age, didn't matter. She turned up when the slack water held its breath. They said she had an accomplice too — a woman just as evil as she was."

The tourist said, "So what did this witch want?"

"Well," said Ally. "If you wanted a favour, all you had to do was ask. If you wanted fame, fortune or someone dead, then Old Meg and her mate was the ones to find."

Ally leaned forward theatrically. "Do you want anybody dead?" She whispered, winking in the direction of the man's wife.

The Frenchman shook his head rapidly. "No, no."

Ally winked.

He said, "But what did she want in return?"

She smiled slow and sort of evil. "Well, your soul of course."

Then she laughed. "Anyway, that's the Water Witch. A pub needs a story. London's good at those." She slid his wine across. "Don't spill the red wine, love; it stains the table."

· · ·

That night, I woke in my bare little room above t*he Water Witch*. I had no idea what woke me. Was it a sound, or was it a feeling? The air felt thin. I was short of breath and cold, and yet it had been mild and damp outside.

I moved the curtain and glanced out of the window. It was deep in the night. I saw barges moored in the river with their night lights on, as quiet against the current as if they were asleep. Over the water I saw the lights of the South Bank. There was thin fog hovering on the water and above it all, between silvered clouds, the full moon shone like an old sixpence.

I heard a noise. Somebody was downstairs. Or had I kidded myself?

I listened hard. Nothing for a while and then a noise from downstairs again. It came from down in the public areas of the pub, maybe the floor below. There was a heavy scraping sound, then another. Like someone was dragging something.

I checked my watch. It was 3:30 a.m. The last customers were long gone. I should know; I'd locked up.

Harry's flat was along the corridor from me. He must hear this and if he did, he would go down. He was the owner.

I waited but there was no sound from Harry's end of the uneven passage.

The dragging went on below, slow and steady. What the hell was it?

My heart was beating fast. It was so loud. Why didn't Harry go down?

And then responsibility hit me, I mean, I worked there so I supposed, I had to do something if Harry wouldn't. I wished Harry would sort it.

I sighed. This was something I really didn't want to do. But I got up, opened my door. I didn't put the light on. I didn't want them to know I was listening. I just stood in the corridor by my open door in my pyjamas. Were they stealing the beer? Most modern casks were aluminium, but Harry's special beer was in wooden barrels. That's what it sounded like.

I sighed. What was the worst that could happen?

I went down the stairs slowly, one hand on the crooked wooden hand- rail, listening all the way.

At the bottom I stopped. Then the stair light snapped on.

Harry was coming up, fully dressed. Mud on his trouser knees and hems. A dark smear on his cuff.

"Harry?" I said. "What's up? What was all that noise?"

"Nothing," he said. "Go to bed."

One good thing about the job was that I got breakfast. Harry did bacon in the pan before opening. Two plates, no fuss. The pub felt nice without customers. The chairs were still up on the tables. He had Radio 2 on low — Terry Wogan chattering on about something.

I said, "About last night. You know I met you on the stairs? I came down because I heard a noise. I thought we were being burgled." I forced a laugh.

He ate, eyes on the plate. "We weren't."

"But all that dragging. Were you moving furniture?"

"I was checking the beer," he said. "We're nearly out."

"At half three?"

He looked up then. "The cellar doesn't care what time it is. It's Halloween tomorrow. We will need beer."

I tried to make it light. "Fair enough. Will you get more in time? Is there a delivery due?"

"I have it in hand," he said. He put more bacon on my plate like that was the end of it

. . .

Lunch was busy. Two coach parties — Japanese and Spanish — pointing at the pump clips and taking photos of themselves with the Halloween Dark Ale. We were run off our feet delivering pints and pies till the room calmed about 2:30 p.m.

About that time, she came in again — the blonde woman. It was the same one. I mean you wouldn't forget a woman like that. She had a different coat, looked like it was from Liberty's. Her lovely long hair spilled over her shoulders, her smile composed as ever. She took the corner by the mirror, the same place as before. She didn't order. Harry brought a glass she hadn't asked for and set it down. He seemed nervous and put the drink down like it was a peace offering. She touched the glass with two fingers and gave him a cold smile.

Harry seemed very on edge. It was like he was reassuring her. He kept his voice low. He was almost pleading. I heard her say, "You know our bargain."

"I know, I know." he said, sharp, then he seemed to remember himself. He took her hand and squeezed it. "I'll sort it, my love. I always do. You know that."

She smiled, stood, and left without drinking. At the door she caught my eye and gave me a small wave and stepped into the autumn cold. Harry saw her wave at me, turned and scowled then told me to check the stock as if that were the problem.

Then it was Halloween day. It was Ally's day off but she'd be back in about 7 p.m. Just me and Harry till then.

He was anxious all morning. I could see it in the way he wiped the bar, same spot over and over, like he was trying to erase something. The way he kept glancing at the door, then at his watch, then back at the door. Another coach party in, different tourists, same cameras, same pointing at the Halloween decorations like they'd never seen a rubber bat before. They ordered the Halloween Dark Ale for the photos, pulled faces at the strength of it, left half their pints. Harry barely noticed. Usually he'd mutter about waste. Not today.

By early afternoon the place was dead. There were a couple of regulars nursing halves in the corner, reading their papers. The kind who could make a drink last two hours and you couldn't shift them if you tried. I didn't mind.

Harry was on edge. He was polishing glasses that didn't need polishing. He put one down, picked up another.

"I was hoping we'd get some tourists in," he said. Not to me in particularly, more like he was talking to himself. Talking off his nerves, . really.

"We've had that bus group in for lunch," I said.

He shook his head, sharp. "No. I mean the ones and twos. The ones who come in on their own."

I shrugged. "It's still early. Halloween night, they'll pile in. Always do, don't they?"

He didn't answer. He was looking at the cellar door like it might open by itself.

"You all right, Harry?" I said.

"Fine." He wasn't. "Need to check something downstairs. You hold the bar."

"Right."

He took the key from his pocket, the small iron one, and went down. I heard the lock turn, then his footsteps on the stairs, careful and slow. Then nothing.

I served one of the regulars another half. There was a weird atmosphere in the pub, sour, like old ale. The boats on the Thames had their lights on and the fog was creeping in early.

Harry came back up after maybe ten minutes. His face was grey.

"Everything all right down there?" I asked.

"Getting low," he said. "Very low."

"You said you were expecting a delivery?"

He looked at me then, properly looked at me, and I felt something cold run down my back. Like when you know someone's deciding something about you.

His tone had suddenly changed. He was more measured now. Not as anxious, as if something had clicked into place. He said, "I'm always expecting a delivery," he said. "I just have to make sure it comes in time."

He went to the window, hands in his pockets, and stared out at the street.

"But you know, we might get a stray tourist." He smiled at me. "That would be best."

"Yeah," I said.

And he kept looking at the pub door. Watching. Waiting.

Five o'clock. No stray tourists. The regulars had gone. We were alone for a minute.

Another change: his composure had gone now Harry was wound tight as a spring. He kept going to the window, coming back, wiping his hands on his trousers. Checking his watch. Looking at me. Looking at me again. I almost thought I had egg on my chin or something.

About fifteen minutes later, I was restocking the bottled beers behind the bar when he said it. "Okay. You'll have to come down to the cellar."

I straightened up. "What for?"

"Beer. For the beer."

"What do you mean?" Then it dawned on me. He said that the special ale was delivered by river.

"The Halloween Dark Ale," he snapped. "Come on."

"What? You need a hand with the barrels? Is there a boat coming?"

"Yeah. Yeah, that." He was already moving towards the cellar door, pulling the key from his pocket. "Come on."

But there was something wrong. The way he said it. The way he wouldn't look at me.

He went down the rickety old steps to the cellar.

And I followed. What else was I going to do? I mean, it was my job.

I followed after him, one hand on the wall. The plaster was cold and irregular and damp. It was gloomy down there. The air got colder with each step. Damper. That smell again, rope and barm and something else. Something organic, like the river at low tide, but more than that.

Harry fumbled with the key. His hands were shaking. The iron clinked against the lock once, twice, before he got it in. He was breathing too fast.

"Harry, you all right?"

"Fine. Fine." The key turned. The lock clicked.

He pushed the door open.

The cellar was flooded. The river had come right in, dark water lapping at the third step, reflecting the single bulb like it was oil. The wooden barrels were floating, turning slowly in the current, bumping gently against each other and the walls.

"Oh," I said. My voice sounded small. "Is the beer spoiled?"

"No. No." Harry's voice was strange. Flat. "Just the river gets like this when she's hungry."

I felt my stomach drop.

He turned and looked at me, and his eyes were desperate and empty all at once. "Go in."

"But it's flooded—."

"I'm sorry," he said. His hand was on my back now, firm, pushing.

I took a step down. The water was at the edge of my shoes. Cold. Then I saw it.

Something moving under the surface. Not the current. Something pale and long, weaving between the barrels. Another one.

Then another. Like thick ropes of flesh, undulating in the black water.

"What the hell is that?" I yelled.

He muttered, "Somebody's got to pay her price. And it ain't going to be me. Sorry, lad. Sorry."

Harry went to shove me, both hands aiming for my shoulders.

I stepped sideways, fast, survival instinct. He missed me and his momentum carried him forward into nothing. He stumbled, arms wheeling, and went face-first into the water with a crash that sent the barrels spinning.

He came up gasping, spluttering, and then the things in the water moved.

Something wrapped round him.

They were fast. Grey tentacles, thick as my arm, erupted from the depths and wrapped round his legs, his waist. He screamed, a sound I'll never forget, high and terrified and somehow surprised, like he'd always known this would happen but never really believed it.

"No! No, please!" He thrashed, clawing at the steps, his fingers scrabbling on the stone. "I brought you...I brought—"

The water churned. More tentacles rose, covered in river-weed and slime, and they pulled him under. Just once, his face surfaced, mouth open, eyes wide and white, and then he was gone.

The water boiled for a moment, thrashing and frothing , then went still. The barrels bobbed gently. One of them spun in a slow circle.

I stood there, frozen, my heart hammering so hard I thought it would crack my ribs.

Then I moved. I slammed the door shut, threw my weight against it. I could hear something on the other side. A wet slithering sound. A soft thump against the wood, patient and curious.

I ran up the stairs, stumbled, caught myself, kept going. I didn't want to be down there. I staggered into the bar. The lights were too bright. The Halloween decorations looked insane, child-ish. I stood there, gasping, my hands on my knees.

What the hell? What the hell had I just seen?

Ally had arrived a bit early. She was behind the bar, tying her apron, hair up with the pencil through it. She looked up and saw my face. "What's the matter, love?"

"Harry." I could barely get the words out. My throat was tight. "Downstairs. In the beer cellar. There was something in the water. I think it came from the river. It was... he was going to..."

She didn't look shocked. She didn't even look surprised. She just reached under the bar and pulled out a glass, filled it from the Halloween Dark Ale tap with a practiced hand.

"Oh, yeah. Have a drink, love. This'll settle you."

I stared at her. "Ally—"

"We're nearly out out of it though," she said, sliding the glass across to me. "We need a refill."

I sat down on the stool because my legs wouldn't hold me anymore. The glass was in front of me, dark as the river water, topped with a thin brown head. I drank it hungrily.

I said, "It was awful. I ran. You should have seen it. It was..."

"Well, finish your drink first, then we'll go down and see what's happened to Harry.." She was wiping glasses, calm as anything. "You know, I've been here longer than Harry. We had another bloke before him. Geoffrey, he was. Nice enough fella. Bit handsy, but harmless. And then before him, what was his name..." She tilted her head, thinking. "Gary Shore. That was him. Gary Shore."

Later, I don't know how much later, but before we got busy, she took me down.

I wasn't brave enough to open the door. My hand was shaking too much, and besides, I could still hear Harry's scream in my head.

Ally did it. She turned the handle like it was nothing, like she'd done it a hundred times before. The door swung open.

The tide had ebbed. Just a few puddles on the stone floor, reflecting the light. The barrels sat quiet and orderly against the wall, no longer floating. The water was gone. The river had taken what it wanted and left.

No sign of Harry. No blood, no body, no torn clothing. Nothing to say he'd ever been there at all except the damp and that smell of rot and blood.

Ally walked down the steps, her shoes splashing softly in the shallow water. She bent down near the bottom step and reached into a puddle. When she straightened up, she was holding something.

The little iron key. Dripping.

She came back up and pressed it into my palm. Her hand was warm. The key was cold and wet.

"You'll be wanting this now," she said.

When we got upstairs we had a flood of customers. We were run off our feet. One of them asked for a Halloween Dark Ale.

I said, "We don't have much left."

But then I saw her, the blonde woman, the beauty. She was standing at the bar. She said, "There's plenty of Halloween Dark Ale now."

"What?" I said.

She smiled at me in her hauntingly beautiful way. "I'll have my usual — I don't drink that beer." She pulled a face. "Harry kept the best champagne on the top shelf in the back room."

Ally was getting someone a gin and tonic beside me. She glared at the blonde and frowned. "You leave the boy alone now, Meg."

The blonde woman laughed. "Oh, come on, Ally. How long have we known each other now?"

"Doesn't matter. He's a good lad. We should let him be."

Meg looked at me and grinned. "Whether I let the boy alone is down to him though, isn't it? "

And I looked back at her and I knew what she'd done. What they'd both done. Old Meg was beautiful. But 'beauty isn't an alibi', my old dad used to say. But for her it was. You'd make any deal with her.

And so our dark bargain was struck: beer for blood. That was years ago, and I'm still here. I always make sure she gets fed.

And after all my protestations, it turns out me and Harry weren't so different after all.

The Frost Fair

TWO FRIENDS PUSHED through the pub door and into the heat and noise, most welcome after the bitter, blistering cold outside. *The Water Witch,* on the north bank of the River Thames in Wapping, was an old pub, 16th Century or earlier, and famous for its dark ale. This is what had drawn them there.

At this time of year, in the deep mid-Winter, the pub was serving up pints of the thick-as-treacle Winter Warmer. Tony, a Londoner for more than fifteen years now, told Mark, a newcomer, that this was exactly what they needed on this cold and frosty Thames-side day.

Looking at them, a stranger would guess that the two men were about the same age, though Tony was slimmer, and more expensively dressed. He sported an expensive camel-hair retro coat and a glittering multi-dialled and multi-jewelled Tag-Heuer watch that was never used as a watch. His friend, Mark, was slightly shorter, but far better muscled. Whereas Tony looked like an ad man, Mark looked like a soldier. He wore a generic puffer jacket and a black-beanie hat that showed no affiliation to brand nor club. He had a small, red enamel poppy pin in his lapel though it was no longer November.

The old timbered bar room of the *Water Witch* held a somehow comforting damp warmth generate by the body-heat of the customers and the outdoor coats gently steaming as they hung on the backs of chairs near the large wood and coal fire that burned in the 18th Century hearth. The wood smoke smell made the place more real, somehow.

As the two threaded their way to the bar, glasses clinked and people laughed. Mark glanced out of the swirly-paned glass window to see the river outside.

"Great here, isn't it?" Tony said, and then, "Hey, I'll get these." Mark was about to say something, but Tony silenced him with an upraised finger. "Don't worry about it. I earn a lot more than you."

Mark accepted with grace. "I'll get the next one. Listen, I'm just grateful to you for sorting me out with that job."

"Honestly, mate, it's nothing. How long have we known each other?"

"Infant's School."

"Yep, Harrington Infants, and you used to give me your bus fare so's I didn't have to walk up the hill when I spent mine on Wagon Wheels."

Mark shrugged. "I lived closer to the school than you."

They were now at the bar. The landlord, a grim, heavy-set, jowly man was standing behind the counter and Tony nodded at him, about to order, but the man scowled and po inted to the blonde barmaid, who was serving someone else. When she was finished, she turned to Tony and said, "What'll you have, love?"

She was slim, about forty, dyed-blonde hair that needed its roots re-touched. She had a staff badge on that said, "Ally."

"Two Winter Warmers and whatever you'll be having."

She offered a practised smile. "Thanks, love. Very generous of you. I'll put it in the tip-jar if you don't mind."

"No, no. fine."

She dragged down the hand-pump, and the dark-brown,

bubble-headed liquid filled the straight glasses. She handed the first to Mark and the second to Tony. They thanked her and went to sit down.

After the first swig of beer, Tony said, "Good stuff, eh? That'll put hairs on your chest." Then he put on his serious face. "Listen, mate, you're one of our nation's heroes. I know the Government doesn't give a shit about you even after what you've done for them, but you're my mate and I do. The job's only in the post room, fine, but at least it's something. It's a beginning."

Mark drank then spoke. "No, mate, it's great. I need something to do. I don't like having too much time on my hands. My mind spins round if I've got nothing to do."

Tony put his hand on his friend's shoulder. "It'll work out, honest."

Mark watched the head of his beer settle. "But I don't really understand this advertising," he said. "What you actually do."

Tony shrugged "It's pretty simple. You've got to stop them thinking and get them feeling. Get them hating, lusting, craving, envying and then they're all yours."

"Sounds a bit immoral."

"At least I don't shoot people, right?" He laughed and punched Mark's arm. "Just joking. Anyway, see, lingerie?"

"What?"

"You know — ladies' underclothes."

"I know what it is. I just don't see the connection."

"Obvious. With lingerie, you've got two emotions to play with. It's lust for him and power for her."

"Oh, yeah. Okay."

"The News?"

"Go on..."

"They pretend they're giving us a public service, but really they're just doing what I do. They make us hate people we've never met, make us covet shit we don't need, make us lust for people we can never have, but most of all make us terrified. Once they've done that, and we're not thinking straight, they can 'nudge' us into making the so-called right choices."

"I don't watch the news."

"They work for the Government, mate, whatever they say. The same Government that told you lads that you were killing and being killed for a greater cause, when the greater cause was only about lining a few a pockets."

Mark grimaced. A pause. They both sipped their beer. "How's your Maria?" Mark said.

"Don't see her now. She ran off with a Spaniard."

"Oh, right. Sorry."

"Nah, water under the bridge, mate. Anyway, you've got to keep on going, haven't you?"

"Sure do."

"I mean you did, didn't you? In Afghan and that?"

"Yeah, yeah."

"You must have seen some things."

"Yep."

"You must have been frightened." Tony studied him. "Or weren't you?"

Mark said. "I was scared-shitless most of the time."

"But you still came through and did your duty," Tony said.

Mark shook his head. "Let's change the subject."

Two women entered. Tony looked over at them. One was younger than the other, a very pretty girl with beautiful copper curls with a permanent wave like she'd come out of the 1940s. She looked to be mid-twenties. The other was an elegant blonde, a bit taller, maybe thirty, dressed very West-End.

The two went to sit in the snug by the mirror. The red-head took off her coat and and wore a vintage blue dress, again very 1940s. She folded her kid-gloves and put them on the table. They must have been well-known in the *Water Witch* because as soon as they sat down, the landlord, the one who'd been miserable to Tony, went to the two pretty girls with a bottle of Bolly and three glasses. The women seemed to know him. He was fawning. It was embarrassing, a man behaving like that. He was old enough to be their dad. They didn't invite him to sit so he waved and backed, off, empty Champagne glass, hidden shyly behind his back.

Tony nudged Mark and nodded to indicate their table. He said, "Those two look all right. Fancy your chances with the blonde?"

Mark laughed. "Out of my league, mate"

Tony sighed. He seemed genuine when he said, "That was always your problem, mate. You always belittled yourself. Either of those two would be lucky to have you. You're decent, you're loyal, you're strong. You don't flinch when others do."

Mark blew out air. "Easy, you'll be wanting to kiss me next."

Tony said. "Okay then, big man. Forget the women, then. Let's focus on beer. Another Winter Warmer?"

Mark said. "Aye, go on then, twist my arm."

Up at the bar, Tony said, "Another two pints of Winter Warmer, please, Ally."

The blonde woman said, "Do I know you?"

"No, I don't think so."

She pulled the pints and handed them to him. "You here before going to the Frost Fair?"

He frowned. "The Frost Fair?"

"Yeah, on the river. Given it's frozen solid this year. It's like being back in the Little Ice Age."

"Must've missed that."

"Not surprised. Last one was in 1814."

. . .

They were nearly finished their second pint and feeling a lot warmer.

"Good beer this," Mark said. "Strong. Tastes very malty."

Tony said, "The Water Witch is famous for its beer. But I reckon it's the same old dark ale rebranded for each season, you know. Winter Warmer, Halloween Dark Ale, Spring Ale. Good marketing, see?"

A movement in the snug caught their eye. The red-head got up and started to put on her coat.

"Our beauties are moving," Tony said.

They could hear the red-head say, "Bye, Meg. Always lovely to see you." The blonde stood, gave her friend a hug, and a double air-kiss. "Off to work now?" she said.

The red-head nodded. "No rest for the wicked."

The blonde one, Meg, said, "Well, you must have been very bad."

Her friend laughed, waved, and went to the door.

Tony stood and drained his pint. "Come on then."

Mark said, "What? I was just settling in."

"No, no. I'm bored. Let's go."

Mark looked at the red-head going out of the door. He frowned. "You're not following that woman? That's well dodgy, mate."

"No, no. Nothing like that. Just bored. Let's go somewhere else."

Mark shrugged and pulled on his jacket and followed his friend out.

The red-head in her warm winter coat was ahead of them, heading down to the river. She ran down some steps. To their right was a sign pointing the way the woman had gone:

"To the Frost Fair! Enjoy the Winter Wonderland! Your life will never be the same again!"

Even before they got onto the river, the wind was bitter cold, and a few feathers of snow drifted from white-lead coloured clouds that sat like a lid over London.

Tony hurried down towards the river. Mark said, "Tony, mate. You can't be following that woman. It's not on."

Tony stopped, turned and smiled. "No, no. I'm going to the Frost Fair. It's the first one since 1814!"

From where they stood, they saw the river was no longer a river any more. Its flow was frozen, locked in ice. From bank to bank, the Thames lay in one solid sheet, thick and opaque, the ice a pale, bluish white under the gathering dusk. Snow had settled on it and drifted into ripples and ridges blown by the winter wind. Here and there, where boots had scuffed the surface, darker ice showed through, hard and glassy.

The river even sounded different. The familiar chop and slap sound of water was gone. Around them, up beyond the embankments the hum of cars and the noise of ambulances went on as usual, but here on the frozen river it was somewhere else. It was focused and silent. It was as if someone had pressed pause on the world.

And there, out on that frozen plain, sat the Frost Fair, like an spun-sugar dream pinned to the ice.

Among the coloured tents, lanterns hung from iron hooks driven into the ice, their amber light smearing on the frozen surface. Overhead, lamps were laced between stalls like glowing beads, swaying and clinking faintly in the wind's hush. The daylight was fading and above even the clouds themselves became hard to see as darkness thickened like black smoke rolling in from the wings of some vast, unseen stage. Snowflakes drifted steadily down, in their ancient rhythm, quiet and slow, catching in Tony's eyelashes and melting into the damp fibres of Mark's beanie.

"I know I'm a cynical ad man, but you have to admit it's beautiful," Tony said. "I mean, look at it! They've nailed it."

Mark did not answer straight away. He was looking past the lanterns, checking the layout. A broad cleared run had been scraped through the snow between the embankment steps and the first line of stalls. Beyond that, the fair spread out in ordered rows, like a market. The tents were arranged with an almost military neatness. There were no crowds pushing and shoving, just clusters of people moving along prescribed paths. He watched where they walked, how far they strayed from the lantern lines, how the ice looked under their feet.

Tony, on the other hand, saw sight-lines and branding. In the lamps' glow the tents showed as blocks of careful colour: deep reds, dark blues, hunter's green. None of the cheap plastic tarpaulins he remembered from shabby Christmas markets. These were canvas, stitched, edged in braid, with little finials at the top. Someone had gone for a late-Victorian Steampunk look. There were pennants too, flapping lazily, each one bearing a name in curly script.

"Very classy," he said. "None of your Poundland tat here. This is premium experience design. Pop-up theatre on the ice. Love it."

Mark grunted. He noted the nearest access ladder cut into the embankment wall. There were two more visible further along, lit with red lamps. He counted the security staff, or what passed for them: thin men in long coats at the perimeter, fluorescent bands on their arms. They had balaclavas pulled over their faces against the cold. Mark watched how fast people came and went. There was a steady trickle onto the ice, and not many leaving.

Tony stepped out first, shoes hitting the surface with a hollow thud. The ice was so thick that it did not move at all. "Come on, soldier boy," he called over his shoulder. "The Empire of Marketing Dreams awaits."

Mark followed him, but cautiously. He felt the cold through the soles of his boots. The air had a flat, dead quality that foretells a heaven full of snow waiting for its time to fall and blanket the world and remake it in its own frigid image.

Near the foot of the cut ice steps that led into the Frost Fair proper, a stall had been set up where a board on an easel read:

Exchange Your Currency for Ice Pennies Here.

Below that, in smaller print:

All Purchases Within the Frost Fair Are Made in Ice Pennies. No Other Tender Accepted.

A waist-high plinth held a flat slab of dark glass, like the self-checkouts in supermarkets. Above it a discreet sign showed the usual contactless symbols and the logos of half a dozen banks and payment apps.

"Of course," Tony said. "They have gone full theme park: Internal currency. I love it."

He tapped the screen. Options came up at once:

£20 / £40 / £60 / Custom Amount.

At the bottom, in friendly letters:

Ice Pennies Are Non-Refundable. Please Choose Wisely.

Mark said, "Wise choice? No choice, they mean."

"You old cynic!" Tony thumbed £40 without hesitation, bumped his phone against the reader, and the machine gave a small mechanical clunk. A drawer opened in the ice beside the plinth with a soft slide, revealing a stack of coins nested in a felt-lined tray.

They were the size of old half-crowns, made of thick glass, each one with a frosted edge and a clear centre. In the middle of every coin, a tiny bubble floated, cloudy and shifting when you tilted it. Inside the bubble was a tiny figure of a man made of what looked like silver but was probably pewter.

"Ice Pennies," Tony said happily, scooping them into his palm. They chimed faintly against each other, cold and solid. "Physical tokens. Tactile. Makes spending fun instead of painful. Also breaks the anchor to real prices. You are not thinking 'this coffee is five quid,' you are thinking 'this is three little magic circles.' You always want to spend the last one, because who wants to walk home with useless glass in their pocket? And then you top up again. Brilliant."

Mark selected £20 and did the same. The machine spat out a smaller stack. The coins were colder than he expected.

"And if something goes wrong," Mark said, weighing the coins, "you've already paid and can't get your money back."

Tony grinned. "Sunk cost, mate. The most powerful spell we have. Come on. Let us see what these little pennies buy us."

They walked inwards, away from river's edge, coins cold in their pockets.

As they got towards the heart of the fair, the details sharpened. On their left stood a tall, narrow pavilion painted in black and white, its awning scalloped like teeth. A sign above the entrance showed a spidery figure in a long coat and brimmed hat, caught mid-step, limbs twisted slightly out of true. Underneath, in looping letters, it read:

JACK FROST

Below that, in smaller writing:

"He Knows What You Regret."

"Now that," Tony said, "is brand alignment. Look at him. He's like a walking anxiety dream. Scare 'em and you've got them fascinated. People love to be scared. Don't know why." He pointed. "You could sell a whole streaming campaign off that image alone."

Mark did not respond. The angular painted figure made him think of nights on patrol when he had seen men caught in the flash of mortar flares, jerking, half in shadow. He didn't like the way the painted eyes seemed to avoid his, as if the figure was deliberately not looking at him.

On the right, a lower stall had been made up as an office, fronted with dark polished wood, brass rails, and a little writing desk. A woman sat behind it wearing a clerk's visor and an old-fashioned blouse, pale sleeves rolled to the elbow. In front of her, a small queue of people waited, hunched in their coats. Above her head hung another sign:

BUREAU OF SILVER LIES
"Terms Apply."

Tony laughed softly. "Genius. Absolute genius."

Mark said, "She must be freezing."

He watched a man in his fifties lean forward to speak to the clerk. She listened, then produced a ledger and made him sign something. As he did, he swayed very slightly, as if the act of writing had taken more effort than it should.

"Looks like a con," Mark said. "All this... paperwork."

"All services are a con," Tony replied cheerfully. "That's capitalism. Everything is made into a monetary transaction, your photographs, your memories..."

Mark said, "Even your dreams?"

"Especially your dreams, mate. They've got a big price tag."

. . .

A little further along, an open-fronted bar had been carved straight into the ice, lined inside with bottles and frost-furred glasses. The female bartender wore a white shirt, black waistcoat and a mask like something from a Disney remake of The Snow Queen meets Thomas Ligotti. Along the top of the stall, in separate 6 inch tall frosted glass letters that caught the lantern light, was spelled out:

DRINK YOUR OWN DEATH
"One for the Road."

"What the hell?" Tony said. He turned to Mark. "The audacity! I wish I could get away with that. Really shock them, you know? But my boss won't let me."

Large glass jars stood on the counter, each holding some pale liquid in which a dark thing floated. At first Mark thought they were bits of fruit. Then he saw one turn slowly and show the outline of a tiny face. It looked like a shrunken head.

Tony jerked back. "Eugh!"

Mark shrugged. It all seemed like arty-farty bullshit to him.

Tony saw his friend's expression. He said, "Oh, come on. That is magnificent. They've gone full immersive. You choose your poison. You get it? You pretend to face your mortality, post it on social. By tomorrow, everyone in London will be bragging about how they 'drank their death' on the Thames. It's amazing."

Mark said, "I don't see why you're impressed. It's all so false."

Beyond the bar, a larger structure rose, easily the biggest in the fair. Its canvas sides were a deep blue that looked almost black in this light, embroidered with silver stars and crescent moons. Along the ridge ran a frill of icicles, real ones, grown long and pointed. At either side of the pavilion door, two young women in silver masks handed out what looked like brochures.

Above the doorway, in tall, elegant letters was spelled out:

THE COURT OF THE WINTER QUEEN
(Queen Mab Attends)

"The promises you broke and the lies you told
Served back to you now, not hot but cold."
<u>Gloves recommended, but not provided.</u>

Tony stopped walking. For a moment even he fell silent.

"You break many promises, Tone?" Mark said.

Tony laughed. "More than I care to remember."

"I won't ask about the lies then."

Tony wagged his finger. "Cheeky! But really," Tony said quietly, "You've got to admit this a perfectly executed pop-up event. They're going to win an award."

Mark wasn't listening. Finally, he said, "It's off,"

Tony glanced at him. "What is?"

"All of this." Mark gestured with his chin. "It's not right. I don't know what's going on, but something is."

"What do you mean?"

Mark said, "Fairs are noisy. People shove. Here everyone walks where they are meant to. Nobody's cutting across the ice. Nobody's mucking about. And those security lads at the edge, they are watching the crowd, not the river. It is like they are keeping people in, not safe."

Tony shrugged. "Health and safety, mate. You can't have people falling down cracks in the ice. Think of the litigation. Anyway, this is curated. That is the whole point. I don't mean to come on all knowledgable and stuff, but this is my world. It's a world dressed up to make you feel apart, away from your normal decision making so you make abnormal, nudged decisions. It's, a socially controlled journey through an artificial, emotionally manipulative world. You are supposed to feel like you are in a different world."

"I do," Mark said.

* * *

Under the lanterns, as the temperature fell, the ice began its quiet enchantment. Frost scaled ropes and stall legs in creeping filigree, in tiny spikes and fronds, so that every post and rail was edged with pale ice flowers. The moment light struck them, they flared like cold stars—sharp, shimmering sparks that vanished when you moved, or even breathed. Everywhere, snow kept falling in fine, steady flakes, turning in the light before settling in the hollows of the many footprints.

Braziers hunched at regular intervals, heavy iron bowls set flat on the ice. Their coals pulsed a deep, drowsy orange, and smoke rose from them in languid ribbons that curled between the lantern ropes. People stood in loose circles around the heat, fingers splayed toward the flames, trying to get warm, their faces fading in and out of the haze. Even so, the braziers' heat barely warmed the air, but the atmosphere was heavy with the perfume of roasted chestnuts and mulled wine: sweet, spicy, smoky— cinnamon, clove, nutmeg, and singed sugar, tangled with the bite of ice and the scent of something nostalgic and without name, Christmas presents and childhood dreams.

The tents were lit from within. Some glowed a simple warm yellow, others pulsed with colour, blue or red or green washing across the canvas in slow ripples. In a few tents, the walls were thin enough that shadows showed on the fabric, black shapes of figures moving within like a magic lantern show.

Once, as they passed, Mark saw a long arm stretch across the inside of a wall and then fold back again. It looked too long to be human, though that might have been the angle. For some reason, he shuddered.

A thin thread of music wound through everything. Was it a hurdy-gurdy somewhere? It wasn't a band, or a tune you could hum, just the mixed sound of the hurdy-gurdy man and a fiddle scraping out a minor and haunting air, like a song you knew in another life but had now forgotten.

The tune came and went as the two men moved, never quite loud enough to grab your full attention. It lingered in the gaps between the people's laughter.

Mark said, "There's no children."

"It's London," Tony said, "the whole city's for kidults now."

"The whole of Western civilisation is."

"It's what you fought for."

"I don't think so."

As they walked past, unlike at real markets where the stall-holders call out for your attention, these ones merely watched. They wore from cold, crystal masks, decorated with filigrees of amethyst with holes for their eyes and holes for their mouths. Some of the eyes behind the masks were clear, some were smoky, and all glittered with an inner life that was barely human.

Mark watched the way the stallholders held their shoulders, the way they turned their heads. He saw tight jaws, chins tucked in, feet always angled so that it would be easy to step away. He noticed how quickly folk moved on if a stallholder looked straight at them, how few lingered anywhere for long. Whatever this was, it was not a party.

"They've thought of everything," Tony said. "Look at it. The controlled lighting, the slow music, the quiet staff, the way people are spaced. It is all about mood. You strip away the chatter, you give them a bit of unease, they lean in. This is immersive done properly."

Mark glanced at a nearby stallholder whose glass mask showed the fire from a brazier in both eyes. He wanted to leave.

"Come on." Tony pointed. "We have to try that one. 'Drink Your Own Death.' You can't walk past a name like that."

They angled back towards the ice bar.

Up close, the bottles behind the counter looked stranger. They were not brands Mark recognised, just tall glass shapes with no labels, lit from beneath by strips of coloured light set into the ice shelf. The light ran up through the liquid so each bottle glowed faintly, green or blue or clear. Frost had crawled over the glass in patterns like fern leaves. Where the light hit it, the frost glittered.

At this end of the bar a girl was serving. She wore a glass half-mask over her eyes and nose, clear except for a thin line of frost running round the edges. Her mouth and cheeks were bare, pale with the cold. Every time she breathed out, a little cloud formed inside the mask and then faded. She wore gloves of gold lamé.

Tony put his elbows on the ice counter. "Two of your finest deaths, please."

She tilted her head, listening. Her voice, when it came, was quiet but perfectly clear, her accent unplaceable.

"How many Ice Pennies have you brought?" she asked.

Tony let the glass coins trickle from one hand to the other with a deliberate chime. "Enough," he said.

"For a full measure," she said, "three pennies each."

Tony flicked six onto the counter without a second thought. They skidded a little on the zinc top.

The girl swept the coins up with a gold-gloved hand and dropped them into the silver cup that hung from her belt. It made a clinking solid sound, like the cup already held plenty.

The girl then took down two squat glasses that had been sitting rim-down on the counter, each one already furred with frozen mist. With a small steel pick she chipped clear shards from a block of ice built into the bar, let them fall into the glasses, then reached for two of the glowing bottles.

The liquid she poured was almost colourless, with a faint, oily sheen when it caught the light. Mark watched it crawl over the ice cubes.

Tony had his phone out now, already framing a vertical shot of the stall sign, the bottles, the girl with her crystal mask and golden gloves. "Frost Fair, London," he murmured. "Drink Your Own Death. Seriously, the production values…"

The girl set the bottles down and reached into a drawer under the bar. When her hand came back up there was a small white packet between her fingers. She tore it open one-handed and took out a slim metal lancet, the kind Mark had seen diabetics use.

"What's that for?" Tony said, at the same moment, trying to keep his tone light.

The girl held the lancet up so they could see it. The frost-light from the bottles flashed on its sharp point.

"For your blood," she said. "Each cocktail is three frost pennies and one drop of your blood."

"That's very theatrical," Tony said.

She merely waited.

"You really mean it?" He said.

"Of course. Everything has to be paid for." She looked at Mark.

"I don't think so," Mark said.

Her eyes were dark behind her mask and strangely alive. "Are you frightened of blood, mister?"

"More than you'd know."

But Tony already extended his hand. "Go on then. I'll pay up."

She jabbed the lancet into the end of his index finger, and a small, red globe of blood welled up.

"I'll take it before it freezes," she said and took his hand and squeezed his finger end so the blood dripped three times into his drink.

"I thought you wanted the blood as payment?" he said.

She shook her head. "Don't believe what I tell you. It's just performance." Then she turned to Mark. "You now, soldier?"

"What do you mean 'soldier'?"

"You look like a soldier," she said. "I like soldiers. They think they're honest."

Mark shook his head. "No thanks. If it costs blood, you can keep the drink."

She slid it closer to him. "No, you can have the drink. Even if you don't pay in blood. Just you won't get the extras."

Tony went to pick up his glass, but she said, "Wait!" and from the zinc counter took a bowl of white crystal that they'd presumed was sugar for coffee. With a silver spoon she sprinkled it into their drinks. "There," she said. "Now you have all the ingredients."

The girl watched them while they hesitated before picking up their ice-cold glasses.

Tony said, "Come on, Mark. Might as well drink it. We've paid for it."

Mark said, "I didn't pay in full," but he drank anyway.

They clinked the glasses. The sound was oddly dull.

The drink burned going down. Not the usual slow whisky burn, but a clean, sudden heat that hit at the back of the throat and then dropped like a stone into the chest. Mark felt it slide behind his breastbone and settle there. It was too, too fast.

"Bloody hell," Tony coughed, blinking. "That's... effective."

Within seconds Mark's face was tingling. A spreading warmth rolled out from his chest to his arms and legs as if somebody had turned a radiator on inside him. His fingers, numb from the cold a moment ago, now buzzed. The air felt thicker. The float of snow in the lantern light seemed to slow further, every flake hanging a little too long before it fell.

He set the empty glass down carefully. The ice cubes inside were shot through with faint red threads now, like veins in marble.

"Strong," he said.

"It's fine," Tony replied, though his voice sounded a fraction looser. "Just what we needed. Blood, sugar and booze. Perfect mix."

"I'm not sure it was sugar," Mark said.

But Tony was already on his phone, watching the little red

hearts tick up on the clip he had just posted. The screen glow painted his face, gave him a waxy look.

* * *

They drifted back towards the tall pavilion without quite meaning to. The drink, the light, the slow drag of the music all seemed to turn them along the main avenue and there it was again: JACK FROST painted in looping letters above the awning, the tilted figure on the sign still caught mid-shiver.

But now a crowd was gathered outside, as if expecting something. From inside the tent came a faint scraping sound, like a chair being dragged across a floor very slowly.

Mark felt the hairs rise on his forearms under his jacket. "What's this, then?"

Tony said. "Showtime."

Tony lifted his phone again, half out of habit, half because this was what places like this were supposed to deliver. Making memories they called it.

The scraping stopped.

"That's weird." he said.

"Just be careful," Mark said.

Tony looked at him quizzically. He thought his friend seemed on edge.

The air seemed to cool suddenly, as if someone had opened a refrigerator door. Mark saw everyone's breath at once, an abrupt cloud rising from the front rank of people.

Then the crowd folded away. It was not a panicked scatter. It was as if two invisible hands had taken hold of the front of the knot of visitors and pulled them neatly to either side, like a zip.

People stepped back without looking round, their feet skidding on the ice. A clear lane opened straight from the tent flap to where Mark and Tony stood.

"Okay," Tony murmured. "That's a nice bit of crowd management."

Something came out of the tent.

Tony saw it first. "Jeez!" he said.

Then Mark looked.

The thing was man-sized. It moved in short, broken jolts, as if every step had three pieces. First the leg, then the knee, then the hip. It was tall, but its height was all wrong: too much in the shins, not enough in the torso. The coat it wore looked like an old frock-coat left in a freezer for a year. The cloth was stiff, the edges furred with frost so that the hems bristled in white spikes. Each motion shook a fine dust of ice from the cuffs.

Its head twitched rather than turned. The chin led and the rest of the skull caught up a fraction too late, like a bad animation. Its hair hung in thin, straggly lengths, each strand stiff, glittering with frost crystals that clicked faintly as they brushed together.

The skin was the worst thing. Where Mark could see the face between the lank hair and the high collar, it looked clear and pale, not quite skin-coloured at all. The nose and cheekbones had the smooth, cloudy look of ice has begun to melt but then refrozen. The thing's mouth was a narrow line that only seemed to find the right position after a couple of tiny corrections.

As it came closer he saw that its eyes were not set straight. One was slightly higher than the other, and both were rimmed with a crust of tiny ice needles that spiked out on the lashes. When it blinked, chips fell.

People were scared.

Every joint in this Jack Frost seemed to give the wrong movement. The shoulders gave a little jerk after each step, the fingers twitched as if pulled by a puppet-master who was getting things wrong. It walked like a marionette directed by someone who knew what walking was supposed to look like but had never quite got the hang of it.

"Christ," Tony breathed. "That is... that is a creature effect. They have gone all in. Look at that gait. That is motion-capture level. Is it a suit? Must be a suit. Or some kind of rig."

His voice sounded odd.

Mark did not see an effect. He saw height, reach, probable weight. He noticed there was no give in the limbs. A man in a suit still had muscle and fat under the padding; there was always some sway, some bounce in the wrists, some slack round the knees. This thing moved like it was all hard inside, like frozen meat on steel rods.

It came straight down the lane formed as people fell back, and as it passed, people turned their faces away. They did not quite flinch, but they did not meet its gaze. Shoulders dipped, hands tucked closer to bodies. This was supposed to be fun, but nobody looked like they were enjoying themselves.

"You seeing this?" Tony whispered, half excited, half uneasy. "The whole crowd behaviour. They're part of the show. This is brilliant. It's like... augmented theatre. The character walks and the extras sell it. I would kill to know who directed this."

Jack Frost turned its head towards them.

The movement stuttered: chin, jaw, eyes, each in its own little hop. When the eyes finally settled, they landed first on Tony, then on Mark. The pupils did not widen or contract; they were already pinpoints, black drilled holes in cloudy ice. It changed direction by degrees, three or four small corrections, people spilled out of its way until the lane it walked led directly to them.

Mark felt his muscles tighten. There was nothing theatrical now. Whatever this was, it was targeting them.

"All right," Mark said quietly. "We're leaving."

Tony gave a short laugh that did not quite come off. "What, because the ghost-train bloke is coming over? Mate, relax. It's supposed to be creepy."

Jack Frost's hands now hung awkwardly at its sides, fingers bent slightly inward. Frost had grown along the knuckles in tiny spikes. It was like there was no body heat inside to melt it. As it came on, the fingers twitched, opening and closing by a fraction, not enough for a full grasp, just testing, like a man flexing a hand after pins and needles. Its fingernails were talons of chipped glass.

"Tony!" Mark said. "Now."

He stepped sideways, meaning to peel them both off down a side path, take any angle that broke the straight line between them and the thing. The row of tents that should have been right there, close enough to brush with his shoulder, seemed a little further away than they had a minute ago. Two strides, three, and the gap did not close as much as it should.

Tony did not move with him.

"I just want one close shot," Tony said, phone lifted, his voice slightly too loud in his own ears. "This is insane. The movement is insane."

Jack Frost was ten yards away, then six. Up close, its face was worse. The ice-skin was not smooth after all. Tiny cracks veined it, hairline fractures running out from the corners of the mouth, the edges of the eye sockets, across the forehead. In those cracks, something darker sat, as if there was old blood frozen in the fissures of ice.

Its head gave a small, sideways jolt, as if something inside had slipped on its supports, and it kept coming.

The thin music of the fair had thinned even further. The fiddle scraped somewhere, too far away now, the hurdy-gurdy player had taken three steps back . The lantern-light stretched; Jack Frost's shadow on the ice moved towards them quicker than its body.

Mark grabbed Tony's arm and yanked. "Come on!"

The phone nearly went flying from Tony's hand, but he recovered it. He swore, but Mark's pull broke whatever had fixed his feet to the spot. Mark turned and walked quickly, hauling Tony with him.

The neat avenues of the fair that had been easy to read from the bank now seemed to shift as they moved. He veered away, boots scraping on the ice, aimed for the line of braziers that marked the main route back.

Behind them, the broken-footed tread followed. Jack Frost was following them. The little three-part rhythm of its step, heel–knee–hip, heel–knee–hip, tapped at his back like fingers.

"Why are we running?" Tony panted, already winded. "It's just a bloke. It's just…"

He did not finish. The word *bloke* did not fit what he had seen up close.

They cut past *Drink Your Own Death*. Mark saw, with a distant jolt of wrongness, the same jar turning on the counter, the same lump of shrunken-head glass rolling slow i nside. The girl was watching them.

They ran blind for a few seconds. Jack Frost's step was still there behind, that three-part knock, jolt, and jerk, but the fair had stopped behaving like a place. It was a dazzling, confusing pattern of black and white lines. Mark yanked Tony sideways at the next gap between tents. A hanging sign swung overhead as they ducked under it:

BUREAU OF SILVER LIES

Before either of them could change their minds, they were inside. The noise dropped at once. No music, no crowd hum. Just the soft rasp of pen on paper and the faint tick of something unseen.

The Bureau was bigger on the inside than the stall front had suggested. A long hall stretched away, floored and walled in grey ice cut flat and smooth. Frost had grown on it in fine lines, like writing that had been half-erased. On both sides stood rows of high-backed chairs, bolted straight into the ice. Most were occupied.

The people in them sat slumped, their heads lolling, their coats open. Each had a padded cuff round one wrist. From the cuff a thin clear tube ran up to the ceiling and joined a slow-moving line of red that crept along a channel cut in the ice overhead. That line split and split again, feeding into glass jars set into niches along the walls. It was like the Fair was feeding off them.

At the far end, the clerk sat behind a wide ice desk. Only here, the ledger in front of her was a block of frozen water with lines and names trapped inside it. Her pen scratched on the surface, and the marks sank slowly down into the block and froze there.

"Jesus," Tony said, voice thin. "This is... okay. Okay. So this is the bit where they overdid it. It's a commentary on... I don't know, capitalism eating time. Very subtle." He laughed once, without humour. "They really don't do things by halves."

A movement at their side made them both turn.

The girl from the bar was there, glass mask, pale mouth, golden-gloved hands. Mark had no idea how she had come in; there was no sound of a door, no draught. She held a tray now. On it, two of the same squat glasses they had already emptied, each one steaming faintly in the cold air.

"Another drink?" she said.

Her eyes behind the mask were bright. Behind her, one of the sleepers in a chair gave a soft sigh as the red line over his head thickened.

Tony actually swayed towards the tray before catching himself.

"No," Mark said, sharply. "We're done."

Then a noise like gunfire cracked under his boots. Not loud, but clear. The ice floor beneath them had gained a new line, thin and white, running from the base of one sleeper's chair out towards the middle of the hall. Another line joined it from the other side, spidering out under the ledgers.

Tony looked down. "Was that the ice?"

Mark said, "Yes. Let's get out of this place."

He took Tony's arm again and steered him back towards the entrance.

The girl did not move to block them. She just watched them pass, her tray steady in her hands.

As they stepped back out into the fair, the crack followed them, crawling under the doorway, faint but growing, like something under glass that had started waking up.

They left the *Bureau of Silver Lies*. Outside, the avenue was almost empty.

Where there had been a slow drift of people before, there were now only a few figures moving with purpose, heads down, cutting across the paths towards the tents. Stall fronts that had been open now showed drawn flaps, lanterns turned low. The braziers still burned, but no one stood round them.

Mark glanced back.

At the far end of the main run, where the tents narrowed towards the middle of the river, a tall shape moved between the lanterns. At this distance Jack Frost looked like a strip of shadow that could now walk. His jerking gait carried him from one pool of light to the next. Each time he passed near a lantern the flame in i t dipped, then flared again with a faint crackle as he passed by.

The stall-holders stepped aside before they reached them. The customers were leaving, disappearing. No one ran. They simply vanished into doorways, ducked under tent flaps. Mark imagined them sinking into chairs in the Bureau, lying back and closing their eyes as the Fair drained their blood. But people were going; the Frost Fair was clearing the stage.

"Right," Mark said. "Let's get out of here and back to the real world."

He had the steps in sight. Down onto the river ice, then up the embankment steps. The lamps on the embankment wall were not far. But between them and the two men, the lanes twisted slightly, just enough that the way back no longer felt like a straight line.

Tony did not look at the steps. His gaze had fixed on the great dark-blue pavilion ahead.

Queen Mab's Pavilion dominated what was left of the fair. Above its entrance, a sign read:

An Audience with the Winter Queen.

With the smaller tents shuttered, Queen Mab's pavilion with its greater height and width stood out starkly. Silver stitching on the canvas caught what light remained, so that patterns of stars and thin moons seemed to hang suspended in the air even where the cloth itself was lost in shadow.

"Let's just go there," Tony said. "It's the culmination, really. I want to see the Queen."

Mark shook his head. "Don't be stupid. This place is dangerous."

The arch of frozen roses round the canvas door of the pavilion of the Winter Queen burned a deeper red now. The buried lamps in each bloom had been turned up, their light thicker, as if something darker than a gel filter was colouring them crimson and garnet. Meltwater ran in slow lines down the stems, pooling at the pavilion's threshold before freezing again.

The two masked attendants with their brochures were gone, but the canvas flaps were tied back, inviting entry.

Still unseen, the hurdy-gurdy man played on. And his plaintive music was joined by the crystal-clear voice of a girl, who sang as the song slid along the ice behind them. Another phrase rose, twisted, almost playful.

Come with us,

You little liars.
You puppet men
Hung on wires.

"Tony," Mark said. "We are not going in there."

"It's the centrepiece," Tony said, as if talking to himself. "This is the whole show. Everything else is build-up. The brand lives in there. Come on."

"No way."

Tony's voice had that bright, thin note he used in pitches when he was over-tired and running on caffeine. His eyes did not leave the pavilion. "Look at it," he went on. "Everything points to it. The currency, the blood gimmick, the creepy tall bloke. It all funnels into the big tent. You don't walk away before the third act. That's bad form."

Mark put a hand on his arm. "Listen to me. Whatever this is, it's feeding now. It wants our blood. Jack Frost is out there somewhere, among all these avenues and tents and everyone else has gone. This is a trap, mate."

Tony smiled, tight. "No, it's performance. You think you're still a soldier, but this is make-believe. You're seeing patterns because that's what you do—threat assessment, lines of fire, exfil routes. I get it. But you also think every alley hides an IED. What I see is professional mastery."

"They've done something to you," Mark said.

"No. This is me. This is really me. It's practically a brief I could have written. If I walk away from this, I'll kick myself for the rest of my life."

The song behind them rose a little, as if amused.

Run if you like.
We have all night.
Go where you will
You're always in sight

Mark sensed Jack Frost's uneven tread that was closer now, stalking them down the lines of closed pavilions. In no hurry, winding round like a spiral, and this was its centre. Mark knew the creature was behind them and he kept his eyes on the embankment lamps, measured the distance, calculated how long it would take to reach safety.

But Tony wasn't coming.

He'd started walking toward the pavilion.

Mark cursed under his breath and went after his friend and Tony stepped under the arch of frozen roses and went in.

The red light caught his face as he passed beneath, drawing new shadows along his cheekbones, his jaw, the shallow hollows under his eyes. He looked ill, but fascinated, drawing his coat tight as he crossed the threshold.

Inside, the air was still, like it was waiting. The ground underfoot was bare ice, perfectly smooth, untouched by snow or boot. Their reflections followed them in ghost-silver, drawn out and warped. The ceiling arched high above like a ribcage of frozen light, each beam rimed with frost and spiked with hoary pendant icicles that chimed faintly without any breeze.

Mark followed two steps behind Tony. The hush closed around them. He didn't like how clearly he could hear the wet scuff of his boots, and the sigh of his own breath, the beating of his own heart.

The pavilion's canvas doors closed behind them though there had been no one there to close them.

In the centre of Queen Mab's pavilion stood a throne. It was carved from a single block of ice, faceted and sharp, diamond-like and glacial, rising in jagged tiers like the seat of a Snow Queen. Frost had formed feathers along its arms, curling upward like wings. At its base, snow gathered in soft drifts, unmarked. From beneath the throne, water dark as blood seeped into the cracks.

And on the throne sat Queen Mab, the red-headed girl from *The Water Witch*. At least she looked like her, but if it was the same woman but she was utterly different now.

This one wore white without warmth—a gown of silvered fabric so fine it seemed spun from frost.

She was the Snow Queen. The embroidery along on her dress caught the light, like roots clutching upward through snow. Her hair was pale copper, and upon her head a crown of quartz, from which a circlet of icicles rose like winter thorns. Each point gleamed, each tip needle-sharp enough to draw blood.

At her throat hung a gem. It was not glass, perhaps it was diamond but it had depth. Inside it, something moved—slowly, like breath beneath water. Mark thought it was a trick of the light, until he saw the outline of a face. A man's face. Pressed inward, as if looking out.

Mab sat motionless. Not lazy or indifferent, but absolutely composed, as if this stillness were the only proper response to worship. Her hands rested lightly on the throne's arms. Her eyes, silver-grey and depthless, found Tony's and held his gaze. Tony stood, stupefied.

She said, "Ah, you're here at last. Two old friends. Both the deceiving and the self-deceived. Bringers of misery at the bidding of others. In fact, your only redeeming feature is the love you have for each other. Most touching — this echo of a lost boyhood before you were corrupted. But that single drop of goodness is not enough to pay the debts you owe me."

Tony was trembling. Mark went to him, held his shoulder.

"My heart melts," Mab said. And she laughed. "You think he is the victim here? You see, my soldier, in some ways, my silver liar here is a more honest man than you. He spun the lies, true, but you pulled the trigger. He knew he was a liar. You thought you were a hero. He lied and you killed — both for the same beast of disenchantment, this beast that is turning the world into money and ashes. You know, your self-delusion would actually be a joke if it were not so tragic."

Mark spoke. "Do I know you?"

"No, but I know you."

Tony shook his head. "You leave my friend alone. He's a million times better than you, you—"

Before he could finish his words, a sound cracked out behind them —a brittle, splintering creak, like fingers breaking.

Tony turned. Mark was already half-turned, fists tight.

Behind them, the pavilion's entrance was opening. One pale, bone-thin, crystalline hand had found the flap. Its joints bent backward slightly as it gripped the edge. Frost bloomed where the fingertips touched. The cloth crackled with ice as it peeled open.

And a long shadow spilled across the floor, outlined in red from the bleeding ice-roses above.

Jack Frost had found them.

It stood in the doorway, then broke into a run, though the motion barely resembled running. It came in lurches, as if dragged forward by invisible hooks—heel, then knee, then hip snapping forward, faster with each disjointed stride. Its arms went up. Frost flew from its cuffs in stinging clouds. Its coat flared like a banner of rot and rime. One moment it was twenty feet away. Then ten. Then it struck.

It went for Tony.

Mark saw the decision happen in real time—the off-kilter eyes flicking from one to the other, landing on the man still watching the throne, still half-listening to the hurdy-gurdy music, still holding a pocketful of Ice Pennies.

Jack Frost launched itself, its full weight crashed into Tony's chest, and he went down. The two hit the ice in a tangle of limbs, Tony's cry snapping short as his back struck the frozen ground driving out his breath. Mark moved without thought. Reflex. Years of training unfolding like muscle memory. He dropped low, jumped, grabbed seized the creature's collar, meaning to pivot and throw it off his friend.. But the coat was stiff with frost, and beneath it there was no slack, no human give—just something locked and immovable, like a post hammered into hard ice. Jack Frost turned its head toward him.

Click. Click. Click.

Its neck moved in jerks, vertebrae snapping into place like misfiring gears. One arm came free from Tony's chest and whipped sideways. The blow landed across Mark's ribs—not a punch but a flat, swinging strike like a frozen branch. Air exploded from his lungs. His boots lost grip.

He slid across the frozen floor.

The cold seized him instantly—back on the ice, breath gone, the whole world narrowed to pain and velocity.

Jack Frost straddled Tony. His hands on his shoulders, long fingers digging in. Frost steamed where its grip met his coat. Tony's breath came in fast pants that hung in the air above his face like smoke. "Get off me," he gasped, trying to twist. One hand beat uselessly at the thing's arm. "Okay, okay, I get it, performance over, you've made your—"

Jack Frost lowered its head.

From inside the tent, from the throne platform, cracks began to spread in the ice below them.

They started as hairline fractures, faint white threads running across the clear floor. The lines moved fast, blooming from the centre outward, racing under the throne, under the arch, out toward the river.

The ice under Tony and Jack Frost crazed in an instant—a spiderweb of fine breaks across the surface. And then it gave completely.

There was no dramatic roar, no cinematic yawning chasm. The sheet under Tony and Jack Frost simply sagged and split. One large slab dipped and went under, taking them both with it.

For a second Tony's hand broke the surface, fingers spread,

reaching for anything, but there was nothing to hold. Then the closing ice clipped his wrist and he was gone.

Cold hit Tony like a hammer striking his chest.

It wasn't gradual. It smashed through his lungs and skin and thoughts in the same instant, so complete that he could not even form the idea of pain. The river swallowed him in a rush of black and white: bubbles, broken ice, the dim smear of the fair's lights above.

His chest locked. Every muscle seized. His body tried to inhale and found only water.

The cold was absolute. It didn't creep into his body, it took it over. It sank claws into his ribs, wrapped iron bands around his heart, filled his skull with white noise. His muscles wouldn't work. His fingers went numb in seconds. His face burned with cold then stopped burning, then stopped feeling anything at all.

The water pressed in from every side, heavier than he'd imagined water could be, squeezing the warmth from him like hands wringing a cloth.

Something was wrapped round him. Jack Frost's arms held him tight in a parody of an embrace, hard and jointed, one forearm under his ribs, the other across his shoulders. Its grip pinned his arms to his sides. Its face came in close beside his, ice-skin scraping his cheek.

It opened its mouth.

What came out was not air.

A stream of water, colder than the river itself—impossibly colder, forcing its way between Tony's lips, a rescue breath that offered no hope of rescue.

The ice-water burned going in, a searing line down his throat that shocked his heart into beating harder. His vision, which had been shrinking to a tunnel, widened for a moment.

He saw the underside of the ice above: thick, greenish, layered in ridges. He saw long, pale roots of frozen water dropping down like stalactites, grown over years where the Thames had frozen and thawed and frozen again. Between them were shadows, narrow black gaps that led deeper.

Jack Frost kicked out with its long legs, driving them both down, deeper down towards the river's bed.

It was so deep, so cold. Pressure built in Tony's skull. His ears rang. The last of the light above shrank to a blurred grey ice penny, then to nothing.

The river closed over his head in full frigid darkness

Every instinct screamed to fight free, to claw upwards, but his limbs would not answer. The cold had stolen the warmth in them. His fingers were distant things, belonging to someone else. His legs hung useless. The thing that held him moved dragged him down.

The cold was eating him from the inside now. He could feel it in his core, in his belly, in the base of his spine. His thoughts came slower. The edges of panic dulled to something softer, almost gentle. Almost welcoming.

Long enough to feel his body reach its limit. Long enough to know that no one was coming. Long enough to understand that the cold would win, that it had always been going to win, that fighting it was just theatre now. Long enough to know that at least that lies would stop.

In the tent above, Mark lay on the pavilion floor, chest heaving, watching the broken oval in the ice knit itself shut. The crack lines thinned and faded. The arch of roses dripped once, then the bloody drops froze into garnet beads.

Mab was watching him. "I know, I know," she said. "You want to die now. To drown in deep icy water too, just like your friend. But you shall not be given that escape. Your punishment is to live, my soldier — to live while others die. And to know, one day we will be back."

The Winter Queen got down from her throne, went towards

the open pavilion door and stepped back over the threshold. She did not spare him a glance.

Outside the music started up again, the whining hurdy-gurdy and the scraping fiddle. The cries of 'Roll up! Roll up!"

The frost fair, lit in amber and diamond, smelling of cinnamon and cloves, began to fill again with more people, more consumers, more liars ready to pay in blood.

PART FIVE

Wales

The Fair Family

Throughout the world there is not a huntsman who can hunt with this dog, except Mabon the son of Modron. He was taken from his mother when three nights old, and it is not known where he now is, nor whether he is living or dead.

FROM THE STORY OF CULHWCH AND OLWEN

THE RAIN BEGAN at Halfway House. It started to spot the windscreen heavily just after Welshpool, and by the time they got to Garthmyl, it was bucketing down.

They'd come down the M6 toll motorway past Birmingham. Dave had begrudged paying the fee, but Angela said you always paid one way or another, either in money or time lost or some other way.

But now they were in Mid-Wales and there wasn't much traffic but what cars and vans there were threw up a lot of spray. The road through the mountains was narrow and full of bends and when Dave got stuck behind a school bus, he couldn't see to overtake, so he sat there crawling along, drumming his fingers on the steering wheel and cursing.

"Overtake here," Angela said.

He shook his head. "Can't see."

"There's nothing coming."

"I'd rather wait."

She sighed. "We'll be late, Catrin will be so upset."

He grunted. "We've got plenty of time."

She exhaled. "No, we haven't."

He muttered, "Quiet. You'll wake Sam."

"It's safe. Just go."

Still he wouldn't. They lapsed into a tense silence.

Samantha, their infant daughter slumbered in her car chair on the seat behind.

As they drove west stuck behind lumbering lorries, the weather got worse. It was September and hadn't been too bad when they drove across from Shrewsbury, but the clouds massed and the sky grew threatening as they entered Wales. Here the wind blew a hooley and the rain lashed and Dave couldn't see the road and he was a cautious driver, anyway. Truth was, he was a cautious man.

A mile later and traffic slowed to a crawl. It was just past Llangurig.

"Are you sure you can't get past them?" Angela said. She pointed through the rain-streaked window.

Dave said "I can't see a thing". The car heater blew warm air on their knees. The glass misted and Dave wiped at it with a micro-fibre cloth that he kept ready on his lap.

"Poor sod. He's worse off than we are," Angela said.

"Eh?"

She pointed through the streaked side window. "That old bloke hitchhiking. He's fifty if he's a day. He shouldn't be out in this weather."

Dave peered, shrugged, leaned forward over the wheel again. "Oh yeah."

"He's hitching," Angela said. "Who hitches these days?"

Dave snorted. "Hell of a day for it."

The traffic inched onward. The old man was stick thin, draped in a ragged-looking black coat, wearing a black hat, of the kind favoured by Roman Catholic priests in the last century. He had a bundle on his back.

"I feel sorry for him," Angela said.

"Yeah, and I feel sorry for us stuck in this traffic." Dave hunched over the wheel.

"Then overtake."

"I can't."

"Well, if you won't put your foot down—"

"—I can't!"

"At least give that bloke a lift. He'll drown in this."

"A lift? He's drenched. He'll soak the car."

She tilted her head. "Please. I feel really bad for him. For him to be out in this weather, he must be in great need."

Dave sucked his teeth. "In great need? He might be a murderer."

Angela laughed. "As if. He's scrawny, and you're a big strong man. You can protect us."

It was true. Dave had played rugby professionally until last year when he'd given up due to a back injury. He'd never regained his nerve to go back on the pitch. He sighed. "I don't really want to stop. It'll wake Samantha."

Angela said, "It's not like we are speeding down the highway. Besides, no good deed goes unrewarded. Please."

And so, because he loved his wife, Dave wound down the window. The rain drove in and cars coming the other way threw up floods against his face but he yelled into the weather. "Mate? Mate! Want a lift?"

Whether he could hear his words or not, the hitch-hiking stranger understood their meaning and smiled and nodded and gingerly picked his way over the streams of rain on the road, avoiding a forestry lorry and a camper van. He approached the car.

"Get in the back. Careful of the little girl." Dave glanced at Angela who beamed at him and squeezed his arm. He'd done a good thing. Angela liked him doing good things. That made him feel marginally better and Dave wound up the window.

The black-clad man brought the tang of damp and rain with him, but as he clunked the door after him, its closing clamped shut on the wind and road noise and they sat as the rain drummed on the car's roof.

The man spoke. "Prynhawn da, Twm Lyn ydw I. Mae'n dda 'da fi gwrdd â chi."

The man, looking more like a vagabond than an everyday traveller, extended a bony, wet hand.

"Ah, we're not from here," Angela said. She gave a mock wince. "English for our sins."

"Ah, English, is it?" The man said. "I'm Twm Lyn — clerwr by trade," he paused and seemed to search for a translation. Finally, he said, "A minstrel."

Angela raised her eyebrows. "A minstrel? That's an unusual profession these days."

The man smiled broadly. "I prefer minstrel to bard. Bards are too common in Wales these days. So many of them on the radio and at their poetry competitions and the Eisteddfod. No, I am a travelling minstrel, I go from town to town, sit down on the kerb, take out my harp, and sing for my supper."

"That's the harp in that bag?" Angela said, pointing.

"Yes. Waterproof too."

"Where are you headed?" Dave asked, as if keen to be shot of the man as soon as possible.

"I'm going to Bryn Ellyll."

Dave shook his head. "I don't know where that is."

"Not many do, but I have family there—old cantankerous relatives from way back. Bryn Ellyll sits on a hill near Goginan just off this main road but many miles on."

Angela offered, "We're going all the way to Aberystwyth, to a christening."

"A christening, is it?" Twm Lyn said. He turned his head, "For this beautiful baby?" He beamed at baby Samantha who hadn't even stirred at his wet and windy entrance.

"No," Dave said. "It's for a mate of mine's kid."

Twm Lyn said, "But we're going the same way at least. Thank you for the lift."

"If we ever get there," Dave said, indicating the barely moving traffic.

Half an hour went by and the traffic hadn't moved. Dave turned the radio on but the surrounding hills and poor weather made reception patchy, and what he could hear was in Welsh.

So far they didn't know what had caused the snarl up. They sat without speaking, Dave impatiently searching for a station that would help him understand why this road was so slow. He cycled between Radio Wales, Radio Cymru and Marcher Sound, between chat shows and easy-listening 80s hits to what sounded like sports commentaries which he didn't understand but from the nods and comments, Twm Lyn did.

They were at a stop. "I need to find out what's going on." Dave snatched at the door handle, pulled it and stepped out. The gale blew in and he was instantly soaked by the September rain. He peered through the spray. The traffic coming the other way had stopped too. It was three p.m. They were running at least an hour late now. He walked forward into the rain, and got to the car in front.

They were tourists by the look of it. He wanted to ask them if they knew what the delay was but the driver avoided his gaze and the door locks engaged. Dave sighed, hugged himself against the rain and cold and went forward to the next vehicle. This was an unladen forest lorry heading west over the mountains on a homeward run. The truck window was high above him. He put his foot on the step, reached up and tapped the glass.

The driver peered out, blinking and blinded by the rain he'd allowed in.

Dave yelled. "Just wondering what the hold-up is."

The man gazed down thoughtfully and Dave hoped he spoke English. They all spoke English, didn't they?

Eventually the man said, "Floods. Floods all along. It's the rain, see?"

Dave saw. He thanked the man and returned to the car.

"Well?" Angela asked.

"Road's flooded. Multiple places apparently."

Angela groaned. "Oh no. What are we going to do?"

Twm Lyn leaned forward. He said, "There's a back road you could take. Little known."

Dave shook his head. "That'll be flooded too."

Twm Lyn said, "It's higher than this road. This main road collects the torrents running off the mountain. The road I'm thinking of runs much higher, away from the flooded valley bottoms."

Dave grimaced. "I'm not sure. I think we'd be better sticking to the main road."

Angela said, "But if we sit here, we'll miss the christening. Let's give it a shot. I don't want to disappoint Catrin. She was my best friend at Uni."

Twm Lyn smiled. "Catrin? A Welsh girl, is it? She would know this mountain way. She would know it is safe."

"Safe?" Dave said. "A minor road through the mountains in this weather doesn't sound safe."

Angela started to cry.

"Awww, babe," Dave said, reaching over to her.

"I was so looking forward to it. It means such a lot to get there. I wanted Samantha to meet her new friend." She reached back and stroked the sleeping infant in her car-seat. Tears ran down Angela's pretty cheeks.

Dave sighed heavily. "I know, but Ange, it's dangerous."

Twm Lyn said, "Do not fear, Englishman; I will be your guide."

Dave shook his head. "But we don't know you. We don't know anything about you."

Angela peered up through damp eyelashes. "Be brave, David."

Twm Lyn laughed uproariously. "Ah, young David; your wife thinks you're chicken – cyw iâr! Prove her wrong!"

Dave paused.

Angela blinked away her tears, brushed her eyes and said, "Please, Dave."

Dave tightened his mouth. "Okay, which way is this other road?"

"Go on about a mile to Ty'n y Bedw and then you'll see a narrow turn-off to the right."

"Go on about a mile? I can't go on an inch."

"Overtake these cars."

"And drive on the wrong side of the road?"

Twm grinned. "There's probably nothing coming anyway. Floods, see?"

Dave gripped the steering wheel with both hands. "It's crazy driving on the wrong side of the road."

"Do it, man." Twm chuckled.

Angela said, "I don't want to miss the christening."

"But we've got Samantha in the back."

Angela pointed. "There's nothing come the other way for fifteen minutes at least."

Twm smiled. "We will all be safe. A christening is a very important thing after all." He looked sideways at little Samantha. "Has your fair young daughter been christened by the way?"

"No," Angela said. "I think it's better for her to make her own mind up about it when she's grown. If she wants to be baptised then, that's up to her."

"Very broad-minded," Twm said with a twinkle in his eye. "I commend you for your modern ways."

"Okay," Dave said. "I'm going." He tipped the stalk by the wheel, and the lights flashed bleary through the streaked window, and Dave pulled the car into the oncoming carriageway. He could hardly see anything through the downpour. He leaned forward and peered, shoulders hunching, fingers gripping the wheel tight, edging forward.

Some of the cars they passed honked their horns, but most didn't. Nothing was coming so far.

"Look out for oncoming traffic, Ange." Dave gulped though he had nothing to swallow.

"Thank you, Dave." She leaned over and kissed his cheek as they drove, going slowly, staring into the rain.

From the back seat, Twm Lyn smiled.

The straights were scary enough, staring through the deluge, blinded by the bucketing water, but the corners were a white knuckle ride. They could see nothing. Dave just had to hope a big timber truck wasn't heading the other way.

They rounded the first corner. Dave exhaled. He could see maybe thirty yards ahead now. He was torn between the terror of speeding and the terror of going too slow, but he stamped his foot on the pedal and they jerked forward. He wanted to zoom down the road and past the long line of stuck cars and wagons and reach the turn as fast as possible.

They ploughed into a deep puddle. The water braked the car, it slowed, struggled and coughed. Dave pushed the pedal. "We're a sitting duck here," he said. The car recovered. "I didn't see that," Dave said.

"You can't see anything, to be fair," Twm Lyn grinned.

"You're doing brilliantly, Dave." Angela stroked his shoulder. "I'm proud of you," and despite the anxiety that coursed through him, Dave smiled at his wife's praise and began to be proud of himself and pushed the accelerator down until the car heaved its way out of the water and onto a marginally drier section of the road.

"There," Twm said. "On the right."

Dave threw his head round. "Where?"

Dave squinted to see. Though it was not night, the heavy clouds and constant rain drained the daylight.

"There!" Twm said.

Dave saw a small turn off where a single-tracked road led away through a stand of conifer trees

"It's tiny. Are you sure that takes us very far?"

"Oh, yes. It's a locals-only road. Only local folk know of it."

"Why is nobody else coming this way?" Angela said.

Twm said, "It's an old road. Memory of it is lost among the young."

"But you know it?"

Twm's eyes glinted. "I am old, ancient you might say. And I am very local." He gestured. "I spring from this ground."

Angela whispered. "We have no option but to trust him."

Dave answered, "Yes, we do. We can turn back and refuse to go up this scrappy, narrow trail."

"But then we'll miss the christening," Angela said.

Twm heard them whispering and laughed. "And to miss a christening is a terrible thing — to miss a christening allows all sorts of wickedness in."

Dave narrowed his eyes. "You don't look very devout. Are you a Christian man then?"

Twm Lyn guffawed. "Oh, I wouldn't go that far. I was around here long before the Nazarene was heard of in these parts, though I admit that I was better known back then, and better honoured. Now I must earn my keep as a wanderer and dabbler in minstrelsy, but master of cynghanedd still, and brilliant-tongued at barddas yet.

"Let's hurry along, Dave. Please." Angela squeezed his arm and Dave took the turn onto the road less travelled, his darling babe Samantha, still slumbering in her seat with its jingle bells a-jangle and its fairy mobiles dangling at her delight.

The narrow road snaked on and up and through the forest revealing sudden precipices and terrors of rocks to their left. Rocks that had once rolled sat now quiet under the drizzling rain.

Up and up they went until it was as if they had entered another country once hidden and now revealed in the bare mountain heart of Wales. On all sides rolling hills rippled away for mile after mile until they were lost in weather wide and wondrous. The land basked in a strange twilight under clouds underlit as if by a thousand will o' the wisps.

The car emerged above the clouds, which melted below them like dirty candy-floss. It was not raining here but this land of marsh and bog and sedge swept away on all sides, and dark water pools decorated with bog cotton and bullrushes glinted and gleamed under an odd sun.

"What a strange colour the sun is," Angela said, pointing. "It's almost as if it were made of brass."

Dave look around him as he drove. "These trees are weird too. Very stunted. I've never seen the like of them,"

In the back, young Samantha slept and Twm Lyn's eyes grew brighter.

"From where the sun is, we're heading west," Dave said. "That's what we want."

Twm Lyn sat forward. "That's the road we travel, yes. From the east to the west, under the sky and over the hill, by sunlight and moonlight, by rain and snow, wind-blown and weather-beaten still, we travel."

Silence grew in the car. A strange atmosphere built until finally, Angela said, almost in a whisper, almost as if she was frightened to ask it, "Who are you really?"

The old minstrel cleared his throat. "I am Twm Lyn, or Son, son of Mother, and I was much younger once, but now am reduced to singing for my supper and earning my scraps in ways that were far beneath me in the days of Gwydion and Llŷr."

"I don't know what you're talking about," Dave said.

"At least the rain has stopped," Angela said and shuddered as she gazed around her at the eerie landscape. "But this is a wild place."

Dave edged the car along a road that twisted and turned at times, and was straight and narrow at others. They saw no other vehicles nor any sign of humankind. They saw no houses nor habitations of men.

They saw the sky turn amber and the land transform from the colour of beaten iron and back again to robin's-egg-blue and salmon-scale-silver.

And they fell into a meditation as they drove. And strange lights appeared ahead and to the sides.

"What are those?" Angela said finally, coming to herself, hand to her throat.

"Nothing to be afeard of," said Twm Lyn. But his eyes searched the mist walls too.

And mist gathered thicker, rolling over the moor and in the fog faint shapes were seen moving.

"What are those things in the mist?" Dave said, foot paralysed on the accelerator as if frightened to go so slow that they might stop yet scared to go so fast that he might by chance come off the road. For if the car rolled onto that odd earth, what strange tendrils would grow up to occupy it? What strange beetles would scuttle in and make it their home?

"Nothing to be afeard of," said Twm Lyn again.

And all this time, little Samantha did not wake.

The fog rolled and thickened and grew close like the cold breath of a dying man. The shapes within it shuffled and shifted and shambled and were never still, but instead they peered from within the mist with blinking eyes, bright and curious and carnal, yet their nature was never clear and their faces always veiled by fog.

Light coruscated within the fog, blues and yellows and reds and greens and purple and gold like a rainbow rippling over the boggy ground.

And then someone was in the road in front of them.

Dave hit the brakes hard and the car skidded forward and came to a stop.

Standing there as if expecting a toll, was a man astride a goat that had eyes like the devil's and a beard like the devil's son's beard and the goat's skin was white as milk and its ears red as blood, and the man on its back was dressed as a king in a fine cloth of gold and his face was sharp and his eyes were black and his eyebrows white and his hair ivory-pale as if he came from Winter.

And stranger still, beside him stood tall and pale his queen, with white hair to her waist and eyes like gems, jewel-bright and fiery-blazing with sapphire for the iris, quartz for the sclera and tourmaline for the apple — or as the Welsh have it: the candle — of her eye. And if the king came from Winter, it was as if this queen came from Spring.

"What the hell?" Dave said with the air of a man who knows he is not where he should be.

The car stood still on the road, engine turning. The king and his queen did not move, but instead spoke in Welsh.

Angela said, "They're demanding something."

"A toll," Twm said. "This is their road."

Dave turned. "You knew. This is a trick. You're in league with them. This is some kind of Welsh mountain Celtic shakedown."

Twm pursed his lips and looked mildly troubled. "They're not always here. Mostly I get away with such trespass."

The King spoke again and brought down his blackthorn staff across the bonnet of the car.

"Hey!" Dave said.

"Get out and have a word with them," Angela said. "Explain. We're strangers."

But Dave didn't move.

Eventually, after a long while, Twm said, "I have an appointment. I can't be lingering here."

Angela turned and whispered, "Help us."

Twm Lyn obviously knew this place and these people. Maybe he could help.

Twm Lyn nodded gravely and reached for the door handle and turned it, pushing open the door and stepping out into the damp air.

From within the car, scared to budge, Dave and Angela huddled together and Angela reached back and put her hand on her beloved baby, Samantha, but Samantha stirred not, and neither did she wake.

Twm Lyn stood tall and ragged as an old crow on the roadway that now seemed crusted in gems rather than stone.

And these gems glinted and gleamed, under the mild fog, in the cold lights that flashed in the strange mist.

And the odd figures in the mist became clearer and crowded closer and Angela gasped and held onto Dave's arm for fair as were the king and queen, ugly and misshapen were their subjects: half-men and half-things, almost vegetal, growing from the ground like stumps of trees or weird fungus or leaf-mould primeval and unnatural and sempiternal.

And as the trespassers sat in their car, these mist-bound monster shapes shuffled and huddled and muttered and watched.

"I'm scared," Angela said.

Dave said, "I knew we shouldn't have come this way. I knew we shouldn't have trusted him."

"Too late now. You should get out. You're a big man. Maybe

if they see there's two of you and you mean business, they'll let us past."

"Or we can pay," Dave said.

"That depends what the price is."

"I'd pay most things to be out of here."

And the goat-riding king spoke: "Henffych, o Fabon mab Modron. Pa bwrpas a ddaeth â chwi yma, a ninnau heb eich gweled ers cyhyd?"

And the pale-eyed queen with eyes like opals and skin like topaz muttered, "Er yn tramgwyddo ar ein tir ni! Tâl sydd i bob trosedd, cofiwch chwi hyn, Fabon."

"A thalu a wna i, frenhines, a chyfarchion i chi, Gwyn ap Nudd, sy'n frenin y fangre hon, ac sydd yn gyfarwydd i mi ers oes oesoedd."

"What are they saying?" hissed Angela.

"How would I know?" Dave said.

Angela trembled. "I feel so foreign here. This isn't our country."

And they were right. It wasn't.

Dave said, "I'm going to go for it. Just drive off."

"You'd leave him?"

"Yes. He brought us here. He's local. They won't harm him."

Tear's rolled down Angela's cheeks. "What if they follow us?"

"We might get away," Dave said.

"But where does this road lead to?"

"Away from here. That's all that matters."

Angela looked at Samantha in the back. "And she's sleeping through it all."

"It's for the best that she sleeps," Dave said.

He looked out. "He's discussing something. Like they're negotiating a bargain."

And the tall, rag-tag man nodded and clucked and grimaced and held out his hands as if he was trying to strike a deal with the strange king and his hostile queen.

And eventually there was nodding and agreement and Twm Lyn came back to the car. "We can go. The King has given us passage through his country."

"I still think you knew he'd be here," Dave said.

"And he's just letting us go?" Angela asked, her brow furrowing as she studied Twm Lyn's lined face.

Twm shrugged. "My words are milk and honey. They work wonders with such as he."

"What is he, anyway?" Angela said. "And what are those?" she pointed through the window at the crowd of gaping monstrosities.

"Those are the fair family," Twm said, "Y Tylwyth Teg. Though they are not fair and only called such for fear of offending them if their true monstrosity was declared. But let us leave now they have allowed us passage. I have to be at Bryn Ellyll before nightfall and you have a christening to go to. You and young Samantha here, who has not herself been christened." Twm leaned and pulled Samantha's blanket so that it covered her face.

Angela didn't stop him.

"So she sleeps better," he explained.

And Dave sighed in relief and set the car off and drove and the mist clung to them and it seemed that the crowd of misshapen beings always kept pace and they could never be free of them until eventually the road pitched downwards and the strange moorland with its rolling colours and roiling mist was left behind.

They were still in wild country but at least it was wild in a way they recognised. Sheep sheltered behind stone walls, and here and there were lonely farmhouses.

"I'll be stopping here," Twm Lyn said quietly.

"Here?" Angela said, "But it's the middle of nowhere."

"Bryn Ellyll, the home of my relations is not far. This will be sufficiently close, as close as such as you can get in fact. My people await me, and thank you for bringing me so far. I am not as late as I feared."

Angela said, "Thank you for helping us out of that awful situation with those strange people."

Dave said, "What bargain did you strike with them that convinced them to let us through?"

Twm smiled. "A toll was asked," Twm said, "And I had to be here by nightfall, and now we are."

"What toll was asked?" Angela said, but Twm Lyn spoke no more.

When the minstrel was gone, Dave started the car. Angela wound the window down to watch Twm Lyn leave and, as he disappeared into the distance, said, "he's carrying something."

"His harp?" Dave said without looking.

"No, that's on his back. He has something in his arms."

Dave grunted and drove on. "I don't know and I don't care. Good riddance to bad rubbish."

The rain had all blown away as they drove down Penglais hill into Aberystwyth. They parked outside the B&B on South Marine Terrace and in a pool of yellow sodium streetlight Angela turned to her baby in the back seat. "I can't believe she hasn't woken through all of this," she said, pulling away the blanket that Twm Lyn had drawn over Samantha's face. She recoiled with a gasp, her hand to her mouth.

"What is it?" said Dave spinning round.

And they both looked at Samantha. But it was not their smiling serene girl child they saw but a toadstool-like thing of misshapen fungus that leaked mucus into the blanket around it.

It had a mouth like a cut and eyes like a wound and it blinked its slow yellow lids looking at Angela, and with its slash of a mouth it said, "Mam, mam."

The Shoemaker

LONG AGO, in the forest of Brechfa, in the small hamlet of Gilfach Wen, during a spell of fine weather in late May, Dafydd Esgidiau, a cobbler of no great fortune but some local renown, stood at the door of his cottage. The morning had passed uneventfully enough until a pedlar, with a pack heavy on his back and a peculiar glint in his eye, approached along the dusty path.

From the first, Dafydd thought there was something unusual about this pedlar. His eyes were too sharp, his ears too pricked, and his mouth too tight. Still, Dafydd thought. He would pass the time of day with the man, even though he didn't know who he was. Manners cost nothing after all, and Dafydd was always alert to a chance of new business.

But the pedlar was a rugged sort, weathered by long roads and rough seasons. He stopped and opened his pack, and despite his look, his wares were a surprising delight—ribbons of vibrant hues, fine cloth from Margam and Tintern, and trinkets that sparkled in his hands. Each one seemed to catch the light, and hold it. These baubles would delight any maid.

Yet, thought Dafydd, there was something unsettling in his manner. His smile seemed too broad for a weary traveller, and his air was far too cheerful for a man burdened by the life of a wayfarer.

As the pedlar laid out his goods, Dafydd's unease deepened. The way he moved, as though he glided rather than walked, and the odd flicker in his golden-brown eyes whispered of something not entirely human. Dafydd remembered the old tales—stories of the Tylwyth Teg, the Fair Folk who walked among mortals in disguise, delighting in games and guile.

It was well known that the Tylwyth Teg were known for their pride and trickery, quick to take offence and swifter to punish it with capricious cruelty. They might sometimes look human, though other times appeared as columns of fire, or trails of sparks, black dogs, or great white hens. The ways of these fairy folk were mysterious, their intentions often hidden, and their gifts when they gave them—never came without cost.

"Good morning, cobbler," the pedlar said, his voice sharp and high, like the notes of a reed pipe.

"And good morning to you, pedlar," Dafydd replied, his tone polite but wary.

The pedlar smiled, his mouth curling in a way that reminded Dafydd of a frog. a little too widely, wider than he'd ever seen a man smile before. "A fine day, isn't it?"

"Aye," said Dafydd. "Fine enough."

"And your health?"

"Good enough."

"Then what more could a man want but fine weather and good health?"

At this, Dafydd laughed, though without conviction. "What more? Money and comfort, perhaps. A man could do without the labour of mending shoes day after day for little reward."

The pedlar's eyes gleamed. "Money and comfort, you say? A reasonable wish. But tell me, would you not also wish for love to accompany your fortune?"

"I have love," Dafydd said, his chest tightening. "But how did you know my name?"

The pedlar's smile widened. "Why, everyone in Brechfa knows of Dafydd Esgidiau, the finest cobbler for miles. They also know of your sweetheart, Eirlys Watcyn."

At the mention of her name, Dafydd's face reddened. "What business have you speaking of Eirlys?"

The pedlar chuckled, his yellowish eyes narrowing. "Only that I hear she loves you dearly and would marry you even in your humble state, yet you refuse her."

"I do not refuse her!" Dafydd snapped. "But I will not wed her until I can give her a life better than this hovel and workshop."

"One should always enjoy the thing one has today, rather than hoping for a better one on a tomorrow that may not come."

"And I see that philosophy has served you well," Dafydd said, glancing at the pedlar's worn shoes and threadbare coat. "No, no. I must work and save and plan today, in the hope that the fruit of my labours will reward me in future."

"Ah," said the pedlar, his tone shifting to one of mild reproach. "And so you labour away, day after day, dreaming of a fortune you have yet to find."

Dafydd frowned, but said nothing.

The pedlar reached into his pack, withdrawing a length of bright ribbon. "But you have a love."

"She loves me, and I love her."

"Perhaps, then, you would like something for her? A gift to show your affection?"

"I will spend no money today, but instead keep what I earn to invest it in our future," Dafydd replied. "One day my work will pay off."

"Is that so?" the pedlar said, with a sly grin. "So you're a gambling man, then?"

"I do not gamble."

"You gamble on times that may not come, it seems to me. But

if you're interested in finding your fortune, why not make it today instead of tomorrow?"

"You begin to tire me, pedlar."

The pedlar smiled his strange wide smile. "Tell me, Dafydd, have you heard the tales of Pant y Garreg Hir?"

Dafydd stiffened. "The old stone circle? What of it?"

"Only that beneath the Stone of Slaughter lies a treasure—a pot of Roman gold. Enough to make a poor cobbler rich beyond his dreams."

"I've heard the tale," Dafydd said gruffly. "And I know it's nonsense. No man would touch such cursed gold."

"Cursed?" the pedlar repeated, his grin growing sharper. "Or merely guarded by those who seek brave and ambitious souls? Are you such a man, Dafydd Esgidiau?"

Dafydd hesitated, feeling the weight of the pedlar's gaze. "I... I do not believe in fairy tales."

"Perhaps not," said the pedlar, shrugging as he slung his pack over his shoulder. "But the moon is full tonight, and brave men find their fortunes beneath its light."

Dafydd felt a flush rise to his cheek. Was he not brave? He felt he must be, though he'd never been put to the test.

"If you'll buy no ribbons, I must be on my way to find some that will, before the night falls and I must make my humble bed amongst the bindweed and ivy." With that, he tipped his hat and walked away, whistling a tune that echoed through the trees.

Dafydd stood for a long while, staring after him. The strange pedlar was gone, yet his words lingered, twisting their way into Dafydd's thoughts like the roots of an ancient tree. As night fell, the temptation of gold grew brighter in his mind, shining like the moon that rose above the forest of Brechfa. Was he not brave?

Night fell over Gilfach Wen, and the moon rose high above the forest of Brechfa, its silver light spilling through the trees and casting long shadows over the cobbler's cottage.

Inside, Dafydd sat at his workbench. A shoe lay in his hand, but his thoughts had wandered far from the stitching.

The pedlar's words rang in his ears. "Brave men find their fortunes beneath the full moon."

Dafydd shook his head. "Nonsense. Fairy tales for old women and children."

But the words sat like a seed in his chest, and as he sat his desire for a better future flowered.

What harm could it do to look?

There would be no gold. Of course not. But if there were…?

He could provide for Eirlys, prove himself worthy of her love, and escape the drudgery of mending other men's shoes for scraps.

So, he put his work aside, and after a supper of bread and cheese, he lit the lantern and pulled on his coat.

The village lay silent, its cottages dark and still. He took the familiar path into the woods, his footsteps muffled by fallen leaves.

The journey to Pant y Garreg Hir was a lonely one. The path wound through dense trees, their gnarled branches clawing at the sky. The wind whispered through the leaves, carrying strange murmurs that made Dafydd glance over his shoulder more than once.

"It's just the wind," he muttered, though his hand tightened on the lantern.

But the wind in Brechfa tells old stories.

At last, he crested the wooded hill and descended into the hollow they called Pant y Garreg Hir. The clearing opened before him, bathed in moonlight. The ancient stones of the circle stood tall and solemn, their dark surfaces gleaming on one side and black as shadows on the other.

In the centre, the Stone of Slaughter lay like a sentinel, its flat surface stark and unyielding.

Dafydd hesitated at the edge of the circle, his heart thudding in his chest.

He had heard the old tales: how the druids of long ago had performed sacrifices on this very slab, how the blood of the dead had seeped into the earth, tainting it forever.

The villagers said the stones whispered at night, warning away intruders.

"Foolishness," he told himself, though his voice wavered.

He stepped into the circle, the lantern casting flickering light over the ancient stones. A soft breeze stirred, carrying faint whispers that made his skin crawl.

He pressed forward, his eyes fixed on the Stone of Slaughter.

"It's just a stone," he muttered, kneeling beside it. His hands, calloused from years of mending shoes, trembled as he touched its rough surface. It was cold, as if it had never known the warmth of the sun.

With a deep breath, he gripped the edge of the slab and pulled.

The stone was heavy—heavier than he had anticipated—and for a moment, it didn't budge.

Dafydd gritted his teeth and tried again, his muscles straining.

The slab groaned, a deep, resonant sound that seemed to echo through the circle.

"It's too heavy," he gasped, sinking back on his heels.

Was he not a strong man?

His hands ached. His arms shook.

He thought of leaving.

Heat rose in his cheeks. He clenched his fists.

With renewed determination, he set his hands to the stone once more. This time, it shifted.

The grating sound of stone on stone sent a shiver down his spine, but he didn't stop.

Inch by inch, he moved the slab, revealing a dark void beneath.

As the stone came to rest, Dafydd leaned over the opening, holding the lantern high.

A black space yawned before him, its depths unseen even in the lantern's glow.

A cold, damp wind rushed up from below, carrying a faint, metallic tang that made him wrinkle his nose.

"What's this?" he whispered.

He thought he heard the sound of tiny bells.

It was a long drop down.

Then, his hand brushed against something solid—wood.

He leaned closer and realised it was a ladder, its rungs worn and splintered with age.

It descended into the darkness, disappearing into the unknown depths below. So he could descend. If he chose to.

For a moment, he faltered. The ladder looked old and precarious — dangerous. And what was down there in the dark?

The stories of curses and spirits whispered louder in his mind.

But the thought of Eirlys and the future he could build with the gold gave him courage.

And then—just for a moment—he thought of a child's voice. Not one he'd heard. One that might one day call him father.

That was enough.

Taking a deep breath, he gripped the ladder tightly and began his descent.

The rungs creaked under his weight, each step accompanied by the faint groan of wood protesting its burden.

The air grew colder as he went down, and the light from the lantern above faded, leaving him surrounded by shadows.

At last, his foot touched solid ground.

He stepped off the ladder and stood still, letting his eyes adjust.

The floor beneath him was cold and damp, the scent of clay and earth thick in the air.

A faint blue light flickered in the distance, like the light of a Corpse Candle, casting eerie shadows on the walls of the cavern.

A strange opalescence glittered in the walls in the light of his lantern, as if gems were buried there.

A path, worn as if by thousands of tiny feet, led on.

Dafydd took a cautious step forward, his breath visible in the chill. As he moved toward the weird light, the sound of finger bells rang softly, their high, tinkling notes reverberating through the chamber.

The cavern was large. As he raised his lantern, the walls shimmered.

The lamplight brushed the bands of agate and amethyst, the stone veined with purples like ink bleeding through silk. Deep red garnets glinted like spilled wine in ancient glass, while jade stitched the seams in delicate, sea-green filaments, like seaweed drifting in captured tidepools.

And he listened. There was a sound in that place as if it the very air were alive, keening a strange unearthly song.

He went on into the tunnel ahead and came to a second chamber. And here, in the heart of this cavern, the source of the light became clear, and of the ethereal singing became clear.

A woman stood waiting.

She was tall and resplendent, her gown shimmering with colours that shifted and danced like sunlight on water.

Her hair flowed in a silver cascade, and her eyes glowed with an intensity that made Dafydd's breath catch.

Her presence was both beautiful and terrible—a force that commanded awe and fear.

"Welcome, Dafydd. I am glad you came in response to my invitation."

"Invitation?"

"Not all invitations are given in plain words," she said, "nor by those who wear the faces they were born with. But that is of no matter."

"Who are you?"

"I am Rhianfellt."

Dafydd knew the name from the old stories.

Rhianfellt—Queen of Lightning—one of the Tylwyth Teg. Some say she was a queen of the People of Peace, others that she had been cast out by them.

Without knowing what else to do, he bowed before this great lady.

"Welcome, Dafydd Esgidiau," she said, her voice like the melody of a harp played in the distance. "I have long expected you."

Rhianfellt's eyes, like great pearls, opalescent and strange, fixed on Dafydd with an intensity that made his knees weak.

"You've come seeking what lies beneath the Stone of Slaughter," she said, her voice soft but carrying an authority to make heroes quail. "And here you stand, bold and trembling all at once. Are you a brave man, Dafydd?"

"I hope I am," he said.

"Perhaps you are. And you've come here in search of a golden tomorrow to replace your threadbare today?"

Dafydd swallowed, his mouth dry. "I—I was curious," he managed, his voice rasping in the charged air. "I've heard tales... of gold."

"Tales?" Her lips curved into a faint smile, though there was no warmth in it. "And what makes you think tales of the gold of the Fair Folk hold any truth, Dafydd Esgidiau?"

He hesitated, the weight of her gaze pressing on him. "Do they hold truth?"

Rhianfellt tilted her head, the light from her hair casting faint patterns on the cavern walls.

"Sometimes they do," she said, her tone light with mockery. "And sometimes they lead men into a merry dance across the moor. Sometimes they lead men to their death. But tell me, cobbler—why would a man like you seek gold?"

Dafydd felt a flicker of defiance. "I want a better life. I want to marry the woman I love and give her more than a leaky roof and patched shoes. I want to be more than a poor cobbler in a poor village."

"A noble desire," she said, though her smile widened, revealing teeth as pale and fine as bone needles. "And what would you give for such a life?"

The words hung between them, thick and still. Dafydd shifted, his hands clenched at his sides. "What do you mean?"

"What I mean," said Rhianfellt, stepping closer, her movements fluid and soundless, "is that nothing we give is given freely. Not here, in the realm of the Tylwyth Teg. You wish for wealth, cobbler? Then you must pay my price."

Dafydd's pulse quickened. "What kind of price?"

"The price of tomorrow against the worth of today."

Rhianfellt's smile lingered as she lifted her hand, her fingers long and pale as the bark of birchwood. In her palm lay a fat, embroidered pouch. The faint chime of bells followed its every movement, though no bells were visible.

"This," she said, "is a pouch of Roman gold. Enough to change your life. Enough to build a future with your Eirlys. Every coin within it carries the weight of centuries."

She loosened the string of the purse so that Dafydd could see the old, yellow coins within.

Dafydd's eyes locked on the pouch. The gold seemed to cast a light of its own that made shapes play on the walls of the cavern, like the shapes cast by a child's moon-lantern.

He saw it all in front of him now. He heard Eirlys's laughter, he felt a warm hearth, and a child's small hand grasping his own. His golden future was within reach.

"But," she continued, with a cold smile. "In exchange for this gold, I shall claim a favour from you. But, don't worry, it need not be paid now."

"A favour?" His voice caught.

"Yes," said Rhianfellt, her smile deepening. "A small thing. A trifle. I will call upon you at a time of my choosing, and you will grant whatever I ask. A fair trade, is it not?"

Dafydd's stomach turned. The cavern seemed to tighten around her words. "What kind of favour?"

Her eyes glittered—too bright, too deep.

"Do not be impertinent, Dafydd Esgidiau. You would seek to bind a queen with your working man's bargains. But Queens are not to be bound by such as you. It is ordained that the future is hidden from us all, even we of the White People. What matters for you is this moment. What matters is always now, not an invisble tomorrow. So this is the offer. The gold for you promise. Will you take it?"

He drew breath, shallow and fast. The cavern spun gently around the pouch in her hand.

"What if I refuse?"

"Then you will climb your little ladder and return to your little life," she said. There was no threat in her voice, only the indifference of cold stone. "And you will patch the shoes of the poor, and doff your hat to the rich, and dream of what might have been."

She frightened him.

She smiled again, "Surely the future is worth a little risk."

The strange music—the song she never sang aloud—grew louder in his head.

His fingers twitched. His thoughts ran in circles.

She was right. Tomorrow belonged to itself. Who knew what tomorrow would bring or whether it would even come at all. So, one day Rhianfellt would call in her promise, but tonight he would carry away her gold.

The pouch rang faintly in her hand, the sound of chiming bells in crystal water. again.

He cleared his throat. "I... I accept."

Rhianfellt's smile widened. She held out her hand.

Dafydd reached for the pouch.

His fingers brushed hers. Cold flooded through him.

The chime of bells rose once more, but now as if she had got inside his own bones.

Her touch was cold. Her skin was not the skin of living women. It felt like winter's breath; it felt like snow falling on the mountain wastes.

But he shook as hand, just as if he were buying sheep at Llandeilo mart.

"The bargain is struck," she said. "Go now, Dafydd Esgidiau. And remember: don't worry about the future. Live your life for today."

Before he could answer, the light dimmed. The cavern folded inward. Stone became smoke and arkness closed like a gate and when he opened his eyes, he was back on the hill.

He stood at the edge of the stone circle. It was as if it had all been a dream. Except, that the pouch of gold was clutched tight in his hand.

Before him, the slab of the Stone of Slaughter was sealed again and the way down was closed, as if it had never existed.

Around him, the forest was silent. Even the owls seemed to be sleeping. The moon still hung overhead.

Dafydd looked down at the pouch. He opened it and touched the coins and in the silver moonlight, their golden glow lit his face. His heart pounded full of joy, and fear and a refusal to think of the price he might have to pay.

Morning light broke over the hamlet of Gilfach Wen, spilling across trellised wildflowers and brightening the rooms through the unshuttered windows.

Dafydd sat at his table, the pouch of gold before him. He had counted the coins twice already, their weight both thrilling and disquieting.

His fingers brushed the embroidered cloth as if to reassure himself it was real. At least it made no sound now— none of that underwater chime from the cavern.

Here, in the thin grey light of his hovel, it was only a pouch.

The future lay open before him, its promise gleaming like the coins. He thought of Eirlys—her smile warm as a summer day. This was the day he would ask for her hand.

After a quick breakfast, Dafydd pocketed the pouch and stepped into the morning air.

The village stirred with its usual rhythms: clattering hens, the lowing of cows, neighbours calling across fences.

But Dafydd heard none of it. His thoughts were fixed on Iwan Watcyn and the task ahead.

The path to Iwan's farm wound through woods and over a stream where sunlight danced on the water.

By the time he reached the stone house, his nerves had drawn tight.

He straightened his coat and knocked on the door.

Iwan Watcyn opened it, his face weathered and wary.

He took in Dafydd's threadbare coat and thin frame.

"Well, cobbler," he said. "What brings you here so early?"

"Good morning, Iwan," Dafydd said, steadying his voice. "I've come to speak with you about Eirlys."

Iwan leaned against the doorframe, arms crossed. "Have you now? And what might you have to say?"

"I wish to ask for your blessing to marry her," Dafydd said. He held the old man's gaze.

Iwan's brow furrowed. "And what do you plan to offer her? You've got little but that leaking roof and a pile of shoes that aren't yours."

Dafydd hesitated. His hand moved toward the pouch.

"I've come into money," he said. "Enough to build a proper home. Enough to give her the life she deserves."

Iwan's eyes narrowed. "Money? From where? I've heard no talk of inheritance, and you've no kin left to leave you one."

"It's a distant inheritance," Dafydd said quickly, looking away.

"It doesn't matter where it came from. What matters is that I can provide for her now."

Iwan studied him. His expression gave nothing away.

"And why my Eirlys? With this money, you could take your pick."

"Because I love her," Dafydd said. "I always have. No amount of gold would change that."

Iwan held him in silence a moment longer. Then, at last, he smiled.

"Well, you've got spirit. Come in, then, and we'll talk."

Inside, the cottage was warm and smelled of woodsmoke and bacon.

They sat at the kitchen table. Iwan poured tea.

He watched Dafydd closely over the rim of his cup.

"You promise to look after her?"

"With all my heart."

"And you swear there's no deceit in this money of yours?"

Dafydd hesitated. His fingers tightened around the cup.

He thought of Rhianfellt's pear bright eyes, and her voice like the sighing wind at on Midwinter's Eve.

"There's no deceit," he said at last, though the words sat heavy on his tongue.

Iwan nodded. "Very well. If you've got the means—and I believe you do—then you have my blessing."

Relief swelled in Dafydd's chest. He stood, bowing his head.

"Thank you, Iwan. You won't regret this."

"See that I don't," Iwan said. Gruff, but not unkind.

Dafydd left the farm with a spring in his step. The sky seemed brighter. The world lighter.

When he reached Eirlys's cottage, she was tending her small garden, hands deep in the earth.

She looked up as he approached, smiling.

"Dafydd," she said, brushing the soil from her palms. "What brings you here?"

He stopped before her, heart hammering.

"Eirlys," he said, voice steady despite the storm inside him. "I've spoken to your father. He's given us his blessing."

Her eyes widened. A hand flew to her mouth.

"Truly?"

"Truly." He reached into his pocket and drew out the pouch.

"With this, we can build a home. A real one."

She stared at it, brow furrowing.

"Dafydd... where did you get that?"

"It doesn't matter," he said quickly, taking her hands.

"What matters is that we can have the life we dreamed of. Say you'll marry me."

She looked into his eyes, searching.

What she sought, he couldn't say.

But then her expression softened. She nodded.

"Yes," she whispered. "Yes, Dafydd. I'll marry you."

He pulled her into his arms, holding her close as the promise of their future rose between them.

But as they stood in the sunlight, the pouch of gold hung heavy at his side.

The morning of Dafydd and Eirlys's wedding broke bright and clear, the air sharp with the scent wildflowers and the fresh tang of the clean river water.

The villagers of Gilfach Wen gathered early at the small stone church, their faces lit with a mix of joy and curiosity.

A wedding was always cause for celebration—and this one had stirred a particular excitement.

Eirlys Watcyn, soon to be Tomos, stood in her cottage as

sunlight spilled through the window across her white dress, simple yet elegant.

Her sister braided ribbons of green and gold into her hair, while her mother fastened a silver brooch at her throat.

"You look beautiful, 'nghariad," her mother said, her voice thick with emotion.

Outside, Dafydd waited with the village men. His coat was new, its fine stitching and weighty fabric a quiet display of the gold he now carried.

He felt their eyes on him—their congratulations tinged with unspoken questions.

The ceremony was plain. Vows were exchanged beneath the carved beams of the church, with the priest presiding.

When Dafydd slid the silver ring onto Eirlys's finger, his hands trembled. And he did not know why.

It was not fear of the moment, but something else. Perhaps the future.

Afterwards, the village feasted on bread, cheese, roasted meats and Welsh cakes, the table crowded with gifts from every household.

Cwrw da flowed freely, fiddles played, laughter rang across the square, and the newlyweds danced beneath swaying lanterns.

Children darted through the crowd. Eirlys's laughter was bright and unguarded. Her hand was warm in Dafydd's.

Yet as the evening wore on, Dafydd's gaze drifted to the edge of the village—toward the dark fringe of woods.

There stood the path to Pant y Garreg Hir, and the stone that covered his bargain.

When the revelry waned and the villagers went to their beds, Dafydd and Eirlys returned to their cottage.

This new house was larger and better built than his old one, its roof sound, its hearth already glowing.

Eirlys, even that first night, made it hers: a vase of flowers on the table, embroidered curtains at the windows.

They sat by the fire, and silence gathered between them.

Eirlys reached out and touched his arm. "Dafydd, what troubles you?"

He hesitated. The weight of the secret pressed on his chest.

"It's nothing," he said at last, too lightly to be believed.

"Don't lie to me," she said gently, her gaze steady. "Not tonight."

He stared into the fire, its light shifting across his face.

At last he sighed. "There's something you should know."

Her fingers tightened around his.

He told her everything.

The pedlar. The journey to Pant y Garreg Hir. The ladder. The Queen beneath the hill.

He spoke of the gold and the favour owed, his voice faltering at the memory of Rhianfellt's gaze and her parting words.

When he finished, silence settled over them again, broken only by the fire's low crackle.

Eirlys's face had gone pale. Her brow was furrowed.

"The Tylwyth Teg are not to be trifled with," she said at last. "You've brought us wealth, Dafydd—but at what cost?"

"I thought it was worth it," he said. "For you. For us. For the life we wanted."

She placed a hand on his cheek. "You meant well," she said. "But you must understand—we'll need to guard against the day they come to claim what's theirs."

Dafydd nodded, his throat tight. "I won't let them hurt you."

Eirlys did not flinch. "We have our love," she said. "We'll face it together."

As the fire sank low and the moon rose high, they sat hand in hand.

Between them, the weight of the bargain lay unspoken—a silent promise of trials still to come.

Outside, the wind stirred the trees.

And far below, in the dark, someone stirred and remembered his name.

The seasons turned in Gilfach Wen, and the days flowed into months. The cottage of Dafydd and Eirlys grew warm with the rhythms of their life together—laughter, firelight, and the scent of baking bread filling its walls.

Yet beneath their happiness, the shadow of Dafydd's bargain with Rhianfellt lingered. Unspoken, but not forgotten.

One crisp autumn morning, as the leaves blazed gold and scarlet, Eirlys stood in the garden, her hands resting on her rounded belly.

She moved slower now, her steps cautious but still graceful.

Dafydd watched her from the doorway, his heart full of joy—and unease.

The sight of her, radiant with the life growing within, filled him with hope.

But also with a strange anxiety.

That evening, as frost laced the windowpanes, Eirlys turned to him. Her voice was steady, but tinged with urgency.

"It's time," she said.

The midwife, Mari Fach Twddyn Amlwg, arrived quickly, her apron still dusted with flour from the bread she'd been kneading when the summons came.

She shooed Dafydd outside with a brisk wave. "Men are more bother than help in these things," she muttered.

Dafydd paced the garden under a sky strewn with stars, his breath clouding in the cold.

From inside came Eirlys's low cries, and Mari's calm voice. The sounds cut through the stillness like a blade.

Time stretched thin. Dafydd gripped the porch rail, his knuckles white—until, at last, a newborn's cry rang out, sudden and clear.

His heart leapt. He ran inside, boots thudding and leaving damp prints on the wooden floor.

In the dim glow of the hearth, Eirlys lay propped on pillows, her face pale, her expression serene.

In her arms: a bundle swaddled in soft wool.

Mari stepped back, her work done. Dafydd approached, unsure, almost afraid to breathe.

"She's beautiful," Eirlys whispered. She tilted the bundle to show the child's face—round and pink, eyes tight shut, a dark tuft of hair crowning her head.

"Meet our daughter, Dafydd."

He knelt beside them. His hands shook as he reached out and touched the baby's fingers.

"Catrin," he said, his voice thick. "Her name is Catrin."

Eirlys nodded, eyes still fixed on the child. "Catrin Tomos," she said, her tone proud and quiet.

The baby's tiny hand curled around his finger.

That small warmth broke something open in him.

All the doubt, the fear, the weight of years—gone in that instant.

Here, at last, was what he had longed for. A family. A future shaped by love.

But as the fire dimmed and silence settled round the cottage, the old unease returned.

Rhianfellt's words echoed in his mind.

"The future always comes."

He looked to Eirlys, asleep at last, and then to Catrin, nestled in her arms.

Outside, the wind whispered through the trees, carrying the scent of frost and fallen leaves.

Above, the stars glittered sharply, bright as eyes.

As if the still folk watched.

And if their queen was waiting.

· · ·

Eirlys and Dafydd returned to the cottage with her heart heavy but their minds set.

"So what are we to do?" Dafydd asked.

"We're going to make a doll," she told him, her voice steady. "A likeness of Catrin that will fool Rhianfellt."

Dafydd stared at her, his brow furrowing. "He is a strange old man. A doll? Eirlys, that sounds—"

She interrupted, her gaze fierce. "Gwilym said it will work. We have to try."

He looked at her for a long moment, then sighed and nodded. "Tell me what you need me to do."

And so, together, they began their desperate work. The fire crackled as they gathered Catrin's clothes, her blanket, and the small toys she loved. Dafydd carved the wooden frame while Eirlys stitched the fabric, her hands moving with care and purpose.

The girl laughed at them as they worked, not knowing the danger she was in.

As they laboured, they spoke to the doll, whispering words of love and memory, weaving their hopes into every thread. The room filled with their quiet voices, the air thick with their determination.

When the doll was finished, it lay in the cradle, dressed in Catrin's clothes and swaddled in her blanket. It was imperfect but, they prayed, close enough to fool the eyes and noses of the Fair Folk.

That night was unnaturally still, the mist thick around the cottage as though it held its breath. Dafydd and Eirlys sat by the hearth, their faces pale and drawn. Catrin slept in the pantry out of sight, her small form wrapped in warm blankets. The doll lay in the cradle by the fire, its tiny face shadowed by the flickering light.

Dafydd gripped the arm of his chair, his knuckles white. "Do you think she'll be fooled by such a thing?" he whispered.

Eirlys stared at the cradle, her hands clasped tightly in her lap.

"We don't have a choice," she said, her voice steadier than she felt. "We must have faith."

Outside, the mist thickened, pressing against the windows like a sluggish cold thing. The air grew colder, and the flames in the hearth flickered weakly, as if shying away from the presence approaching the door.

The latch lifted without a sound, and Rhianfellt stepped into the room. Her silver hair shimmered like frost, her luminous eyes scanning the space. She moved with a grace that was both mesmerizing and terrifying, her gown trailing behind her like a veil of moonlight.

"Good evening, Dafydd Esgidiau," she said, her voice soft and cold. Her gaze shifted to Eirlys. "And you, Eirlys. How touching to see you together. Often I am entranced by this thing that mortals call love. We on the other side are hungry for it, but cannot create it ourselves. And so we come to you as the beekeeper comes for honey."

Eirlys rose slowly, her knees trembling beneath her skirts. "You've come for the child," she said, her voice firm despite the fear clawing at her throat. "Then take her."

Rhianfellt's lips curved into a faint smile. "Indeed," she said. Her sharp gaze flicked to the cradle. "And there she is."

Dafydd stood, his body tense. "She's sleeping," he said quickly. "Be gentle with her."

The fairy queen tilted her head, amusement flickering in her eyes. "This thing love again! How considerate of you," she said. She stepped toward the cradle, her movements silent as a shadow.

Eirlys held her breath as Rhianfellt bent over the doll. The fairy queen's fingers brushed the fabric of the blanket, and her eyes narrowed slightly. She tilted her head, studying the tiny form with a faint frown.

"She is warm," Rhianfellt murmured. She reached out and gently touched the doll's cheek. "And so full of love. It warms my cold silver skin and my empty moonlit heart."

Eirlys's heart thundered in her chest. She willed herself to remain calm, to keep her hands from trembling.

Rhianfellt straightened, the frown on her face softening into a smile. "You have cared for her well," she said, her voice almost kind.

Eirlys nodded, her throat tight. "She is precious to us," she said softly.

The fairy queen gathered the doll into her arms, cradling it as though it were truly a child. "She will thrive in my realm. I will give her gold and silver and milk and honey, and she will dance under the stars from where we fell," she said, turning toward the door.

Dafydd and Eirlys exchanged a glance, their fear mingling with a fragile hope.

But as Rhianfellt reached the threshold, she paused. Her sharp eyes flicked back to them, narrowing. "You have been quiet," she said, her tone thoughtful. "Strangely quiet."

Eirlys forced herself to meet Rhianfellt's gaze. "What more could we say?" she asked, her voice trembling but steady enough. "You've taken what was promised. We've kept our part of the bargain."

Rhianfellt's eyes lingered on her for a moment longer, and the silence stretched unbearably. Then, with a faint smile, she turned and stepped into the mist.

The door swung shut behind her, and the oppressive cold lifted. The room seemed to exhale, the fire flaring brighter as warmth returned.

Eirlys sagged into her chair, her hands covering her face. "She's gone," she whispered.

Dafydd ran to the pantry, his hands trembling as he opened the door. Inside, Catrin stirred in her blankets, her tiny hands flexing as she yawned.

"She's safe," Dafydd said, his voice breaking. He lifted her into his arms, cradling her close as relief washed over him.

Eirlys crossed the room and wrapped her arms around them both, her tears falling silently.

Outside, the mist began to thin, retreating into the woods. But the faint sound of Rhianfellt's laughter lingered on the air, a haunting reminder that the Fair Folk were not so easily fooled.

The village of Gilfach Wen stirred with anticipation as Nos Galan Gaeaf approached, the time when the veil between worlds grew thin, the night the English call Halloween. The crisp autumn air carried the scent of woodsmoke and fallen leaves, and the villagers prepared for the traditional honouring of the dead and the turning of the year. Lanterns carved from turnips lined the paths, their flickering light casting strange shadows across the cottages.

In Dafydd and Eirlys's home, the warmth of the hearth glowed brighter than ever. Little Catrin, now a lively infant, gurgled in her mother's arms as Eirlys hung garlands of dried autumn flowers above the windows. Dafydd sat nearby, carving a small wooden rattle for Catrin, his knife moving with practiced ease. Yet beneath the peace of that moment, unease lay coiled like a snake sleeping through winter, waiting for a day when it would wake again

As the sun dipped below the horizon, the shadows lengthened and the village came alive with masked figures and bonfires. Children darted between the flames, their laughter mingling with the sharp crackle of kindling. Villagers told stories of the Tylwyth Teg, the bwci bo, and the danger of straying too far on such a night— when the Fair Folk walked abroad, and not always unseen.

Dafydd stood at the threshold of his cottage, pipe in hand, watching the flicker of bonfires in the distance. The air felt heavier than usual, charged with a hush that raised the hairs on his arms. He drew on his pipe, the smoke curling into the still air. But then, a sudden chill swept over him, cutting through the warmth like water through wool.

The mist came without warning. It rolled over the ground like breath, thick and slow and strangely alive. It coiled about the cottage, muffling the sounds of revelry. One by one, the Halloween lanterns went out, smothered by the fog.

From within that whiteness, a figure emerged. Where she stepped, the grass shone faintly under her feet. Rhianfellt stood amidst the swirling mist. Her silver hair shimmered like moonlight on ice, and her eyes, pale as as white opals, gleamed with terrible purpose. Her gown flowed like a river, its hues shifting with every breath of the air.

"Dafydd Esgidiau," she said, her voice soft and sharp as a harp-string. "It is time to pay the price of our bargain, struck beneath the Stone of Slaughter."

"I am not ready," he said.

She laughed. "It does not matter whether you are ready or not. Did I not tell you the future always comes? And here it is."

Dafydd's throat tightened. His pipe slipped from his fingers and struck the threshold. "My lady," he whispered, "what is it you want?"

She stepped closer. Her gaze did not waver. "You had the gold. You spent it gladly. Now I take what I foresaw before it ever came to pass—what lives now in your fine house and calls you father. The gold was never free. I have come to claim what is mine."

Dafydd stumbled back. "Not my Catrin. You can't—I won't let you—"

Rhianfellt raised one long hand, and the words died on his tongue. "I have come for the child. Catrin is mine. She is the price."

"No!" Dafydd's voice cracked. "She's ours—she belongs to us!"

At that moment, Eirlys appeared in the doorway, her face pale and her eyes bright. She held Catrin tightly to her chest. The child stirred in her arms, sensing the cold in the air.

"You will not take her," Eirlys said, her voice low and unwavering. "She is ours, born of our love, not of your gold."

Rhianfellt turned her gaze to her. A faint smile touched her lips. "A sweet, Eirlys. A mother's defiance. Touching. But it changes nothing. The child was paid for, and I will have her."

Eirlys stepped forward. "You think you hold all power, fine lady, but you misjudge the strength of a mother's love. You will not take her."

The fairy queen tilted her head, sharp eyes narrowing. "And what will you do to stop me, mortal woman?"

Eirlys did not answer. She turned and ran into the cottage, the door slamming behind her.

Dafydd stood frozen. The mist swirled about his boots. Rhianfellt's eyes found his again. "I dislike using force, but a bargain is a bargain," she said. "I will return, when your wife has seen the truth of our agreement and realises then what you owe."

Then Rhianfellt was gone. The fog outside, thinned but did not roll away, blanketing the village in silence and cold.

Inside, Dafydd heard Eirlys whispering to the baby. He shut the front door and turned the bolt.

The mist lingered through the night and into the grey light of All Souls' Day, curling along the window sills, slow and reluctant to leave. Dafydd and Eirlys sat by the hearth, pale and sleepless. Catrin lay in her cradle, dreaming and laughingg].

Eirlys clasped her hands. "You saw how she looked at Catrin. She will come again."

Dafydd stared into the embers. "I know. But I don't know how to stop her."

But Eirlys lifted her head. "If we don't know, we must ask someone who does."

"Who?"

"Gwilym Hen," she said. "The cunning man."

Dafydd frowned. "He's not a respectable man."

"Gwilym knows their ways," said Eirlys. "And we need help."

"If he can help us, I'll give him every coin we have."

"So give it. What is gold," she said, "against love?"

She stood, took her shawl from the peg, and lifted Catrin into her arms. The three stepped out into the mist. The path was half-lost in fog. The child whimpered, but Dafydd lifted her and held her tight.

Gwilym Hen's cottage stood on the village's edge, roof sagging, chimney crooked. The scent of damp herbs hung in the still air. Eirlys knocked.

The door creaked open. Gwilym Hen blinked down at her, his eyes bright under bushy brows. "Eirlys Watcyn."

"Tomos now," she said.

His eyes shifted to Dafydd, then to Catrin. "Ah," he said. "And Dafydd Tomos. Henffych, and come in, all of you."

The interior of the Cunning Man's cottage was dim and fragrant, steeped in smoke and secrets. Bundles of drying herbs hung from the rafters in clusters—mugwort, brushed Dafydd's head as he entered. Twists of betony, with its crumpled purple blooms, hung beside sprigs of meadowsweet.. A thick rope of rowan berries, bright as blood, dangled near the hearth, their juice dried to the consistency of wax. Vervain, slender and brittle, crackled faintly in the heat, and from a beam above the fire hung a bundle of wild thyme, gathered from Mynydd Mawr, its scent strong and clean.

Shelves lined the walls, laden with stoppered jars and yellowing paper packets labelled in a cramped, looping hand—boneset, self-heal, solomon's seal, eyebright, and things in darker corners that Dafydd didn't try to read. Over the fire hung a blackened kettle and a cast-iron cauldron, while a row of foxglove heads, dry and papery, fluttered softly whenever the door creaked or the wind shifted.

A carved wooden mask with no eyes watched from the wall. The place smelled of peat smoke, beeswax, and the old man's tobacco.

He bid them sit by the fire.

"It's about our Catrin," said Eirlys. "The fairy queen has come for her. She says Dafydd owes her a debt."

They told him everything. He listened without interrupting.

"Aye," he said at last. "They never forget. And Rhianfellt—she's not the worst, but near it. She delights in causing unease among we ordinary folk."

"What can we do?" asked Eirlys. "How do we stop her?"

He leaned back. "The Fair Folk are old Clever, but not always wise. They are proud and they can be tricked, if you know how to use their arrogance against them."

Eirlys leaned forward. "How?"

"They are not flesh and blood. Not truly. They look like us, but they are nearer fire and storm. They do not know us as well as they pretend. For instance, they cannot always tell a child from a likeness—if the likeness carries love."

"What do you mean?"

"If you were to create a likeness of Catrin, and then hold it as if it were her, feeling the love you feel for the real Catrin."

"You mean make a doll?"

"Yes. A changeling in reverse," he said. "Clothe it in her clothes. Stitch it with her scent. Weave your love into every thread. Talk to it. Let it carry her memory."

Eirlys flinched. "And if it doesn't work?"

Eirlys stood. Her eyes shone.. "Then we'll make it. We'll do it now."

Gwilym laid a hand on her arm. "Go carefully. Their kind look for cracks in your courage. They will try to make you frightened. But love is your shield. Let it be stronger than fear."

Eirlys and Dafydd returned to the cottage, her heart heavy but their minds set.

"So what are we to do?" Dafydd asked.

"We're going to make a doll," she said, her voice steady. "A likeness of Catrin that will fool Rhianfellt."

Dafydd stared at her. "He's a strange old man, that Gwilym. Folk say he's crazy. I mean, a doll? Eirlys, that sounds—"

She cut him off, her gaze fierce. "Gwilym said it will work. We have to try."

He hesitated, then nodded. "Tell me what to do."

Together, they began. The fire crackled as they gathered Catrin's clothes, her blanket, and the toys she loved. Dafydd carved the wooden legs and the wooden arms, and used a wooden ball for its head; Eirlys stitched the fabric, her hands precise and trembling.

Catrin laughed from her bed as they worked, unaware of the danger hovering just beyond the hearth.

They whispered to the doll as they built it, naming it, praising it, murmuring their love into its seams. The room filled with a quiet intensity as they stitched fear into cloth and hope into wood.

When it was done, the doll lay in the cradle, dressed in Catrin's clothes, swaddled in her blanket. Imperfect, but perhaps close enough.

That night, the world held its breath. The mist pressed against the cottage like a living thing. Catrin slept in the pantry, wrapped in quilts, hidden from view. The doll lay by the fire, its face shadowed by flickering light.

Dafydd gripped the chair's arm, white-knuckled. "Do you think she'll be fooled?"

Eirlys kept her eyes on the cradle. "We must have faith."

The flames guttered. The mist thickened. The latch lifted without a sound.

Rhianfellt entered. Her silver hair shimmered in the firelight, her gaze sweeping the room. She moved like something conjured from snow and silence.

"Good evening, Dafydd Esgidiau," she said softly. Her eyes

turned to Eirlys. "And you, Eirlys. It moves me to see you both. Mortals love so deeply, and we cannot make such things ourselves. We come for love as the beekeeper comes for honey."

Eirlys rose, legs unsteady. "You've come for the child. Then take her."

Rhianfellt smiled. "Indeed. And there she is."

Dafydd stood, tense. "She's sleeping. Be gentle."

"How tender," Rhianfellt said with mild amusement.

She crossed to the cradle and bent over the doll. Her fingers brushed the blanket. Her eyes narrowed.

"She is warm," she murmured. She touched the doll's cheek. "And full of love. It warms my silver skin and my empty moonlit heart."

Eirlys forced herself to stay still.

Rhianfellt straightened. Her smile deepened. "You've cared for her well."

"She is precious to us," Eirlys said.

The Queen gathered the doll into her arms. "She will thrive in my realm. I'll give her gold and silver, milk and honey. She will dance beneath the stars from which we fell."

She turned toward the door.

But then she paused.

"You've been quiet," she said, thoughtful. "Strangely quiet."

Eirlys met her gaze. "What more could we say? You've taken what was promised. We kept the bargain."

Rhianfellt stared at her for a long moment. Then she smiled and stepped into the mist.

The door swung shut. Warmth returned. The fire rose. The cottage breathed again.

Eirlys sank into her chair, hands over her face. "She's gone."

Dafydd ran to the pantry. Catrin stirred, yawning. He lifted her, cradling her close. "She's safe."

Eirlys crossed the room and embraced them both, tears slipping down her cheeks.

Outside, the mist ebbed into the trees. But the sound of Rhianfellt's laughter lingered, faint and cold—a warning that the Fair Folk are not so easily fooled.

Dafydd and Eirlys sat close by the hearth, their breath shallow and their eyes red from a night spent waiting for the Fairy Queen to return. The mist had lifted and the weather was cold with hoar frost bearding the glass and sugaring their windows. The cottage lay quiet, and neither dared to sleep. Little Catrin rested against Eirlys's chest, warm and safe in her mother's arms. She slept peacefully, unaware of how close she had come to being taken.

"Do you think she'll return?" Dafydd asked.

Eirlys tightened her hold on Catrin. "She thinks she has what she came for," she said quietly, though doubt clung to her voice. "If we put enough love into the doll—loved it as if it were our child, even for a single day—and if what Gwilym said is true, that they cannot tell the living from the likeness, then surely she won't come back."

When the first light crept through the windowpanes, Dafydd rose to stoke the fire, seeking solace in the familiar rhythm of ordinary things. But before he could lay another log, a sound stopped him—a faint chime, delicate as bells caught in a passing breeze.

Both turned toward the door, their hearts held fast as the latch lifted. Rhianfellt stepped inside, her silver hair catching the morning light, her eyes glimmering with an unreadable warmth. She paused at the threshold, her presence transforming the modest room into something more like a court.

Eirlys stood, holding Catrin close. "You've taken the doll," she said, her voice steady. "It held the love you sought. What more do you want?"

Rhianfellt's lips curved into a faint smile, neither cruel nor kind. "I have not come to take," she said, her voice lilting with amusement. "I have come to give."

Dafydd stepped forward, fists clenched. "What trick is this? Haven't you tormented us enough?"

Rhianfellt tilted her head, her luminous eyes narrowing. "Tormented you?" she repeated, puzzled. "You mistake me, cobbler. I am not mortal to bear grudges. Your cunning amused me. Few dare deceive the Tylwyth Teg. Fewer still succeed."

Eirlys exchanged a wary glance with Dafydd. "What do you mean to give us?" she asked.

The Queen stepped further in and reached into the folds of her gown. She drew out a silver box no larger than her palm, patterned with stars and creeping vines. A faint light pulsed from within, casting shifting shadows across the walls. She placed it gently on the table.

"What is it?" Dafydd asked, his tone wary.

"A gift," said Rhianfellt. "A token of my amusement. And of my respect."

Eirlys frowned. "Why would you give us a gift after what we've done?"

Rhianfellt's smile widened. Her teeth caught the firelight, sharp as frost. "Because I can. Because I choose to. And because we Fair Folk are not as predictable as you mortals like to think. Don't trouble yourself trying to grasp my reasons, Eirlys Tomos. We are not you, as you are not us."

Eirlys shifted Catrin in her arms. Her voice dropped. "What's inside the box?"

Rhianfellt's laughter rang out, cold and clear. "That, dear mother, is for you to discover—when the time is right. Perhaps it holds treasures. Perhaps answers. Or perhaps nothing at all. The gift matters less than how you choose to receive it."

Dafydd's gaze flicked from box to Queen, his suspicion unrelieved. "And what of Catrin? Have you truly left her alone?"

Rhianfellt looked to the sleeping child, and her gaze softened. "If I cannot be her foster-mother, then I shall be her fairy godmother," she said. "She will walk in your world for the length of her mortal life. And when that life is done, she will come to my halls. She will dance beneath the hollow hill, and the Tylwyth Teg will make her welcome."

Eirlys shivered at the thought. But Rhianfellt's voice held no cruelty—only certainty. Catrin would not live as a human soul lives, nor die as a human soul dies. Perhaps that was a blessing, for which mortal girl would like not to die and to dance in the fairy halls forever?

Rhianfellt turned to the door. Her gown shimmered like ice. At the threshold, she glanced back.

"Guard her well, Dafydd Esgidiau and Eirlys Fwyn," she said, her eyes glinting. "But rest easy. She has my protection now."

Then she stepped into the mist. The air cleared. Frost melted from the windowpanes. Her laughter hung a moment in the doorway, and then it, too, was gone.

Dafydd and Eirlys stared at the silver box, its light still pulsing —faintly, steadily—as though it breathed.

Years passed in the hamlet of Gilfach Wen, and Catrin grew into a radiant young woman. Her golden hair caught the sunlight like spun silk, and her laughter lit the meadows with joy. Dafydd and Eirlys watched her with pride and love, though always with a shadow of unease. The memory of Rhianfellt lingered. Her gift sat untouched on the mantelpiece in its silver box, waiting for the moment they might dare to open it.

On the evening of her sixteenth birthday, Catrin sat by the hearth, the firelight warming her face. Her parents brought down the box, its engraved patterns glinting in the dim glow. Catrin's eyes sparkled with curiosity.

"What is it?" she asked, her voice full of wonder.

Eirlys and Dafydd exchanged a glance.

"It's a gift," Eirlys said softly, placing it in her hands. "From your godmother."

Catrin tilted her head. "My godmother? I didn't know I had one."

Dafydd's voice was quiet. "She's not like other godmothers. But she's always watched over you—even when unseen."

Catrin looked between them, unease flickering beneath her curiosity. "Who is she?"

Eirlys brushed a strand of hair from her daughter's brow. "She belongs to another world. But you need not fear her."

Catrin ran her fingers over the box, its surface cool beneath her touch. "May I open it?"

Dafydd nodded. "You're old enough now. It was always meant for you."

Catrin lifted the latch. The box opened with a faint chime, like distant bells in the wind. Inside, resting on a cushion of deep blue velvet, lay a silver comb. Its teeth were slender and smooth, shaped like the branches of a winter tree. The handle was engraved with stars and curling vines that shimmered faintly in the firelight.

"It's beautiful," Catrin murmured, her fingers hovering over it. "What does it do?"

Eirlys leaned forward. "We don't know. But we trust it was given in goodwill."

Catrin's eyes widened. "It's magic?"

Dafydd nodded. "I think so."

She picked up the comb. It was cool and oddly comforting in her hand. As she held it, warmth bloomed through her—a quiet clarity, as if some hidden strength had stirred. She ran it through her hair, and the sensation was strange and soothing, as though something long asleep had woken.

She set the comb back in its box and looked at her parents. "Why did she give this to me? What does she expect in return?"

Dafydd placed a hand on hers. "Because she chose to. The Fair Folk don't think as we do. Maybe she was amused. Maybe she saw something worth guarding."

Eirlys's voice was uncertain. "Or perhaps she meant you to be ready—whatever the road ahead may bring. The future is always unknown."

"But it always comes," Dafydd added.

Catrin stared at the comb a moment longer. Then she smiled and closed the lid. "If she's watching me, then I thank her," she said simply.

Over the years, Catrin grew into a young woman of rare beauty and grace. Her golden hair shone like sunlight, and her laughter rang clear as birdsong. Yet it was her wisdom—gifted, perhaps, by her godmother—that truly set her apart. She saw through others as clearly as shifting skies and carried herself with a calm assurance that left people hushed in her presence.

One bright spring morning, word reached the village that Lord Rhys of Dinefwr, famed for his ambition and generosity, was travelling through the region. His retinue arrived in splendour, banners snapping in the breeze, horses gleaming with fine tack. The villagers gathered as the nobleman dismounted in the square, his presence cool and commanding, his gaze sweeping the crowd and expecting the bows and curtsies he saw.

It was not long before he approached Dafydd's cottage. With his usual courtesy, Dafydd stepped outside to meet him, his lined face composed. Eirlys stood in the doorway, her arm around Catrin, who watched the nobleman with quiet curiosity.

"Dafydd Tomos, I have heard of your family," Lord Rhys began, his voice smooth. "And of your daughter's beauty and grace. Such qualities deserve to be nurtured in noble company. Let her serve as a lady-in-waiting at my court, and she shall know only privilege and safety."

Dafydd hesitated. The memory of past bargains burned behind his eyes. He glanced at Eirlys, who bit her lip—torn between pride that such a great lord would seek out her daughter, and fear that his offer was not as innocent as it seemed.

"My lord," Dafydd said carefully, "we are honoured. But we are simple folk. She is a good girl, but Catrin belongs here. This is her home."

Lord Rhys raised an eyebrow, more curious than offended. "Are you certain? What I offer is a life of refinement—education, fine company, the protection of noble walls. Surely that is better than the toil of village life."

Eirlys looked at her daughter. It should be Catrin's decision. "What do you think, cariad?" she asked softly. "It could be a great opportunity."

Catrin stepped forward, her eyes bright and steady. She curtsied with grace, then spoke in a voice quiet but clear. "Thank you, my lord, for your kindness and for honouring my family. But I will not leave my home."

Eirlys caught her breath. "Are you sure, Catrin?" she whispered, "This is a rare chance—"

Lord Rhys smiled. "It is rare indeed, but so is her beauty."

Catrin turned to her parents, her tone gentle but firm. "You've always taught me that happiness lives not in riches or promises of tomorrow, but in love and truth, here and now. And I belong here, with you, among those I love."

Lord Rhys studied her for a long moment. Then, to everyone's surprise, he smiled.

"You are wise beyond your years, Catrin of Gilfach Wen," he said. "Few speak so plainly. Fewer still speak from the heart. Your family is fortunate to have such a wise daughter."

He bowed, a gesture of rare respect for a lord so great as he, then mounted his horse. His retinue followed, and the sound of hooves faded into the hills.

And somewhere, beyond the veil of the mortal world, Rhianfellt watched. Her silver hair glinted like starlight, and she smiled —because Catrin was not like her father. Not at all.

PART SIX

Brittany

PART TWO

The Tower of Ker-Zu

Thirteen

MAY TIME WAS HERE, and the Forest of Brec'helean was heavy with blossom as Tristan bade farewell to the fortress of Ker-Wenn. The mayflower's sweet scent haunted the avenues between the trees, and small birds flitted from shade to sunshine through the undergrowth while Tristan Mab Bennog rode his bay mare Jezebel and hummed a song of his own composing. It was a song of love and loss, for he had loved, and they had lost.

His long fingers danced over the strings of the lute cradled in his left arm. Sitting back on his head was a wide-brimmed hat with a jay's feather in its band. This hat served to keep the sun out of his eyes while he played, though the sun was yet low and screened by thick undergrowth. A bird called raucously from the bushes. It seemed that all in the world was yet well.

Early that morning, the Lady of Ker-Wenn slipped a note under his door. The message warned him that her husband suspected their dalliance and that if Tristan valued his head, he should leave before breakfast. Tristan had sighed: They made excellent breakfasts there. And he had craved one last kiss from her apple-red lips. But Tristan was fly enough to know Fate's breeze blew in his face, not at his back so long as he lingered. So, slipping to the stable below, he saddled fleet Jezebel and fled.

Tristan made a practice of moving at Lady Luck's prompting, and in this way kept her favour. From the stone bridge outside the castle, he waved a fond farewell to his latest married ladylove and left. The dawn mist lifted from the clear-running River Arzh as he rode east, choosing to take the forest track.

They said that Brec'helean Forest was haunted. Tristan himself didn't fear ghosts, but he knew others did. Even brave men, handy with a sword, avoided the haunted glades of Brec'helean, and that could be handy for a fugitive.

And Tristan was often a fugitive from love, running from husbands at least once a month, so he knew the forest well.

He rode on, playing a chord progression on the lute and guiding Jezebel with his knees. The horse seemed to need little direction to keep on the path. She was used to his inattention. Tristan's head was always full of music or fair maidens, but the mare was the only constant female in his life. Tristan was a free spirit. He was a troubadour and bard by profession, but more than his work, his true passion was women.

As he strummed a whimsical chord sequence, his memory returned to that last lady. She, whom he would forever remember fondly, though sadly never see again, and whose name grew vaguer by the mile, had one day asked him whether he loved her.

When a woman asked that particular question, Tristan pushed back his hat with its feather, grasped her white hand between both of his, and said, "How could you doubt my love for you?"

He feigned an expression to suggest infinite hurt and melt her heart. Their hearts always melted. Hers did too.

Tristan would deny that there was any bad faith in this: in his own way, he loved all the women he bedded. He loved them intensely until it was time to leave.

How could he be expected to settle with one woman? The

world was filled with beautiful girls. And time and time again, he proved them ready to undo their bodices for the right song.

He knew other men were jealous of his success. He had what these louts lacked: his dark brown hair, his sea-blue eyes, his height, his lean muscled frame. Above all, he had his skill at words and music and indeed at every other art requiring delicacy of fingers or tongue.

To his mild annoyance, the last lady, one night after loving when he had intimated he had soon to move on, told him, "You should treat women better." What could she mean? When he was with them, they had his full attention and his temporary love. In any case, lady what's-her-name was the last adventure: the next lay ahead.

Jezebel plodded down the forest path where wayside flowers in yellows, blues and reds opened to the beauty of the May morning. As the mare went along, Tristran tried runs of notes that sang out sweet to his ears as his skipping fingertips strummed the catgut strings. He pushed back his hat and swept his dark hair from his brow so he could better see the frets. His finger danced, encircled by rings of silver and gold.

His placid mare strolled on. The day was warm, and the season was pleasant. For a long time, they rode along the forest road beside the brook that ran fast and clear over its bed of pebbles. Trout darted in the deep pools. Flies buzzed under the trees.

Tristan was so absorbed in his composition, that he didn't notice he was being watched. Sly faces stared from thickets, and glittering eyes watched from holes in the ground.

Then, when the day was nearly half done, his stomach told him he should soon eat. Jezebel would be glad of a chance to graze on the lush grass growing. The sun was not quite at noon, but they had started early. Tristan slung the lute on his back and leaned forward to stroke his mare's neck. "We will stop soon, Jezebel."

And then he saw a perfect place ahead. The trees widened out to his left. Here lay meadow, ankle-deep in grass, graced with yellow Tormentil and blue Speedwell. Dew starred the grass, and the meadow basked in the benediction of the morning sun.

Tristan clicked his tongue, and Jezebel neighed and slowed to a stop. Tristan slid from the saddle and took Jezebel's rein, strolling with her to the meadow. The mare grazed on the sweet grass, and he unpacked his food from the saddlebag. Here was white bread, ripe tomatoes with dried meat and dainty cakes all packed for him with love by his last lady.

He left Jezebel munching grass and sat on a flat stone by the stream. Shadowy fish darted from hiding places under rocks, and blue and crimson Kingfishers hunted them with beaks like spears, while green-gold dragonflies and iridescent damselflies darted over the rushing water. It was bliss. The words of the song that would woo his next woman came to his mind, and he sang them to the mild breeze.

Voices raised in anger broke the peace, and Tristan looked round for their source. He heard two or three gruff voices and one clearer one. Someone was being set upon out of sight. Tristan sighed and put down his bread and meat. He dusted flour off his palms and stood. Was this really his fight?

Tristan looked at his boots. They were a little scuffed. He glanced at the sky and tried to concentrate on the few puffy white clouds. Then he studied the butterflies that danced around the wild iris by the stream. But it was no good. His conscience would not let him stand by while some innocent person suffered: he would have to intervene. Tristan pulled his jerkin straight and squeezed the cramp from his neck.

Jezebel had pricked up her ears and was looking in the direction from which the shouting was coming. He patted her flank. His sword was tied to his pack and still sheathed, so he reached and pulled the blade from its scabbard. As he drew it, the sun gleamed on the sword.

For a minute, he hefted the weight of the sword in his hand, trying practice feints. The shouts of the victim grew more frantic. Facing their direction, Tristan moved forward.

He pushed a weave of hazel leaves and entered another clearing. This glade was a satellite to the large meadow he had come from, smaller with one entrance. All the other sides were hedged in by thorn bushes.

Three ugly men in dirty leather armour had blades drawn a knife, a sword and an axe. A boy, with short red hair, stood at bay. Against the knife, sword and axe, the lad held only a staff.

Tristan stepped forward, swept his hair from his face and saw how the sunlight struck his sword. He took a minute to admire the decorated hilt and a further few seconds to consider how his silver and gold rings gleamed in the sun, smiling as he recalled the lovers who'd donated each one. He lifted his hand, so the gems sparkled in the sun—yes they were gorgeous, then he cleared his throat and yelled, "What's going on here? It seems a little unfair for three to be fighting one."

An ugly man turned. He had black stubble, dark bags under his eyes, a scar running down his left cheek. When he spoke, his mouth revealed only a few rotten teeth. From his air, he appeared to be their leader. "Fuck off," he said. "This ain't your fight."

"It is if I make it mine," Tristan said to the boy. "Need a hand?"

The boy nodded. "These brigands set on me as I was walking home."

Seeing the lad distracted, a brigand rushed the boy. The boy raised his staff, and the poorly aimed blow went awry. The brigand leader ran, screaming at Tristan. Tristan sidestepped. The man went past, and Tristan smacked his arse with the flat of his sword. This enraged the man who turned and swung again. But the swing was wild and undisciplined, and Tristan's same sidestep tricked him again. Another blow to the arse, but this time edge on to cut. The brigand yelped like a dog.

Tristan yawned. He could do this all day, but looking over his shoulder, he saw the boy was hard-pressed by the other two brigands. Time to finish it. When his assailant ran at him again, Tristan gutted him with the ease of a butcher filleting steak.

The man fell to his knees, a surprised look on his brutish face. He collapsed sideways, fresh blood staining his filthy jerkin.

But the boy was being beaten. Tristan narrowed his eyes, picked his target and rushed the closest brigand. The oaf turned and saw him too late, then gasped as he took the point of Tristan's sword in the eye.

They were now down to one enemy.

Tristan smiled encouragingly at the boy, and the last brigand, with a glance at each of his erstwhile comrades, turned and fled.

The boy yelled and ran after the thief waving his staff, but the man had the fear of death upon him, and the boy knew danger was past. The brigand ran for his life while the boy stopped short, panting.

When the boy came back, Tristan was cleaning the blood off his sword on the grass.

"Thank you." The boy gasped, finally getting most of his breath back. "You saved my life."

"You're welcome," Tristan said. He winked. "Though it did interrupt my lunch."

The boy grinned. "Come back with me, and I'll make sure you get a good dinner."

Tristan sheathed his sword. "That sounds inviting. I think."

Catching sight of the rings on Tristan's hands, the boy said, "You must be rich. You should be careful in the forest."

"I'm not so rich," Tristan said. "And I can look after myself."

"I noticed." The boy extended his hand. "I'm Yann."

"A grand name," Tristan said, giving the hand a shake.

"My father had grand plans for me," said Yann. "I am named after the famous king, Yann Mab Yrien. He thought I would go to Court and win favour with the Duke."

"And you didn't?"

Yann shook his head. "Not yet."

"The Duke is overrated!" Tristan said.

"I'm surprised you dare say that."

Tristan made a show of peering around him. "I don't think his spies stretch this far."

Yann said, "You don't know who has eyes in the forest."

"The Duke?"

"Worse than the Duke."

Tristan smiled. "Come on, lead me to where I will get this dinner. And a comfortable bed, I hope?"

Yann said, "My father owns 'An Den Glas'—the Green Man —it's a famous inn in these parts." Then he paused. "The only inn in these parts."

They walked back towards where Jezebel was grazing again.

"Lovely horse," said Yann. "I look after the horses at the inn. I know a fine mare when I see one."

"She is a fine mare," Tristan said, stroking the blaze on Jezebel's brown nose. The horse snickered. Tristan felt her soft, warm breath on his palm and then stroked her nose.

"You're only light," Tristan said, looking at Yann. "I'm sure she can bear us both."

Both of them climbed on Jezebel's back, who set off without complaint to be carrying two.

The afternoon was still warm. Tristan was hungry again. "Is it far?" he said.

"Not so far."

"The forest is beautiful," Tristan said.

"She pretends to be," said the boy.

"The forest pretends to be beautiful?" Tristan said, puzzled.

"She has different moods," said the boy. "Just now she's kind and beautiful. But when the mood strikes her, she's vindictive and cruel."

"Sounds like a woman," Tristan said, smiling. The boy didn't speak. Perhaps he didn't know as much about women as Tristan did. Tristan leaned down from the saddle and plucked a long stem of grass. He chewed it thoughtfully as the horse ambled on.

"What are you doing here?" said Yann. "If I may be impertinent. I only ask because we get few visitors in these parts."

"But you run an inn!"

"Interesting visitors, I mean. We make our living selling ale to the locals and the odd bed for the night to passing merchants. Those who find the lure of profit stronger than the fear of the forest."

"Fear of the forest?" Tristan said. "Everyone talks about the haunted forest, but it's never bothered me. What's so frightening about it? Apart from brigands."

"The brigands are the least dangerous thing here." Yann paused and looked serious, sitting behind Tristan. He said, "The forest is filled with spirits."

"What kind of spirits? Brandy? Whisky? Schnapps?"

Yann frowned. "There is a tower in the middle of the forest. Though no man can find it unless the Lady of that place wishes him to."

"That sounds interesting," Tristan said. "I've never had any difficulty in making a woman want to find me."

"You're very sure of yourself."

Tristan laughed. "And who is this Lady?"

"She is a witch, but worse than that."

"Worse than a witch?"

Yann nodded. "She is a demon. If she was once human, she is not now."

"But she's still a woman, so she can be won over. Believe me." Tristan grinned.

Yann furrowed his brow. "She's no joke."

"I treat everything as a joke," Tristan said.

"Be careful," replied the young man. "One day, your pride will backfire, and someone will stop you laughing."

"You're too serious," Tristan said. He took off his jay-feather hat and twirled it around his finger. "Tell me more about this demon woman."

Yann shook his head. "She is very evil, the lady of the Dark Tower."

"And what is her name?"

"They call her the Lady Melusin."

"I will consider it a personal challenge to make her want to meet me," Tristan said.

The Green Man Inn stood by a crossroads in the middle of the forest. It took them an hour to ride there. The summer trees in their green raiment swayed in the slight breeze. There were a few dwelling houses nearby as well as an ostler, a blacksmith and a general provisions store. The cottages of the woodcutters and trappers crowded round the Green Man as if for safety. Around the hamlet's perimeter was a fence of sharpened wooden palings.

"What's the fence for?" Tristan said as he and Yann rode through the gate on the back of Jezebel.

"To keep the wolves and bears out. And the brigands," Yann said.

"But not the Lady Melusin?"

Yann whispered, "Don't joke about her. She might hear you."

Fourteen

THEY ARRIVED at the wide wooden door of the Green Man. The building was timber-framed and stood three storeys. There was a stable around the back, and Yann yelled for the stable lad's attention. When the boy came, Tristan commended Jezebel to him and slid a few deniers into his hand, telling him to take excellent care of his horse.

"Now. I'd like you to meet my parents," Yann said.

"My honour," Tristan said as they trotted up the wooden steps to the inn's front door.

Inside, a maid fetched a middle-aged man and woman. They looked like country sorts. They nodded at Tristan but initially said nothing.

Yann put his arm around Tristan's shoulder. "This man saved my life."

Tristan bowed.

Yann's parents listened with grave faces as the boy told them about the attack and Tristan's rescue of their son from the terrifying brigands.

Yann's mother dabbed her cheeks with her linen handkerchief. "We are eternally grateful."

"We are eternally in your debt," Yann's father said. "You must stay here as our guest as long as you wish."

Tristan bowed. "I'm not much of a stayer anywhere. But I will tarry awhile in this welcoming inn, and while I'm here, I won't stay for free—I will pay you with my music."

Yann's mother raised both eyebrows." You're a minstrel?" She turned to her husband. "I do not remember us ever having a visit from a minstrel!"

Her husband clasped her hands. "It will be a great treat for the Green Man and all our customers."

Tristan bowed again. "A bard, a troubadour, a minstrel, yes. And I will sing for you tonight."

It was then that a slender blonde girl caught Tristan's eye. From habit, he beamed at her. She glanced away shyly. Tristan nudged Yann and said, "You haven't introduced me to this lovely creature."

Yann smiled but his brow furrowed. "This is my fiancée, Arc'hantael."

Tristan bowed to Arc'hantael who had stepped closer. She studied Tristan without meeting his eye.

Tristan swept his jay-feathered hat down low. "I have seen many beautiful things today, but you are the fairest by far."

The girl blushed, She didn't take her eyes off him. "It's not often we get gallant strangers here."

Tristan guessed there were plenty of rough huntsmen passing through, eager for the summer ale and a grope of her bum if she didn't move deftly out of their way and then there were the fat merchants who might try to see how far they could get if they dropped a little gold. But intelligent, lyrical, handsome artists would be few and far between in this out of the way clearing in the forest. That was his trump card.

Arc'hantael suddenly glanced at Yann, who was staring at her. He turned and clapped Tristan on the shoulder and moved him away from the girl. "Come, let me show you the rest of the inn," he said.

The guest bedrooms were on the first floor above the bar. Yann explained that the family had their quarters on the storey above that. He showed Tristan to his room. The floor was of wooden beams, planed and then varnished. It was spotless. The walls were panelled in the same wood. There was a large bed with crisp white linen sheets and heavy woollen blankets, unlikely to be needed on these summer nights. Tristan went to the window. He looked out through the trees whose leaves were fine gold as the sun shone through them. The sky was still blue, and the clouds had all but disappeared. The sunshine was turning the rich butter yellow of evening as the golden orb began to dip in the west. Butterflies and honeybees buzzed around marigolds that grew in pots set outside the window on the sill.

"What a lovely place," Tristan said. "You're very lucky to live here." He turned, "And you're fortunate to be engaged to such a beautiful young woman. She'd be a rare gem in the city, but there won't be many like her for many miles around here."

Yann frowned. "Thank you. I am fortunate, as you say."

"She's beautiful." Tristan grinned. "Have you...?"

Yann reddened. "No, it's not our way. She remains a virgin."

Tristan slapped him on the back and laughed. "Good for you."

Yann sighed. "I love her. But I worry I bore her. Her head's always full of stories, and she has ideas of travelling to Roazhon and seeing the Duke."

"You could do that," Tristan said. "Roazhon is lovely: the tall castle on the hill above the city made of gleaming white stone and the way the red-roofed houses crowd on the tongue of land between the three rivers where they come to the silver sea."

Yann said, "My future is here in this village." He sighed. "But if I were able to talk like you, Arc'hantael wouldn't find me boring."

"You have other qualities," Tristan said. "You're brave and courteous for a start."

But Yann wasn't listening. "I know it would be easy for you to take her from me. I saw her looking at you."

Tristan sighed. "It wouldn't be the act of a friend to steal another man's betrothed."

Yann said, "Thank you. I do believe you to be an honourable man. You came to save me, involving yourself in my trouble."

Tristan said, "Anyone would have done the same."

Yann shook his head. "No, most people would have walked away. I know you will always do the right thing." Yann walked to the door. As he was going out, he hesitated. "But I guess you have stolen many a man's woman."

"That was different. They weren't my friends," Tristan said. "Anyway, what time do we eat?"

After Tristan napped, he got up, washed and dressed. With the coming of evening, the forest grew cold. Through the window, the pinpricks of the stars pierced the dark blue sky. Tristan left his room, not bothering to lock it, and went down to the inn's common room.

He had his lute with him. There were long wooden trestle tables across the bar, and huge log fire burned in the hearth. Yann greeted him warmly and showed him to his table. Tristan saw that Arc'hantael was working—taking the food to the tables. Trying to be discreet, he admired her long blonde hair and her slender figure. Despite his attempt at discretion, Yann saw him looking and frowned. Not good.

Arc'hantael brought him roast pork with sweet potatoes and carrots and onions from the garden behind the inn. Then she brought him a flagon of brown ale.

She lingered as if wanting to chat. He thanked her with a smile but cut the conversation short for Yann's sake. Then he watched her walk away, and he sighed and lifted the ale to his mouth. She was stunning, and she was interested. But a promise was a promise.

Tristan glanced over to where Yann stood next to his father by the bar. Yann looked back at him with slow anger in his eyes. Tristan smiled, but the young man did not return his smile. He was doing his best not to encourage Arc'hantael. He couldn't help that she found him attractive.

Tristan smiled and mouthed, "The food was great." This time, Yann smiled back, but it was with effort, and he looked troubled.

And when he finished his meal, Yann showed him to a stool so he could play. Tristan took the lute and began to tune it, plucking at the strings and running up scales and arpeggios until he was content that the instrument sounded its best. And then, while the folk in the bar waited with quiet anticipation, he struck the first chord and sang.

Tristan's rich baritone voice rang out. He sang a song of loving and losing. His voice was rich and deep, and all the women fell in love with him with his dark hair and his clever fingers. The instrument flowed as sweet as honey and as clear as water. And then when their hearts were full of love, he sang a song of warring and winning, and their spirits grew proud with honour and camerarderie and loyalty fast unto death. All the women loved him, and all the men envied him.

Tristan sang for an hour. People bought him drinks, and he grew merrier and sang songs that made the audience laugh. Then he sang for an hour more. It was near midnight. The candles burned low and the fire went to embers and the mood changed and the shadows grew in the corners, and Tristan sang about *An Itron Gaer Zidruez,* who in French is the *La Belle Dame Sans Merci*: the beautiful woman with no kindness.

"That's a story about the Lady Melusin," a rustic chap with a leather tankard in his fist yelled. The others hissed him to be quiet. "But it is," he said, but shame-faced for speaking her name.

Another one, half-drunk said, "This singer thinks he's a charmer, but she's one woman he could never win round."

Yann's father suddenly spoke up. "Don't talk about Lady Melusin. We don't want the Green Man to become a target of her ill-favour."

Tristan sang another song gathering nuts and kissing in the hazel bushes. Then another song, then another until the drunks were drunker than before and the lonely hearts even more misty-eyed.

And as the owls called from the trees outside, the evening's entertainment drew to a close. People applauded. They crowded round him as if they wanted to take some of him home with them —the young girls with bright eyes, the middle-aged married women with lustful ones. The men clapped him on the back and said they'd love to hear him play again sometime.

"Well, Tristan?" said Yann. "Will you stay another night?" He said it in a way that sounded as if that was the last thing he wanted.

Arc'hantael stood close by Tristan, and Yann moved to block her, but still the candles of her eyes flared when Tristan looked at her. "Please?" she said.

Tristan shrugged. "I think I'll be off tomorrow."

Yann exhaled with relief. Arc'hantael squeezed her fingers as if she was about to ask him to reconsider, but Yann turned to her, and she fell quiet. She looked at her feet then back at Tristan. Her cheeks were flushed.

Tristan thought it was time to say goodnight. He made to get up.

Arc'hantael put her hand on his arm and said, "Do you have to go to bed yet? Perhaps you could play some more?"

"It's late," Yann said.

"Aye, it's late," Tristan agreed. "I should go to bed."

"Or if you are too tired to play more, you could tell us some stories."

Arc'hantael was almost pleading.

Tristan sighed.

The bar was nearly empty now. Yann's mother was clearing up behind the bar. His father was in the kitchen. Arc'hantael sat down next to Tristan. "Tell me about Roazhon. Yann says, you know the city well. Tell me about the Duke, and especially the Duchess. Is it true that you know her?"

Yann stood behind her with eyes like thunder. "Tristan must be tired."

"Sing me a song of far off places. Somewhere you've been." Hers were misty.

"I'm tired," Tristan said, smiling.

Yann glowered at both of them for a second, and then he stalked off.

"I don't think Yann is pleased," Tristan said.

"He's jealous," said Arc'hantael, her head cocked, ignoring her fiancé and staring at Tristan as if she'd found something rare and beautiful.

Tristan said softly, "I don't want him to be jealous."

"I don't have much experience of the world," said Arc'hantael, "but I've never known anyone like you." Her voice was full of yearning. "All the boys here are farmers or woodcutters. We don't have any singers," she said with a dismissive wave of her hand. "Nobody like you."

"I was born the lowest of the low," Tristan said.

She looked at the rings on his hand, and she reached out and touched them. "To us, you seem rich."

He made a fist. "These? All gifts."

"You earned them with your talent."

He smiled thinly and said, "Yes. But not with my musical talent."

She laughed. "Then which talent?"

He thought how naïve she was and tried to shock her to scare her off. "With my talent at seduction," he said finally.

"Ah." Her speedwell-blue eyes remained on him. His comment had had the opposite effect entirely to what he'd hoped.

"I'm a virgin," she said, head down.

"And you shall stay that way, as far as I'm concerned."

Just then, Yann came to the door and barked into the room. "I thought you were going to bed, Tristan, and you have work tomorrow, Arc'hantael!"

Tristan looked up at the boy. "I am going up now," he said, his tone conciliatory.

"And you're still leaving tomorrow?" asked Arc'hantael.

"Tomorrow, I've decided I'm going to find the Lady Melusin."

Arc'hantael's eyes widened. She put her hand to her throat.

Yann shook his head scornfully. "Then you go to your death."

"I don't mind danger," Tristan said mildly.

"So how do you plan to find her?" said Arc'hantael. "They say you can't find her unless she wants you to."

"I can make her want to meet me," he said.

"You're very arrogant," Yann said.

"It suits him", Arc'hantael said. Yann watched her do it. "Be careful," she said. "Melusin likes pretty men."

"This is a very foolish thing to do." Yann said. "But it is your decision to make."

"I will head into the heart of the forest. I'm sure to find her there," Tristan said.

Yann nodded. "I disagree with you going. It's pointless throwing your life away in your silly arrogance. Melusin is wicked and cruel."

"They say no man can defeat her," said Arc'hantael.

Tristan laughed. "She'll fall as they all do—after all, she's only a woman."

In the morning, Tristan ate a leisurely breakfast sitting outside the Green Man at the back, perched on a stump of wood. Arc'hantael brought him his food and offered him beer, but he accepted only water drawn from the inn's well.

"I'm sorry you're leaving," said Arc'hantael. Her blue eyes fixed him as she stood, blonde tresses falling over her shoulders. She waited there, half-nervous, half-entranced by him. "I don't think you should go looking for trouble," she said.

He shrugged and stood. "Trouble is an adventure."

"Nobody here has much thirst for adventure."

"It's not for me to judge others," Tristan said, standing. He looked toward the stable. "Jezebel has eaten?"

"Why don't you take me with you?" She said it as if it was a joke, but he knew she was serious. "We could see all the cities and the sea and the stars over Jerusalem. Things I'd never see if I stayed here and married Yann."

Tristan smiled, trying to be kind. "Maybe I'll come back here."

Quickly, she said, "I'd like that. But you won't."

She was right. Tristan would never come back. He knew coming back would cause heartbreak, and he didn't want to hurt her or Yann. He put on his jay-feather hat and twisted the rings on his fingers, so the various runes and glittering stones faced upwards and were straight.

"Yann is bringing your horse," Arc'hantael said. "I can meet you outside the village if you wait."

"You're a bright and beautiful young woman, but your path isn't with me."

She said quietly, "Have you had a lot of women?"

He smiled but didn't answer.

"Did you ever fall in love with any of them?" she said.

He shook his head. "I've never been in love."

"So you have never lost your heart?"

"No."

"I've lost mine," she said.

She turned and reached to the rose bush behind her. The green leaves were still beaded with dew. Red roses grew on it, some in full bloom and others still buds. She plucked a bud. "Here," she said. "Remember me when you look at this."

He took the rose but said, "It will fade."

"As I will fade from your memory."

They turned to see Yann appear, leading Jezebel. Tristan stepped away from Arc'hantael. He called his horse. She looked well-rested and whinnied when she saw her master.

"Thank you," Tristan said, offering the boy a coin. Yann looked at it but did not reach out his hand. "I won't accept money from the man who saved my life."

Tristan bowed. "Thank you for your hospitality. And thank your mother and father on my behalf."

Yann bowed. "And if you ever come this way again..." Tristan knew he didn't mean it. He saw Yann glance at Arc'hantael from the corner of his eye. She stared at Tristan. No, Tristan said to himself — I won't be back.

Then Tristan mounted Jezebel. He clicked his tongue, and she moved off. Arc'hantael watched him as he disappeared into the forest, the lute on his back, a jay's feather in his broad-brimmed hat.

Fifteen

TRISTAN AND JEZEBEL made their way into the heart of the wood, and soon they were far away from the Green Man and their only companions were the trees and the animals. The path here was much less used and more overgrown than the broad one they had taken to the inn the previous day.

With his head full of music and thoughts full of escape, Tristan forgot his quest to look for the Lady Melusin. Jezebel trotted on. Tristan was a flighty man, whose interests changed as quickly as the buzzing bees move from flowerhead to flowerhead. He now considered making his way to another castle, singing for his supper and having some fun.

Often, Tristan thought making love to a knight's bored wife was a duty. Usually, the wives were well educated, but ill-matched with a drunken boor. Always, they lapped up his news of Court, and Duke, and the city of Roazhon. Unfailingly, his music won their hearts and loosened their vows.

Tristan liked women. He liked to seduce them and make them love him. So why not Arc'hantael? He could have stayed at The Green Man a few more days.

In fact, why didn't he have his way with her and move on as

usual? She had a fine body, and he knew he could please her in bed. Sadly, please her better than Yann ever would.

And as he thought this, Tristan cursed himself for a rogue — Arc'hantael was different. She was as innocent as all the other women had been worldly. He said out loud to the breeze. "Maybe I'm developing a conscience?"

He remembered his boast to make the dark lady of the forest come to him. He had spoken with bravado at the time, but in truth, when he said it, he doubted she existed — just another peasant fear of the dark.

This was no time to think of shadows and fears. It was a fine summer morning. He thought that he would head east for the town of Trec'horanteg where he would find the lovely dark-haired Klervi or her sister Solen. If he were lucky, one or both of their husbands might be away hunting.

Around lunchtime, Tristan came across a deep river. He thought this must be the River Muc'huz, named after jet because it ran almost black. An ancient bridge arched over it, of ancient appearance, built of pink granite, and below it a pool where the water ran dark from the peat in the hills from where it rose.

Tristan dismounted and opened the packet of food that Arc'hantael had prepared for him. She had put cakes and apple from Penn ar Bed as well as cuts of spicy sausage and cheese from Penn ar Menez. She had also put little violets on top of the food. He remembered that those were the flowers given by country maids to the lads they loved, and he smiled and shook his head.

Tristan sat on the bridge, dangling his legs and eating his lunch while Jezebel grazed behind him and buzzards circled on currents of air high above, the quiet broken only by their mewing cries. Bees and flies fussed around the nearby flowers, and the air hung sweet with the fragrance of purple clover and the perfume of roses and honeysuckle that came from the bushes on the other side of the bridge.

Tristan was hot. He decided to swim. He took off his jerkin

and then his cambric shirt. He removed his calf-length soft leather boots and then his trousers. He then stripped of his undergarments and stood, enjoying the feel of the sun on his flesh. He was lean and long. His muscles were well defined but not bulky. His feet were strong and graced by a few sprouts of curly brown hair on their tops and on his toes. Not bad, he thought.

He dived from the bridge, and the cold of the stream shocked him. He ducked his head and swam underwater to where the river was deep, stopping at the granite margin which the water had worn away through ten thousand winter floods.

Languidly, he turned on his back and took a few backstrokes to take him where he had jumped in. He played a game, just kicking and using his hands enough to keep steady against the current as he stared at a blue sky framed by the foliage of the summer trees.

And then he heard Jezebel whinny. He raised his head, the water running from his ears and hair.

"What's the matter, my lass?" he shouted.

The horse whinnied again. It was probably nothing, but, now alert, Tristan swam to the stream's edge and pulled himself out. He stood on the pebbles, naked, water streaming down his chest and arms. He could see no one, but he sensed a presence. He walked stealthily towards Jezebel and, still naked, pulled his sword from its sheath.

At the corner of his eye, something moved. Tristan spun around, brandishing his blade before him. But nothing again. Nothing at all.

Or was there?

The undergrowth fluttered He peered into the dim forest, over-canopied by oaks and ashes. It was darker there than it should have been—as if night had visited day. Someone had been there, and it was a woman.

But now, she was gone. Tristan scanned the undergrowth on

all sides, but she was nowhere to be seen. He let the warm sun dry him. Then he put his clothes back on.

Tristan mounted Jezebel and set off along the path. After a while, the track seemed to peter out.

Grass stood tall in the middle of the trail and, as he rode, all over until it was a trail no more. The ground grew rushy and damp. Low tree branches blocked it, and Tristan had to dismount. He led Jezebel by her rein, looking for any gap in the trees that might suggest better passage. He decided they had taken a wrong turn and would need to retrace their steps. But he could not find any way back to retrace nor anything that looked like a proper way.

"Hmm," he said, stroking his horse's neck. "Jezebel, I think we're lost."

They stumbled around in the wood for half an hour, then an hour, and then two hours. Tristan became more and more frustrated. He ate what was left of the food. It seemed that whatever direction he took, the woods grew thicker. And it was getting unaccountably dark.

At this time of the year in Brittany, the days were long, and the sun should not set until much later. But here, it was gloomy. He got a shiver between his shoulder blades — a feeling he was being watched.

Even Jezebel seemed wary of the shifting shadows.

"I don't like this place, my girl," Tristan said.

When the dusk was thick and the forest heavy with the stink of wild garlic, at last, they struck upon a roadway of some kind. This path was wide and well-appointed. It must come from somewhere and go to somewhere else, but still, he was suspicious. To what danger did it lead? To wander around in the darkening wood was feebleminded, but Tristan worried that taking that dim way was foolish as well. He waited a while without moving.

"What choice do we have?" he said finally to the horse.

The trail was clear enough from stray branches for him to mount now, so he swung up onto Jezebel's saddle. As they walked forward, he kept one hand on the pommel of his sword. He and Jezebel plodded their way down the track while crows cawed from their hiding places in the funereal trees that lined their road. It was too dark. Dark far sooner than it should have been.

"This is most unnatural, Jezebel," he said.

The mare whinnied and shook her mane.

The undergrowth changed. The trees were no longer the happy oaks of the wide summer forest, but instead, weed-hung things whose name Tristan did not know.

The ground either side of the path was choked in briars and bramble but here and there bloomed the bright berries of the deadly nightshade.

They walked the path for the best part of an hour, Tristan starting at shadows and drawing his sword more than once at sounds and screeches in the shadow-haunted woods.

And then, ahead of him, the battlements of a stone tower appeared. The tower rose tall above the trees, red-black and riven from volcanic rock, bloody and flat in colour, drenched in dark moods and pregnant with great melancholy. Windows ran up its length, but they lay lightless. A great door stood at the bottom, fashioned of dark wood and studded with bosses of black metal. As he grew closer, Tristan saw a heavy knocker —a twisted iron ring painted black, shaped like a serpent, and this snake's body was held in an iron devil's mouth.

"I think I've found the Dark Lady's house," he said.

Tristan dismounted and stepped over to the door. Behind him, Jezebel stood. She stamped her fore-hoof and shifted as he approached the massive door. Tristan hesitated then took the iron ring in his hand. It was full night, with not even a ghostly remembrance of day lingering in the western sky and there were no stars. Tristan thudded the ring against the thick wooden door. The blow echoed in the gloomy grove. Crows croaked and lifted into the air at the sound, but no human answered. He lifted the ring again and again struck the door with it. The same dull sound rang out. Disquiet possessed him as if the knocker spoke a secret name, and that name summoned something that a god-fearing man should never call. The crows flapped around the clearing, their wings fluttered in the tenebrous air above his head.

Still no one came. He turned to Jezebel. "The place must be empty."

The horse didn't answer.

"So what do I do now?" Tristan mused. He retired from the door and back to Jezebel. She was still stamping and rolling her eyes. The horse seemed keen to leave the place. Tristan looked ahead. The track they had been on led on further past the castle, going to who knows where. But who knows where might be better than here that he now knew too well. He was about to mount into the saddle when he turned to see the door to the tower open soundlessly.

"What witchcraft is this?" he said aloud. Tristan reached for his sword. He drew it from his sheath. Even in the dark, the metal shone, and that gave him comfort for he knew the sword's keen edge, and he was confident in his skill to wield it.

From nowhere, a woman's voice whispered, "Your blade will be no use to you here, minstrel."

The voice that called out to Tristan from the gloom around the tower was soft as balm and sonorous. Its tone was like a song that draws deep emotions from the hearer. At first, he couldn't see the bearer of the voice, but as his eyes stared into the darkness, the shadows became a woman, and she stood, imperious and bold, beside the gate.

She was tall with sable hair, black as the raven's wing: fuliginous, lustrous, wondrous and rich. Her hair reached down her back even unto her waist, her skin was pale as January snow, and her lips were red and ripe as crimson haws.

Her teeth gleamed white and sharp, and her eyes burned so dark that they might be midnight's font and origin. This woman's black eyes followed every move Tristan made, and there was a hypnotic power in her gaze. Tristan felt a strange flood of emotions in his gut: fear, yes, but lust also, and a peculiar humility that was unfamiliar to him.

"I'm sorry, my lady. I didn't see you at first," Tristan said, but his hand still gripped the sword. He tried to unsheathe it, but his movements were dull and uncoordinated. He couldn't make his hand do what he wanted it to, and he knew she was the cause of it.

"Welcome to my home Tristan Mab Bennog," she said, "I heard you were looking for me."

"Forgive me, lady, but you are?"

She laughed. "You well know who I am. Some of your comments about me were over boastful."

He felt himself blush. How did she know that? Maybe she did have spies everywhere.

"You wanted me to come to you, so I came to find you," she said. "I enjoyed watching you swim. Your naked form pleased me."

"You know my name," Tristan said, trying to recover his composure. "But I don't know yours."

The woman laughed, mocking him gently. "I think you do. I am the Lady Melusin. I believe you said that I was *only a woman* with the implication that I would be overpowered by your beauty and wit and soon become another of your conquests."

She mocked him, and he felt a cold in his throat. Her power was almost palpable and there was something sinister and threatening about her. He as far away from any help. He tried to speak, but he was tongue-tied. He could not use his eloquence. The words that were his tools and gift stuttered, refusing to leave his mouth. A chill of fear rose in his chest, its cold reaching even to his blinking eyes, and he fought to stop it showing.

Melusin watched him with cruel amusement. "I think I will invite you into my house, where you can keep me entertained." She beckoned him with her long black-nailed finger. And Tristan walked, not of his own will, but by hers, through the heavy oak door and up the stone steps of the tower, sword still in hand, but now useless.

Despite the summer he had not long left, the tower was filled with the chill of winter. They climbed the stone spiral stairs, turn after turn until they were very high. She opened a door and led him in.

Tristan stood in a stone chamber, its walls covered by tapestries depicting murder and crucifixion. The stone floor was carpeted with rich rugs of reds and orange and brown. Wooden chairs and sofas furnished the room, draped in the furs of wolves and bears. There was a fire set in the wall. Flames of blue and white blazed around glowing coals in a deep-set stone hearth. There was only one window, a narrow slit, and by it, a perch upon which a raven sat watching him with bright eyes.

Candles burned and dripped black wax, their light flickering and throwing shadows on the stone walls.

The Lady Melusin stood watching him. She pointed to the sword in his hand and said, "You will not need that."

He looked at his sword as if just remembering it. His mind felt sluggish, thick with some intoxicant. He let the sword drop, and it hit the rug below his feet with a muffled noise.

"My horse?" he said.

The Lady Melusin smiled, her incisors were sharp, and their white enamel gleamed, her moist lips red as blood. He was close to her now. "Sit," she said.

And he sat.

In her chambers she was not disguised with shadows and he saw her clearly for the first time. She wore a cloak of raven's feathers, glittering iridescently as she moved. The pale flesh of her throat and shoulders was bare. Her gown was of a crimson samite, and sewn into it with gold thread were the images of winged demons with hawks' faces. A line of pearl buttons ran down from her pale chest. Around her wrists were bangles of gold encrusted with gems and on her fingers rings of jade and platinum. Her nails were sharp and black. He stood befuddled while she walked towards him. Standing close, she towered over him. Her beauty filled his vision and was all he could think of.

She tilted her head and said, "And now, minstrel, will you play for me?"

"My lute is on the horse," he said.

She indicated with her eyes that his lute was beside him.

His brow furrowed. "How?"

"My servants brought it."

"I saw no servants."

She shrugged, her lustrous hair sweeping across her bare shoulders. "Servants are not to be seen."

Tristan fumbled for his lute. Though his mind felt slowed, his fingers were nimble; it seemed her magic allowed that. Quickly he ran through intricate webs of notes. He played high, and then his fingers slid to play low. He played melodies so beautiful that they brought sadness deeper than tears, a sadness that choked the listener. Though not her.

He played rapid rills of notes that resembled rain; he played quick torrents of chords to conjure flowing birdsong. Melusin watched, inscrutable, her eyes never leaving him. Sometimes she watched his fingers, and sometimes she watched his face. As he played, his mind began to clear.

He looked to see whether he pleased her, but he could not read past the faint smile on her alabaster face. He paused.

She clapped. "Bravo, you have played of life."

He bowed, smiling.

Her face grew cold, "But now," she said, "play of death."

And his fingers moved without him willing it, finding deep chords that were strange to him. The rhythm was strong and pulsing, bringing to mind the sound the oars make when we are ferried across the final river.

Tristan's skin went icy-cold as if he were dragging his fingers through the water of the river of death. The room darkened until the only thing he could see was her face — her slanted cheekbones, her full mouth and above the mouth, her awful black eyes.

He played on. Then he did not know if he was still playing, but he heard the music yet. The lute lay discarded to his side. And she was close to him, and her hands undressed him. They ran over his broad shoulders, examining them, admiring his muscles and they caressed his brown arms.

Then she undressed, dropping cloak and gown to fall around her feet. Her flesh was the white of bone against his tanned skin. Her breasts swelled like a young woman's, though she could not be young. Her nipples were red as dark grapes, and they stiffened and brushed his chest. She lent in to kiss him, and he felt the soft weight of her long hair over his face and shoulders. She settled on his thigh, and he felt her sex press against him. He felt the moist warmth of her eagerness.

The touch of her fingers was like ice; it shocked and thrilled him as her hands ran over his face. He desired her cold more than any heat he'd ever had. She was the pale moon, and for her touch, he would forsake the sun. But while her fingers and her mouth and her skin were chill, her sex was a pit of burning ice. Her fingers reached down and grasped his hardness.

How proud he was of its length and girth. How the girls had whispered of it and how they chased after him, eager to feel it inside them. The Lady Melusin guided and lowered herself onto him, sheathing it like a sword in a scabbard. All Tristan's arrogance in his skilful lovemaking was gone. First, she rode him; then she took him as a mare takes a stallion. When he was spent, she demanded more. Despite the cold of her skin, he sweated. And when he had ridden her more times than he had ridden any woman, she let him rest. He lay there, his head on her breast, and she stroked his hair like he was her pet.

"You satisfy me, Tristan."

He said nothing. He was weak from her. He was a mouse in the presence of a cat. She was the Lady Melusin, and she had taken him between her legs, but on her terms, and he knew when he failed to please her, his life would end.

Then he felt pain at his neck. He put his fingers there and drew them away covered in red. In the heat of their mating, he had not noticed, but now he looked and saw he was bleeding. The blood ran from his throat to his chest.

He stared at the red on his fingers. "What have you done?".

Melusin looked at Tristan with an emotion in her eyes that was almost like affection, if a predator can have affection for its prey.

She ran her fingers through his brown hair. "I feed from your life, my little Tristan. With one hand, she reached and cupped his balls. "I take this," Then with the other hand, she adrew her fingers down the line of his jugular vein, "And this."

She smiled with her, and he saw the trace of his dried blood around her lips. "But in return, you get this." She stroked her mons pubis with its covering of hair black and soft as sable. "A good trade?"

He struggled to sit. He fought to wake from this dream of sex and death.

She allowed him to stand. He pulled on his trousers.

She laughed softly. "You have abused women all your life, Tristan. And now you begrudge one abusing you?"

He shook his head as he pulled on his shirt. "I abused no woman. All of them came of their own free will."

"Mostly true," she said. "But their free will was influenced by your little tricks. The way you told the ugly girls they were pretty and the way you told the pretty girls they were clever. And then your music and the honeyed promises you never meant to keep: *I love only you... You are the most beautiful... I dream of you, my love...* And to the virgin girls, you sneaked from their father's houses you'd say: *How can it be bad if we both want it?*"

"And to the married women you laid in their husband's beds, you'd whisper: *Your husband doesn't need to know... Don't you deserve some pleasure too?* Yes, Tristan, you have used your talents well. It's just a pity they were always for your own selfish ends."

Tristan pulled on his boots. He bowed, trying to muster his charm and manners. "I have enjoyed our time together, my lady." He frowned. "Indeed, I have never known lovemaking so intoxicating. But I must leave."

She was still naked. She sat, legs akimbo. The swell of her breasts, her wide hips and her sex plump and dark as a well-fed cat stiffened him again. But now his lust was sharpened by fear. He was arrogant. He had thought his charm could overcome any woman, but Melusin was different. He had no power over her.

She stood languidly and walked over to the fireplace. He watched her swaying stroll, her full buttocks, her waist, and the way her hair moved as she walked. She reached up to a crystal decanter filled with red wine.

It had not been there before: her servants again. He wondered what else they'd seen, or even if they had any interest in what their mistress did.

Melusin poured the red liquid into a crystal glass. She handed it to him, taking her his hand in hers and pressing the glass into his palm. She closed his fingers around it. "Drink."

"I must leave, my lady," he said, but took the glass anyway. He felt her influence on him again. She made him do what she wanted, not what he knew was best. He sipped. The liquid was not cold as he expected, and it was not wine. It was warm. It tasted of salt and iron. He spat it out. "Blood!"

She laughed. "I thought you needed some to replace what I took."

He wiped his mouth and put the glass on a nearby table. "This is my blood?"

She took his glass and swallowed what was left of the blood. She licked her lips, lasciviously with her pink tongue. "No, it's the blood of a virgin. Which, you cannot claim to be," she said. She found the whole thing amusing as if his revulsion was a joke.

And then the raven on its perch, which had been quiet through all their lovemaking, squawked. Tristan turned around, but the bird was looking not at him, but at the opening door.

Sixteen

TRISTAN HEARD steps outside the chamber, and then the door swung open. Wearing lacquered armour with a scimitar at his hip, a tall black-haired man entered. He gazed at Tristan and his lip curled with disdain. The man's eyes were red as fire, and his teeth were cruel and sharp, protruding over his swollen lips. His face was misshapen and evil radiated from him.

Tristan stepped back.

The naked Lady Melusin said, "Tristan, bid good day to my husband."

The man glowered at her nakedness then snarled at Tristan, "You are a brave man indeed to come here, or a foolish one."

"Perhaps both,' Lady Melusin said.

Tristan bowed. "I'm sorry my Lord; you have the advantage of me. I don't know your name."

The man showed rows of vicious teeth that ran down his throat like those of a shark, multiple and keen as razors. His incisors were as long as a snake's and his eyes burned with red hate for humanity.

The Lady Melusin smiled and said, "This is the Lord Iblis."

The man said disdainfully, "It seems you have just cuckolded me. You should know there is a price to pay for that."

Melusin raised a warning finger. "He's mine, and it's not the first time you've been cuckolded."

"No, you wanton. Nor the hundredth. But still, I will bleed him until his flesh is white," Lord Iblis snarled.

Melusin shook her head. "It is I who will bleed him in my own good time."

Iblis stalked fully into the room, and his armour chinked with each step. He walked with a strange grace, and Tristan felt his hair prickle as an ancient fear gripped him. He stood before humankind's predator, and terror filled him in its presence. Fighting to keep his voice steady, fixing the thing with an unblinking gaze, he muttered, "As I said, I'll be leaving."

He stooped to pick up the sword where he'd dropped it, forgotten while Melusin took her pleasure with him.

As Tristan bent, he felt Iblis's eyes burning into him, and painful fire ran down every vein of his body. Glancing up to see the cause of his pain, the monster's eyes held him, and he felt the sword fall from his numb fingers. Tristan tried to walk to the door —he forced his legs to move, but they did not obey him, it was as if they were someone else's limbs. He budged them slowly by a massive effort of will, but the distance he walked was small. His feet were heavy and unbiddable. Then his legs stopped moving altogether.

Iblis sneered, "Now, worm, you will pray to me," and Tristan felt his hands moving and forming the attitude of supplication before the thing that stood before him. Iblis laughed, showing his teeth like a cobra. Tristan struggled, but he had no power against Iblis's mocking gaze.

"Leave him," Melusin said. "He pleases me."

Her husband snapped. "Cover yourself—you disgust me."

Melusin dressed slowly, drawing out each movement to taunt

him. Tristan feared that if she made him too angry, Iblis would use his will to snap him like a dry stick and upset her that way.

"There," Melusin said, buttoning up her dress and pulling the cloak of feathers onto her shoulders. "I am dressed. Now leave him."

Iblis let Tristan slump and the minstrel fell backwards onto a chair, his ringed fingers heavy and hanging; his handsome face pale, a slick of hair over his damp brow.

"If I let you keep him, what will you give me?" said Iblis to his wife.

Melusin sighed and came over to Tristan. She stood behind him and stroked his head as if he were her pet dog. "What do you want?" she said.

"I want the blonde virgin and her lover—the ones you caught today."

Melusin exhaled impatiently. "I have hardly tasted them yet."

"Give me them or I will kill your minstrel now."

With an air of terrible boredom, Melusin said, "Very well, you can have the boy. I will keep the girl."

"I want them both."

"You are greedy."

"Surely this," Iblis pointed at Tristan, "is more valuable to you than both of them together?"

Melusin considered Tristan, running her fingers over his shoulders, massaging him. "He is a fine specimen." She smiled. "My minstrel boy."

"Then the boy and the girl are both mine?" said Iblis.

She shrugged. "Very well."

Iblis smiled his evil smile. "Where are they?"

"In cells off the lower dungeon."

"I will go and visit them," Iblis said. "I hunger."

. . .

When Iblis had gone, Tristan felt relief sweep over him. He sat heavily.

Melusin said, "Do not leave this chamber while I am away. You are safe only here. Whatever he says, he will kill you, just to upset me."

But Tristan's mind was on other things. A thought occurred to him. He said, "Who are the boy and girl?"

Melusin seemed uninterested. "I don't know. They strayed near the tower today, just before you came. They are from one of the villages, though it is unusual for them to come so near. Still, it saved me the work of going looking for blood."

"Do you know their names?"

"No," Melusin said frowning. "Why would I? They are merely food. Do you ask the names of the cows that provide your beef?"

"You said the girl was blonde and a virgin."

Melusin laughed, "Indeed, she told me that as if her purity and innocence would protect her. Perhaps she thought I would feel a motherly regard for her? But I am no mother."

Tristan wanted to ask Melusin more, but she dismissed his question with a wave. "Enough of them. They'll be dead soon. Iblis doesn't draw out his kills as I do." She came and stood directly in front of Tristan. "I will sleep soon, and I want you again before I do."

Tristan said, "And what are your plans for me after that?"

Melusin took off her dress, "I will kill you eventually. But the longer you please me, the longer I will keep you alive. Think of it like Scheherezade in A Thousand and One Nights."

"But she only told stories!"

Melusin smiled and pointed. "Then tell me a story each time with that."

She laid her dress over the chair behind her. She was again naked before him. Even though he wished it would not, he felt her wicked beauty arousing him. She came close so he could smell her musk.

"So this is my fate?" he said.

"I would have thought you would have relished the challenge. The more inventive you are in bed, the longer and harder you please me, the longer you will live." She stroked his cheek, and her hand slipped to his shirt. He watched as she unbuttoned it.

"But you will still kill me in the end."

She said, absentmindedly, as she stripped him, "You are a very talented musician, you know."

He said nothing.

"Your music has great power. Perhaps instead of killing you, I could teach you magic — to enable you to use your music to conjure the dark and to bend people to your will." Melusin seemed taken with the idea. She mused "Yes, we can ride out together to the villages, and you can use the tunes I teach you to ensnare my prey."

"I would never do that," he said.

"You silly man," she said. "How late in life to develop morals."

He was naked now; his penis stiff. He hated her, but she excited him more than any woman had.

She looked down approvingly and stroked his hard length. "Stop talking and let us make love."

He stood up and pushed her down onto the furs that lay on the floor below the fire. He forced her legs apart with his knees. She laughed at his demonstration of power, and he knew that she was allowing him to take her, and if the whim struck her, she would crush him like an insect on a board.

She opened herself, her hands on his buttocks. As he pushed into her and she groaned with pleasure, he knew what he had to do: he had to rescue Arc'hantael and Yann. He was sure it was they that had come to the tower. And he guessed that somehow Arc'hantael had followed him and got herself ensnared and that Yann had followed her because he loved her.

Tristan thrust roughly in Melusin, wanting to punish her, but each time he sunk into her, she squeezed her legs around him and moaned in delight. And, he thought, I will find a way to kill you too, you evil bitch.

She made him couple with her another twice. And then she released him. "I go to sleep now," she said. He was exhausted. He lay without energy on the furs, naked and limp.

"When I sleep, the day comes; when I wake it flees," she said. "You might prefer the day, but I counsel you to sleep at the same time as me, for when I am awake, I will need you, and I will not let you rest."

"Where do I sleep?" he said.

She pointed to a door he had not taken account of before. "Through there is a bedroom. There are heavy curtains at the window. They will keep the sunlight out."

He stood and grabbed his clothes. He walked to the door. When he got there, she was at the main door about to go out.

She turned and said, "I like you, Tristan." He hoped she did not want him to reciprocate. She looked thoughtful for a second and said, "In some ways you remind me of Iblis."

He shook his head. "What?"

"Whatever you think, like him you take whom you want and you care little for their fate, only for your own pleasure."

"That's not true. I am nothing like him."

"If you say so."

He said coldly, "I don't love you, Melusin. I never will."

"We shall see about that," she said and blew him a kiss. Then she left and closed the door.

When she was gone, Tristan went over to the heavy blue drape that was pulled over the slit in the stone wall that served as a window. He drew it back and light came spilling in. Outside, the sun was high. He could hear the small birds flitting and calling from the trees around the tower.

He walked over to the door of his bedroom and pulled it open. Inside there was a four-poster bed hung with sombre fabric. He touched the sheets; they were crisp, clean linen. On an oaken dresser, stood a ewer and jug filled with fresh cold water for him to wash. There was a fireplace stacked with logs and ready to be kindled at any time he should need it. He wondered with what. He guessed the tower's invisible servants would light the fire at his bidding, or more likely at hers.

He turned and walked out of the room. Whatever she said, he could sleep later. He walked through the chamber where he had been with Melusin. Through the door was the stairwell of the tower. He hesitated, thinking of her warning. But he reasoned, when she slept, so would Iblis. They were of the same kind. Surely it would be safe to leave his room? The thought of being a prisoner sickened him so he stepped from the chamber onto the stairs.

Grey stone steps wound up and down, spiralling out of sight in both directions. As he walked down the spiral, there were other doors off the staircase, but they were locked. Then he got to the enormous front door. He pulled back the iron bolts and lifted the metal bars across it. He pulled it. Nothing happened. There should be no reason for it not to open, but it would not. He put his shoulder to it and pushed with all his strength. Still, it would not budge. He cursed the door. It was held by sorcery.

Then he looked down the stairs that descended yet further. They delved into bedrock, and he heard the drip of water. Tristan went down the steps. Torches were in sconces on the wall, flickering with unseen drafts of wind and their smoky smell tainted with the reek of the pitch they had been dipped in.

Tristan felt uneasy, and his hand strayed to the hilt of his sword, though he knew it would do no good against the lord and lady or their invisible servants. He stepped down slowly, one step at a time. The dripping water grew louder, and he saw that the steps ended and a tunnel stretched away, worse lit than above, with few torches, some burned out and others fluttering.

This was the dungeon. This was where Melusin and Iblis locked their prey.

Tristan prowled forward, his sword half drawn now. Ahead of him on the left were a series of doors. The tunnel here was cold, and the rain that had soaked through the bedrock created a damp sheen on the walls and the floor.

He came to the first door. It was wooden with a barred window. He peered through and saw it was a prison cell. A skeleton, brown-boned, long-dead, picked clean by rats or worse, lay on the floor in irons. He felt a chill of fear of that place, but he told himself not to give in to such feelings.

He looked through the next cell window and saw Yann sat on a stone shelf and laid out with her head on his knee, Arc'hantael. She looked pale and ill and was sleeping. At first, the boy did not notice him, but when he saw a face at the door, he shouted, "What? Are you here to torture us again so soon?"

"Yann," said the minstrel. "It is I—Tristan."

"Tristan?" the boy's voice sounded suddenly full of hope. "I thought it was him again," he muttered. "The Lord Iblis, who has nearly killed my Arc'hantael."

"How did you get here?" Tristan said.

Yann's voice was full of subdued anger. "It was your fault. You cast your spell on Arc'hantael. After you left, you were all she could talk about. She said she was going to follow you and that you would love her and you would live together happily in some city." Yann spat. "But her foolishness has brought us both death."

"But you got here quicker than me," Tristan said.

The boy shrugged. "The path led us straight here. We did not mean to stop at the tower, but the Lady Melusin appeared and offered us refreshment. In her passion and hurry to find you,

Arc'hantael had not thought about bringing food, and we were hungry and thirsty."

"And you accepted Melusin's offer?"

"Arc'hantael did. I said I was afraid of the lady, and she told me to be a man. She said you would not have feared Melusin. I was stung. I couldn't let her go into the tower alone."

"I'm very sorry. But this is not my fault."

The boy laughed bitterly. "Perhaps you didn't tell her to come, but you knew she was fascinated with you. You made her love you as a game to entertain yourself. It is your fault."

"That's not true," Tristan said.

"Then why else do you seduce women? You don't want them. You only want them to want you, and when they do, and your ego is satisfied, you leave."

"You make me sound as much of a monster as the Lord and Lady of this place," Tristan said.

"I think you are." Yann hung his head, and his tears fell on Arc'hantael's sleeping face. "It doesn't matter," Yann said finally. "We will all be dead soon. You are here in the Tower, so you are their prisoner too, never mind that you are not in a cage. I take it the Lady Melusin captured you? After your boast that you would win her over, the joke is now on you."

Tristan felt shame rise through him. What the boy said was true. He said, "I will rescue you."

"And how will you do that?" said Yann dryly.

Tristan said, "I don't know how I will rescue us all yet. But I will think of a way."

"Then it had better come soon, for my Arc'hantael has lost much blood. The vampire drank deep from her neck."

"I will return soon."

"I don't believe you. Perhaps you even think you will, but when your life is at stake, I think you will leave to save yourself, for you are the only person you ever truly loved."

Tristan turned away. He would be back, whatever the boy said. And he somehow would deliver them from this evil.

Tristan found the Tower's entrance hall. This huge door led to the outside. He tried to turn the heavy iron ring, but the door was locked against him. He heaved and shoved and hammered. He looked all around for a key, but there was none. He was indeed trapped in here.

Head hanging, trailing his fingers along the cold stone as he walked, he returned to his room. The birds still sang outside, and the sun still shone. Tristan looked from the window in his bedroom across the broad forest of Brec'helean. The sun stood high and free in the blue sky, but for all that Tristan could see this beautiful world outside the tower; he could not reach it.

He went back to his bed and lay on the comfortable mattress of goose down. He stretched over for his lute and began to play, singing along in a low voice. But he could not settle — even with his music, a thing that usually gave him such pleasure.

He sighed and stood up. Visions of the Lady Melusin kept coming to his mind. He thrust them away, but her image would return, and with the thoughts, his heart beat faster. He hated himself for it, but he wanted to see her again. A kind of infatuation had stolen over him.

Tristan sang to distract himself, but all the love songs were about Melusin. His rational mind knew this was some kind of sorcery, but still, the longing for her tugged at him. He threw the lute on the bed in disgust. What was the matter with him? What spell was she weaving to draw his thoughts always to her?

Or was it really love? An emotion unfamiliar to him—something he'd never felt in his life: love for a woman. Maybe love was what infected his mind. He went to the window again, but the vision of the vast forest only tantalised him. And then he walked into the hall where the raven still sat on its perch.

"You're as much a prisoner as I am," he said to the bird, but the bright-eyed creature did not reply.

He turned again. Restlessly he paced from the window around the room to the door onto the stairwell. He looked up the stone steps. She would be up there sleeping. He thought he would go and look on her resting face. Maybe he'd even wake her so she would come back to him sooner. He felt disgust, but longing too.

As he mounted the steps, he was filled with terrible jealousy towards her husband, the Lord Iblis. He ran through fantasies of how he would destroy Iblis and have Melusin to himself. And then he realised, the further he got up the stairs and the closer to her he was, the stronger his infatuation for her grew. He was near the top of the tower now. Just above him was a door where the staircase stopped. Her presence felt very strong here, but strong too was the burning fear that emanated from Lord Iblis.

Tristan stepped up to the door. He pushed at it, and it swung open on oiled hinges. The room revealed was small and square. On the wooden floor were two sarcophagi. Between them burned a single torch, its restless light lending a strange liveliness to the sculpted representations of lord and lady that decorated the coffins' tops. The coffins were carved from smooth alabaster.

Tristan walked over to them and stroked the stone face of Lady Melusin. It was exact — a perfect representation of her beauty in stone. But it was not enough to touch a carving of her. He longed to see her again. He put his weight against the sarcophagus lid and shoved. It moved far more easily than he had suspected. The stone shifted slowly with a grating sound and the inside of the casket became visible. He could see the edge of a rosewood coffin, lined with cream silk.

Tristan pushed the lid further and revealed another inch; now he saw her dark hair, but instead of the lustre it held when she was with him, it was dry and lifeless. He pushed the lid a further inch and saw half her face and gave out a cry he could not control.

Melusin's face was dry and desiccated, skin like old parchment stretched too tight on decrepit bone, sunken eyes like thumb-squeezed apples, yellow teeth on receded gums. She was dead.

His heart was beating. He didn't even know how to name the emotion—was this grief? Bereavement? Disgust? He had made love to this dead thing. He began to retch, but he had eaten nothing, and there was nothing for him to throw up. With shaking hands, he dragged the sarcophagus lid shut. Revulsion filled him, and he fled from the room.

Seventeen

BY THE TIME Tristan got to his room, his shaking had steadied. He found a meal set for him on a table placed in his room by unseen hands. There was chicken and rice with peppers and a fresh tomato sauce. It was hot and set out on a crystal, with a knife and fork of antique silver, handles chased in heavy gold, on either side of the plate. By the plate, too was a golden goblet filled with crisp white wine.

Despite the gnawing of hunger in his belly, he could not face the food, but he drank the wine. He gulped it too quickly, guzzling it to quieten his nerves. Feelings hatched in his heart that she had laid like a cuckoo's egg inside him. He loved her, the Lady Melusin, but that love was not a natural growth. Like a hybrid, hothouse orchid, she had forced it. These were not his feelings, though they felt more real than any emotion he had ever known.

He placed the goblet on the table and watched amazed as it filled itself again with wine. And he thought of where he was and how he had come to this end. When he examined himself, what emotions had he ever felt other than pride at his own cleverness? How he enjoyed his beauty and talent and the fact that everyone he charmed fawned around him, congratulating him and wanting to be his friend?

Tears formed in his eyes and fell down his cheeks, but even these were tears for himself. He left the food to go cold and stepped again to his window.

He cursed his false feelings for Melusin, and he thought of Yann and Arc'hantael chained to a wall in the prison cell, and then he felt the flowering of another strange emotion — pity, and he knelt by his bed, and he prayed to a God he had long forgotten. All he said was simply, "Father, let me do good for once."

He noticed the light from the window suddenly fade as if the sun was eclipsed. A strange wind grew in the treetops outside, and the birds fell silent. The unnatural night had returned, and Tristan knew that Melusin would soon come back to him.

Melusin came like a dark wind. The curtains over the window flapped as her presence sucked away the daylight. Tristan looked up from where he was to see the book of music she had provided for him flutter as she entered the room.

And there she was—no longer the dried dead thing he had seen in the coffin, but vibrant and living in her funereal majesty. Her dress now was dark blue edged with gold, sparkling diamonds sewn into it like glittering seeds. Her flesh was pale as a mountain snowfall, her eyes terrible as a storm. She smiled.

Against his will, his heart thrilled, and he stood to greet her. He found he was smiling back at her, and then he corrected the smile to a frown.

She was amused. "You almost looked pleased to see me, Tristan," she said. She picked up the golden goblet of wine, which was all he had taken from the meal. She said, "Good that you drank my wine. But you ate nothing, and my servants will be upset. They will take it as a personal slight."

"I wasn't hungry," he muttered.

"Love steals the appetite," she said.

"I don't love you," he said and then regretted rising to her bait.

She laughed. "Not yet, my darling. But soon."

He shook his head. He would never admit the feelings she had seeded in him. He felt like a petulant child because she was beautiful, and she was intelligent. She was magnanimous too; she forgave his petty moods. She forgave him the scoundrel he had been. Why should he not love her? He put his hands to his head as if to take the thoughts out. He knew it was the drug of her presence that made him feel like this. And the drug of her absence too, when she hadn't been there. She was the intoxicant, a dark liquor made of blood and longing.

She had gone to the raven and was stroking it. It allowed itself to be petted by her, apparently enjoying the touch. "Has Bran kept you company while I slept?" she said.

"The raven? No. He said nothing."

She smiled again, showing the tips of her teeth. "But he sees everything."

"I had supposed you had your spies," he said.

"Everywhere," she smiled. She came close to him and ran her nails across his face; lightly in a way that did not break the skin but reminded him that she was in her power. "How did you amuse yourself while I was gone?" she said.

"I explored."

"I told you not to wander."

"I found the door, but I can't get out."

"No, that is true and is my intent."

"I found the dungeons. The young couple in there."

She looked at him evenly.

"The girl will die soon," he said. "Could you not release them?"

"Why?" She seemed genuinely puzzled.

"For me. If you care about me as you say, you could release them for me."

She gazed at him. "It's true I do care for you. But those creatures are our food."

"They are people, not food!" he spat.

She explained to him slowly, as if speaking to a stupid child of whom she was fond. He had the impression that she was being particularly indulgent. She said simply, "People are my nourishment."

"That's disgusting," he said.

She spoke in the same even tone. "Do you pity the hens and the pigs you eat?"

"It's not the same."

"If you weren't so sentimental, you would see this more clearly." She stroked his arm. "But I like your sentimentality."

"So you will drink their blood until they are drained, and then they die."

She nodded. "Let's talk of something else. I don't want to fall out. Did you look at the music book?"

He shook his head and continued. "I beg you, Lady, let them go free. Find other victims."

"Ah," she said, in sudden realisation. "You knew them before, I think. They mean something to you."

"I hardly know them. I met them briefly."

"The girl is beautiful. Did you...?"

He shook his head, angrily. "No, of course not."

"Of course not?" She laughed.

His furrowed brow showed his anger.

Melusin continued. "But somehow you feel responsibility..." Then she fixed him with her piercing gaze. "I see. They came here because of you. The girl loves you!" She laughed out loud. "That is delicious. Are you sure you didn't seduce her behind her lover's back?"

Tristan shook his head vehemently. "I told you, no."

"Ah, you've changed then?" She was still mocking him.

He was serious. "I have changed," he said.

Her hand was still on his arm. He didn't pull it away.

"And what has caused this tremendous change in you?"

He bowed his head. "She changed me. Her innocence."

"The girl?" Melusin's voice was suddenly icy. "I like her less now. I won't have a rival, especially a silly human girl."

"And you've changed me too," he said.

She raised an eyebrow. "Really? How?"

"I learned what it was to be someone's plaything. To be treated not as a person but as an object."

"That is hardly fair, Tristan. I treat you well. You are my favourite pet."

Tristan stepped away from her. He went to the fire that blazed with an unnatural blue light. Still, it gave off warmth, and he stood in front of it, trying to rid himself of the chill Melusin's presence always caused. "I looked at the music," he said eventually.

She appeared pleased. "Will you play me something from it?"

He nodded. He went to his room and fetched his lute. Then he sat near her and tuned it. She observed, admiring the way his deft hands plucked the strings and made the chords. Almost shyly, he began to play one of the tunes.

She listened as he played with great emotion. When the last notes died away, she applauded. "That was my father's favourite tune."

"Your father?"

She said quietly. "Yes, I had a father. Did you think I was always thus?" She gestured to herself. She stood. "No, I was human like you before Iblis found me."

Tristan frowned. "I didn't realise."

"Our kind is made, not born. Iblis told me I was beautiful, and I believed him. I was very innocent."

"You are beautiful," Tristan said.

"Thank you," she said. "But he said he would make me more

beautiful. And terrible. And I would live forever. I was seduced." She shrugged.

"Do you regret it?"

"I am past regrets, Tristan. I am what I am. I listened to him. I believed he loved me. He offered me the blood kiss, and I took it." She lowered her gaze. "That was a long time ago."

Tristan watched her as she walked over to the raven. It cocked its head and let her stroke it. She seemed deeply sad. She smiled at him, and he thought he had never seen a more beautiful woman. To see her vulnerability was too much. He could not resist her in her regret, and perhaps that was what this was all about— another trick to win him? And then he saw the tears on her cheeks were real.

"Melusin," he said, rising.

She put up her hand to stop him. "You make me feel strange things, Tristan. I have not cried for centuries. Not since I became this."

He offered her his linen handkerchief. It was a trick of his to listen to his lady loves and provide them with a handkerchief and make them believe in his great sensitivity. But this time his empathy was real.

Melusin took the handkerchief "What are we doing, Tristan? Two monsters like us. Are we becoming human?"

"I don't know."

"I joke," she said. "It is too late for me to become human. But you, you have the gift of humanity, but you have squandered it with your selfishness."

"I will change. I have changed," he said.

"But you don't have much time," she said, "Because I will kill you. No matter how much I come to care for you, I will kill you. It is my nature."

. . .

Melusin took Tristan with her out of the Tower. It was night. She mounted on a black stallion and he on his faithful Jezebel. The horse had been well fed but was pleased to see him. As they rode from the tower into the night-clad forest, Tristan said, "Where's Iblis?"

"Lord Iblis is hunting," she replied. "But we are not going to find him."

"I don't think he likes me," Tristan said. His mood was lighter now. He began to play his lute to amuse them as they rode.

Melusin laughed. "Do you blame him? He is very possessive of me and jealous of you. Normally I find a man and take him and kill him within the first hour. But it's different with you, and he doesn't like it."

"But you will kill me. You said you would."

"Don't let's talk of that," she said. "Not now."

The horses trotted down the forest road. All around the trees slept a drugged sleep as if the coming of the Lady Melusin overwhelmed even them. Even the stream flowing beside the road ran sluggish and slowly, iced over with a coverlet of snow-crystals until it too was locked up by Melusin's magic.

"Where are we going?" asked Tristan.

"To the hamlet. It's just a few houses, a place called called Tregerec."

"I don't know it."

"No."

They rode on, and then Tristan saw a cluster of rude huts — roughly made dwellings of wattle and daub with thatch roofs. When they came up to the nearest house, Melusin dismounted.

"Leave your horse here," she said.

Tristan tethered Jezebel to the rail on the house's balcony.

"Come," Melusin said.

Tristan followed her. She looked at the first house and gave a curious movement of her head as if she were sniffing. "Not this one," she said.

She walked on. They came to the second, then the third house, and still she didn't find what she wanted. Then she said, "This one."

She went to the door and tried it. "Locked," she said. "They must have been afraid I would come." There was a cross on the door.

"Good Christians," Tristan said.

"I do not fear the cross," Melusin said. "Wait while I open the door." She stood as if preparing a charm, and then she said, "No. I have a better idea."

She smiled at him. "I told you I would teach you how to weave magic into your music. Play this." She hummed a series of notes. They were simple enough, but Tristan heard strange sounds behind the ordinary music. There were notes of opening and revealing. They hung in the air like the thrumming of tuning forks.

Tristan went back to Jezebel and fetched his lute. He played the music she had sung, copying it note for note, but it was deeper and stranger than any music he had played before. It was as if the door listened to the music, and when he was finished, the door swung open. Tristan stood open-mouthed.

Melusin said, "I could have opened it with a charm, but I want to teach you the power you could have. When I have taught you, you will be able to achieve anything with the sounds of your art."

"But why make me powerful?"

"I will answer that later. Soon we will go into the house, but first I want to teach you a tune of sleeping."

And she taught him the tune. He was talented and learned it as quickly as the tune of opening. Once he had mastered it, she said, "Come."

Tristan followed Melusin into the rough peasant house and felt the inhabitants' eyes watching them with a silent terror. He heard the sudden animal sobbing of the daughter. Then he saw the woman of the house holding her infant daughter in her arms. Her face was twisted in pleading. Tears ran down her cheeks. Her husband stood, shaking and silent but brave, holding a pitchfork as if that could ward them off.

"Melusin..." Tristan said.

"Play!" she commanded.

He played his lute, and the eyes of the peasants grew heavily and finally closed. Soon they fell asleep, chins lolling on chests, snores erupting comically and incongruously, given what was about to happen.

"It's kinder for them to sleep," Melusin said. "I bear them no ill will."

"Kinder? Like stunning animals in an abattoir before the slaughter?" he said icily.

"I know you are being sarcastic," Melusin said, "but yes. Exactly. I will take only the father. The children need their mother."

"The children need their father too."

She shrugged. "I need to feed, or I will die. Will you watch?"

"No," he said. He was powerless to stop her, and he knew it. But worse than that, he understood why she did what she did. She was like any predator. Melusin didn't hate her prey; she drank their blood so that she did not die herself.

Tristan went outside. His head was whirling. And then his stomach heaved, but he had hardly eaten, and all he managed to throw up was bile.

Melusin came out around fifteen minutes later. There was blood around her mouth and her eyes were cold as she watched him. "I did not think you were so weak."

"For being sick? What did you expect? Why did you bring me here, anyhow?"

"I wanted to test you."

"To test me? For what?"

She was lost in thought for a second as if debating whether to say what was on her mind.

He said sharply. "What?"

It seemed she thought better of speaking. "Come on," she said, "back to the horses."

They walked, and he said again, "What?"

She looked at him as they walked. "I have considered offering you the blood kiss. I have never made another vampire. Iblis did not allow it."

"And why would he allow you to give it to me?"

"He wouldn't."

"Well, then."

"Help me mount," she said.

He made a cradle for her foot with his hands. Melusin could mount the horse without his aid, but it was another test of his servitude, or perhaps his devotion to her.

"Tristan, you are not a stupid man." She was hinting at something, and he was missing it.

He was baffled. "Speak plain."

She stared at him. "I want you to kill Iblis and become my mate."

They did not speak of it again until they returned to the Tower. Invisible servants took the horses. Tristan noted carefully where the horses went, to the right of the tower. He thought that he would find the stable that way. Then Tristan and Melusin went to the room where they had first met. There was food for him—ripe red apples and grapes. Tristan took a quick bite from a crisp apple, and where the blood-red skin broke, he saw the white flesh underneath.

If Iblis was in the Tower, there was no sign of him. Tristan went to the door, opened it and looked down the stone stairs. He could only imagine the state of Arc'hantael and Yann in the dungeons below. Iblis might be with them now. He hoped they still survived, but he knew Melusin would not allow him to check and any demonstration of his care for them would be used by her against them.

Melusin decided she wanted to play chess. Tristan saw for the first time there was a chessboard in the room. The squares were made of ebony and ivory, and the pieces were of gold.

Melusin played well. He didn't. He was close to losing and frustrated at his inability to concentrate on the game.

She said, "It's a pity you are squeamish about blood."

He snorted. "Why a pity?"

She reached out and stroked his hand. "Because I will live forever and you will die, unless I make you like me."

"Unless I accept your blood kiss?"

She took his hand almost tenderly. Her black eyes were filled with love. It seemed as if she had charmed him, but he had won her dark heart in return.

Then he said, "How do I kill him?"

"Not so loud!" she hissed. "The walls have ears; so does the raven."

Behind her, the bird shifted on its perch. "Though he loves me best," she added, turning to look at it. She lowered her voice. "This is what you must do. Go into the forest, cut a branch of rowan wood. Sharpen it. Then come to him while he sleeps."

"I can't get out of the Tower when you sleep."

"I think you can."

He realised she meant the musical charm of opening she had taught him.

"I could kill you too," Tristan said. "While you sleep."

"You could."

"Do you trust me with your life?" he asked.

She let go of his hand. She seemed surprised at herself. "I must do."

"Then you are very foolish," he said.

She chuckled. "Or cleverer than you think."

For the first time, she made him laugh spontaneously.

"I'm pleased I can make you laugh," she said. "But it won't stop me beating you." She moved her queen and checkmated his king. "And now, days comes and I sleep. There are rowan trees along the path to the north. About two hundred yards."

Eighteen

AND WHEN SHE LEFT, the night left with her. Sunshine streamed in through the narrow window, casting an oblong glow on the floor and across the wall. Tristan was very tired. He hadn't slept for hours. He looked at the bed and longed for it, but he had to go out into the forest. He took his lute with him. When he got to the gate of the Tower, it was still locked. This time, instead of pushing with his shoulder, he plucked the strings of his lute, and he wove the magic sound that Melusin had taught him. The Song of Opening echoed in the stone entrance hall, and as its notes died away, the door clicked and slowly, of its own volition, swung open.

Outside the summer sun reigned. There were rabbits on the grass outside which fled as Tristan stepped out. Though he meant them no harm, they did not know that.

Swallows and swifts twittered and shrieked around the tower as they dived and jinked, hunting midges. First, Tristan went around the back of the Tower. Jezebel neighed before he saw her and he went into the stall and fetched her, leading her out and then walking her to the start of the trail that led away from the Dark Tower.

Tristan mounted Jezebel and rode a short distance before he recognised the rowan's serrated leaves and glowing-red berries. He knew it was a wood thought to have magical properties, said to be powerful against witchery and supernatural evil.

Tristan cut a stem as thick as a spear and used his knife to sharpen it and then, carrying it as a weapon, rode Jezebel back to the tower. He tied the mare to a tree in the clearing in front. "Wait here, my lass," he said, stroking her noble head.

He left his sword but took his lute in his left hand, and in his right hand, carried the sharpened rowan stake.

From the tower's entrance hall, he descended the stone steps to the dungeon. He went anxiously, fearful of what he might find. Before he came to the door, he called. "Arc'hantael? Yann?"

Yann answered. "She is dead." The boy's voice was heavy with sorrow.

"I'm so sorry," Tristan said. He stopped at the first door, not wanting to go further so that he did not have to see the girl's lifeless body. But he took a breath and stepped forward. Through the barred window. he saw there Yann cradling the limp form of his love, and Arc'hantael's blonde hair draped over his knees and fallen to the floor. Yann was staring at her as if he thought she might move again.

"He said that he would kill me next," said Yann. "But I don't care. There is no life for me now Arc'hantael is is dead."

"I have come to take you home," Tristan said quietly.

The boy laughed, but it was a hollow and dry sound. "I'm locked in, or haven't you noticed?"

Tristan took his lute and, once again, he played the Song of Opening. As the music played, its melody entered the door's lock, and twisted it open.

Yann's jaw dropped. "How did you do that?"

"It doesn't matter. Now let us leave. Quickly. I do not know how long we have before Iblis and Melusin awake, or whether they can wake when it is still daylight."

"I can't leave her."

"No," Tristan said. "We will take her back to her family." He went and helped Yann carry the dead Arc'hantael. She was light and, slowly and with reverence, they carried her out of the Tower. They laid her on the grass. Tristan said, "There is a black stallion in the stables around the back of the Tower. Go and fetch it and you can ride it home with me."

Yann didn't move. He was staring at Arc'hantael as she lay among the grass and woodland flowers. "She loved you," said Yann. "But you didn't care for her."

"That's not true," Tristan said.

"She's dead because she followed you here; I'll never forgive you for that."

Tristan couldn't meet the boy's eyes. "And I will never forgive myself." He said finally. He turned and walked to the door of the Tower. As he was about to enter, he called back. "Get ready to leave. I won't be long."

Tristan mounted the steps up to the top of the tower. He had the sharpened stake in his hand.

Tristan opened the door to the chamber where Melusin and Iblis slept. He pushed the door cautiously as if afraid they might wake and kill him.

But there was no sound, not even the sound of breathing. And the two were not slumbering in bed, they were dead in their coffins.

In the room were the twin sarcophagi, the reliefs on them cast in flickering shadows by the single torch. Tristan went to Melusin's tomb. He placed the rowan stake on the floor and pushed the lid.

Even though he had seen it before, revulsion at her dry, dead face, seized him. He stepped back but, forcing himself to do a task that disgusted and frightened him, pushed the lid further open.

The sound of the stone grating open resonated in the room. Melusin's hands were folded over her chest.

Above them, he saw her robe where it covered her heart. That was where he would strike. He picked up the stake then. He had it ready to push into her dry body. Then he hesitated. Sweat beaded on his face, running into his eyes. He wiped them with the back of his shirtsleeve.

"The other first," he said to the quiet room.

He turned to Lord Iblis's tomb. Pushing pushed aside the lid, and the fierce demonic face stared up at him. He gasped, and his hand trembled. Iblis was more terrifying in death even than it was in life.

Tristan hesitated, but then he gained his resolve. Raising the stake, he plunged it into the sleeping vampire's breast. The thing shrieked loud with a noise that split the silence of the room. The scream echoed throughout every room of the tower. In final death, the vampire's hands reached to grasp the stake as if to pull it out. His eyes opened, and his mouth twisted in a frenzy of hate. But it was too late for Lord Iblis. The magical rowan wood burned the creature, and Lord Iblis's form, held together by sorcery, collapsed in on itself until it was only dust and bones, wrapped in a rich red robe.

And now it was Melusin's turn. Tristan removed the stake from the ruins of Lord Iblis's body. He examined it and found that despite the conflagration that had consumed Iblis, the wooden stake was not even scorched. Tristan walked to Melusin's tomb with deliberate tread.

The thing in the coffin was not the Melusin who had made love to him, who seemed to care about him in her own malefic way. He would end her. He had to rid the forest of her evil. He raised the stake and stood ready to plunge the rowan wood spike into her chest, but he hesitated again.

He suddenly thought of her tears when she stood regretful of the thing she had become. He thought of her innocence and how she had accepted the blood kiss from Iblis, not understanding what it was and what it would make her. Tenderness filled him. He thought of her eyes and her mouth, not dead like this, but animated and full of passion and humour, and he forgave her and lowered the stake.

"Maybe I do love you," he whispered. "Monster that you are. But I should be merciful if I would be shown mercy by others. I was no less monster than thee, Melusin. I was a vampire of kinds, not a drinker of blood, but a taker of honour, a seducer who treated all women as if they were merely prey. I owe you something for teaching me that at least."

He dropped the stake, and it clattered on the stone floor. He turned and left the room, running down the stairs to where Yann waited.

The afternoon drew on, and Melusin would wake soon, he knew. Perhaps she would forgive him for not killing her.

Tristan stood outside the Tower door and saw Yann had fetched a wagon.

"I found it in the stables."

On the waggon, wrapped in a rich tapestry, torn down from the tower wall as a makeshift shroud, lay Arc'hantael, pale and dead.

The two horses were yoked, harnessed and ready to pull.

"Let's hurry," Tristan said. They jumped onto the wagon.

"The village should be this way," said Yann.

Yann pulled on the reins, and the horses set off. He urged them into a gallop. When they were rumbling down the path, he turned. "Did you kill them?"

Tristan studied his be-ringed fingers. "Not both."

"Not both?" said Yann. There was fear in his voice. "Which did you not kill?"

"I left Melusin."

"Why would you do that?"

"I don't know if I can explain," Tristan said.

"I can explain it — she has bewitched you."

"Maybe."

Yann was shaking. "She will come and kill us both now."

Tristan shook his head. "I don't think so." He turned and gazed back at the Dark Tower. "Though I think I will meet her again."

May time was gone, and the first flush of summer had left the Forest of Brec'helean as Tristan rode away from the the Dark Tower of Ker-Zu. They had found Yann's father out looking for him and once Tristan was sure that Yann and his dead love Arc'hantael bound for home, he took his own road, not knowing where he was going.

Drooping poppies studded the verges of the path, like a crimson army among the emerald stalks of wild grass. The sweet scent of musk rose haunted the avenues between the trees, and songbirds flitted from shade to sunshine through the under-growth while Tristan Mab Bennog rode his bay mare Jezebel and hummed a song of his own composing. It was a song of love and loss, for he had loved, and he had lost.

9 781739 559694